ATLAS SERIES
BOX SET

BECCA C. SMITH

Published by Red Frog Publishing a division of Red Frog Media

Visit our website at www.redfrogpublishing.com

Cover by Stephan Szpak-Fleet

First published in 2013, 2014, 2016

ISBN 9781949877540

Printed in the United States of America

ATLAS

Chapter One

PUNCH!

Crap, Kala Hicks reprimanded herself. *Another bar fight? What's wrong with me? Seriously!*

She just couldn't seem to stop herself. Some jerk would try and hit on her and BAM! Kala was either throwing a punch or kicking a groin. Kala couldn't figure out what offended her most: guys that wanted to have sex with her or guys that wanted to have a relationship with her. Both made her furious beyond measure.

This particular asshole tried to grab her waist and pull her close. Before he could reach his hand around her, Kala's fist split his nose.

The man was screaming to high heaven.

"Relax, dude, I'm a girl." Kala was even more offended at how much of a baby this guy was. But she knew she was being unfair. Kala was a trained Navy Seal sniper with two black belts, one in Aikido and one in Tae Kwon Do. A punch in the face from Kala was the equivalent of a punch in the face from any man (probably worse, since they never seemed to expect it from a woman). Kala was five six and only 120 pounds, her shoulder length auburn hair framed a straight nose, giant green eyes and perfectly shaped lips. The girl was stunning. Jack Norbin, her commanding officer, would often assign Kala undercover missions because her looks were so unassumingly "safe," while her fighting skills were deadly. Though as the team's sniper, Kala usually found herself holed up in a room lying on a table with her rifle and an earpiece telling her who to put a hole into. Either way, Jack never worried about Kala's ability to defend herself.

On the other hand, Jack *did* have to worry about Kala getting into unnecessary fights.

Like now.

"You bitch!" the man wailed. He tried to punch Kala back since the whole bar was laughing at him.

And by laughing at him, it was more that they were laughing at Kala's short fuse. Kala's fights were quite the amusement for the other bar regulars. Just a way for Kala to blow off steam, and if it entertained them at the same time, they were all for it.

Kala easily dodged the man's fist and sent another blow to his chest.

The man gasped for air.

"Just walk away," Kala sighed. She was bored already and the thought of beating the crap out of this guy until he stopped trying to fight back was not something she was in the mood for tonight.

Next time, walk away yourself, idiot, Kala grumbled to herself.

Kala wished she had more self-control, but she'd been like this her entire life. Her mother abandoned Kala in a dumpster as soon as she gave birth to her. She was discovered the next morning and taken to the hospital. Kala ended up being one of the unlucky kids who was never adopted, a childhood spent moving from foster home to foster home. The only family that Kala ever gave a damn about were the Johnsons. She was sent to them when she was fifteen years old. Owen and Linda Johnson. Owen was in the Navy and drilled respect into a very unruly

Kala. She loved him for it and followed in his footsteps by joining the Navy. When she started her training, the Seals nabbed her right away. Kala's test and target practice scores were off the charts, always deadly accurate. A few years of exemplary service later and she was nabbed again by Jack. Kala had been on his team ever since, working secret government missions that usually required a lot of killing and mayhem.

For a smart girl, Kala often wondered how she could be so dumb. A question her fellow soldiers wondered sometimes as well.

"You okay, Kala?" Derek yelled from the back of the bar.

Even if Jack was the commanding officer, Derek Echols was the big brother in their little crew of two women and two men: Kala, Lali, Derek and Jack. They were never too far apart from each other, even in off duty time. It kept their minds in the game — because they never knew when they'd be summoned to perform a mission. Though currently only Derek was around.

"Fine, thanks," Kala half-waved to Derek.

CRACK!

He did not just do that!

Kala felt the wooden bar stool hit her lower back with a loud crunch.

Seriously! Ouch!

Kala was pissed now.

But not as pissed as Derek.

Kala almost felt sorry for the poor guy as Derek jumped up on his table and charged like a bull, leaping from table to table until he slammed full force into the guy's chest. Derek picked the man up by his neck and flopped him on the surface of the bar, breaking every glass that had happened to be resting there.

"Trust me, you'd be worse off if I had let *her* get a hold of you," Derek said in the man's ear. "But then again…"

Derek shoved the man so hard the guy slid all the way to the end of the twenty-foot bar and toppled off the end in a heap. The man's friends hurried to his side, then carried him out of the bar before he was stupid enough to try coming back for more.

Kala rolled her eyes at Derek. "I had that under control."

"Yeah, you were a complete lady." Derek handed the bartender a wad of cash to pay for the damages. The bartender didn't flinch: apparently fights in there were commonplace. If you paid what you owed, he was just fine with that.

Kala laughed. "Yeah, yeah."

"What did he do? Ask for your number?" Derek motioned the bartender for two shots.

Before Kala could blink, the shots were ready.

"Worse, he tried to have a conversation." Kala drank her shot with Derek.

"The nerve," Derek chuckled.

Derek was tall, well over six feet, and all muscle. He wore his hair shaved, which suited his dark complexion. Derek was always dressed in military fatigues, and Kala wouldn't have been surprised if he slept in them as well. She had never seen anyone so loyal to their country. Derek lived and breathed America. He had been a marine before he was recruited to be on Jack's team, and Derek was *Semper Fi* all the way. Kala knew he would take a bullet for any one of them.

Kala picked up the rickety bar stool that had served as a tennis racket to her back and sat down. "I'm going to be sore tomorrow," she moaned, rubbing her back. It wasn't painful yet, but that was probably because she'd already had four shots of tequila that evening.

Derek touched his forehead. "I think I hit my head when I slammed him into the bar."

"Idiot."

"Moron."

Derek and Kala both started to laugh. Pulling up a bar stool, Derek ordered two more shots of tequila and the two of them slammed them back like pros.

"Sooner or later you're going to have to let someone in," Derek said this carefully. He knew he risked injury by bringing up the touchy subject.

But Kala was too drunk to get mad. More importantly, she was too scared that Derek would figure out that not only had Kala "let someone in," but the person she had let in was their commanding officer, Jack. She could barely admit it to herself, let alone any of her team.

Even Jack was in the dark at how much Kala truly cared about him. And it was more than just *caring*. Kala was in love with him.

The 'L' word didn't come naturally to Kala. It always felt forced and fake when she thought about saying it out loud. She was jealous at how effortlessly it came to most people. Some people said it as easily as "good-bye" in a conversation. It made Kala feel like she was some kind of alien, incapable of human emotion. Kala made Jack think that he was her "booty call," but that was a lie, because Jack was so much more to Kala. The intensity of their relationship scared her more than anything in her entire life, and that was saying something considering she was a part of the most elite special ops team ever assembled.

"Not if I can help it," Kala picked up a newly refilled shot glass and toasted Derek, who shook his head.

At that moment Kala's cell phone buzzed. She stared down at it. It was a text from Jack simply stating: *you coming over tonight?*

Kala's chest tightened. She felt like a teenager. The guy gave her butterflies and she really despised that. But she texted back: *be there in 20.* Kala groaned internally at her own weakness. It looked like tonight Kala was *Jack's* booty call and not the other way around. She should have been strong and said no. Sleeping with your commanding officer broke about a hundred rules, but Kala didn't care. Being with Jack was one of the few true things she had in her life. Any time with him beat tequila shots in the wee hours of the morning. Period.

"Gotta go," Kala informed Derek. "Thanks for taking out the trash for me."

Derek motioned the bartender for another drink. "See ya tomorrow."

Kala casually saluted and walked out of the bar.

The cold January air felt amazing after the stuffiness of the bar. It had rained that morning, giving the air a fresh-after-the-rain smell that Kala loved. Being stationed in D.C. wasn't exactly Kala's first choice of homes, but after the last three years she had learned to appreciate the little things. Kala's foster-jumping life was in Los Angeles so she had been raised in sunshine. Seasons were an entirely foreign concept to her when she joined the Navy. Her first winter was in Virginia Beach and even though everyone kept telling her that 48 degrees was mild, it felt like she had been stuffed inside a freezer. Kala wasn't one to complain, but a part of her would always miss L.A. for the weather.

Kala's beat up maroon '73 Buick Apollo sat in the back of the bar's parking lot, but she knew she was in no condition to drive. At least she didn't have to worry about anyone stealing it: though sentimentally Kala felt that her Apollo was the best car ever made, no one else seemed to agree with her, especially thieves. Luckily, Gordo's Bar was near the center of town off of 16th street, so hailing a cab wouldn't be a problem, especially if you looked like Kala. She wasn't exactly dressed for a night out, but her t-shirt and jeans with a black leather form-fitting motorcycle jacket showed off her figure to any man with eyes.

Hailing the first cab that drove by, Kala slid into the back seat and gave the driver Jack's address. Even as she said the numbers out loud her chest squeezed again. She was ready to punch herself for being such a sap. Kala knew more about her sniper rifle than she did about love. The military was a welcome distraction whenever things got too complicated for her emotionally. Kala was blessed with the innate ability to hit her target no matter what the distance or the trajectory. So being a sniper was a no brainer. Kala had no idea where she inherited this gift and she often wondered if her mom or dad had been soldiers themselves. Knowing her luck, they'd probably been homeless crazy people who were really good at darts.

Owen had taught her how to shoot tin cans in their backyard. It was the first real moment she ever had with anyone before in her life.

No one had ever given her the time of day, always writing her off as the problem kid they wanted to get rid of. But Owen treated Kala like his daughter that day. He patiently taught her how to safely use a gun. Kala would never forget the glimmer of pride shining in his eyes when she had hit five cans on her first try. After a few weeks of training with Kala consistently hitting every target Owen put in front of her, he entered her into a shooting range competition. Kala came in first place and Owen and Linda were so proud of her they kept Kala's trophy displayed in the foyer of their house for everyone to see.

The cab stopped in front of Jack's brownstone. Kala paid the man, giving him a sizeable tip. The cabbie was more than thrilled and tipped his hat to her as she left for Jack's front door.

Kala was almost sobered up, or at least only slightly above tipsy, but her training still kept her aware of her surroundings no matter how fuzzy her state of mind.

Jack's brownstone always seemed to reach out and welcome Kala more than her own apartment. There was just something so inviting about the building's old architecture with its dark brickwork, arched windows and stone stairway leading up to a wrought-iron entry.

Kala hopped her way up the stairs and knocked on Jack's door. Even though her heart raced and her palms were sweated, an outside observer would never know. Kala knew this emotional "camouflage" was a blessing and a curse. A blessing because it kept her safe from getting hurt. A curse because she could never let the people she cared about really know how she felt.

The clacking sound of someone walking by caused Kala to turn and look.

It was a woman wearing a business suit with a tailored trench, holding a briefcase in her hand.

There was nothing special about her by all outward appearances, but something about this woman made Kala's skin crawl. Enough so that she felt for her gun, but quickly remembered she wasn't armed.

The woman didn't look at Kala as she walked past Jack's brownstone, but Kala had the feeling that the woman could see her all the same. It was an eerie feeling that Kala couldn't shake, as if the woman had eyes on the side of her head. If she weren't so creepy, the woman would actually be quite stunning. High cheekbones framed a chiseled youthful face. A long nose, full lips and gigantic brown eyes made the picture complete. With her stark black hair pulled back in a loose bun, and tailored pants suit, any observer would think that she was a businesswoman coming home from a long day at the office.

But not to Kala.

Kala couldn't stop staring.

This was another reason why this woman was alarming her. If someone had been staring at Kala the way Kala was staring at this woman, Kala would have stared right back, and let's face it, she probably would have ended up in some kind of violent confrontation. Or at least a verbal one.

It was hard for Kala to let things go.

But this woman walked off down the street without a single glance.

"What is it?" Jack's voice broke Kala out of her stare down.

Kala turned to him and tried to shake her paranoia. "Nothing. Just some lady. She gave me the willies."

Jack pulled Kala in and kissed her, then pulled away with a smile. "Someone actually gave *you* the willies? Now that's someone I'd like to meet."

Kala shrugged, which normally would make any guy annoyed at her obvious lack of affection, but Jack was used to it. He nodded his head toward the inside of his house to invite Kala in.

Kala moved past Jack and entered inside his apartment. After Jack's knee-buckling kiss she wanted to jump him in the doorway, but her stubborn pride wouldn't let her.

"You got anything to drink?" Kala took her jacket off and threw it over one of Jack's plushy armchairs.

The inside of the brownstone was just as cozy. From the golden hardwood floors to its soft cushioned furniture, Jack's place was as warm and inviting as the outside. There was a brick fireplace framing the living room, with a dining room and kitchen right behind it. On the mantle were pictures of his family: brothers, sisters, parents, nieces and nephews. Jack was seriously the All-American Boy. Everything about him was perfect. He had a perfect life with a perfect family and was just well… perfect. Being a Navy Seal himself, Jack's physique was all tone and muscle. Sometimes Kala couldn't look at him for too long, his face was gorgeous in a scrappy-sexy kind of way, and his shaved head was always a weakness for her. And it certainly didn't help that he was only wearing his A-shirt and boxers.

"What would you like? I have scotch or vodka." Jack walked over to the kitchen and pulled down the two aforementioned bottles.

In that moment, Kala no longer wanted anything to drink. She just wanted Jack.

There was something so sexy about a polite guy. Bad boys were never her thing, probably because *she* was the "bad" one in most relationships. And being twenty-eight years old, Kala had had more terrible relationships than she cared to admit. But Jack. Jack was different. He was kind and protective *and* a bad ass to top it off.

And did she mention he was gorgeous?

Kala walked to the kitchen and grabbed Jack by his shirt, pulling him in for a passionate kiss. Jack was easily persuaded away from the alcohol as Kala led him up the stairs and into his bedroom. Being with Jack sexually was the most intense experience Kala had ever felt. As closed off as she was, sex never meant anything to her before, it was just a means to an end. There was never a guy Kala felt was worth her time. But Jack was different. He was attentive — and cared more about her experience than his own. The hardest part for Kala was not letting Jack see how intense her feelings were for him.

Jack lowered her to the bed and the two of them ripped off each other's clothes like they had acid on them. Kala flipped Jack over so she was on top, which Jack didn't mind in the least. She leaned down and they kissed with some force, as if they couldn't get enough of each other. Kala loved the way Jack kissed her. His kisses were the perfect combination of light and forceful that made Kala's whole body tingle.

Jack reached over and turned out the lights as the two of them proceeded to have a good time.

***

Kala listened to Jack's heavy breathing as he slept beside her. Normally, this was her cue to sneak out, but for some reason she didn't want to leave just yet. He looked so peaceful lying there with the down comforter keeping him warm on this cold winter's night. Jack never asked her to leave. He never asked her to pretend they weren't seeing each other. He completely gave Kala her space and time. Never pressuring. Always respectful. Who was this guy? Jack was flawless.

That was what scared Kala the most.

There must be something wrong with him. No one was that perfect.

Kala tried to resist the urge to snoop, but since it was in her nature, she carefully crawled out of bed and walked to Jack's dresser. She had probably been in Jack's room over a hundred times and over a hundred times Kala had done exactly the same thing she was doing now: looking for anything that would confirm that there was no way on the planet someone like Jack could exist.

After a few minutes of searching, she came up with what she always came up with:

Nothing.

Kala didn't know why it was so hard for her to trust men she was in relationships with. Sure she had a crappy childhood, but once she met Owen and Linda, her life had turned around ten-fold. When it came to combat, Kala never had a single trust problem. She knew her fellow soldiers would die for her and that she would do the same for them. But for some reason when it came to relationships, Kala never really cared about the guy, not like Jack, who she figured had to be some sort of robot or clone.

She took a deep breath, then went to the window to feel the cold against the glass. Sometimes just holding her hand against the pane and feeling the cold air hovering on its surface calmed Kala down. Pulling the sheer curtain aside, she looked outside. Kala's heart jumped in her throat.

The woman from before stood across the street, staring straight at Kala.

Kala threw the curtain aside and instinctively grabbed Jack's gun out of his side table.

Jack was up instantly.

"What is it?" He jumped out of bed, poised for action like a trained soldier.

"That creepy woman is out there, staring at your apartment," Kala said while cocking the gun.

Jack carefully took the gun from her hands. "What are you going to do? Kill her for staring?"

Kala shook her head. What *had* she been thinking? It wasn't like her to grab a weapon just because someone creeped her out.

Then again, Kala never got creeped out.

So what was it about this woman that made Kala's skin crawl? The person down there was a businesswoman for God's sake. Carrying a briefcase.

Or a bomb.

Maybe that was what set Kala's teeth on edge. Her instinct that this woman was a terrorist.

Kala grabbed back Jack's gun and looked him in the eye. "She has a briefcase and I'm checking it out."

Jack didn't argue. He pulled the curtain open further to get a look at the mystery woman himself. "Where is she?"

Kala was putting her jeans on, but dashed back to the window.

The woman was gone.

And really gone.

No sign of her anywhere.

Jack wrapped his arms around Kala from behind and kissed her neck. "Are you sure you weren't imagining things?"

Was she?

Could she have possibly made up the whole thing in her head? It definitely wasn't like her, but it was late and now that Kala looked outside…

She pulled away from Jack and placed his gun down on the dresser, then she rejoined him at the window. "You think I'm crazy," she accused.

Jack smiled. "My kind of crazy."

Kala relaxed and smiled back as Jack leaned down, giving her a kiss that made her knees wobble.

A loud buzzing interrupted them.

Kala mumbled into Jack's lips, "That's your phone."

Jack finished the kiss, then pulled away and picked up the phone by his bedside.

Kala watched as Jack's face revealed something she'd never seen in him before. Ever.

Fear.

It was so foreign to her she didn't know how to react.

"What is it?" she asked and found that her voice was shaky.

When Jack looked up at Kala, all signs of fear were gone.

Kala started to wonder if she was going insane. First the woman appearing-disappearing, then Jack being scared? Her eyes were playing tricks on her. Or her brain was. Or maybe it was all that tequila.

"We've got an assignment." Jack put his phone down and started to get dressed.

Kala was a bit taken aback. Usually when the team was called in all their phones went off at the same time like a universal alarm.

Kala's phone hadn't made a peep.

A slow inkling of doubt began to creep up in her brain. Was Jack lying to her? Why would he when she could easily catch him in a lie like that?

"Are you going to get dressed?" Jack was transitioning into "commander mode."

"Yeah," Kala said and since she already had her jeans on she reached for her t-shirt on the floor.

Both their phones went off at the same time.

Kala grabbed her phone off the dresser and checked the message:

Compound A.S.A.P.

Kala tried not to show what she was feeling. Something was weird. And something was off. Jack received a message almost two minutes before the rest of the team received orders to report in. It was nearly impossible for Kala not to be suspicious. In the three years that Kala had served in Jack's company, Jack never received orders first. Orders came from General Turner and they were simultaneously sent to everyone on the team. So who had given Jack the heads up? And why?

Kala desperately wanted to grab Jack's phone and see who the first message was from.

Jack was fully dressed and tossed Kala her jacket. "Let's get going."

"I took a cab." Kala was horrified. The last thing she wanted to do was arrive at headquarters with Jack. Derek and Lali would know right away about their affair. It was extremely difficult to hide anything from the two of them and Kala was positive Lali was already suspicious. But to arrive together at three in the morning? They wouldn't be fooling anyone.

"Your choices are simple: take another cab or come with me. What will it be?" Jack had a kind of hopeful look in his eyes, and Kala knew he wanted her to come with him.

"I'll call a cab." Kala just couldn't. She wasn't ready.

Jack seemed to be okay with this as he smiled knowingly at her. "Stubborn as ever."

Kala just nodded, called a cab and headed for the front door.

Jack went with her. Before he walked towards his car he leaned down and kissed her. "See you there."

Kala nodded back and watched as Jack got into his car and drove away, toward the Compound. She waited for her cab as patiently as she could, but patience wasn't exactly her strong suit.

Then she saw the woman again.

She was down the street, standing there, holding her briefcase. The woman couldn't have been more than three hundred feet from where Kala stood.

Kala wasn't going to let it pass this time. Unarmed, Kala ran toward the woman.

The woman didn't move. It was like she wanted Kala to confront her.

When Kala was within ten feet of the woman, she slowed to a stop.

"What do you want?!" Kala yelled at the woman aggressively.

The woman smiled at Kala and Kala felt the hairs on the back of her neck rise.

"Not you, dear," the woman said as if sharing some inside joke with no one in particular.

Kala walked slowly toward the woman.

Eight feet.

Six feet.

Four feet.

The woman held her hand out to stop Kala from coming any closer. "That's far enough, Ms. Hicks."

Shouldn't have said her name.

Kala leapt the final three feet and had this woman in a headlock before the woman could react. "How do you know my name?" Kala whispered harshly in the woman's ear.

"Stay away from Jack," the woman warned.

Though Kala had the upper hand, hearing this made her push the woman away from her.

"Are you sleeping with him?!" Kala accused. Now she was pissed. If this woman was a scorned lover, or worse, another lover, Kala would have finally figured out what was wrong with Mr. Perfect. Jerk!

Before Kala could move, the woman was suddenly in her face. Her eyes were bright blue and *glowed* slightly.

Glowed! Kala had never seen anyone's eyes glow before!

What the hell was in that tequila?

Hallucinogens. Definitely hallucinogens.

Kala instinctively moved like a cat and was behind the woman, holding the psycho's arms behind her back.

The woman seemed shocked that Kala was able to capture her. "I get what Jack sees in you," the woman admitted.

"Let's take a look inside your briefcase." Kala grabbed the case and shoved the woman away.

Kala opened it despite her years of training that taught her to take it to the Compound where they could handle it safely.

Aside from a pen and a single piece of paper, there was nothing in the case.

Nothing.

Kala tossed it aside and wondered how her instincts could be so off. Then she said what she dreaded the most, "So what? You two a couple?"

"No," the woman answered simply. "But we will be if you don't ruin it for him."

Great, a stalker, Kala thought to herself.

The woman's eyes glowed again.

What was going on?

Kala stood in attack stance.

"Not this time, little one," the woman scolded Kala like she was three-years old.

Before Kala had a chance to make a move, the woman disappeared.

Completely.

Kala thought she was going nuts. One minute this woman stood in front of her and the next Kala was by herself on the sidewalk.

"You call a cab?"

Kala turned to the street to see a taxi waiting for her.

"Um, yeah," she said, reeling from what just happened.

Kala still wasn't sure what *had* just happened. She sat down in the taxi and told the cabbie the Compound address.

The driver nodded and they drove off.

Chapter Two

Kala stared out the taxi replaying the last ten minutes. The woman had seemed obsessed with Jack. Warning Kala to stay away from him was the standard jealous girlfriend threat. But it had seemed like more than that.

And her eyes freaking *glowed*! Kala still didn't believe that she'd seen that right. Maybe the street lamp had hit this woman's eyes at an angle that made it look like they were glowing?

But then she vanished from thin air.

By the time she arrived at the Compound gates, Kala was convinced that someone had slipped her acid or some kind of drug at the bar. What she'd seen was impossible. Kala wouldn't be surprised if she had made up the whole lady thing in her head. Kala was a jealous person. It made sense that she'd hallucinate a stalker business lady with glowing eyes that could disappear on cue.

Seriously?!

Kala shook her head. She needed to clear her mind before she went in. Missions required full and complete concentration. For the sake of her fellow soldiers she needed to file this incident away immediately. Kala was tempted to report the possibility that she had been drugged, but she knew there'd be testing required and she wouldn't be able to go on the mission. That was something Kala wasn't willing to give up.

And, secretly, she was worried that the tests would come up clean and that maybe what Kala saw wasn't drug-induced, which would indicate that she might be crazy.

Kala paid off the cab driver and walked up to the front gate entrance. From the outside the buildings appeared to be a series of warehouses and hangars. Nothing special. No one knew that those buildings were just fronts for what lay beneath. An enormous underground compound almost a square mile in size, housing the highest level of military combat and technology on the planet. The base was a half a mile underground, encased in walls made of a special metal that was undetectable by satellites and radar. Kala still felt a surge of pride every time she entered the structure that was known only as the Compound. She was one of the few chosen to be a part of something so important. Kala kept on wondering when they'd realize they'd made a mistake and boot her out, erasing her memories or something dramatic like that. But, so far, her sniper skills had kept her invaluable to the team.

Kala arrived at the gate, where three armed guards stood attentively in a small booth. She flashed them her badge and they waved her through, buzzing for the gate to open.

A jeep awaited Kala as she moved closer to the warehouses. Derek was driving.

"I saw your Apollo in the parking lot and figured you'd take a cab. How's the head?" he asked sympathetically.

Kala hopped in the jeep and shook her head. "I don't know what the hell they put in the tequila, but I swear to God I've been seeing weird crap." Kala secretly hoped Derek would volunteer that he had had similar hallucination issues, but he just chuckled.

"Must be lack of sleep, kiddo. Aside from this monstrous headache, I just had one hell of a buzz." Derek drove them through a pair of enormous doors and straight into one of the unassuming hangars.

There were a couple of jeeps parked inside the gigantic hangar, though other than that, it was completely empty.

Derek and Kala jumped out of the jeep and walked to the center of the room.

A holographic circle rose up from the ground around them, surrounding the pair, then rotating and scanning their bodies with beams of light. Kala could see her and Derek's stats appearing on the rotating hologram with chains of DNA circling their bodies and then the words IDENTIIES CONFIRMED flashed. The hologram vanished and the floor became a platform that began lowering them underground.

The one weakness Kala had in terms of physical endurance was motion sickness. No matter how hard she tried to fight it, something about her equilibrium just couldn't handle fast motion. And the platform they were on was descending fast. It flew down into the bowels of the Compound, slick black walls flying by them at frightening speed.

Derek looked over at Kala and tried to hide a grin, but Kala noticed.

"Shut up," she groaned.

"How many times have you been on this thing?" Derek was highly amused.

"You suck." Kala took a deep breath, trying to steady her stomach. It didn't help that she still had half a bottle of tequila in her system.

Within seconds the platform stopped and two doors slid open. Kala shook off her queasiness with a couple more deep breaths and walked inside.

Kala was still amazed every time she entered the Compound: holographic images rotating on computer consoles, smart screens, shelves stacked with every kind of gun imaginable. It was like the military had puked on a science fiction novel. The same slick black metal made up the floors, walls, ceilings and doors.

The Compound was an entire city built underground. The section that Kala and Derek had arrived in was just the Research area, a mixture of scientists and soldiers, each with their own agendas working at various stations.

Lali came up behind Kala.

"You guys get your orders yet?" She was already dressed in full combat gear. Lali was shorter than Kala by a few inches, but what she lacked in height, she made up for in muscle. Kala wondered how Lali's shoulders could be bigger than most men's, but Lali managed to pull it off and still look like a girl. Lali had short bobbed black hair with blue eyes. She smiled at Derek, but talked to Kala, "We're on the stealth carrier tonight."

They shared their little joke at Kala's "air-sick" expense. Kala shrugged like she wasn't concerned, but that only made the two of them laugh.

"You guys love this," Kala grumbled at her two teammates. "I'll make sure I vomit on the both of you."

"Let's suit up," Derek grinned.

The three of them walked down a series of hallways until they reached their ready room. It was a typical locker room, except all the lockers were made of the same black metal as everything else in the Compound. Kala and Derek started to suit up in their combat clothes.

"Change of plans." Jack entered dressed in a black body suit that almost looked like scuba gear.

Kala's stomach fell. She knew what his clothing meant, and Jack quickly confirmed it.

"Phase-suits tonight," he announced and Kala groaned.

No one really liked phase-suits, but Kala hated them the most. Mainly because it aggravated her motion sickness, but also the whole idea just felt unnatural. She could never get used to the sensation of walking through walls. The new phase-suit was better than the last with only minimal disorientation, but if any part of the body wasn't covered, it would be left behind.

As in not being attached to the body anymore.

Last year, Lali lost an ear when the team took down the terrorist leader John Graverstin. The seam on her hood popped open from the impact of running through a thick security wall and when she stepped into Graverstin's bunker, Lali's left ear didn't come with her. Kala had to give it to Lali though. She hadn't made a peep. Lali only grunted slightly from the initial shock and pain, then she was all business. In less than ten minutes, Kala's team had taken down Graverstin's entire base of operation. Kala barely noticed Lali's missing ear anymore, since she always kept it covered with her hair.

Kala reluctantly slipped into a black bodysuit. The suit itself was made from a special kind of stretch material, like a thick spandex. It was mainly there to make sure everyone's body parts stayed covered so that when they put on the phase-suit nothing would be showing. It was tight and uncomfortable and Kala felt like Catwoman in it. And not in a good way. Showing off her womanly curves always made her self-conscious. In combat situations she wanted to be seen as tough, not sexy.

From the passing glance she just saw coming from Jack, she was out of luck.

Reason number one thousand why she shouldn't have let herself get involved with her commanding officer.

After everyone was suited up the four of them headed toward the Cog, where all the fancy military gear was housed. You had to have a level five clearance just to enter the Cog, and considering that the highest clearance level was six, that was saying a lot. Jack's team was all given level five clearance, only Jack had six.

Kala walked second to last in the group order and felt like she was wearing a big onesie. Not only were her hands covered with tight-fitting gloves, but the suit covered her feet as well. To top it off, their suits had face hugging hoods currently hanging behind their necks. With no heavy shoes, the four of them hardly made a noise as they walked through the black metal hallways toward their destination.

They reached the double doors of the Cog a few minutes later. The four stood in front of the doors and a holographic wall shot up in front of them like it did for Kala and Derek on the elevator. It scanned each person individually, their profiles rotating in front of them, until they were all cleared for passage.

The black doors silently slid open.

The Cog. Home for every imaginable and unimaginable piece of military gear owned and invented by the government.

Kala knew that one of the head honchos of the whole compound, General Geoffrey Turner, was responsible for it all. He and his partner, General Harry Clifton, started the secret OPS program years ago and were pretty much given free reign to do whatever was needed to protect the country. Kala had never met General Turner, but she had heard stories of his greatness. Turner had been a Seal himself, so Kala always felt a little extra pride that they had once been a part of the same team. General Turner basically scoured the earth for the best and brightest and he was pretty much allowed access to whatever he needed to use for experimentation. The results were astounding, the phase-suit being Turner's greatest accomplishment so far.

The Cog itself was a giant circle with smooth walls. Upon first glance the room appeared empty. Its black marble floor was the only reflective surface in the space.

Next to the door, Jack typed into a small panel.

A piece of the flat wall opened up and a metal rod with four phase-suits slid outward. Kala was always a little disappointed at not being able to find out what lay beyond the surface of the walls. She had only seen about a quarter of the high-tech inventions that were stored in the Cog. Kala wished she could spend a day exploring everything in there, but only Generals Turner and Clifton had that kind of clearance.

Kala walked with the others to the phase-suits and took hers off the rack. Phase-suits were lighter than they looked, but still weighed at least five pounds. They were constructed with a thick charcoal grey material that made the uniforms ideal for night missions. The cloth felt almost rubbery to the touch, but the surface was smooth. It was one piece that zipped up all the way to the top. Like the black undersuit, a hood made up of a mesh version of the phase-material dangled on the back. It covered the entire head, snapping into place around the neck so no area was exposed, but still making it possible to see.

The second part of the suits was the most important to Kala: the vests. This was where the guns were stored. Kala threw hers on and neatly tucked her two side arms into the inside of the vest. Not her beloved sniper rifle, but with this kind of mission, Kala had to settle for handguns. Kala hated these type of jobs. Phase-suits meant *up close and personal* and Kala much preferred aiming out a window at a target hundreds of feet away. It wasn't that she couldn't take care of herself. Kala held her own. It was more that she liked to observe and prepare for all possible outcomes. Hand-to-hand missions were the equivalent of a smash-and-grab to a thug. Sloppy. Kala hated sloppy.

It meant more things could go wrong.

Chapter Three

Kala and the team quickly finished suiting up. Once fully dressed, Kala shuddered to think of how, if anyone ran across her unit in a dark alley, they'd run screaming. The team was quite an intimidating vision, and without being able to see their faces, Kala thought they looked a little bit like an invasion force of aliens.

Jack led the team to the hangar deck where a stealth carrier awaited them. Within the darkness of night and the dimly lit space, Kala had to squint, trying to peer through the mesh of her hood and see the ship better. Smooth black matte metal made up the surface of the airplane. Though the wings and nose of the plane were slick and aerodynamic, the "carrier" part made the plane look like a pregnant fighter jet. Hydraulic hinges opened the mouth of the beast, acting as a ramp for Kala and the others. Right up the fat belly, Kala entered the ship and quickly strapped herself in the row of seats bolted into the side of the plane's wall. There was an identical row of seats across from her in which Lali and Jack strapped in. Derek sat next to Kala like a pillar of hardened stone.

Kala took a deep breath as the metal walkway shut closed. As the carrier was taxiing out of the hangar and onto the runway, Kala tried to stay as calm as possible. The last thing she needed was to get airsick. The sound of the jet engine was barely audible as the plane raced down the runway and into the sky.

After about ten minutes of being in the air, Kala tried to keep from puking. She leaned her head back on the cold surface of the craft to distract herself from the sensation.

Kala could feel the plane vibrate as it moved through the air at an impossible speed. It was a specially designed stealth plane that was undetectable to all radar systems. This wasn't the first time Kala had flown in this plane, but she could never quite get used to the ride.

Jack motioned to the team that they should listen, "Our mission is on Air Force One."

Kala pushed aside all feelings of nausea and focused on the task at hand.

"Air Force One?" she asked with surprise. Normally, Kala kept quiet, but hearing their destination and all the implications that it held was a little jarring.

Jack nodded. "The President is being held hostage. We need to take the terrorists out and gain back control of the plane. The President's life is our top priority."

Kala was used to high priority missions, but the *President*? Everything came in sharp focus for her. How often did anyone get to save the President!

"Get ready to jump," Jack barked. He unstrapped himself from his seat and hit the button that opened up the door.

Cold air rushed into the cabin. The team climbed out of their chairs and stood in a line on the edge of the plane.

Staring into the night with wind blowing all around, Kala saw Air Force One flying below them. The stealth craft was keeping pace with the larger plane to try and make the jump as smooth as possible.

Jack handed everyone a small device the size of a lipstick container. Oxygen.

Kala took hers and opened up the bottom of the mesh face-covering, placing the mini-oxygen tank in her mouth. Being this high up, the pressure alone was substantial, but trying to breathe would be impossible. Plus, there was never a guarantee that their team could keep Air Force One in flight. If anything happened to jeopardize the cabin pressure, they'd need oxygen there as well.

"Kala, you first," Jack yelled over roaring wind.

Jack always had Kala go first because of her ability to adjust after passing through the walls. She may have motion sickness, but when it came to phasing, Kala was the first to snap out of the disorientation stage.

Kala nodded. She hit the small button on the upper right shoulder of her phase-suit turning it on.

When Kala heard the familiar buzzing sound of the suit coming to life, she jumped.

Adrenaline coursed through her as the tearing wind surrounded her body. Jumping mid-air going 700 miles per hour wasn't exactly something Kala enjoyed, but she felt the rush regardless. She hoped the speed of the jump wouldn't interfere with the suit's pass-through capabilities. The last thing anyone needed was to lose a body part on this mission. Especially if that body part ended up being a *head*.

It took less than five seconds to reach the tail end of Air Force One and once Kala hit the surface of the ceiling she closed her eyes. Traveling through walls was always a surreal experience, but doing it 3,000 feet in the air made it all the more bizarre. Every fiber of her body felt liquid, as if for just a second Kala had been turned into water. A millisecond later, Kala belly-flopped onto the floor of the back cabin. Recovering almost immediately, she was quickly on her feet and drawing out the two guns from her vest.

Kala pulled back the mesh face-covering and spit out her oxygen device, pocketing it inside her vest. She squeezed her eyes open and shut a few times to regain her bearings. There was always a moment of disorientation no matter how disciplined she was, but Kala shook her head to keep focused. The last thing she needed was to be caught unaware by the terrorists who'd taken over the plane. Kala was still in shock that she was in Air Force One. As many high-ranking covert Ops she'd been a part of, Kala had never met the President. This wasn't exactly the way she wanted to meet him, but saving his life from terrorists had a certain heroic majesty to it that Kala could appreciate.

Aside from the urge to vomit up all the tequila she'd downed earlier that evening, Kala was ready to go. She'd landed in the back of the plane, in a room where office supplies were stored. Perfect place to rendezvous and take stock of the situation. A single door led to the main cabin in front of her, but it was closed. While Kala was waiting for the others to arrive, she crept up to the door and opened it a crack.

The belly of the plane consisted of cushy leather chairs that looked like they belonged in a house, not on an airplane. They were arranged in rows, all facing a podium. Obviously the Press section of the plane. Kala cursed to herself. Normally in missions the whole team would be fully briefed of the location they were entering. But this?

The orders from the higher-ups must have been fast and panicked for the operation to be this disorganized.

Kala surveyed the area. The room was empty. She just hoped that Jack had a little more information to go on since the team was pretty much riding blind on this one.

As if in answer to her request, Jack thumped to the ground behind her. The guy even managed to look graceful when doing a face-plant from the ceiling drop. For Kala there was no way to land with any kind of decorum when falling through a flying plane in a phase-suit. Kala had learned to take her SPLATs with a certain amount of humbleness.

Jack was on his feet in seconds, shaking his arms and legs to rid himself of the disorientation. He pulled back his face-covering and spit out his oxygen mouth piece. Jack made eye contact with Kala, giving her a slight smile. "You good?" he asked.

With all the adrenaline rushing through her system, Kala smiled back. "Yeah. The next room is clear. Where's the President?"

"In his main office. It's at the forward end of the plane," Jack answered.

Kala knew then that Jack was privy to a lot more details of this mission than he had let on. She trusted him with her life, so as much as she wanted to inundate him with questions, Kala kept quiet.

The rest of the crew hit the floor shortly thereafter. A few minutes of adjustment time and they were ready to go.

Jack took the lead. The team went into their standard formation, which consisted of Jack up front, Kala, Derek and Lali in the back.

Jack led them into the empty Press section. Everyone had their guns out and ready. Only Kala held both her guns, she felt more comfortable with two, ready to take down the men who held the President hostage.

As they passed through the bolted leather recliners, Kala looked outside the small round windows. She realized that the plane was headed toward a large grid of lights: Washington D.C. The goal of these terrorists might be to crash the plane somewhere in the Capital. They needed to gain control of the plane immediately.

Kala made brief eye contact with Derek behind her. She could tell he was thinking the same thing. An understanding passed between them. Kala knew that they'd both do anything to stop these crazies. *Anything.*

Jack took them through five more sections of the aircraft, all empty. The whole situation reeked of strange. Normally, there'd be guards stationed along the way. Maybe the terrorists thought that a rescue mission would be impossible once in the air. Either way, something just felt off to Kala.

She eyed Jack in front of her. He looked extra nervous as well. It wasn't like Jack to show any kind of emotion in an operation, but he looked downright petrified as he motioned the team forward into the galley. Seeing him like that made Kala even more wigged out. Something was definitely *wrong* about this whole thing.

Kala tucked her second gun inside her vest. She felt like she needed a free hand.

Jack stood in front of the closed galley door leading to the next room. He whispered, "The next room is Medical and then the President's office. Intel says he's being held in the latter. We'll go in fast. Head shots only. We don't want to hit a window and lose cabin pressure."

Which meant no random firing. This wasn't a problem for Kala, but Lali had a bit of a trigger-finger problem. And now that the plane was flying directly over the country's capital, they couldn't let it go down.

Kala noticed that Jack was sweating. For any other person, this wouldn't be an issue, but Jack never sweated. Kala knew it was probably because this mission was way bigger than anything they'd ever done before, but instinct told her there was more to it than that. Jack was scared, and it had nothing to do with terrorists.

Jack slowly cracked open the galley door and Kala could see through the opening that there were at least five men in Medical. All with guns.

To everyone's surprise, Jack swung the door open wide announcing their presence to the bad guys.

But that was just it.

The men in Medical were Secret Service.

Their guns were up and pointed at the team, but upon recognizing their uniforms' military insignia, they lowered their weapons.

The door to the President's office was shut.

Kala and the others filed into the galley to confer with the Secret Service men. Kala had counted correctly, there were five of them. Wardrobe was typical of government bodyguards: black suits and ties. The five of them had obviously been preparing to siege the next room, loading guns and conferring in a small huddle.

When Jack and his team joined them, their leader spoke up, "I'm agent Ford. I'm assuming you're Turner's squad?" Ford directed his statement at Jack.

Jack nodded, "Jack Norbin. What are we looking at here?"

"The situation is delicate…" Ford paused, looking like he was unsure of how to continue.

"Delicate how?" Kala asked when Jack hadn't.

It was as if Jack already knew what was happening and Kala and the rest of team were the only ones in the dark. It still struck her as odd that he wasn't confiding in them. They were such a tight-knit group and to have their leader acting so aloof made Kala ill at ease.

"There are no terrorists on this plane," Ford stated carefully.

Huh?

Kala didn't think she'd heard him correctly. "A hoax?"

"This is the worst crank call ever," Derek grumbled to himself.

Ford shook his head in the negative. A look passed between him and his men.

Something was very wrong.

And Derek was growing impatient. "Are we all going to stand around here like we're at the water cooler or something? Or are we going to save the President?"

Kala felt the same way. A bunch of elite military and Secret Service huddled like they were about to play flag football. Everyone's side arms out and ready to shoot. And more importantly, Kala was ready to shoot.

"That's just it," Agent Ford glanced at Derek, "The President *is* the threat."

Kala and her team stared blankly at the Secret Service agent.

"Excuse me?" Lali asked. Normally, the girl kept her mouth shut, but claiming that the President himself was the actual threat was preposterous.

Ford wiped sweat off his brow and explained. "The President has five bars of C-4 strapped to his chest hooked up to a bomb with a remote trigger that only he holds." Ford was obviously freaked. No wonder Ford and his guys had been conferring in the Galley. What could they do? Shoot the President?

That was what Jack's team was for.

Kala took a deep breath, trying to calm herself down. This was an impossible situation. She wondered why in the hell the President would want to blow himself up!? And over Washington D.C.! He could kill thousands of innocent lives.

"Do we take him out?" Jack asked Ford. And not with the incredulity that Kala would have expected from Jack. It was almost as if he was asking for Ford's permission.

Ford's eyes were practically bugging out of his head. "We've been arguing about that for the last twenty minutes! It's the President of the United States for God's sake!"

Jack placed a hand on Ford's shoulder, "That's what we're here for. You swore an oath to protect him at all costs. We didn't."

Kala was pretty shocked at how calmly Jack said that. It was in that moment that she knew something with absolute certainty.

Jack was there to kill the President.

He had known what his mission was way before they suited up, and Jack had been mentally preparing for it the whole time.

Jack nodded to Ford. "We've got it from here."

Ford's demeanor had slowly deteriorated since Kala's crew arrived. He was an utter mess: sweating, shaking and clenched. Ford ordered his men to stand aside.

Jack motioned to Kala to stay behind him, and the others followed in their standard formation.

Very carefully, Jack opened the door that led to the President's office.

What awaited them was terrifying.

President Jareth Wilton stood behind his desk. He was wearing a vest that held five grey bars of C-4 wired into a bomb. Wilton was a tall man, well over six feet with stark black hair and a long face. He was a young President, only fifty years old, but he looked like he'd aged twenty years since the last time Kala had seen him at a press conference, with dark rings under his eyes and worry lines on his forehead.

But his smile was what made the scene surreal and horrific. His thin lips were grinning as if he'd just climbed Mt. Everest.

President Wilton stared directly at Jack as the door swung open the rest of the way. "I figured it out! I figured out how to break it! No one will ever have to do what I've had to do again! Do you realize what this means?"

Kala knew then and there that the man was cracked. Figured what out? Break what? He was rambling like a mad man.

But the more frightening moment came when Jack responded back to Wilton. "Killing yourself is impossible. People have tried that in the past."

Not only was President Wilton talking crazy, but apparently Jack knew his language and was responding accordingly.

Kala noticed that Wilton's eyes lit up when Jack spoke. "You're the one they sent to replace me."

Jack nodded.

What? Kala was seriously confused.

Kala spoke up, "What's going on Jack?"

Replace him for what?

Jack didn't acknowledge Kala or the rest of the team, which was shifting uncomfortably behind him.

Wilton shook his head, serious. "You can't do it. You have to let me detonate this bomb. We have to crash the plane! It's the only way to stop it!"

"You can't stop it!" Jack yelled back.

"I can and I will!" Wilton talked into an earpiece. "NOW!"

The plane nose-dived.

Everyone jolted forward and stumbled from the force of it.

Jack barked orders, "Lali get up to the Flight Deck and by any means necessary take over this plane!"

Lali paused for a second, she looked more confused than Kala felt, but after a moment to gain her bearings as the plane was falling fast, she managed to high-tail it out of the room and up to the Flight Deck.

Kala was sure they'd hit ground at any moment.

Jack aimed his gun at the President's head.

Wilton was frantic. He ducked behind his large oak desk that was bolted to the ground.

"You can't kill me! You'll ruin everything!" Wilton yelled.

Jack turned to Kala and Derek. "No one shoots him but me!"

Kala kind of nodded, but she was in shock at the fact that they were about to flatten a part of the capital with Air Force One. She really didn't care what Jack was saying. She couldn't let President Wilton set off that bomb and kill thousands.

Jack shot at the desk, trying to hit the president, but he didn't come close.

Only Kala could make a shot like that and not get them all killed from shooting a hole through the plane.

Kala and Derek made eye contact. Kala could tell Derek was thinking the same thing. He whispered so only Kala could hear, "Do it."

Kala's nod was barely perceptible.

Jack saw her and his eyes went wide. "Kala STOP!"

Kala shrugged. "I can't let him do this, Jack. I'm sorry."

Only the top of Wilton's head was showing.

It was enough.

Kala took her shot.

Chapter Four

"**M**y, my, this is quite a surprise. Welcome," President Wilton said, offering Kala a seat.

Kala was sure that she was either dreaming or dead.

In front of her was President Wilton. He was at a small café, sitting in an intricately ornate iron-wrought chair, with an equally ornate table in front of him. A small espresso rested on the table. The café looked old, like they were in France or Italy, made of aged brick and ivy growing up the walls of the building. Cobblestone sidewalks and streets lined the whole area, making Kala feel like she'd walked into an old painting.

There was absolutely no one in sight except for Wilton, not even inside the café. It was like there'd been some sort of evacuation and only the President and Kala had been left behind.

An identical chair to the President's sat empty across from him. "Trust me, you're going to want to sit down."

Kala knew it had to be some sort of delusion or dream. The plane must have lost oxygen or air pressure and Kala probably passed out.

The President no longer had a C-4 bomb strapped around his chest. In fact, he looked quite relaxed in his dress shirt unbuttoned a few buttons and his khakis. Being the last person Kala saw before she blacked out, it made sense that she'd see Wilton here.

"You're not dreaming. I assure you this is all quite real. I'm not the President though unfortunately that's how you'll see me. You should have seen what I looked like before Mr. Wilton took over. I was quite the Adonis," Wilton said jovially.

Kala reluctantly sat down because at this point what else could she do? If this were a dream she'd wake up at some point. If she were dead… Well, she might as well enjoy the illusion of being alive for a bit.

Wilton looked happy that Kala complied and sat down. "You still think you're dreaming, don't you." It wasn't a question.

Kala didn't answer. She didn't feel the need to respond to a figment of her imagination.

Wilton sighed in amused frustration. "No one has come here *by accident* before. Every replacement is vetted from birth and trained their whole lives to do this job. By the time they get to me, I simply give them the explanation on how everything works and send them on their way. But you…" He left the thought hanging.

Wilton's face went from amused to angry in about a millisecond. "SPEAK!" he screamed.

It was so real, Kala jumped back in her seat. "Why? You seem to be pretty comfortable doing all the talking." Kala's sarcasm never failed her.

Wilton laughed. "You're going to be interesting, I can tell."

Kala wished she'd wake up. This dream was getting weird.

Wilton was serious once more. "How many times do I have to tell you: you're not dreaming!" His voice was insistent.

"You can scream 'til the cows come home, but there's no way this is real," Kala said, hoping this would jolt her awake.

She felt her throat close, like invisible hands were strangling her.

Kala clasped onto her neck, trying to pry off the force, but no air was coming through her passageways.

She knew then.

Wherever *this* was: it *was* real.

Kala nodded to Wilton, showing him that she believed him.

Her airways opened up, letting a flood of oxygen into her lungs.

Definitely real.

All sorts of scenarios ran through Kala's head. Had she passed out and been dumped here? Where was the rest of her team? Why was the President of the United States talking to her at a café in the middle of nowhere? It just *couldn't* be real. This had to be some sort of psychotic break from reality. But everything: from the feel of the metal chair beneath her, to the warm breeze on her face, to the…

…Ouch. She pinched herself.

Kala thought that maybe she was in some kind of "experiment" from the Compound. She had heard about all the different kinds of "research" being done by Generals Clifton and Turner in what was only known as the Black Wing. It was the only reasonable explanation for what Kala was experiencing. How could everything be so real, if it was perfectly obvious that none of it actually was?

"Have you just about finished that little debate in your head?" Wilton asked with a sly grin.

Kala wasn't sure how she should respond to that. After all, if this were real, how would President Wilton know what she was thinking? This was insane!

But she responded, "Yes."

Wilton didn't look convinced, but he smiled regardless. "How much do you know about Greek mythology?"

Okay. Not at all what Kala expected to hear from the guy, but she answered him anyway.

"Just what I learned in high school," she confessed. Kala was never much for history class. Aside from the battles, Greek mythology was too wordy and poetic for her taste. It was like watching a Shakespeare movie. By the end of it, Kala knew what was happening, but the language confused her. It almost felt foreign at times.

"Know anything about Atlas?" Wilton raised an eyebrow, obvious to Kala that he hoped she'd say yes.

"Wasn't he the guy that had to hold up some pillars or something?" Kala was pretty impressed with herself that she remembered that much. Of course, there was a more than fifty/fifty chance that she was confusing Atlas with someone else, but still, at least she had an answer.

Wilton sat back in his chair and took a sip of his cappuccino. He kind of laughed at the word *pillars*. "I suppose that's one of the legends, yes, but there's always a kernel of truth in fiction. The story had to come from somewhere, right?"

"Usually, I go on the assumption it came from someone's imagination." She wasn't sure where Wilton was going with this line of thought, but when Kala thought of the word *Atlas*, her mind pictured maps and globes, not a Greek god or whatever.

"Well, Atlas *was* real. I'm him. Hello," Wilton waved like he was a little kid greeting Kala.

Then he continued, "And I didn't hold up pillars or the world as some histories profess. Like every piece of history, the stories are taken too literally." Wilton explained this as if he were discussing a topic Kala would actually be interested in.

"Is there a point here?" Kala asked, her impatience getting the best of her.

Kala really wished she hadn't said that.

If smoke could have come out of Wilton's nose and ears it would have.

Kala placed her hands up in supplication. "Calm down. Don't choke me or torture me, I'm just asking what the hell the President of the United States has to do with some old myth? I'm very confused." Kala threw that last bit out to try and calm Wilton down. This whole situation was weird to say the least and to have to deal with Wilton's temper tantrums every five minutes wasn't something Kala wanted to do.

Wilton visibly calmed down. "I'm not the President, I told you: this is just the current incarnation of who I am. I'm Atlas. I'm a Titan. An Elder god, the first gods, not like the puny Olympic gods, though, to be fair, they defeated us, but I digress..." He paused and eyed Kala carefully. "And I'm sorry if I'm boring you, but we're talking about the rest of *your* life here and I thought you should know your back story."

Huh? Kala thought to herself.

"The rest of *my* life? What does some forgotten god have to do with my life?" Upon seeing Wilton breathing fire at the mention of the word *forgotten* Kala quickly said, "*Misunderstood* god, I mean."

This brought an amused chuckle out of Wilton. "Because *you* are going to do my job for me."

Kala stared at Wilton for a few moments, waiting for him to elaborate. When he didn't she said, "Excuse me?"

Wilton threw up his hands, way more amused than Kala felt he had the right to be. "Yep, congratulations, you're the new Chosen One."

Kala felt like her brain was a skipped record that couldn't find the next groove. "Chosen One?"

Wilton nodded, "Yup."

After a few more moments of awkward silence, Kala sighed heavily. "Explain, please." If this *was* an experiment being conducted by Clifton or Turner, then whatever Wilton or Atlas or whoever said might be related to a mission she'd have to take on. Kala figured she might as well play along and hear out her orders so that she could get back to the real world.

"When I betrayed the Olympian gods and sided with my brothers the Titans, my punishment was to bear the weight of the world on my shoulders. Do you understand what that means?" Wilton asked Kala.

Kala felt like she was in high school when a teacher would call on her to answer a question that she had no clue what the answer was. She didn't like being perceived as uneducated or what she translated to as *stupid*. It was her biggest insecurity. That was why she made sure she was an expert in everything pertaining to her job, from guns to fighting techniques to thrill-seeking-bravery. Kala was the best at what she did. But if Wilton was trying to elusively tell her about a new mission, Kala wasn't getting it.

She answered tentatively, "I don't understand what that means in regards to me." Kala figured if she worded it in a way that personalized the message, then she wouldn't sound as dumb as she felt.

"It means, dear one, that carrying the weight of the world means something very different than actually *carrying* the world. It means that unless you do exactly what you're told to do, there will be a domino effect, and the world will end."

Kala sat there not sure how to respond to that.

If this was a test from Turner and Clifton she wasn't going to fail now.

"What do I have to do?" Kala thought she'd ask for details.

"Nothing you want to. I'm sorry, but you're going to have to do some pretty horrific things in order to keep the world safe. Every four days. One act of atrocity. For the greater good." Wilton took another sip from his espresso cup.

Kala felt this was all a little too dramatic. "An act of *atrocity*? That sounds ominous. What? I have to assassinate some terrorist who plans on blowing the world to smithereens? I think I can handle that." She had done it before and if taking out bad people was her only job description from now on, Kala was just fine with that.

Wilton laughed. "It wouldn't be an act of atrocity if you were killing bad guys, now would it?"

Kala's defenses immediately went up. "I'm not killing innocents. You can find someone else for that."

"You'll do what you're told, or the world will burn. That's a fact. There has to be a balance between good and bad. And that was my punishment. I'm the balancer. Without me there is only chaos," Wilton said each word like he was driving in a nail.

"If it's your job, then you do it." Kala shrugged defensively.

Wilton smiled a Cheshire-cat grin. "I don't have to. That's what you humans are for. I tricked one of you thousands of years ago into taking my place and not one of you has figured out how to break it ever since." Wilton took a sip of his espresso with extreme pleasure. "Now I can sit back and let you guys do my job. I like to think of it as retirement."

Kala sat back in her chair and ran her hands through her hair. *Atlas? Really?* It sounded so preposterous, she didn't know whether to laugh or admit herself into the nearest mental ward. Assuming of course she could find a mental ward outside of the abandoned town she was in.

Kala tried to steady her pounding heart. She had to think of this as a mission from General Turner or General Clifton or an extremely vivid dream. There simply was no other explanation for it. Kala didn't think she could go through with whatever the two Generals had in mind, but she knew it would do no good to argue with… the President.

Kala forced a smile. "I'll do what you want. Can I go now?"

Wilton stared at Kala with eyes that said he completely saw through her, but he slowly nodded his head. "You'll have to see for yourself, I guess."

He took a deep breath, "You're going to be hunted by things you don't even know exist. Our time is short, so here are the rules. First, you are technically what I would call my surrogate, which means you'll have all of my responsibilities, but none of my powers." He annoyingly flexed a muscle. "I'm pretty strong in the outside world."

"Awesome." Kala tried very hard to hide the snark from her tone, but failed miserably. One thing she knew for sure, if he really was a god, then gods were irritating.

Of course Atlas/Wilton ignored her completely. "Second, you should see your mission right away in a vision. It may come to you in a dream, it may come to you in a fish bowl; it all depends on how your brain wants to see it."

This was already way over Kala's head, but she just wanted it to be over at this point so she muttered, "Okay."

"Third, you can't get out of this deal. So don't try. The only way out is to have someone kill you so that they become the next Atlas. And trust me, there are a lot of people and non-people out there that want to be the next Atlas."

Non-people? Kala really didn't want to know.

"I've already taken too long explaining. You'll have to learn on your own. I hate to say it, but I don't think you'll survive your first mission. I'll be meeting with the new Chosen One tomorrow, or a couple of days from now if you're lucky."

"Thanks for the confidence," Kala mumbled sarcastically. Whether or not this was all happening in her brain, her competitive nature actually took offense at Wilton's lack of faith in her.

Kala stood up and made forced eye contact with Wilton. "I'll complete my mission and there isn't a thing on earth that I can't shoot. Believe me, I've shot plenty."

Wilton grinned. "Me being no exception," he said and the bullet hole that Kala gave him materialized on his forehead, gushing blood. "Clock starts now."

A giant round clock, well over ten feet in diameter, suddenly appeared in the air above them. Instead of twelve numbers there were four, each with twenty-four hour segments in-between counting down. A second hand moved almost too slow to notice, starting on day 3, hour 23, minute 59, second 59...58...57...

Wilton shrugged as if to say he was sorry, but his eyes showed that he wasn't sorry at all. He was amused. "I hope you last. I find you quite entertaining."

"Thanks?" Kala wasn't sure how to respond.

Wilton's face turned serious. "Time to go."

A flash of white light engulfed Kala completely, and she felt like she was dying.

DAY ONE

Chapter Five

Everything came into quick focus as the white light dimmed enough for Kala to see she was lying on a bed in the infirmary. She sat up with a jolt and took in deep breaths as if she had just woken up from a bad dream and needed to calm herself. Then Kala realized that she probably *had* woken up from a bad dream and began to relax.

"You're awake," Derek's voice sounded from behind her.

Kala turned her head to see Derek's smiling face looking down at her.

"How long have I been out?" Kala asked.

"An hour, maybe two," Derek answered gently.

Kala rolled the dream over and over in her head. The insanity of it all was actually quite funny if she thought hard enough about it. She couldn't figure out how her brain managed to think up a mash-up of Greek mythology and elite mission assignments, but it wasn't that much of a stretch considering…

"The President?" she asked tentatively.

Derek shook his head. "Dead. Jack and Lali are in with General Turner and General Clifton now explaining what happened. I wanted to make sure someone was here when you woke up."

Kala leaned back into her pillows. "Am I going to be executed or something?" She really hoped the answer wasn't going to be yes.

"Not if Jack has anything to say about it. I was there too, you know. Wilton made his intentions clear: he was going to kill a lot of innocents if you hadn't taken him out." Derek's loyalty knew no bounds and apparently that included her shooting the President.

Kala rubbed her hand over her face trying to wake herself up. "I had the craziest dream when I was out."

Derek plopped down on a chair next to Kala and smiled. "After what we just went through? I'll bet."

Kala looked around the infirmary and remembered why she hated this place so much. It felt like a sterile bandage made into a room. White and chrome. All the sheets and blankets reeked of bleach and felt scratchy against Kala's skin. There were a hundred beds filling up the room in three even rows — all empty except for Kala's. Her bed was in the back row near the side exit, which was a small comfort that at least Kala could make a run for it if Turner and Clifton decided she needed to be axed. She hated to be paranoid, but she *did* shoot the President. No matter how crazy the circumstances, Kala didn't think she'd get off that easy.

There was a digital clock on the wall behind her and she craned her neck around to see exactly what time it was.

Her heart stopped.

Kala blinked her eyes several times, hoping to see something different than what she was seeing.

Derek looked at her with worry. "What is it?"

"What does that clock say to you?" Kala's voice was breathless.

"5:07 A.M.," Derek said, studying Kala carefully. "Why?"

Kala blinked over and over, trying to see what Derek saw.

But it wasn't going away.

The clock was counting down.

3d 23h 53m 42s.

41…40…39…38…

Kala turned her head around and grabbed her chest.

Derek stood up and held her shoulder with concern, "Kala, you're freaking me out right now."

Kala turned away from the clock, then looked back at it, praying it would just show her the time like it was supposed to.

But the countdown continued.

"Let me see your cell?" Kala demanded impatiently.

Derek eyed her worriedly. Kala could tell he was trying to figure out why his friend was acting bonkers. Little did he know just how bonkers she was, but Kala didn't want to fall into a full-blown panic attack without checking a few things first.

"You know we're in a dead zone, right?" Derek prodded cautiously.

"Would you just please let me see your phone?" Kala tried to sound as calm and casual as possible.

But she could tell she wasn't fooling Derek for a second. He knew her too well.

He handed over his cell phone.

Kala closed her eyes taking the phone from his hand blindly, terrified at what she would see.

"You ask to see my phone and yet you have your eyes closed," Derek's voice sounded incredulous.

Kala opened her eyes fast, like tearing off a bandage. She swiped the phone open and she felt like she wanted to cry.

Just like the clock behind her, Derek's cell phone displayed the same countdown instead of the time.

It hadn't been a dream at all.

Or…

Kala felt a shred of hope race through her.

"Have there been any reported side effects to phase-suits? Besides losing body parts?" Kala's eyes were wide as she asked Derek.

Derek just stared at her, obviously trying to figure out where Kala's brain was. "Not that I know of, but we could ask one of the technicians. What is all this about? You've been acting funny all night. First, you think the tequila is making you hallucinate and now you're obsessed with clocks."

Kala tried to hide her emotions.

She *had* been hallucinating all night. The woman with the glowing eyes, the café in the middle of nowhere with the President, and now all clocks seemed to be counting down. It couldn't be the phase-suits.

She took a deep breath. "I need General Turner to test me for drugs. I think I was slipped something at the bar. I've been seeing things that aren't there all night."

Even with Derek's dark complexion, his face paled. "You can't do that," he said, real fear etched into his voice.

Kala knew why he was so upset. If she asked to be tested and her blood came back positive for drugs, she would most undoubtedly be executed for the death of the President. But Kala had to know. She had to know what was happening to her. She just couldn't accept that she was now working for some mythological god that wanted her to keep the world from destroying itself. It was too crazy to consider.

"Look, I know someone who can test your blood, but you're not telling either General. You are not, you hear me?" Derek was adamant.

"Take it now and it's a deal." Kala wasn't about to leave that room until Derek had a sample of her blood in hand.

He nodded and left the room for a few minutes, returning with a syringe. Derek sloppily took a sample of Kala's blood. Their whole team had been medically trained for the field, but they rarely had to use any of their skills, and Derek wasn't exactly the smoothest when it came to needles. Still, he managed to get the job done, though Kala knew she'd have a giant bruise on the inside of her arm where he punctured her with the needle.

At that moment, Jack walked in with a somber expression on his face.

Derek hid the sample of blood in one of his cargo pants pockets.

Kala's heart beat faster when she saw Jack looking at her with concern in his eyes.

"You okay?" he asked.

Kala wanted to jump out of her bed and run into Jack's arms, but Derek was there and now more than ever she didn't want anyone knowing of their affair. After what she'd done to the President, it was better to keep everything as professional as possible.

Jack walked over to her bedside and placed his hand on Kala's forehead as if he was checking for a fever, but she knew he just needed to touch her. The light touch of his hand sent a thrill down her spine. It took every ounce of self-restraint Kala possessed not to pull him down and kiss him. Jack must have felt the same because he quickly took his hand away and turned his attention to Derek.

"Can we have a few minutes?" Jack ordered more than asked.

Derek nodded, giving Kala one last look of support and tapping the pocket that held her blood sample. At least she would know if that tequila had been laced with some kind of drug. It would explain so much, although Kala didn't know if she could live with herself if she had assassinated the President because she had been on drugs. She needed to know from Jack that she had done the right thing, hallucinogens or not.

After Derek left the room, Jack leaned down and kissed Kala with as much passion as she had ever felt. She could literally feel her arms forming goose bumps it was so intense. When Jack pulled away it was torturous, her lips ached for him to kiss her like that again.

Jack gently stroked her cheek with his hand. "Why did you kill him? I told you he was my responsibility to take out."

Kala could see that Jack was truly hurt by her actions. What she couldn't figure out was why? What did it matter if she killed him over Jack? She decided to give him a tactical answer. "I'm a better shot and I had an opening, you didn't."

Jack closed his eyes as if her answer pained him.

For some reason, Jack's response upset her more than it should. "Why are you so upset? They're going to execute me, aren't they?" Kala suspected it before, but seeing Jack's intense pain only solidified it. She was going to pay for what she did. Right or wrong, an American does not harm the President. Period.

Jack opened his eyes, surprised. "No, of course not. I gave my report and so did the others, including the entire Secret Service on board. No one faults you. It was… it was just… it was *my* job. That's all." He turned his eyes away to avoid contact.

"What is going on with you, Jack?" Kala was confused: if she wasn't going to be punished, then why was Jack so upset? And why had he been so adamant to have the kill shot, she was the sniper of the team for God's sake! It was her job to take impossible shots. Why would it be any different in this situation?

The look Jack gave Kala was so full of fear and indecision it made Kala flinch.

Then she saw flash of… what? Anger? Regret? Panic?

"Jack?" Kala's voice was barely a whisper. She couldn't explain it, but for a second it almost looked like Jack was going to hurt her. It was such a shock, Kala froze.

And just as suddenly, Jack was leaning in and kissing Kala once more. It was desperate like he was saying good-bye.

Kala pulled back, but held Jack's face in her hands, forcing eye contact. "What is going on? You're acting really weird."

Jack reached out and rested a hand on top of Kala's. "Nothing. I'm just glad you're safe." He gently removed her hands from his face and kissed them lovingly. "General Turner and General Clifton want to debrief you personally."

That jolted Kala out of the mood.

Kala had never met either general, and they scared the bejeezus out of her. She knew with the gravity of what had happened that she'd have to explain herself to the big guns, but it still made her nervous.

Kala just hoped they wouldn't kill her.

Chapter Six

After changing out of the hospital gown and into her fatigues, Kala made her way down a long black hallway to the assigned debriefing room, trying not to sweat. For a super-elite soldier, Kala felt like a wimp. It didn't matter what job someone did, explaining yourself to your boss was always a nerve-wracking ordeal.

Especially if you've shot the President in the head. Kala thought to herself. She didn't care how much reassurance she'd had from Derek and Jack, Kala still wasn't sure she wasn't about to be shot herself.

Kala arrived at the door leading to her doom. At least that was what it felt like. She took a deep breath and opened the metal door.

It was hard not to gulp when she entered the room.

Dead center was a small metal table with two men sitting behind it. And they looked angry.

There were no windows and only one door, which happened to be the one Kala was walking through. The walls were made of the same black metal that the Compound was built with. Sleek overhead lights barely lit up the room, making the two generals appear almost dark and sinister.

General Turner sat on Kala's left, looking angry with a hint of amusement in his eyes. Kala thought he was a handsome man. He was in his forties, young for his position. He had only slight hints of gray in his dark hair and his face was chiseled with a strong chin and straight nose. Turner radiated power. He was almost too intimidating to look at, let alone have a conversation with. On Kala's right was General Clifton. Though Kala knew they were around the same age, General Clifton appeared older to her with his cropped gray hair and overly tanned skin. Being out on desert missions for so long had given him a kind of leathery look, like he'd been weather-proofed. He was intimidating as well, not because he emanated power, but because he looked mean. If anyone was going to call for Kala's head, it would be Clifton.

Kala respectfully saluted the two generals. Neither general saluted her back, which made her immediately on edge.

"Please, sit." General Turner motioned to the empty chair across from them.

Kala immediately did as she was told and sat down in the metal chair. She knew better than to talk first, being so vastly outranked, so she waited for one of them to speak.

It felt as if hours passed, waiting there in silence, but Kala knew it had only been seconds when General Turner spoke again. "Lieutenant Hicks, please tell us your side of the events."

Kala told them everything that happened from when she phased through the wall to when she blacked out. She refrained from telling them about having a cup of espresso with the dead President and how all clocks looked like a four-day countdown. No sense in giving them any more reason to call for a rope and a tree!

When she finished, General Clifton leaned forward. "You're not telling us everything."

His eyes were cold and calculating and Kala wasn't sure how to respond. She knew he was right, she *was* holding back, but what was she going to say? *I think I was drugged. Yes, I shot the President, drugged. Oh, and after he was dead he told me he was Atlas, yes, Atlas from Greek mythology.* Kala felt sick at the thought.

"I told you everything I know, sirs," Kala said lamely.

Turner didn't look angry like Clifton, he just looked like he was studying every facet of Kala's face. After a moment he said, "I'm inclined to agree with General Clifton here. You're definitely hiding something. If every last soldier hadn't just come in here and told the exact same story you did, we'd be having you executed right now."

Kala said nothing. She still wasn't convinced that she was going to leave the Compound alive.

Turner sat back, never breaking eye contact with Kala. "You do realize that the whole purpose of this operation here is to be the President's right arm?"

Kala nodded, terrified to say anything.

"And you killed him," Turner drove his point home.

"Yes, sir," Kala responded. What else could she say? They were going to do whatever they wanted with her and nothing she said would change that.

Clifton shook his head, disgusted. "We've informed the White House that the President was killed in the plane crash."

"The plane crashed, sir?" Kala asked before she could stop herself. Kala didn't know what happened after she blacked out, but a crash? How did everyone survive?

Clifton shot an annoyed expression at Kala, whereas Turner simply answered her question. "Lieutenant Lali Mills landed the plane in the ocean. Once everyone was evacuated, Harry had it torched."

Kala realized that *Harry* was General Clifton. He didn't look like a Harry. Harry's were supposed to be good-old-boys, not scary looking a-holes. This Harry looked like the kind of guy who would enjoy torching things. But Kala wasn't about to share her opinion of her superiors right this moment, she was just thankful they couldn't read minds.

So they had faked a plane crash. It wasn't the first time, but Kala felt a small shred of relief because no one would be looking for an assassin. If the public thought it was an accident, then her odds of surviving the night seemed better than she had first hoped.

Turner unexpectedly turned to Clifton and asked quietly, "Could you give us a few minutes?"

General Clifton took a few seconds before he nodded. Kala thought he looked pissed, as if taking orders from Turner was like swallowing nails. She knew they were close, but obviously there was some tension between them. Kala recognized Clifton's green shade of jealousy. There was no contest, Turner just carried himself in a way that set him apart from most people. Kala thought Turner could be President himself he was so intimidating. And for a guy like Clifton, who didn't come close to Turner's presence, it had to eat away at him, no matter how close they were.

General Clifton stood up and walked past Kala, avoiding her as he exited the room. She was surprised she didn't hear him huff from pouting. She couldn't believe what a baby that guy was.

Of course, now she was left alone with *Mister Scary*. General Turner didn't say a thing, he simply stared at Kala. She waited patiently for him to make his move. Turner was the one with the real power and Kala was sure he was the man who would ultimately decide her fate.

SMASH!

Kala jumped out of her chair as Turner violently flipped over the table between them, crashing it against the wall. It was so shocking that Kala didn't know what to do. Rage fired hot in Turner's eyes. Kala knew this was it. General Turner was going to reach for her neck and squeeze until she died.

But instead, he just stood there, his eyes boring into hers.

Kala couldn't move. The chair behind her teetered and fell on its back from the force of her standing. It was an eerie CLANK in the silence.

"What aren't you telling me?" Turner seethed.

Kala knew he wasn't the kind of man that liked secrets. She suspected the reason he was in the position he was in today was because he knew how to extract information when necessary.

"You'll think I'm crazy," Kala blurted out the words before she could stop herself.

A part of Kala desperately wanted to tell someone of her insane hallucinations, but her boss? She knew it would be a huge mistake, but she couldn't seem to stop herself. "I blacked out, and I was drinking coffee with the President and he told me I'd have to do something horrible to save the world and he said he was Atlas and that I was the new Atlas and then I woke up," Kala rambled like the crazy person she felt she was.

After a few long moments, Turner started to laugh. Really laugh.

Hearing and seeing him so amused by her confession made Kala really think about what she had just said. To her surprise she found herself starting to laugh, too. Saying it all out loud made it sound like exactly what it was: ridiculous.

Turner reached out and shook Kala's hand warmly. "This was what you were hiding." He said it as a statement of fact. Somehow, he was able to tell that Kala had told him everything she knew.

"Now that I said it, it sounds idiotic, doesn't it, sir?" Kala felt comforted by Turner's hand in hers, like he was her lifeline to sanity.

Turner gently pulled his hand away and waved to the flipped table. "We can all be a bit dramatic at times."

Kala smiled and felt like she could tell General Turner anything. There was a warmth to him that reminded her of her foster dad. He oozed a charisma that made Kala proud that she was a part of his team. Of course, seconds before, she had been terrified of the man, but seeing him look at her with relief and kindness made her wonder how she could have ever been scared of him in the first place. She guessed the mixture of both were the reasons Turner was in the position he was in today.

The General motioned toward the door. "Dismissed, lieutenant."

Kala saluted and was about to turn around to exit when Turner added, "People have been known to black out using the phase-suits, and this was the first time they'd been used jumping into a moving plane. The air pressure alone could have caused you to black out."

Kala nodded in appreciation at Turner's explanation to make her feel better. "What about hallucinations, sir?" She thought she'd ask the source. As much as Kala would love to blame the air pressure and the phase-suits, it didn't explain why she was *still* hallucinating.

Turner thought a second, then shook his head. "You just had a bad dream. It wasn't real or a hallucination."

Not wanting to admit her current predicament with the clocks, Kala saluted General Turner once more and left. As she walked down the hallway, Kala wondered how long it would take before General Clifton would try and undermine Turner's decision to let her live. There was a tension between the two of those men. At some point it would come to a head, Kala just prayed the head wouldn't be hers.

Chapter Seven

After changing out of the hospital gown and into her fatigues, Kala made her way down a long black hallway to the assigned debriefing room, trying not to sweat. For a super-elite soldier, Kala felt like a wimp. It didn't matter what job someone did, explaining yourself to your boss was always a nerve-wracking ordeal.

Especially if you've shot the President in the head. Kala thought to herself. She didn't care how much reassurance she'd had from Derek and Jack, Kala still wasn't sure she wasn't about to be shot herself.

Kala arrived at the door leading to her doom. At least that was what it felt like. She took a deep breath and opened the metal door.

It was hard not to gulp when she entered the room.

Dead center was a small metal table with two men sitting behind it. And they looked angry.

There were no windows and only one door, which happened to be the one Kala was walking through. The walls were made of the same black metal that the Compound was built with. Sleek overhead lights barely lit up the room, making the two generals appear almost dark and sinister.

General Turner sat on Kala's left, looking angry with a hint of amusement in his eyes. Kala thought he was a handsome man. He was in his forties, young for his position. He had only slight hints of gray in his dark hair and his face was chiseled with a strong chin and straight nose. Turner radiated power. He was almost too intimidating to look at, let alone have a conversation with. On Kala's right was General Clifton. Though Kala knew they were around the same age, General Clifton appeared older to her with his cropped gray hair and overly tanned skin. Being out on desert missions for so long had given him a kind of leathery look, like he'd been weather-proofed. He was intimidating as well, not because he emanated power, but because he looked mean. If anyone was going to call for Kala's head, it would be Clifton.

Kala respectfully saluted the two generals. Neither general saluted her back, which made her immediately on edge.

"Please, sit." General Turner motioned to the empty chair across from them.

Kala immediately did as she was told and sat down in the metal chair. She knew better than to talk first, being so vastly outranked, so she waited for one of them to speak.

It felt as if hours passed, waiting there in silence, but Kala knew it had only been seconds when General Turner spoke again. "Lieutenant Hicks, please tell us your side of the events."

Kala told them everything that happened from when she phased through the wall to when she blacked out. She refrained from telling them about having a cup of espresso with the dead President and how all clocks looked like a four-day countdown. No sense in giving them any more reason to call for a rope and a tree!

When she finished, General Clifton leaned forward. "You're not telling us everything."

His eyes were cold and calculating and Kala wasn't sure how to respond. She knew he was right, she *was* holding back, but what was she going to say? *I think I was drugged. Yes, I shot the President, drugged. Oh, and after he was dead he told me he was Atlas, yes, Atlas from Greek mythology.* Kala felt sick at the thought.

"I told you everything I know, sirs," Kala said lamely.

Turner didn't look angry like Clifton, he just looked like he was studying every facet of Kala's face. After a moment he said, "I'm inclined to agree with General Clifton here. You're definitely hiding something. If every last soldier hadn't just come in here and told the exact same story you did, we'd be having you executed right now."

Kala said nothing. She still wasn't convinced that she was going to leave the Compound alive.

Turner sat back, never breaking eye contact with Kala. "You do realize that the whole purpose of this operation here is to be the President's right arm?"

Kala nodded, terrified to say anything.

"And you killed him," Turner drove his point home.

"Yes, sir," Kala responded. What else could she say? They were going to do whatever they wanted with her and nothing she said would change that.

Clifton shook his head, disgusted. "We've informed the White House that the President was killed in the plane crash."

"The plane crashed, sir?" Kala asked before she could stop herself. Kala didn't know what happened after she blacked out, but a crash? How did everyone survive?

Clifton shot an annoyed expression at Kala, whereas Turner simply answered her question. "Lieutenant Lali Mills landed the plane in the ocean. Once everyone was evacuated, Harry had it torched."

Kala realized that *Harry* was General Clifton. He didn't look like a Harry. Harry's were supposed to be good-old-boys, not scary looking a-holes. This Harry looked like the kind of guy who would enjoy torching things. But Kala wasn't about to share her opinion of her superiors right this moment, she was just thankful they couldn't read minds.

So they had faked a plane crash. It wasn't the first time, but Kala felt a small shred of relief because no one would be looking for an assassin. If the public thought it was an accident, then her odds of surviving the night seemed better than she had first hoped.

Turner unexpectedly turned to Clifton and asked quietly, "Could you give us a few minutes?"

General Clifton took a few seconds before he nodded. Kala thought he looked pissed, as if taking orders from Turner was like swallowing nails. She knew they were close, but obviously there was some tension between them. Kala recognized Clifton's green shade of jealousy. There was no contest, Turner just carried himself in a way that set him apart from most people. Kala thought Turner could be President himself he was so intimidating. And for a guy like Clifton, who didn't come close to Turner's presence, it had to eat away at him, no matter how close they were.

General Clifton stood up and walked past Kala, avoiding her as he exited the room. She was surprised she didn't hear him huff from pouting. She couldn't believe what a baby that guy was.

Of course, now she was left alone with *Mister Scary*. General Turner didn't say a thing, he simply stared at Kala. She waited patiently for him to make his move. Turner was the one with the real power and Kala was sure he was the man who would ultimately decide her fate.

SMASH!

Kala jumped out of her chair as Turner violently flipped over the table between them, crashing it against the wall. It was so shocking that Kala didn't know what to do. Rage fired hot in Turner's eyes. Kala knew this was it. General Turner was going to reach for her neck and squeeze until she died.

But instead, he just stood there, his eyes boring into hers.

Kala couldn't move. The chair behind her teetered and fell on its back from the force of her standing. It was an eerie CLANK in the silence.

"What aren't you telling me?" Turner seethed.

Kala knew he wasn't the kind of man that liked secrets. She suspected the reason he was in the position he was in today was because he knew how to extract information when necessary.

"You'll think I'm crazy," Kala blurted out the words before she could stop herself.

A part of Kala desperately wanted to tell someone of her insane hallucinations, but her boss? She knew it would be a huge mistake, but she couldn't seem to stop herself. "I blacked out, and I was drinking coffee with the President and he told me I'd have to do something horrible to save the world and he said he was Atlas and that I was the new Atlas and then I woke up," Kala rambled like the crazy person she felt she was.

After a few long moments, Turner started to laugh. Really laugh.

Hearing and seeing him so amused by her confession made Kala really think about what she had just said. To her surprise she found herself starting to laugh, too. Saying it all out loud made it sound like exactly what it was: ridiculous.

Turner reached out and shook Kala's hand warmly. "This was what you were hiding." He said it as a statement of fact. Somehow, he was able to tell that Kala had told him everything she knew.

"Now that I said it, it sounds idiotic, doesn't it, sir?" Kala felt comforted by Turner's hand in hers, like he was her lifeline to sanity.

Turner gently pulled his hand away and waved to the flipped table. "We can all be a bit dramatic at times."

Kala smiled and felt like she could tell General Turner anything. There was a warmth to him that reminded her of her foster dad. He oozed a charisma that made Kala proud that she was a part of his team. Of course, seconds before, she had been terrified of the man, but seeing him look at her with relief and kindness made her wonder how she could have ever been scared of him in the first place. She guessed the mixture of both were the reasons Turner was in the position he was in today.

The General motioned toward the door. "Dismissed, lieutenant."

Kala saluted and was about to turn around to exit when Turner added, "People have been known to black out using the phase-suits, and this was the first time they'd been used jumping into a moving plane. The air pressure alone could have caused you to black out."

Kala nodded in appreciation at Turner's explanation to make her feel better. "What about hallucinations, sir?" She thought she'd ask the source. As much as Kala would love to blame the air pressure and the phase-suits, it didn't explain why she was *still* hallucinating.

Turner thought a second, then shook his head. "You just had a bad dream. It wasn't real or a hallucination."

Not wanting to admit her current predicament with the clocks, Kala saluted General Turner once more and left. As she walked down the hallway, Kala wondered how long it would take before General Clifton would try and undermine Turner's decision to let her live. There was a tension between the two of those men. At some point it would come to a head, Kala just prayed the head wouldn't be hers.

Chapter Eight

Kala was so stunned she didn't move. The woman wore her wavy black hair down today, which only brought out her high cheekbones and chiseled face. Her blue eyes stared at Kala with annoyance. A part of Kala wondered if this woman was just another part of her crazy train. After all, the hallucinations *did* start with her glowing blue eyes.

"Are you going to let me in?" The woman looked agitated, giving the impression that the last place she wanted to be was anywhere near Kala Hicks.

"I'm still deciding if you're real or not." Kala decided to be honest. If this woman really wasn't real, then Kala was simply talking to herself anyway.

"Really? You're one of those?" The woman shook her head at Kala.

Kala wanted to punch her just because it would make her feel good, in fact…

PUNCH!

Right in the nose.

And it felt great.

To Kala's surprise the woman didn't try to tackle her to the ground like she'd secretly hoped. One thing that always made Kala feel better was a good fistfight. But this lady wasn't biting.

"Are you quite done?" the woman asked, annoyed.

Kala shrugged and held her hand out for the woman to enter.

After sneering in disgust at the state of Kala's abode, the woman said plainly, "It's time to get your things in order. Do you have any family you'd like to say goodbye to? A will? Anything like that?"

On instinct Kala reached into a kitchen drawer and pulled out her Beretta, pointing it at the woman. The silencer wasn't on it, so a shot would definitely alert the neighbors, but Kala wasn't about to let this ridiculous woman take her down. Albeit, it was the nicest way anyone had ever threatened Kala's life, which just made it all the more strange.

"Get out before I hurt you," Kala warned.

"Oh relax, I'm not going to kill you. I physically can't. But Jack is and he's on his way over." The woman said it so matter-of-factly that Kala almost missed the part where she said that Jack was coming to kill her.

Kala dropped her gun to her side in shocked confusion. "Wait. What?"

"This whole thing was an unfortunate mistake. Jack is the Chosen One, not you. You killed the Atlas, which is why *you are* the Atlas. Once Jack kills you the burden will fall on him. But unlike you, he's prepared for it," the woman said with an air of arrogance. "He's trained his whole life for this moment and you stole it from him. So, really, it's your fault you have to die."

Kala lifted her gun once more, wanting to shoot this lady just to keep her from talking. There it was again, this whole Atlas thing. She closed her eyes tightly and opened them quickly, hoping the woman would disappear. Kala's brain could not wrap around any of this as truth. It was just too much. Too weird. Too insane.

"Jack would never kill me," Kala said. She was surprised to hear the desperateness in her voice. The images of what she'd seen on the television still played in her head. If all this was true, then killing Jack was her "duty" as the new Atlas, whatever that meant. But there was no way she would ever hurt Jack, and Kala was positive there was no way he could hurt her either.

The woman laughed. "He'll do what he's told. The only reason I'm here is because I fell for his sappy plea to let you say good-bye to your family and put your affairs in order, yadda yadda. If it were up to me, he would have killed you in your sleep this morning and been done with it."

Kala couldn't seem to grasp everything that this woman was saying. All she knew was that insane-o lady wanted her dead and wanted Jack to do it. "Who are you?" Kala decided to ask finally.

This appeared to catch the woman off-guard as if she didn't introduce herself that often. "Penny," she said after a pause, then she looked at her watch impatiently. "If Jack doesn't get here promptly I'm afraid I'll have to take you to a safe house until he can kill you. You've made quite a mess in your wake."

Kala leveled her gun. "I'm not going anywhere with you."

Penny apparently had had enough of Kala and her gun. She walked over to Kala and made Kala pull the trigger straight into her forehead.

BAM!

After the gun fired, Kala dropped the Beretta in shock. Why would this woman want Kala to kill her?

But instead of a dead body, Penny stood in front of Kala with the same indignant look on her face. The newly made bullet hole closed up and healed before Kala's eyes as the bullet popped out of Penny's head, falling to the floor.

Penny shook her head. "I can't be killed, so don't bother trying to threaten me. It's annoying."

A strange screeching noise sounded from outside Kala's apartment. Kala turned to the window wondering what on earth would make such a sound.

Penny's face went pale. "Asmodeus."

Kala turned to Penny. "What's Asmodeus?"

"Not someone I ever want you to meet. You've really screwed things up, you know? If you hadn't blabbed that confession to your superior and whined about seeing the countdown, then we could have kept this whole thing under wraps. But now both sides know who the Atlas is. Know who *you* are. That's never happened before. EVER." Penny was beside herself with anger, but Kala noticed it was more than that. Penny was terrified.

Kala had zero idea of how to respond to any of this. The screeching sounded again and it chilled her to the bone. Whatever this Asmodeus was didn't sound friendly.

"I may not be able to kill you, but I'm sure as hell not going to sit around and wait for my boyfriend to kill me." Kala punched Penny as hard as she could and made a run for the door.

Penny was too fast. She was already blocking the door before Kala could reach the knob. Kala went for another swing, but Penny grabbed Kala's fist before it landed.

"I'm trying to help you," Penny scolded.

"You just said you were basically babysitting me until Jack came to take me out," Kala accused incredulously.

Penny tilted her head in grudging agreement, "Well, temporarily help you until he gets here."

Kala shook her head in frustration and tried to shove Penny aside using one of her Aikido moves, but Penny was inhumanly strong. She pushed Kala to the floor.

The screeching again, but this time sounding just outside the window.

Penny pulled Kala to her feet. She placed Kala behind her body protectively. This whole situation was completely surreal. For someone who claimed to want Kala dead, Penny was certainly acting as if she wanted to save her.

"Does this Asmodeus want me dead too?" Kala asked. She found that she wasn't really scared. It felt like she was in combat and under attack. Nothing felt more natural to her. It was when Kala did her best thinking.

Penny on the other hand was shaking with fear. "No, he wants you to fail. He wants the world to end."

Kala was sure this sentence would scare most people, but to her it was information on how to survive the upcoming attack. Whoever this Asmodeus was, he didn't want her to die. Not yet anyway, Penny on the other hand was counting down the minutes until Jack arrived to kill Kala. So Kala's choices were, Asmodeus, Penny or Jack?

It wasn't a question: Jack. This Penny girl might think Jack would kill Kala, but Kala knew Jack. He'd never let anything happen to her.

Taking advantage of standing behind Penny, Kala picked up the discarded gun and shot seven rounds into the back of Penny's head. Kala knew it wouldn't kill the woman, but she was sure it was give her at least a few seconds to escape. Penny dropped to the floor from the shock and probably pain of it.

Kala ran out the door and into the hallway at breakneck speed.

And sure enough, apparently healing fast, she heard Penny scream her name in rage.

Running down the exit stairs four at a time, Kala was surprised she didn't tumble to her death. The screeching penetrated through the walls and Kala began to know real fear. She'd been in countless combat attacks, but there was something about that sound...

It wasn't human.

Penny's pursuing footfalls thudded down the stairs above Kala. Kala knew Penny would be on her in seconds. Hitting the bottom floor, Kala pushed open the exit door and ran into the alleyway that lay between her apartment complex and the one next door.

The screeching was deafening outside. Whatever it was, it was close.

Asmodeus. *Whatever* or *whoever* that was.

Kala ran past her neighbors, who had run out of the apartment building thinking the noise was some kind of fire alarm. At least now she knew she wasn't making it up in her head, unless her hallucinations included imagining confused neighbors. No, Kala had survived her whole life trusting her instincts. And her instincts told her all of this was happening. She just wasn't sure what "all of this" actually was yet. Oh how she wished for the simple stress of countdown clocks!

Jack's car squealed to a halt in the parking lot. "GET IN!" he screamed at Kala.

Kala looked behind her to see Penny running out of the apartment building. When she saw Kala, her eyes flared blue.

Uh oh. Kala gulped. What was worse was how Penny was looking at Jack. I guess she didn't like the fact that Jack had come to rescue Kala and not kill her. Kala couldn't resist being smug.

As she opened the passenger door to get in, Kala smiled at Penny triumphantly.

Penny screamed in outrage and started to charge the car.

Kala slammed the car door shut as Jack hit the gas full throttle. Looking back through the window, Kala nearly gasped as a blur of black smoke completely engulfed Penny, followed by the screeching.

It appeared that Asmodeus was going to have to satisfy himself with Penny for the moment.

Flipping back around, Kala looked at Jack. He turned to her and his smile was slow and meaningful.

He simply said, "We need to talk."

Chapter Nine

"That's an understatement," Kala replied. She took a deep breath to steady herself, adrenaline pumping through her veins a mile a minute. It felt as if she had just cheated death, the biggest rush there was. Kala knew she needed to calm herself enough to process what was happening.

"What happened to you when you killed the President?" Jack asked.

Kala had been ready for explanations not questions, but the question jarred her a bit. If what Penny had said was true, then Jack had been preparing to kill the next Atlas his whole life and Kala had taken that away from him.

"I'll share all the details after you tell me what you know. That Penny girl says you have to kill me. Are you going to kill me, Jack?" Kala needed to see his response. To see if Jack was who she thought he was.

Jack didn't hesitate. "Never."

Kala took a few seconds to take that in, then she nodded. "Tell me what you know."

"Let's get somewhere safe first."

They drove the rest of the way in silence.

Kala took the trip as a breather to think about everything that had happened to her. She still couldn't quite grasp that what she had seen with the President was real, but so far everything that she'd witnessed made her come to some kind of truce with herself that she'd listen to Jack with an open mind. The one thing she didn't want to think about was the fact that, if all of this was real, then her "mission" was to kill Jack. That was not something Kala could do. Ever. So ultimately that meant she was going to fail. She just hoped that failing didn't mean what the President said it would mean: world destruction.

And, now that she was really thinking about it: WTF? Some screeching smoke monster named Asmodeus just engulfed an annoying woman named Penny that somehow can survive a round of bullets to the head. Kala guessed it wasn't any more farfetched than being an ancient Greek god that was saving the planet every four days, but still... Looney bin time.

After about a half hour of driving, Jack pulled into a diner on the outskirts of town. There wasn't anything special about the restaurant, it looked almost comforting to Kala after the ordeal she'd just been through. Large glass windows wrapped around the rectangular-shaped buildings and an old seventies style neon sign simply said: Nora's Diner. Kala didn't know who Nora was, but she had to be nicer than Penny.

Turning off the car engine, Jack turned to Kala. He grabbed her and pulled her close, kissing her passionately. Kala lost herself in that kiss. She let all the craziness of the past twenty-four hours wash away in the solace of Jack pressing up against her. It almost felt like they were teenagers sneaking away to a make-out-point the way they were going at it in the front seat of Jack's car. But Kala didn't care, she didn't want it to stop. Because she knew, when it did, more insanity would try and to suffocate her life.

Agonizingly, Jack finally pulled away, but he kept his hand on Kala's cheek. "I love you."

Jack kissed Kala gently, then drew back so their faces were only inches from each other. His eyes were intense — sad, happy, scared — anything and everything was going on behind them. So much so that Kala didn't know how to respond to his declaration. She wanted to tell him she loved him too, but her fear was a much stronger combatant, so she waited for him to say more.

His lips were still inches from hers, which made Kala want to pull him in for another kiss, but Jack spoke instead. "You don't have to say anything back. I don't expect you to, but Kala, you have to know that I love you and that I'll never let anything happen to you. I don't care what they want. Do you trust me?"

Kala found that she couldn't say much of anything, let alone confess her true feelings for Jack, so she simply nodded.

"Let's get something to eat." Jack tilted his head toward the diner. As if he couldn't resist himself, he kissed Kala one more time.

Kala was the first to break the kiss, and she smiled at Jack. "I'm starving."

The two of them entered Nora's Diner and found it almost empty. The décor was exactly what Kala expected: 70s vinyl booths with Formica table tops, black and white checkered linoleum floor, and the smell of grease. A large platter of steak fries and a cholesterol-filled patty melt was exactly what the doctor ordered. Kala looked up at the clock and had to do a double take. The countdown was more annoying now than freaky. Doing the math in her head was not something Kala was particularly good at. It said: 3d 18h 45m 21s. After what felt like an eternity, she finally asked Jack. "What the hell time is it?"

Jack gave her a momentary look of confusion, then understanding dawned on him. "Do all clocks countdown for you?"

Kala wasn't sure how she felt about Jack knowing so much more about her situation than she did, but she nodded anyway without her usual snarky comeback.

"It's 11:15," Jack answered. He motioned to the booth in the back of the diner and the two of them sat down.

After the waitress took their order, Jack took a deep breath as he looked at Kala. She felt the weight of his stare like an anvil of guilt. He finally spoke, "You must think you're going crazy."

Kala laughed at that. "I haven't ruled that out completely yet."

Jack reached across the table and held Kala's hands in his. She didn't pull away. "This is something I've been training for my whole life. My parents have been dreading and waiting for this day since I was born. And when it came down to it I choked."

"You didn't choke, I just had a better shot." Kala found that her first instinct was to make Jack feel better, not strangle him and ask him what the hell he was talking about. Sometimes she felt like such a girl! Kala decided to remedy that. "What have you been training for your whole life? This Atlas thing, or whatever?" Oh the elegance.

"Sounds mental, doesn't it?" Jack took his hands away when the waitress came to drop off their food.

Kala bit into the greasy deliciousness that was her patty melt and everything felt a little better. "It sounds more than mental, it sounds like a cheesy fairytale."

"Stories and myths always come from somewhere." Jack bit into his healthier turkey club.

"I was pretty solid on the fact that they came from writers," Kala couldn't resist the attitude. Like the scorpion and the frog, it was just in her nature.

"Not this time." Jack sighed. "Now they want me to kill you so I can be what everyone thinks I was destined to be."

"So, the only way to make a new Atlas is to kill the old one?" Kala decided to get a few things clarified.

Jack nodded, "But the Demons would rather the Atlases not accomplish their mission and let the world slip into chaos after the four-day time clock."

"Hold up. Demons?" Kala needed a bit of a rewind. Demons? Being a foster kid, religion was always forced down her throat before she lived with Owen and Linda. And Demons had always scared her the most. The thought of something so evil actually existing made her skin crawl.

Jack sat back, shaking his head. "There's so much you don't know. I had a whole lifetime to learn it. Yes, Demons. There are two sides: the Malaks and the Demons. The Malaks are the good guys like Penny. They're fighting for balance. But the Demons live for chaos and destruction. Asmodeus is their leader."

"First, off, Penny is not a good guy, she's a bitch. And second, Demons?" Kala still couldn't wrap her head around the fact that Demons were real. Not only that, but their leader was just at her apartment trying to… Kala didn't even know what exactly he was trying to do.

"Have you had your vision yet? The task you're supposed to complete to keep the balance?" Jack looked at Kala with genuine concern.

Kala sat there quietly. She couldn't tell him. How could she? What was she supposed to say, *Yes, my mission to save the world is to murder you.* Then again, Jack was completely honest about *his* mission to kill her and his refusal to carry it through.

"Not yet," Kala lied. There had to be some way out of this mess. This retired Atlas guy had underestimated Kala's tenacity to weasel out of situations. If there was a loop hole, Kala would find it.

As if on cue to Kala's misery, the waitress turned on the television. Sure enough, the scene of Kala shooting Jack in the head played again and again until Kala had to shield her eyes with her hand to stop from seeing it.

"You don't like car commercials?" Jack glanced at the TV and smiled.

"Not that one." Kala moved her hand away and kept her focus on Jack to distract her from the television.

"Normally the Demons have no knowledge of who the Atlas is. This is the first time both sides know who you are." Jack's voice was laced with worry.

"That's what Penny said. Is it because I told Turner?" Kala knew what the answer was, but she had to ask anyway.

Jack nodded. "Your confession went on record, including the part where you told the General about being the new Atlas. Information like that didn't take long to get into Asmodeus's hands. Now that the Demons know about you, they won't stop until they have you." Jack pushed away his sandwich as if the thought made him lose his appetite.

"Why wouldn't they just kill me, be the new Atlas and then wait out the apocalypse." Kala sounded a little too rational for her taste.

"Honestly? We don't know. We think it's because Demons don't know what would happen if they killed an Atlas. And what they don't know is dangerous, so locking you up in a hole for four days is a much safer bet," Jack explained. "It's the Malaks you have to watch out for. Right now they're focused on me being the next Atlas, but once they realize I'm not going to kill you, they'll bring in the next in line. Some other poor kid who's been raised to think they're the Chosen One. Penny is still fighting for me, but after the stunt I just pulled, she won't be able to defend my position much longer."

"So what you're telling me is that 'the good guys' are the ones trying to kill me and 'the bad guys' are too scared to kill me so they're just going to lock me up?" Kala asked incredulously. In her book, 'the bad guys' sounded like a much better alternative. Especially since Kala wouldn't have to kill Jack if they got their way. "Isn't there some way to break this curse?" Kala asked.

Jack didn't outright say Yes or No, he actually seemed to be thinking on it, finally admitting, "I don't know, Kala. I wish I could say 'yes,' but I don't see a way out. President Wilton seemed to think he'd figured out a way, but all I saw was a guy that was going to try and kill himself along with a butt load of people."

"I really wish we would have let him tell us his plan, maybe it could have worked." Kala would never have agreed to kill innocents.

"Maybe, but I've been told that there have been Atlases in the past who have tried to stop the cycle by killing themselves. But that's a part of the curse. You can't kill yourself. Anyone on the planet can kill you, but if *you* try to put a bullet to your head. Nothing. It would pop right out and heal."

"Like dear old Penny. Why can't she be killed?" Kala wanted to know. Honestly, knowing that she couldn't kill herself didn't make much difference to Kala since she would never in a million years try to commit suicide. She didn't care how bad things got, suicide was never the answer. Not for her anyway. But Penny? That girl couldn't be killed, by anyone. That was way more interesting!

"There's a lot more to Penny than even I know. She was my trainer when I was a kid and she looks exactly the same." Jack's face had a kind of far-off expression as if he were remembering better times.

"You know I unloaded my Beretta into the back of her head, right?" Kala made the *guilty face*. Though Penny wanted her dead, Kala still felt weirdly horrible about shooting a "good guy."

Jack smiled. "I'm sure that pissed her off." Then he looked serious. "Did you know she couldn't die before or after you shot?"

"Before! Geez." Kala defended herself, but she could see that Jack was teasing her. Kala inwardly rolled her eyes at the fact that they could tease each other about shooting people.

They could hear the screeching again. It was far off, but Kala knew with certainty that it had picked up their scent and was coming for her.

Jack knew it too. "Asmodeus. The Demons won't stop until they have you. Being the first time they've ever known who an Atlas is, they must be salivating. We have to get you out of here. As soon as you know what your mission is, you *have* to complete it. No matter how difficult. Agreed?"

Kala found it hard to hide her expression of horror at that statement, but she nodded. "Agreed." Lie. Glancing at the television playing Jack's death on repeat-o didn't exactly put her mind at ease either.

Then a terrifying thought hit her. "Is this going to be my life forever? Running from Demons and doing horrible things?"

Jack didn't answer, which to Kala was a resounding yes. She definitely needed to get herself out of this situation and pronto before it changed her life for good. The thought of being on the run for the rest of her life scared her. It was too much like her childhood, being placed in home after home, never feeling like she belonged anywhere. Owen and Linda changed all that for her and gave her a place in this world. And after leaving home, the military had become a sanctuary for her. To lose it all… for what? For *this*? A nightmare that Kala could barely believe was actually true. It was like someone telling her Santa Claus was actually real. Her rational mind wanted to laugh at the absurdity, but her instincts told her to run before the forces of nature swallowed her whole.

Kala followed Jack out of the diner and they headed to his car. "Seriously, where is safe?" Kala couldn't see a way out of confronting this Asmodeus Demon.

They jumped into Jack's car and Jack drove out of the parking lot and onto the road. Jack hadn't answered Kala's question, which made Kala think that he didn't have an answer.

"Jack, where are we going?" Kala wished she was driving, not that she knew where she would go, but it would give her more control.

"I don't know. The Compound? That's as secure as you can get," Jack suggested.

"We're not allowed in when we're not on missions," Kala reminded him. She found it funny that she was the calm and rational one in this situation. Jack seemed frazzled and scared, two things Kala never saw in him before last night. But he knew a lot more about what was happening than she did. Ignorance was bliss, or at least more easily coped with.

"I know a place," Jack said as if a light bulb just went off in his head. They were well outside the city now, on the highway headed to the middle of Virginia. Jack exited on a side road that led to a forested area.

"We're going to hide out in trees?" Kala asked skeptically. She was a city girl: the thought of hiding in nature was actually less appealing than facing this head Demon guy. There was something about being in the dark in a forest that was so much eerier than being in an alley at night. The alley, it was a familiarity, a feeling of being able to escape. In a city Kala always had an escape plan no matter where she was, but nature? What could she do? Climb a tree? It was starting to upset her more than she cared to admit. "Do you have any guns? I need guns."

"Guns don't work on Demons or Malaks, you're kind of screwed in that department," Jack informed her.

"Then how am I supposed to defend myself? How were you going to defend yourself?" Guns were her safety net. Being told that her one form of defense wouldn't work on what was chasing her made Kala feel vulnerable.

"There are other ways. I'll show you. There's a cabin up here in the woods that I was planning on making my base. It's yours now," Jack said.

Kala couldn't help but feel Jack was playing the "mentor" role. Worse, he seemed to be enjoying it. Jack dodged a bullet when Kala shot the President. This life that she was experiencing was supposed to be his. What horrible thing would Jack have had to do if he had completed his mission and became the next Atlas? It wouldn't have been to kill himself, since being the Atlas meant you couldn't actually kill yourself. That made Kala think. Why did she have to kill Jack? *He* was supposed to be the Chosen One, the champion, so why would killing him save the world? It didn't make sense. None of it did.

They were driving on dirt roads now, traveling deep into the woods. Luckily, it was early afternoon so it wasn't nearly as scary. It would almost be beautiful if Kala didn't hate nature so much. To Kala outdoors equaled bugs, wild animals, birds (Kala hated birds!), weird smelling air and an eternal dampness that she could never seem to shake.

But Kala didn't have to worry about it long.

The black smoke that swallowed Penny earlier suddenly appeared in front of their car.

Jack floored the gas pedal to try and drive through it, but the smoke engulfed the entire car like a black fog. Kala couldn't see out the window, but she could feel that the car had stopped. Or rather, the tires were rotating wildly, but the smoke lifted the car off the road so all Kala could feel was the vibration of spinning wheels.

Kala looked at Jack as if he would have some answer of what to do next. Before Jack could say anything the screeching sound came back full force. Kala had to cover her ears it was so deafening.

"Okay, we get it! You have me, now shut the hell up!" Kala screamed.

Nothing like pissing off the leader of the Demons. But Kala didn't care, she just wanted the noise to stop. It was making every one of her nerves raw and she thought her head would explode.

To Kala's surprise and relief, the screeching stopped.

The car thudded to the ground with a jolting THWAP, and the black smoke dissipated. Jack hit the gas, but the car was dead, as in, click… click… click went the starter.

Kala watched through the front windshield as the black smoke started to take shape into…

…a really hot guy.

Chapter Ten

Kala hadn't been sure what she was going to see, but a guy that looked like he stepped out of a GQ Magazine definitely wasn't it. When she heard the word *Demon* she expected horns or red skin or something devil-y. Asmodeus was well over six feet tall and Kala could see he was completely cut underneath his "little too low" v-neck t-shirt and perfectly faded jeans. Kala wondered when Demons had the time to work out. The thought would have made her laugh if she wasn't so freaked out. His hair was sandy brown and cut in a faux-hawk style. It framed his perfectly chiseled face with a perfectly straight nose, slightly full lips that were in permanent sexy-pout mode, and bright brown eyes that were currently staring at Kala.

"Are you coming out?" Asmodeus asked like he was talking to a naughty child trying to evade punishment.

"Don't go," Jack warned.

Kala shook her head at Jack. "He's not going to kill me. Just watch my back." At least she hoped Asmodeus wasn't going to kill her. Kala was betting on a theory, but at this point she didn't feel she had much choice. She was always a leap-before-she-even-knew-if-there-was-a-net kind of girl.

Before Jack could argue, Kala exited the car.

Kala could feel Asmodeus's eyes follow her every move as she warily approached him. Though he looked like a human, his presence was ominous. Every fiber of Kala's being wanted to run into the trees and hide he was so intimidating. It just seemed to radiate off him like waves of power. Kala felt a surge of panic race through her. She was trying to comprehend the fact that she had just watched black fog turn into a human being. A Demon. What did that mean anyway? He looked so normal. Like a million guys Kala had seen before. Like a million guys that had hit on her before. If only there was a bar stool to hit him with.

"What's up?" Kala said before she could stop herself. *Really? What's up?*

Asmodeus smiled, but there was no humor in it. "I finally get to meet an Atlas and you're an idiot. So disappointing."

"About as disappointing as finding out the leader of the Demons looks like a frat boy douche bag. You might as well be wearing Ed Hardy, dude." Kala's attitude was a reflex when someone insulted her.

"Interesting," Asmodeus said. He didn't look offended, but he didn't look happy either. "It's *King* by the way. King of Demons."

Kala knew the only way to figure out how to permanently throw Asmodeus off her trail was to find out as much about him as she could. More importantly, she needed to learn how he was tracking her. Of course, none of that would be possible if she kept putting her foot in her mouth, so she decided to play nice.

"Well, you've got me, your highness. Now what?" That was about as nice as Kala could muster.

Kala could hear Jack trying to get out of the car, but somehow Asmodeus had sealed the doors shut. She glanced at Jack and knew she was on her own.

Asmodeus stepped forward and caressed his hand against Kala's cheek. It was so sudden and unexpected, Kala just stood there staring up at Asmodeus's brown eyes. If she didn't know he was a Demon, Kala would have kicked him where it counts. But did Demons even have private parts? She knew they had powers and that was all that mattered in this moment. Kala didn't want Asmodeus to hurt Jack. Or her for that matter.

"You are a beautiful creature," Asmodeus smiled at Kala, examining her like a prize horse.

Kala took a step back so Asmodeus was out of reach. "No touching, perv." She just couldn't seem to stop herself.

Asmodeus looked shocked at Kala's behavior. She knew in that moment that no one had ever turned this guy down before. He was apparently used to women falling at his feet, drooling over his good looks. Kala never cared for conceited guys. They cared more about mirrors than they did anything else. She liked a little humble with the men she was attracted to. Like Jack. Gorgeous, but didn't know it, or didn't care. This guy… or Demon… or whatever… was completely full of himself, thinking he was god's gift to all women (or men for all Kala knew).

Asmodeus moved forward, grabbing Kala's arm. Instinct kicked in and she flipped him on his back, her knee to his throat. Instead of trying to release himself from her pin-down, Asmodeus laughed. "A fighter. I like it."

Asmodeus touched her leg…

…And Kala found her surroundings shift out of focus. Jack, the car, the forest and Asmodeus all disappeared in a flash. She felt like she was on a terrible acid trip, or at least what she thought an acid trip would feel like.

Just as abruptly, everything snapped back into focus.

Well, Kala definitely wasn't in nature anymore, and she was completely alone. Kala wasn't sure where she was, but it was definitely in some kind of high-rise. An entire wall made up of tinted windows overlooked a vast cityscape. Kala knew that cityscape. It was New York! The fact that this Asmodeus dude transported her from the forests of Virginia to New York City in about two seconds was beyond Kala's comprehension. In fact, this whole day was beyond her comprehension. The room (or she should say floor) itself was abandoned. There wasn't any furniture, there wasn't anything in it at all, just a steel gray industrial carpet and windows. Somehow this wasn't what she imagined a "Demon lair" to look like. There was only one door, and it looked like it was made of titanium. A small keypad was bolted on the wall next to it. Kala had seen that kind of keypad before at the Compound. It might be easy to crack. She couldn't be sure until she looked at it.

But Kala's problem wasn't breaking out of the room (she was certain she could do that), it was what she would do after she escaped. This Asmodeus guy could find her anywhere and apparently transport her 200 miles in a few seconds. Kala had no idea how she was going to keep him from finding her over and over. Maybe there was some kind of super high-tech suit or device at the Compound that would do the trick. But even if there were, she'd have to convince General Turner that she needed to use it, and somehow that seemed more impossible than her current situation. After all, when she had confessed what happened to her, he flat out laughed out loud. So did she, but things had changed since the last time they met.

The bottom line: Kala had no intention of going through with her mission, so really Asmodeus had nothing to worry about. Maybe she could use that.

Kala called out to air. "I don't know if you can hear me, but you don't have to keep me locked up. I'm not going to do what they want me to do."

Nothing.

"Hello?" Kala was really hoping she wasn't talking to herself. She had to assume that Asmodeus wouldn't leave her completely unattended. The place had to be bugged or have some kind of spying capabilities, even if they were supernatural ones.

Then a sudden thought hit her. "We could help each other out. I saw my vision. The one that tells me what I have to do in order to stop the world from collapsing or whatever. But I'm not going to do it, and you could help me protect who they want me to kill."

Like a cheesy magician, Asmodeus formed out of a puff of black smoke in front of her. Kala almost wanted to laugh. She guessed he had taken her "douche-bag" fashion comments seriously because he was now dressed in dark looser-fitting jeans and a nice button up shirt with only one button unbuttoned. Of course, now he looked like a Banana Republic model, but at least he was putting in an effort. Although Kala didn't know if she should be scared or flattered that he cared enough to listen to her insults. Maybe he needed adoration more than she had guessed. The fact that she had no interest in him whatsoever must have really bothered him.

Good, she thought to herself. *Even Demons are typical males.*

"What is your task?" Asmodeus asked Kala with curiosity. Kala could tell that having one of these Atlases in front of him was extremely exciting to Asmodeus. She figured he'd probably been hunting them down for decades, maybe thousands of years, so to have one standing in front of him, must have been mind-blowing.

Kala decided she'd just be honest. She really believed that Asmodeus was the key to saving Jack. "To kill Jack."

Kala looked Asmodeus in the eye and with as much intensity as she could muster added, "And I will *never* do that. Will you help protect him and get us somewhere safe?" she asked.

A plan was forming in Kala's head as she talked. If Asmodeus could find her anywhere, maybe he could disguise her anywhere, too. At this point, Kala just wanted this whole thing to be over. And to be completely honest, Kala felt that if she didn't kill Jack the world wouldn't end. Maybe this would be the way to break the Atlas curse: not do anything. Kala just wanted Jack to be safe, and though it was hard for her to admit, she wanted to be safe with him. Jack had said he loved her and she had said nothing back. Kala wanted to show him how much she loved him. By saving him.

Asmodeus stared at Kala in dumb shock. After a moment he finally spoke, "You're serious."

"Deadly," Kala confirmed. "I didn't ask for this. I still don't believe I'm not having the most surreal roofie trip of my life. But, trip or not, I'm not killing Jack." Kala felt tears welling up in her eyes. Just saying the words *killing Jack* out loud were painful. In that moment she didn't care if the world did collapse, as long Jack was alive. It was the first time Kala truly understood why someone would pick 'the one' over 'the many.'

Asmodeus smiled at Kala and she found it frightening. Though she had expected Demons to look like horned devils, having a stunning looking man stare at her with ancient eyes was way more terrifying. "This is not at all what I expected. It makes me wonder how many Atlases I could have made deals with, if I could have found them."

"How did you find me? Do I have a smell or something?" Kala wanted his help, but she also wanted to ditch the guy.

"Smell?" Asmodeus laughed. Kala had to admit, he looked almost normal when he laughed. "No. Once I touch a human, I can find them anywhere in the world. People are all unique, like a signature."

"Signatures can be forged." Kala tried to punch a hole in his theory, or at least tried to think of a way to disguise her "signature."

"But souls cannot." Asmodeus grinned maliciously.

He had her there. How could Kala disguise her soul? Yeah, that wouldn't be hard at all!

"Does Penny have the same ability to track me as you do? Can you hide me from her and the Molonies or whatever?" Kala worried about "the good guys" finding them and trying to force Jack to kill her, or worse, trying to make her kill him, or even worse, finding out her mission and killing Jack themselves!

"Malaks," he corrected Kala. "And yes, they have the same ability, but I can hide you from them. *Rearrange* your soul, if you will. I can shift your DNA slightly so you won't be recognized. Of course, if they see you by sight, there's nothing I can do, but I'd assign a couple of my Demons to protect you." Asmodeus was watching Kala like a cat eyeing a toy.

She wasn't exactly sure what that meant, "rearrange your soul," but Kala decided to give him the benefit of the doubt. What choice did she have? "Let's do this, then." Kala rubbed her hands together, ready to go.

Asmodeus paused. "You haven't noticed my new appearance."

"I noticed." Kala didn't know why, but she liked messing with Asmodeus. She was still fascinated by the fact that he actually cared what she thought of his appearance.

"And?" Asmodeus prodded.

Kala could tell that he was irked, but he was still trying to squeeze a compliment out of her. This was the wrong tactic on a girl like Kala.

"Are we going to get Jack or what?" Kala evaded Asmodeus's baiting on purpose.

Asmodeus's eyes grew round with rage, but he managed to stay calm as he said, "I can make you mine if I want."

"If you did that then I wouldn't care if Jack died or not. I might actually try and complete my mission," Kala said as if Asmodeus's threat was the most ridiculous thing she ever heard. But his threat scared her. She didn't want to lose the only real feelings she ever had for anyone, and Kala had no doubt that Asmodeus could erase Jack from her brain with a snap of his fingers.

Asmodeus stepped closer to Kala and pulled her in, kissing her. Kala did not kiss back. She had been in this situation before and she decided to find out if Demons had private parts. Kala kneed him in the groin, when Asmodeus keeled over, she punched him in the face with both hands clasped together. Asmodeus flew backward and landed on his rump. His face was etched in pure shock. He stared at Kala like she was a foreign object he'd never seen before.

"That's the second time you've attacked me," he said as if the idea was unfathomable to him.

"Quit trying to kiss me! I'm not interested." Kala wanted to be as clear as possible. She thought being around for thousands of years a guy could take a hint. Apparently not.

Asmodeus got back up as gracefully as possible after being leveled by Kala.

"I'm going to help you. But not in the way you want." Asmodeus's eyes were alight with malice.

"What's that supposed to mean?" Kala froze in place from fear.

"Sleep," Asmodeus said.

Kala dropped to the floor.

DAY TWO

Chapter Eleven

Kala woke up in her bed with a start. She threw back the sheets and jumped out like a rat had crawled over her feet. It took her a few seconds to calm herself down as she surveyed her surroundings. Kala was definitely at home. This was definitely her bedroom. And through the doorway was definitely the rest of her apartment.

She sat down on the mattress with a huge sigh.

It had been a dream.

A horrible, vivid dream.

Kala tried to remember the details of it all, but the dream was slipping away from her, as most dreams do. It had felt so real at the time, but the more she tried to focus on remembering, the less she could remember. In fact, Kala couldn't seem to recall what she was supposed to do at all. Did she have a job? Did she have friends? She couldn't remember any of it. Kala thought this should make her panic, but it didn't. It was somehow comforting not knowing anything. She wondered how she could have been so upset about a stupid dream.

A knock on the door brought her out of her reverie.

Kala wondered who it could be? She was sure she didn't know a soul.

Throwing on a t-shirt and jeans, Kala walked to the front door and opened it.

A beautiful man stood in front of her, dressed in jeans and a t-shirt. His sandy brown hair was perfectly messy, framing his chiseled features. He looked at Kala with stunning brown eyes that seemed to pierce her very soul. "Are you going to let me in?" he asked as if they were the best of friends.

And then it occurred to Kala, that this was Asmodeus, her amazingly gorgeous boyfriend. How could she have forgotten? She felt incredibly guilty. Kala thought she must have had one too many drinks the night before to forget Asmodeus. He was always so kind to her and she remembered how much she loved him.

Not knowing why, Kala gagged a little. She figured she must be hungover.

Kala waved him in with a smile. "Of course, come in."

Asmodeus walked in with a confidence that made Kala remember why he was her boyfriend. He grinned at her like he had just won some kind of contest.

"What's that look for?" Kala teased him.

Asmodeus pulled Kala into his arms and kissed her lightly. "Just happy to see you," he replied softly.

Kala thought that was so sweet. She gagged again. "I must have something caught in my throat." She left Asmodeus's loving arms and walked to the kitchen to grab a bottle of water.

Jack.

The name flashed in Kala's head like an eye-blink bolt of lightning. When she tried to figure out what it meant, it didn't seem so important anymore. After a few seconds she completely forgot what had shocked her so badly. Picking up a bottle of water, Kala drank deeply. If she was having a hangover, water was always the best cure.

Asmodeus sat on Kala's recliner in front of the television. He patted his lap, "Come sit with me."

Kala put the water bottle down on the counter and walked over to Asmodeus, sitting on his lap. He wrapped his arms around her waist and pulled her in tighter. "Better?" he asked.

Kala nodded, though internally she felt like something was off. She immediately felt horrible like she was the worst girlfriend ever. But Kala couldn't seem to shake the feeling that Asmodeus's hands did not belong on her body.

As if Asmodeus could sense her thoughts, he kindly reached up and touched her face gently. "What's wrong, buttercup?"

There went the gagging again. Kala wondered if she was coming down with the flu, but she didn't want to offend Asmodeus so she said, "Nothing, just feeling a bit off today."

"Let me fix it," Asmodeus said in a deep, reassuring voice.

Kala instantly felt relaxed. She practically melted into him as Asmodeus pulled her head down to his and kissed her passionately. Kala felt the intensity of the kiss as Asmodeus's lips moved with hers. She would have categorized it as a pretty mind-blowing experience, except that Kala began sensing that "off" feeling again. Asmodeus's hands were firm around her waist as he pulled her in for a deeper kiss. Kala tried to let herself enjoy the moment but...

...Before Kala knew it, her fist was punching Asmodeus in the face.

Kala's eyes grew round in mortification. "I'm so sorry! I have no idea why I did that!" Kala leapt off of Asmodeus's lap and she immediately examined the damage. "I don't know what got into me."

To Kala's surprise Asmodeus didn't look mad, he just looked shocked and a little bit amused. "You're something else, you know that?"

"Is that good or bad?" Kala asked. She was worried she had hurt Asmodeus's feelings, and she couldn't really blame him! She had punched him in the face!

But, somehow, punching him felt right. Really right. Like he deserved it or something. But that was impossible. Asmodeus was always such a gentlemen, and Kala truly loved him.

Okay, the gagging was getting out of control.

But it was enough to make her pause. Why *did* Kala gag every time she thought something nice about Asmodeus. Was it her subconscious trying to warn her about her boyfriend? Kala knew she was on to something.

Then she felt her thoughts start to shift slightly. It was as if every time Kala began to intuit some kind of truth, her own mind would try to steer her away from it.

She didn't think she'd ever felt that way before. Kala couldn't seem to remember anything past this current encounter with Asmodeus. It was as if her life started the moment she woke up this morning. Normally, Kala assumed that would be a terrifying prospect, but something prevented her from panicking. Like she was being controlled by something or…

…someone.

"You," Kala accused. "You're doing something to my brain." She tried to hold onto this belief before it would run away from her and she'd be kissing this freak again.

This freak? Her mind rebelled against the thought. How could she feel that way about someone she loved?

Because you don't love him! A small voice screamed in her head.

Kala felt like her brain was going to explode into a sloppy mess all over her living room floor.

Asmodeus rose from the chair. He stood in front of Kala and reached for her face.

Kala flinched away, but Asmodeus gently held her face anyway. "Relax, I'm going to fix you."

As soon as Asmodeus's hand touched the sides of her head, all Kala's memories flushed through her like a mudslide of emotion. She fell to her knees from the force of it, and gasped for breath.

Instead of throwing a fit or a punch for that matter, Kala felt terror. Asmodeus had made her forget everything. *Everything*. That was far more dangerous than any military operation she'd experienced. The ability to alter someone's mind was something Kala had no defense for. At least on a mission she had her weapons, her guns, and they could protect her. Her ability to use them made her feel safe. But this magic mumbo jumbo was so foreign to anything Kala had ever experienced before, she found it difficult to slip into "strategy" mode like she normally would because how could she strategize a way out of magic?

Kala's flight or fight mode was kicking in big time, but she'd never known someone as powerful as Asmodeus, and she could do neither. Slowly, Kala regained her composure and stood up.

Asmodeus smiled at her in an oh-so-condescending way. "I've never met a human with so much will power before. Impressive."

"It wasn't that hard, considering how every time I thought of being with you I gagged." Kala had to wipe that condescending smirk off of his face.

Before Kala could react, Asmodeus clasped his hand around her neck, choking her. "I was being nice," he snarled. "I could wipe everything from your little pea-brain and you'd just be a drooling vegetable. You wouldn't be able to perform your little task and the world would end, just like I want."

Kala couldn't think of a single reason why Asmodeus wouldn't do exactly that. Then she realized why: ego. Asmodeus was a Demon, but he was still a man, and Kala was fast becoming the ultimate "hard to get." Placing her into a coma would be admitting that he wasn't capable of winning her over. Kala decided to test her theory and she choked out, "What you want is for me to like you without tricks."

Asmodeus released her neck and tossed her to the side. She stumbled a few steps and massaged her throat, facing him. "I'm right, aren't I? I can't possibly be the first girl to turn you down."

That seemed to anger Asmodeus more. "As a matter of fact: you are."

"Ha!" Kala laughed. "I find that hard to believe."

When Asmodeus looked like he was going to charge her a second time, she put her hand up in a placating manner. "Hold up, big boy. I'm into someone else. I'm kind of loyal that way. It's nothing against you."

"But when I wiped your mind of him, you still fought against me." Asmodeus was genuinely perplexed, which Kala found almost endearing.

"I'm stubborn, what can I say?" Kala couldn't believe she was actually trying to make the king of Demons feel better about her rejecting him. Normally, she would tell the guy to quit being such a baby and get over it already, but Kala didn't want to run the risk of him lobotomizing her.

This seemed to make Asmodeus relax a little.

Kala sighed. "You had no intention of hiding me and Jack, did you?"

Asmodeus shrugged. "Why would I go through all that trouble when I can just keep you here for the next three days? You underestimate my laziness."

"You went through the trouble of bringing me all the way home," Kala pointed out.

"Oh that," Asmodeus smirked. He waved a hand and Kala's apartment transformed back into the empty room on top of the sky rise.

They hadn't gone anywhere.

"Did you even shift my DNA thingy? Or was that just bull too?" Kala wished she had a shot of tequila right about now.

"You'll never know," Asmodeus grinned.

"You sound like a five-year-old." Kala crossed her arms.

THWAP! THWAP!

Kala's body spun in a full circle as two bullets hit her shoulder and arm and she fell to the floor.

Chapter Twelve

A sniper? Really? That was all that went through Kala's head. That was *her* job! She wasn't supposed to be killed by a freaking sniper! The pain in her shoulder and arm wasn't as bad as she thought it would be. Surprisingly, Kala had never been shot before. In her line of work that was quite an accomplishment. She had always imagined that gunshots would be excruciatingly painful, but Kala was so angry at being shot at in the first place, she barely felt them.

Asmodeus screamed so loudly at the broken window through which the shots fired in his oh-so-screeching-manner, Kala had to cover her ears. He was pissed. Kala didn't think Asmodeus was used to being attacked on his home turf, or at least in his high-rise-hideout. He kneeled down next to her and placed his hands on Kala's bullet wounds.

Heat burned Kala where Asmodeus touched her and she yelled out in pain, but after a few moments of burning anguish, she felt as good as new. Asmodeus tossed the two bullets that he extracted from Kala's body aside in disgust. Kala looked through the bullet hole tears in her shirt and saw baby pink unbroken skin underneath.

"Thanks," Kala found herself saying before she realized who she was thanking.

Asmodeus leaned down and kissed her lightly on the mouth. Kala wanted to punch him for it, but after his "healing-stunt" she restrained herself.

"Anytime, buttercup," Asmodeus smiled mischievously.

Kala had to chuckle at that. "Calling me buttercup is what probably broke your little spell on me."

Asmodeus teasingly pinched Kala's nose. "I think it's more than fitting."

THWAP! THWAP! More bullets.

"Time to go." Asmodeus was about to grab Kala's shoulders when...

SWOOSH!

Asmodeus's body was thrown all the way to the back wall.

SNAP!

Kala cringed as something definitely cracked in Asmodeus's body from the impact.

The entire wall of windows shattered completely.

A lone figure appeared on the edge of the floor. The man was dark: dark clothing, dark hair and dark skin. He looked at Kala with piercing brown eyes, and pointed a Glock with silencer at her. She'd almost be impressed with the gun if it wasn't aimed at her head. But it was a *gun*. Kala felt the first stirrings of hope. If she could just get her hands on that Glock.

Asmodeus was back on his feet as if he hadn't been touched. "Grautlin! A gun? So beneath you."

The man named Grautlin turned away from Kala and focused on Asmodeus. "Guns kill humans as easy as anything else."

"Yes, but why? You're a Malak for God's sake. You don't honestly want to be the next Atlas?" Asmodeus seemed appalled at the idea.

Grautlin took a step toward Asmodeus, determined. "A Malak is the perfect being for Atlas. Humans are fragile, but a Malak?" To prove his point, Grautlin lifted his hand and made Asmodeus fly across the room again.

But there was no impact this time. Asmodeus disappeared completely in mid-air.

Kala realized that the Demon probably decided she wasn't worth his hide and teleported his ass out of there. She could hardly blame him, but Kala was now stuck with a Malak who had a gun.

Grautlin appeared to have come to the same conclusion as he turned to Kala and looked at her with a serious expression. "You are not worthy of being the Atlas. I will take your place." Grautlin lifted the gun.

Kala went into mission-mode and dove for cover behind one of the support columns.

Asmodeus appeared directly in front of Grautlin. "Surprise," he grinned.

Before Grautlin could defend himself, Asmodeus used his powers to propel Grautlin out the open wall and into the air beyond.

Kala couldn't say she was exactly shocked to see that Grautlin didn't fall; instead he flew straight back in the building, tackling Asmodeus to the floor with a sickening crunch.

Upside? Grautlin dropped his gun in the process.

Downside? A Demon and a Malak were rolling around in tackle-mode on top of it.

Kala debated whether or not it was worth it to try and snag the gun, but decided escape was higher on the priority list. She stealthily made her way to the only exit on the floor and hoped it wouldn't be too hard to break the code. Once Kala was face to face with the digital security panel, she tried to remember all she could about how to crack it. She turned the door handle first, just for kicks, but was not surprised when the door didn't open.

The amount of smashing and cracking Kala heard in the room behind her back made her palms sweat. At least they weren't attacking her; Kala didn't think she'd survive a single smash to the wall, let alone the kind of pounding the two of them were slugging at each other. In a sad sort of way, Kala was actually rooting for Asmodeus, at least he didn't want to kill her. He did, however, want to lock Kala up and make her his love slave, which might be just as bad.

Kala concentrated on the keypad. Intense, life-threatening situations were her forté. It was where she thrived. She went through all the protocols in her head and wished Jack was there. He was always the brains of their team. Kala sometimes felt that all the rest of them were just there as muscle. A part of her training at the Compound consisted of codes, not breaking them, just memorizing numbers that would set an alarm back to its factory settings. There were thousands, but only about ten that were commonly used in most domestic security systems. It wasn't "breaking" the code, but it would open the door and that was all Kala cared about at the moment.

Punching in several numbers, Kala tried to tune out the epic fight behind her. If her life wasn't on the line, she might actually enjoy watching two mythical beings she didn't know existed until two days ago having a massive throw down.

Finally, Kala typed in the right sequence of numbers to reset the machine.

The door swung open and Kala slid through it, sealing it shut behind her.

Luckily, that appeared to be the only security to speak of. Kala found herself in a standard high-rise office area filled with a sea of cubicles. They were all empty of course, which was a disadvantage to Kala. She wasn't sure how long she had before Asmodeus and Grautlin finished their fight and realized their "prize" was gone. Hiding amongst a busy office place would have been great cover. Instead she made her way through the graveyard of cubicles to the stairs. Being at least fifty stories up, the flight down would take a while, and Kala's military instinct didn't want her to be stuck in an elevator where too many things could go wrong.

Kala took the stairs three at a time, using the railings to keep from falling. She knew she was running on borrowed time. There was no way they could still be fighting. Kala just hoped Asmodeus wouldn't POP in front of her when she was so close to getting out of this building.

Reaching the last floor, Kala pushed open the exit door, rushed outside — and nearly slammed into a businessman. In her excitement she had forgotten about the throng of people always walking on the Manhattan sidewalks. With an immense sigh of relief, Kala blended into the mass of people and made her way toward the first crosswalk she could see.

Kala felt the hand on her arm yank her out of the crowd and into a deserted doorway.

On guard, Kala grabbed the hand and had it pinned behind the attacker's back before the attacker could react.

Penny.

Kala let go of her before Penny's eyes glowed blue and fried her where she stood. Kala didn't exactly know if that was possible, but with everything that she had seen in the last two days, she didn't want to take the chance.

Kala groaned. "Great. Are *you* going to try and kill me now?"

Penny looked genuinely alarmed at that statement. "Asmodeus tried to kill you?"

"No, he just wanted to sleep with me. That Malak guy tried to kill me. Look, they're in the middle of some kind of Demon/Angel battle to the death right now, but as soon as they're done, they're coming after me. So, if you can help in any way?" Kala tried to hide the desperate hope out of her voice.

Penny, though, was apparently still stuck on Kala's previous statement. "Did this Malak have a name?"

"Grautlin. He said I was weak and that a Malak should be the next Atlas. If it didn't mean me having to die, I'd have to agree with him. He's seriously kicking Asmodeus's ass." Even while talking, Kala surveyed the area like a soldier, preparing for an attack. She was still chastising herself for not seeing Penny before she pulled her off the street. Kala had been so focused on the crosswalk she had let her guard down temporarily. She promised herself that she'd never do that again.

Penny reached out and touched Kala's forehead.

Kala felt a kind of shimmering flow through her body. "What was that?" she asked.

"A disguise of sorts," Penny said cryptically. "I would have done it earlier, but Asmodeus already knew where you were."

"You mean the DNA switcheroo thing? Asmodeus told me all about it," Kala said it with confidence just to see the look on Penny's face. She wasn't disappointed, Penny was stunned.

"He confided that in you?" Penny's voice was small with shock.

"I told you, all the guy wants to do is get in my pants," Kala replied. "Can you do that whole 'teleport' thing, or did you have to drive here?"

"I have my little tricks, like turning invisible on cue, but only Demons and Malaks have the power to teleport. I'm neither," Penny stated tersely.

"Good to know." Kala knew she only had a small window of opportunity before Asmodeus or Grautlin started tracking her, so she tried something she wasn't sure would work.

She snapped Penny's neck.

Kala heard a passerby scream at the sight. More importantly, Penny actually dropped to the ground unconscious. Before Penny could wake up, or a crowd could mob Kala for "murder," she ran for the crosswalk.

DNA fixed and Penny couldn't teleport. Check.

Kala was almost home free.

Chapter Thirteen

Kala knew Penny would soon be on her trail if she didn't get out of the area as soon as possible. Having never been to New York before, Kala found that the city was easy to maneuver.

Traversing through the busy streets of people and cars, Kala had that overwhelming feeling again that this was going to be the rest of her life. She'd be running forever. The thought made her feel more lonely than she ever had been in her life, and as a foster kid that was saying something.

Her first instinct was to call Jack. He was more involved in this Atlas thing than she was. Actually *being* the Atlas obviously made her as involved as one could get, but Kala still couldn't fully commit to this being reality. After everything she had witnessed, Kala knew she was crazy for doubting, not crazy for believing. Nevertheless, the rational part of her brain just didn't want to accept what was happening.

When Kala was sure she lost Penny (at least temporarily), she dipped into a small Internet café. Kala couldn't do this alone. She needed help. Against her better judgment, Kala sat down at an empty station and signed into an email account she'd never planned on using. It was an emergency account she and Derek set up when they were first recruited to the team. Her connection with Derek had been instant. He was like the big brother she never had. Kala was sure Derek thought she was suffering from some kind of brain disease, but she also knew that he had her back no matter what (even if she was a raving lunatic). Deciding to be short and sweet, Kala simply wrote: *Meet in our spot in four hours.* She clicked send and stared at the screen, wondering if she had done the right thing.

Bringing Derek into the fold was very selfish of her, but Kala needed help.

In less than a minute a return email popped up with Derek's response: *I'll be there.* Almost every muscle in Kala's body relaxed when she read Derek's words. It brought tears to her eyes. The fiercest loyalty surged through her. She couldn't wait to see him.

Groaning in resignation at the three hour train ride Kala had ahead of her, she headed out of the café. To avoid any unseen delays, Kala had added an hour to the meeting time, just in case. Shaking her head in frustration, Kala felt a moment of rage. Being transported to New York was a pain in the butt. Asmodeus was a royal a-hole. Kala found herself grumbling, something she rarely did.

Walking out onto the crowded streets, Kala asked someone where the train station was and was directed a few blocks away. She kept her eye out for Penny, knowing full well that whatever that woman was, she wasn't human. Penny may not be able to teleport, but the lady always had a knack for finding Kala somehow.

Minutes later, Kala arrived at Grand Central Station. She'd always wanted to see the New York landmark, but not under these circumstances. At the moment she wanted to be as far away from this place as possible. The station was packed, yet even in the enormity of the cavernous room Kala still felt claustrophobic. The only saving grace was the light coming in through the Station's arched windows, providing an illusion of some kind of openness to the outside.

Reading the list of trains to D.C., Kala found one that left in twenty minutes. If she was late to the meeting, Kala knew Derek would wait until she arrived.

Paying cash for the ticket, Kala hopped on the train and sat in the rear of a passenger car, where she could have a view of anyone that came in or out. Kala tried to relax as much as possible, but sitting in a train for three hours just made her nervous. It wasn't like she actually had a weapon or anything, but Kala figured a gun wouldn't exactly help her against a Malak or a Demon anyway. At this point, it was about getting away, not experimenting in supernatural battles.

Exhaustion was slowly started to overtake Kala. She fought to keep her eyes open. Running on adrenaline only worked when you were running. Fortunately, this wasn't the first time Kala had to keep herself awake while dead tired. Being a sniper meant hours of sitting and lying around, waiting for a target to show up: caffeine and stimulants only worked so much. Kala had trained her body to do small exercises like clenching and unclenching her legs and arms in order to stay awake. It seemed to be working for the time being right now, too, but Kala knew she'd need to take a nap soon. Though Asmodeus knocked her out for… how long had she been out? Kala wondered.

Searching the train's cabin, Kala spotted an old fashioned clock with antique wrought-iron hands. Of course, to Kala the standard numbers were gone and replaced with the countdown: 2d 19h 10m 33s. Doing quick math in her head, Kala was pretty sure that meant it was almost 11 A.M. So, she was on day two and only had two days left to kill Jack to save the world. Whatever that meant. Kala wondered what was the worst that could happen? A flood, a hurricane, a nuclear bomb? She shrugged and thought that worse things had happened before and people survived. The world would have to fend for itself as far as she was concerned.

Kala rubbed her hand over her face in frustration. To make the leap that the world would literally end seemed a little much.

It also seemed ludicrous to think that other Atlases in the past hadn't refused to do their duty, and the world certainly didn't end. It could've been times in history like Pompeii or Hiroshima or other terrible moments in history.

Kala started to feel a sense of relief at the thought. Those were horrendous events, yes. And Kala certainly didn't want to be responsible for anything that terrifying. But it really wouldn't be her fault. It was the Curse's fault, or whatever it was. No one could blame her.

But Jack would.

Jack had trained his whole life to be the next Atlas. He had been ready to do whatever it took to make the world whole. He'd never forgive her if he knew. But what if he knew that the only way to save the world was for Kala to kill him?

Kala shoved the thought from her mind. She knew exactly what he would do. He'd tell her to pull the trigger.

But she couldn't.

She just couldn't.

A woman entered the cabin from the adjoining train car. It was the entrance on the opposite side from where Kala sat so Kala had a perfect view. There was something about this woman that made the hairs on Kala's neck stand up. Picking up a magazine from the seat in front of her, Kala pretended to thumb through it while following the woman's progress through the corner of her eye.

Surveilling the room, Kala noted that there were five other passengers in various seats, either reading or sleeping. Only this woman was moving, and she was headed towards Kala.

Exits.

Aside from the front and end of the passenger car, all the windows could be opened or broken if needed.

Next, Kala's opponent.

If this woman was a Malak or a Demon, Kala would be in trouble — but if she was human, Kala could take her easy. Or at least, easier. If this kind of thing was Kala's life now, she was going to have to learn some kind of defense against the supernatural. Definitely not something they prepped you for in Seal training. Guns had no effect, except maybe to slow them down, and neck snapping only worked if Kala could take them by surprise. Both those options were out considering Kala didn't have a gun and this woman was already stalking her.

As the woman approached, Kala kept her guard up while pretending to read the magazine.

"Is this seat taken?" the woman asked.

Kala smiled as warmly as she could muster, "No, go ahead."

The woman smiled back and sat down across from Kala. Kala's nerve endings were on overload. Something was definitely *wrong* with the woman. Since she wasn't attacking, Kala sat there, waited, analyzed and strategized.

Information.

Whether it was made up or not, Kala decided to ask this girl some questions. You could tell a lot about a person by the way they lie.

"Where you headed?" Kala inquired as conversationally as possible.

"D.C.," she replied softly. The woman sat back, trying to look relaxed.

But Kala noticed her hands were slightly clenched, a sure sign of being on the offensive. As if sensing Kala's observation, the woman unclenched one hand and pulled a stray strand of hair behind her ear. She was average looking in the face, but Kala could see this woman was in shape. Medium length hair framed her face, and Kala wasn't opposed to some serious hair pulling if need be. Her clothes were comfortable and flexible, khakis and a long sleeved stretch shirt.

Kala wished she was in similar attire, but she still wore her blue jeans from yesterday. They had some flex, but let's face it, denim was always a little stiff and tight. Maneuverability was the key and this lady had the advantage.

"D.C.? Me too," Kala said in a friendly tone. "I'm Jenny by the way," Kala lied. She knew any name she heard back from this woman would be a lie as well, but Kala wanted to keep her talking to distract her, to disrupt her concentration as much as possible.

"I'm Virginia," the woman said.

Virginia? Kala thought to herself. It was an old-fashioned name. Could be a Malak or Demon too out of touch to think of a modern name. Or the lady could have just thought of the state they were heading towards.

"What brings you to D.C.?" Kala asked as she casually rolled the magazine with one hand. Any weapon was better than nothing. She would swat her like a fly if she had to.

Virginia placed her hands in her lap in a seemingly casual way, but her arms were tensed. "Work," she said with a half-smile.

"Work with no bag or even a purse?" Kala pointed out Virginia's obvious lack of personal items.

SLASH!

Virginia swung a small club that sparked blue at Kala's head. A taser-club.

Kala had been ready for an attack so she easily leaned back in her seat. It was the basics of Aikido, using the force of your opponent's momentum to your advantage. When Virginia leaned forward and didn't meet the expected resistance of Kala's face, Kala used the force of Virginia's fall and slammed Virginia's hand hard on the seat next to her. The club was fully embedded in the wood framing from the force of Kala's blow and electrocuting the seat. Kala wished she had turned it on Virginia as she could tell the thing was officially broken.

Virginia quickly recovered and tried to punch Kala in the face. Kala slammed the side of her open hand directly on Virginia's throat.

Gasping for air, Virginia used her sitting position to an advantage by kicking out at Kala with both legs. Kala dove into the aisle, barely escaping Virginia's stomping feet.

At this point the three passengers who were quietly reading noticed the outright brawl starting to take over their cabin. Kala knew it wouldn't be long before one of them ran for help.

From the woman's mundane fighting style, Kala at least knew she was fighting a human. She could already tell that Virginia was no match for her, but Kala needed information.

"How did you find me?" Kala said as she elbow-punched Virginia's face.

Virginia was livid as she shrugged off the blow. "Grand Central Station? Really? It's called surveillance." She tried to upper-cut Kala's chin, but Kala blocked it easily.

"They shouldn't have sent a human. This isn't even a challenge." To make her point, Kala side-kicked Virginia in the chest sending her flying backwards to land forcefully against the exit door.

At this point the sleepyheads were awake, too, and making their way to the opposite exit. Kala knew security would be there any minute. She needed to get as much information out of her opponent as she could, then dump her off the train.

Virginia jumped to her feet, arms and hands rotating in a defensive position. "You really are off your meds. Human? What else would I be? An alien?"

This made Kala freeze. "Wait. Who sent you?"

Virginia took advantage of Kala's momentary indecision and kicked Kala in the gut. "The mother ship, psycho."

Kala felt the air escape her lungs as Virginia's foot made contact. But Kala was always quick to recover. It was in her DNA (assuming her DNA disguise hadn't changed it too much!).

Punching Virginia in the throat, Kala watched Virginia collapse onto the floor, trying to breath.

This was the moment when Virginia was most vulnerable. Just like her training taught her, Kala took one knee and pinned Virginia down with it. Virginia grabbed onto Kala's leg, trying to remove the stabbing knee from her chest, but Kala had done this too many times to budge. To make her point, Kala put more pressure on Virginia's ribs, causing a scream of pain.

"Who sent you?" Kala demanded through gritted teeth.

Virginia grunted in agony. "Who do you think?!"

"I don't want to think. I want you to tell me." Kala drove her knee in harder for emphasis.

Virginia screamed in response. "General Clifton!"

Kala froze.

"Why?"

"Because you killed the President and left town!" Virginia was trying her hardest to remove Kala's knee from her chest.

Kala had heard enough. She punched Virginia hard in the face causing Virginia's head to hit the floor, knocking her unconscious. Before the slowest-security-ever arrived, Kala quickly stood up and dragged Virginia's body to the exit. The train was going fast, but Virginia would survive. Kala hated being so cold, but she couldn't have Virginia waking up in the next few hours to start attacking her again.

Kicking open the door, Kala lifted Virginia up through the arms and tossed her off the train. With a couple of painful looking thumps, Virginia landed in an empty field of grass.

Then Kala calmly entered the adjoining train car, away from the direction her frightened fellow-passengers had fled. Just to be safe, she moved through five more cabins before she settled on the last one. No one seemed to pay her any mind, so she figured she was safe for the moment. Sitting down near the back exit again, Kala stared out the window at the passing landscape.

I'm so screwed.

Chapter Fourteen

The last two hours of the train ride made Kala's brain hurt. Like she didn't have enough to worry about with this whole *Atlas* thing, now she had to watch her back with her own people?

The thought was terrifying. On the run from Demons and Angels is one thing (one very insane thing), but on the run from her own government, too? From an elite team that hunted down criminals in their sleep? *That* was real.

Being a part of that team, Kala knew that staying off the grid would be nearly impossible. How could she explain why she left D.C.? *Oh sorry, General Clifton, I was teleported by Asmodeus, the king of Demons, to New York City. You understand. Those pesky Demons, there's just no controlling them.*

Kala groaned.

Getting to Derek was the only ray of brightness that Kala could hold on to. He would tell her how much trouble she was in.

Over and over in her head, Kala kept wondering what General Clifton intended to do with her. Maybe he just wanted to question her again. Kala remembered how he'd looked at General Turner before leaving the interrogation room. Clifton was jealous, he was angry, it was like he wanted to do the opposite of what Turner wanted just to be contrary. At the time, though, Kala thought that Clifton might let it go, that the scandal of the President's assassination would be too much to deal with. She obviously underestimated his competitive nature. Clifton needed to be right. More importantly, he needed Turner to be wrong. What better way to prove Turner wrong than to expose the President's assassin as a guilty runaway?

Kala just needed to explain.

But explain what? What on Earth could she possibly say?

Kala still hadn't figured it out as the train came to a stop in D.C.

Looking at the clock: 2d 14h 31m 22s: 2:30. She was getting better at this. Kala only had about a half hour to rendezvous with Derek. Kala hurried off the train and made her way to the line of cabs parked in the front of the station. Hailing one over, she slid in the back seat and told the cab driver where to go.

There was a small television implanted in the back of the driver's seat and it was playing something. Kala assumed it was the local news, but all she saw was herself shooting Jack in the face over and over. It was a relief when the driver finally arrived at her destination. Paying the cab fare in cash, Kala hurried out of the vehicle and away from the TV monitor.

Kala kept her head ducked down as she made her way to the designated meeting place: Tapper's Storage. Lot 22 to be precise. Derek and Kala always figured that meeting in a storage locker was remote enough that no one would be the wiser, and Tapper's was the twistiest-turniest storage facility in the area. Even knowing exactly where unit 22 was it was still difficult to locate. After making her way through the maze of doors, garages and hallways, Kala finally arrived at the accordion door labeled 22. She nearly held back a cry of joy when she saw Derek there waiting for her.

Kala couldn't control herself, she hugged him tightly when she saw him. Derek's arms held her close and Kala never felt safer in her life.

"Whoa, girl, what's going on? You're never this affectionate," Derek chuckled.

Kala pulled away and smiled a smile of relief. "It's just nice to see a friendly face."

"Where have you been?" Derek asked, concerned.

"New York. Not by choice, believe me. Have you seen Jack?" Kala wanted to know if Jack had told Derek anything. From the look on Derek's face, he hadn't.

Derek shook his head, "Jack's been closed-up in interrogation since last night. Kala, when you disappeared, General Clifton re-opened the investigation of the President's death. They're looking for you."

"I know. I kicked the crap out of the poor girl Clifton sent after me. I didn't know she was bringing me in. She attacked me, so I defended myself." Kala didn't bother telling Derek that she had thought Virginia might have been a Malak or a Demon. No sense in stirring the pot.

"Where is she now?" Derek asked.

Kala paused, not sure how Derek would take the news. "I kind of threw her off the train."

"You what?!" Derek's eyes bugged out.

"I didn't want her attacking me again. I'm not sure I trust Clifton. I think he's out for me, whether he thinks I'm innocent or guilty," Kala confessed her suspicion. The more she analyzed the situation, the more she felt like a pawn.

"That may be true, but Turner has your back. I talked to him myself. They just want you to come in," Derek explained.

Kala took a step back. "You didn't tell them you were meeting me, did you?"

"Of course not, but I did tell them I'd bring you in." Derek reached forward and gently touched Kala's arm. "No one is going to hurt you. You know I'd never let them do anything to you. Jack is already at the Compound. We'll protect you," Derek tried to reassure her.

But Kala wasn't having it. "Derek, I get it. I get that you're doing your job, but I'm not sure it's a good idea for me to go back just yet." Kala couldn't explain it, but her gut told her that General Clifton wasn't going to let her go easily no matter what assurances Derek gave.

"Running makes you look guilty, you know that." Derek's dark eyes were intense as he tried to reach Kala on an emotional level.

"Derek, I *am* guilty. I *did* shoot the President. That's on record, from everyone that was there, including you, including me. The fact that they haven't executed me yet is a miracle no matter how justified I was in doing it."

Kala couldn't believe what she was thinking. She suddenly knew with perfect clarity that she needed to leave Jack's team. There was no forgiveness. Someone had to go down, whether they told the public that the President died in plane crash or not. Kala had pulled the trigger, so Kala would be the one punished. And though Kala had no intention of fulfilling her duties as an Atlas or whatever, she didn't want to die. She wasn't that heroic, and she definitely was not a martyr. Kala knew she'd die to save Derek, Jack or Lali, but she'd never willingly sacrifice herself so that the bureaucrats would be satisfied. Kala was not a fan of the hierarchy: dying to please them was not something her brain could compute.

"Derek, I have to go." Kala looked him in the eye and she could see that he knew she was saying good-bye.

"Kala, just come in with me," Derek pleaded. "Everything will be okay, you'll see."

"I can't. It's complicated, but I have to keep on the run. I'll contact you when I can." Kala grabbed Derek's hand and squeezed it gently. "Bye Derek."

Derek closed his eyes in pain. "I'm sorry, Kala."

Derek's apology only meant one thing.

He wasn't letting her leave.

Kala turned to make a run for it, but Derek snatched her and pulled her close to him. Before Kala could fight back, the smell of chloroform reached her nostrils and everything turned woozy. She felt so betrayed. She knew Derek was doing what he thought best for her, but Kala hated the fact that he didn't trust her to make her own decisions. Duty first, friends second.

After a few seconds of struggle, Kala welcomed the black abyss.

At least she wouldn't have to think about anything for a while…

Chapter Fifteen

Kala woke up in a blacked-out van handcuffed to a metal bench. She knew they were on their way to the Compound. Derek sat next to her like a protective lion, not letting any of the other seven soldiers near her.

"Handcuffs? Really?" Kala inquired groggily.

Derek looked down at Kala, his eyes full of determination, but laced with guilt. "This is for the best, trust me."

"You were the only one I thought I could trust. Sucks to be wrong." Kala knew it was harsh, and she knew it would sting, but she couldn't help it. She felt betrayed. Derek was her family, and he chose the government over her. It made her stomach turn.

Derek looked away, not saying a word. Kala knew he felt like crap too. As horrible as it sounded, that gave her some comfort.

The bigger picture? Either Kala would be executed for the assassination of the President, or Asmodeus would search for her at the Compound. Both options weren't terribly appealing. How many times would she need to have some supernatural creature shift her DNA or whatever?

Then it hit her.

DNA.

That was how Kala gained entrance into the Compound. The machine used DNA to match the identity of the person entering. If Penny had truly changed her DNA, then Kala wouldn't register in the system. This was bad.

"Um, Derek?" Kala hoped he would actually talk to her after her little insult.

Derek's expression of hopefulness made Kala feel horrible. He really felt like an a-hole, Kala realized. "We're almost there," he said, a comforting tone in his voice trying to soothe the situation.

"I know this is going to sound crazy, but I'm not going to pass the DNA scan." Kala didn't know why she was confessing to this. It probably would have been easier just to let it happen, but Kala was certain that once she failed the DNA match General Clifton would use it as an excuse for immediate execution.

Instead of Derek looking shocked or curious, he looked at Kala with sympathy.

Kala knew Derek genuinely thought she had lost her mind.

She couldn't really blame him, not when she thought about how she'd been acting after the mission. Kala hadn't even told him the truth! Imagine if she had? He'd really think she was a nut job. Although, now that she thought about it, Derek had probably already heard about her conversation with Turner. Gossip like that was hard to keep quiet.

"They say it might be the phase-suit. It could have messed with your brain a little. They're going to fix you, Kala." Derek squeezed her hand in support.

"It's not the phase-suit," Kala said under her breath, but she might as well have been talking to a lamppost.

Kala knew that Derek was convinced something had happened to her and that she needed to be *fixed*. A part of her wished he was right. *Maybe this is how crazy people think.* Kala remembered the few times she had run away from foster care and lived on the streets. Some of the homeless people were truly fried in the brain, but they believed what they were screaming in her face. Kala wondered if this was how it started, trying to convince friends and loved ones, then when they turn you over to the psych ward, you end up yelling at anyone who will listen.

Kala almost wished she was losing her marbles. That way, no one would get hurt, and she could be with Jack the rest of her life. If Clifton or Turner could prove that some kind of brain damage caused her to hallucinate everything that she'd seen so far, then Kala was sure she could fake being sane. And if she could fake it, she could live a normal life, never having to do anything horrible ever again.

The van slowed to a stop.

"Here we are," Derek announced.

Kala tried hard not to panic. This was it. One DNA scan and she was toast.

Derek took her arm gently and led her out of the van.

Sure enough they were standing in front of the worn down warehouses that served as a cover for the Compound. Just inside those doors was the platform scanner that would seal her doom.

Instead of fighting, Kala kept her head down, stayed silent and let Derek guide her to the warehouse.

"Hello, Kala."

Kala looked up to see Jack standing next to the platform standing next to…

Gulp…

Penny.

And she looked pissed.

Jack stepped forward, taking Kala from Derek. "Kala, this is Dr. Rosen. She's a neurologist and she's going to take a look at you."

Penny hid her anger well as she smiled at Kala, "Pleased to meet you, Ms. Hicks. We're going to make sure everything's working as it should."

"Great." Kala found that this was the only word she could think of.

What do you say to the girl you killed twice?

"I'll take her from here," Penny advised. As Penny touched Kala's arm, Kala felt the familiar tingling sensation that she had felt before when Penny had altered her DNA.

Jack had yet to let go of Kala's other arm, so together Penny and Jack led Kala to the scanning platform, followed by Derek and five guards from the van. Feeling the circular scan around her body, Kala hoped Penny knew what she was doing. When everyone came up as a MATCH, Kala felt relieved.

Of course, that was short-lived when she realized Asmodeus now had a green light to pop in and take her away. Kala only hoped that the Compound and all its technology was enough to keep him away. After she left, assuming Kala would be able to leave, she'd need Penny to work her DNA mojo again. (Assuming Penny would help her at all.) There were a lot of assumptions going on, and none of them seemed too promising at the moment.

The platform whizzed its way down to the belly of the compound. Kala fought her motion sickness as the elevator dropped farther down than she'd ever gone before. She knew that couldn't be a good sign, but somehow having Penny next to her gave Kala some weird kind of comfort, though she couldn't really explain why. Yes, Penny wanted Jack to kill her and become the next Atlas, but Kala knew Jack wouldn't do that, so where did that leave Penny? For the time being, Kala was pretty sure it meant that Penny would keep her safe. Or at least not let her get killed by the U.S. government. Kala knew that Penny thought of her as the "enemy she knew," and being executed was not on the menu.

The platform finally stopped. The black metal doors slid open. No one had said a word the entire trip down and no one was starting now. Kala made brief eye contact with Jack as they were greeted by a soldier who led them through a dimly lit hallway. Her heart fluttered as Jack's eyes revealed what looked like encouragement. They had been on enough missions for Kala to read Jack: his quick expression told her that he had a plan. Kala gave him one of her looks that said she'd follow him anywhere, and he answered with a smile.

No matter what happened, Kala knew that Jack was on her side.

Penny didn't look too happy by the exchange, but she only grimaced as if to say she was getting used to the idea of Kala being around. The thought made Kala scared. Penny didn't know the mission was to assassinate Jack. Kala wondered how Penny would feel if she knew. It was one thing to reluctantly agree with Jack to support Kala as the new Atlas, but when your golden boy is the target…

Kala knew Penny would kill Jack herself if she knew.

That's why she'll never know, Kala vowed to herself.

Derek walked behind her like a bull dog. As mad as Kala was with Derek, she still knew he would die before he let anyone hurt her.

Following the soldier down the never ending hallway was starting to make Kala a bit anxious. A part of her military training was to always have an exit, but with one really long hallway, that made the elevator platform the only exit and that was hundreds of feet away. Plus, no doors anywhere. Wherever this hallway ended up would be the safest place in the Compound since this long tube they were walking down was essentially, a bottleneck. If an army could find their way down here, they could be held off forever with nowhere to go. With enough fire power it would be a quick slaughter.

Kala was never more grateful for having someone like Penny who couldn't be killed on her side, or at least sort of on her side.

Finally after at least a half hour of walking the group came to a metal door with a digital keypad. The soldier typed in a series of numbers and a green light scanned his eye. With a click and a clank, the door swung open.

General Clifton and General Turner were inside a fairly large room standing next to the strangest machine Kala had ever seen. It looked like a chair with hundreds of tubes attached to some kind of helmet hanging from the ceiling. A row of computers were hooked up to the whole contraption. Kala had the sinking feeling that this machine was meant for her.

Turner spoke first, "Please. Come in. This machine is a prototype, but it should tell us if there's anything wrong with your brain."

"My brain?" Kala gulped.

Turner walked over to Kala, then looked at Jack and Penny still holding her respective arms. "You can let go of her now, I promise I won't bite." Then he motioned to Derek. "Uncuff her please."

Derek immediately complied. As he unlocked the cuffs, Kala felt his hand squeeze hers. She squeezed back. No matter what was happening she still considered Derek her family: just in case this machine fried her brain, she wanted him to know she wasn't mad.

Turner smiled in a weird kind of excited smile and motioned to the chair. "Please. You'll be the first. Our respective guinea pig."

"Fantastic," Kala muttered. Normally, Kala would never be so disrespectful to a senior officer, but the last two days had made her a little immune to decorum.

Unfortunately, General Clifton wasn't very forgiving of that fact. Kala felt his hand grab her neck as he reached forward and threw her onto the chair. "You will address the General as 'Sir' or 'General'."

"Yes, sir," Kala responded. She wanted to break Clifton's neck, but a part of her agreed with his anger. Kala was proud of the fact that she was a good soldier. She didn't like it when she lapsed back into old habits.

Turner didn't seem fazed by Clifton's actions, nor by the fact that Kala hadn't given him a title of respect. He was far more interested in hooking Kala up to his newest toy. He placed the helmet on her head and Kala instantly felt her brain buzzing.

"Whoa," she said. Her teeth started rattling.

Turner turned a knob on one of the computers and the vibrating lessened enough for her teeth to relax. "Better?" he asked.

"Yes, sir," Kala responded. But *no* would have been more truthful.

"This is my domain, General," Penny pushed her way next to Turner.

Turner looked like a kicked puppy, but didn't argue. "Of course, Doctor. I'm just excited to see my baby out for a test run."

"Your *baby* needs to be monitored by a professional or you'll put this girl into a coma." Penny examined the machine and the monitors next to it. "I'll run a few tests and we'll see if she's had any damage from the phase-suits."

Kala was watching Penny fiddle with the machine when everything went black.

Kala wasn't unconscious, it was like she was blind, but at the same time she knew she wasn't.

"Can you hear me, Kala?" Penny's voice sounded in the darkness.

"Yes," Kala responded. She felt as if she was in a dark room rather than simply going blind. She could feel herself standing in the blackness. Dark, like an interrogation room or somewhere else in the Compound. Kala wondered if Penny had lied to her before and really could teleport her. Maybe Penny had teleported her to some dark lair that she could never escape from. At least Asmodeus gave her a skyline to look at.

With a snap of the fingers, the space lit up to reveal a whole lot of nothing. It was brighter, but like a grayish-white fog all around. Kala could see her own body, but then was startled to notice that she was slightly transparent. Penny appeared in front of her. She was also somewhat translucent.

"We're in this machine of his," Penny said in disgust. She was obviously referring to General Turner, but Kala could tell she didn't like him very much.

"Do they know we're having this conversation?" Kala asked.

Penny looked at Kala like she was a total idiot. "Of course not. That man doesn't know how this machine works. I don't like all this technology he's building, it's dangerous."

"More dangerous than Demons or Malaks?" Kala found that she wanted to defend the General. It felt like an "Us versus Them" situation, *Us* being humans and *Them* being whatever the hell Penny was.

"Of course not, but that's the point isn't it? With all of the General's *toys*, he has the potential to do some real damage. I wouldn't be surprised if his death was your mission, or at least a future mission. Speaking of which, do you have your mission yet?"

Here we go. Kala thought to herself. She knew Penny must be dying to know what the new Atlas was supposed to do this time around. She probably was expecting to be a part of Jack's missions and help him make the world a better place or whatever. Kala knew the last thing Penny expected was to be in some kind of brain machine trying to fish out information from a stranger.

"Nothing yet," Kala lied. "When is that supposed to happen anyway? I mean, I only have two days, right?"

Kala pushed too hard. She could see that Penny knew she was B.S.'ing her.

"You already know," Penny accused, demanding furiously, "What is it? Tell me!"

Though Kala knew neither one of them were really there, she still took a step back, thinking fast, trying to cover her flub. "I said I don't know."

"I may not know what your mission is, but I can tell you with certainty that if you don't do it, this world as you know it is over," Penny said with finality.

Kala groaned. "Yeah, yeah, but what does that really mean anyway? A new disease? War? Been there, done that, and the world ended up being just fine."

"You stupid fool." Penny shook her head. "Those events that you think the world survived? Those are the moments in time where certain Atlases thought like you did. They didn't do their job…"

Kala interrupted, "And see? We recovered. Humans are resilient like that…"

Penny came face to face with Kala, fury in her eyes. "Those events occurred after the countdown had expired, yes, but if the Atlas hadn't finally snapped out of it and performed their duty, those horrible things that you're so proud of surviving were only the beginning. Imagine what would have happened if the Atlas had done nothing?"

"You don't know, that could have been the worst of it. No one will ever know now," Kala rationalized. She just couldn't accept that the *world would end* if she didn't kill Jack. It didn't make any logical sense. Not like anything that was happening made any sense. Even the stuff that was *real* like this machine she was strapped into had a surrealness to it.

Still, Kala knew she'd have to at least pretend to go along with Penny in order to get her off her back. Before Penny could enter into another tirade, Kala stopped her. "Fine. I'll do it. I don't have to tell you what it is though, do I?"

Penny visibly relaxed. "No, of course not. So you do know what your mission is?"

"Yes," Kala confirmed. "And I'm assuming you're not trying to have Jack kill me anymore?"

Penny nodded, "For the time being, yes. But others of my order will not agree, if they can't persuade Jack to kill you, they'll send others. People they deem more worthy of the title. People who won't flinch at their duty."

"You don't know what they want me to do," Kala said before she could stop herself.

"It's always something unthinkable. That's the nature of the curse." Penny actually looked sympathetic.

"And why do people volunteer for a curse?" Kala asked sarcastically.

Penny smiled. "Because you're a hero now. You're saving the whole planet every four days. Some people like being heroes."

Like Jack.

Jack was definitely more suited for this job than she was. Kala was never interested in being a hero. She enjoyed being one of the good guys, but being part of an elite military team was more for the excitement rather than the good. And let's face it, some of the things they had done were questionable. There were a few missions that Kala definitely felt like she was on the wrong side of things. But it was her duty…

Her duty.

Wasn't this her duty now?

No. Kala pushed aside her thoughts. Killing Jack was a line she didn't want to cross.

"Now what?" Kala asked.

"Now I wake you up out of this contraption and give you a clean bill of health," Penny answered.

"Before you go, who exactly are you if you're not a Malak or Demon?" Kala decided she'd try again to find out who or what Penny was.

"It's complicated, another time. Time to wake up."

Kala opened her eyes to see the same group of people standing around her chair. General Turner was beyond excited as he looked at all the read-outs on the computer screens. Kala wasn't sure he knew what he was reading, but he appeared thrilled at the results.

Penny pointed out a few wavy looking graphs to Turner and Clifton. "As you can see here, there's no brain damage. There is nothing here to show that Ms. Hicks has had any kind of episode."

General Clifton eyed Kala with venom, then turned to Penny. "So you're saying she's of sound mind?"

"Yes, General, Ms. Hicks is fit for duty," Penny replied confidently.

"Soldiers!" General Clifton pointed to the four men behind Derek and Jack. The four men marched forward. "Execute the prisoner."

Chapter Sixteen

Kala was too stunned to respond.

Derek wasn't.

The man turned into an enraged animal as he threw the two men closest to him aside like he was parting tall grass in a jungle. The next two guards whirled around to fight their opponent.

General Clifton pulled out his gun and aimed it at Kala's head. "Time to say good night, sweetie." Clifton pulled the trigger.

BAM!

The gunshot blasted from the gun, but Kala didn't feel the impact.

That was because Asmodeus suddenly appeared between her and the bullet. The bullet fell harmlessly off his back.

"Miss me?" he smiled at Kala.

"At this moment, yes, I definitely missed you." Kala had to give it to him. Blocking a bullet gave him some mad credit in her book.

"I couldn't let that ass be the next Atlas, he would actually enjoy doing horribly vicious things. Wouldn't you agree, Pandora?" Asmodeus looked up at Penny.

Pandora? Kala wasn't sure if she had heard correctly. After all, Derek was making a meal of the remaining soldiers, causing a lot of noise and mayhem.

In the middle of it all, Turner didn't look upset. Instead, he stared intensely at Asmodeus. Kala guessed teleporting wasn't in his realm of science yet, and deflecting bullets with his skin well… let's just say Turner looked beyond intrigued.

Kala felt Jack's hand in hers and he pulled her away from Asmodeus. Apparently, Jack didn't like Asmodeus touching his girlfriend, let alone being her savior.

Asmodeus, on the other hand, didn't like the fact that Kala only had eyes for Jack. He reached out to touch Kala's shoulder.

Kala knew with certainty it was to teleport her away. As tempting as it was to leave the Compound clean, Kala didn't think she could manage an escape from Asmodeus's clutches again. Malak-distractions aside, the guy was too powerful. She jerked away before he could touch her.

Clifton unloaded his entire bullet cartridge in Asmodeus's back. The bullets deflected off his skin like pebbles hitting a wall, the shells clattering to the floor like a musical symphony of clinking.

Asmodeus whirled around to face Clifton, annoyed. "You done, little man?"

General Clifton was at a loss. He looked genuinely shaken. "What kind of material is that shirt made of?"

Clifton obviously assumed Asmodeus was wearing some kind of super fabric that would deflect bullets. Kala guessed that Clifton must have thought Asmodeus's teleporting skills were from a rival country's technological advances as opposed to the king of Demons popping in to take her away.

"97% cotton, 3% lycra," Asmodeus said as if he were in a commercial. Then without warning he lifted his hand and Clifton lifted with it. Asmodeus flicked his wrist causing Clifton to fly backward and slam against the wall with crunching impact.

Even Kala had to flinch at the sound. General Clifton slid to the ground, out cold.

Derek knocked out the last two guards by smashing their heads into the wall simultaneously. Kala was always amazed at how strong the guy was! Her heart sang with joy at his loyalty to her, but it sank at the same time, knowing that he would now be a fugitive like her.

Asmodeus turned his attention to Kala like she was the only one in the room. "You ready to leave, my love?"

"I'm not going anywhere with you," Kala responded, though she wasn't sure how she could stop him.

"And don't call her 'your love'," Jack practically snarled.

Kala loved the fact that Jack was jealous, but she didn't love the fact that Asmodeus could pop Jack's head like a grape if he wanted to. Her only ray of hope was the fact that Asmodeus knew her mission was to kill Jack, so that made Jack somewhat safe.

"You're not taking her, Asmodeus," Penny stepped in front of Kala.

"And *you're* going to stop me?" Asmodeus didn't seem concerned at all.

"Yes," Penny answered with such authority that Asmodeus paused. Penny turned to Kala. "Remember, you promised to fulfill your mission. I'm trusting you."

Guilt much? Kala simply nodded, though she was lying.

Then Kala saw a look of confusion on Asmodeus's face as Penny's eyes glowed blue. Penny leapt forward, wrapping her arms around his chest. They both disappeared in a flash.

It was so sudden that no one in the room moved.

Kala didn't know what to do next. She was now officially an enemy of the state and she was pretty sure Derek and Jack were, too.

Jack appeared to be having the same thought process as Kala as he looked at Turner, waiting for him to respond.

They had him outnumbered, yet Kala still felt the need to be deferential. This was the guy in charge: whether or not they tied him up or hurt him, this would be the man that hunted them down afterward. Clifton was scary, but Turner was terrifying.

Turner seemed to know this as well, though he was much more fascinated by Asmodeus and what he thought was a neurologist disappear before his eyes.

"So," Turner said, looking directly at Kala. "You're the cause of a lot of trouble, aren't you?"

Kala nodded, not sure what she should or shouldn't say.

Derek walked over one of the unconscious guards, standing protectively next to Kala. Kala wanted to give him a big hug for doing what he'd done, but now was definitely not the time.

"I'm assuming Harry will be okay?" Turner nodded towards General Clifton, still lying in a heap on the floor.

It was strange to hear General Clifton called by his first name.

Jack quickly checked Clifton's pulse. "He's just unconscious. Asmodeus didn't kill him." Jack walked back to stand beside Kala.

"Asmodeus, huh? What kind of a name is that? Arabic?" Turner was trying to work things out.

Kala noticed Jack making eye contact with Derek. They were planning a coup if they had to, she could tell. She didn't want them to be on the run their whole lives, not if she could help it. "General Turner, I acted alone in all this, Jack and Derek are just trying to protect me out of loyalty. Please don't punish them."

Turner shook his head. "I'm not punishing anyone."

Kala waited for the "just kidding" part of the conversation. When she didn't hear it she asked, "You're not?"

"No. Unfortunately for you, Harry will come after you no matter what I order. I can keep you off the official records as a fugitive, but that won't stop Harry." Turner eyed his friend with a kind of resignation. Then turned to Jack and Derek. "As for Colonel Norbin and Lieutenant Echols: they will stay in their command positions here at the Compound.

Harry won't argue." Turner nodded toward Derek, "Harry likes loyalty, just make him think that Lieutenant Hicks deceived you and that you're loyal only to him. The man loves his ego stroked."

"I don't know if I can…" Derek began.

But Kala finished his sentence for him, "Derek will do it. Thank you, General."

Kala looked up at Derek with as much determination as she could muster. "This is my problem, Derek. I don't want you involved any more. If you were executed because of me, I'd never forgive myself."

Derek didn't argue, but Kala could see that he knew better than to argue in front of Turner.

Jack looked at his clock. "I don't mean to break this up, but Penny can only hold off Asmodeus for so long. He'll be back soon and when he does none of us can stop him from taking Kala."

Turner looked around the room at all his unconscious soldiers in annoyance. "My soldiers can't even win against Lieutenant Echols, what chance do they have against…?" He left the sentence hanging waiting for someone to finish it. When no one did, Turner said simply, "I'm not letting you go until you tell me who he is."

"You wouldn't believe us if we told you." Kala wasn't sure how much she should tell Turner.

"You'd be amazed at what I'd believe. I'm working on projects right now that would blow your mind. They will literally change the world as we know it. I can believe quite a bit." Turner shrugged. "Besides, like I said, I can keep you here as long as I want until you tell me."

"That's the point, General, you can't," Jack corrected him. "Asmodeus knows where Kala is and as long as he knows he can pop back in and pop back out with her before you can utter *Stop*."

Turner took a moment to evaluate that in his head, then finally nodded in agreement. "Just tell me what I'm dealing with so I can come up with some kind of defense in the future."

Kala could see that Turner had complete confidence in his ability do just that. So much so that she felt the sudden need to tell Turner everything on the off chance that he could develop something to help her fight Asmodeus. "He's a Demon, sir."

"A Demon?" Turner repeated.

Derek looked at Kala like he was in on a joke. She knew he didn't believe it for a second. He thought she was lying to Turner.

So when Jack said what he said, Derek's face went from amused to confused in about a second.

Jack confirmed, "Asmodeus is the *King* of the Demons, General. He's the most powerful being on the planet, and I can't stop him. I can't slow him down. And if we don't get Kala out of here, it's over."

Turner nodded. He tapped the brain machine as if it held all the answers. "If this Asmodeus is after you, then you must be something *different*. I have all the results I need to research *what* you are." He looked directly at Kala. "You *do* want me to help you, don't you?"

Kala wasn't sure how to respond, but help from General Turner the mastermind behind every crazy invention she'd ever seen, sounded like a godsend. "If you think you can, sir. I could use all the help I can get."

"Good. Now that that's settled, you two," he pointed to Jack and Derek. "I'm assuming you're useless against this Demon?"

Jack admitted, "Yes, sir."

Though Derek still looked distraught at where the conversation had gone, he said boldly, "I could take him, General."

Jack intervened, "No, Derek, you couldn't."

Derek had had enough. "What the hell is going on here?! Are we really having a serious conversation about *Demons*? This is bull!"

"Oh my," Turner said, then he handed Derek a small round object the size of a marble.

Derek took it. "What's this?"

A flash of light from the object and Derek dropped to the floor, unconscious.

Kala's instincts overrode her good sense: she grabbed a gun from the floor and pointed it at Turner.

"Relax," Turner looked more annoyed at her behavior than worried. "He's out cold. These events were a little too much for our friend here. It's better for your Lieutenant Echols' cover story if he wakes up with Harry. And you Jack, you need to stay here, too, if you don't want to be on Harry's hit list. You have the best chance to convince him that you are still loyal, since you didn't fight any of the soldiers."

That was the first time Kala realized Jack hadn't fought at all. In fact, he'd just stood there. Derek had been the loyal-monster-machine. If Asmodeus hadn't shown up to save her, would Jack have let her die? A ball of emotion churned in her stomach. Maybe it would have been better if Kala had been killed. That way if Clifton became the next Atlas, Jack would have no problem taking him out. Jack just couldn't take her out.

It was a conflicting thought. On one hand Jack couldn't kill her, on the other hand he could let someone else.

Kala pushed the notion aside. Maybe Jack froze like she had. Maybe she was thinking too much. Being abandoned her whole life made the girl paranoid.

"Lieutenant Hicks, you're coming with me," Turner ordered.

Chapter Seventeen

Kala followed General Turner down the long hallway feeling like she was in grade school walking to the principal's office. It wouldn't matter if Kala had super powers like Asmodeus, Turner would always make her feel intimidated. Although Kala had to admit that he was taking all of this quite well. Nothing seemed to faze the guy. The more crazy the explanation, the more intrigued he became. Kala figured that it was just the way his brain worked. Turner was an inventor or, at least, he hired brilliant people to invent things for him: either way, he saw the world differently than most people. Kala knew enough about history to know that people like Turner really did change the world.

Turner slowed down enough so that Kala was walking beside him. "I'm assuming everything that you told me before is true as well? About the whole Atlas thing?"

Kala nodded yes, not quite sure why she was confessing. Still, if the General thought he could help, then at this point she was desperate.

"Interesting," was all Turner said.

When Kala couldn't think of anything to say, she ended up simply putting one foot in front of the other to whatever destination Turner had in store for her.

After a few twists and turns through the Compound, Turner spoke again. "This Demon character, he can just appear at any time? Does he use some kind of device or is it a power?"

"Definitely a power, and yes, he can jump in whenever he wants to. That's how I ended up in New York," Kala explained.

"And you escaped this… Asmodeus?" Turner prodded.

Kala realized she'd have to bring up the Malaks as well. "I escaped while he was distracted with a Malak."

"An Angel?" Turner asked curiously.

"They call themselves Malaks," Kala said, impressed at Turner's knowledge. "But yeah, I guess they're Angels."

"Yes, the word Malak means Angel in Arabic. This is old magic," Turner said as if categorizing Kala's particular situation in a filing bin in his head.

"Magic?" Kala asked timidly.

"Oh yes." Turner appeared to be opening up at the excitement of all the day's new revelations. "My wife Roberta is a student of all kinds of magic. She's quite an expert. Vodun is her strongest suit, but she's dabbled in old magic from the Greeks and the Arabs. She'll be very interested to hear about all this."

"Maybe we shouldn't be talking about this too much. Wouldn't General Clifton try and have us all executed or committed to a psychiatric ward?" Kala didn't like the idea of Turner telling people, even if it was his wife, about her situation. She barely understood it herself and she figured in two days when she didn't accomplish her mission Turner would have enough on his hands trying to save the world.

"Let me handle Harry. I won't be able to stop him from hunting you, but I will be able to help you hide. I'm developing a system now for tracking people and making people disappear. They go hand-in-hand as you might guess. As for this Demon fellow, how is he tracking you?" Turner was in business-mode and Kala felt a surge of hope that maybe good old-fashioned science might help her through this, rather than crazy-magic-DNA-transformation like Penny had done to her before.

"Supposedly, once he knows who I am he can track me anywhere in the world. He said I have a distinct signature. Penny said it was my DNA and she was actually able to shift my DNA profile enough to hide me from him," Kala explained as best she could. She still wasn't quite sure how all this worked.

Turner was genuinely flabbergasted. "Shifting DNA? Interesting. I'll have to tell Fortski. He'll definitely be interested in hearing about this."

Kala had no idea who Fortski was, but she assumed he was one of Turner's main scientist-inventors for Turner to mention him by name.

"Do you think anything you have will help hide me from Asmodeus?" Kala wanted to know if there was a chance at success here.

"Possibly." They arrived at a sealed metal door. "Through here." Turner opened the secured door with a biometric scan of his eye and they entered the most insane room Kala had ever seen.

The room itself was the size of a football field jammed packed with enough electronics to make Kala's head spin. It was hard to focus on any one thing at a time. Almost every inch of space was taken by some kind of machine or computer, all with wires, blinking lights and robotic parts. She saw a few of those brain-machines that had been used on her sitting empty against the wall.

After averting her eyes from all the flashing lights, Kala finally noticed a handful of scientists busy at work at various stations. None of them looked up at the two of them as Turner led her to the middle of the room.

"Here we are." Turner stopped in front of a small metal pedestal that came up to Kala's waist. There was what looked like a type of tranquilizer gun resting on top, a row of tubes filled with red liquid next to it.

"Is that blood?" Kala asked about the red tubes. She really didn't want it to be blood, but the closer she examined it, the more she knew what Turner would say.

"Every type, yes," Turner confirmed her suspicions. "This is the prototype. You'd be one of the first human volunteers."

"Awesome," Kala said, trying to hide the sarcasm from her tone. "What does it do?"

"It uses nanotechnology. Inside the blood are the teeniest tiniest devices, not even the size of a single blood cell. The devices are GPS trackers, once injected into the bloodstream, we'd be able to find that person anywhere on the globe, but we found that the GPS trackers mutated in the specimens and it had the opposite effect. The nanos completely hid the injected volunteer from any tracking system available today."

"Why?" Kala was curious.

"No idea. We're still trying to figure it out."

Kala was skeptical, but tried to be hopeful. "So you think it might work on me?"

"To be candid, I have no clue, but it's worth a shot, right?" Turner was acting more like a concerned friend than Kala's superior officer, but she found his attitude reassuring.

Fighting magic with science. It was something Kala felt she could have faith in. Having to admit that Demons and Angels were real was a hard pill to swallow, but now, maybe with this room of craziness, she'd have a real shot at some kind of defense. Being a soldier with no way to protect herself was new to Kala. She hated feeling so helpless. Growing up, helpless was all she'd ever felt, and it bothered her that she was back in a situation that she couldn't control. Enlisting in the Navy had been one of the ways that helped her achieve a sense of stability in her life. This whole Atlas-thing was beyond her imagination.

Of course, the room she was standing in was beyond her imagination as well, but it still felt more *real* than what she had experienced in the last two days.

"But will the Compound be able to track me with this?" Kala didn't want General Clifton being able to pinpoint her exact location when he regained consciousness.

"Not if you have the same reaction as the other volunteers." Turner picked up the injection gun. "Shall we?" He smiled. He was enjoying this way too much.

"Too late."

Kala cringed as she recognized Asmodeus's voice behind her.

Don't touch me! Kala yelled in her head.

Before turning around to see Asmodeus's smug face, Kala leapt forward, jumping behind a particularly large machine. She had no idea what purpose it served, but right now, it served as a barrier between her and *Teleport Boy.*

"Really?" Asmodeus seemed more amused than thwarted. "You don't even *want* to complete your mission. I'm just going to take you to a place where you can't for two days. Is that so bad?" Asmodeus acted as if he and Kala were the only two in the room.

Kala peeked behind the large square of a machine to see that Turner was gone. He must have ducked and run when Kala had. She couldn't worry about the General at the moment, though, since Asmodeus was ten feet away and staring straight at her.

"After the world ends or whatever, what do you plan on doing with me then?" Kala already knew the answer, which was why she wasn't going anywhere with the king of Demons.

Asmodeus looked like he was weighing the pros and cons of what to say next, then he finally shrugged in resignation. "Okay, I'll probably kill you. But not because I don't find you irresistible."

"Comforting." Kala wished she could punch him. And yet he truly seemed conflicted about his attraction to her. Even Demons always wanted what they couldn't have.

Kala decided to pull out the charm, from a distance of course, since Asmodeus hadn't moved from where he had popped in. Kala smiled the smile that had gotten her free drinks since she was seventeen. "If I'm dead, you'll never know if I would have chosen to be with you."

Mission accomplished. Asmodeus's face looked stricken. It really did bother him that Kala wasn't interested. Like, a lot.

"I really can't," Asmodeus said this as if he was turning Kala down for something simple like a date rather than her death. "You have to die and you have to die by ritual," he sighed like it was out of his hands. "It's only because Atlas needs to grow a pair and show himself after 2,000 years of tricking you idiots into doing his job." Asmodeus appeared to need to explain himself.

Kala wasn't expecting that tidbit of insight into her current employment situation, but any information was good. "I'm not going with you." Kala stared him straight in the eye.

"You don't really have a choice." Asmodeus stared back.

"Yes, she does." Turner appeared from seemingly nowhere. He said a few words in a language that Kala didn't recognize and injected Asmodeus's neck with something from the tracker gun he held earlier. Kala could see from where she stood, that it wasn't one of the blood vials, it looked like a vial of black ooze.

To Kala's surprise, Asmodeus screamed in anguish, clutching his neck like it was on fire.

In the mayhem of Asmodeus thrashing wildly around the room, desperately trying to gain control of himself, Turner hurried to Kala's side.

"What was that?" Kala asked in shock.

"Unfortunately for you I can't explain in time. You have to get out of here. I called my wife and she told me what to do on the fly, but I'm not sure how long he'll be in that state."

Asmodeus had resorted to his screeching cry that made the hairs on Kala's arm stick up. It was much nicer when he was a frat-boy-douche-bag than a screeching Demon-lord.

Turner grabbed Kala by the hand and guided her through a maze of machines toward the opposite end of the room. Kala noticed that the scientists had evacuated the lab. It made her marvel at how quickly employees of the Compound reacted to intrusions. Kala wondered how many times the Compound had been compromised. Until today, she would have said zero, but the way everyone responded made her re-think that.

When the two of them arrived at the door, Turner pulled Kala in close so he could whisper. "Roberta says Demons have incredible hearing. Even in his current state, Asmodeus will be trying to listen to us. Here." Kala finally noticed the small duffel Turner had slung over one shoulder. He pulled out the injection gun and loaded it with a vial of blood. "B positive. We have your medical records here."

Kala leaned her head down so Turner could inject her neck. As the gun deposited its contents into Kala's bloodstream, Kala felt a small flush of warmth course through her.

Then nothing. Back to normal.

Turner shrugged with an encouraging smile, "Let's hope it works."

Asmodeus's screaming intensified and the sound of crashing equipment made Kala jump in spite of herself.

Turner appeared very impressed with himself. "It's lasting longer than I expected." The General handed Kala the duffel. "I have two shots left of the stuff I injected our friend with. It's some kind of concoction Roberta made and you have to say these three words as you inject it." Turner gave Kala a piece of paper with three words she didn't recognize on it. "I spelled them out phonetically." There was also an address written on the paper. "Stay there tonight. If that anti-tracker works, you should be safe there. My wife will meet you in a few hours. She'll teach you some tricks."

Kala took the duffel, feeling a little bit better about her situation than before. From the sound of Asmodeus's screeching and flailing. Turner's wife obviously knew some kind of magic defense measures.

Opening the secured exit, Turner motioned for Kala to leave. "The platform is down the hall and two exits to your right. I've informed the guards on duty to expect you. You won't be stopped." Turner placed a hand on Kala's shoulder and squeezed it supportively. "Good luck, Lieutenant Hicks."

Kala saluted General Turner. "Thank you, General." She slung the duffel over her shoulder and ran down the hallway.

Chapter Eighteen

Kala arrived at the address scribbled on the piece of paper General Turner had given her with relative ease. She figured the anti-tracker must have worked since Asmodeus hadn't reared his annoyingly attractive head since she'd left the Compound. Kala also figured that if Asmodeus did catch up with her he'd be extremely pissed. She had probably lost all leverage with the Demon. Somehow she doubted he wanted a girl who was partially responsible for causing him some serious pain. (Although, with Asmodeus, she never knew.)

Leaving Derek and Jack behind was the hardest part of it all. Kala felt especially bad for Derek. He had been so confused by what had happened, it made Kala feel horribly guilty. At least Jack knew about Demons and Malaks and Atlas and Ugh, Kala didn't want to think about it anymore.

Kala held on to the duffel Turner had given her like it was a lifeline. To see Asmodeus debilitated like that filled her with happiness. She didn't want to be cruel, but he *was* the king of Demons and he *did* want to kill her for some 'ritual' or whatever.

The address Turner gave her was a typical looking brownstone off of 10th street. The neighborhood wasn't great, but it wasn't bad either. It was exactly the definition of ordinary.

Hiding in plain sight, Kala figured as she walked up the cracked cement stairs to the wooden door leading inside.

Kala turned the doorknob.

Locked.

Expecting this, Kala pulled out two paper clips that Turner had placed in the duffel. She had wondered why they were in there, and now her suspicions were confirmed. A part of Kala's training involved picking locks and doing it on very little. Instead of leaving a key that could be traceable, Turner had left the paper clips, relying on Kala's skills to get her in. After a few minutes of grumbling, Kala heard the click of the door unlocking.

Inside was just as ordinary as the outside, simple leather furniture, hardwood floors, wood-framed non-descript paintings and a couple of fake houseplants. Overall, brown was the way Kala would describe it, lots and lots of brown. The couch sung out to Kala's exhaustion like a siren calling her prey. She plopped down on the faded leather and nothing felt so plushy and soft as that couch did in that moment.

Looking around for a clock, Kala finally spotted an old fashioned grandfather clock against the far wall adjacent to a brick fireplace. She was getting used to seeing time in terms of her mission. A countdown to an epic failure, but a countdown none-the-less.

2d 07h 05m 13s: 10:53PM.

Sometimes being a *simple human* wasn't exactly ideal. Kala wanted to curl up into a ball and sleep, but she knew she needed to wait for Turner's wife, Roberta. If she could teach Kala a trick or two, Kala would be a very happy girl.

After a half hour of lying down on the couch trying desperately not to fall asleep, Kala heard the click of the front door opening. She was instantly on guard, peeling off the couch and plastering herself against the wall. She wanted the advantage if the visitor wasn't Roberta.

"You can come out in the open, I'm here to help," a female voice came from the hallway.

Kala stepped out to see a very beautiful older woman walking toward her. Though the woman was a little too botoxed for Kala's preference, and maybe a little young in Kala's opinion to have a face-lift, she still looked great. Long black hair fell to her shoulders in perfect waves, and her eyes were almost the same color, both in stark contrast to her pale skin. Kala imagined that Roberta Turner must have been quite a stunner in her younger years and figured that was why Roberta was going a little overboard trying to keep her youthful appearance. Any more surgeries, though, and she'd start to look like a cat. Her expression was sharp, but there was kindness behind it as well. Kala immediately liked her without explanation. There was just something in the way Roberta held herself, a kind of confidence that Kala respected. That and the fact that Kala knew this lady was responsible for causing frat-demon-boy pain. Definitely a power to be reckoned with.

When Roberta arrived at Kala's side she handed her a large leather satchel. "Put that on the table, we have a lot to talk about."

Kala did as she was told and placed the bag and its precious contents on the round wooden table situated between the couch and the kitchen. "I'm Kala by the way," she said in a friendly tone.

Roberta took a second before she responded, then she smiled and shook her head. "I apologize, I'm still reeling about what Geoffrey told me. I completely forgot my manners. I'm Roberta, General Turner's wife." Roberta put her hand out in greeting.

Kala took it and when her hand clasped Roberta's she felt a warmth. From the look in Roberta's eyes, she felt it as well. "We're going to get along just fine," Roberta said what Kala was thinking.

Taking the duffel Turner had given her, Kala plopped it next to the leather satchel. "The General gave me the black ooze gun, along with what words to say. What is this stuff anyway?" Kala pulled out a vial and examined it.

Roberta sat down and motioned for Kala to do the same. After they were both situated, Roberta started taking out smaller leather pouches from her bag. The pouches were tied shut, but Kala could smell odd odors coming from them. Roberta explained, "The 'ooze' is made up of these various herbs and other ingredients. I'll give you a list for the future. Combined with the right spell, you can cause a lot of havoc to Demons and Angels." Roberta looked at Kala thoughtfully. "Geoffrey only told me a little of what's happening, so you'll have to fill me in if you really want me to help you. And believe me, I'm one of the few people on this planet who can really help you."

At this point Kala felt like she had nothing to lose. She told Roberta everything. Everything except the fact that Kala's mission was to kill her boyfriend, and the fact that she wasn't going to complete it. But everything else she told Roberta, and after she finished Roberta's eyes were alight with anticipation.

"I've been telling Geoffrey for years that Demons and… 'Malaks' you call them?" Roberta continued when Kala nodded her head in confirmation. "I've been a practitioner of magic since I was a girl, but Geoffrey only paid it little mind until today. He's lucky I look out for him and stock his lab or he wouldn't have had the proper ingredients to banish that Demon."

"Asmodeus didn't go anywhere though, he just screamed in pain and couldn't seem to snap out of it." Kala tried to paint Roberta a picture of what she had seen happen.

"If I had been there, I could have banished him. Geoffrey barely believed it would work. I think it was only his faith in me that made the spell have any success. Magic is about belief, the stronger the belief, the stronger the practitioner," Roberta explained.

Kala's mind was spinning. *Magic?* Until two days ago, Kala didn't believe in an afterlife, let alone freaking magic! If magic was based on belief then Kala would be an epic fail. And now, this woman was telling her that she could actually fight back against both Demons and Malaks, but the only way to do that was to *believe*. Well, Kala definitely couldn't deny what was happening to her, but was it the same thing as belief?

"I'm not sure I'll be good at this," Kala voiced her fears.

Roberta smiled again as she took out the rest of the leather pouches. "Nonsense. I'll teach you. There's not much we can do tonight. Magic takes time to learn and I'm good, but I'm not *that* good. I might be able to show you a few tricks, but you'll have to rely on the 'ooze' gun for now. Guns should be somewhat of a reassurance for you, right?" Roberta added in a comforting tone.

"You're going to leave?" Kala logically knew Roberta wouldn't be able to stay long, but she was feeling the need for a security blanket. Roberta fit the bill alarmingly well.

"Our visits will have to be limited due to your current 'status' with the government. Geoffrey can't have Harry finding out that I'm meeting with the enemy. We'll have to meet somewhere new every time, but you need my help, trust me on that." Roberta appeared very confident in that fact and Kala tended to agree with her. Just seeing Asmodeus as helpless as he was from an injection and a few simple words was proof enough.

"What if magic isn't my thing?" Kala asked what she feared most. What if the one defense against Demons and Malaks was something she was incapable of?

"Anyone can practice magic," Roberta smiled. "And you'll get better over time. Remember, this Asmodeus character is the king of the Demons, meaning he's the most powerful, and if Geoffrey can squeeze an ounce of pain out of him, you'll be able to do the same."

"I hope so." Kala wasn't convinced. "Because I'd really like to cause that ass-hat some serious pain."

Roberta raised her eyebrow in curiosity. "You don't like Asmodeus, do you?"

"That's an understatement," Kala confided.

"Well, I'll go over everything I can with you, and maybe we can squeeze in some kind of Demon-torture-spell for you to use." Roberta seemed genuinely pleased at the prospect.

"I appreciate it," Kala said gratefully. She was still shocked that she had any help at all. Kala didn't want to admit to Roberta that she wouldn't need anyone's help for much longer anyway. Once the next two days had passed and whatever disaster hit the planet, Kala knew that Roberta and Turner would know that she failed the mission and would want nothing to do with her. As much as Kala liked the woman sitting in front of her, she knew she'd have to pump Roberta for her knowledge and skills and then get out of Dodge fast.

"I have one more thing here," Roberta said. She reached into her satchel and pulled out an old leather-bound book that looked like the pages were about to fall out of it. The cover was so faded Kala couldn't read the title, but she guessed that this book was probably where the "spells" came from. Roberta held the book like it was the Holy Grail: with reverence and delicacy.

"I have others, but this one focuses on Demon protection. It was written over six hundred years ago after the Black Death ravaged Europe. It speaks of the time of Demons roaming free and feeding off the plague. At first I thought it was more of a metaphor for the disease running rampant. But the spells in here are so specific that I started to wonder if any of the Demon stories were true. I performed some of the spells just to see what would happen: I could feel the power in them, but it wasn't until I cast *this* spell that I was certain Demons were real." Roberta reopened the book to a specific page and handed it to Kala.

Kala read the title of the spell: Infusing Demonic Essence.

Whoa. That sounded bad, but Kala had no idea what it actually meant. "What happened when you did it?"

Roberta carefully took the book back and her eyes lit up from the memory.

"Exactly what it says: I infused the power of a Demon inside me. I stole its power for a time. It was both terrifying and exhilarating. It only lasted for a short while, maybe an hour at the most, but I realized that the spell must be used in conjunction with other spells to amplify them. Basically, harnessing Demon energy to be as powerful as the Demons are." Roberta let that last thought hang there a bit.

"Um." Kala was at a loss for words. She felt like her brain was going to explode with all this new information. And not just information, but insane-holy-crap-what-the-hell-happened-to-my-life information!

Roberta didn't appear fazed by Kala's reaction at all. She simply placed the book down and reached across the table to touch Kala's arm supportively. "This is all a bit overwhelming. I can't imagine what you're going through, but the fact is that Demons are real and they're coming after you."

"Angels, too." Kala added, not knowing why she needed to add an extra stressor to the already stressed out situation.

"Angels, too." Roberta smiled and took her hand away. "Unfortunately, there's nothing about protecting yourself against an Angel directly, but if we can teach you to harness the Demon energy…"

Kala cut her off. "No."

"No?" Roberta looked at her quizzically. "No *what?*"

"No, I don't want to 'harness Demon energy'. I don't want to have anything to do with Demons, let alone take their power. I may not be religious, but it just feels wrong on so many levels."

To Kala's surprise, Roberta didn't bat an eye. Kala thought she might have offended Roberta by making her protestations, but Roberta simply smiled and gave Kala an encouraging nod. "I'll let you stew some more on that topic. You may change your mind later down the road. Besides, the spell is far too advanced to learn in a few hours. It would take time, years even, to really learn how to perform it. I just want you to know it's an option, okay?" Roberta stated carefully.

Kala knew Roberta was only trying to help and she was relieved that the woman wasn't pressuring her. And Roberta was right, maybe in time,

Kala would be desperate enough to want to use a spell like that…

It doesn't matter anyway, because I'm not killing Jack, Kala reminded herself. She kept on letting her mind plan for a future of fighting Demons and Malaks as if she were actually taking the Atlas gig. What did it matter if she said yes or no to Roberta if the spell took years to learn? She'd probably never see Roberta again after tonight.

"Let's start out small, then. Shall we? I'll teach you the trick I taught Geoffrey. I'm not sure what it'll do against an Angel, but it might be enough for you to run away to safety."

And so began the next few hours of Roberta teaching Kala all about different herbs and ingredients that were a part of spell-making. At times it felt like Kala was in Chemistry class, the measurements had to be so exact, but after a while, she started to get the hang of all the different meanings of each ingredient. Together they prepared an entire bowl of the black ooze that had incapacitated Asmodeus. The consistency was thick and disgusting, although creating it really did feel more like science than magic.

It wasn't until Kala performed her first spell that she realized it was one thing to talk about magic, but it was entirely different to experience it.

The spell was a levitation spell. Kala always wished she had super powers growing up, so she volunteered to try this one first. She figured if she got really good at it, she could throw everything including the kitchen sink at whoever was trying to attack her. It might not hurt them, but Kala was under no illusions that she could actually hurt a supernatural being. Though Roberta kept insisting that Kala could, Kala just didn't believe it. Then, after her third try, Kala levitated a nickel. She had to recite the words from the book, which she committed to memory, but it was one of the few spells that didn't require any concoctions.

Roberta appeared to be very impressed with Kala's progress (or, at least, she acted like she was). Kala didn't know if Roberta was just being nice, or if she genuinely thought Kala was doing a good job, but either way, Roberta seemed very happy to have a fellow "magic-friend."

After another hour of trying to perfect the levitation spell, Kala was barely able to lift the nickel three inches off the table. But, to Kala's surprise, Roberta was thrilled, gushing at what a natural Kala was, while Kala felt like a complete failure.

"A nickel won't do much damage against a Demon," Kala vented her frustration.

"It's not the object that you're lifting that I'm impressed with, it's the spell. Levitation spells are very complicated because of the fact that you have to rely solely on the practitioner. You don't have potions or herbs to help you," Roberta said encouragingly. "And you would be amazed at what a nickel could do when moving fast enough."

Kala conceded the point. She'd done a lot of damage with far less when out in the field. Maybe in time...

But, right now, Roberta grabbed the black ooze they'd concocted. "Let's put this in vials." She pulled out ten empty vial cartridges specially made for the tranquilizer gun.

Kala and Roberta worked together to pour the black mixture into the vials. Kala loaded one on the gun, ready for an attack.

"I should make a holster for this gun," Kala thought out loud.

"You'll find everything you need in that closet." Roberta nodded to a door under the staircase as she finished filling the vials.

Kala walked to the closet door and opened it. Inside was gear central: gun belts, holsters, flak jackets, even some extra clothing if she needed it. Though everything was obviously for guys, but Kala would make do.

"I have clothes for you upstairs, but take what you need," Roberta replied as if reading Kala's thoughts.

Grabbing a holster that looked like it would do the trick, Kala brought it back to the table. She picked up the tranquilizer gun and placed it inside the leather cradle. Perfect. Exhaustion finally caught up with Kala. She didn't think she could keep her eyelids open a second longer. Roberta picked up on this when Kala plopped down on her chair, almost missing it entirely.

"Let's get you to bed," Roberta said softly.

"No, I need to learn more," Kala protested weakly, unable to mask the tiredness in her voice.

"You have enough here to help you survive the next two days. I'll send word for our next meeting place." Roberta helped Kala to her feet and led her up the wooden staircase to a small bedroom with a queen-sized bed inside.

"How will you send word?" Kala wanted to know. If she was trying to stay hidden from the supernatural, she didn't think Roberta would be able to locate her.

"I have my ways," Roberta smiled.

Kala wanted to ask her more, but couldn't stay awake. She just needed a few hours rest, then she could think clearly again.

As soon as her head hit the fluffy feather pillow, Kala fell fast asleep.

DAY THREE

Chapter Nineteen

Kala woke up not knowing where she was. It took her a few moments to figure it out, and when she did, she wished she were back asleep. At least when she was unconscious she didn't have to accept the reality she was currently living. Glancing over at the alarm clock only solidified that belief as she saw the countdown.

1d 21h 12m 32s. 8:39 a.m.

Her heart jumped at seeing a 1 in the day slot. Time was running out and though Kala had vowed not to kill Jack, a part of her still felt the stress of not completing a task. It wasn't in Kala's nature to not see a mission through. A part of her was energized by being a rebel and the other part wanted to crawl under a rock from guilt. She didn't know how she was going to live with herself if something truly horrible happened as a result of not completing her mission. Being trained her whole military career that the good of the world far outweighed a single soldier's life, Kala hated that she was still struggling with the decision she'd made.

Killing Jack couldn't be an option for her.

The thought of pulling the trigger eased her doubts about that choice. It was not something she was capable of. Besides, Kala still wasn't totally convinced that anything bad *would* happen. This whole situation felt more like a fantasy. She wouldn't believe it until she saw it.

"Roberta!" Kala called out as she thumped her feet on the floor to get ready for the day.

When no answer came, Kala noticed a fresh set of clothes lying perfectly folded on the foot of her bed. She quickly dressed herself in the jeans and pull-over sweater and hurried down the stairs to see if Roberta was still there.

Kala felt a stab of disappointment when she realized Roberta was gone. Roberta was the first person on this whole journey that had made her feel somewhat empowered. Just having a handful full of ooze-ammo and a gun to shoot it with made Kala feel more confident if she ever ran across Asmodeus again. And maybe she could get better at the levitation spell. It might just be throwing things with her mind and a few choice words, but the more she learned, the more it leveled the playing field.

Kala wondered if other Atlases had known sorcery or magic or whatever. Kala certainly felt like it should be a job requirement, since no amount of mundane weapons or martial arts appeared to have any effect on the supernatural. Kala felt a surge of frustration at that thought. She had worked her whole adult life to be practically indestructible, the best of the best, so much so that she was chosen for Turner and Clifton's elite team. To be virtually defenseless made Kala's head implode. It was grossly unfair. At least the tranq gun made her feel a little like her old self. She put on the gun holster and placed the gun inside.

Kala sighed. She should be used to the unfairness of life, but it always seemed to knock her on her butt whether she expected it or not.

Still.

Kala wondered how Roberta was going to make contact once she left this place. Roberta said she "had her ways," but Kala was losing hope that she'd ever have another encounter with the woman again. There was so much more to learn and Kala didn't know the first thing about how to figure it out. If Roberta was able to contact her, she probably wouldn't want to after Kala deliberately failed her mission.

Kala walked to the refrigerator for breakfast.

After a giant meal of eggs, bacon and pancakes, Kala felt ready to face the day. A part of her wanted to hole up in this hideout, but she was sure that this wouldn't be a safe house for long. Staying on the move was the best bet for survival.

Kala put on a baseball cap and tucked her hair up inside. She figured if General Clifton had her on his radar, he'd use every surveillance camera available. That meant keeping her head down so not even traffic cams could readily recognize her.

Kala put on her jacket, making sure the holster was out of sight. Grabbing her bag, Kala left the brownstone and headed for a place where she could find a computer. There was a lot of research to do, mainly about Atlas. She was sure most of what she'd find would be the typical mythology stuff, but maybe, just maybe, someone who actually knew about the real job position would have written something over the years.

A thought hit her like lightning.

Asmodeus's words: "*You have to die and you have to die by ritual. It's only because Atlas needs to grow a pair and show himself after 2,000 years of tricking you idiots into doing his job.*"

Something about what he said struck a chord with Kala. If Atlas tricked humans into doing his job, maybe a human could trick *him* into taking it back. Though Atlas himself had said this wasn't possible, the thought still made her head giddy with possibilities. But just as suddenly a horrible thought overwhelmed her: if she didn't kill Jack, then Atlas would. Escaping from the burden of this job wasn't the answer because the answer was always the same: Jack and a bullet through his head.

Kala decided to file away what Asmodeus said for another time. It was definitely important information, Kala just couldn't process it at that moment, not if it meant thinking about murdering her boyfriend.

Making her way past row upon row of brownstones, Kala reached a busy street crowded with restaurants, stores and, more importantly an Internet café. She picked the closest one to her and paid the clerk for two hours of computer time. She ordered an iced mocha, feeling like she needed a little sugar and caffeine to jump start her day. Sidling up on a bar stool, Kala signed in to the computer with the username and password the clerk had given her.

After a few agonizingly long moments, Kala was finally on the Internet and felt like an idiot when she typed in "History of Atlas": almost every page was about the history of the atlas books, as in maps. Although she had a moment of feeling justified when she remembered thinking this in the presence of the real Atlas. Most people did think of the map kind of atlas before they thought of the Greek god Atlas. So Kala refined her search to: Greek god Atlas history. She found out right away he was a Titan and that Titans were the first Greek pantheon known as the Elder Gods, just as Atlas had told her. Atlas was a second generation Titan being the son of Iapetus, but Kala wondered if there really was a big difference between first and second generations. Everything she read was all the same: he led a fight against Zeus and lost and his punishment was holding up the world or in some legends guarding the pillars that kept the earth and sky apart, either way he was definitely guardian of the earth. Or at least the guy that kept the earth from crumbling. It made an odd sense, everything that Kala had been told from the real Atlas. The histories were a watered-down version of what was true. In order for the world to function properly, Atlas had the burden of making it happen.

Now that burden was hers.

And she was completely ignoring it.

There were also a couple of pages that said Atlas taught humans astronomy, and a story about how he tricked Hercules into taking his burden…

Kala froze.

Tricked Hercules into taking his burden!!

Kala suddenly knew that the Hercules story was actually the truth. Sure, she knew Hercules probably wasn't real, or honestly, she couldn't really say that with confidence anymore, but that must have been the moment Atlas was set free. Hercules may have been Zeus's son, but he was also half human, which meant Atlas tricked a mortal into doing his job.

After her two hours were up, Kala felt like she knew a little more about Greek mythology than she did before, but she still felt way out of her depth. She had fiddled around looking up what she could on Hercules, but mostly it was stories about his bravery and valor. It said he tricked Atlas back into taking the pillars again. If that were true, maybe it meant that Hercules was the first to shove Atlas's job back in his face. Maybe Atlas tricked a full-blown human after that. Kala had no idea, and no one to ask. Everything was just one big guess at this point.

Throwing her bag over her shoulder, Kala left the café and made sure she kept her hat down, hiding her face from any cameras that might be above her. It was weird hiding from the people she trusted most. The Ops team had been her family and as far as she was concerned they still were, but Clifton had it out for her. Talk about pissing off the wrong guy. Kala felt that she was a pawn thrown into the middle of a fight between Turner and Clifton, but either way, the most elite force in the government and probably the world now had her face as enemy number one. The person who assassinated the President.

The worst mistake she had ever made.

"Kala Hicks?" A man's voice sounded behind her.

Kala kept walking. She didn't respond or react. Kala hoped that maybe whoever it was would think they confused her with someone else. A part of her was curious as to who called out her name. If it was one of Clifton's guys, she'd be captured already, or at least, in the process of *trying* to be captured. It had to be someone from her past who honestly thought they were reuniting with a friend.

As if from thin air, a man stepped in front of Kala. "I've been looking for you," he snarled.

And Kala recognized him right away.

It was the Malak, Grautlin.

Kala switched into military-mode. He was a Malak — he'd be too fast if he saw her going for the gun, so she tried distraction. "How did you find me?"

Grautlin seemed very impressed with himself. "Security camera in the café. You can't disguise yourself from a Malak."

Kala pretended to act scared. She pretended to cry dramatically, covering her face with her hands. Anything to disguise what she was about to do.

"You're pathetic," Grautlin sneered. "I'll enjoy killing you."

Before Grautlin could move, Kala had her gun out of the holster and shoved into Grautlin's stomach. She pulled the trigger and recited the words from the spell.

Grautlin shrieked, holding his head in pain.

Kala ran.

She didn't know how long the spell would last.

Kala was just relieved that it had worked at all! And on a Malak!

While she ran Kala reached in her bag and pulled out another ooze-vial, loading it onto the gun. Knowing that Grautlin would do anything in his power not to let her have another chance to inject him, Kala kept the gun out and ready.

Kala cursed all surveillance cameras and hoped that Clifton's face recognition software wasn't as advanced as the Malaks' ability to spot her.

Grautlin's screams from behind her stopped abruptly.

Kala shoved her way past people walking down the sidewalk, ignoring their stares of suspicion and fear.

Grautlin popped up in front of her, reaching for her neck to snap.

On instinct, Kala canted the levitation words she had memorized and to her amazement made a garbage can lift off the ground and smash into Grautlin. She knew she didn't have time to inject him again, so she ran as fast as she could down the street and into a nearby alley.

Kala's adrenaline was pumping fast and she realized she was running aimlessly. Where did she think she was going? Where could she run? A part of her was impressed with herself that she'd managed to levitate the garbage can so easily. Maybe she did have a knack for magic. It excited her a bit.

Just as Kala turned the corner, Grautlin appeared and roared in anger.

"I would kill you slowly if I had my choice," the Malak raged.

"You could try." Kala leapt to a set of fire escape stairs on the side of the alley. She was halfway up the second flight of stairs when Grautlin materialized in front of her.

Kala groaned in frustration. "I hate that trick." She injected Grautlin again, but before she could finish the spell, he backhanded her off the fire escape.

Waiting for the inevitable impact of the cement lasted longer than Kala expected. Just before she reached bottom, it was as if a force of wind slowed her fall. She landed on the ground with a light thump.

Looking around for whatever or whomever had cushioned her landing, Kala laid eyes on a man entering the alley.

Grautlin saw him too and screamed in fury. "She's mine, Malak!"

Great, another Malak. Kala had had enough of the supposed "good guys" trying to kill her.

But the man didn't make any sudden moves toward her, he just stared at Grautlin with anger. "Leave, Grautlin, before you regret it," the man warned.

"Who are you?" Grautlin didn't look worried at this stranger's threats in the least.

"It doesn't matter," the man said calmly. "Leave the girl and live."

Kala suddenly felt like she was standing in the middle of an old-style western gun fight.

She took it as a cue and made a run for the opposite exit.

Grautlin materialized in front of Kala so suddenly she almost smacked into him. She managed to stop herself just inches from Grautlin's body.

"Time to die," he grinned.

And that was exactly what happened.

BOOM!

Grautlin's body exploded in front of Kala.

She waited for the splattering of Angel guts to hit her, but in a large POOF there was no evidence that Grautlin ever existed.

Instinct took over. Kala whirled around to face the stranger who stood there like the Angel of Death. The fact that this Malak had just obliterated one of his own kind scared Kala in a way she couldn't describe. Not even Asmodeus had that kind of power and he was the king of the Demons.

And if this stranger could do that to a Malak, Kala knew she was a dead woman.

But Kala was a fighter. She focused on the dumpster next to her, levitation spell already on her lips. Before she could utter a syllable, however, the Malak lifted his finger and placed it on her mouth. Kala tried to say the words of the spell, but nothing came out. A surge of panic ran through her: this man had taken away her ability to speak. Her only defense against the supernatural taken in one touch. She was beyond furious, she was terrified.

"Relax," the Angel said softly, calmly. "I'll give you back your voice. I just need to talk to you before you attack me with a dumpster," he said with a slight smile.

Kala was close enough to shoot. She placed the gun on his chest and was about to pull the trigger when the gun dissolved in her hand. Within seconds her whole defense system was literally dust blowing in the wind. Just like Grautlin.

It took Kala a few seconds to gain her bearings. In this new life of hers she figured she'd listen to anyone who had more power while she quietly devised a plan of escape. First goal: get her voice back. She nodded and tried to look as defeated as possible so he would think she was ready to listen.

Although under normal circumstances it would be quite easy to listen to the Malak standing before her. He was very attractive with short light brown hair in a messy-sexy-swoop, blue eyes and bone structure for days. He was wearing a black, tight-fitted biker jacket with a white t-shirt and jeans. Supermodel anyone?

Why did Malaks and Demons have to be so freakin' gorgeous! Supreme beings, Kala guessed, but it still annoyed her. Couldn't the bad guys be ugly or something, so she could at least tell them apart from the good guys?

The man gave her a look that suggested he wasn't buying her supplication for a second. Instead of being angry, though, he looked amused. "I think I'm going to explain myself first before I give you your voice back. I don't trust you… yet."

The way he said *yet* made Kala pause.

Things that she knew: A. He'd just saved her life. Maybe he did this to become the next Atlas himself, but he did it all the same. B. He hadn't actually tried to kill her and at this point, having taken her voice, he could so very easily. C. If he wanted to teleport her to some dungeon to kill her there, he could have done it a hundred times over by now.

Kala really did want to hear what this *creature* had to say. It was easier calling him a creature, it made his good looks feel more unnatural and less attractive.

Trying not to have too much snark, Kala waved her hand in front of her gesturing her impatience as if to say, *Get on with it*.

The man smiled, enjoying Kala's attitude. "Let's go somewhere less… public."

Kala didn't like the sound of going anywhere with this guy, though she did agree that being in an alley near a busy street left her vulnerable to Clifton, and apparently the forces of Malaks and Demons as well. She didn't have much choice anyway, though, as the man touched her arm and Kala's surroundings blurred in front of her eyes.

Everything came back into focus as Kala and the man materialized in a small apartment overlooking the Capitol Building, with the Washington Monument in the distance. Kala quickly did the math and realized they were somewhere in the Capitol Hill area. She was relieved that they were still in D.C., but Kala really hated this whole teleporting business. Travel of any kind made Kala a little squeamish, but teleporting made her downright nauseous. She would have given this guy a piece of her mind, but as she couldn't speak she simply plopped down on the brown linen couch that was resting against the far wall.

The apartment was a studio with a small kitchenette, hardwood floors, a couch, matching recliner chair and a ginormous flat screen television, at least sixty inches, maybe bigger. What a Malak needed with a TV Kala had no idea, but she wasn't in a position to fault the guy for it. It only reminded her of the fact that she'd never be able to watch television again without seeing herself murder Jack on repeat. A thought that was extremely depressing.

Kala noticed that there wasn't a bed, not even a mattress. She guessed the supernatural didn't need to sleep. *The more information the better*, she shrugged.

Kala gave the man a look that suggested she wasn't playing anymore. If she could have put words to it, she would have said, *Speak or die, asshole.*

The stranger got the message, though he didn't appear threatened at all by Kala, she noticed with irritation. He took off his jacket and laid it on the back of the recliner as he sat down across from Kala. "Sorry about the theatrics and the teleporting. I can see your face is a beautiful tinge of green," he started in a friendly tone.

For some reason this annoyed Kala even more. She raised one of her eyebrows and gave him the stink eye while crossing her arms in a huff.

He continued, "I'm going to give you your voice back, but if you try any spells I'll have to block you again. Understand?"

Kala nodded, though she felt as if she was being addressed like a four-year-old. To be fair, Kala figured that this guy was probably thousands of years old while Kala was only a speck of dust on the map of time to him.

A fuzzy rushed sensation flowed through her chest and Kala cleared her throat, relieved to hear sound. "What do you want with me?" Thought she'd get that out of the way first.

"I'm what humans call an Angel," he responded. He reminded Kala of her fifth grade science teacher in the way he answered so patiently, like if he was clear and concise enough, Kala wouldn't get behind in the conversation.

"I thought you guys were called Malaks." Kala uncrossed her arms and sighed. She hated being in situations that she couldn't control. She was tempted to ignore his threat of voice control by making the recliner flip him backwards, but Kala knew he'd stop her in mid-sentence. A new trick she couldn't even use.

Awesome.

The man shook his head. "I'm a different kind of Angel. Malaks want you dead. Grautlin was a Malak, I'm not."

Kala shrugged then nodded. "But you're both Angels?"

"I'm of a different order, the Grigori. We were sent down to teach humans how to be civilized back when you were barely above the ape-stage of your existence, but the powers-that-be decided we were over-stepping our bounds and banished us from earth."

"Over-stepping?" Kala was curious. Up until now history lessons had been a bore to her, but lately, history lessons meant ammunition for future death matches. Not to be too dramatic, but that was how it felt to Kala.

"We were supposed to start you humans with the basics— fire, cooking, hunting — but we saw the raw potential in you. We began showing you magic, science, technology, and you soaked it up like you were born to it." The stranger lit up with the memory, making Kala realize he was probably one of the actual Grigori that existed back then.

How old did that make him? Kala would have to look up the Grigori on the Internet since her *historical-fact* knowledge was spotty. But one word stuck out to her more than the others. "Magic?" she asked.

The man smiled. "Yes. Much more advanced than the primitive stuff you practice, though. The woman you trained with is the best I've ever seen, but she only scratched the surface when teaching you."

"It was only one night, geez." Kala found that she was a little defensive at being called primitive. Levitating crap and throwing it at people was quite impressive in her book.

"I didn't mean to offend you. I just meant I can teach you much more." He seemed genuinely polite about the whole thing.

"Who are you anyway?" Kala became conscious of the fact that she didn't know this Grigori Angel guy's name.

"I apologize. My name is Talan."

"Of course it is." Kala smirked. *Talan?* Talk about your romance novel name. The fact that he had the looks to back it up only made it more absurd.

"I fail to see why you think my name is obvious." Talan stared at Kala with a curiosity that made her feel uncomfortable.

"Why am I here?" Kala changed the subject.

"I'm here to help you carry out your mission. This is the third day and you're running out of time." Talan's blue eyes looked at her intensely.

"I don't need your help. I can do it just fine on my own." Kala skirted the issue that she wasn't planning on carrying out any mission.

"You're lying," Talan said matter-of-factly. "You don't want to do what you were shown."

Kala didn't answer, which she realized only confirmed Talan's statement.

He laughed. "It's understandable, Kala. Not a single Atlas has *ever* wanted to complete a mission. The first one is always the hardest, but they do get easier."

Kala's defenses kicked in big time. She stood up in a huff. "What would you know about it? Were you ever an Atlas?"

Talan stood up with her, but his demeanor was calm, comforting. He placed his hand on Kala's arm to steady her.

Kala did not want to be touched, especially from this guy. She shrugged his hand off and stepped away from the couch. She would have made a break for it if she didn't know that Talan could easily find her and bring her right back.

"How did you find me anyway? I thought that anti-tracker made it impossible for your kind to find me. It worked on Asmodeus anyway." Again with the changing subjects, Kala was good at that.

"The same way Grautlin did, the café surveillance tape," he said.

Kala groaned. She'd have to steer clear of all civilization at this point!

Talan continued, "And the anti-tracker does work. The Turner family is very powerful. They are much more advanced than most humans, him with his science and her with the magic. The supernatural world has no idea how far the Turners have come and it'll be too late to do anything about it by the time they figure it out." Talan almost seemed proud of Turner and Roberta, as if they had reached some level of nirvana that he was somehow responsible for. Like a proud teacher...

"*You've* been showing them! You said yourself that you Grigori guys got in trouble for teaching magic and science. You've been sneaking in some tutoring behind the collective Demon and Angels' asses!" Kala knew she was right and everything made total sense. "The Turners have no idea what you are though, do they?"

Talan didn't deny Kala's accusations, he only confirmed them by saying, "To Roberta I come as an older Cajun man and master of Voodoo. To Turner I'm one of his top scientists. But they have such raw talent on their own! It will take them far."

Talan's eyes were proud as he added, "I wouldn't be surprised if they end up ruling the world someday."

Kala shrugged. "It wouldn't be such a bad world if they did. So far, they've helped me more than I could have ever imagined. And maybe they could..." she didn't finish her thought.

But Talan did, "Maybe they could fix what you destroy when you don't complete your Atlas mission?"

Kala's eyes met Talan's, and she knew she'd given herself away in one look. That was exactly what she was going to say.

Talan stepped toward her again. This time Kala didn't pull away. He touched her arm gently, his eyes were big round blue abysses of intensity as he looked at her. Kala was attracted to him, though she hated herself for it. Though he looked human, there was something unnaturally beautiful about him.

Maybe the fact that he's an Angel? Kala chastised herself.

"Tell me what you have to do," Talan asked calmly.

They were so close at this point it was making Kala aware of Talan's body heat, radiating off of him like a freaking space heater. It was the first time since meeting Jack that Kala physically felt this kind of chemistry, and she didn't like it.

"I'm not telling you." Kala wanted to back away, but found herself frozen in place, as if she needed to feel the heat from Talan's body.

"I won't complete your mission if that's what you're afraid of, but if you tell me what it is I can show you what will happen if you don't complete it." Talan's face was so close to Kala's it was making her legs shaky. Not just because of the chemistry she was feeling, but because of what he was offering her.

A chance to see what would happen if she didn't kill Jack.

But she didn't trust him. She didn't know Talan. He claimed he wouldn't go out and kill Jack, but if he decided he wanted to, there was nothing she could do about it.

"I don't trust you, and I have no way of stopping you if you're lying to me." Kala decided the honest approach was her best option.

Talan stared at her a few more moments, then backed away with his hands up in mock surrender. "I'll tell you anything you want to know. Better yet, I'll show you."

Kala found that she was disappointed when Talan stepped away from her. She hated herself for entertaining any kind of desire toward Talan, but chemistry wasn't something she could control.

She could, however, control herself — and Jack meant more to Kala than anything she could think of. No *Angel* would stand in the way of that.

Then what Talan said registered in her brain. "Show me?" she asked.

He nodded. "The same way I will be able to show you the future, I can show you the past. My past."

Kala's one weakness in life was her insatiable curiosity. Being able to see what an Angel's life was like was too tempting to turn down. She looked Talan in the eye and nodded quickly before she could chicken out.

"Show me," she said.

Chapter Twenty

Talan reached out and took Kala's hand. She had to repress a shiver that went down her spine at his touch. Kala wanted to punch herself in the face for her reaction to Talan, but she shoved down her emotions instead. Just like always. She was good at that.

Talan led her back to the couch and they both sat down facing each other.

"Close your eyes," he instructed.

Kala closed her eyes and felt Talan take her other hand so that he held them both.

Relax. Kala scolded herself, but her heart raced with excruciating anticipation of what was going to happen next.

A flood of images drowned Kala's senses to the point where she had to open her eyes from the onslaught.

Talan quietly instructed, "You have to close your eyes. The images will slow down. Relax and calm down."

Kala wanted to grumble in annoyance, but kept her opinion to herself. She never liked to be told to calm down. For some reason just the words made her want to choke someone. But in this instance Kala figured Talan was right. She was trying very hard not to panic, which was completely new to her. Being a Navy Seal, panic wasn't exactly one of her regular sensations. Kala was always cool under pressure, but these were very different circumstances. She couldn't shoot her way out of this one.

Closing her eyes, Kala let the melee of images fly past her. If she tried to focus on any one of them it zoomed by too fast to really tell what it was. Taking a deep breath, Kala steadied her nerves, calming herself to the point of relaxation.

The images slowed down.

Kala could start making out what she was seeing.

People and landscapes, from cavemen to the modern age. Kala saw flash photos of manmade progress in technology, science and agriculture. She would have fallen asleep of boredom if it weren't for the giant nuclear explosion that drew her attention.

Talan's voice sounded like a narrator as the still images stopped and rapidly morphed into moving visions. "My first task was to teach people how to protect themselves." It was almost like watching documentaries in history class, but it felt so real, like Kala was actually there. She was seeing Talan showing a group of humans, or what Kala thought were humans, more like cavemen, how to use fire. But it wasn't as simple as showing them how it worked, Talan was showing them darker things. He was throwing ingredients into the blaze that turned the fire black, then purple, then a bright burning yellow.

Magic. Kala understood. And not the levitation stuff she'd learned. This was darker, more intense.

The fire finally turned a whitish color and Talan-from-the-past nodded. One of the humans closed his eyes, concentrating, and the others followed. The flames responded by rising higher and higher. The humans opened their eyes and stared at the growing flames in awe. Kala noticed, though, that they also looked at the flames with greed. As if the power was intoxicating. The man who was their leader, his eyes turned milky white as he concentrated on the fire.

In one flash of light, the fire rose up from the ground and flew *into the eyes* of all that stood around it!

Then the fire completely snuffed out.

It was now living inside them.

"The spell gave them strength." Talan sounded proud of his work as the scenery changed and turned into a wide view of the humans, charged with the power the fire gave them, attacking beasts who were invading their homes. These were not prehistoric animals that Kala could recognize. She began to realize that much of the mythology in history books was closer to reality than anyone ever dreamed.

The beasts that were attacking the people had heads that looked like bulls with overly large horns protruding from their temples. They had human bodies that were muscular and bulky.

"Minotaurs," Talan answered Kala's unasked question.

She'd seen them in movies and books, but to see them in front of her like this, so real and vivid, was freaking her out. The concept of fighting mythological beasts was not something Kala had ever considered. At least Demons and Angels looked like people. This *Minotaur* was out of a nightmare. Although a part of her thought that her sniper rifle would do very nicely against a creature like that. She imagined herself on a nearby cliff, popping them off one at a time.

But when she saw what the humans did, Kala realized her rifle paled in comparison.

The fire that the people had captured through their ritual burst out of their eyes and mouths with deadly force, slamming into the Minotaurs with frightening accuracy. The Minotaurs were completely engulfed in the fire, screaming in agony as flames stuck to them like tar. Every time a Minotaur tried to douse the fire, the humans poured on more flames, making the Minotaurs suffer in a fiery prison.

After watching the horror of these creatures burning in front of her, Kala found herself relieved when the Minotaurs finally fell to their deaths, black charred corpses. The grotesqueness of their final expressions of agony was forever etched into Kala's brain.

Free of the fire, the humans looked normal again. They started to celebrate their victory as the scenery changed again…

…to a place that Kala's brain couldn't comprehend.

It felt as if she were in outer space, yet standing on solid ground. There were stars all around her as if she had stepped into the center of the Milky Way. Swirling red mist creeped across from where she stood; upon closer inspection she saw that it was made of tiny red rocks. She felt them prick her skin as the cloud flew by. Where she stood was almost blinding from the intensity of light against utter darkness.

"This was the Grigori's punishment for teaching you humans magic, banished here for eternity." Talan's voice sounded as if he were standing next to her.

"Poor you," Kala could hear the sarcasm dripping gooeyly out of her mouth. As far as prisons went, this place was stunning. A bit overwhelming, but Kala didn't think she'd ever get tired of watching the universe up close like this.

"We didn't deserve it. We were only trying to protect your species. Most of my brethren are still stuck here, but a few of us managed to escape. Open your eyes," Talan instructed.

Kala opened her eyes to see Talan still across from her, still holding her hands. He was looking at her cautiously, like he wasn't sure how she would react, but Kala's reaction was simple. "That's it?"

Confusion crossed his features, "What do you mean?"

"You said you'd show me who you are. All you showed me was some psycho humans blazing up some Minotaurs and a crazy-ass space prison. I still don't know anything about you." Kala wasn't sure what Talan had wanted to prove by showing her those memories.

Talan was taken aback by Kala's response, at least, that was what it looked like to Kala. He pulled his hands away and appeared as if he were taking a moment to reflect.

After an awkward silence he finally said, "My point was to show you the kind of magic I can teach you to survive. The few of us who escaped our prison have been teaching select humans we believe can change the world. We've only been back a little over two-hundred years and had to be careful so as to not be caught and forced back into exile. But didn't you ever wonder why humans have grown so fast technologically in the past hundred years as opposed to the thousands of years before? It's because of the Grigori. We're finally able to complete our mission." Talan's blue eyes searched Kala's for some kind of appreciation or awe.

Kala wasn't that kind of girl.

"Fine, so because of you I have my iPad. Do you want a medal or something?" Kala knew she was being a jerk, but it was her one way of distancing herself from someone she was attracted to. Be mean. Always worked.

To her surprise, Talan laughed. "Do you want my help or not?"

Put in those terms, Kala was frozen with indecision. That fire spell looked pretty effective. She wondered if it would work on Demons and Angels.

But all this magic mumbo jumbo made her head hurt. "Of course I want your help. Apparently, I was getting it filtered through Roberta anyway, so better to learn from the source, I guess."

"You should still train with Roberta, she's very special. She's learned things even I have never seen. It's one of the things that drew me to her in the first place. She has raw power almost as formidable as any Demon or Angel. She's not aware of how powerful she is, though. If Roberta and Geoffrey ever have children I can only imagine how strong they would be," Talan mused.

"I still don't know if I can trust you," Kala admitted.

"You're going to have to trust someone." Talan looked at Kala carefully, then stated simply, "You can't do this job alone. The ones who have tried never lasted very long."

"I'm not going to do it. I'm not going to be the Atlas. The world will just have to end I guess." Kala didn't exactly say that last bit with too much conviction. The world ending was a little severe even for her, and she didn't believe it would happen anyway.

Talan seemed to pick up on this. "You say this, but if you could see what will happen if you don't complete your task, you'd change your mind. I promise you."

Kala didn't want to see. She was afraid of how she would feel if she did. Kala didn't want to consider killing Jack. But seeing what would happen if she didn't? It would be too much. At this point Kala had built an entire city in Denial-land.

Standing up, Kala avoided eye contact with Talan as she walked to the window to look at the distant peak of the Washington Monument. She wished she could spear her chest with it and save everyone the trouble. She almost laughed when she remembered that being the Atlas meant she was invincible when it came to self-destruction. It was only when others were trying to kill her that she was vulnerable.

Kala could hear Talan walk up behind her, then she felt his hand rest on her shoulder. "I'm hiding too. The Demons and Malaks would try and capture my brothers and I if they knew we were back. We're more powerful, but we're outnumbered."

Kala turned around fast enough to shrug his hand off and looked at him. "Why do you want to help me? What do you care about the stupid Atlas?"

Talan reached over and touched her hand. Kala couldn't believe she was letting him, but his touch was electrifying. "We've worked too hard to create this new world and we've only just begun. I think I've found my champions in the Turners, but if you fail all of it goes away. Everything the Grigori have worked for will be destroyed. So, yes, I have more than a passing interest in your safety."

Kala grabbed his hand and angrily shoved it off hers. "Don't touch me," she snarled. "And why don't you kill me and become the Atlas yourself if you're so worried about this *End of Days* scenario?" For just a second Kala almost wanted him to. Death seemed an easier choice than killing the only man she ever gave a damn about besides her foster dad.

Talan didn't look offended at Kala's violent rejection. He simply stared at her with eyes that suggested he wanted more from her. Kala knew that look all too well. Yet another supernatural being that wanted to get into her pants. Kala didn't like it, especially since she had been flitting with the idea herself. But making it with an Angel wasn't exactly on her bucket list. It seemed kind of gross and a little bit sacrilegious.

"I can't kill you," Talan said simply.

Kala waited a few more seconds before she realized he wasn't going to elaborate. "Can't or won't?"

"Both." Then before Kala could react, Talan reached out and held her arms in his hands, his expression one of wonder and desire. "I know you can feel it too. We're tied to one another. We're bound. Killing you would be like killing a part of me."

"Whoa, dude, rein it in." Kala easily shoved her way out of Talan's grasp, but didn't move away either. "Chemistry: maybe. And that's a big maybe, but you're acting like we're freaking soul mates. I'm spoken for. Seriously spoken for." Kala made sure she said those last two sentences with as much clarity as possible. She didn't want a Grigori stalker, Asmodeus was bad enough.

"I can wait. As the Atlas, you won't be able to stay with your boyfriend. Even if you ignore your duties, he'll be destroyed in the aftermath anyway," Talan said this as if he were waiting for a pesky fly to die.

It pissed Kala off.

"Saving Jack is exactly what I'm going to do. We're going to hide somewhere until this whole *apocalypse* blows over. I'm not letting anything happen to him!" Kala felt like kicking Talan in the crotch for emphasis, but decided against it.

Talan's eyes lit up as if he discovered some secret surprise. "That's your mission."

Kala froze. She swallowed hard, trying not to reveal anything in her expression, but she knew her pause gave everything away. "What are you talking about?" She tried to add as much attitude as possible to her voice to throw Talan off.

Then he closed his eyes as if in extreme pain.

When he opened them, Kala almost flinched from the amount of concern on his face. "I'm so sorry," was all he said.

Kala suddenly needed to walk away. She shoved past him and headed toward the door. "What are you sorry about?" Kala heard the choke in her voice before she could stop it. Having Talan guess what her mission was made it real for her. Though she hadn't admitted it yet, just hearing the words from another person caused her immense pain.

Talan was promptly by her side. He wrapped his arms around her and held Kala close. Kala wanted to push Talan away for trying to hug her, but at that moment it was something she needed. Before she could stop herself she had wrapped her arms around Talan and buried her head in his chest, trying to hold back tears. It wasn't romantic or sexual; it was Kala trying to take some comfort from another living soul over everything that had happened to her in the last couple of days.

Finally Kala pulled away. She looked up at Talan with desperation, "You're not going to kill him are you?"

Talan didn't try and pull Kala back in towards him, somehow sensing her unease at his closeness. He shook his head, "I told you: I won't do that. You either complete your mission or it doesn't get completed."

Kala wanted to believe him, but her innate distrust for...well... everyone... wouldn't let her. "It's not like I can stop you, but if you kill Jack I swear I'll make Roberta show me how to hurt you." It was an empty threat, but Kala felt desperate. The fact that Talan knew her mission scared her beyond measure. There was nothing to stop him from killing Jack. Except her. And Kala would die trying.

"You don't have to threaten me, Kala Hicks. I told you I'm bound to you: that means more than saving the world my brothers and I are creating. It also means I can't stop them either. It's no secret that you are the Atlas. They'll hunt you down and either kill you to take your job, or make you do your job. But know this, I will fight every one of them to protect you," Talan said these words in warning, but Kala could see the genuine fierceness in his eyes when he talked about protecting her.

"I need to get Jack and get out of town. Just a few days until this all blows over." Kala backed away from Talan, toward the door. His intenseness scared her, mainly because she felt it back and that made her mad at herself, like she was betraying Jack somehow.

Talan shook his head sadly. "Kala."

The way he said her name made her pause. It was as if eons of pain were shoved into that one word.

"Don't try and stop me. I don't care how you *think* you feel about me. I only want Jack." Kala couldn't seem to turn around to leave. She just kept backing up so that she was always looking directly at Talan. It wasn't like Kala thought he'd hurt her, it was just that she felt an indescribable need to face him.

Talan spoke gently, "At least let me show you what will happen if you don't kill him."

Kala could tell he wasn't trying to push, that he genuinely wanted to help her see the consequences of ignoring her duty. Kala flinched when she called it her *duty*. The word burned like acid. How could it be her *duty* to kill the man she loved? Kala knew she could not say no to seeing the potential future. It wasn't in her nature. If she was going to make the decision to run, she had to know the costs.

Kala nodded.

Chapter Twenty-One

Talan approached Kala slowly and carefully took her hands in his.

A rush of images flew through her head. She closed her eyes to try and see them more clearly.

The first scene filled her with joy. It was Kala and Jack, together, in a small apartment she didn't recognize. They were resting comfortably in bed. Kala was already feeling pretty good about her decision. Not killing Jack seemed like a good thing after all. The fact that an apartment existed seemed like a good sign to her. Kala had been expecting to see some kind of zombie apocalypse or something.

Then Kala's chest squeezed in pain as she realized that she and Jack were visibly upset. She tried to think of any reason other than a looming apocalypse that would make them both so sad, but it was obvious from their expressions that Jack knew what her mission was.

Jack begged Kala to kill him, telling her that he didn't want to be responsible for killing billions of lives, but Kala ran out of the room.

Jack grabbed his gun from the side table next to the bed and quickly followed her, but she was gone, out the front door.

Jack raced down the stairs and out onto the street. He had the gun tucked behind his pants. He searched for Kala, but he couldn't find her anywhere.

The only ray of hope Kala could think of was the fact that the streets looked normal. No destruction. No bombs. No plagues. Maybe it wouldn't be that bad...

Kala's breath caught in her throat as she watched Penny step out of the shadows of an alley to face Jack. She looked sad to see him.

"Where is she?" Penny asked.

"I don't know," Jack admitted weakly.

Kala knew they were talking about her.

"You're the next Atlas, Jack, the sooner you realize that the better. We only have minutes before she fails. You have to kill her," Penny pleaded.

Minutes?

Kala realized that this was all happening before the countdown was over. There was no apocalypse because she hadn't failed yet.

"It's your destiny. You were born to be the next Atlas. It is written in the holy texts, Jack. This girl is a fluke, an accident. It's sacrilegious that she even exists." Penny tried to get through to him.

Jack looked at Penny with tears in his eyes. "But I'm her mission, Penny. She has to kill me or billions will die." Jack spoke as if quoting a book, "One cannot live, while the other one exists. A new Atlas shall reign; and the potential must die. A beginning to the end; and an end to the beginning. A new paradise shall be born. The Fated One will be the last."

"Don't quote the texts to me, Jack. I know them better than you." Penny shook her head. "She can't be the one! You were supposed to bring us salvation. *You!*"

Jack looked down at his watch. "Time's up."

Kala saw the time from her vantage point: 0d 00h 00m 03s.

...2...1...

BOOM!

Kala felt the ground shake, even in the vision. A deafening roar filled the air like the earth was screaming. Kala grew up in L.A., this was an earthquake. A big one.

Penny shook her head, tears in her eyes. "Jack, no!"

"If Kala can't kill me, you have to," Jack pleaded with her. "I can't kill myself. I tried, but I'm a coward."

Penny was on the verge of sobbing as she stepped forward, taking Jack's gun.

Suddenly, Asmodeus popped up with a large grin. "Demon hearing is so useful these days. I can't let you kill the man, not when things are about to get fun."

And POP! Asmodeus disappeared with Penny.

Jack was alone in the alley.

Kala's point of view zoomed out, away from Jack. She saw the city, shaking and crumbling to the ground.

Zooming out again, Kala saw a sea of tornadoes ravaging the middle of the country all the way to Arizona.

Zooming out again, fires raged in Europe, black swirling clouds blanketed the entire continent of Asia.

Zooming out again, Kala was now in space, watching nature tear apart the planet like an enraged animal.

Kala's eyes opened and she was back in Talan's apartment. Her legs shook violently and she let him lead her to the couch.

"What was that?!" Kala choked. She knew what she'd seen, but she didn't understand it. Kala had figured the reason why Jack had been chosen as her target was because of something that he'd do. She had secretly hoped that, once she found out exactly what he was supposed to do that was so bad, then she, she would prevent Jack from doing it. It was the only way out she could see.

But this…

Talan's eyes were wide with wonder as he looked at Kala. She knew that whatever Talan saw impressed him immensely. "You're the Fated One," was all Talan could say.

Too much.

Kala stood up at his words. "Fated One? Seriously? That's freaking cheesy." Kala started to feel panicked.

What she had witnessed…

Talan stood up with her. "Cheesy or not, it's the truth. You and Jack cannot exist together. One of you has to be sacrificed or the world will collapse in on itself. When you became Atlas you sealed your fate and Jack's. He's the potential, you're the Fated One."

"But…" Kala couldn't finish her sentence. She had no argument. How could she argue things she knew nothing about? "But…" That seemed to be the only word capable of coming out of her mouth. Finally, she said softly, "I was going to save him." Kala had really believed that, whether she was going to hide Jack or fix his potential mistakes. She truly hadn't considered any other alternative.

Kala felt numb.

All she wanted to do was curl into a little ball and collapse on Talan's floor until the world ended because she still couldn't imagine killing Jack.

Pulling the trigger…

Kala looked at Talan, desperate for someone to tell her this was all a mistake and that she wouldn't have to do the unthinkable.

But Talan only had sympathy in his eyes. "I'm sorry."

"I can't…" Kala hardly ever cried, but the tears formed against her will. She couldn't look at him anymore. Talan was just another reminder of how far off the reservation her life had gone. "I won't."

Talan gently held her arms with his hands, forcing eye contact with her. "Hey," he prodded kindly until Kala met his eyes again. "I'll help you through this."

Kala's sadness turned to anger, "*Help me through this?* We're not talking about rehab here, we're talking about killing the only man I ever loved!"

"I know," Talan admitted. His grip tightened on Kala's arms, "But it has to be done. I will keep you safe, but there are others who will try to kill you to have the honor of killing Jack."

Kala breathed in deep to steady herself. "I know." She didn't know what to say. Normally, she'd have shoved Talan off her by now, but feeling his hands gripped tight around her arms gave her a sense of stability. Kala was afraid she'd fall over if he let go.

"So, let's think this through. What are you good at?" Talan managed to situate Kala back down on the couch, sensing her shakiness.

"What?" Kala felt like she was in a surreal nightmare that she couldn't escape from and every question from Talan felt ridiculous. "You mean like cards?"

"No. *Think*," Talan urged.

"I don't know," Kala said defensively. "Drinking?" She wasn't sure where Talan was going with this. Was he trying to change the subject to get her mind off of Jack? Was this some sort of re-grouping technique?

"You're a sniper." Talan finally revealed his intentions.

Kala's brain stopped. "You want me to snipe Jack?"

Chapter Twenty-Two

Kala couldn't wrap her head around what Talan was suggesting. "He'll be defenseless." It was such an odd thing for a trained sniper to say, Kala was surprised she said it, but killing Jack like that seemed evil. It made her question everything she'd been taught to do. Kala had only killed a handful of people in her life, but she had been trained to think of them as the enemy. Targets, nothing more. They needed to be taken out in order for her team to complete their missions. Kala hadn't thought of them as people. She hadn't thought of them at all.

But to kill Jack like that? Someone she loved.

Looking at him through the scope…

Talan brushed a stray hair out of Kala's eye. The way that he looked at Kala was the way that Jack looked at her.

"You just met me, don't look at me like that. And stop touching me." Kala's voice sounded weak. She wanted to push Talan away, but she couldn't. No matter how presumptuous Talan was being, he was genuinely trying to help her. Kala couldn't explain it, but she trusted Talan.

She didn't like it, but Kala let it go.

Their relationship would never be romantic to her no matter how much she was attracted to him. Kala loved Jack not Talan, no matter what Talan wanted.

Alive or dead Jack was her soul mate. That thought hit Kala hard.

Talan didn't appeared fazed by Kala's biting remarks. It was like he could see right through her defensive façade. Yet another thing to be annoyed at him for. He lifted his hands in supplication. "I promise I won't touch you again."

The way he said it made Kala shiver. She really despised chemistry. Another thing she couldn't control! But she *could* control her actions. "Good, keep it that way."

"If you can't kill him face to face, then shooting him at a distance may be the only way," Talan offered gently.

Kala shook her hand in front of her face for Talan to be quiet. "Can we focus on you teaching me how to protect myself from *creatures* like you?"

Talan took a moment, then sighed, standing up. "Yes, of course. Why don't we start with that fire spell I showed you?"

Kala raised her eyebrow in surprise. She didn't expect Talan to change topics so easily, but he could probably see how hard it was for Kala to discuss killing Jack, and decided to make her feel better about her situation. And besides, scorching Minotaurs sounded pretty awesome right about now, even if they were in the shape of an ass-hat named Asmodeus. Kala could pretend, couldn't she?

The next few hours were spent almost burning down Talan's apartment. Luckily, he had crazy powers that could extinguish flames in less than a second. They were using a small outdoor grill the size of a footstool for the fire itself. Talan had a stack of newspaper that he'd light with his freaking mind whenever Kala attempted the spell.

The spell itself was all about thought. Kala had never had to concentrate so hard in her life. She thought training with Roberta had been hard. She soon realized that Roberta had been going easy on her.

The first step was to absorb the fire into her being. If Kala hadn't seen this in the vision she wouldn't have believed it was possible, and like Roberta had taught her, magic was mostly about belief. It was almost like breathing the fire in without letting it touch your skin.

The first few attempts resulted in massive coughing fits and a case of heartburn that Kala didn't feel would ever go away. But Talan waved his hand over her face and chest and Kala had instant relief. He would definitely come in handy after a hard night of drinking and binging on fast food. The fourth attempt was a success. Kala felt a rush of adrenaline and shock at her victory. As she imagined herself breathing in the fire, Kala saw the flames snuff out of the grill and then she felt it dance inside her stomach and esophagus. The fire didn't burn. It felt tingly and strangely soothing. When the sensation didn't go away, a part of her started to panic slightly.

"Is it stuck in me now?" she asked.

Talan smiled. "Until you decide to release the flames, yes. Roberta was right, you have a natural gift for magic. The people you saw in the past took years to learn this spell and it only took you a few hours."

Kala looked up at the clock on Talan's wall: 1d 14h 15m 41s.

3:45 P.M.

The day was half over, and Kala only had one day left.

She wanted to expel this fire before she burped and accidently fried some poor squirrel or something. "How do I get rid of it?"

"Focus and release. It's that simple. Try it on my couch," Talan instructed.

"Grills and tabletops are one thing? But a couch? Can you put it out in time?" Kala couldn't help but doubt Talan's skills.

"I can handle a burning couch," Talan answered Kala's skepticism with an entertained smirk.

Kala shrugged and went for it. She looked at the couch and felt the rush of fire leave her stomach and mouth. She almost fell over from the shock and terror of seeing real flames shooting out of her mouth and surrounding the couch in a giant fireball. She wondered if her eyes were white like the people from Talan's vision. Kala took a few steps back from the heat wave that hit her full force.

Talan blew about as hard as if he were blowing out a birthday candle and the fire went out. The couch was a blackened carcass, but there were no residual flames. "You don't have to expel the fire from your mouth," Talan waved his hand at the couch and it transformed from a charred lump into a brand new sofa. "You can channel it through your hands."

"Really?" It felt like some kind of video game power, from fire breathing dragons to exploding hand fireballs, Kala was definitely out of the realm of her comfort zone.

"The people you saw were only able to perform the spell in its most simplistic form, that's why the mouth, but *you…*" Talan's eyes shined with admiration, "you are truly a wonder."

"All right, quit with the googly eyes." Kala wasn't comfortable with Talan's obvious affection for her, especially since there was a part of her that felt the same pull he did.

"No more *googly* eyes, I promise," Talan said with amusement. He lit the grill with the snap of his fingers. "Now, take in the fire and extract it through your hands."

"Yeah, no problem," Kala retorted sarcastically. She knew that both Roberta and now Talan thought she was some sort of prodigy, but this magic thing was hard. It was exhausting and took way more concentration than Kala had at the moment. She had to go into sniper mode to keep her focus up. Her training was coming in handy. Spending hours in a room looking through a rifle scope, you needed a lot of stamina and ability to be extremely attentive. Kala had to use every ounce of that particular skill with this magic stuff. It was one of the hardest thing she'd ever done. Not to say she wasn't enjoying it. Being able to breathe fire was a bit of a power rush, especially when she imagined scorching the crap out of Asmodeus's cocky face.

Kala looked at the small fire and focused on transferring it inside of her.

So weird. The strangeness of it all would hit Kala sometimes. If someone had asked her about breathing in fire a week ago, only the circus would have come to mind.

Taking a deep breath, Kala opened her eyes and stared at the flames intensely. Within seconds she felt the tingling sensation of the fire entering inside her while watching the grill snuff out. Her natural impulse was to blow it out the way in came in, hence the mouth breathing fire technique. But she believed Talan when he said she could channel the fire in other ways. She closed her eyes again and focused on the tingling sensation. Whereas she had only been aware of the sensation in her chest and stomach before, now she experienced it tingling all through her body. It felt like recovering from an arm falling asleep, tiny pinpricks in every part of her.

This time when she opened her eyes Kala knew what she was capable of. Her innate gift of aim didn't have to be used for guns alone. The magic that coursed through her veins amplified all her senses, but mostly her eyes. It was like her eyes had turned into a magnifying glass. Kala looked out the window to test her theory. Sure enough, Kala focused on the tip of the Washington Monument miles away, and like a rifle scope, Kala was able to zoom in until she could see a tiny fly landing on the top of the monument.

Before Kala could think rationally about her decision, she pointed her finger at the fly. Fire burst in a laser-like line, searing a tiny hole through the window and traveling the ten or so miles until it reached its destination. The fly never had a chance.

Kala realized that if anyone had looked up they would have seen a strange line of orange attacking the top of the Washington Monument.

"No one saw it, and if they did, they wouldn't know what it was." Talan was already trying to comfort her, sensing her anxiety.

Kala turned to Talan and stopped when she saw the pure and utter fascination written all over his face.

Before Kala could say anything he tossed her a lighter. "Constant source of fire."

"It's so tiny."

"It's all you need. The size of the fire doesn't matter."

"Then why on earth did we use a grill? We could have used this thing the whole time!" Kala was annoyed that Talan felt the need to tell her this after the fact that she had been using pretty sizeable fires to practice on.

"For novices, the bigger the fire the better, but after seeing *that*," Talan nodded toward the tiny hole in his window, "you don't need much."

Kala examined the lighter more carefully. It was pretty stylish as far as lighters went, tarnished silver with intricate engravings etched on its surface that were black from lack of polishing. Kala didn't recognize the pattern of the engraving, but knowing that an Angel gave it to her, she figured it meant something. "The engravings?" she asked.

"Grigorian," Talan replied with a nod. "Guaranteed to always light." He smiled.

Kala smiled back. "That's handy." She pocketed the lighter. "Please tell me this fire spell works on Demons."

"It technically works on everything, but it won't kill a Demon or an Angel, if that's what you're hoping for. Just Minotaurs." Talan smiled again.

He was joking with her, she realized. Kala didn't realize how much she needed a little bit of lightness to brighten up the darkness of her situation. He was trying to make Kala laugh about what her life had become. All Kala could give him was a smile, but it was a genuine one and it lifted her spirits immeasurably.

"Well, if any Minotaurs attack me, I guess I'm set," Kala responded.

"It *will* hurt Demons and Angels though, buying enough time for you to escape. And with your control, you could do some serious damage." Kala saw that he was toning down the "gush" factor for her sake.

"What's next?" Kala asked. The longer she trained with Talan the longer she wouldn't have to deal with her mission.

Talan was on to her. "Kala, you saw what would happen after the countdown is over. The Atlas is given four days as a courtesy, not a luxury. You have to think of it as a suspension of time. The repercussions of Jack existing with you is put on hold essentially, but at the second the four days are up, the Universe tries to right itself."

Kala *had* seen, but she didn't want to acknowledge that it was true.

The destruction of everything.

It was hard to ignore.

Talan waved his hand over the counter and Kala's sniper rifle appeared. Normally, Kala felt comforted by her guns, but this time it made her stomach twist in a giant knot. The rifle itself could shoot accurately from over a mile away. Maybe if Kala were far enough away from Jack it would be easier…

Kala's head pounded just imagining it.

"I don't think I can," Kala repeated her fears out loud.

"You always have a choice, Kala," Talan said softly, "but he'll die anyway. You're indecision will be for nothing and billions of people will die because of it."

Kala thought he sounded like he was talking to someone about to jump off a ledge, gentle but forceful. The more she thought about it, the more she realized he was trying to do the opposite. Talan was trying to talk Kala *into* jumping off the ledge. He'd provided Kala with her gun and he wanted her to shoot.

"I don't know where he is," Kala mumbled lamely and she wished she hadn't.

Suddenly her entire world shifted.

Chapter Twenty-Three

Before Kala could move, her surroundings changed: she was standing on the roof of Union Station in the center of D.C. with the sniper rifle in her hands.

"Holy crap!" Kala flattened herself on the roof, placing her gun next to her to try and hide it. "A little warning would have been nice." Kala was furious that Talan would drop her and her rifle onto a national monument with thousands of people moving in and out all day. Nothing says terrorist like a single shooter with a sniper rifle on top of a building in Washington D.C.! Kala wanted to scream.

Talan stood beside her, not bothering to try and hide himself. "No one can see you. I'm hiding us from view," Talan said this as if Kala should have known better.

Not quite trusting that this information was true, Kala stayed where she was. "Why here?"

Talan pointed to the grass and brick-worked courtyard in front of the station. There were several benches and fountains creating warm and inviting images for people exiting the station. Kala got to her knees and peered over the side.

And there was Jack.

From this vantage point she could easily see him sitting on a bench. He was reading a newspaper, but Kala knew better. Jack was waiting for someone. She could tell by the way he held the paper, just low enough that he could keep his eyes on his surroundings. Every few seconds or so, Kala watched as Jack glanced in a different direction so no one could take him by surprise.

It was a clear, clean shot.

"He'll never feel a thing. You can do it quickly, painlessly." Talan leaned down on his knees to be level with Kala. "I know this is the hardest thing you'll ever do, but you know it's right."

Kala moved away from him. "The more you try and convince me, the less I want to do this. In fact, you know what?" Kala stood up and started to walk away, leaving her gun behind. "I'm leaving."

Talan was by her side in seconds, his eyes soft, pleading. "Kala, I'm sorry. I don't know what to say to make the consequences clear to you."

"I know the freaking consequences, okay? I'm not stupid! Killing someone you love may be easy for you, but it's not for me. It's not in me!" Kala knew she was being unfair to Talan, but she didn't care.

But like always, Talan didn't show an ounce of hurt from Kala's words. She could tell he wanted to reach out and hold her, but he was respecting her wishes of a *no touch zone*. "Kala, it's time and you know it."

The way Talan said it made her skin crawl, mainly because Kala knew he was right. There were no words she could say, everything would sound insincere and trite. She never thought of herself as a murderer though she had killed people before on missions. Her rational mind told her that killing Jack was another mission, but it was still murder. Plain and simple: killing Jack would make her a monster.

A monster that saved the planet, but a monster nonetheless.

Kala didn't make eye contact with Talan as she walked back to her rifle. She went into military-mode and began setting up her rifle stand on the cement ledge, locking the scope onto the rifle. Lining it up with the park bench, she looked through the scope.

It took her a few seconds to put Jack's head in her crosshairs, but when he was, Kala wanted to vomit. A single shot to the head and the world would be saved, but Jack would be dead. All she had to do was pull the trigger. It would be so simple.

Kala just had to squeeze.

One little squeeze.

It would all be over.

Jack turned his head.

Through the scope it seemed like he was looking straight at Kala.

His eyes.

His gentle, kind eyes.

Before Kala could think, she stood up and left the rifle behind.

"Kala, wait," Talan called after her.

Kala whirled around and had the lighter lit before Talan had stood up. "It may not kill you, but it will hurt. Don't follow me."

Kala didn't wait for Talan's response. She knew if he wanted to he could pop up right in front of her and teleport her to the moon. But she had to do something. She had to see Jack, to talk to him, to tell him what she saw, anything.

After a few seconds of searching, Kala found the exit from the roof and rushed down to the service entrance of Union Station. Feeling like a zombie, Kala kept moving forward, hurrying her steps as she thought of talking to Jack. Barely noticing anything, Kala pushed her way through the beautiful latticed architecture of the station's main hall, through the throng of people and through the double exit doors.

Seeing Jack on the bench with his fake newspaper disguise made her heart jump into her throat. Kala wanted nothing more than to hold on to Jack and never let go. She hurried over to him, but Jack saw her a hundred feet before she arrived and was waiting with open arms.

They didn't need to say a word as Kala and Jack embraced. Emotion threatened to choke her as she felt his arms wrap around her. How could she have ever considered killing this man? Kala started to doubt everything. Maybe Talan was evil, showing her a future that wasn't real? How could she know if he was an Angel or a Demon? She was simply taking his word for it. Showing her how to do magic could have been a way to discover how powerful she was. But she knew that wasn't true. If Talan was evil he could have killed her a hundred times over. The fact that he hadn't stopped her from seeing Jack also proved that Talan was giving Kala time with the one she loved. Kala decided not to think about any of it. She just stood there, in Jack's arms, soaking in every second of it.

Jack leaned down and whispered in her ear, "I was so worried. I thought someone might have…" He left that sentence unfinished.

Kala finished it for him, "Killed me? It is *me* we're talking about here."

Kala suddenly saw the person Jack had been waiting to meet arrive. Penny.

"Now!" Penny said with authority.

Jack looked down at Kala, anguish in his eyes.

Now meant *kill*, Kala had no doubt.

"Jack," was all that Kala could utter.

Jack's arms stayed locked around Kala and Kala's around him. He was struggling as hard as she had been.

Penny pleaded, "Jack, you have to."

Kala turned her gaze to Penny. "You and Talan are like a broken record: *Jack kill Kala, Kala kill Jack.* Shut up already!"

Penny's eyes widened. Kala had never seen her so scared, so shocked. "Did you say *Talan*?"

Kala remembered that maybe she was supposed to keep the whole Grigori thing a secret. Oops! Since she couldn't successfully backtrack, Kala decided to stay silent instead.

"Impossible! The Grigori have been banished for all of time." Penny looked like she was on the verge of panic. "And why would Talan tell you to kill Jack?"

Both Jack and Penny picked up on the reasoning behind that in about two seconds.

Surprisingly, Jack leaned down and kissed Kala's forehead. There was a strange kind of relief in his eyes. "I'm your mission." He made it a statement of fact.

"She's the potential, Jack. She has to die." Penny was becoming a little too scary for Kala's taste.

Jack and Kala looked at each other; Kala could read Jack's thoughts like they were her own. He wasn't going to kill her, and she wasn't going to kill him. But they did need to occupy Penny while they made their escape.

Kala reached into her pocket while still in Jack's embrace and sparked the lighter. Jack's eyebrows furrowed in curiosity. Kala tried to prepare him for what he was about to see. "Get ready for a shock."

Faster than she expected, Kala sucked in the fire and shot it out of her hand, completely engulfing Penny in a cocoon of fire.

Penny screeched in anger — but not anguish: Penny knew what this meant and she was pissed. Meanwhile, people around the courtyard panicked and screamed when seeing Penny on fire.

Jack was definitely shocked, but he was a soldier first and knew when an opportunity to retreat presented itself. He grabbed Kala's hand and they ran to Union Station. There was no talking between them as Jack bought the tickets. Kala didn't hear where they were headed, just as long as they were headed out of there. Their hands never left each other's as Jack led the way to the departing train. Kala figured that at least no one would wonder why they were running since the train was about to leave the station.

Finally, they leapt onto the train and were in one of the main cabins just as the platform loudspeakers announced that no more passengers could board. Kala plopped down on an empty booth; Jack slid in beside her.

"I was just on one of these things yesterday," Kala observed.

"We won't be on long. This train is to Alexandria. It's a twenty-minute ride and there's a train going there every half hour. We'll be hard to track." Jack wouldn't let go of Kala's hand.

Kala didn't mind, though she had tried to brush a stray hair out of her face and found that Jack wasn't budging. She couldn't imagine what was going on in his head.

Jack obviously knew he was the target, but there was so much he didn't know.

Kala could tell that her *Grigori* slip meant nothing to Jack. Penny, however, seemed to know who Talan was, and she definitely looked scared. It gave Kala a smug satisfaction that Talan scared Penny. Kala felt a strange sort of loyalty to her new Angel friend. Of course, she had abandoned him and threatened to light him on fire, but Kala knew that Talan forgave her. There probably wasn't anything Kala could do to truly anger Talan. Still, she wondered why he hadn't popped up to take her away.

Kala sighed in defeat when it hit her.

Talan was giving her the time to kill Jack because he believed she would eventually cave in and go through with it. He was probably watching her somehow, like an annoying stalker-spy.

"Is that true?" Jack spoke. "Killing me is your missin?"

Kala looked up at Jack sitting next to her, his eyes were full of fear and worry.

She nodded. "I didn't want to tell you, but I'll never do it. You don't have to worry."

"Kala, you have to. If it means saving the world, my life is worth nothing," Jack said in a deadly serious tone.

"I'm working on a way out of this," Kala lied. There was still a tiny part of Kala's brain that thought of what Asmodeus had said about some ritual to summon Atlas by killing her. If she could pull it off without actually dying... Maybe if she was able to trick Atlas into taking the power back, then Jack would be safe. After all, the only reason why the earth ended in Talan's vision was because *she* was the Atlas and Jack wasn't. They couldn't exist together in the same space. If a god became a god again, maybe that problem would cease to be.

"There is no way." Jack seemed convinced. "I won't kill you either... if you're worried."

"I'm not." Kala squeezed Jack's hand for emphasis, but internally, there was a part of her that wasn't as confident as she pretended to be. Jack had trained all his life to become an Atlas, he was a true believer, and he looked like he had considered killing her. Maybe Kala had imagined it. A part of her wasn't sure.

Relief flooded Jack's face. Regardless of whether or not he had been tempted to take Kala out, Jack had chosen not to, and Kala's words of faith obviously made him feel better.

"Where are we going?" Kala needed to know if Jack had a plan.

"There's an apartment in Alexandria that I use for emergencies. No one knows about it. Not even Penny." Jack lifted their clasped hands and kissed Kala's as if taking comfort from her presence.

"Emergencies?" Kala inquired with curiosity.

Jack explained, "A part of my training growing up was about Demons and Angels tracking me. As long as the fact that I was the Atlas was hidden I'd be safe, but I wanted a couple places just in case, like the place in the forest where I was going to take you before Asmodeus grabbed you. Somewhere where no one would look for me."

Kala didn't want to burst Jack's bubble about his place being safe. She knew Talan could show up at any minute. Once an Angel or Demon had Kala's *signature* they could find her anywhere. The more time Kala spent away from Talan, the less angry she was with him. She knew the vision he showed her was true. She just didn't care. But Kala didn't really want to bring up Talan at the moment. She was just grateful that Asmodeus hadn't figured out where she was yet. It was definitely a *yet*. Kala had no doubt the Demon would use any means necessary to find her.

"You've had so much time to prepare for this." Kala felt jealous. Jack knew exactly what had been in store for him. He'd had years to prepare. Kala was thrown into this mess without a life preserver and expected to swim like an Olympian.

"I'm sorry this is happening. I really am." Jack finally released his grip on her hand and reached up to touch her face. "I love you, Kala."

Kala grabbed the back of Jack's head and pulled him into the most intense kiss they ever had. Every part of her tingled from his touch. No one made her feel like Jack did. The more they kissed the more Kala wanted. If she could have ripped his clothes off right then and there, she would have, and from the way Jack grabbed her waist, he felt the same. It was as if all the pent-up frustrations from last three craptastic days were suddenly being released into this one kiss.

"Excuse me, but the train has stopped." A voice jolted them out of the moment.

A very disapproving passenger was the culprit and he gave the two of them a dirty look as he exited the train car.

Jack smiled shyly and took Kala's hand once more. "Let's get out of here."

Kala smiled back and let Jack lead her once more.

It took them less than a half hour to reach their destination: a small apartment complex. Kala was reminded of Jack's brownstone only because of the older brickwork and black trim of the windows. The building was three stories high and looked like it was built in the late 1800s. It had the same warmth as Jack's apartment, making it feel like home. Once they were inside, Kala smiled at the décor. It was very similar to Jack's apartment, old-fashioned furniture with a pleasant worn-in look that always screamed *cozy* to Kala.

"I think I have some food in here." Jack let go of Kala's hand to search the cupboards. "Mac and cheese?" He poked his head out from the cupboard door.

"That actually sounds amazing." Kala couldn't remember the last time she ate, but she was starving.

"Agreed." Jack started boiling the water for their *nutritious* meal.

Kala walked over to him and he pulled her in for an embrace. She rested her head on Jack's chest while his hands wrapped around her small frame.

He kissed the top of her head. "We're in serious trouble, aren't we." It wasn't a question.

"Yeah." Kala didn't know what else to say.

"So what's your plan? You said you had one." Jack pulled away to dump the macaroni noodles into the boiling water.

Kala told him about what Asmodeus had said.

"Do you think you could pull it off, tricking Atlas? Do you think *dying by ritual* is the only way to contact him?"

Kala was happy Jack hadn't dismissed the plan altogether. If she were being honest with herself, they were grasping at straws. But maybe Jack wanted to grasp at the same straws. Maybe together they could pull it off.

"I need to talk to Asmodeus again," Kala admitted. She couldn't believe those words had actually come out of her mouth. If she met with him it would have to be soon because when the countdown was up, Asmodeus planned on killing her by performing whatever the stupid ritual was. The whole thing made her head hurt.

"No way." Jack fell immediately into protective mode. "He's a Demon, Kala. You have no defense against a Demon. Remember the Compound?"

"Remember Penny?" Kala hated being snarky, and she didn't really want to go into her training sessions with Roberta and Talan. Especially Talan. Talking about him in front of Jack seemed wrong. She felt guilty, like she had somehow cheated on Jack or something. Grumbling to herself, Kala wished she could punch Talan at the moment.

"You think fire would hurt a Demon?" Jack was unconvinced of Kala's newly learned powers, though he had seen them firsthand. Apparently scorching Penny wasn't impressive enough for him.

"Just trust me, I can handle myself." Kala tried to sound as persuasive as possible so Jack would drop it.

"What was all that stuff about a gigi, or jambili? Penny looked pretty freaked." Jack was fishing, Kala could tell.

"Grigori. He's a type of Angel and he taught me that fire trick." Kala hoped Jack would leave it at that.

Nope.

"*He*? Why did he want to help you? Shouldn't he want to kill you to be the next Atlas?" Jack watched Kala like a hawk, waiting for her face to reveal something.

Kala had dealt with jealous boyfriends before so she knew how to keep her face casual and dismissive as she spoke of another man. "The Grigori are some group of Angels who were banned from earth for teaching humans magic. He escaped somehow and just wants the Atlas to do its job so he can stay here. It's not that complicated." Kala widened her eyes with mock-annoyance, like talking about Talan was a horrible chore she didn't want to think about it.

It worked.

Jack's whole demeanor relaxed. "He must be powerful if Penny was scared of him. Did he teach you anything else?"

Kala didn't want to admit that the answer was no, so she nodded. "Yup. I'm all set if Asmodeus arrives unannounced." Lies.

Jack breathed a sigh of relief and finished preparing the mac and cheese. They plopped on the couch and each ate a giant bowl of the stuff.

"Feels kind of normal, huh?" Jack said after scraping the bowl clean.

"Weird, right?" The familiarity of it all was almost intoxicating because of its normalcy.

Jack looked around the apartment. "I never thought anyone but me would visit this place. I was preparing for a pretty lonely life."

"I don't know, it's been non-stop introductions to freakshows for me. You underestimated the social networking of the supernatural." Kala tried to make light of the situation.

Jack chuckled slightly, then turned serious once more. "It's been pretty horrible for you, hasn't it?"

He looked so guilty and beaten in that moment that Kala couldn't complain, not that she would have anyway. Kala watched Jack as he sat there with his empty bowl looking so vulnerable. She wasn't used to seeing him that way. He was always her commander, so powerful and decisive. It was nice seeing this other side to him. It made her realize how much she loved him.

Without thinking, Kala put her bowl down, stood up and sat in Jack's lap, leaning in for a kiss. Jack immediately responded by grabbing Kala's waist and pulling her toward him so their stomachs were touching. He kissed her as if his life depended on it. A part of Kala thought that Jack actually believed that. That every kiss may be their last because one of them might give in and kill the other. It somehow made the moment more passionate, more dangerous.

Grabbing onto Kala's legs, Jack lifted her up and carried her upstairs. Kala was so blinded by the intensity of their kissing, she was amazed that Jack found his way to the bedroom without tripping over something. Like a gentleman, Jack laid Kala on the bed as if she was made of glass. It was one of the things she loved most about Jack, his ability to be both gentle and rough. Always the perfect mixture. As if reading her mind, Jack ripped open Kala's shirt as if it was made of paper.

Kala let out a gasp of desire as Jack's hands pulled her in close. When their mouths touched again, Jack's kiss was firm, with just enough tenderness to make Kala quiver in anticipation. She knew she'd never find anyone that could kiss like Jack. It was a serious skill and not many people had it, but when they did… mind blown.

All time stopped and all worries melted from Kala's head as the two of them made love.

***

Kala watched Jack sleeping beside her and smiled. She wished she could bottle up this moment and keep it forever, because she knew it wouldn't last long. Looking at the clock on her nightstand, Kala shuddered.

1d 08h 04m 21s.

9:56 P.M.

Sleeping wasn't an option at this point. Kala had only one more day. One day. It still didn't feel like it was actually happening. If it hadn't been for floating inanimate objects and breathing fire, Kala might have been able to write it off to a bunch of cult crazies predicting the end of days. Even as she thought it, Kala knew that was a lie. What she was going through was real. Too real. No amount of hiding would change that.

Kala picked up what was left of her t-shirt that Jack had ripped in half and tossed it on the ground. Sliding out of bed, she walked over to a small black dresser across from the bed. A drawer full of neatly stacked t-shirts lay perfectly inside. Grabbing a simple v-cut white one, Kala pulled it over her head.

At that moment she really noticed the bedroom.

Kala froze in her tracks when she realized she was standing in the bedroom of Talan's apocalypse vision. This was the bed that she and Jack had woke up from…

Shaking herself out her paralysis, Kala grabbed her jeans from the floor and put them on. She needed to get out of there, away from Jack, away from the memory of what was to come. Kala leaned down and kissed Jack's forehead.

He mumbled something unintelligible.

Kala whispered to him, "I'm going to get some air. I'll be back soon."

"Love you," Jack muttered, then was back asleep.

Kala touched Jack's face gently. She meant to say she loved him back, but stopped herself. He wouldn't hear her anyway. And Kala wanted the first time she told Jack to be special. Kala had never told any man that she loved him, not even her foster father whom she loved with all her being. She wished the 'L' word wasn't so hard for her, but it was and there was nothing she could do about it at the moment. But at least after today, Kala figured he would know how she felt. The fact that she wouldn't kill Jack to save the world had to be proof to him. What else could she do to convince him?

Grabbing her jacket, Kala left the apartment and walked down the sidewalk. The neighborhood was on the older side with lots of brick buildings and old-fashioned street lamps posted every fifty feet or so. It almost felt like Kala was on vacation, the area was so pristine and quaint. Maybe for just a second she could pretend that her life didn't suck.

She walked with purpose, following the path that Jack took in her vision. It hadn't been her plan to do this, but once she was outside and recognized the scenery, Kala couldn't help herself. She passed a coffee shop and stopped when she arrived at the alley Penny had stepped out of.

Kala could almost see Jack and Penny, though it was dark and not morning light like it had been in the vision.

"Thought you could hide from my master?" A voice called out from the alley.

A silhouette soon turned into…

Lali?

Chapter Twenty-Four

"Lali?" Kala thought she might be dreaming. It was a surreal moment to see her fellow soldier walking out of the shadows. "Shouldn't you be back at the Compound?" Kala couldn't seem to get past her confusion. Though Lali was a few inches shorter than Kala, she was still an imposing figure. Her short black hair almost disappeared into the shadows of the alley, but her bright blue eyes stared at Kala with…

…hatred.

Thought you could hide from my master…

The words finally hit Kala.

Master?

"Who's your master?" Kala decided to assess the situation by keeping a conversation going with Lali.

There were several things that bothered Kala about her current predicament. The first of which was *How in the hell is Lali a part of all this?* The second being: *Which side is Lali on?* Malaks or Demons?

"You know who," Lali snarled. "I'll be rewarded for finding you."

Kala figured it was a good bet that Lali was a Demon based on the fact that Asmodeus wanted her alive and a Malak would probably want her dead. Unless…

"Does your master want to kill me?" Kala took a few steps back as Lali took a few steps forward. Kala didn't really want to have a fist fight with Lali in an alley. Lali was a formidable fighter as a human, if she was some kind of supernatural being, Kala didn't want to get her butt kicked. Or teleported.

"Stalling," Lali accused.

Kala threw up her hands in exasperation. "Are you a freaking Demon or Malak? Just tell me Lali." Kala didn't really expect Lali to give her a straight answer, but she might as well try.

"Demon, duh." Lali looked at Kala like she was a moron.

"It's not that easy to tell, ass-hat," Kala responded defensively. She was suddenly struck by the fact that, aside from the topic, this conversation was almost *normal*. "How did you find me?"

Kala knew that Lali couldn't resist the urge to brag, it was one of her more annoying traits. Knowing now that she was a Demon, it kind of made sense.

"I followed Jack. I knew it wouldn't be long until the two of you hooked up again." Lali had a look of superiority on her face. "You guys thought you were hiding it from the rest of us, but it was obvious."

"Why were you a part of the unit? Did you know who Jack was?" Kala wondered what a Demon was doing in an elite military team.

Kala recognized that look on Lali's face: confusion.

Lali had no idea what Kala was talking about. "Jack? Why would I give a crap about Jack? Corn-fed Iowa boy. That boy was born a do-gooder. He's insignificant. I was there to watch Turner."

Kala actually thought that was pretty logical. "That makes sense."

Lali went into attack stance. "I'm taking you to Asmodeus."

"You can try." Kala knew that sounded obnoxious. "If you were following us, then you know what I can do."

"The fire thing? Yeah, not worried." Lali pounced.

Kala sparked the lighter, sucked in the flame and shot it out her hands.

Lali was a goner when it came to Kala's aim, though Lali had tried to duck out of the way in time. The Demon screamed in pain as the flames engulfed her whole body.

Kala ran as fast as she could away from the alley and the burning Lali. As she hurried her way through the streets, she could hear people reacting to the flaming woman with screams of terror. She realized two bodies torched in one day would be front-page news. D.C. would think there was a serial pyro-killer on the loose. Knowing that neither Penny nor Lali would die from it, or frankly, be hurt by it, didn't help the fact that Kala was responsible for both incidents. She just hoped there were no cameras around to make the hunt for her expand to the police!

It didn't matter anyway, because Lali was coming up behind her fast. The fire was out and she looked furious. Kala chanted the words that made a man's briefcase fly out of his hands and smack into Lali's annoyed face. The man looked at his hands, slightly horrified, like he thought *he* had thrown his briefcase at Lali. If Kala hadn't been more than a little hurried she would have found it amusing.

Kala knew it wouldn't stop her, but she just needed to get to safety, wherever that was! She didn't know how long she would have to run, or where she was running to, Kala just needed to create some distance between her and Lali.

Since it was late at night there weren't that many people out, but Kala could see their stares out of the corner of her eye. She could tell they were debating whether or not to stop her, probably assuming she had stolen Lali's purse from the expression on her former teammate's face. It didn't help that Lali's clothes were charred black from being set on fire. If Kala had been in their place, she would have kicked her own ass by now.

Kala still couldn't believe Lali was a Demon! How many Demons were out there? Kala had trusted Lali. They had a bond. Two females picked for such an elite job, it was a badge of honor. To find out that the girl was just there to spy on Turner… One thing was for sure: Lali did not know anything about Jack training his whole life to be the next Atlas. All Lali apparently knew was that Asmodeus wanted Kala, and that Kala had unfortunately taken on the role of the shmuck-o god.

The only advantage Kala had at the moment was that it appeared Lali was acting alone. Kala didn't know if Demons had some sort of telepathic way of communicating with each other, but she figured Asmodeus would be here already if Lali had been able to tell him.

Lali screamed in rage as Kala stayed just out of reach. Demon or not, Lali had short legs, and Kala knew she could outrun her. The question was: could she lose her? All it would take was one touch from Lali and Kala would be teleported straight to Asmodeus. Or at least somewhere where Lali could hold her until Asmodeus arrived.

Kala dodged, cars, people, alleys and small animals. She didn't think she could keep this up much longer.

Lali screeched.

Kala turned around and saw Talan with his hand around Lali's throat.

Kala had to admit, it was kind of sexy. She stopped running to catch her breath and see what Talan planned to do with the Demon.

Lali's eyes were wide with fear and confusion.

"Burns, doesn't it?" Talan asked Lali.

Kala could see the tiny wisps of smoke floating up from Talan's hand wrapped around Lali's neck. She could hear a slight sizzling.

"How?" Was all Lali choked out.

Talan leaned in close and Kala saw the intense anger in his eyes. "*You are a lesser being.*"

Lali's voice rasped in terror. "Malaks are lesser…beings." She couldn't seem to wrap her mind around how Talan was causing her so much pain.

Talan smiled. "I'm Grigorian."

Lali's eyes grew even rounder. "It can't be."

"People keep saying that, yet here I am," Talan answered.

SNAP!

Lali's head came clear off her shoulders.

Talan turned to a shocked Kala standing ten feet away. No one was around, but Kala knew that wouldn't be the case much longer. A decapitated body wouldn't exactly escape notice.

"Can you hide that with one of those magic spells?" Kala asked. It hadn't hit her yet that the woman she thought was her friend was actually a Demon, and now dead because of her. Not only dead, but headless. Not only headless, but headless on a public street.

"Are you okay?" Talan asked, his face full of concern.

"Oh, she's just fine, *Malak*."

Kala knew that voice.

Asmodeus.

"It's a shame to lose Lali, she was a well-placed servant, but ultimately she proved very useful." He stepped out of the shadows, right behind Kala.

Before she could think to move, Kala felt Asmodeus's hand on her shoulder.

All Kala saw was a large beam of light pouring out of Talan's eyes before her world shifted.

DAY FOUR

Chapter Twenty-Five

Kala slowly came to. She was in a hotel bed, Kala could tell by the uncomfortable blankets and the too tightly tucked-in sheets. Daylight poured in from the windows.

Last day, Kala realized with a surge of panic.

"What in the hell was that?" Asmodeus's voice sounded genuinely curious.

Kala looked outside.

"Are you kidding me? Los Angeles?" Kala stared out the window of a luxury hotel in downtown Los Angeles.

Asmodeus shrugged. "I figured that, even if you escape, you probably can't get back to D.C. in time from here. Now back to my question: what was that?"

Kala crawled out of bed and plopped down on a floral chaise. She looked at Asmodeus like he was an annoying cousin, "What was *what*?"

"That Malak. He was beaming light out of his eyes. I've never seen a Malak do that, and I've been around a long time." Asmodeus leaned against a cherry wood desk set across from the chaise. Kala was surprised Asmodeus was there with her. She figured he'd kidnap her, drop her in a hole, and then leave. Since there was no sign of Talan, Kala knew that Asmodeus had shifted her DNA or whatever it was that supernatural creatures did to hide her.

"He wasn't a Malak," Kala said vaguely. She liked lording information over Asmodeus, it made her happy to watch him suffer.

Asmodeus had none of it. "Of course he was. I can tell the difference between an Angel and a Demon."

"Oh, he's an Angel all right." Kala didn't elaborate again. It was driving Asmodeus insane, she could tell. More happiness.

Asmodeus stared at Kala, waiting for her to continue. When she refused, he looked downright appalled. "I could torture it out of you."

"But you won't," Kala replied with a confidence she didn't feel.

It was enough.

Asmodeus's expression was filled with intrigue. He may be old, but he fell for the easiest "girl" manipulations on the planet.

"No, I won't. I'm sad enough over having to kill you tomorrow."

"Let's worry about tomorrow *tomorrow*." Kala changed the subject. Survive today, that was the only goal she cared about at the moment.

Speaking of which: Kala looked at the digital clock by the bedside.

0d 21h 55m 18s.

8:05 A.M.

Seeing the zero made Kala's chest squeeze. Less than twenty-four hours. Being stuck in Los Angeles gave her a twinge of relief. It was home at least. A part of her wanted to see her foster parents Owen and Linda before…

Before the end of the world? Her inner voice chided.

By not Killing Jack, she'd be killing Owen and Linda.

The thought created a giant lump in her throat. She couldn't think of it that way.

Why not? It's the truth.

"Are you going to tell me about this Malak or what?" Asmodeus brought Kala out of her reverie.

Kala wasn't surprised that Asmodeus hadn't noticed she was upset. She shook herself out of the downward spiral of responsibility-misery that she felt.

Analyzing Asmodeus's reaction very carefully, Kala hit him with, "He's Grigori."

Asmodeus looked startled. Kala knew he'd never show true fear, not in front of her, but the shock of this information threw him off guard. Kala felt a moment of pride. Talan was on her team and so far all the super-mojo-supernaturals were running scared. It was the first time she was actually happy about having a stalker.

"Liar," Asmodeus hissed.

Kala felt the hairs on her neck raise. Asmodeus looked at her like he was going to kill her, but she kept her cool. "His name is Talan."

Again, Asmodeus's face revealed more than he probably wanted: both seething and frightened at the same time. "Talan," he said his name like he was warding off bad spirits. "Is it just him?"

"Grigori? No, he said they were all back," Kala lied. She liked scaring the bejeezus out of Asmodeus. It was fast becoming a favorite pastime.

"I have to warn the Elders." Asmodeus looked…official. It was the only word Kala could think of to describe him. He wasn't Mr. Playboy anymore, he was all business and *official looking*. She liked this side of him more than the other side though Kala guessed that an all-business king of Demons probably meant bad news for her.

"Elders?" Kala pried. "I thought you were king or something." Kala remembered when she first met Atlas and he had said that Titans were *Elder gods* now it sounded like there were Demon Elders as well? Too many *Elders*.

Asmodeus looked at Kala like he had just noticed she was there, he was so caught up in his thinking. "The Elders make Malaks and Demons look like humans compared to their power. But the Grigori…" Asmodeus showed a flash of fear again, but quickly hid it. "Let's just say they were banished to the fifth heaven for a reason. The Elders used their combined power to do it."

"If the world ends, what does it matter?" Kala was starting to wonder just how powerful Talan actually was. And seeing how this was rattling Asmodeus, she didn't want to tell him that as far as she knew only a few Grigori had escaped the fifth heaven. Kala had seen this "heaven" first hand and had thought it was breathtaking for a prison. If the Elders were strong enough to send a bunch of Grigori to some kind of heaven jail, Kala wondered what chance *she* would have if she ever had to confront them.

"The world as we know would end," Asmodeus corrected her. "What will be left will be chaos and mayhem for centuries. Hell on earth as they say, which is heaven for a Demon." Asmodeus reached over to brush his hand on Kala's arm.

She resisted the urge to slap his hand away. Pissing off Asmodeus would only hurt her cause. Kala needed him wrapped around her finger to get anything from the guy. She put on her pouty-seductive charm and said, "If there's chaos for centuries, why do you have to kill me? Can't you protect me instead?" Kala knew the answer was 'no' before Asmodeus could say it, but she hoped he would reveal a tidbit of information about the ceremony he wanted to perform on her. If she could find a way to trap Atlas then maybe she could force him to take his job back.

If Asmodeus knew Kala was faking her attraction he was too much of an egomaniac to notice. He sighed, "The only way to make sure the world never rights itself again is to kill Atlas. The only way to kill Atlas is to force him to make an appearance. The only way to force him to make an appearance is to kill you."

"I see," Kala tried to sound as sad as possible, but internally she felt energized by the information. Kala remembered a few years back, General Turner had given the whole team a shot of some kind of serum that had stopped their vitals so that they could be transported into enemy territory as corpses. Though they weren't really dead, maybe it would be *dead enough* for Kala to contact Atlas.

Asmodeus looked at Kala with frustration. "Just when you were starting to like me."

"Oh, I don't like you," Kala gave him the *you're a leper* look. "I just need information from you and stroking your ego seems to be the only way to get it." Kala wanted to smack herself. Why did she get so defensive when men claimed that she liked them? It was quite possibly the worst thing anyone could say to her. Kala couldn't even tell Jack, the man she actually loved, that she loved him. But Asmodeus? A Demon she despised? She just couldn't hide her dislike any longer.

"I don't believe you." Asmodeus wasn't angry. *Yet.*

This was where Kala should have backed down to fool the guy into thinking that, in fact, she *did* like him. Nope, couldn't do it. "I really don't care what you believe. You may be a gagillion years old, but you can't seem to take a hint."

Asmodeus stood up angrily. "You are the most infuriating human I've ever met. I'm looking forward to killing you tomorrow."

"No you're not because if I die you'll know that there was one girl in all of time that you couldn't get. You couldn't convince me to like you when you wiped my brain. If I die you'll never know if you could have changed my mind or not." Kala figured she was grasping at straws. What did a Demon care if one freaking human didn't want him?

But by the way that Asmodeus stared at Kala, she could tell that he definitely cared. It was downright eating him alive. "I would have convinced you," he said lamely.

"Dream on, buddy." Kala crossed her arms and smiled at him a little too cruelly even for her.

Asmodeus was becoming more shocked than furious, but it was a close toss up. "The fact that I allow you to live after speaking to me like that astounds me. I should kill you right now. I'd have to wait another four days, but it might just be worth it."

Kala stood up and faced him, all bravado, but her insides were shaking in fear. "No, I don't think you would. I don't think you *can* kill me. I think that if you could kill me, you would have done it already. Why wait four days on an unpredictable *human* that may or may not complete her mission when you can guarantee that *you* would let the four days pass so you can have your '*utter destruction*'." Kala air-quoted that last part. She hated people that air-quoted, but it somehow felt extremely appropriate right then. Kala had no idea if her theory was correct, since she was making it up on the fly, but it was one of those arguments that felt right as it came out of her mouth. Like a part of her had been working it out since she first met Asmodeus.

Asmodeus lost all his anger as he raised his eyebrow in fascination of Kala. "Interesting theory. Care to bet your life on it?"

Go big or go home... or die... "Absolutely," Kala responded without blinking an eye. She wished she were as confident as she sounded.

A good minute passed as the two of them stared each other down, each waiting for the other to blink.

Finally Asmodeus spoke, "I cannot confirm or deny your theory, but let's just say it's a bit more complicated than what you suggest."

"I'm sure it is, but bottom line is: you're not killing me, and I'm also willing to bet that no other Demon is either."

Asmodeus didn't speak. He looked genuinely baffled.

"I'll take your silence as a yes. Now, do something useful and hand me that room service menu." Kala whirled around before Asmodeus could decide she wasn't worth the trouble and send her to some kind of torture cell. But she was relying on the fact that so far Asmodeus had acted like the quintessential male who loved a woman who played hard to get, and that he would appreciate Kala's bossiness.

When she turned around and sat on the foot of the bed, Asmodeus handed her the menu with a smile. "You know this room is protected by Demon wards, right? So don't even think about hopping a ride on the room service cart to get out of here."

"Wouldn't dream of it." Kala took the menu and pretended to thumb through it. That was *exactly* what she had hoped for, but at least she knew the place was rigged with *Demon wards*, whatever that meant. "You going to order something? Do Demons eat?" Kala examined the menu, feeling her stomach growl.

"Yeah, we eat. Let me see that." Asmodeus plopped down next to Kala and if it weren't for the fact that he was the king of Demons and generally the epitome of evil, it almost felt like two friends ordering room service.

"Burger sounds good," Kala mused.

"Fifty bucks for a burger?" Asmodeus sounded appalled. His complaining about the cost of food made Kala feel normal for a second.

"Won't be able to charge that tomorrow," Kala joked.

Asmodeus laughed.

Kala chuckled back. It was actually a real moment between the two of them.

"Can I ask you a question?" Kala turned to Asmodeus seriously.

Asmodeus looked at Kala with thoughtful eyes. "Shoot."

"Since I'm going to die tomorrow anyway, can I see my foster parents? They live here in L.A., you know." Kala had the sudden urge to see Owen and Linda. If she couldn't be with Jack, then spending her last hours with the only parents she'd ever known was the only thing she wanted to do.

"I can't let you do that." He didn't say it in a cruel way; it was almost as if it were out of his hands.

"Why not?" Kala decided to be direct.

"Because, if you see them, it may change your mind about your mission."

That had been a fleeting thought before, but when Asmodeus said it, it hit Kala hard. The only reason he would say that was because he knew they'd probably die tomorrow too and if Kala could stop that from happening, she would try.

Meaning:

In the end, Kala might have to kill Jack after all.

But now that she thought about seeing Owen and Linda, Kala knew she wouldn't rest until Asmodeus took her to them. "You have me imprisoned, and Jack is on the other side of the country. I think you're safe on the me-completing-my-mission front."

"Malaks have the same teleporting power I do. So do Grigori. If Talan or one of his men finds you, you'll be back on the east coast in seconds." Asmodeus didn't mind admitting his weaknesses, Kala realized. She hadn't really thought about that. As quickly as it took Asmodeus to get her here to L.A., going back to D.C. would be just as easy.

"Look, I accept my death. I accept being your prisoner. I accept not doing my duty as an Atlas. I know you're supposed to be evil or something, but I know there's more to you than that. I've seen it." Not really, but Kala would say anything to convince him.

Asmodeus stared at Kala for a few more seconds, then agreed. "Fine. But only for an hour."

Kala smiled, genuinely happy. "Thank you." She meant it.

Asmodeus pointed his finger at Kala, trying to be tough, but failing miserably. "Only for an hour."

Kala nodded emphatically, afraid he would change his mind.

Asmodeus smiled back at Kala as he touched her arm gently.

Chapter Twenty-Six

Kala felt the now-familiar dizziness of teleportation as the scenery around her came into focus.

With Asmodeus by her side, Kala stood in front of her foster parents' home in the L.A. suburb of Sherman Oaks. She felt nostalgic at seeing the old place with its blue exterior and white wood-slat shutters. The lawn was perfectly manicured, but the trees were slightly overgrown. The biggest tree was in the center of the grass: a ten-foot peach tree full of ripe peaches, a good portion of which had already fallen to the ground. The other trees were fruit trees as well and they lined the front of the house. Lemons, oranges and avocados, all in abundance, and much larger than Kala remembered.

It made her realize that she hadn't visited Owen and Linda's house in years. The only times she'd seen them lately was when they had come to visit her in D.C.

Kala took a deep breath and headed for the front door. Asmodeus followed.

Kala stopped. "You're not coming in."

"Relax, just tell them I'm your boyfriend."

"You wish." Kala put her hand on Asmodeus's chest. "No way. I've never introduced any guy to them before. They'll think we're serious."

"For someone who's going to die tomorrow, you certainly care a lot about what people think. Besides, if you're gone wouldn't you want them to think that you had a bit of happiness in your life before you died?" Asmodeus caressed the hand Kala had pressed on his chest.

She pulled her hand away. "You suck." That was Kala's usual response when she didn't have an argument. Not mature, but it was all she had.

"I won't eat them, I swear." Asmodeus smiled wickedly.

Kala was pretty sure he was kidding, but as he was a Demon she had to ask. "Do you *eat* humans?"

"Only the tasty ones." Asmodeus gave her a knowing glance.

"So. Gross." Kala shook her head. Turning her back on the Demon, Kala approached the front door.

She felt nervous as she knocked gently on the wooden surface.

After a few moments, Kala heard footsteps approach from inside. Asmodeus reached down and clasped his hand in hers.

Just as Kala was prying his hand away, the door opened to reveal Linda standing there. When she saw Kala her eyes lit up with such happiness it made Kala's spirit soar.

"Hi, Linda," Kala smiled. Though every part of her wanted to call her foster parents *mom* and *dad*, Kala still couldn't. It was like saying *love*, it wasn't in her nature.

Linda's arms were around Kala in an instant, squeezing her so tight she could barely breathe. "We've missed you!" Linda spoke in Kala's ear.

When Linda pulled away, she looked at Asmodeus for the first time. "And who is this?"

Kala was about to say his name then realized how crazy his name sounded. "Frank. This is Frank. He's my… boyfriend." The words burned in her mouth.

What burned even worse was the grin that Asmodeus had on his face after she used the "B" word.

Linda was beside herself with glee. She immediately hugged Asmodeus with almost as much fervor as she'd hugged Kala. "So nice to meet you, Frank."

When Linda pulled away, Asmodeus didn't miss a beat. "I'm so happy to finally meet you, too. Kala has told me so much about you."

Mock-scolding, Linda eyed Kala. "I wish I could say the same about you, Frank."

Kala squirmed uncomfortably. "You're meeting him now. You know I like surprises."

Linda reached out and squeezed Kala's hand affectionately. "I'm just kidding you. Now, come on in before we let in the flies."

"Wouldn't want to do that," Asmodeus agreed and re-captured Kala's hand. Kala wanted to punch Asmodeus in the stomach with the hand he was holding, but her foster mom's excited grin at the sight of them made her curb her violent thoughts.

The house felt as cozy on the inside as it looked on the outside, with blonde hardwood floors and plush linen furniture. Even the dining table was in the blonde wood family, with chairs to match. Starting in the living room and passing through the dining room, it all led to the heart of the house: the kitchen. Kala noticed that it had been recently remodeled with new black granite countertops and the same blonde wood cupboards as the flooring.

"Did you grow up here?" Asmodeus asked. "It's lovely."

Kala wanted to kick him in the shins, knowing full well that the king of Demons could care less about home décor, but she answered anyway. "Owen and Linda took me in at fifteen, remember? I grew up in foster homes before that."

Asmodeus didn't miss a beat. "I just meant is this the house you lived in when you met your mom and dad?"

The fact that Asmodeus had now called Owen and Linda *mom* and *dad* before she did made Kala suddenly furious. She was about to say something nasty in true Kala fashion when Linda mouthed to her so only Kala could see, "Gorgeous!"

Kala smiled back, trying to let Linda enjoy the moment she thought she was having: her daughter bringing home her first serious boyfriend. Inside she was screaming: he's a freaking Demon, Mom, but Kala let it slide. Kala knew her mother was just excited and besides, Asmodeus was gorgeous. That was what made him so annoying.

"Can I make you something to eat?" Linda asked as they arrived at the kitchen.

Kala and Asmodeus sat down on the stools at the island breakfast bar.

Asmodeus nodded enthusiastically. "I'd love a sandwich."

Linda picked up on Kala's annoyance at Asmodeus's request. "Kala, it's no fuss, I'll make you both a sandwich."

When Linda turned to open the fridge and retrieve the ingredients, Kala turned to Asmodeus and mouthed, "Really?"

He mouthed back, "What?"

Kala ignored him and turned her attention back to Linda. "Where's Owen?"

Linda started to make three sandwiches, laying everything out on the island in front of them. "He should be back any minute. He just went out to pick up a few things at the grocery store."

After a few more minutes the sandwiches were made and properly eaten by all parties. Kala had never had a more satisfying meal, probably because she had been starving.

"How long are you in town?" Linda was already clearing off the plates.

"Just this afternoon. We're on a mission. I just wanted to stop in and see you guys." Kala found herself welling up with emotion. She tried to hide it as best she could, but she knew Linda could see right through her.

"Kala, what is it? Is it dangerous?" Linda came around the island and put her arm around Kala supportively.

Though Kala wasn't a touchy person, Linda's embrace made her feel immediately better and worse at the same time. Asmodeus's fears were right: seeing Linda like this made Kala terrified that if she didn't kill Jack her foster parents would die.

Kala wrapped her arms around Linda and held her close. Linda squeezed tighter and Kala heard her mother's slight choking sound as she held back tears. "Oh Kala, you're really scaring me."

Pulling away, Kala forced a smile. "It's okay. I'll be fine. Just some jitters, that's all."

Linda held Kala's chin with her hand looking her straight in the eye. "I am so proud of you, Kala. You save the world every day and I just want you to know how amazing I think you are. You're my little girl and I love you more than anything."

Normally, Linda's praise would lift Kala's spirits beyond measure, but today, it just hurt. She wasn't saving the world, she was ending it.

"Mom… I…" Kala couldn't finish. She didn't know what to say. She was ashamed of herself.

Linda's eyes filled with tears at Kala calling her 'mom.' Kala had been so wrapped up in the emotion, she hadn't thought about it. Then she realized, she hadn't thought about it because it *was* natural for her to say, Kala had just been too stubborn to admit it.

"Kala, Linda, step away from that man. NOW!" Owen's voice sounded from the front door.

Turning to see her dad, Kala saw that he had dropped the four bags of groceries he had been carrying and was staring daggers at Asmodeus's back.

Asmodeus slowly turned around to see who had spoken. When he saw Owen he smiled maliciously. "Malak."

"Wait, what?" Kala said in shock.

"Try *Grigori*, Demon King. Leave now, while you still can."

"Wait, what?" Kala was even more shocked.

But Asmodeus was downright scared.

Owen turned to Kala. "I mean it, Kala. Step away from *it*. Take your mother and lock yourself in the bedroom."

Linda was visibly shaken at Owen's words. "Owen, this is Frank. He's Kala's new boyfriend."

"No, he's not." Kala knew now was not the time to lie. If her foster father was a Grigori, then he could potentially kick Asmodeus's ass. And that was not something Kala wanted to miss.

Linda looked at Kala, rattled. "What do you mean? Who is he?"

Kala took Owen's advice and started to move Linda away.

Asmodeus turned to Kala, venom in his eyes. "Don't go anywhere. You're coming with me."

Owen stepped forward. "She is *not* going with you. Leave this house before I turn you to dust."

"I'd like to see you try." Asmodeus was out of his seat in seconds, facing Owen.

"I don't have to try." Owen's eyes lit up a bright white, like Talan's had before Asmodeus had teleported Kala away.

Asmodeus leapt at Owen, squeezing his arms around Owen's body like a vise.

Owen laughed. "You may be king, but you're still just a Demon." He barely shrugged his arms and Asmodeus flew off his body like a rubber band that had just snapped. He soared backward across the room, his back hitting the granite-topped kitchen island with a large CRACK!

Kala flinched at the sound, but kept moving her terrified mother backward.

All Asmodeus needed was one touch, then he could take her anywhere.

Asmodeus seemed to realize this, too, as he turned to Kala with a look of determined desperation burning in his eyes. He jumped toward her.

White light streaked across the room, a glowing snake of lightning, hitting Asmodeus before he could touch Kala. He screamed in pain as the light engulfed him. His skin started to disintegrate. Kala knew she should be happy, but a tiny part of her had grown kind of used to the jerk. Seeing him die wasn't as satisfying as she thought it would be.

Through his screams, Asmodeus saw what must have been concern on Kala's face. It made him smile. "Don't worry, I don't die that easy."

"Oh you *do* die easy, little king, but not today. Go tell your Elders, the Grigori are back and they should be scared." Owen turned his hand, which twisted the white light tightly around Asmodeus, causing him to screech in agony. Kala had forgotten how disturbing his screeching was.

Then in a quick bright flash Asmodeus disappeared.

The light popped out.

For a second Kala wasn't sure if this was a trick — that Asmodeus wasn't actually gone, but when Owen reached her side he confirmed, "He's gone."

Kala realized that she'd been shaking as she and Linda both embraced Owen tightly.

After a moment, he pulled away and looked at the two of them. "Are you two okay? He didn't hurt you, did he?"

"I made him a sandwich," Linda muttered nervously.

It struck Kala as funny through all this chaos and she laughed. Soon Owen and Linda were laughing as well, breaking the tension of the last five minutes.

"You know what a Grigori is?" Owen asked Kala.

They both looked at her for an answer. Kala wondered if Linda knew, but then saw in her expression that she knew who her husband was.

Kala nodded. "I met another one of you. His name is Talan, he helped me."

Owen's face showed relief. "Talan. Good. Why didn't he protect you against Asmodeus? And why does Asmodeus care about you? What kind of missions are you doing over there with Turner?"

It took a few seconds for Kala to respond as she was soaking in Owen's statement. He knew Talan, he knew Asmodeus by name, and he knew Turner was her boss. Not to mention the fact that her foster dad was a *Grigori*! "I need to sit."

"Of course." Owen was all concern as he led Kala back to a stool.

The granite was cracked down the middle of the island as if a boulder had landed on it, a reminder of how much stronger Demons and Angels were compared to her fragile human self. There was no way Kala would have survived a tossing like that.

"It was all a mistake," Kala said. She was with her parents now. For the first time since this whole thing started, she felt safe, like they could fix everything. "I didn't mean to. I really didn't." Kala felt the need to preface what she was about to confess.

"We know you wouldn't do anything intentional, just tell us what happened," Owen encouraged.

Always on her side, Kala felt a twist of overwhelming emotion. She felt ashamed then, knowing they wouldn't be on her side much longer. Not when she told them what she planned to do or, more accurately, *not* do. But they'd find out sooner or later. If Owen was a Grigori, and the world started to crack, he'd know why. He'd find out the Atlas failed. Then he'd find out the Atlas was his daughter. It hurt her on such a deep level, for the first time since she was five-years-old Kala cried.

Linda's arms were immediately around her. Kala grabbed her back, desperate for contact. It somehow made her feel better for what she was about to say.

"Was it Asmodeus?" Owen sounded protective. "I should have killed him. I've gotten soft over the years. What did he do?"

Kala pulled out of the embrace and wiped her tears away. "It wasn't Asmodeus, although you probably should have killed him."

"Agreed," Owen grumbled.

"You guys are going to hate me." Kala took a deep breath.

"We'd never hate you, Kala, just tell us so we can help," Owen urged.

Kala nodded and took another calming breath. "I'm Atlas."

Chapter Twenty-Seven

Linda looked at Kala with confusion. "As in the Titan god?"

Owen, on the other hand, had gone completely white. "No," he said in a small voice.

"Yeah." Kala and Owen shared a pained look.

Saying it out loud had an effect on Kala she wasn't expecting. Being Atlas, the job itself, the actual position, had always felt like a far-off dream that she could ignore until it went away. Admitting it to her foster parents, saying the actual words, brought it all into the spotlight.

"You both look like death warmed over, so it must be bad. Tell me what this means." Linda stroked her daughter's hair comfortingly.

Kala told them everything. From how Jack was supposed to kill the President, to how Kala took the shot, to her mission to kill Jack.

"Oh sweetie," Linda said. There was pain and sympathy in her eyes. "You love this Jack, don't you?"

Tears welled up in Kala's eyes again and she felt like punching herself for being so emotional. Unable to speak, she simply nodded.

Then Kala remembered her shred of hope. "But I have an idea. I think I can stop this whole thing, or at least my part in it."

"There's no way out of this, Kala," Owen replied firmly, but he looked inconsolable for having to tell her that.

Kala started to ramble. If she just said it fast enough, Owen couldn't veto the plan. "General Turner. He gave us drugs that made us appear dead, in fact, we were almost dead, but the drug revived us after a certain amount of time. It's the only way to meet with the original Atlas. Dying. You can see him when an old Atlas dies and a new one takes his place. I could trick him, or beg him, or something. If I could just talk to him, convince him somehow, even for one day, it would be enough. The cycle would break and Jack and I wouldn't be causing some paradox by existing together at the same time. We could both live. Don't you see?" Kala knew she sounded crazed, desperate, but she didn't care. She had to try.

Owen nodded slowly.

Kala was too stunned to speak or move.

Owen held Kala's face in his hands, his eyes intense. "I understand why you need to try, and I won't interfere because I don't want this for you. If I could pick one job on earth that I would never want for my child, it would be Atlas. But he's been tricked before and if anyone can do it, you can. But Kala," Owen dropped his hands and placed them on her shoulders, "If you end up staying the Atlas, you *have* to complete your mission."

Kala looked away. She couldn't face Owen knowing she couldn't kill Jack. "I can't."

Owen forced eye contact with Kala by lifting her chin with his finger. "If you don't, it will kill billions of innocent people. Kala, I know you. You'd never be able to live with yourself if that happened, not even for the love of your life."

"I don't know how." Kala was honest. Even if she agreed and thought it was the right thing to do, she didn't think she could go through with it. And having to watch the video on repeat every time a television was on only made it more surreal, and more unfathomable.

"When the time is right, you will. I have faith in you." Owen leaned down and kissed Kala's forehead, then stood back to look at her. "I can finally tell you how I found you. I never dreamed I'd be able to."

"I thought I was sent to you through the foster system." Kala was happy to change the subject.

Owen shook his head. "Kala, Grigori see humans differently. We can see what you would call auras, I guess. Most people are pretty boring, the color of their aura is in line with what they're good at, and let's face it: most people never discover what they're good at. They simple lead mundane lives, never living up to their potential. But the truly special people have auras that are almost blinding. These are the people Grigori seek out to teach, because they're destined for great things. You are one of those people, Kala. Your aura was so bright I saw it from miles away, and when I found you, you were in a terrible home."

Kala remembered that home. The home of Harold and June Slater. They were the kind of foster family that was only in it for the monthly paycheck, pretty much leaving the kids to fend for themselves. Kala remembered having an all-out war with one of the other kids for the last hot pocket. When the officer arrived and took Kala to Owen and Linda's home it was a huge relief. Having three meals a day without having to fight for it was a perk alone, but to have foster parents that gave a damn was priceless.

Owen continued: "I nurtured your talents, which seemed to be with your ability to target things. But it is so much more than that: you have an innate ability to see things others can't. That's why your aim is so precise. My job as a Grigori was to bring you to your full potential, but Kala, your potential is limitless. Every time I tapped into one talent another one would present itself. I've never seen anything like it." Owen placed his hand on Kala's arm, looking at her with pride. "Kala, what I'm trying to tell you is that you are special. I've always known that you were destined for great things, it's why I made sure you were placed in

Turner's army. He's also destined for greatness, *he* will change the world, but you, *you* will keep it safe. I think it was your destiny to be the next Atlas, whether you want to believe that or not."

Owen's words made Kala's head spin. Owen was the only father she'd ever known and his approval meant everything to her. To see this pride for her radiating from his entire body made Kala feel both happy and devastated all at once. "I have to try to save Jack first," was all that came out of her mouth. Kala felt like a broken record, but there was nothing else she could give. That was all she had.

Owen held her once more and Kala clung to him. "I'll help you any way I can. I love you, Kala."

Linda came in for the hug as well. "We both do."

And for the first time Kala was too defeated to feel awkward about the "L" word. "I love you guys, too." It felt right. It felt good. And she meant it with every fiber of her being. Foster care or not, these two people were her parents. Her *real* parents.

And she wouldn't let anything happen to them. Kala knew it in her soul. If it came down to it, she'd save them at any cost. It brought another lump to her throat, but Kala was tired of chastising herself for feeling emotional. At this point, she earned every tear that fell from her eyes.

"Am I interrupting?" Kala recognized Talan's voice immediately. Though she had only spent a brief time with him, one thing she couldn't argue was the fact that they had some kind of connection.

The trio separated from the hug to see Talan standing in their living room, his expression concerned and humbled.

When Owen saw Talan he quickly walked over to him and embraced him like he was family. "Talan." Kala could hear so many different meanings in the way he said Talan's name. It was a mixture of relief, happiness, and confidence all combined into one.

"Owen."

Kala could see that the two of them hadn't seen each other in a long time.

"Talan this is Linda, my wife."

Talan walked over to Linda and hugged her. She looked thrilled at meeting him. "So nice to meet you."

Talan pulled out of the hug and looked at Kala. He was so respectful it made Kala's chest hurt. Talan was still abiding her wish not to be touched. But in this moment, finding out that Owen was a Grigori, that Talan was his friend; it made Kala feel an overwhelming sense of emotion. Like Talan was a friend for life, like he would protect her until the end of days, like he was… family.

Before Kala knew what she was doing, she wrapped her arms around Talan and squeezed. She felt his arms firmly hold her and his touch gave her goosebumps.

Oh yeah, that's why I don't want him touching me. Kala suddenly remembered and extracted herself from his embrace. "Okay, that's enough touching."

Owen hid a smile, but Kala saw it. She knew she was being her normal ornery self, but she couldn't help it. Talan was dangerous to her *because* of the way he made her feel.

"How did you find me?" Kala asked.

"I knew Asmodeus had you so when I felt Owen use a banishment spell on him I used it to come here," Talan explained. He turned to Owen. "Where did you banish him?" Talan asked.

"I sent him to the Elders," Owen chuckled.

Talan smiled, extremely amused. "He probably hasn't been to the 5th in a long time. I wish I could see his face."

The two of them looked like they were sharing some kind of inside joke, so Kala asked, "What is the 5th?"

"The 5th level of Hell. It's not somewhere you ever want to be," Owen answered.

"Isn't he like a king of Hell or something? Why would he care about being down there, or up there, or wherever it is?"

Talan explained to Kala, "Asmodeus is the self-proclaimed king, which I'll admit, he's earned. He's definitely the strongest Demon I've ever seen and over time he's grown more powerful. But the 5th level of Hell? That place is deadly to all supernatural beings if they're not careful. It's why the Elders live there: for protection. Only the Grigori are powerful enough to destroy them and even then they'd give us a run for our money, especially since there are only five Grigori on the planet. The rest of our brothers are still trapped in the fifth Heaven as I showed you."

"You showed her our prison?" Owen asked Talan. When he nodded, Owen turned to Kala. "For you to have met two Grigori in your lifetime shows the strength of your potential."

Kala couldn't listen to another speech on how great she was. "Owen, seriously, I get it, I'm full of potential, but I'd rather use it to take down terrorists with my sniper rifle than to kill Jack. So, can we try my plan or not?"

Owen nodded and filled Talan in on what Kala wanted to do.

To Kala's relief, Talan didn't dismiss the idea either. "It might work."

"Might is better than impossible. Now, will one of you take me to Turner or what?"

Chapter Twenty-Eight

After an argument of *Dad* versus *soul mate* (soul mate according to Talan, not Kala) soul mate won. Talan convinced Owen to move locations, since Asmodeus would certainly be back with reinforcements. It was sad that they'd have to leave the only home Kala ever knew, but Kala wanted her parents safe and, after all, it was just a house. After promising to meet up in a few days, Kala and Talan were finally ready to leave.

Linda and Owen gave Kala and Talan one last hug before they popped out of the living room to who-knows-where.

Talan turned to Kala. "Ready?"

"As I'll ever be," Kala said with more confidence than she felt.

Talan touched Kala's arm and her parents' house was just a memory.

With a disorientating SLAM! Kala and Talan were in a beautifully decorated living room. The design was of the Victorian era with antique furniture made up of ornate wood and brown velvets. There was a small love seat and a large couch, both with rounded individual backs tacked in with intricate studs. To say the fireplace was large would be an understatement, it was almost big enough that Kala could stand in it. For a second, Kala thought Talan had teleported her back in time to some rich person's mansion, but when Turner and his wife Roberta entered the room, Kala knew she was at their house.

"Kala, this is a surprise," Turner stated with a kind of amusement. "I'm not going to pretend that I'm particularly happy that you didn't set off at least one alarm breaking in here, but I did hire you for your *talents* after all. I trust my injection worked for you?"

Kala knew he was referring to the anti-tracker, which had worked great until Lali had decided to find her the old-fashioned way by following her. "Lali was a Demon. She tracked me down."

Turner couldn't hide his disappointment at the news. "Lali? A Demon? Can you tell me if I've employed any other supernatural beings?" Turner seemed disturbed by this news.

"No, but *he* can." Kala nodded toward Talan and found it hard to not think about the fact that Turner already worked with Talan in a different form.

Roberta apparently had enough small talk and she went up to Kala and hugged her. "I'm so happy to see you safe. Now tell us who he is."

Kala hadn't been sure if Talan would show himself to Roberta and Turner in his current form. He had told her before that he came to Roberta as an old black man and to Turner as a scientist; Kala had thought Talan might come to them in either of those forms. The more she thought about it, though, the more Kala realized that Talan wasn't ready to retire his two disguises. He wasn't done with the couple yet.

"This is Talan. He's an Angel." Kala knew that sounded absurd, but she also knew that at least the couple believed in Demons and Angels. And she didn't want to get into the whole *Grigori* thing.

Turner's head jerked back, startled slightly. "Really?"

Kala looked directly at Turner. "I need your help."

But it was Roberta that answered, "Anything."

It was then that Kala saw the kind of symbiosis Turner and Roberta shared in their relationship. It was almost like they were one person. Whereas Turner may have been on the verge of objection, by Roberta promising her help Turner was completely on board, no questions asked. Kala wondered what Turner would do if he was in Kala's position and was asked to kill his wife.

"I need to die," Kala stated simply.

Turner raised his eyebrow in curiosity. "That can be arranged."

After Kala explained her plan, Turner and Roberta brought Kala and Talan to the basement of their mansion. Floor after floor of the house made Kala dizzy. She could never live in that much space, she'd get lost for sure. Her one bedroom apartment was plenty. As Kala glanced in each passing room, she realized that Turner and Roberta needed the space. Catching glimpses of electronic equipment and scientific gear, made Kala want to stay out of their business altogether.

Kala glanced over at Talan. She knew he was probably responsible for most of their scientific discoveries, but Turner had obviously taken the research to a whole new level. Talan's eyes met Kala's as if he felt her looking at him. He smiled gently. She looked away. Kala couldn't handle Talan being so supportive and nice right now. It made her annoyed for some reason though she was grateful for his help. The opposing thoughts confused the crap out of her so she figured it was best just to avoid as much contact with Talan as possible.

When they stepped into an elevator, Kala was impressed. An elevator in a house?! It blew her mind. The elevator went down four more floors to reach the basement. Exiting the elevator, Kala stepped into a giant room full of lab tables. It looked like a college chemistry lab, from the size of the room and the beakers, Bunsen burners, and sinks at every seven-foot long table. With all the steam and bubbling, Kala expected to see at least a handful of scientists at work, but she only saw one. He came hurrying up to them.

The man was short-ish with gray hair and brown eyes. His features were overly small, making him almost rodent-like in appearance. Although he had gray hair, his face still looked relatively young, perhaps only in his mid-forties. Turner introduced him to Kala and Talan. "Ms. Hicks, Mr. Talan, this is John Fortski."

Kala shook his hand and noticed when Talan shook John's hand that Talan knew him. It was just a small moment, a flash of pride, but it was enough to give Kala a surge of relief. If Talan had trained this guy, then Fortski would be good.

"John is the man who devised the 'death cocktail' you took before. John, you can explain it better." Turner gave the floor to Fortski.

Fortski looked extremely nervous, especially around Roberta, furtively looking at her as if she was likely to scream at him any moment. Then he focused his attention back on Kala. "The drug I gave your team slows the heart rate down so slowly that any EKG will register it as stopped. It has a time release adrenaline shot that jolts you back to the living. I can make the time release up to two hours, but anything after that, you could run the risk of actually dying."

Kala looked at the clock.

0d 13h 55m 23s.

4:05 P.M.

Time was flying. Kala had less than twelve hours to fail or complete her mission, but she needed enough time with Atlas to either trick him or convince him to take his job back. If Kala ever needed the talent of negotiation it was right now.

"Give me an hour to be safe," Kala qualified.

"I'll set the parameters." Fortski nodded. He went back to the table he had been working at when they arrived.

Turner nodded toward the back of the lab. "We'll set you up back here. I had a cot brought down."

The four of them walked to the area, where Kala found a standard issue army cot, which was somewhat comforting. It was familiar and familiar felt good at the moment. Kala lay down on the hard mattress and tried to calm herself for what was about to happen. Talan kneeled down beside her.

"Are you sure you want to do this?" Talan asked with concern.

"Yes, positive." Kala had no doubts. This was her one shot to save Jack: she was going to take it no matter what.

Fortski walked over with a metal plate and syringe resting on top. "Here we are."

Kala knew the procedure, having experienced it before, but it still gave her a bout of butterflies.

Fortski knelt down next to Kala on the opposite side of where Talan was. Kala figured Fortski thought that Talan was her support system and didn't want to deprive her of him.

"Should I invoke a protection spell?" Roberta asked Talan.

"Yes, I'll help. We need to keep Demons and Malaks out, Malaks especially, since they'll want to kill Kala directly. Demons will just want to take her," Talan qualified. "I shifted her DNA, but once she's in a mortal state, she may be trackable."

Roberta seemed to light up at this new knowledge being presented to her. She obviously knew about Demons and Angels already, since she had learned to harness their powers, but to be working directly with one was definitely making her happy. Little did she realize, she'd been working with Talan for years and just didn't know it.

Talan squeezed Kala's hand before she could scold him for it. "We'll keep you safe, just do your thing and don't worry."

Kala reluctantly squeezed Talan's hand back and grudgingly mumbled, "Thanks."

Talan stood up and went to Roberta's side.

Kala heard them start to chant in a language she didn't recognize. In seconds Kala physically felt some kind of invisible force laying on top of her like a blanket. It was a strange sensation, like waving your hands over goose-pimpled hairs. She didn't know if it would protect her or not, but she figured it couldn't hurt.

Looking up at Turner, he seemed fascinated by the whole *magic* thing. Kala could tell that this was new to him as well. She guessed that

Turner hadn't taken it as seriously as he should have and now, witnessing it in action, he was seeing some of its uses.

Talan's observations about the Turners suddenly rang true for Kala, thinking that the combination of their magic and science would make them unstoppable. Kala was just relieved she was on their good side. She'd hate to think of the poor sap that got on their bad side.

Fortski gave Kala a nervous smile as he readied the syringe. "You should only feel a slight prick."

"Yeah, yeah, just do it." Kala wanted it over and done with.

Not having to be told twice, Fortski injected Kala with the serum.

It felt the same as before: cold liquid entering her blood stream. It was almost soothing in a way, like an I.V. drip after being dehydrated. Then the fun began. Kala felt the sweat beading on her forehead as her heart physically started to slow down. The drug was forcing her to relax, which instinctively made Kala a prisoner in her own body. Slower and slower her heart pounded, loud in her ears. The last thing Kala saw was Talan's face as she entered into darkness…

"Well, well, isn't this interesting." Kala heard her own voice talking — to herself.

She opened her eyes. Kala stood on a white sand beach with bright turquoise waters lapping gently on the shore. Sitting on a beach chair was *herself* drinking some kind of fruity tropical drink. A large umbrella dug into the sand providing generous shade for the other Kala. An empty identical beach chair lay under the umbrella set out for the real Kala.

"Atlas?" Kala asked her doppelganger.

"In the flesh, or in *your* flesh I should say. How on earth did you pull this one off? I give you kudos, this is definitely new. I've never talked to an Atlas in their own form before." Atlas looked genuinely amazed.

It was strange talking to a mirror image of oneself, but Kala knew better than to dwell on it for long. She didn't have much time and didn't want to waste any of it. She sat down next to Atlas and an identical fruity drink appeared in Kala's hand.

"Drink up. Enjoy yourself while you can because when you wake up, it's back to business." Atlas toasted Kala, then took a drink herself.

"That's what I wanted to talk to you about," Kala started, "I tried to tell you before, this was a huge mistake. I wasn't meant to do your job. In fact, I'm *not* going to do your job. The world will end. You don't want that, do you?" Kala said in a rush.

"You think you're the first to shirk their duty?" Atlas laughed as she took another drink. "The longest an Atlas went without completing their mission was two years. You *do* remember the Black Death, don't you? That Atlas hid in a hole until the next Chosen One tracked him down and killed him. It took the world almost 150 years to recover from that little mishap."

"But this is different, it's not just going to be a horrible event that humanity can recover from. A Grigori Angel showed me the future, he showed me that I was something called the *Fated One* and Jack is a *potential* or something. We can't exist together. It's written in some kind of scroll thingy." Kala sarcastically commended herself on her eloquence.

Atlas stared at Kala without saying a word. Watching the image of herself looking at her made Kala's skin crawl. Still there was one advantage to Atlas taking on her form: Kala could read Atlas's facial expression because it was an expression Kala had felt many times before: doubt.

"We're running out of time. You have to stop this," Kala pleaded. Kala had figured if Atlas knew what was at stake, he (or she at the moment) would be willing to switch back.

"How dare you," Atlas seethed.

When Atlas didn't elaborate, Kala stood up. "How dare I? How dare you! You're going to let this planet die all because you're too lazy to do your own freaking job!"

Atlas stood to face her, eyes full of fury. "No, *you're* going to let this planet die for not doing your job!"

Everything that had happened to Kala finally reached its peak, and her fury matched Atlas's. "You're weak and pathetic! You're supposed to be a god!"

"I didn't want to be a god!" Atlas shouted back. "I still don't want to! And do you think I care what a measly *human* thinks of me? You're the one who's weak and pathetic, crawling to me, begging for me to let you out of your responsibility. One task. One simple task and you save the whole world. That's a *gift* not a curse! You ungrateful peon!"

Rage burned through Kala like a fire. Atlas wasn't going to release her. Atlas was going to sit and drink Mai Tai's until the world collapsed around him. Kala had thought for a moment that the real threat of the world ending would make Atlas do the right thing. But Kala could see now that Atlas *wanted* the world to end. He just wanted it to be over.

"Then you don't deserve this *gift*," Kala raged.

Terror flashed in Atlas's eyes. "What are you doing?"

Something inside Kala was terrified as well, but the stronger part of her took over. It was as if she were accessing some secret file somewhere hidden inside her. Though her conscious brain had no idea what she was doing, Kala's subconscious took over.

"You are no longer worthy, and you *will* be punished." The words came out of Kala's mouth, but she had no idea where they came from. A tiny part of her was screaming for herself to stop.

Atlas started to back away, his body shifting into something else. He looked human. But something more as well, he was almost alien-like in his perfectly symmetrical features, like a living statue. And he grew. Grew so large he was well over twenty feet. Standing in front of Kala was a god.

And it meant nothing to Kala.

Towering over her, Atlas was still puny to her.

Atlas cowered, whimpering like a caged animal.

He knew what was coming, even if Kala hadn't figured it out yet.

From deep inside Kala, she screamed, "I AM TAKING WHAT'S MINE!"

Kala couldn't stop herself, she didn't know what she was doing.

Atlas howled in shock and fear as his body started turning into a white swirling smoke.

And that was when it happened.

Kala opened her mouth and devoured him.

The white smoke poured inside her body like ice in her veins. Kala felt as if she was swallowing a giant snake that wouldn't end. The more she consumed, the more power she felt growing in every cell of her body. When the last wisps of smoke that were Atlas were swallowed, the realization of what Kala had just done hit her like an explosion of torment.

Kala was a god.

Kala was Atlas.

Chapter Twenty-Nine

Kala's eyes opened and she sat up in the cot like a lightning bolt had shot through her back. She could barely hear Fortski's panicked voice as she tried to regain her senses, "The adrenaline shot must have activated too early."

"Relax, John, we'll figure it out later," Turner's voice tried to calm Fortski.

Kala had to stand up and pace. The enormity of what just happened wasn't processing in her brain yet. She had *consumed* a god. Of course, Kala hadn't known what she was doing at the time, but there was obviously a part of her deep down that knew *exactly* what she was doing. Her body tingled all over like she was having a panic attack, but Kala knew that wasn't true. The tingling was her human body adjusting to becoming a supernatural one.

Her brain could not seem to wrap around the fact that she was now Atlas. Not a human being tricked into taking on the job, but the real Atlas. So many questions raced through her mind. How did she know how to devour a god? A Titan? *Why* did she do it? Where had those words of power come from? Could she take it back? Vomit him out or something? What did being a god mean? Did she have powers? Could she be killed? Kala instinctively knew the rules were different now that she was no longer an emissary of the god, she just didn't know the specifics.

Kala felt a hand on her shoulder. It brought her mind back into focus.

Everyone in the room watched her intently, Talan being the most concerned hence the hand belonged to him. "Kala," he said her name in shock.

Kala could tell from his face that he knew what she had done. Seeing him there, not knowing what to do, so worried for her, Kala fell into his arms.

Kala looked up at Talan. "Am I what I think I am?" She hoped he would tell her it was all a dream.

Talan nodded.

"How did that happen?" was all she could think to ask.

Talan held her close and spoke quietly in her ear. "I don't know. It's never happened before, Kala. *Never.*"

His words scared her even more. When she had said the words to consume Atlas, it had felt like remembering the lyrics to an old song. At first she didn't think she knew what to say, but then the words came out of her mouth in perfect formation.

Kala's body suddenly jerked backward in Talan's arms. She screamed from the pain. It felt like her cells were fighting against each other. "What's happening to me?"

Fortski was at her side next to Talan, feeling like he was the most "doctorly" of the bunch. "Maybe it's the adrenaline kicking in. Come sit down."

Turner and Roberta were arm in arm, watching Kala with concern, though Turner looked more fascinated than worried.

Another jolt of energy surged through Kala and she arched her back in anguish. "Talan, make it stop!"

"I can't!" Talan's face was wracked with agony. "Kala, your body is trying to fuse both sides together. The human part of you is rejecting the power of the Titan."

"Am I dying?" Kala screamed as another jolt of pain surged through her.

"Humans aren't meant to have a god's power Kala," Talan looked at her with grief in his eyes.

"So that's a yes." Kala shrugged him off and let Fortski sit her back down on the cot. She screamed again. It felt like her blood was on fire.

Kala took deep, calming breaths.

Roberta knelt beside Kala and Talan. "What can I do?" she asked.

Talan shook his head. "She's trying to integrate with a god and her body won't allow it."

Kala fought the urge to scream again as the pain intensified.

"So we have to find a way for Kala's body not to reject this god's… power? Aura? What?" Roberta was obviously trying to get a clearer picture of the situation.

"His *being*. The Titan has died and Kala consumed his energy. It's not like there will be two people living inside her, she is becoming the god itself," Talan tried to explain.

Kala could barely listen to their conversation. It started to feel like every cell in her body was popping like popcorn.

Roberta grabbed Kala's hand. "Squeeze as hard as you like."

Kala obliged and felt bad when she heard a slight gasp from Roberta.

Roberta asked Talan, "I've been working on ways to astral project. Do you know what that is?"

"Traveling from one body to another through dreams." Talan nodded.

"Yes, through dreams, but in waking as well. I can go inside Kala's head to try and connect the two entities together," Roberta offered.

Turner spoke up at that suggestion. "Roberta, that's way too dangerous. I won't allow it."

Roberta turned to Turner, determined. "We have to try, Geoffrey."

Kala wasn't sure she liked the idea of someone poking around in her head, but the pain was so intense she would try anything to make it stop. "Please," she begged.

Turner gave his wife a look that said he trusted her judgment.

Talan looked at Roberta doubtfully. "I'm not sure it would do any good."

"Listen, her brain is unfocused right now, she's giving in to the pain and fighting it at the same time. If I can go in there, I can make Kala relax enough for the two souls to integrate." Roberta tried to convince Talan.

Kala screamed again in agony.

Talan nodded. "Do it."

Kala was ready to scrape her eyes out from pain — then...

A sudden calm melted through her.

She heard Roberta's voice in her head, soothing, "Relax. Let him in, Kala. Let him in and calm yourself."

Kala felt another squeeze of fire in her chest, but Roberta's voice grew louder. "Give in, Kala. Relax."

With every word, a sense of serenity started to take the place of the pain.

Just when Kala thought she had given in to the calm completely, her body seized in a fit of pain. She screamed.

Roberta's voice echoed in her head and spread through her entire being. "Calm."

It was so gentle...

The pain stopped.

Kala looked at Roberta who seemed to be coming out of a trance. When Roberta's eyes met hers, Roberta said in awe, "Such power."

Coursing through her veins, Kala felt exactly what Roberta was talking about. Kala had never felt more alive in her life. She felt as if she had been injected with a double dose of adrenaline. Her heart pounded in her chest and Kala could feel the blood pumping through her veins like millions of tubes connecting her body together. Kala's senses were on overdrive. She heard everyone breathing as clearly as if they were snoring. She smelled every chemical in the lab as if it was right under her nose. And Talan's hand. Kala felt the pores and tiny hairs of his hand like they were craters.

It made her want to panic and fly at the same time. Kala settled on standing.

Roberta and Talan stood with her.

Talan's face was wide-eyed. "You shouldn't have been able to survive that."

Kala took deep breaths to calm both her excitement and nerves. "Roberta helped me."

Roberta still looked dazed, but she smiled at Kala warmly. Turner searched his wife for wounds as if she had been in some kind of battle.

"Roberta kept you calm, yes, but physically, Kala... you shouldn't have survived that." Talan shook his head. "To integrate with a god...a human..."

"Yes, I'm very special. But am I safe? What does this mean Talan?" Kala still had so many questions and Talan was the only one who was remotely qualified to answer.

"I'm not sure, but the rules have definitely changed. You're no longer an emissary of Atlas, which means if anyone kills you, they won't become the next Atlas. I'm fairly certain it means you cannot be killed by a mortal." Talan was apparently trying to work everything out himself.

"And Demons and Malaks?" Kala was more worried about the supernatural than an overzealous human.

"Gods can be killed, yes, Kala. You've just done it. Why do you think Atlas has been in hiding all these years, tricking humans into doing his job? As far as Demons go, you're in more danger now than you were before. They'll want to kill you once and for all so the world will be in chaos forever. The only advantage you may have is the fact that the Malaks will want you safe at all costs now, since no one can become a new Atlas." Talan shrugged. "Angels are like that, they only see in black and white."

"Aren't you running out of time?" Turner asked Kala.

His words cut her like a knife.

Kala had sealed her own fate.

There was no tricking Atlas into taking his job back. She *was* Atlas.

She could either kill Jack or let the world destroy itself.

There was no turning back now and frankly, Kala still hadn't decided yet.

Kala turned to Turner. "What would you do? If your mission was to kill Roberta or the world would end?"

Turner didn't hesitate. "I'd let it burn." Turner nodded to Fortski to leave and helped his wife toward the exit. "I'm assuming you two can leave the way you came, unless you need any more help from me?"

"No. Thank you for everything." Kala still reeled from Turner's words.

Talan reached out and took Kala's hand. "To Jack?"

Kala closed her eyes in confusion, but slowly nodded.

When her eyes opened she was in Jack's bedroom at the hideout he had taken her to. Jack was asleep, the sheets and blanket in a tangled knot from his restlessness.

Talan was gone, letting her decide what to do on her own.

Seeing the room made a lump form in Kala's throat. It was just like the vision Talan had shown her. Tomorrow morning Jack would go to the alley and seek out Penny and the world would destroy itself.

"I made sure he would sleep the night." Penny's voice came from behind Kala.

Kala whirled around to see the woman step out of the shadows.

When she made eye contact with Kala, Penny took a step back. "Impossible."

"Possible," Kala corrected. She didn't feel like getting into it with Penny right now. She just wanted to be alone with Jack.

But Penny had a different idea. Penny charged at Kala with her hands outstretched.

Kala blocked Penny using a simple Aikido move. She pulled Penny's energy into her, then pushed it back into Penny's chest with an open palm.

To Kala's shock Penny flew across the room and smashed into the wall, causing it to crumble into a Penny-sized crater.

"Whoa," Kala said in surprise. Being a god meant super strength.

Penny recovered quickly, but instead of attacking, she slumped her shoulders and looked on the verge of tears. "Possible," she whispered.

It was as much of an apology as Kala was ever going to get. Kala walked over to Penny and put her hand out to help her up. After a few moments of hesitation, Penny finally accept Kala's offer and stood.

"Sorry about shooting you… and breaking your neck… and lighting you on fire… and smashing you into a wall." Kala felt the need to apologize.

"Jack can't become Atlas anymore, can he?" Penny asked, brushing past Kala's apology.

"No. No one can." Kala sighed.

"You're the Fated One." Penny didn't sound happy, but she didn't sound angry anymore either.

"Looks like," Kala answered.

Penny's voice cracked. "Is Jack the Potential?"

Kala felt tears in her eyes. She simply nodded.

Penny closed her eyes in pain, then opened them, looking at Kala with sympathy. "I'm sorry."

"Me too." Kala turned to watch Jack sleeping peacefully. Then she focused back on Penny. "Asmodeus called you Pandora. You're not the *real* Pandora are you?"

Penny nodded. "I've been training Atlases for centuries. I thought Jack was the Fated One. I didn't know what the scrolls meant, but seeing you…" She left the thought unfinished.

Kala knew what she meant. She hadn't expected this outcome, either. After everything Kala had been through, finding out that Penny was Pandora just seemed to be another layer to a very large cake. Something to be filed away for later.

"I want to be alone with him," Kala asked of Penny.

Penny didn't argue. "If you need my help in the future…"

Kala nodded.

Penny left the apartment.

Kala took a moment before she walked over to the bed. A part of her wanted to wake Jack up to spend as much time with him as possible before she'd have to make her life-altering decision. Instead, Kala snuggled up behind him and wrapped her arm over his chest. Even in his sleep Jack instinctively clasped on to Kala's hand and held her tight. It made her want to scream it was so emotionally painful.

Kala glanced at the clock.

0d 06h 04m 12s.

11:56 P.M.

Kala closed her eyes, letting sleep take her.

***

"Kala, wake up."

Kala opened her eyes to see Jack's face staring down at her. He leaned down and kissed her deeply. "Where have you been?" he asked between kisses.

Feeling his body on hers and his kisses made Kala want to forget everything, but instinctively she pulled away and checked the clock.

0d 00h 03m 3s.

5:57 A.M.

Three minutes until the end of the world.

Kala jumped out of bed. "Jack."

Jack was up next to her. "What is it? Did you talk to Atlas? Did you get him to fix it?"

Kala shook her head, not wanting to accept what was happening. "Jack."

Jack stood there, staring at Kala, obviously trying to process the situation.

"I've seen it, Jack. We can't exist together. If one of us doesn't die, the world will instead. But I won't do it. I can't. I can't kill you!" Kala was almost in hysterics. Standing in front of Jack, imagining shooting him…

Kala looked around the room.

It wasn't just the same room from Talan's vision, it was the room where she saw herself in every television killing Jack.

"We have to get out of here." Kala grabbed Jack's hand and started to pull him out of the bedroom, but Jack didn't budge.

"I knew it," he finally spoke.

"Jack, I mean it, we have to leave. We have two minutes," Kala pleaded.

Jack grabbed Kala's other hand so he was holding them both. "Listen to me, Kala: I *knew* it. I knew it from the beginning. You have to do this."

"WHAT? NO WAY!" Kala couldn't calm herself down no matter how hard she tried.

"Kala," Jack's voice cracked.

It smashed Kala's heart into a million pieces.

This was the moment. The moment of Talan's vision where Kala ran out of the room and Jack couldn't find her. A part of her wanted to do it. To run and never look back. Never have to do what she knew she must.

But Kala stayed where she was.

"Jack," her voice was so small she could barely hear it.

"I was never made for this. I let you kill the President. *I* couldn't do it. I didn't want to." Jack seemed to feel the need to confess to Kala, but Kala didn't want to hear it. She just wanted to throw him over her shoulder and hide him somewhere until… until what?

As if in answer, the ground started to shake.

"It's starting," Kala swallowed hard.

0d 00h 01m 10s.

"Kala, it was always supposed to be you." Jack's eyes were so full of light and hope it made Kala want to cry.

"I can't do it!" she screamed.

The ground shook harder, almost causing them to stumble.

Jack went to his bedside and pulled out his gun.

The gun.

The gun from Kala's vision.

"No, Jack." Kala shook her head. This wasn't happening.

Jack carefully placed the gun in Kala's hand and knelt in front of her.

Everything was the same.

Everything was the same, except Kala couldn't shoot him!

A jolt nearly toppled Kala to the ground.

"Kala, you have to," Jack pleaded.

"Jack," was all Kala could utter.

"Please. Don't let billions die to save me. I'm not worth it."

"Yes, you are!" Kala was crying now.

"No, Kala. I'm not. No one is."

"Jack."

"Kala, please."

Kala couldn't breathe.

She couldn't think.

Everything hurt too much.

"I won't," she choked.

Her head was spinning.

Kala felt the metal of the gun as if it was made of burning ice.

No.

"Please," Jack begged.

No.

Numb.

"Kala."

No.

"I love you, Jack."

Kala pulled the trigger.

GRIGORI
RETURNED

DAY ONE

Chapter One

Kala watched Jack's body drop to the floor with a small thud.

She was frozen in place.

Her mind completely comatose.

She stared at the pool of blood forming on the ground from the hole in Jack's head.

He was gone.

Forever.

And she had been the one who did it.

Kala killed the only man she ever loved.

The gun dropped from her hand.

The gun that had killed Jack.

Jack.

Her eyes couldn't look away. The blood crept across the wood floor and surrounded Kala's feet. Jack's face was slack, empty of all life. No more smiles. No more sparkling eyes. No more kisses.

Dead.

Kala felt like if she moved, her whole brain would crack. She'd end up curled in a ball sobbing until her body would give up and die.

If she hadn't been so still, Kala probably wouldn't have felt the slight brushing of a hand on her arm.

"We need to go." Penny's voice sounded small in the silence.

Kala still couldn't move. She continued to stare at Jack laying at her feet.

"I can't," Kala managed to say.

"You have to," Penny said with some urgency. "It'll be harder to kill you now, but you can definitely be tortured and imprisoned. Asmodeus will be here any second. I won't be able to protect you."

"My dad banished him to the 5th Level of Hell. He and Talan both seem to think Asmodeus will be there for a while." Kala's brain started to feel like it was thawing. Talking about two very powerful Grigori angels: her foster father, Owen, and her stalker, Talan, began to bring her back into reality. Using the word *reality* in the same sentence as angels still made her feel nuts, but the last four days had been a crash course on what was *real* in the world she lived in.

Besides, seeing Penny's face at the mention of Talan, and now her dad, was all worth it. The supernatural world had no idea the Grigori were back and it scared them to pieces. Though Penny claimed to be on Kala's side now, she had been a royal pain in her butt since the beginning of the *Atlas* ride. Making her squirm gave Kala a small surge of happiness in this darkest moment of her life.

"Impossible." Penny sounded terrified.

Good.

"You keep saying that," Kala pointed out with a little bit of snark. Right now, panicking Penny helped her break out of the shock-coma she was in.

"Because it is!" Penny exclaimed.

"Relax," Kala scolded, finally looking away from Jack's body to stare down Penny. "Why is it so *impossible* that the Grigori are back? Asmodeus was just as freaked. Are they really that powerful?" At this point Kala was fishing. She didn't know much about the Grigori except that there were only a handful of them that had escaped some kind of "Heaven prison." She *did,* however, have a firsthand account at some of their tricks. Talan had made a Malak explode with the touch of his hand, and had taught her a pretty nifty fire trick that allowed her to set Malaks and Demons into a fiery blaze. But her foster dad, Owen, had never revealed his true nature, so aside from banishing the king of Demons to the 5th Level of Hell, she had no idea the extent of his power.

Penny shook her head. "It's too much to explain. Please. I can't bear to see him like that." Her voice broke.

It brought tears to Kala's eyes. Hearing Penny so hurt at Jack's death only reminded her that she was the one who had killed him. Kala felt a surge of overwhelming emotion. She didn't think she could contain it much longer.

So she nodded.

Penny left first.

Kala forced herself to look at Jack one more time, knowing this was the last time she'd ever see him. Watching him lying there, the pool of blood now a lake surrounding his body, Kala hoped that Jack was in a place like the heaven Talan had shown her. It may have been a prison to the Grigori, but it was the most beautiful place Kala had ever seen. Jack was the best person she had ever known and if anyone deserved to be in an eternal paradise it was him.

Tearing her eyes away, Kala followed Penny out of the building.

As she walked through the exit door, Kala fell to her knees.

A flash of light and she was suddenly in a gigantic chamber. There was a throne the size of a large house at the end of the enormous space. Pillars lined the walls on both sides. A man sat on the throne, surrounded by five men on his right and six women on his left. They were huge! Well over twenty feet tall.

Kala looked down at her body and noticed that she wasn't in *her body*. She was in a man's body.

As she viewed the giants more carefully, Kala realized that she actually knew them.

With a certainty that fascinated her more than scared her, Kala realized that she was seeing one of Atlas's memories. Somehow when she had swallowed the Titan whole, she had apparently swallowed his memories as well.

It was Cronus sitting on the throne, with his sisters and brothers beside him.

Kala immediately recognized Atlas's father, Iapetus, by his disapproving glare. Then Kala cringed as she sorted out Atlas's lineage in her head. All the Titans that stood in front of her were brothers and sisters. But this was where Kala's disgusted-bell went off. Iapetus's brother and sister, Oceanus and Tethys, had a daughter, Asia, and Atlas was the offspring of Iapetus and Asia. So Atlas was the product of some serious inbreeding. Kala shuddered. There were only twelve of them around back then and the pickings were slim, but still.

Asia was nowhere to be found, but Grandma and Grandpa were scowling at Atlas/Kala in the same way that Pops was.

At first glance Kala had registered the twelve figures as human, but the more she looked at them, the more otherworldly they seemed. Aside from their size, they had a deep blue glow around them as if they were outlined in light. Their faces looked like they were carved in stone, they were so symmetrical. Their presence was intimidating for Kala, but she could feel it even more so for Atlas. In this memory, he was downright terrified.

Kala took a deep breath.

This was who she was now.

Atlas's past was her past.

This must be a part of the integration process, she rationalized. *But why this memory?*

Kala had the sneaking suspicion she was about to be scolded by some serious mojo-toting gods. She tried to remember the rest of it so she wouldn't have to go through it in real-time, but it wasn't working. She even tried calling out for Penny, hoping she could pull her out of this dream-state. Kala probably still stood in the doorway to Jack's hideout, drooling in the sun, or collapsed on the front porch.

But nothing worked. She was there to stay.

Kala shrugged.

It looked like she'd have to take her licks. She just hoped it wouldn't last long.

Then Kala spoke, or at least, Atlas spoke. Kala was just along for the ride in this flashback.

"They threatened me! I didn't have a choice!" Atlas whined like a baby. Kala wished she could change the memory and say what was really on Atlas's mind. He was furious that his plan hadn't worked. Apparently, there had been another war between the Titans and the Olympians and Atlas had picked the wrong side.

Again.

Kala was really starting to hate the fact that she had to share any part of herself with Atlas. To her, he was a coward. A guy who picked the team he thought would win with no loyalty. And when he inevitably lost, he groveled. Kala despised people who did that. She had seen enough soldiers like Atlas to make her skin crawl.

Cronus, apparently, felt the same way as Kala, because he leaned forward in his throne. "You are pathetic, Atlas. A sniveling rat who begs for his life after betraying your father."

Kala wished she could shut Atlas up, but as this wasn't her memory, she cringed when he yelled, "*You* castrated your father to take over the world!" Kala felt Atlas calming himself. "I just sided with your son. Is that really a crime?"

The other Titans stayed silent, waiting for Cronus to speak on their behalf. "Yes, Atlas, it *is* a crime."

"May I remind you that I have to do my job or you won't have a world to rule." Kala could tell Atlas was trying to remind the Titans that he had some value.

Cronus nodded and laughed. "That was your punishment for siding with us, your true family. If you had stayed loyal, we could have made Zeus lift this burden from you."

Atlas must have seen something in Cronus's eyes that Kala couldn't, because his fear level jumped drastically. "It's fine, really. I like my burden. Just doing my part to keep the earth spinning and such…" Atlas started to back away.

Kala began to see what Atlas saw. Cronus's smile turned into a wickedly cruel snarl, as if he had just swallowed a canary. "Atlas!" Cronus announced as if he were making a decree. "The next time you complete the cycle, you will be stripped of all your protections, and we'll see how you fare against everyone you've wronged. The four-day curse is still your burden, and after this cycle we will no longer hide you from the ones who want to stop you."

Kala searched her brain for any kind of thought or memory as to what happened to Atlas after he completed his next cycle, but she came up with nothing.

She could feel Atlas in a complete panic. "But if I fail, you lose everything! Why would you risk that?" Atlas couldn't fathom why the Titans would drop their protections over him when it could mean the end of the world.

"Making you live in constant fear and shame over what you did is worth the risk. We can always find another if you fail. We'll have to force my son Zeus to comply since he is the one who created the curse, but torturing him will be extremely satisfying." Cronus stopped smiling as if he were now officially bored with this conversation. He leaned back in his throne. "Go. Do whatever it is you're supposed to do."

Cronus snapped his fingers.

Kala's eyes opened and she found herself sitting on the front steps of Jack's hideout, leaning against the iron railing.

Penny was next to her. "What happened?" she asked, more curious than concerned.

"Memories," Kala grumbled. "So am I going to pass out every time I have a new flashback of Atlas's?" Kala stood up, annoyed.

Penny joined her and motioned for Kala to walk with her. "Something like this has never happened before, so I have no idea. What did you see?"

Kala followed Penny's lead as they walked down the street toward the train station.

"Some big-ass Titans scolding Atlas for switching sides. They said they were going to take away his 'protections' as punishment. What happened to Atlas after that? Please tell me he got his butt kicked." Even though Kala was officially the same person, she still despised him. He represented the complete opposite of who she was.

Penny was silent for a few moments, then she spoke quietly. "That's when I took him into hiding and showed him how to trick the first human. He never lost his protections from the Titans because he never completed the next cycle on his own, his surrogates did."

Kala rolled her eyes. "Of course he didn't. What a dick."

"You're missing the point here, Kala. *You're* Atlas now." Penny stared at her knowingly.

But Kala didn't understand what Penny was trying to imply. "Yeah, so?"

"So, *this* is the next cycle. After it's over, it'll be *you* that loses those 'protections'."

Kala groaned.

Chapter Two

Kala didn't say a word after that information bomb. She had too many other things to think about anyway. First off, the most important piece of knowledge she gained from her trip down memory lane was the fact that Zeus had created the four-day curse and was the only one who could break it. It literally tore her insides to shreds to think that there might have been a way to stop killing Jack. She blamed herself for not finding out about Zeus and the curse earlier. It had never occurred to her that Zeus even existed let alone was hanging around somewhere and she could have forced him into taking Atlas's curse away. Of course, that probably would have required handing over Atlas as opposed to what she had done when she swallowed him whole.

Thinking about that moment brought a chill to her bones. Kala hadn't had any idea what she was saying when she confronted Atlas. It was as if someone else had been speaking, like she was a puppet on strings. Kala started to remember the words of the prophecy Penny had been so sure was about Jack, but ultimately had been about Kala. *One cannot live while the other one exists. A new Atlas shall reign; and the potential must die. A beginning to the end; and an end to the beginning. A new paradise shall be born. The Fated One will be the last.*

Kala felt a surge of hope. If she was the Fated One and the Fated One would be the last, then maybe that meant she'd talk Zeus into letting her out of this four-day contract. The prophecy did mention paradise being born, that had to be good, right? Kala's head started hurting. Her whole life was making her sick.

"In here." Penny nodded towards a small brick building.

It was nondescript and blended into the blocks and blocks of brick row housing. If Penny hadn't stopped, Kala wouldn't have even noticed it had been there. Penny opened the door. Inside was completely empty except for a twin mattress on the floor and a small desk in the corner with papers stacked on top.

"Is this yours?" Kala asked with curiosity. Somehow, she had imagined Penny living in some plush, fancy penthouse somewhere in the swanky part of D.C., not this grungy heap of squalor in Alexandria.

"What did you expect?" Penny walked over to the desk and started shuffling through the papers looking for something.

"Not this." Kala shrugged. "What are you looking for?"

"I have a copy of the Ancient Texts. Now that we know you're the Fated One, we need to know everything we can about the rest of the prophecy," Penny said as she continued her search.

"Wait. There's more to the prophecy?" Kala would have gulped if she had it in her. But Kala still grasped onto the words *paradise* and *the last*. Maybe the rest was just details on how to corner Zeus and make him lift the curse.

"Of course there's more," Penny snapped. "We need details." Penny didn't even look up.

Kala could see that Penny was frantic, as in, something personal was at stake. There was no way Penny was this concerned about Kala, of that she was certain. Kala gathered that her being the Fated One meant something more to Penny, more than she was letting on anyway.

Kala walked over to Penny and grabbed her arm. "Hey, what's all this about?"

Penny shrugged her off and practically scowled. "I thought *you* of all people would want to know what your destiny is?"

"At this point, I'm thinking I find Zeus and beat the crap out of him until he breaks the curse. I was hoping you'd point me in the right direction seeing as you're his… what… niece or something?" Kala's grasp of Greek mythology was still lacking, but from the family chart in Kala's brain from her brief encounter with the Titan memory, it was a safe bet that Penny or Pandora… Pandora…

Penny had confirmed that she was the one and only Pandora to Kala before she had to kill Jack. Kala's brain hadn't had time to process what that meant or if it was of any importance to her at all. But her curiosity got the best of her. "Was there ever a box?" Kala asked referring to the one legend she *did* know. Pandora was given a box and opened it, despite being told not to and that was how all the evils of the universe were released. Supposedly, Pandora closed the box before it all leaked out and hope was still contained inside.

"No. Like most of your human histories, it's more of a symbolic version of the truth. The box or jar, whichever legend you go by, was my part in helping Atlas trick the humans into taking his job. So, in a sense, I did release all the evils of the world onto humanity, by making people responsible for keeping the balance of good and evil in check," Penny said as if she had prepared to answer that question a long time ago. "And, no, I'm not Zeus's niece. I'm his granddaughter. Hephaestus is Zeus's son and Hephaestus is my father, and if we don't figure this out, he is going to die." Then Penny looked at Kala like she was a nut job. "And even with Atlas's super strength, Zeus could crush you, so I wouldn't be too keen on picking a fight with the guy. Besides, the Titans keep him locked up in the 5th, so good luck trying to get to him."

"Wait a minute. The 5th? As in the 5th Level of Hell? That place my dad sent Asmodeus? Isn't that where the Elders or whatever are?" All these new places and vocabulary were making Kala's head spin.

Penny stared at Kala as if she were an irritating gnat. "Who do you think the Elders are?"

"Some kind of old super Demons or something?" Kala had figured that, since Asmodeus was the king of Demons, he answered to… other Demons. She hadn't given it much thought.

"The Elders are Titans, Kala, as in Elder gods. It's in your human history books." Penny went back to searching the papers. "Your daddy and grandparents waged war against the entire supernatural existence and won. They rule from the 5th to protect themselves from rebellion. If they find out the Grigori are back after all the energy they spent banishing them, they're going to be furious. And you don't want to see Cronus furious."

Kala remembered Atlas's memory. "Yeah, he seemed like a dick."

Penny briefly glanced up at Kala and a hint of a smile showed on her face, then she shook her head. "He is. A dangerous one." Penny grabbed a piece of paper with triumph. "Here it is."

Kala fought the urge to grab it out of Penny's hand. It was about her after all, but she let Penny scan through it first.

"So the Titans banished the Grigori? How'd they manage that?" Kala wondered.

Penny focused on the paper and it took a moment for her to respond. "The Olympians had a weapon that drained the Grigori of their powers, but the Titans secretly spelled the weapon to drain the Olympians too. The Olympians didn't even know what hit them. But even then, it wasn't enough. You asked how powerful the Grigori are? It took the combined strength of the Olympians and the Titans to banish them. Now that the Titans have the Demons on their side, they may be able to fight back the Grigori, but I'm just not sure." Penny gave Kala an exasperated groan. "Can't you access Atlas's memories so I don't have to be your walking encyclopedia?"

Kala tried to take as much sarcasm out of her voice as she could. "Well, I'd love to, but it's not exactly something I can control…"

***

Great.

Kala had no idea where she was, but it wasn't like any place she'd ever been to on earth. She could be anywhere really, considering this was Atlas's past she was visiting. It looked like she was in the center of a nebula with purple and blue gasses swirling around her. It was a strange sensation being inside someone else's body, and frankly, Kala hated it. Being knocked unconscious just to have a flashback was extremely dangerous in Kala's position. The soldier in her despised that. She was trained to always have an exit, but Kala had no control over her own brain. That left her vulnerable. The only plus side: now Kala was an actual Titan. She couldn't be killed that easily or even at all (she still wasn't convinced of that one). It was a mental adjustment she hadn't quite accepted yet. She still thought of herself as human. And as a human, her body could easily be killed. But as a Titan, she was… less killable.

The first thing Kala noticed in this blast from the past was that she was not alone. She was standing next to…

Asmodeus.

Could she ever get away from this guy?

At least he wasn't lusting after her Atlas form. Kala was spared that. Not that she minded necessarily, the Demon was definitely a hottie, but he was such a jerk about it. In this memory, Asmodeus wore all black and his sandy brown hair wasn't in the modern day swoop cut that Kala was used to. It was longer and pulled back, which only made his chiseled face all the more chiseled. With his straight nose, slightly full lips, and completely ripped physique, the guy looked like he had just walked off a romance novel cover.

Currently, Asmodeus looked at Atlas as if he were a leper. "Are you sure about this Atlas? If you're lying, you know what I'll do to you."

Kala felt herself speak. "I'm a Titan. I can squash you, Demon King."

Asmodeus yawned. "Please. You're a second generation Titan. And I'm more than willing to see who would win the fight. How about you?"

Kala experienced a thrill of fear run through Atlas. He may be threatening Asmodeus, but even he didn't believe he could best the Demon King. Kala inwardly moaned. Atlas was such a wuss! "I'm telling the truth. The Olympians will take down the Titans once and for all."

"I'd like to hear that from someone besides the weasel that switches sides like he's a hot potato." Asmodeus crossed his arms. He looked like he was about to leave if Atlas didn't say something convincing enough for him to stay.

"Listen, Zeus is gathering his army against Cronus. It's only the Grigori that stand in their way. I made the mistake of siding with my father in the last war and look where it got me. With the Demons on our side, we'll crush Cronus and the Titans once and for all." Kala could sense the determination in Atlas. He really thought the Olympians would win.

Asmodeus spat. "The Grigori? They can't be defeated. Not even the Olympians can hurt them."

"They can, I swear on my life." Atlas tried to convince Asmodeus.

"What's in this for you?" Asmodeus eyed Atlas carefully.

It took a few moments before Atlas finally responded, "Zeus promises to relieve me of my curse if I help him."

But Kala knew Asmodeus better than Atlas because she could read that snarky look on his face. Asmodeus was simply gathering information. He had no intention of helping Atlas or Zeus, and Atlas was clueless. He was spilling state secrets like a fool.

"You and that curse." Asmodeus chuckled. "Zeus's biggest mistake. Tearing out the balance of the universe as if it were made of fabric and turning it into a neat little curse. Now that's abusing power. He's my kind of god."

Kala felt the hope rise in Atlas at Asmodeus's words. Kala waited for the inevitable letdown that was about to come.

Asmodeus shook his head as if he felt sorry for Atlas. "Thanks for being an idiot. You never disappoint, Atlas. While we stand here, the battle has already begun. It's too late for you to warn them. It's too late for anything. You gods love your double-crosses. I'll be sure to tell your daddy you said hello."

Kala woke up in Penny's dingy apartment. She lay on the twin mattress while Penny sat on the edge of the bed, completely engrossed in reading the prophecy and ignoring Kala entirely.

"I'm back," Kala announced. Not that Penny cared.

Penny turned to Kala with a frustrated expression on her face. "Good. Read this. See if it makes any sense to you."

Kala took the proffered paper from Penny. Though the actual paper itself came from the nearest office supply store, the copy of the text on the page was obviously from a really old document. It was handwritten in calligraphy, making it very difficult for Kala to decipher. Kala grew up with computer keyboards, not handwriting, let alone the fancy kind. The text took up half the page, making Kala's heart sink. If this was all they had to go on, it wasn't much.

After a few moments of squinting and rotating the paper every which way, Kala finally sighed, "You might have to help me with this."

Penny snatched the document back with a roll of her eyes and pointed to a specific sentence. "This top part you already know, but this is the rest of it." Penny read out loud, "*The cost will be great, and the immortals will reign. The one that knows death will release the curse of balance.*"

WTF? "What does that mean?" Kala asked aloud more gracefully than what she had thought in her head.

"I don't know," Penny answered honestly. "Does anything resonate with you? I think we've established that you're the Fated One at this point. I thought you'd be able to translate."

"Not a clue. Sorry." Kala tried to read the prophecy herself. Now that she knew what it said, it was a little easier to navigate through the calligraphy. "*The one that knows death will release the curse of balance.* In my memory flashback, Asmodeus said that Zeus created Atlas's curse by ripping out the balance of the universe. Is this talking about that same curse or are there other crazy-ass curses you haven't told me about? Do you think *the one that knows death* will break *my* curse? Cronus seemed to think Zeus was the only one who could undo it, maybe Zeus is *the one that knows death?*" Kala brainstormed more to herself than expecting any real answers from Penny.

Penny had a kind of helpless expression on her face that said it all to Kala. Penny was as confused as she was, but more apparent was the fact that Penny looked defeated. "I'm never going to find him."

The tone in Penny's voice made Kala's heart squeeze. "Your dad?"

Penny nodded and turned away just as her eyes welled up, not wanting Kala to see.

And even though she mostly hated Penny, Kala found herself saying, "Look, I'll help you find your dad. Maybe he's being held with Zeus or something." It took a few seconds to register in Kala's brain what she had just said aloud. Granted, everything that had happened to her in the last four days left little room for doubt of the supernatural, but it still wasn't normal for her to have a conversation about Greek gods in a serious way.

"We can't go to the 5th Level of Hell!" Penny exclaimed in fear and shock. "We'd be killed or tortured for eternity!"

"I can take you there."

Kala and Penny whirled around to see who spoke.

Standing in the doorway was Talan.

Chapter Three

Kala didn't know if she wanted to run into his arms or kick him in the groin. Both options seemed satisfying at the moment. Instead, she chose to stay where she was on the mattress. Kala wasn't mad at Talan; in fact, he had been the perfect gentlemen in the most difficult moment of her life. It was the fact that he thought they were destined to be together and wasn't shy about telling her. Talan's admission made her angry, like he was belittling how she felt about Jack. And now, by looking at her with nothing but love, it felt like he was disrespecting the dead. Kala had killed her one true love and Talan stared at her as if *he* were her one true love. She wanted to punch him in the throat, and now that she had Atlas's strength, she was seriously considering it.

Penny stood up, terror in her eyes. "Talan."

Talan nodded kindly. "Hello, Pandora."

It wasn't hard for Kala to figure out that the two of them had a history. "You two know each other?"

Penny gave Kala a look of annoyed disgust. "Mind your own business."

Kala took that as a yes. She stood up and walked over to Talan. "How can you get us to the 5th Level of Hell?"

Talan's eyes bored into Kala with so much concern she had to turn away. He started to reach out to touch her arm, but stopped himself. "Are you okay?"

The way he asked made Kala's heart squeeze, but she didn't want to cry, not in front of him and definitely not in front of Penny. "I'm fine. Can you get us there or not?"

Penny apparently had felt like she needed more answers. "Talan. How are you back? And how long has it been?"

Talan kept his eyes on Kala as if waiting to make sure she was all right before he talked to Penny. Kala didn't like his intensity, she wasn't ready for it, but she nodded nevertheless. "Go ahead. I'll back your play," Kala said to Talan, letting him know that if he chose to lie about how many Grigori had escaped their prison, she'd go along with it. As far as Kala knew only a handful of the Grigori made it through, but she wasn't sure if Talan wanted Penny to know that. If her dad was the Olympian god Hepha-something, that may put Penny on the ally-at-a-distance list. Penny had tried to make Jack kill her for the last four days, and Kala was a grudge-holder.

And friends? Seriously? Talan and Penny? She couldn't imagine it. Did they *hang* out? It was hard for Kala to picture the two of them doing anything casual. What the heck was Penny anyway? A god? Demi-god? Thinking of them together annoyed Kala even though every fiber of her body didn't want to care either way.

Talan spoke to Penny. "You should have known that the prison wouldn't be strong enough to hold the Grigori. Haven't you wondered why technology has grown exponentially in the last century? The Elders imprisoned the Grigori for involving ourselves with humans, but they were just scared that the humans would surpass them. And trust me, Pandora, they *will*," he said passionately. Kala could tell Talan was angry and he took it all out on Penny.

Penny yelled back just as vehemently. "Don't kid yourself. The Titans banished you because they were afraid of the Grigori. You're stronger than they are. Stronger than the Olympians. And, Talan, you *were* making humans too powerful. You had to be stopped! If you hadn't…"

Kala answered for her, "Then *humans* would be able to kick the gods' collective asses."

"It doesn't matter." Penny crossed her arms defensively. "The prophecy says very clearly that *the immortals will reign*. So teach away. The humans will always be weak no matter how many weapons you show them how to create."

"We'll see." Talan eyed Penny as if he would smite her where she stood.

It gave Kala a perverse satisfaction, and she understood his sentiment. Kala had, after all, done her fair share of *smiting* Penny. From shooting her to snapping her neck to lighting her on fire, Penny's immortality had protected her from any real harm, but Kala hated to admit that it had helped get out all her aggression toward the girl.

Instead of attacking Penny, Talan focused all his attention on Kala. "How are you integrating?"

Penny felt the need to chime in snootily, "If you mean she keeps passing out every five minutes from memory flashbacks, then the girl is doing fantastic."

Talan's eyes never left Kala's. "Is that true?"

Kala nodded, a little embarrassed at her obvious lack of control over her own consciousness. "I can handle it," Kala lied. The truth was, the blackouts were becoming more than she could manage. What if she blacked out in the 5th? It was a level of Hell after all. Kala took another second to re-live *that* sentence, then turned to Talan. "How long do you think it will keep happening?"

Talan finally moved from the doorway and led Kala back to the mattress. He acted as if Penny wasn't even in the room with them. Penny didn't seem to want to force the issue of her presence either, so she stayed planted where she was with her arms still crossed.

"Lie down," Talan instructed Kala. "I'm going to need to touch your forehead." He awaited her approval.

Kala nodded. She had made Talan promise not to touch her, and he had held true to his word. When his hand pressed down on her forehead, Kala felt her whole body shiver. It was *the* reason why she didn't want him to touch her. Chemistry. They had it. Kala didn't like it. It made her feel guilty about Jack. End of story.

The shiver turned into something more physical, as in actual heat. Talan was doing something to Kala, something *Grigori*.

Kala suddenly cried out in pain as a flood of images rushed before her eyes. They were moving so fast she couldn't focus on any single one. It was the same as when Talan had shown her memories of his past. And also when he had shown Kala her possible future if she didn't kill Jack. But unlike both those instances, there were too many images flying past her to slow it down.

Talan's voice calmed her as he spoke. "Don't try to focus on any of the images. I'm releasing them from where they are stored in your brain. There are too many memories for you to integrate all at once. Atlas is thousands of years old and your mind locked the memories away so you wouldn't go insane."

"My *mind* locked them away or Roberta did?" Kala grunted through clenched teeth. When Kala had consumed Atlas, her human body tried to reject the god's essence. If it hadn't been for her commanding general, Geoffrey Turner and his wife Roberta, Kala would have died soon after. But Roberta had used her own magic—or what she had called astral projection—to help Kala take Atlas in and assimilate him into her body.

"Either way, that's why you lose consciousness when recalling Atlas's memories. They're stored in a spot that takes too much effort to access," Talan explained.

"Aren't you going to kill me by releasing them all?" Kala asked, trying to rein in the throbbing.

"No," Talan replied gently. "I'm putting the memories in your frontal cortex so you can retrieve them at will, but not remember them all at once."

The images stopped and her head no longer hurt. Kala didn't feel any different. She didn't remember anything new. Sitting up, she looked at Talan, confused. "I don't remember any of Atlas's past."

Talan smiled warmly. "You will. It'll be like any of your old memories, you'll see something familiar, and a single recollection will be triggered. No more blackouts."

Kala didn't argue. One thing she knew for certain: she trusted Talan. And if he said she wasn't going to black out anymore, then she believed him. Kala felt an enormous sense of relief. This whole "integration" process was annoying. So far being a god sucked.

Talan rose to his feet, holding his hand out to help Kala stand. She ignored it and stood up herself.

"So are we going to the 5th or what?" Kala said, ready for a fight.

Chapter Four

"What about your mission? Have you seen what you have to do yet?" Talan asked.

"Oh that," Kala complained. "No. I haven't had time. It's been what? An hour since I killed Jack? Relax!" Kala spat in anger. She hoped she could avoid her Atlas duties entirely. Talking about breaking into what equated to a high-security dimension of Hell and possibly fighting Titans sounded like fun to Kala. Being a soldier was everything she had ever known and now that she was a god, she wanted to try out some of her new abilities. So far, Kala only knew she had super strength because of the way she'd tossed Penny across the room the night before, but Kala was eager to see if her Atlas powers could do anything else.

Penny chimed in with an attitude, "Well, you'd better figure out what it is. You saw a glimpse of what will happen if you don't go through with it."

Kala wanted to elbow Penny in the mouth for even speaking. The girl grated on Kala's every nerve. "I have four days," Kala said as if this were a defense.

"It doesn't mean you have to take the full four days," Penny sniped back.

"Listen." Kala stood up and pointed her finger at Penny's chest. "If I have to *commit acts of atrocity* every freaking day I'll go insane. I'm going to take the four days, so get over it." Kala figured that there was a reason four days were given to complete the mission. Even Zeus knew that gods had their limits. Four days wasn't a lot of time to recover from doing the horrible things the Atlas job required, but it was something. And Kala intended on taking full advantage.

Still. A part of Kala was curious as to what insidious thing the universe needed her to do in order to stop the world from ending. Maybe it wouldn't be that bad this time. Nothing could be worse than killing Jack. Nothing. Her stomach turned at the thought of Jack's blood pooling at her feet.

Kala blinked away tears. "I need to see a TV. That's how I see the visions." Kala hid all evidence of her emotions as she stared Penny in the eye. "Let's get this over with."

Talan snapped his fingers and a flat screen television appeared on the wall.

"Does that come with free cable as well?" Kala joked at Talan's ability to make expensive televisions suddenly appear in crappy apartments.

"Whatever you need," Talan answered seriously, "But you probably only need a signal to see the vision."

Kala sighed heavily. "Just turn it on."

The power light went from red to green and the sight made Kala's heart skip a beat.

She wasn't ready to see.

Kala shook out her arms and legs and rolled her neck like she was about to enter a boxing ring. Anything to calm her down. A fight she could handle. She could control. But waiting for a TV to turn on so she could watch some horrendous thing that she'd have to do: nauseating.

The screen on the television finally came into focus. Kala tilted her head to try to figure out what she was seeing. It looked like a close-up of some kind of document.

"Can you turn the station?" Penny asked Talan.

"No. Be quiet." Talan didn't even look at Penny.

If Kala weren't so concentrated on the television, she would have smiled at Talan's dismissiveness toward Penny. It seemed Penny irritated him as much as she irritated Kala.

Kala knew that what the two of them were seeing was completely different from what she was seeing. To them, the television was playing whatever show was currently airing. But to Kala, this was how she saw her Atlas missions. Television screens. From streaming on a phone to the Jumbotron at a football game, the vision of her mission always played on repeat.

Kala fought back tears again as she remembered the last four days and having to re-live the nightmare of killing Jack every time she was near a television. She had thought she could fight it. Stop it somehow...

Shaking off her emotions, Kala focused on the screen.

It was definitely some kind of document. The writing was a series of equations, and that was all Kala could make out. She wasn't great at math, but she had taken enough classes in high school to know that these equations were way over her head. As if a camera was filming the whole event, Kala's view zoomed out to reveal a man that she recognized: John Fortski. The scientist that worked for General Turner. Kala knew almost nothing about the man except for the fact that Turner had a lot of insanely advanced technology and she figured Fortski was probably responsible for inventing a lot of it. On the screen, Fortski was panicked, shaking his head.

Kala cringed. *Please tell me I don't have to kill this guy.* Taking out someone who basically equated to the Albert Einstein of her time made her head hurt. Although a small part of her knew it would be easier than killing Jack. Being a sniper, Kala had killed before, so she knew she could do it again, but she had lost the stomach for it after Jack.

On screen, Kala walked into view. She was holding a gun, but she wasn't pointing it at Fortski. Kala recognized her stance. She wanted

Fortski to believe that she'd kill him if necessary, but she could see that the Kala in the vision had zero intentions of hurting him.

They were in some kind of laboratory, filled with metal tables stacked with ongoing experiments. Only Kala and Fortski were in the room.

There were three computers next to Fortski and vision/Kala. All of them were destroyed, their hard drives pulled out and smashed. Apparently, the documents in Fortski's hands were all that was left of whatever was on the computers because the Kala on the TV leapt forward and grabbed the papers from his hand.

Fortski screamed, "Please! You can't! That's the only copy."

"I know. I destroyed all the hard drives." Vision/Kala said somberly. "I have to do this. Trust me. It's for the best."

"No, please!" Fortski pleaded. "Do you know how many lives I can save with that? Thousands! Millions even!"

Vision/Kala shook her head. "I have to."

"Didn't you ever know anyone with cancer? You can save them! You'll be destroying the cure! Do you understand? You're destroying the only copy I have! I can't memorize equations like this! Turner will kill you for this!" Fortski was in a total panic now.

But Vision/Kala looked determined. Calm even. "No, he won't," Vision/Kala said confidently. Then she pulled out the lighter that Talan had given her and set the documents on fire.

Fortski screamed and leapt at her, but Vision/Kala didn't use her gun, she simply shoved him hard. The push from a god made Fortski fly across the room and smash against the back wall. There he slumped to the ground, crying.

When the scene started to repeat, Kala turned the TV off.

"Really?" Kala exclaimed incredulously.

"What did you see?" Penny asked.

The look in Penny's eyes was a little too greedy for Kala's taste.

"I have the mission, that's all you two need to know." Kala decided against telling either one of them. Talan she trusted, but Penny was another story.

Talan didn't seem fazed or offended at all. *Of course!* But Penny... she appeared downright annoyed.

"How can we help you if we don't know what you're supposed to do?" Penny practically harrumphed.

"Just let me handle it," Kala demanded.

Then it truly struck her. She was going to have to *destroy* the cure for cancer. The cure for freaking cancer! Fortski was brilliant enough to discover the cure and the universe wanted Atlas to demolish it? Why? Why would any force of good want something like that to happen? It rocked Kala. Maybe she wasn't a force of good; maybe the job of Atlas was evil. It certainly felt that way. Kala had to remind herself that killing Jack saved billions of lives. But curing cancer? How could destroying something so important be the right thing to do? By not letting Fortski release the cure, it would kill more people than it could possibly save. Wouldn't it?

Glass crashed.

The muted THWAP of a silenced gunshot reached Kala's ears.

She felt the bullet smack her square in the heart.

It took Kala a second to comprehend that a sniper had just shot her! She watched in shock as the bullet popped out of her chest and clattered to the floor.

A rain of muted bullets followed.

Kala screamed over the strange noise. "It's Clifton!"

Before any more bullets could find their way into their bodies, Talan lifted his hand. A clear dome formed over their heads, the ammunitions bouncing harmlessly off its surface.

"I'll get us out of here," Talan reached out to touch both Penny and Kala.

Kala took a step back. "I have to see who it is for sure."

Hundreds of bullets battered the protective dome like metal hail. It even sounded like hail. Kala remembered lying in bed listening to the frozen rain hit the roof when she had first arrived at Owen and Linda's home. She had felt safe for the first time in her life. She was safe now too. If this was Clifton's military team coming to get her, they were way out of their league. General Clifton was Turner's partner, but they didn't share the same opinion of Kala. Turner was on her side and believed in the unexplainable, whereas Clifton was bitter and jealous and wanted Kala dead because he didn't like or trust her. And he had the power to send elite military squads to attempt to take her out.

Through the bouncing bullets, Kala tried to see where the shooters were. She spotted them through the broken window and across the street in the adjacent building. The more she focused the easier it was to see the snipers. It was as if her eyes were binoculars. She almost lost focus it was such a new and strange sensation, but she needed to see who she was up against.

Her view was now close-up, as if she were in the same room with the shooters. There were four. She recognized two, and they were definitely Clifton's guys.

The snipers stopped after seeing Kala's protection. They probably thought she had some state-of-the-art bullet shield. They'd never guess that a Grigori angel was using his powers to protect her.

Within seconds, five soldiers busted down the door and entered the room, guns drawn and pointed at Kala, Penny and...

Where was Talan?

There wasn't a shred of doubt that the angel was still there, it just threw Kala off as to why he'd hide himself.

Teleporting was out of the question. Clifton had already seen Asmodeus *pop* into the Compound. He'd be convinced that some other country owned teleportation technology. And he'd most likely do anything to get it.

"Kala Hicks, you are under arrest by the United States government for treason and the assassination of President Wilkins," the lead soldier shouted. Kala noticed that her head never left his gun site.

Kala knew the five soldiers would bump into an invisible wall in about five feet, or at least she hoped so. A remote part of her kind of wanted to see that happen. It was a surreal moment to hear a fellow soldier accuse her of treason. The one thing Kala had always been proud of was her service to her country. Killing the president had been an extremely difficult decision for her, but when he was threatening to murder thousands, Kala felt she had no choice. Little did she know at the time that President Wilkins had actually been the current Atlas and by killing him, Kala ended up stuck with the job.

"Whose orders?" Kala yelled back.

The lead soldier ignored Kala's question and bellowed, "You're surrounded. Raise your hands and walk over to me."

Kala sighed and noticed that Penny watched the whole situation with mild curiosity as if the soldiers were animals in a zoo. Talan stayed hidden. Kala seriously hoped he was still there and keeping the bullet-barrier up. Not that she could die apparently, but with enough bullets in her, Kala could definitely be put out of commission for a while. Or not. She had no idea. But she didn't want to find out. Somehow being shot in the chest a hundred times didn't appeal to her. The once was enough.

Kala spoke more calmly, "Name and rank."

The lead soldier snarled, "I don't have to answer to you. You are a traitor to this country and I should shoot you where you stand. I could always report that you died while trying to escape." He paused, then smiled. "But who am I to deprive the Compound of a good hanging?" He was genuinely salivating at the thought.

"You talk too much," Kala reprimanded, "And by telling me about the Compound I know Clifton sent you. He put the order out and the public still thinks the president died in an accident." Kala said this with such confidence even she believed it. She was trying to put out feelers as to how often she'd be evading super-soldiers. If it were just Clifton, it would be in small pockets like the men in front of her. But if Turner had decided she was a liability, then Kala would have a lot more to worry about than these guys. Dealing with Clifton was like dealing with a five-year-old bully, whereas dealing with Turner was like dealing with Napoleon, a brilliant military strategist.

Kala could handle Clifton. She wasn't so sure about Turner. He knew too much about her.

The soldier looked miffed at Kala's accusation. "If I have to repeat myself one more time, I'm going to shoot you."

Penny popped out of sight.

The soldiers' training kicked in and a rain of gunfire smacked full force into the invisible wall.

The noise was even louder at this close range.

Kala shouted over the noise. "What are you doing, Penny?" She knew Penny's disappearing trick well. Penny had pulled it on her a few times. Penny's motivation was a mystery to her. They were safely behind the barrier after all, so why disappear? If anything, it would just make the soldiers think she teleported, something Talan had just tried to avoid.

Then Kala figured it out. She turned her head away from the soldiers to see the stack of papers and texts that Penny held dear start to disappear from view. Penny was hiding any kind of evidence of who or what they all were. It would be complete mumbo jumbo to someone like Clifton, but Kala didn't want him to be a bigger problem than he already was.

One by one, the soldiers stopped shooting. Kala thought it was because of the futileness of the protective barrier, or maybe they ran out of bullets.

But when she turned to see why, her heart stopped.

Snapping the necks of each soldier daring to try to kill Kala was...

Derek.

Chapter Five

Kala's whole body filled with happiness at the sight of Derek, her one true friend in this world, then she comprehended that three soldiers lay dead at his feet. "Don't kill all of them!" Kala called out.

At that point, Derek couldn't hear. He was in the middle of a fistfight with the last two soldiers, one of which was the lead a-hole.

Kala ran to help him, but slammed up against the barrier. Apparently, it went both ways. She screamed, "Talan! Let me out right now!"

Kala slammed her fist against the barrier and it dissolved.

Derek cold-cocked the soldier next to him with the soldier's own gun. Before Derek could focus the rest of his rage on the lead soldier, Kala grabbed the man first. She lifted the lead soldier up by his neck as if he were a rag doll and tossed him across the room. The man flew fast and hard, slamming against the far wall with enough impact to shake a piece of the ceiling loose. He was out cold.

Derek's eyes were round at seeing Kala's strength, but his expression quickly turned to awe. "Impressive," he smiled.

That smile almost brought tears to her eyes. Kala fell into Derek's open arms and they hugged each other fiercely. "Derek," was all Kala could say.

After a moment, Derek gently pulled out of the embrace and affectionately moved a strand of Kala's auburn hair away from her eye. "So. What's up?"

Kala shook her head and nudged him adoringly. "Nothing much. I'm a god now, so that's new."

"You're not kidding, are you?" Derek's eyes were full of affection, but Kala could see the doubt there as well. She knew there was a part of Derek that couldn't accept what was really going on. She couldn't blame him. If it hadn't happened to her, she wouldn't be able to conceive of it either. But she needed Derek to believe. It hurt too much to have her closest friend think she was looney tunes.

As if in answer to Derek's question, Talan and Penny materialized inside the room.

Derek's gun was leveled and ready, always the soldier.

Kala reached up and lowered Derek's revolver. "They're with me."

"I can tell." Derek gave Talan a disapproving glare.

Talan couldn't seem to hide the way he felt about Kala. She guessed that existing before the age of time took the edge off caring what people thought of you. Kala knew that even though Derek was staring daggers at Talan, inside he was probably happy that she had some supernatural backup.

Derek turned his focus to Kala. She could sense so many conflicting thoughts racing around in his brain. Kala stared back and admired Derek's flawless features. He was well over six feet with a dark complexion, full lips, and a shaved head. Derek used to be a marine before he joined Kala's elite crew, and he was one of the biggest assets to the team.

A thought suddenly occurred to Kala. "Derek. Why are you killing Clifton's men? Have you gone rogue?" Kala's worst nightmare was coming to fruition: that because of her, Derek's life was ruined. He'd be on the run for the rest of his days. And he wouldn't have superpowers like her to protect himself.

Derek holstered his gun and surveyed the room as if waiting for more soldiers to arrive. He shook his head in the negative. "I'm working for General Turner."

"But Turner and Clifton are on the same team," Kala voiced her confusion. "Isn't Turner going to be pissed that you took out his men?"

Derek smiled. "After Clifton tried to have you killed two days ago, I woke up in Turner's house. He didn't think Clifton would ever trust me again after I went against his orders and clobbered his men."

"Turner's probably right about that." Kala remembered it well. Two days! It felt as if it had been a lifetime ago! When General Clifton had ordered Kala's death, Derek went berserk. He took down Clifton's men in seconds. Asmodeus had almost taken her, but Penny somehow managed to teleport the Demon King out of there. Kala figured she must have used the Demon's own teleportation powers against him, because Kala knew that Penny didn't have the capability herself to teleport. Derek had seen it all, but refused to believe what was happening in front of his own eyes. Kala had even told him that Asmodeus was a Demon and at that point, Derek's alarmed response had prompted Turner to knock him out.

"Turner told me in these exact words, 'protect Kala Hicks by any means necessary. I will back up all collateral damage, just make sure Harry doesn't touch her.'" Derek motioned to the dead and unconscious soldiers. "That's what I did."

Talan stepped forward. "She doesn't need your help." He turned to Kala. "Your friend will die trying to protect you. Is that what you want?"

Derek's eyes never left Kala's. "Do you want me to eliminate this guy?"

Kala raised her eyebrow as if considering the offer, but she shook her head. "He's right, Derek. You'll get yourself killed. Soldiers are one thing, but you have no defense against Demons and Malaks." Kala didn't like Talan's condescending delivery, but his message was true. Though a selfish part of her wanted to keep Derek close, she loved him too much to put him in that kind of danger.

"Turner's wife stocked me up." Derek pulled off his tight fitting backpack and opened it up for Kala to see. Inside was a stack of plastic vials filled with black goop next to a gun that looked like a tranquilizer. Kala recognized the ooze straightaway. It was a concoction made by Roberta that incapacitated Malaks and Demons.

Kala understood at that moment that Derek not only believed, but he was prepared for battle. She turned to Talan. "This stuff works. He can help."

Talan walked over to Derek and touched him.

Derek disappeared.

"Dick!" Kala spun on Talan with an uncontrollable fury. "What the hell did you just do?"

"You would never have sent him away," Talan stated confidently.

Penny added, "You wouldn't have."

"Shut up, Penny!" But Kala kept her eyes on Talan. "Where is he?!"

Talan stayed calm, which only made Kala angrier. "He's safe. I sent him back to Turner. Roberta and Turner should know you're still alive."

Kala couldn't control her rage. She wanted to lash out and attack Talan. "How could you do that? Derek is the only person I trust! I needed him!"

Penny was livid now herself. "Get over it! Were you planning on taking him to the *5th Level of Hell*? I don't care if those play guns hurt Malaks and Demons, they'll do nothing against the creatures there."

"You know what? Screw you both!" Kala had reached her limit. She stormed toward the door. Talan reached out and touched her arm, but Kala shrugged it off. "Don't touch me!" Kala was out the door before Talan or Penny could stop her.

Kala had no idea where she was going, but she kept walking down the street. Remembering that Clifton had every surveillance camera in existence on the lookout for her, Kala brushed her auburn hair forward lamely. She was a sitting duck out here and she knew it. Not that Clifton's men could kill her, but Kala didn't feel like dealing with bullets. She didn't feel like dealing with anything.

Seeing Derek had given Kala a moment of happiness and peace, and Talan had ripped that from her. Derek was all she had left of her past. Of Jack. The fact that Talan had the nerve to make decisions for her made Kala furious. It was bad enough that her brain was still reeling from Jack's death.

She trusted Derek in a fight much more than stupid-dumb-face Talan.

Kala knew she was overreacting, but it felt good to loathe someone. To have someone to blame for everything. And Talan was an easy target.

Walking by a small electronics store, Kala tried to ignore the televisions replaying the vision of destroying Fortski's cure. She needed to keep it together. The idea of what she had to do was unfathomable to her. Kala had thought that killing Jack would be the worst thing she'd ever have to do. That whatever Atlas task she'd do next would be cake compared to murdering the only man she ever loved. But by destroying that cure, thousands would die. Even though she'd never see their faces, it would still feel like she had pulled the trigger on them all. No matter how much she tried to rationalize what possible benefit destroying the cure for cancer would have for the greater good, Kala came up with zilch. She started to feel like her job was evil and not a *balancer* as everyone claimed it was. Zeus was a genuine jerk for coming up with this punishment.

Kala rounded a corner and smacked right into…

Talan.

Kala didn't even stop, shoving past him. "Go away." She made sure he could hear her.

But instead of having the decency to act human and run to catch up, he materialized in front of her instead. "You're not safe," he replied calmly.

Kala stopped in her tracks. "You think?" she responded sarcastically.

"Gee, I'm so glad you popped in to tell me that. I had no idea. I've only been chased by Demons, Malaks, gods, and my own freaking government for the past four days. I'm so glad you warned me. Thank you so much. You're such a savior. What are you Grigori or something?" Kala pushed her way past him again. It felt good to go into a tirade.

But Talan was persistent. He kept teleporting in front of her so she'd almost smack into him every time. So. Annoying.

"Kala, I understand that you're angry, and I'm sorry I didn't give you a choice in the matter of your friend." Talan let the apology sit there for a moment, apparently thinking it would make a difference in Kala's mood, then he continued, "But if the Demons didn't know where you were before that fire fight, they do now. Extracting that bullet from your chest took magic. *Your* magic. Atlas's magic. It was like a beacon."

Kala grudgingly listened, her mood starting to thaw a bit. Just a bit.

Talan seemed to pick up on this. "I know you think Derek can handle himself, and yes, Roberta's magic would give him some protection, but in about five minutes this whole area is going to be crawling with Demons searching for you. He wouldn't have survived. I was trying to save him," Talan pleaded. "I know how much he means to you," he finished softly.

Damn him. Kala softened. But she had to make one thing clear before she let it go. "You could have told me that and let me have the choice. Even if it ends up being the same choice. I need to be the one to decide. Okay?"

Talan nodded solemnly. "Deal."

Kala ran her hand through her hair and sighed heavily. "Where's Penny?"

"I sent her to a safe place. I'll take you there now." Talan started to reach out to touch Kala…

…When his face grimaced in pain. Kala glimpsed the tip of a blade protruding from Talan's stomach, then it was yanked out viciously. Blood poured from the wound causing Talan to stumble slightly.

A man had materialized behind Talan, and he held a gnarly looking knife covered in Talan's blood. Talan grabbed his gut from the newly inflicted gash. The fact that a metal blade could actually hurt Talan momentarily threw Kala off.

Talan turned to face his attacker. "Miss me, *Brother*?" The man smiled wickedly.

Chapter Six

"**R**otoph." Talan looked horrified.

Kala's training kicked in.

She studied Rotoph as an enemy combatant. He referred to Talan as *brother,* so that told her he was Grigori.

A flash in her memory.

Or Atlas's memory...

Atlas knew Rotoph, or at least knew of him. Kala couldn't seem to pull any memories together in the heat of the moment.

The Grigori's expression was cold and calculating, though his bright green eyes twinkled with evil delight at stabbing Talan. Short, brown hair framed his angular face, making his long crooked nose the centerpiece. He was undeniably handsome. Not the ethereal beauty of the Angels and Demons that Kala was used to, but he was definitely easy on the eyes in a rugged kind of way.

Seeing Talan clutching his stomach and Rotoph's triumphant grin made Kala angry beyond belief. She could be mad at Talan all she wanted, but no way was she going to let this jerk hurt him.

She took advantage of the classic mistake Rotoph was making: enjoying the kill.

Before he could respond, Kala snatched the bloody weapon from his hand and slashed Rotoph's throat. Rotoph's hands grabbed futilely at his neck, trying to stem the bleeding, his eyes rounded from the shock of Kala's move.

He dropped to his knees and gargled his own blood. Within seconds, Rotoph was lying face first on the cement, completely still.

Kala pocketed the knife and supported Talan with her weight. "We have to get you someplace safe. Are you okay?"

Talan nodded then pulled away. "I'm okay. Look." Talan pulled away his bloody slashed shirt to reveal smooth skin free of any injury. "That knife doesn't kill. Nothing can kill a Grigori. It does, however, take away my powers."

"For good?" Kala was appalled.

Talan shook his head. "No. At least an hour though." Then he looked over at Rotoph's still form. His face was angry. "You did well. Cutting him like that will make him powerless too."

Rotoph's body stirred. He was healing. Power or not, the guy wasn't someone Kala wanted to have around. "We should get out of here." Kala took Talan's hand and pulled. He didn't budge.

"I have to face him." Talan looked resolute.

"Actually, you don't." Kala yanked harder and Talan reluctantly went with her.

When they were halfway down the street, Kala heard Rotoph's voice. "Talan!" he screamed. Kala recognized that tone. He was pissed.

Talan let go of Kala's hand and turned to face Rotoph.

Rotoph's throat was bloody, but there was no wound.

With Talan's bloody shirt and Rotoph's horror-movie neck, people were staring. No one seemed to be calling the police though, which wasn't a surprise to Kala. She found that most people didn't believe what was in front of them, as if there were some other explanation for bloody throats and shirts. They would rather look the other way, too scared to get involved. Kala knew it wouldn't last long. Especially since she planned to cause a scene.

As Rotoph neared the two of them, his eyes never left Talan. "So you have a Titan as your bodyguard now?" He nodded to Kala. "Nice move by the way."

Kala leveled the knife at Rotoph. "I can repeat it if you like."

Okay. Kala saw someone dialing their cell phone. It wouldn't be long before another crew of Clifton's men would be on their way. Not to mention real cops.

Rotoph looked like he was a cat about to pounce.

Kala was far too good of a soldier to let some amateur fighter take her weapon from her. The guy may have super Grigori powers but, according to Talan, Rotoph was running on empty. That made it an even playing field to her human self. But she was a god now so Kala could do some real damage.

Rotoph leapt forward to grab the knife.

Idiot. Kala wanted to roll her eyes, but she went into fighter-mode instead.

As Rotoph's hand grabbed at the blade, Kala swung her body to the side: now she could use Rotoph's momentum to her benefit. When his hand didn't grab onto the intended target, Rotoph had nothing but air for support. He stumbled forward. Kala took advantage of the opening, used her Atlas-strength, and elbowed Rotoph hard in the small of his back.

He screamed in anguish as he collapsed to the ground.

"You Grigori are babies without your powers." Kala rested her foot on Rotoph's back to keep him down. "I'm keeping this knife. So stop trying to take it back."

It was mayhem now. People were screaming and running away. Sirens echoed in the distance.

Kala viewed the knife more closely. Every part of its surface was covered in strange runic markings. It was a stunning piece of work. The blade itself was slightly curved with a jagged edge on the outside and a smooth sharpness on the inside. The handle was made of bone. "How can this knife take your powers away?" Kala asked Talan as if Rotoph weren't there.

"There used to be twelve of them. One for each Olympian. How do you think the Grigori were banished? The gods needed help, so the Titans had Hephaestus forge them," Talan shared.

Kala remembered now Penny mentioning a weapon that drained both the Grigori and the Olympians of their powers. This blade must be it.

Talan nodded toward the screaming pedestrians. "I'd teleport us out of here…"

"But you can't. Right. What about him? Do we take him with us?" Kala asked.

Rotoph responded. "This wasn't how I planned my morning."

Kala dug her foot in harder into his back, making Rotoph groan. "Did I say you could talk?" She turned to Talan. "Well? He's your family. What would Owen do with him?" Kala asked of her foster father.

Talan didn't even blink. "He'd kill him if he could."

"Right." That was all Kala needed to hear. She leaned down to Rotoph's ear and whispered. "This is for my dad."

"Dad?"

But before Rotoph could utter another word, Kala slit his throat again. She knew it wouldn't kill him, but the mayhem of her stabbing him so publicly would give her and Talan enough time to escape.

The area was filling up with quite a crowd. The audible screams and gasps when Kala cut Rotoph made her feel as if she was a gladiator in some kind of ancient Roman stadium.

Talan grabbed Kala's hand and they were off down the first alley they ran past. Before long, they had twisted and turned so many times Kala wouldn't have been surprised if they had made a giant circle. But Talan knew his way around and he led her into a small hole-in-the-wall bar at least a mile away.

It was still morning, so there were only a few patrons inside. The place was darkly lit and barely fit six small tables. There was a seven-foot bar on the left where a plump, balding bartender served his only customers. He nodded at Talan as if they knew one another. Talan gave a friendly wave back and the two of them sat at the table farthest from the door.

Always the soldier, Kala sat facing the entrance so she could see whoever entered the establishment.

She knew they were hiding out, but she felt she could really use a drink. "I'm ordering, so get over it."

As if on cue, a waitress arrived at their table.

Kala got right to it. "Glenlivet on the rocks and some fries. You serve fries, right?" The waitress nodded. "Make it a double order then."

"Coming right up," the waitress chirped warmly.

"You're paying," Kala replied pointedly.

"With what? My good looks?" Talan said with an ample amount of sarcasm.

Kala was impressed. "You have a sense of humor. Noted." She patted her pockets looking for money. "I'm not into dining and dashing so if I don't have cash I'm cancelling my order." Being a foster kid, Kala had lived in some pretty sketchy homes. Some of the other foster kids would make a habit out of going to seedy diners, eating, and then taking off without paying the bill before anyone could stop them. Kala always cringed when a new set of kids *dined and dashed*. When she refused to go along with it, Kala ended up washing dishes or cleaning toilets for a week as a result. It just wasn't in her to do something like that.

A few seconds later, Kala pulled out a fifty-dollar bill from her back pocket. She couldn't remember how it got there, but she was happy she found it. Fries and scotch sounded like the perfect breakfast. Kala wondered if her constitution would be much different as a god. Maybe horribly unhealthy foods wouldn't give her indigestion. At least she knew she wouldn't die from it. Kala didn't think Titans had to worry about cholesterol much.

Kala waved the fifty bucks triumphantly, then asked, "Did you want anything?" She paused. "Do angels eat?"

Talan replied, "We don't have to, but we like to. I'm sure you saw Owen eating once or twice."

"True," Kala acknowledged. Mentioning Owen brought her back to reality. "Who was that guy? I gathered that he's Grigori, but I thought all of you were best pals or something."

"Like you're *best pals* with General Clifton? Grigori are no different than any other species. We don't all get along. Rotoph betrayed the Grigori and will never be forgiven, nor does he want to be," Talan stated as if he were an offended child.

Kala raised her eyebrow in fascination. She wasn't used to seeing Talan in this light. He was normally so calm, cool, and collected. To see him almost human was actually quite comforting. "Where'd he get the knife? You said Penny's dad made them. Was that the weapon that the Titan's spelled?"

Before Talan could answer, a memory took shape before Kala's eyes. She was relieved that she was still conscious, but it was still more jarring that a normal *human* memory. It was as if she was in two places at once. A part of her sat in front of Talan in a bar, while another part of her was Atlas standing in front of Hephaestus on a beach overlooking the ocean. Hephaestus was both familiar and new to Kala. Logically, this was because Atlas knew Hephaestus, but it still tripped her out. He was tall, but not like Cronus and the other Titans. Kala guessed that the Olympian gods, being the next round of offspring, were smaller. His hair was black, long, and curly and there was a lot of it. Even his beard went down to his flat belly. The Olympian was in shape, Kala gave him that. Her Atlas memory bank told her it was because he was the god of fire and spent most of his time blacksmithing. His arms were like tree trunks he was so built. Derek had nothing on this guy and Derek was seriously cut. Atlas/Kala was eye-to-eye with Hephaestus and she could sense that Atlas was excited by the meeting.

"I'm here," a familiar voice called out.

Kala recognized Rotoph as he walked up to Atlas and Hephaestus.

From thin air, Hephaestus produced a long ebony box. He opened it in front of Atlas and Rotoph.

Inside, resting on black satin, were twelve knives identical to the one Kala had stolen from Rotoph.

Except one thing: there were no runic markings.

The blades were a beauty to behold without the engravings, but the more Kala watched the more she understood why Owen and Talan hated Rotoph.

Hephaestus handed the box to Rotoph. "Your turn," he said. Though Atlas couldn't see it, Kala could – Hephaestus didn't trust Rotoph.

Poor, pathetic Atlas did, of course. He really believed that the Olympians were going to double-cross the Titans after they took down the Grigori, and that Rotoph was like him: willing to turn on his own kind to save his skin.

Kala watched as Rotoph took the box and recited an ancient spell. As each word fell out of his mouth, a new rune would appear on all twelve knives until they looked like the blade Kala currently had stashed in her jacket.

"It's done." Rotoph nodded. "One cut to a Grigori and they are powerless for a time. Make sure it's enough to banish them or, god or not, they will destroy you."

Hephaestus looked worried. He definitely feared the Grigori. "Are you sure the blades will work?"

"They'll work," Rotoph replied flatly. "Just make sure you're ready."

The memory faded. Kala came back into focus. Fries and a glass of scotch had been placed in front of her.

Talan watched her carefully. "A memory?"

Kala nodded. "Atlas knew Rotoph."

"Rotoph betrayed Atlas and the Olympians worse than any of us. The whole time he was really working for Cronus. He made them believe that he engraved the knives to help the Olympians take down the Grigori and then in turn kill the Titans once and for all.

"Zeus fell right into Cronus's hands. He was so focused on double-crossing his father, he didn't see Cronus's true plan coming until it was too late.

"Cronus had convinced Zeus that the Titans were still weak from their last war, that the Olympians needed to take down the Grigori because they were stronger. Zeus suspected his father was up to something, but he didn't know what. He thought having Hephaestus make the blades would protect them. He never suspected Rotoph would be working for Cronus." Talan motioned for Kala to pull out the knife. "Let me show you something."

Kala took out the knife and placed it on the table. Talan pointed to a small rune in the shape of a slanted "F," on the bone handle. "See that there? Rotoph seared it into every handle so that it would drain the power from the user. The more the Olympians used the blades, the weaker they became." Talan sat back as he stole a fry from Kala's plate. "Weakening the Olympians worked too quickly and the Grigori almost escaped banishment, but the Titans stepped in and used their combined powers to capture and torture the Olympians and seal us into the 5th Heaven."

"A lot of fives going on: 5th Heaven, 5th Level of Hell. What about one through four? Aren't they any good?" Kala didn't bother hiding the snark from her voice. She sipped her scotch and sighed in bliss. Just what she needed.

"Five is a powerful number. Look at your human religions. The Torah contains five books, Jesus had five wounds, there are five pillars of Islam, the five sacred Sikh symbols. I could go on, but I can see the drool forming around your mouth." Talan stole another fry.

Kala liked this side of her stalker angel. Attitude and sarcasm went a long way with her. "Cute." She grabbed some fries herself and began eating. They were greasy and scrumptious. Kala added thoughtfully, "Let me get this straight, the Titans spent too much energy destroying the Olympians and banishing you guys, so they hid in the 5th Level of Hell? Couldn't the Demons or Malaks take them down at that point?"

"A weakened Titan is still more powerful than any Demon or Malak," Talan stated frankly.

"What about a second generation Titan?" Kala asked of herself.

"Thousands of years later? Yes, there *are* some Demons and Malaks who could challenge you, but you still have the advantage. Plus, you have two Grigori on your side. Not to mention Turner's toys if you need them." Talan finished off her fries.

Talk of Turner reminded Kala of her Atlas task. She could tell Talan. "Turner may hate me after I complete my mission."

"You don't have to kill Roberta, do you?" Talan's face paled.

"No. No killings…" But Kala didn't get to finish her sentence.

Through the door walked Rotoph, but this time he had company. Though they looked human, Kala knew that they were Demons. Three of them. Kala was surprised that she could now tell the difference between humans and Demons. It wasn't anything she could put her finger on. She simply looked at them and knew what they were. She wondered if it would be the same for Malaks.

After Rotoph and the three Demons entered the bar, she got her answer.

Behind them, entered two Malaks.

"It's about to get ugly," she muttered under her breath.

Kala was on her feet, holding the Grigori blade. She knew she couldn't rely on it too much though. If it could drain the power of an Olympian, it could most certainly drain the power of a baby Titan.

Talan took her lead and stood beside her.

"Power?" she asked.

"I'd say I'm up to half strength," Talan answered.

"It'll have to do. And, by the way, this situation right here is why

I wanted Derek with me. No one can win a bar fight like that man," Kala reprimanded. Derek had always been her back up and she'd pretty much needed it on a daily basis. Bar fights were what Kala did best. She just felt sorry for the handful of people that were still in this joint. They were about to see quite a show.

Kala watched the group of six make their way toward her. It was an intimidating sight for all the patrons to watch.

The bartender stuttered weakly, "I don't want any trouble."

One of the Demons waved his hand in the general direction of the barkeep and the poor man flew into the air, smashing against the wall of bottled alcohol behind him. Glass and liquid shattered and poured over his unconscious body.

That was enough for the rest of the people in the bar. They took their cue and ran out the front door.

Kala eyed the Malaks behind Rotoph and the Demons. She hadn't had much luck with Malaks, seeing as the only one she ever met tried to kill her… twice. But these two stared at Rotoph with pure hatred.

"Oh, don't think these two will help you. They're under my complete control." Rotoph smiled.

The Malaks looked positively enraged but didn't say or do anything to contradict Rotoph's words.

Kala did the math in her head. If Talan was only at half strength, then Rotoph should be even less since she'd stabbed him later. Nevertheless, the fact that he could control two Malaks testified as to how powerful the Grigori really were.

"What's your deal, Dude? Why are you even here?" Kala gave him a look that diminished most men where they stood. But to Rotoph, Kala was simply irritating.

"I'm here for *him*." Rotoph pointed at Talan.

Kala was surprised by that. "Talan? You seriously aren't after *me*?" She looked at Talan and shrugged. "That's surprisingly refreshing."

"Why me?" Talan asked Rotoph.

Kala knew Talan's curiosity was his Achilles heel. A part of being Grigori she guessed. She just wished he could focus on taking these beasts down as opposed to having a conversation with them. But Kala could use it to her advantage. As long as they were talking, they were off guard. And from the steaming piles of hatred radiating off the Malaks, Kala knew she'd have allies if she could break Rotoph's hold over them.

"Simple, Brother. I want you to help me free the Grigori from their prison."

Chapter Seven

"**W**ait. What?" Kala felt the need to join in this conversation. "You were the one to trap the Grigori in the first place." She turned to Talan. "Don't trust this guy."

"I don't plan to." Talan kept his eyes on Rotoph.

Kala felt the need to drive her point home despite Talan's agreement. "And! You stabbed him in the back. Not really a way to show you're a good guy."

"I don't need to explain myself to a reject Titan who has a nasty habit of picking the losing team," Rotoph snarled.

Kala decided to try a little bluff. "Atlas *was* weak, and this *lowly* human consumed him. I might just do the same to you." She didn't think she could perform a repeat of the act. Nor did she want to. Having to integrate with one schmuck was difficult enough. But she needed to make Rotoph believe it. And from the look on his face, it worked.

Kala decided to hammer the last nail in the coffin. "Being raised by a Grigori gave me everything I needed."

That did it.

Rotoph took a step back.

The three Demons didn't like the way this confrontation was going. *They* obviously wanted a fight.

More importantly, they wanted to fight Kala.

The Demon on Rotoph's right leapt at Kala full force.

Kala was prepared. She shifted her weight to the side and avoided impact. As the Demon flew by her, she grabbed the back of his shirt and threw him against the wall. Dust and plaster fell in chunks to the floor where his body made contact.

Rotoph ordered, "Attack her!"

The remaining four Demons and Malaks came at Kala in a pack. Kala knelt down and tucked herself into a ball as their groping hands reached for her. She rolled away, causing them to smash against each other.

Rotoph used the distraction to reach for his brother. He was about to teleport Talan, Kala knew with certainty. She couldn't let that happen. The little angel had grown on her, doe-eyed and all.

The Demons and Malaks didn't take long to regroup. The Demon closest to Kala grabbed for her throat. She used an Aikido move by rotating her arm to deflect the blow. Being fast kept her out of their grasp.

Kala spun and jumped toward Rotoph before he could touch Talan.

But Talan was on it.

He threw his hand out: Rotoph grabbed his own throat, writhing, as if he were choking from invisible hands.

Within seconds, Rotoph shook off the attack. Being Grigori himself, he knew all the tricks and how to counter them. Even at half power.

Half power. Kala let the words roll in her head. She looked at the blade she was holding and immediately felt foolish.

Vaulting onto a table, Kala kicked the nearest Demon in the face.

Her Titan strength caused him to jolt backwards giving her enough time to leap to the next table.

With only a few inches separating her from Rotoph, Kala slashed the knife forward.

It was enough.

A trickle of blood formed on the side of Rotoph's arm from where Kala nicked him.

Whirling around to see if her idea worked, Kala smiled.

The two Malaks grinned at her triumphantly. Rotoph had no powers now, which meant no control over the Malaks.

The first Malak called out, "We've got it from here. Go. Accomplish your mission."

The Demons snarled at their new opponents while the Malaks finally looked like they were fighting the right enemies.

It sounded like a catfight breaking out as the Demons and Malaks tried to rip each other to pieces.

Kala stayed on the table, watching as if she were witnessing a train wreck.

Demons and Malaks didn't fight elegantly. They fought like animals. They fought to destroy.

Kala filed that away in her arsenal. Always know your opponent. And Kala was pretty sure she would be fighting a lot of Demons in the days to come.

Rotoph reeled on her, furious, yelling over the noise of the destruction of the bar. "I stabbed Talan so that he would listen!"

"Yeah, that's smart, stab the guy you want to talk to. It's too late to explain yourself, jackass. Next time don't look like you enjoyed it." Kala jumped down from the table and stood next to Talan. "Powers up?"

Talan nodded. "Ready to go."

"Take us to Penny. I actually miss her." Kala shrugged.

Rotoph reached out, his face pleading. "Talan, please! Listen to me. I want to free our brothers and sisters! I just did something that could get me killed, but it won't be worth a thing if you don't help me!"

Talan shook his head. "You turned against your own kind and left us in that prison to rot."

"Rot is a strong word," Kala interjected, remembering the beauty of the Grigori pokey.

But Talan and Rotoph ignored her. Talan looked at his brother with a genuinely hurt expression. "Why should I listen to a word you say, Rotoph?"

Before Rotoph could respond, the two Malaks came at him from both sides.

Then Kala noticed what was left of the three Demons laying on the ground. It was as if a bear had broken into the bar and mauled the three of them. Kala figured that was probably what the headlines would read when the bodies were found.

Rotoph had no defenses.

The Malaks ripped into him like savages.

"Is he going to end up like these three?" Kala had a momentary pang of sympathy.

Talan shook his head. "Grigori can't be killed. Even powerless." He turned to her, eyes sad. "Shall we?"

Kala nodded wishing she could say something to make Talan feel better, but her mind came up blank. "Let's go."

Talan reached over and held her hand.

Kala's surroundings blurred for a second. They re-focused sharply moments later when they teleported into Talan's apartment. Kala felt a strange solace being back in Talan's lair. Even though it was a tiny studio with the simplest of décor – a couch, recliner, super-sized flat screen and a small kitchenette – it still felt a little bit like home.

Penny sat on the couch thumbing through her stack of papers. She looked up when hearing them arrive. "What took you so long?" Then she noticed the blood on Talan's shirt. "What happened?" She hurried over to examine Talan.

Talan waved her away. "I'm fine."

"Your shirt is covered in blood and it's slashed. What kind of Demon could get the jump on you like that? Did *she* distract you?" Penny's eyes barely glanced in Kala's direction.

Kala took back reminiscing about Penny. "His brother, Rotoph, had the privilege, thank you very much." Kala pulled out the knife from her jacket. "Using this beauty."

Penny's face turned about three shades of white. "Where did you get that?" She turned to Talan as if Kala had made up the whole thing. "Is that true? Rotoph attacked you?"

Talan apparently didn't feel like confiding in Penny, or maybe he just didn't want to re-live it. "Yes, Rotoph stabbed me." Talan's eyes glanced at Kala.

Kala was shocked that she knew exactly what he was telling her without him saying a word. He didn't want Penny to know that not all the Grigori had escaped. Talan wanted to keep her in the dark, and by telling her that Rotoph needed Talan's help to break out his brethren would reveal too much. Kala had no idea *how* she knew Talan's thoughts, but she didn't question it. Once she decided she could trust someone, Kala stuck by their side to the bitter end.

And in Talan's case, that could be very dangerous.

Penny crossed her arms in annoyance. "Are you going to elaborate?"

Kala stepped in front of her. "Why don't you stop acting like a jealous girlfriend and do something useful. Did you find anything else in your scrolls?" Kala nodded to the stack of papers on the couch.

Penny pursed her lips from anger and walked over to the couch. "No. Just more of the same." She eyed the knife. "That doesn't belong to you. My father made that knife, you should give it to me."

Kala laughed. "Yeah, right."

Penny turned to Talan for support. "You don't honestly trust her with that blade, do you? She could rip your powers from you anytime she wants!"

Talan was livid. He moved so that he was inches from Penny's face. "I trust Kala with my life. The knife stays with her."

Penny didn't argue. She looked positively shocked. Then her face softened as she turned to Kala. "I'm sorry. You've more than proved your loyalty. I'm just not used to everything being so out of control." Penny laughed nervously. "I never thought I'd think of my days with the Atlas as easy, but compared to this?"

Talan eased up on his attitude as well. "That's the nature of prophecies. They come with a lot of destruction."

Penny sighed deeply and said to Kala, "The 5th and Zeus can wait. How can I help you fulfill your mission?"

Her mission. Kala didn't want to think about her mission. She wanted to find Zeus and force him to break the curse. The last thing on the planet Kala wanted to do was find Fortski and destroy his life's work. If the curse was broken and *balance* went back to happening on its own, then Fortski's cure for cancer would somehow be destroyed if that was what the universe wanted. Kala just didn't want to have to be the one to do it. It was hard enough adjusting to the fact that she was a Titan. Without the curse, what would that mean? Maybe Turner would take her back and she'd be some kind of super soldier with her Titan strength.

Kala felt like she deserved to be condemned to this life after what she did to Jack. But if Zeus broke the curse, then killing him would have been for nothing. It would just be murder. It left a gaping empty hole in her chest that was too painful to contemplate. If she continued to do Atlas's job, then at least Jack died for something.

Penny grabbed her attention once more. "Can you tell us your mission?"

Kala snapped out of her reverie. "No. I told you: I'm not ready yet. I want to confront Zeus first. Besides, didn't you say you wanted to save your dad? What exactly are we saving him from?"

Penny couldn't hide her emotion. "Hephaestus is being held against his will by Cronus. He's being forced to make weapons for the Titans and Demons. Rotoph sears the runes into them like he did with that knife. The fact that you managed to steal that blade is a small miracle."

"Not really a miracle, more like bad planning on his part." Kala examined the knife more carefully. "This rune drains the power of the user. Can we get rid of it or something?"

Penny and Kala both looked at Talan for an answer. He gently took the blade from Kala and touched the power-sucking rune. When he pulled his hand away, the rune still remained. Talan shook his head. "Rotoph always had a knack for this kind of thing. Owen might be able to remove it."

Kala took the blade back and tucked it into her jacket. "I don't care if it drains me. I haven't felt anything so far and I've used it twice. I'm thinking the Olympians did a lot more than just a few slices."

Talan's eyes flared with bitterness. He nodded. "My brothers and sisters were hacked into pieces. Only a few of us managed to fight back, but even the injuries I sustained kept me weak enough for Cronus to banish us all. When the dimension sealed shut, there was nothing any of us could do."

Unsure of how to respond, Kala felt for Talan. Her rage grew every time she thought of Cronus and his lackeys hacking up angels. The supernatural were egotistical jerk-offs. Kala didn't want to have anything to do with them. Of course, she was one now, too, and that only made her angrier.

Kala imagined seeing Owen lying in pieces…

"If we have this knife, where are the other eleven?" Kala decided to be tactical instead of emotional. It helped her in life when she didn't want to deal with feelings she wasn't ready to face.

Penny was very sure of herself, "Cronus has them. After the banishment, Cronus sealed the blades away in the 5th Level of Hell. Rotoph and my father have been working for him ever since. I don't think Rotoph knew what he had gotten himself into when he betrayed his kind."

Talan responded thoughtfully, "I don't either."

When he didn't continue, Penny plopped down on the couch. "If we're not going to complete Kala's mission, then she should rest before we go to the 5th."

"Rest? Let's go now." Kala's adrenaline was pumping, and she was raring for a fight.

Talan turned to Kala and looked at her like she was the only one in the room. "Pandora is right. You need to sleep. You may be a Titan now, but you're human as well. Your body is still transitioning."

"I'm not tired," Kala protested. And lame. She had thought that being a god would mean she wouldn't be susceptible to sleeping and eating and *human* things. The thought had been pretty darn exciting. Kala hated that she had to eat and sleep. She often times wished that she could do without. It wasn't that Kala didn't like food and rest; it was just frustrating that it was essential to living. It seemed like such a waste to her. She always thought about how much more she could get done if she didn't have to stop her life for *human fuel*. "What time is it anyway?" Kala looked over at Talan's digital clock.

Kala had almost forgotten that she couldn't see time in a normal way anymore. The countdown startled her momentarily.

3d 11h 13m 45s.

Realizing what time it was startled her even more.

5:47 P.M.

Where had the day gone? "Look, I don't feel like taking a *nap* when I could be breaking this damn curse…"

Talan touched her forehead mid-sentence. Before she could utter a profanity aimed at him, Kala was out cold.

Chapter Eight

Kala awoke to find herself feeling pretty darn good. She hadn't felt that way in a long time. Even before her life had turned to the crazy ride it was, Kala had been a horrible sleeper. Always having to be on alert did that to a person, especially to a sniper. Catnaps were more her thing. Getting rest while she could on a mission or even in life. It was a skill she was proud of, but now?

Pulling the blanket back, Kala slid out of bed feeling more rested than she had ever been in her life. "Was that some kind of Grigori sleeping pill? Holy crap." Kala stretched her arms.

Talan and Penny were on the couch watching television. It was so normal that Kala had to remind herself that the two of them were supernatural beings. Kala grunted when she tried to see what they were watching. She'd never know. The vision of Kala destroying Fortski's cure re-played itself over and over.

"Would you turn that off?" Kala asked.

Talan looked at the TV and it shut off. Apparently, Grigori didn't need remote controls.

Kala looked at the time.

3d 01h 03m 34s.

3:53 A.M.

Kala clutched her chest in panic. "You let me sleep for thirteen hours! Are you insane?!"

Talan was instantly by her side. "You needed it, trust me. Your body is still trying to assimilate to a Titan. You'll thank me later."

As good as Kala felt, she didn't think she would thank Talan anytime soon. So much time lost. Kala was only an hour away from Day Two and that made her stomach drop and churn into a giant stress ball. Sleep was her enemy. It made time pass too quickly. Kala vowed not to sleep again until she made Zeus break the curse. If she had to go through with her vision of destroying the cure for cancer, Kala didn't want it to come sooner than it had to.

"Enough rest. I'm ready to go." Kala stood up and Talan joined her.

Penny walked over to the two of them.

Talan nodded. He reached out and clasped Kala's hand.

Then he turned to Penny. "Sorry, Pandora."

Kala saw a glimpse of shock and betrayal as Penny's face popped out of view.

***

Kala fell to her knees coughing uncontrollably. The air was filled with the smell of sulfur and rotted flesh. Kala had been around enough dead bodies in her life to recognize the stench. It reminded her of cinnamon, which was why she'd always cringe whenever someone was chewing cinnamon gum or had the nerve to eat Red Hots in front of her.

Talan touched her chest and she could breathe again.

The smells were still there, but at least she wasn't choking on them anymore.

"Lovely," Kala observed.

Her surroundings were oddly beautiful in a terrifying kind of way. Kala oftentimes found beauty in the grotesque, if just for its sheer uniqueness. The ground reminded her of lava, as if she was standing inside a volcano, but with no heat. She and Talan were in some kind of hallway with hundred foot ceilings and walls that were a width of at least that long, all covered in sharp spikes.

It was the sound that set Kala's teeth on edge. It was as if a trillion snakes were slithering around them, hissing and spitting. She kept glancing over her shoulder expecting to see a python coming her way. It threw her instincts off, which kept her guard up even more.

Aside from the two of them, there was no one to be seen. No gods, no Demons, no nothing. If it weren't for the noise, scenery, and stench, Kala would have wondered if they were in the right place.

"We're at the gateway," Talan spoke over the hissing. "I'm going to need your help to enter unseen."

If this was the gateway, Kala wondered what the rest of the joint was like. The quicker they found Zeus, the better.

"How can *I* help?" The fact that Kala wasn't on Earth started to sink in. She figured her ability to cope with the situation was a combination of military training and Atlas's memory of this place. Though she couldn't remember the specifics, a part of her knew that she had been here before.

"You're a Titan now, Kala. And this is a *Titans-only* place." Talan led her down the long hallway.

The uneven ground felt awkward under her feet. "Why didn't you bring Penny?" Kala decided she would broach the topic. She had been certain that Penny was along for the entire ride, but just like that, Talan had left the girl behind.

"I don't trust her to make smart decisions," Talan spoke with a finality that left Kala chilled.

"Ouch. Okay," Kala responded.

Talan stopped and turned to Kala, concern etched in every feature.

"Pandora has been trying to rescue her father for several thousand years now. She put Atlas in hiding because he was the only link she had to finding him. She knows Hephaestus is in the 5th. Kala, she'd do *anything* to save him."

"Anything? As in, sell us out?" Kala asked.

Talan nodded.

"The girl bugs me, but I understand her need to rescue her father. I'd do anything for Owen and I would have done anything to save Jack," Kala admitted.

Talan looked away. "I'm sorry."

Kala sighed. She didn't want to discuss it with Talan. It made her angry. "Let's just find Zeus."

Talan walked ahead without another word. There wasn't much to say anyway. After a few minutes trudging down the awkward landscape, Kala was ready to tear her ears off from the sound of hissing and spitting on constant repeat. Motioning Kala to halt at a spot that felt the same as any other, Talan pointed to an area on the sharp spiked wall. He instructed, "Touch here and imagine a doorway."

Kala looked at Talan, incredulous. "Really? Imagine a door and it appears?"

"I'm not sure it will work since technically you're only half Titan, but it's our only option. Only Titans are allowed into the inner sanctum. Any other being needs permission," Talan warned.

"What? You're saying a big powerful Grigori couldn't bust through?" Kala half-teased but was actually curious as to the answer.

"Oh yes, I could break in, but then we'd have every Titan on us in seconds. I could take two maybe three on my own, but all twelve? I'd rather slip in under the radar," Talan confided.

Kala's military training forced her to agree with the guy. "Okay." She placed her hand on the designated spot and closed her eyes. It was easier to play make-believe with her eyes closed. Creativity wasn't her strong suit, unless she was trying to win a fight. Kala could think of all kinds of crazy when she needed an exit during a failed mission. She pictured the door to Owen and Linda's house. It was the only home she had ever known and the easiest for her to visualize. Kala imagined reaching forward and turning the knob.

"We're in," Talan's voice sounded next to her.

Kala opened her eyes and saw the opening before her. It looked like a black hole formed out of the spiked wall. Normally, Kala wouldn't even consider walking through something so sketchy, but when Talan moved forward, she knew she had to follow.

Kala looked down at her watch.

3d 00h 02m 53s.

Day One was almost up.

Kala didn't want to be stuck in Hell when Day Four rolled around. She took a deep breath and entered the blackness. There was a moment of utter darkness as Kala passed through the gateway. When she arrived at the other side, her breath caught in her throat.

An enormous cavern spread out before Kala with stunning brilliance. This was nothing like the hellish hallway she had just left. It felt as if entering into the inside of geode rock. The walls, ceiling, and ground were crystallized purple, each crystal glowing from its own light source. It was as bright as daylight, but with no sun. There were dozens of archways carved into the walls, all leading to different parts of the 5th Level of Hell, Kala assumed. She was utterly speechless as she took in the beauty of the cavern.

Talan's voice broke the silence. "If Zeus is being held anywhere, it would be in The Pit. It's this door over here." Talan headed left toward one of the entryways.

Kala shook her head as she followed Talan. She couldn't wrap her brain around the fact that this was the 5th level of any kind of Hell. It was too beautiful. She had expected more of what she saw when they first arrived: sulfur, hissing, and lava spikes. But this? This was stunning!

She suddenly heard a voice that made her skin crawl.

"Buttercup, you came to save me."

In the corner of the cavern, hidden in the shadow of one of the arched doorways, was someone Kala hadn't expected to see.

Chained to the wall and grinning at Kala like a lion about to pounce on its prey was Asmodeus.

63

DAY TWO

Chapter Nine

Kala audibly grumbled.

Talan's face lit up with a kind of happiness Kala had never seen before. "I see the Titans punished you for your ineptitude."

Asmodeus ignored Talan completely and focused entirely on Kala. "Are you going to let me down from here or what?" he said with as much charisma as a man chained to a wall could have.

"Actually, no." Kala didn't know how much clearer she could be. "You're much safer tied up."

"I'd much more prefer it if *you* tied me up instead." Asmodeus smiled slyly. "Now, seriously, you're not going to leave me here are you?"

"Yes. Yes, I am." Kala couldn't believe the king of Demons actually expected her to help him escape. She turned to Talan. "Please, lead the way."

Talan had a satisfied expression on his face. "My pleasure."

Talan began walking toward the archway that supposedly led to *The Pit*.

Asmodeus called out, "I know you love following your little Angel-boy there, but Zeus isn't in The Pit."

Kala stopped. She knew she shouldn't. She knew Asmodeus was probably lying. Trying anything to keep her there to help free him. But her gut told her he was telling the truth.

Apparently, Talan felt the same, because he turned to Asmodeus with irritation in his eyes. "Let me guess: you won't tell us where he is unless we unchain you?"

"Grigori were always known for their intelligence." Asmodeus finally acknowledged Talan's presence. "In my experience that was just a rumor."

"Har-de-har-har." Kala had no patience for Asmodeus's quips. "Why should we believe anything you say?"

"Have I ever lied to you before?" Though his tone was light, his eyes were intense. "Besides, when I wiped your brain," he added with a sly smile. "Technically, I never said I was your boyfriend, I just implanted it."

"So you made me lie to myself and therefore it shouldn't count?" Kala rolled her eyes. "If I drastically stretch my imagination, then no, you never lied to me. But there's a first time for everything, and I'll never really trust you."

"I'm not asking you to trust me. I'm asking you to break me out in exchange for the location of Zeus. Why do you want to see him anyway? You think he'll release you from that curse? Only the true Atlas could…" As the words were leaving Asmodeus's mouth, he started to focus on Kala. His eyes widened. "You didn't… How?" He turned to Talan, shocked. "How did she do that?"

Talan shrugged. "She's stronger than you think."

Asmodeus's gaze veered back to Kala with utter surprise and admiration. Kala noticed with annoyance that her joining with a Titan made the Demon even more attracted to her. "*How* did you do it?" he asked, amazed. "I must know."

"You must, huh?" Kala grunted. "I have no freaking clue. But the more memories I have of the guy, the more I realize what a loser he was."

Then she added, a little embarrassed, "I ate him." Kala had never talked much about the details of her experience, and confessing to Asmodeus wasn't something she planned to do, but the raise of his eyebrow said it all.

"I knew I had a feeling about you," he said.

Talan stepped in. "Tell us where Zeus is and we let you live." Talan apparently had enough of confession time.

Kala assumed it was because he didn't like her interacting with Asmodeus, but she was relieved not to share anymore. Somehow Asmodeus had the ability to make her spill her guts and she didn't like that about him one bit. It was dangerous. It made her feel weak.

"You can't kill me." Asmodeus didn't look worried at all. "And I do know where Zeus is being held. You need me, Grigori."

"I could snap your soul into pieces," Talan warned.

Kala had never seen Talan look so vicious.

"I may be serving my punishment, but the Titans still protect me," Asmodeus snarled.

Before the Angel/Demon testosterone level reached epic heights, Kala yanked Talan to the side to talk to him privately. "Look. Can you find Zeus or what?"

It took a few moments for Talan to calm himself enough to focus on Kala. Then he nodded slowly. "Eventually, yes."

"Eventually?"

Asmodeus chimed in making the *private* meeting not so private. "It could take days, weeks, months. The world will have ended by then. What is your task this time anyway?"

"Shut it, Demon," Kala snapped.

"Demon? So impersonal." Asmodeus huffed, but when seeing Kala's disapproving glare, he looked away. "Fine. I'll just stay here, then. Let you two work it out."

Kala focused back on Talan. "Is that true?"

Talan stared at her frustrated. "Yes, but I wouldn't let you fail your mission. We can always jump back here and keep looking."

Kala shook her head and turned to Asmodeus. "Tell us where Zeus is and Talan will zap you back to earth. Deal?"

"Deal," Asmodeus agreed happily.

Talan shook his head. "I can't agree to that, Kala."

Kala should have known Talan would continue to balk at freeing Asmodeus, but Kala needed to talk to Zeus and Asmodeus appeared to be the only one with immediate knowledge of his whereabouts. Asmodeus wasn't trustworthy, but he was familiar. Kala could read him pretty easily. Definitely an evil she knew.

Asmodeus joined in helpfully. "He doesn't have to send me back, just get me out of these chains and I'll do the rest."

Kala was immediately suspicious of Asmodeus's perky nature, but she chalked it off to excitement at being released. She turned to Talan. "Just the chains?"

Talan took a few minutes to think. Finally, he nodded. He walked over to Asmodeus and touched the heavy chains that kept him captive. They disappeared.

Kala kept her guard up as Asmodeus massaged his wrists. "Much better, thank you."

"Zeus." Kala kept Asmodeus on target.

"Ah, yes, Zeus." Asmodeus held his arm out for Kala to take.

"Not happening." Kala deflected Asmodeus's flirting tactics. Even in the 5th Level of Hell, the guy tried to have game.

"No?" He acted mock-offended. "A little privacy perhaps?"

Both Kala and Talan looked at each other, unsure of Asmodeus's intentions.

Asmodeus snapped his fingers.

A ten-foot snarling dog appeared in the giant cavern.

Kala stared at the enormous dog growling in front of her. He looked like a cross between a Doberman pincher and a Pit-bull, except his teeth were black and had razor edges.

"Say hello to Spot, Grigori. Created by the Titans to eat little pesky angels like yourself." Asmodeus was quite pleased with himself.

Kala didn't move for fear of the giant beast gobbling her up, but she was more than livid. "Were you ever going to take me to Zeus?"

"Oh, buttercup, I'm still taking you to Zeus. I just don't want the third wheel tagging along."

Spot apparently didn't feel like waiting around for a conversation: his enormous head lunged toward Talan.

Talan plunged his hands forward and fire flowed out of his body with laser-like precision. The ray of fire engulfed Spot's left eye causing the dog to screech in pain.

Asmodeus tried to grab Kala to get her out of there, but there was no way she was going to leave Talan defenseless.

Kala leapt at Spot and grabbed the dog's head between her hands. It was like holding the front end of Volkswagen Beetle it was so huge. Then she used all her Titan might and threw Spot clear across the cavern. His body smashed against the purple rock and a few shattered pieces fell to the ground.

Spot was up in seconds, but instead of running toward Kala like she wanted, he ran full force toward Talan. Asmodeus was right. This dog was bred to hunt Grigori. She could beat him until he died, but he wouldn't attack her because she was a Titan.

Kala shrugged. She'd have to kill the poor bastard. Kala loved animals, even ten-foot supernatural ones, but if it meant Talan getting hurt or worse, the dog would have to go.

Spot took a running leap straight at Talan, but Talan threw his hands out and water flowed out of his fingers this time. As it touched the dog's body, it turned to ice. In less than a second, Spot had turned into a Popsicle.

"Well, that was disappointing," Asmodeus observed.

Spot shook loose of the ice.

And now he was pissed.

Kala ran full force at the dog and knocked him right into Asmodeus's smug face. It felt pretty good to hear both Asmodeus and the dog yelp from the impact.

Talan took advantage of the moment and sent another wave of fire toward Spot. This time there were large flames designed to burn. The fire engulfed Spot and turned him into a fiery ball of teeth and fur.

The dog quickly rid himself of the burning blaze with a full body shake.

Spot had had enough.

Before Talan or Kala could retaliate, Spot's gigantic head snapped forward and swallowed Talan whole.

As in: no more Talan.

Legs and all.

Kala was too dazed to register what had happened.

One minute they were fighting the Titan's guard dog, the next moment Talan was kibble.

Kala was about to break off a piece of purple rock and slice Spot's stomach open when she felt Asmodeus's hand on her shoulder.

Oh crap! Kala thought to herself as her surroundings blurred from Asmodeus teleporting her away.

Chapter Ten

Apparently, teleporting in Hell was the same as teleporting on earth. It took a few moments for Kala to adjust her eyes, but when she did, she smacked Asmodeus in the chest.

"Take me back!" Kala yelled at the Demon.

Asmodeus looked at her as if she were a child who didn't understand something. "Relax. Your boyfriend will be fine."

"He's not my boyfriend! And I don't believe you. Take me back now or I swear to God…" Kala started in anger.

But Asmodeus cut her off. "You'll what? Punch me with your Titan strength?" He grabbed Kala's hand and kissed it before she could react. "I'd much rather you use that strength for something more fun."

That was it.

Kala punched Asmodeus with as much force as she could. His whole body flew across the room, but before he made impact he used his Demon powers to stop himself and land on his feet. He massaged his jaw with a smile. "Look around you. Familiar?"

Kala did as he asked out of military habit, more than any command from Asmodeus.

Memories from Atlas flooded back to her as she recognized where she stood. It was a chamber made of what looked like shredded steel on the walls and ceiling. The ground was some kind of rusted metal. The combination of old and new only emphasized the contrast between the two metals. There was a single closed door at the end of the rectangular-shaped room and Kala knew where it led:

Zeus's prison.

Her Atlas memory remembered vividly. She knew that when she opened the door, Zeus would be chained inside a cell lined with the same shredded steel that surrounded her out here.

Kala threw up her hands. "Fine. You're a Demon of your word. I'm here. Now take me back."

Asmodeus casually walked over to Kala and put his hand out. "See for yourself." A holographic image hovered above his hand. It was like watching security footage, supernatural-style. Talan was in the cavern they had just left, covered in Spot guts. What was left of the beast coated most of the purple rock. It looked as if there had been a hurricane made of dog entrails and Talan stood in the aftermath.

"How do I know this isn't fake?" Kala asked suspiciously.

"Because you know. Am I wrong?" Asmodeus moved his hand and the image disappeared.

Though Kala couldn't explain why, she *did* know. It gave her a sense of relief, but also made her furious. "Bring him here right now!" she threatened.

"Now why would I do that?" Asmodeus replied as if Kala wasn't in her right mind. "The only reason I was not put in chains the second Talan freed me is because I turned him in. Turn in a Grigori and apparently all is forgiven." Asmodeus was pleased with himself again.

"Is he with the Titans now?" Kala was incredulous. "We have to save him!"

"Talan won't stay long enough for them to capture him. He's probably teleporting back to earth as we speak." Asmodeus reached toward Kala's head in what she could only assume was to touch her face or hair in some way. She smacked his hand away.

"Just keep your distance." Kala couldn't really argue with Asmodeus's logic. Talan wouldn't stay. He couldn't travel without causing more alarm anyway.

Then a horrible thought struck her. Talan was convinced that the two of them were soul mates. Kala knew he would throw caution to the wind and fight his way to her.

She had to get a message to him somehow. Tell him she was okay. That he *should* leave the 5th.

This would be a good time to find out that Atlas has some kind of telepathy power. Anything? Kala sighed inwardly. She knew Turner's wife Roberta had powers like that. The woman had entered Kala's brain to help her fuse Atlas's essence with hers. Without Roberta, Kala would have died.

Kala? Roberta's voice sounded in Kala's head.

Kala stood very still. Was she crazy? Or did she just hear Roberta in her brain?

Asmodeus was apparently growing impatient. "Look, we'll talk to Zeus, then I'll take you back to earth…"

Kala put her hand up sharply. "Shut it. I'm listening."

Asmodeus looked around the room confused but, to Kala's relief, did as he was told.

Kala tried talking to herself, hoping she wasn't imagining Roberta. *I'm here. I need your help.*

What do you need? Roberta answered fast.

Whoa. Kala thought. *Is this real?*

You and I have a connection now. Anytime you open your mind to me, I can enter and you can do the same to me. Roberta's voice sounded as clearly as if they were in the same room.

Kala wasn't sure if she liked this new development, but she didn't want to lose Talan to the Titans. *The old Voodoo guy that teaches you magic, he's really that angel I brought with me when I became Atlas.* Talan probably wouldn't appreciate her telling Roberta about his disguise, but Kala wanted him safe, so she rolled the dice.

Interesting. Roberta sounded intrigued. *He needs help?*

Yes. How do you normally contact him? Kala asked.

The same way we're communicating now. Remember what I told you the night I taught you the telekinesis spell? About contacting you?

Kala thought back to that night, when she had asked Roberta how to reach her in the future, Roberta had replied *I have my ways.* Kala figured it was a pretty good guess that *this* was the way.

That's how you were going to find me? Kala had wondered how Roberta would track her down.

Helping you assimilate with Atlas made that a lot easier. Roberta confirmed. *Now, what can I do for Pierre?*

Contact him. Tell him you know he's Talan, and that I'm okay. He needs to leave the 5th, Roberta. He'll die or be imprisoned if he doesn't. Just make sure he knows I'm fine and that I have Asmodeus in check. Can you do that?

Of course. Roberta responded. *I'll do it now.*

Before Kala could answer back, she physically felt Roberta's essence leave her mind. It was light, like a small breeze.

"What was that about?" Asmodeus asked.

Kala didn't want to tell him. "Sometimes when I have memories from Atlas's past, I zone out a bit." It wasn't a lie. She did zone out when she experienced Atlas's recollections.

Now that Roberta was hopefully making sure Talan was safe and not playing hero, Kala decided to actually figure out what Atlas could recall about this place. Separating Atlas's memory from the present moment was a little bit more difficult for her after the mind-melding experience with Roberta. Regardless, she tried to focus on what Atlas remembered.

Atlas had come here to make Zeus fulfill his promise after the Titans captured all the Olympians. Atlas still couldn't believe the war was over, not after picking the wrong side for a second time. If he could just talk to Zeus, Zeus could free him of his curse. It wasn't fair that Atlas helped the Olympians and was still being punished. Helping Zeus should be enough to make him break the curse. It wasn't Atlas's fault that the Olympians had lost.

Kala really hated the way Atlas thought. It was such a weasel thing to think. But Atlas was a part of her now and she had to accept it. It was hard enough dealing with her own regret, now she had to deal with Atlas's too?!

The memory became more vivid when Atlas opened the door to see Zeus chained to the shredded steel wall. The Olympian looked weak, skinny, and pale. Not at all what a powerful god should look like. He barely glanced at Atlas.

"I'm here to help you escape," Atlas lied. He figured if Zeus thought he was going to free him, he might be more likely to break the curse.

Zeus may have appeared weak, but when he spoke, his words were pure power. "You betrayed us!" Zeus accused.

Atlas had not been prepared for that. "I did not! I did everything you asked! How was I to know that Cronus was two steps ahead of you? It's not my fault your father is manipulative and evil!" Atlas felt his chances of Zeus helping him slip away.

Zeus growled, "You were always loyal to my father! I deserve this punishment for being so foolish as to trust you!"

Atlas panicked. "I swear to you, Zeus, I did nothing! Now break this curse! I did everything you asked!"

Zeus laughed. "You are despicable, Atlas. Groveling to me when it's your fault I stand here chained for all eternity. I'll never lift that curse. *Never!*"

The force of Zeus's words jolted Kala out of the memory.

When she blinked her eyes to re-focus on the present, she was suddenly face to face with Asmodeus, his hands cradling her waist as he stared down at her.

Kala pushed him away. "Seriously? You need to find some nice Demon queen to settle down with, because *we're* never going to happen."

"When you've lived as long as I have, never say never." Asmodeus smiled.

That brought Kala back to Zeus's threat of keeping Atlas cursed forever. "I actually hope you're right about that." Seeing Asmodeus's eyebrows rise in sudden hope, Kala quashed it. "About never saying never, not about hooking up."

Asmodeus seemed pleased by this anyway. "What's the difference?"

Kala didn't want to argue semantics with the guy, so she plowed toward the door.

Once she reached it, Kala wondered if it was locked. If this place was a super prison, shouldn't it be much harder to get to the prisoners? She paused in front of the entrance, not wanting to rush into any potential traps or surprises.

Asmodeus stepped next to her, a little close for her taste, but she was too on guard to do anything about it. "You know it's unlocked, right?" Asmodeus peered down at Kala obviously curious as to why she had paused. "Or are we having another flashback?"

Before Asmodeus could wrap his hand around her waist in hopes she was in spaced-out-memory-lane mode, Kala smacked his hand away. "Why aren't there any guards? What's stopping Zeus from escaping?"

Asmodeus laughed out loud. "Because he's in the same chains I was just in. Only Titans and Grigori can break them. And you saw for yourself: Grigori can't get into the 5th without the help of a Titan."

"But they can transport your ass here." Kala pretty much verbally bitch-slapped Asmodeus. Her foster father, Owen, had banished the king of Demons to the 5th like it was child's play.

Asmodeus lost his smile and shrugged. "True. But look how stupid your boyfriend was to free me."

"Stop calling him my boyfriend," Kala responded, not knowing why she always rose to the bait with the Demon. "Come on, let's see what

Zeus has to say for himself."

Kala breathed in deep and opened the door.

The cell was as Atlas had remembered it. Except for one thing.

Zeus was no longer there.

Chapter Eleven

"**W**ell, that's a surprise," Asmodeus observed. "The Elders are not going to like that."

Kala was in shock for all of two seconds then her emotions turned to anger. "Do you think they moved him? Maybe when they realized I was here they took him somewhere else?" Breaking her curse was starting to feel like it was getting farther and farther out of reach.

"Anything is possible, but why move him after 2,000 years? Just because a half-breed – no offense – comes to interrogate Zeus is hardly cause for panic. Really? What could you possibly do?" Asmodeus mused.

"Thanks," Kala retorted sarcastically. Nothing like the Demon King to make her feel completely inadequate. It was a new sensation for her not to be respected as a soldier. She was used to being the elite of the elite, and to be thrown into a world where she was lower than the bottom of the totem pole was very humbling. "If not the Titans then did he escape on his own?"

Asmodeus shook his head. "I told you: only a Titan or Grigori could break that chain."

Kala had a sinking sensation in her stomach. *I just did something that could get me killed, but it won't be worth a thing if you don't help me.* Rotoph's words echoed in Kala's head. She was starting to imagine that Rotoph's *something* had been freeing Zeus. But she wanted to see what Asmodeus would say about her suspicions first. "You don't think a Grigori…"

"How? The Elder alarms would go off if they got anywhere near his cell. No. You were right the first time. They must have moved him. Maybe they're more scared of you than I thought."

"What about Rotoph? Doesn't he work for the Titans? He could have done it." The more Kala thought about it, the more she knew that Rotoph showing up yesterday morning was more than just a Grigori reunion. He had probably released Zeus and ran to the only person he thought would give him the time of day: Talan.

"How do you know about Rotoph? Never mind. Don't tell me. Listen, sweetie," Asmodeus said seriously, "Rotoph is not someone you can trust. He's dangerous."

"Ha! This coming from you?" Kala guffawed. But Asmodeus's concern made her pause. "I stabbed him a couple of times." Kala felt like defending herself.

"Really?" Asmodeus raised his eyebrow, impressed. Then his face turned ashen. "Stabbed him with what?"

Kala pulled out the Grigori blade.

Asmodeus's eyes widened. "Where did you get that?"

"I stole it from Rotoph." Kala was careful as to what she wanted to reveal to Asmodeus. She knew there were certain things she could trust the Demon with, but knowledge of Rotoph's plan to free the Grigori wasn't one of them. If Rotoph had helped Zeus escape, then Kala recognized that he had been sincere in his plea for Talan's help. He really did want to free the other Grigori.

And Kala had left him vulnerable. Oops.

By the way he looked at Kala, Asmodeus was definitely impressed. "You are just full of surprises." He eyed the knife again. "You know that drains your powers, right?"

Kala shrugged. "So far I've used it three times and I haven't noticed anything. Maybe I need to use it excessively to trigger the power-sucking rune," Kala voiced her theory.

"Maybe." Asmodeus looked thoughtfully at Kala. "Or maybe the fact that you're a walking anomaly gives you a certain amount of protection."

Kala had never thought of that possibility. The fact that she was a human who had consumed a god apparently never happened before. Asmodeus might be right. Maybe her *differences* would protect her from things that would normally hurt a god. Only time would tell, but Kala decided to rest on the cautious side for now. "I don't plan on hacking up any Grigori in the near future, so we'll never find out if this knife drains me, will we?"

Asmodeus smirked as if hiding something.

"What was that look?" Kala didn't like a smirking Asmodeus.

"Nothing. Good on you. No more stabbing Grigori." Asmodeus led Kala out of the cell and back into the adjoining room. "We should get you back to earth."

"Oh no, stop right there." Now Kala was certain that Asmodeus was keeping something from her. "Spill."

"Just tuck that away, and let's get out of here." Asmodeus eyed the knife with disdain.

Kala peered down at the blade. Kala couldn't figure out if Asmodeus didn't like her talking about not killing Grigori or the knife itself. But he was definitely acting squirmy. "If you don't tell me what you're hiding, I'll have to stab you with this myself."

"Is this what our relationship has turned into? Stabbing me if I don't share my most intimate secrets?" Asmodeus smiled mockingly.

But Kala noticed he kept his distance.

It was all she needed.

"Ha!" Kala laughed. "I can read you so easily. This blade hurts *anything* supernatural, doesn't it?"

Asmodeus didn't look upset by Kala's revelation. If anything, the hearts in his eyes appeared to grow even larger. "You *can* read me, can't you?" Asmodeus obviously felt it was worth the risk of a good stabbing because he reached out and pulled Kala to him.

Kala debated whether or not to gut the Demon to escape his grasp, but his hands were loose enough around the small of her back that she could free herself easily. And letting Asmodeus feel like he was getting closer to her only made him reveal more information. There was another teeny part of her that was trying to ignore the tiny thrill that went through her at his touch. Something she wished she could squash from her brain entirely. "Tell me about the blade," Kala said with as much seduction as she could muster.

It worked.

Asmodeus wore the same expression of every other guy Kala had ever lured into her bed when she wanted a one-night stand. Until she met Jack, Kala only believed in one-night-only deals. They were easy, no emotions, and it got the job done. And no one could deny the thrill of the chase.

Kala let Asmodeus tuck the hair back behind her ear. "You're right. It hurts all supernatural beings."

"Even Titans?" Kala cooed.

Asmodeus leaned in close so that their lips were inches from each other.

If Kala wasn't in interrogation mode, she would have been tempted to have rebound sex with Asmodeus. Talk about no strings attached. At least for her. And the chemistry she was feeling between them was intoxicating. She could almost feel his lips on hers.

Asmodeus's voice was almost a whisper, "Yes, even Titans. It's why they kept the blades under lock and key after the Grigori and Olympians were disposed of. But it doesn't strip them of their power like it does for Grigori. It only makes them weaker."

Though the tension was palpable, this new information brought Kala out of the lust fest she almost dove into. She now had a weapon that she could use against all her enemies. And, hey, a knife worked on human enemies as well.

Kala pulled away from Asmodeus, more to clear her head, than anything else. "All right, let's get back to…earth." That sounded weird. Those weren't words she ever expected to come out of her mouth.

Asmodeus was still half-leaning down for the kiss he expected. It was as if Kala pulling away was particularly torturous for him. "Right." He surveyed the metal room with seeming understanding. "You want to go somewhere more comfortable."

"You keep believing that." Kala turned on the coldness that had propelled her into many fistfights with grown men.

But Asmodeus was different. His face showed that he kind of liked Kala's refusals. It had become a game to him. A game that he apparently was enjoying thoroughly.

"As you wish." He bowed. Asmodeus gently reached out and touched Kala's arm.

Nothing happened.

Asmodeus was just as confused as Kala.

He touched her again.

Nothing.

"Uh, oh." Asmodeus cringed.

Kala's scenery warped and swirled until she stood in the same throne room that had been in Atlas's memory, but this time only one Titan was in the room.

Sitting on the throne with an expression of rage was Cronus.

Chapter Twelve

"**H**ey." Kala lamely nodded her head in greeting.

The room was much bigger to Kala in person. Though her Atlas memories felt as vivid as if she were experiencing them in person, for some reason *actually* being in the same location live felt different. It was almost as if her surroundings were extra sharp.

It was difficult to imagine fighting Cronus, since, of course, that was what Kala was trying to figure out. She had the Grigori blade tucked safely in her jacket. Knowing that it could hurt the Titan was enough for her; it was simply about how to land a hit.

Cronus's voice rumbled as he spoke. "How dare you enter my realm."

"Neat trick with the voice. Is that supposed to intimidate me or something?" It absolutely *did* intimidate Kala, but she wouldn't let Cronus know that. Keep him off guard. It was the only way she could see of having a remote chance to escape.

"It should intimidate you because I could crush you with a mere thought," Cronus bellowed.

Kala was an excellent poker player: she knew a bluff when she saw one. "If that were true, I'd be dead already. So why don't we get to the point. What do you want from me?" Kala hoped the terror that she felt inside didn't show. Unlike Cronus, bluffing was one of her strong suits so she crossed her fingers that he was buying it. And if she could garner information out of the guy, then hey, bonus.

Cronus studied Kala. She knew that look. She had certainly seen it enough when people couldn't figure her out: surprise. She puzzled the Titan. "I see Atlas inside of you, but you are nothing like him." He may have been thrown off by Kala's responses, but his face was still etched with fury. Cronus didn't like being caught off guard any more than he liked intruders. She was the enemy and he was weighing his options. Kala just hoped he didn't pick the *crush her* option.

"I may have devoured your little Titan nephew or whatever, but I'm still me. And Atlas was a *douche*," Kala responded defensively. Sure the superpowers were awesome, but having memories that made her feel like a total wimp were devastating.

"I'm not sure what a douche is, but it seems to describe Atlas accurately." Cronus sat back on his throne, his eyes full of rage. "You are a conundrum."

"Is that good or bad?" Kala tried to gauge if Cronus was preparing to hurt her or not.

"I haven't decided yet," he mused, his voice laced with anger.

"I vote for good." Kala eyed her surroundings, waiting for anything Cronus might throw at her.

Cronus stared at Kala, his eyes fuming. Maybe he always looked like that. Either way, it made Kala nervous. She felt like a very tiny mouse near the maw of a very large cat. "Atlas's blood runs in your veins. I can smell it."

Rub it in.

"That's what happens when you swallow a god, I guess," Kala answered sarcastically. "Why did you bring me here?"

"How did you consume him?" Cronus leaned forward, examining Kala as if she were a lab rat. "HOW?!"

The room shook violently.

Kala stumbled but kept her footing. She tried not to sweat. This was way out of her comfort zone. What she wouldn't give for a sniper rifle and target. Kala had thought her life was hard then. Looking back, that was just child's play.

"I'll never tell you." Probably because Kala had no idea *how* she ate the Titan, but she wasn't about to tell Cronus that. *I don't know* never sounded as good at *I'll never tell.*

Cronus leapt out of his chair and in one swipe of his arm, Kala flew through the air, her body smacking a nearby pillar.

Surprisingly, it didn't hurt as much as she thought it would. All her limbs were still intact despite the crater her body had just created. But Kala knew how to fight better than anyone. And this was just a very odd fistfight.

Kala pretended to be knocked out from the blow. The way she situated her body was strategic. Her legs were bent for an easy stand-and-run while her hand rested on the hilt of the Grigori blade.

"Your human form makes you pathetic," Cronus crowed, overconfident.

Exactly what Kala needed him to be.

Kala heard, then felt, Cronus walking up to her still form.

A slight nudging of her body from Cronus's foot told her that he bought her unconsciousness act.

The Titan leaned down and Kala felt his hand as Cronus turned her head to examine her face.

Right where she wanted him.

Here goes nothing.

Kala flipped her body and thrust the knife hard into Cronus's gut.

The Titan screamed in anguish, reeling back from shock as Kala twisted the Grigori blade for added damage.

Kala knew she had to act fast. Her momentum would be gone in milliseconds. Pulling out the Grigori knife, Kala slid across the floor and slashed Cronus's Achilles tendon on his left foot as she went.

Cronus howled in rage.

He was so much faster than Kala could have imagined.

Cronus's hand was around her neck before Kala could make her next move. He tossed her like a rag doll clear across the giant hall. Remembering how graceful Asmodeus had been when Kala threw him, Kala tried to land with some kind of decorum.

Nope.

She was all limbs as she smashed into the marble wall. Another crater.

Cronus was on her fast. He lifted her up by her hair this time and crashed her down on the floor.

It shocked Kala that she was still alive. Not only alive, but only slightly beat up. The Atlas part of her could apparently take quite a beating. The human part of her wanted to demolish the Titan.

She started to understand why everyone hated Cronus.

He appeared to have healed completely from the wounds Kala inflicted. She knew she had been reaching, but she had to try.

As Cronus made her fly across the room again, Kala had enough sense to survey the chamber at startling speeds. She looked for an exit. Kala had no idea how to get out of the 5th Level of Hell, but she was a resourceful girl. She'd find a way. As her body collided with Cronus's throne, she saw the entrance at the other end of the hall.

Wracking her brain for Atlas's memories of this place, she suddenly recalled that there was a room outside this chamber than led to Iapetus's chambers. Kala knew Atlas's relationship with his father was strained, but she was technically Atlas now, so maybe she could make amends enough to ask Iapetus to teleport her back down to earth.

It was all she had.

Desperate, but Kala had to try.

Cronus charged.

This time Kala used a simple Aikido move on him. Using the momentum of his advance, Kala leaned in, blocked his grasping hand with her arm, and used his own force to throw him into a pillar.

Where Kala's body had left a small dent, Cronus's snapped it in two.

He was utterly surprised at the blow.

When Kala rushed him, she suddenly found she couldn't move.

"That's enough." Cronus dusted himself off as he stood.

No matter how hard she tried to break free, she wasn't budging.

"Afraid of a fight?" Kala couldn't stop herself from taunting even if she wanted to. "You have to use some kind of spell to stop me? You're a bigger 'fraidy cat than I thought." Kala laughed. "Hiding in the 5th? Afraid of Grigori? Afraid of everyone! You're the pathetic one!"

Cronus was all fire.

He stood in front of Kala. Ten feet of raging fury.

"I'm afraid of nothing," Cronus roared.

"Sure, buddy, and I have some swamp land in Florida I can sell you." Kala rolled her eyes.

Chances were the Florida joke went way over his head, but he must have surmised the meaning because he spat, "I could never be afraid of a puny Titan like you. You're not even worthy of my presence."

"Then why am I here? Send me to earth if I annoy this much." Kala decided to make a Hail Mary move. Briar Patch anyone?

Cronus smiled wickedly. "So, you'd abandon your Grigori boyfriend just to get back to earth. Where's the loyalty? Oh yes, I've forgotten to whom I'm speaking. You may have another skin, Atlas, but you're still the same traitor you've always been."

Kala struggled hard at that, but she was still frozen in place. "What did you do to Talan?"

Ignoring the traitor talk, Kala's heart sunk. Roberta must not have been able to reach him. Or worse, Talan had decided to stay and look for Kala despite her assurances.

"What I plan on doing to all Grigori," Cronus snarled.

A pile of what looked like thick logs appeared above Cronus's head. With a flick of his wrist, the logs flew at Kala's still form and dropped at her feet.

Talan.

Hacked.

In pieces.

His head staring at her, lifeless.

His limbs were bloodless, as if they were frozen.

"YOU KILLED HIM!" Rage burned inside Kala like lava.

Cronus laughed. "You're not the only one with a Grigori blade. And I have the other eleven. Speaking of which…" Using his Titan-telekinesis, Cronus pulled the knife from Kala's unmoving hand and into his own.

She barely noticed.

Kala couldn't see straight.

She'd never been this furious before.

Kala stared at the most powerful Titan of them all and felt no fear.

"YOU WILL PAY!" she screamed.

Cronus started to laugh again, but stopped when the whole chamber started to shake violently. His looked around in disbelief. "How are you…"

BOOM!

The invisible bonds that secured Kala in place exploded with a deafening roar.

Cronus was downright mystified and to Kala's delight…

Scared.

The ground shook even harder.

Pillars crashed to the floor.

Cronus's throne shattered into a million pieces.

"NOW YOU WILL DIE!" Kala's voice was not her own. It was like the moment when she had consumed Atlas. Something deep inside her, speaking for her, saying words she didn't understand.

Cronus's eyes filled with terror as part of the ceiling crashed down on him. "The Grigori is still alive. They can't be killed. Another Grigori can put him back together," Cronus sputtered in a panic.

Kala wanted to give into this inner voice. This inner depth that could crush Cronus where he stood, but she knew that it was wrong.

Talan was alive. In pieces but alive.

The bellowing rage disappeared. Whatever was inside her, crawled back down to her subconscious.

But one thing it left her with.

Knowledge.

Knowledge of powers Kala hadn't been aware of.

For one: telekinesis.

"I'll be taking what's mine," Kala said and made the Grigori blade fly back into her hand.

Cronus stared at her, afraid she would destroy him.

And for another: she could teleport.

Kneeling down next to the mound of body parts that were Talan, Kala gave Cronus one last snarky grin. "Later." She saluted.

Kala touched Talan's body and they vanished.

Chapter Thirteen

In a sudden rush, Kala landed in the last place she imagined.

The Compound.

More specifically, General Turner's lab. Kala remembered this room. It was where Turner introduced her to the tranquilizer gun that helped her fight Malaks and Demons. The actual size of the room was huge, almost the size of a football field. There were computers, wires, electronics, and robotic parts covering almost every inch of the place. After teleporting herself for the first time, Kala felt a little dizzy from the onslaught of metal and lights. She was still kneeling with Talan's body parts at her feet.

"Lieutenant Hicks?"

Kala looked up, General Turner stood above her. He appeared more curious than shocked. Something she was getting used to with the man. When he saw Talan's bloodless limbs, he glanced at her with concern. "Is that a person?"

Kala stood up, shaking her head. "It's Talan, the angel you met before. And, apparently he's not dead. He just needs to be put back together."

Turner nodded to two scientists working at their respective stations. They walked over like mindless servants.

Inspecting the room, Kala noticed that aside from the two scientists, there were only three others in the giant space.

"Get a table and put him on it," Turner ordered. As the two men left, he turned to Kala. "This is the angel that you wanted Roberta to contact?"

"Yes." Kala tried to use as few words as possible. Her mind still reeled from what had just happened.

Turner scrutinized *the Talan pile*. "Fascinating. You said this is the same man who appears to my wife as Pierre?"

Kala nodded. Revealing *that* might not have been a great idea, but desperation had made the decision for her. And for no reason it appeared. Kala damned Talan for being stubborn and loyal, traits she normally admired, but now made her feel horribly guilty.

"Pierre taught my wife powerful magic. That's where she learned how to make that ooze that works so well on Demons." Turner seemed quite chipper for someone who stood next to a pile of body parts. He was definitely an odd one. Then he said something that made her pause. "I'm assuming he's actually Dr. Fortski as well?"

Kala laughed, it threw her off so much. Her mission was to destroy Fortski's work, but he was so brilliant Turner thought that the doc had to be supernatural. "Nope. Fortski's the real deal." Kala didn't elaborate because she didn't want to reveal her mission. She also didn't want to divulge any more of Talan's secrets. He'd be mad enough at her for the whole *Pierre* thing. Nice name by the way. Wonder how long it took him to come up with that one.

The two scientists returned with a metal table on wheels and began piecing Talan together. After a few moments, they had loosely connected his body together. They left without a word, returning to their stations.

The current circumstances were bizarre enough, but the two scientists only added to the weirdness factor.

Kala detached herself from the situation to keep her head on straight. Having Talan thrown at her by Cronus awoke something inside her. It terrified Kala. She couldn't admit that to anyone but herself. The supernatural world needed to believe that she was not only unshakeable, but someone to be feared. Her legs shook from the confrontation. Not because of the fight, but because she didn't know where her power came from. Kala had consumed Atlas and if she was honest with herself, she knew that she could have done the same thing with Cronus.

He knew and she knew it.

And he was scared.

…But so was she.

"Clifton can't know I'm here."

Turner threw Kala a look that suggested he wasn't an idiot. "If I can hide Mr. Echolls under Clifton's nose, I think I can hide you. And I'm assuming after you've put Humpty Dumpty back together again you'll be on your way?" Turner examined Talan with fascination.

Derek.

"Is Derek okay?"

Turner kept studying Talan's body parts with fascination as he talked with Kala. "Mr. Echolls is fine. I thought you would make more use out of him."

"Trust me, that wasn't my idea. Talan thought Derek would be safer, and considering what happened to *him* I think it was the right call." Kala's heart squeezed as she stared at Talan.

Turner nodded at the disassembled body. "It appears so."

Kala ran her hand through her hair, observing the room. "I don't even know how I got here. I've just discovered that I apparently have teleportation powers and it was a quick exit. I guess my brain sent me somewhere familiar," Kala rationalized.

"Well, you've only been to this lab once, but I'd say it was a pretty productive trip the last time you were here," Turner observed.

He was right. It was the first time Kala had witnessed a *regular old human* actually hurt Asmodeus. Turner had used the tranq gun filled with Roberta's mojo juice and injected it into the Demon. Asmodeus turned into a crying baby, giving Kala enough time to escape. Kala had felt like she had a fighting chance after that. It made sense that her mind would take her here.

Maybe Turner had some more toys she could use.

Kala couldn't stop staring at Talan's broken form.

Even though she logically told herself that Talan was still alive, part of her doubted Cronus. What if Talan really was dead? It bothered her more than she liked. The guy had been her backup throughout this whole ordeal. She may not share the same feelings for him that he had for her, but Kala cared about him. Talan had helped her when he shouldn't have and saved her when it would have been safer for him to let her die.

Only one person could help Talan now.

Owen.

"I need to get someone here who can help," Kala announced to Turner.

Turner waved to her encouragingly. "By all means. You can come and go as you please apparently."

"I don't think I have to. I think I can bring him here." Kala had no idea how to pinpoint her foster father and teleport to him. She figured that whole mind-speech thing that Roberta did would work better. She just needed to figure out how to use it with someone besides Roberta. "I have to concentrate." Kala turned away from Talan's body.

Now what?

Kala closed her eyes.

Owen? Kala felt like an idiot. Why did she think this would work?

Because it works with Roberta. Kala scolded herself.

And when was talking to herself a good idea?

Kala wanted to scream. She needed Owen and she had no idea how to connect with him, let alone contact him in any other form.

OWEN! Kala screamed in her head.

"I'm here, Kala."

Kala opened her eyes. Standing in front of her was her foster father, Owen. She fell into his arms, relief flooding through every vein. Kala only recently found out that Owen was a Grigori angel like Talan, but it didn't make her look at him any differently. Owen and Linda had saved her life as a foster kid. They were the first two people who ever showed her what it meant to love. Kala might not be related to them by blood, but they were her parents. Period.

Owen's arms felt like the most comfortable place on the planet right then. Kala wished she could stay there forever. But eventually Owen pulled away to look her in the eye.

"What is it, Kala? Are you okay?" His face was all concern.

Kala nodded behind her at Talan.

Owen looked over her shoulder and his eyes widened. He hurried to Talan's body. "Who did this?"

"Cronus," Kala answered. She couldn't help but notice Turner's eyebrow raise at that. Kala admired the fact that Turner knew when to be quiet, not in the sense of being polite, more like he was observing and gathering information. No wonder Talan sought him out. The guy was a sponge.

Owen stared at Kala even more shocked. "How did you escape without Talan to help you?"

Kala turned to Turner. "I'm not sure how much I should say with some of these guys in the room." She gestured toward the handful of scientists. Sure, they seemed pre-occupied, but if just one of them was a spy for Clifton – or worse a Demon – Kala didn't want to say too much.

Turner shrugged, not concerned. "They're loyal only to me. You can say anything you like."

Kala wasn't convinced. "You can't guarantee that."

Owen gave Turner a knowing look. "Yes, he can."

Kala looked at Owen, surprised. "You know something I don't?"

Owen said pointedly, "Let's just say these workers couldn't say anything even if they wanted to."

"Magic?" Kala asked. Maybe Roberta had put them in some kind of worker-bee spell. It would explain their drone-like behavior.

Owen nodded. "Something like that. The point is you can trust them. Now, tell me what happened with Cronus?"

"I'm not sure." Which was the truth. Kala still wasn't positive what had happened, but she told Owen and Turner everything that took place. Maybe one of them would have some insight.

Turner didn't look fazed at all, probably because all this talk of Titans and angels wasn't in his wheelhouse of experience. Turner was a science guy. Magic and mythology was more his wife's cup of tea. Though from the expression on his face, his curiosity was definitely piqued.

Owen, however, appeared rocked. His eyes didn't seem like they'd ever blink again. "Kala," was all that came out.

"What does it mean?" Kala was afraid of the answer, but she had to ask.

"I can't say for sure." Owen's voice was hoarse as if what Kala had said took the wind out of him. "There are so many things about you that are impossible. We've just added another one to the list." Owen managed a smile. "You still have the blade?" Owen asked. Kala pulled it out and he nodded in approval. "You hold onto that. We may need to use it."

Kala tucked it back into her jacket.

Kala knew Owen's smile was to make her feel better, but she also knew that he was seriously freaked. He turned his attention back to Talan. "Maybe Talan will know. Let's put him back together."

Turner asked Owen, "Is there anything you need from me?"

Owen motioned to Talan's shredded clothing. "He's going to need something to wear."

"Of course." Turner motioned to one of his zombie-scientists to fetch some clothes.

Owen suddenly looked self-conscious as he turned to Kala. "We're going to have to strip him down. Maybe you should turn around."

"I've seen a naked man before." Kala shook her head with a smile. It reminded her that Owen was still her dad and she would always be his little girl.

Owen looked embarrassed. "Right. Good to know."

But Kala knew it wasn't really *good to know*. Owen didn't want to discuss Kala's love life any more than she did. He was actually blushing. It was hilarious.

"Let's get this done." Kala took the initiative and ripped off what was left of Talan's clothing. She let Owen take care of the crotch area. No need to mortify him any more than she had to.

In order to cope with the disturbing sight, Kala made herself see Talan as a disassembled mannequin.

At this point, Kala and Turner were just by-standers. Neither one of them could turn away from what was happening.

Owen began at Talan's feet. His hands glowed a warm hue of gold. When Owen touched the gap between Talan's feet and the bottom part of his legs, the two fused together. It was quick work after that: each body part reattached with Owen's glowing hands, until finally all that was left was Talan's head.

It all came down to this moment for Kala. She trusted Owen's abilities implicitly, but part of her doubted that Talan could be saved. The concept of a real person being chopped up into pieces and reassembled without a scratch on them was a thing of fiction to Kala. She knew Talan wasn't *human*, but that was how she saw him.

Kala held her breath as Owen laid his glowing hands on Talan's neck.

Talan shot up to sitting position, gasping for air.

Before Kala could think better of it, she reached over and pulled Talan into a hug. Feeling his arms around her made her feel immense relief. He was okay. He was alive.

He was naked.

Kala pulled away and kept her eyes focused on Talan's. She didn't want her view roaming to… other places.

Talan apparently could care less about his nakedness. His eyes were alight with his feelings for Kala. No matter how many times Kala put him in his place, Talan couldn't hide his emotions for her.

And at that exact second, it felt good. Kala had never thought she'd see him look at her ever again. Let alone with so much affection.

"Clothes." Turner handed Talan a stack of folded attire.

Fatigues and a white t-shirt. It fit perfectly. A little too perfectly. The boy looked good. The shoes were standard issue army boots.

Kala had to admire that a Grigori angel could look like a boot camp grunt.

Talan was on his feet. He embraced Owen and shook hands with Turner.

"We should leave." Talan took charge. To Turner he said, "Thank you for your hospitality, but this place isn't safe for Kala."

"I couldn't agree more. Three levels above us Clifton is planning an all-out manhunt for Ms. Hicks here. The sooner you leave, the better." Turner was on the same page as Talan.

Kala asked, "Where to?"

Owen responded first. "Your mother wants to see you."

That sounded amazing to Kala. The thought of seeing Linda made Kala feel like her heart might be able to start to mend. There was nothing like the healing embrace of a mother.

Kala and Talan agreed.

Owen reached out and touched the two of them.

Nothing.

Kala was having flashbacks from the 5th. What? Did Cronus stop teleporting in the Compound as well?

Talan touched Owen and Kala, trying to use his teleporting power instead.

Nothing.

"What's happening?" Owen focused on Turner.

Turner was genuinely baffled. "I have no idea."

Before Kala could truly process her situation…

General Clifton and a team of his men marched into the room.

Their guns were raised and they were all pointed at Kala.

Chapter Fourteen

Clifton's smug expression made Kala's skin crawl. "After our last teleporting visitor, I made some changes to our defenses."

Turner looked impressed. "How did you pull that off, Harry?"

Harry didn't even look mad at Turner. Their relationship went beyond Kala's understanding. She could see that she wasn't going to get any help from Turner though, not when Clifton was standing next to him. He had to protect his own neck.

Clifton shrugged. "You have your scientists, I have mine."

"I'd like to meet yours." Turner raised an eyebrow in curiosity.

"I bet you would," Clifton guffawed.

Watching their exchange was fascinating. But Kala didn't want to kill soldiers, she just wanted to get out of there.

"You know you can't hurt us, right?" Kala wanted to wipe the triumphant smirk off Clifton's face.

The smirk didn't go away. He didn't believe her. "I saw the security footage from yesterday's attack. I know about your shielding technology.

And you're not leaving here until we get it from you."

Clifton included Turner in his *we*. The sad part was that Turner knew Talan's *shielding technology* was supernatural.

"Good luck with that. He used magic." Kala loved that it sounded absurd. And she loved that it was true.

Kala couldn't believe she had been scared of Clifton as her superior. He was such a tool. Of course, the fact that she was an immortal Titan helped curb the fear of ten guns being pointed at her, but still. It was nice standing up to him. He reminded Kala of every bully she'd ever encountered in her life.

As her boss, she had to put up with it.

As a god, not so much.

Clifton didn't buy Kala's *magic* comment for a second. He didn't live in that reality. He lived in the reality where rival governments were constantly developing new and cutting edge weapons. Clifton thought she was a smart ass (which she was), and he didn't like it.

"We're leaving." Kala turned to Turner. "Where did you get me out last time?" She knew she shouldn't remind Clifton of the fact that Turner helped her escape, but it was so hard not to want to take him down a few notches.

Turner sighed. "You know I can't tell you that."

Kala saw Turner touch the face of his watch. If she hadn't been staring at him, she wouldn't have noticed. No one else seemed to. Was he giving her a signal? Was he trying to say something about time? Kala was immortal, so she didn't have to worry about dying, but the Compound was miles deep and miles wide. There was no way she was getting out of there without help. Kala had limited knowledge of the layout of the Compound. She had only been allowed into a few designated areas. It was a maze that Kala did not have a key to.

"Enough!" Clifton bellowed. "Take them. If they resist, kill them."

The guy was a fool.

Clifton's men kept their guns raised as they closed the distance between themselves and Kala.

Kala knew they were just doing their job. She also knew that these soldiers weren't about to capture two Grigori and a Titan. In military-mode, Kala loved to use any advantage available to her. And being a god was definitely an advantage.

Owen barely moved his hand: Clifton and his men dropped to the floor.

"Okay," Kala observed. "That was easy."

"They're out cold for a few hours." Owen focused his attention on Turner, who looked quite amused. "A way out?"

"Right." Turner eyed Clifton's unconscious body, contemplating. "I'm afraid the escape route Ms. Hicks left through the last time has been closed off. Harry's security measures. But, since I clearly didn't realize how fast you'd take care of *this* situation, I already called for backup."

As if on cue, Derek entered the room, gun at the ready. Seeing Clifton and his men sprawled on the ground, he lowered his weapon and placed it in its holster. He smiled at Kala. "I knew you had this handled." Derek recognized Owen and saluted. "Sir. Good to see you again."

Owen saluted back. "I know you've been looking out for my daughter, and I'm eternally grateful."

"I'm not sure how much I've really done to help, but I'll always have Kala's back," Derek responded.

Drawing Derek into a hug, she whispered, "Thank you." As she pulled away she said, "And teleporting you away was not my idea."

"I figured. Can you even do that?" Derek treaded on territory Kala wasn't so sure he wanted to know about.

But she was honest with him. "Apparently so."

Talan was surprised, and Kala responded, "How do you think I got you out of the 5th?"

"I figured Owen answered Roberta's call and rescued you," Talan admitted.

Owen stepped in. "It's far greater than that, Talan. What Kala is capable of…" he didn't finish his thought. Kala could tell it was because he was afraid she couldn't handle it. Such a dad.

"We can discuss my *amazing* powers later." Kala glanced at Derek and Turner. "Get us out of here."

Derek liked orders. He had confided in Kala once that orders made him feel grounded. In their line of work, there was too much chaos in the world and having a chain of command made the terrifying easier to cope with.

Nodding for them to follow, Derek led Kala, Talan, and Owen through the giant research lab to the exit door. Kala remembered coming in through this same door just a few days ago to get away from Asmodeus. She was amazed that Derek knew where he was going since this part of the Compound was a complete labyrinth to her.

Once outside the room, they entered a series of hallways. The walls used the same black metal that most of the Compound was constructed from. Whatever ingredient was in it supposedly made the entire structure invisible to radar. Being that this place housed devices that most of the public was unaware existed, secrecy was the highest priority.

Kala followed Derek closely, with Talan and Owen trailing. Soldiers' weapons weren't a threat to the three of them, so they walked with confidence. Derek was the only vulnerable member of their party, but Kala and her two Grigori would keep him safe.

No, the real mystery was how Clifton had managed to prevent teleportation out of the Compound. Clifton saw Asmodeus's surprise arrival as a weapon, so somehow he had found a way to block supernatural activity without even knowing it. Kala had to find out how. If she could stop Malaks and Demons from popping in or out any time they felt like wreaking havoc on her, it would be invaluable. Turner would find out. And when he found out, she'd find out.

Turner and Roberta turned out to be strong allies. It shouldn't be surprising, considering Talan had picked the two of them to train. It just surprised Kala because Turner had been so intimidating when he was her boss. It was amazing how becoming a Titan relieved all fears of Clifton and Turner. Power could do that. Before, with a snap of their fingers, Kala could be dead.

Now, they couldn't touch her.

Apparently, the only thing they *could* do was prevent her from leaving.

And after she had just learned to teleport.

Figured.

Several elevator rides and staircases later, Derek steered them deeper into the bowels of the Compound.

"Shouldn't we be going *up*?" Kala asked as they entered yet another elevator going down.

"We have to go down to go up," Derek answered. "Trust me. This is the best way to avoid Clifton and his lackeys."

"I'm not really worried about them," Kala admitted honestly. "I just want to get out of here."

Derek shook his head. "I get that. But I'm still working for Turner and *I* need to get in and out of here on a daily basis."

"You're right, sorry." Kala hadn't thought about that.

"No worries. We're almost there," Derek informed her.

Kala sighed inwardly. She was so involved in what was happening to her, she hadn't even considered how Derek was managing to survive. Working for Turner required being at the Compound – and the Compound was half Clifton's. *Of course* Derek needed a stealthy way of entering and leaving the high-tech structure.

And it was all her fault.

If Kala had never become the next Atlas, then Derek would still be an elite soldier working for Turner *and* Clifton. Not one side against the other. There was nothing she could do about that, but it still hurt. Derek was a better friend than she was.

Kala vowed then and there to keep Derek safe at all costs.

Speaking of *safe*, Kala wondered why the Compound appeared to be deserted. They hadn't run into a single person on their long trek into the depths of the building. It didn't shock Kala, since the whole building was a giant security entity, but a part of her was a little surprised at the lack of people.

Another long hallway and one metal staircase later they arrived at a steel door. It had a retinal scan security lock. Derek placed his eye in the proper location and the tiny lasers scanned his eyeball.

With a loud KERCHUNK, the door opened.

Derek explained, "This is Turner's private lab. Clifton leaves it alone so it's safe for me. The exit to the surface is in here."

Kala entered with the rest of them.

Her heart stopped.

Kala stood in the lab from her vision.

This was where she was supposed to destroy Fortski's research and his cure for cancer.

"Okay. *Really* need to leave." Kala gulped.

Chapter Fifteen

"**W**hat? Labs freak you out now?" Derek teased.

"Yes. Yes, they do." Kala didn't want to elaborate. She tried to hide the emotions she felt. From the tables to the computers to the experiments, it was identical to her vision. The only thing different was the fact that Fortski's three computers were intact and not destroyed.

The place reminded Kala of the lab in Roberta and Turner's house, where Fortski had injected her with a drug that allowed her to confront Atlas. Of course, it was this confrontation that led to Kala consuming the Titan, but that wasn't Fortski's fault.

As if thinking of the man made him appear, Fortski walked into view. He appeared to be the only person in the room. It had been the same at Roberta and Turner's. Apparently, the guy liked to work alone.

Which was the key factor to making her mission easier. If Fortski was this private in his working environment, he was most likely even more private when sharing his research. Destroying his computers would be enough.

Just as her vision showed her.

A part of her wanted to do it now. Get it over with. This was only her second Atlas mission, but when she had been a soldier, her missions had never been given to her on a silver platter like now. Derek would think she was crazy, but Talan and Owen could hold him off.

But what would be next?

The clock would reset.

Kala glanced at the clock on one of the walls: 2d 03h 12m 43s

1:48 AM!

Almost to Day Three!

But maybe in those two days she could find Zeus and force him to take this curse away from her. Then she'd never have to ruin the research of the most brilliant man alive that would save millions of lives.

No. Kala couldn't perform her task now.

Not when there was a shred of hope.

It might only be a shred, but it was enough.

Killing Jack had destroyed her in ways she couldn't comprehend yet, and he was only one life.

Destroying the cure for cancer would kill so many innocent people. And she would be responsible. Maybe indirectly, but that was semantics to Kala. She'd feel the weight of every loss of life as if she had shot them herself.

Despite the fact that Jack was supposed to be Atlas's surrogate and not her, Kala had to believe that he would want the universe to be in the hands of the *universe*. Not in one person. The curse shouldn't exist. Zeus was an idiot.

And Kala was going to make the Olympian make amends.

Fortski seemed a little surprised at the unexpected guests, but when he saw Kala and Talan, he managed a friendly smile. "Ms. Hicks, Mr. Talan, good to see you again. I trust all your issues have been resolved?" he asked pointedly at Kala.

Fortski had a front row seat in the battle to integrate Atlas into

Kala's human form. As a scientist, he must have found the whole thing fascinating, but at the time, he was at a loss. Kala wasn't even sure he truly understood what had happened. Even if he did, he may not believe it. His work was about curing diseases.

Or was it?

It suddenly occurred to Kala that she had no idea what Fortski's work was about. Sure, she knew he had just found the cure for cancer, but had that been his goal? He was employed by a covert military general. Somehow cancer research didn't seem a likely topic of interest for him.

But Kala could only go on what she knew. And what she knew was that, whether intentional or not, Fortski had found the cure for cancer and Kala's job was to destroy it.

Kala responded to Fortski's greeting with a smile of her own. "Dr. Fortski. Good to see you again. I'm doing fine, thank you."

"Good. Good to hear it," Fortski replied jovially.

There was something about Fortski that Kala really liked. He had an air of discovery about him that showed in his enthusiastic expression. It was almost painful for Kala to see, knowing what she might have to do…

"We really need to leave." Kala's patience was at an end. She couldn't be in this lab a second longer.

Owen glanced at Kala with a look of worry. "There's something here that scares you. What is it, Kala? Is it this man?"

Always the protective father, Owen was misreading Kala's desire to save Fortski's work as being wary of the scientist.

Kala was never very good at hiding her emotions from the people that knew her. "I'm fine. I just want to get away from this place and find Zeus."

Fortski's eyes widened. "As in the god Zeus?"

Kala grasped how ridiculous that would sound to someone like Fortski, but she was surprised to see that he was genuinely asking. Maybe he actually believed her infusion into a Titan god. Working for Turner and Roberta, the guy had to have seen some pretty crazy things.

"I know that sounds insane," Kala began.

But Fortski shook his head. "Not at all. Geoffrey explained everything to me. Some of my research is based on the results we found in your brain scan, Ms. Hicks. That was before you completely integrated with the deity, of course, but the results were quite fascinating nonetheless."

Owen didn't let Kala change the subject. "I know that look, Kala. What's wrong?"

Derek and Talan stared at Kala as well. The more scrutiny, the harder it was to keep up her poker face. "Just leave it alone." To Derek, she pleaded, "Out. Now."

It was Talan who spoke next. "Your mission. It's in this room."

"What!" Kala exclaimed a little too loudly. "You're crazy." To Derek she added urgently, "Seriously, Derek, let's go."

Kala walked ahead even though she had no idea where she was going. She just needed to move. The last thing she wanted to do was to have a blowout with two angels and Derek.

Fortski seemed intrigued by the suggestion. "Mission? In here? What kind of mission?"

Kala spun around, defensive. "There is no mission. Can we drop it, please?"

Owen stepped toward her. "Kala, we can help you. Just tell us what it is."

"I said, drop it!" Kala's temper got the best of her.

Derek knew better than to push Kala. He nodded toward the north side of the room. "This way."

"Thank you!" Kala harrumphed.

Before Kala could follow Derek to the exit, she felt Owen's hand on her arm. "Kala, stop." His voice was calm and steady. "It might be easier with us here."

Kala's panic flared. "I can't!"

"What are the odds that you'd be in the very spot of your mission? How do you expect to get back in here?"

Owen tried to be rational, but Kala didn't want to hear it. "As we know, I can teleport in, I just can't teleport out!" she said with the attitude of an unruly teenager.

Derek stepped in at this point. "I think we should go. She obviously doesn't want to do whatever it is you guys are talking about."

Fortski piped in, "Maybe I can help you?"

His words made Kala even more upset. All she could see was the look of anguish that would be in Fortski's face when she destroyed all his work from her vision.

"You definitely can not help." Kala needed space. She took a few steps back from everyone and ran her hand through her hair nervously.

"Kala…" Talan began.

She cut him off. "Talan, don't." Kala turned to Owen. "I still have two days. Two days to get out of this curse. Please, just give me those two days."

"I'll give you all the time you want. That's not the issue. You have an opportunity to complete your task with people who love you. You're not alone." Owen looked like he wanted to hug her, but Kala kept her distance.

"If you knew what it was…" She shook her head.

"Tell us, then," Owen prodded.

"NO! Just trust me. You don't want me to do this. And if Zeus can release me of this curse, then it won't need to happen and the universe can do its own damn work. Let the chips fall as they may." Kala stared at Owen. "Please don't make me."

Owen nodded. He turned to Derek. "Let's go."

Fortski wasn't ready for them to leave. "I really can help. Anything you need."

Kala turned to the scientist and smiled sadly. "Hopefully, you'll never see me again."

Apparently, the way Kala said it made Fortski's face turn white. "I see."

Kala didn't want to wait for another response from Fortski. She glanced at Derek. He may not know what was going on, but with everything he had seen over the last few days, Derek knew it was something big. And his first priority was to save his friend.

"Follow me," Derek directed. He led them across the room, leaving Fortski behind.

Kala hoped she wouldn't have to come back there, but her mission-based side was comforted by the fact that at least she knew where to go if need be. She was less than two hours away from Day Three, but Kala was determined to find Zeus. Forty-eight hours had to be enough. She was running on no sleep, but adrenaline was keeping her alert. Not knowing how long that would last, she concentrated on leaving the Compound.

Derek ushered them out a door that in turn led them up a long staircase. Steps that kept going and going and going. Kala was surprised at the fact that she was hardly winded at all. Granted, she was as in-shape as an elite soldier could be, but even under ideal circumstances this many stairs would exhaust a marathon runner. Kala heard Derek panting, slightly out of breath, and he was the healthiest guy she knew.

Besides Jack.

The thought grabbed her chest and made it tighten.

Jack should be beside her, and he never would be.

Kala compartmentalized before she broke down. Swallowing up her emotions was second nature for her. Being an abandoned child, she learned this skill early on. Facing her feelings was completely new to her and Kala wasn't very good at it. Shoving everything down felt natural, normal. It might be unhealthy, but it was what made her a good soldier.

Looking back at Talan and Owen, they hadn't even broken a sweat. Evidently, Grigori were immune to exertion as well.

Derek informed them in the dark, "About a hundred feet to the surface."

The last set of stairs went quickly. They came to a top hatch with another eye scanner. Derek placed his eye in front of it and the device lit up green. Pushing with his right shoulder, Derek lifted the round door and flopped it onto the concrete above.

Stepping into the early morning air felt more amazing than Kala could describe. From being stuck in the 5th for an entire day to being in the bellows of the Compound, Kala missed fresh air. It felt crisp and chilled her cheeks. She took in a deep breath as Talan and Owen exited the Compound to join her.

Kala knew where they were: about a mile from the main entrance point to the Compound. She could see the dilapidated warehouses in the distance, perfect cover for the military base. Since the underground facility was made of untraceable metal, any enemy flying overhead would see abandoned buildings, nothing more.

Derek shut the top hatch and it blended in perfectly with the ground. "We're exposed out here. Behind that set of trees is my jeep." Derek moved swiftly towards his car.

The landscape was cracked dirt and shrubbery with a few pockets of trees here and there. It had the appearance of a dump. But it was an exit, and that was all that mattered.

Within a few seconds they all arrived at Derek's jeep. It was covered in a camouflage mesh tarp, which he quickly bundled up and tossed in the back.

Before Derek could enter his car, Talan put up his hand for him to halt. "We may not need to drive. Let's see how far Clifton's teleport-shield goes." Talan reached over and touched Derek.

Nothing.

"That's crazy." Kala was shocked. "How can he restrict teleporting out, but not in? He's not that smart. And if he had any scientists that were that smart, Turner would know about it!"

"He had help," a voice sounded from behind them.

Kala knew that voice.

Turning around, she came face to face with Rotoph.

But what really made her furious was the person standing next to him.

Penny.

Chapter Sixteen

"**W**e leave you behind and you turn to the enemy? Shocker," Kala accused Penny. She had started to like the girl, but Rotoph? Was Penny really that stupid?

Penny kept her eyes on Kala. "Just listen. Rotoph is on *our* side."

Before Kala could utter a hearty laugh, Owen moved faster than Kala would have thought possible. He had Rotoph in a chokehold before anyone could move.

Rotoph teleported out of Owen's grasp, reappearing a few feet away. "Owen! I need to talk to you."

Before Owen could attack a second time, Kala put her hand up to stop him. She pulled out the Grigori blade and nodded toward Rotoph. "Will you agree to let me take your powers away so we can talk?" She decided to be diplomatic since she suspected that Rotoph may have freed Zeus from the 5th. Plus, the sight of her foster father getting into a brawl with another Grigori wasn't something Kala wanted to see.

Rotoph nodded his agreement.

Owen still looked like he was on the verge of pouncing, but he stayed where he was.

Kala carefully walked over to Rotoph with the blade in hand.

Rotoph gave her a small smile. "Not the throat this time."

"If it weren't for the fact that we need you to talk…" Kala gently sliced a nick on Rotoph's wrist. "Okay. You've got five minutes."

Owen went to Kala's side. "We don't need five minutes. Now that his powers are gone we can teleport out of here."

Kala had never thought of that. They could leave right now before Clifton awoke from the Grigori-sleep-bomb and caused them more trouble. If Rotoph was the one helping Clifton, then teleportation was back on the table.

But there was something to the fact that Rotoph let himself be disarmed. Whatever he wanted to say, Rotoph thought they'd want to hear it. And if her suspicions were correct about Rotoph and Zeus…

"Let's just listen," Kala suggested cautiously.

Owen shook his head. "Kala you don't know him. We listened to him before and he betrayed us. He engraved that knife you're holding. A knife like that one that tore Talan into pieces. Trust me, Rotoph is our enemy."

"Owen…" Rotoph began, but Kala stopped him.

"Don't speak. You're not helping your cause." Kala turned to Owen. "You have a personal beef with this guy, I get that, but something tells me we should listen. If we don't like what he has to say, we leave him here. Without his powers, he's not going anywhere."

Owen paused. After a few moments of thinking, he gave a slight nod.

Rotoph looked relieved. He focused his attention on Kala since she appeared to be the only one willing to listen. "I know my brothers will never believe me, but I'm trying to make amends for the mistake I made. I was power hungry, and Cronus offered me the world, and I took it. But he fooled me like he fooled the Olympians. I've been his slave for the past 2,000 years…"

Talan interrupted with anger, "Are we supposed to feel sorry for you?

You're not telling us anything we don't already know."

Talan had been so quiet during this whole confrontation Kala had almost forgotten he was there. But apparently, hearing Rotoph complain about being Cronus's bitch was too much for him.

Rotoph was annoyed. "Yeah, because the 5th Heaven was so horrible. I made sure you were banished in paradise!" he shouted the last part.

Kala had to agree. She had seen the Grigori prison and it was spectacularly beautiful. At this very moment though, she didn't want to take Rotoph's side in front of Talan and Owen. "Just continue, please," she prodded Rotoph.

"Prison is prison!" Talan wasn't letting it go. He turned to Owen. "Why are we still listening to him?"

Rotoph forced eye contact with Talan, then Owen. "Because I'm the one who freed you."

Pin drop.

Rotoph took advantage of the silence to continue, "Didn't you ever wonder how you were able to break out? Did you really think you were powerful enough to escape a prison that strips you of all your powers?" He looked at them as if they were ludicrous to even consider the notion.

His answer was more silence, which indicated to Kala that they hadn't really considered that they'd had help from the outside.

Owen was the first to speak. "Only five of us were able to leave."

Rotoph nodded. "The strongest. Yes, I know. I've kept tabs on all of you for the entire two hundred years you've been out. I need you to free our brothers and sisters, but it's Talan's skills I need most. Please. Help me."

Talan started to soften. "I want to trust you, Rotoph."

"What possible motivation would I have to trick you? There are only five of you. The Titans could crush you if they pooled their resources. I was a fool. Please. Let me prove myself to you," Rotoph begged.

Kala had to admit that Rotoph seemed sincere.

Derek was on a time crunch because he said, "I may be the only *human* here, and I get that you guys could probably stop any military attack, but I really don't want to be around to see it. Can we have this conversation somewhere else?" He air-quoted "human," of course.

It must have been strange for Derek not to consider Kala human, but he was the kind of soldier that took everything in and went with it. Derek's period of adjustment on the *stranger than fiction* table was over and he was on board with anything that came his way. Derek was also practical. As much as he wanted to help Kala's cause, his future safety was at stake. "This is my only way into the Compound and if it's compromised, I'm screwed."

Kala wasn't about to let her friend be in the lurch like that. "Let's go. Now."

All of sudden Penny decided she wanted to be a part of the conversation. "No. We take care of this now." She turned to Rotoph. "You promised!"

Kala could hear Derek groan. He always hated hysterics. Kala had to agree. It was annoying.

Owen was the calm one, though. "Promised what, Pandora?"

Even Owen knew who she truly was. It didn't surprise Kala, but it made her wonder how small a circle this whole gods/angel/demon thing was.

"Tell them!" Penny ordered Rotoph.

Rotoph looked directly at Kala when he said, "I can take you to Zeus. I'm the one who freed him." When Penny continued to stare him down, he added, "And Hephaestus."

Hephaestus was definitely for Penny's sake, but Zeus? Kala could feel the stirrings of hope rise up in her. Her guess had been correct: Rotoph had freed Zeus from the 5th Level of Hell. And now Kala would have a chance to confront him and make him take away her curse.

"When do we leave?" Kala was in full mission-mode.

Rotoph had an apologetic expression on his face. "I'd love to, but someone took away my powers."

Kala wanted to punch something, but she knew there was nothing anyone could do. Only Rotoph knew the location and only *he* could teleport them there. They'd have to wait out the effects of the Grigori blade.

But not there.

"To your place?" Kala asked Talan.

Talan nodded and motioned for the small group to gather around him. "Everyone, grab on."

At the same time, Kala and the others touched Talan's shoulders.

A disorienting moment later, they all stood in Talan's small apartment.

Derek's face showed little of the discomfort Kala was certain he was in.

It was crowded in the tiny space and the situation struck Kala as funny somehow. Three Grigori, Pandora (as in the actual Pandora), a Titan, and Derek all in a Washington D.C. apartment overlooking the Washington Monument. It felt like the beginning of some awful joke.

"How long before we leave?" Kala asked Rotoph.

"An hour, maybe two." Rotoph plopped on the couch before anyone else could.

Kala looked at the time: 2d 01h 20m 12s

3:40 AM.

An hour and twenty minutes until Day Three.

Kala's life was all about time now. Always a race. She hoped Zeus was the key.

Since everyone stood around awkwardly, Kala took Rotoph's cue and sat down beside him. She needed to be off her feet even if it was for just a few seconds. Being a Titan didn't mean she couldn't get tired.

Rotoph looked surprised by Kala's presence right next to him, but seemed pleased at the same time. "I've heard about you," he confided.

"Good for you." Kala didn't feel like talking about herself, least of all to a Grigori traitor. He was a means to an end. Kala's way to Zeus. Being pals wasn't on the agenda.

"Your attitude being the most prominent." Rotoph sounded amused. "I had the same reputation amongst the other Grigori."

"Please don't compare yourself to me." Kala started to feel like she'd made a bad decision sitting next to him.

"No? I had a destiny I didn't want to fulfill so I banished my own people. You have a destiny to fulfill, and you're running to Zeus to get out of it. We're not that different." Rotoph leaned his head back against the couch.

"The difference is I have to do it every four days," Kala complained. She couldn't be mad at Rotoph. He saw things the way he saw things; nothing she said would change his mind. Rotoph needed to connect with someone from this little posse and apparently, he had chosen Kala as his willing victim. "What was your *destiny* that you felt the need to imprison your entire family?" Kala was curious.

"That's a story for another time. I'm surprised Owen or Talan hasn't told you," Rotoph sighed.

"To be honest, I didn't ask." Kala suddenly felt guilty for not trying to know more about Owen and Talan's history, Owen especially. Owen and Linda were the closest people in the world to her. Granted, Kala had no idea Owen was an angel before three days ago, but she chastised herself for being so self-centered. She already felt like a horrible human being for killing Jack, this just added salt to the wound.

Rotoph smiled widely. "We *are* more alike than you'd think."

Kala didn't argue. A part of her figured he was probably right.

"Look, I'm going to close my eyes for a few minutes. Wake me up when it's time to go." Kala didn't wait for a response. She closed her eyes and nodded off.

***

Rotoph gently shook her awake in what felt like a second later. "It's time," he announced.

Owen and Talan stood next to her by the couch. Holding his hand out for Kala to accept, Owen helped her to her feet.

"Where's Derek?" She suddenly noticed his absence.

It was Rotoph who spoke. "No human can go where we're going, and you seemed rather attached to the fellow."

Talan reassured her, "I sent him to his safe house. We'll contact him when we get back."

Kala was tired of her supernatural buddies moving Derek around like he was Kala's teddy bear that she couldn't live without. Derek was a formidable opponent against anyone, supernatural or not, and an asset to any team. It bothered her that it seemed as though they thought Derek was an anchor rather than a strength.

But if he really couldn't go where Zeus was located then she was happy he was safe.

"Let's do it." Kala eyed Rotoph, knowing he was the man in charge of this mission.

Penny positively beamed and even Kala cracked a small smile. Being without her father for thousands of years obviously had taken its toll. Now that Penny was about to see him again, she was radiant. Kala secretly hoped it would improve her personality, but she didn't hold her breath.

Talan and Owen acted as her pillars while Rotoph stood in the middle.

"Everyone grab hold," Rotoph instructed.

As soon as Kala touched Rotoph's arm the room disappeared.

They all stood in a small cavern. It was lit by a red/yellow glow from a few rotating orb-like devices above them. Most of the rock was smooth, but there were a few stalagmites draping from the ceiling here and there.

A gasp from Penny made Kala's head turn.

Behind them, two men were near a stone table.

Kala recognized Hephaestus from Atlas's vision. He looked over parchments and maps, his muscular form obvious even through his heavy armor. The second was Zeus. He had his head in his hands as if he were sleeping. He sat on the floor with his back propped up against the wall.

When Hephaestus saw Penny, his eyes lit up.

In seconds the two were reunited, Penny's small cries of happiness were muffled in his enormous chest.

Kala didn't want to intrude. Seeing Zeus so close, she inched her way around the happy reunion and approached the most powerful Olympian alive. "Zeus?" She felt ridiculous asking.

Zeus peered up at Kala through parted fingers.

And that was when she knew…

He was completely out of his mind.

"Pretty girl stands before me. About to die. About to die," Zeus cackled.

Kala didn't like the sound of that. But part of her didn't feel quite right since they had arrived. Kind of like she had eaten one too many burritos.

"Zeus," Kala tried to reason with the god. "You have to break the curse on Atlas. I'm Atlas."

Zeus laughed hysterically. "Atlas would survive this place, but you won't!" He randomly picked up rocks and mashed them in his hair.

"What does he mean?" Kala turned to ask anyone who'd answer. Then a sharp pain stabbed her in the gut. Kala clasped it with her hand.

Talan was immediately by her side. "Are you okay?"

Kala felt like barfing. "I'm fine." She pushed him away and turned back to Zeus. She couldn't lose this opportunity. "Break the curse! You're the only one who can!" she pleaded desperately.

"Die. Die. Die. Die," Zeus kept repeating creepily.

Kala puked. And it wasn't her last meal that came up.

It was blood.

"Is he killing me?" Kala asked Talan.

Hephaestus stepped forward, pulling himself away from Penny. "A part of you is still human. You have to leave here."

"Not without him!" Kala pointed at the mad god. Then she vomited blood again. The pain was like nothing she'd ever experienced, but her stubbornness wouldn't let her go without an answer from Zeus.

"Kala, I promise you, I will find out everything Zeus knows, but you'll die if you stay. You have to get out of here. Owen will take you," Talan begged.

Kala knew she had to go, but she wanted to grill Zeus more. "I'll leave. Just find me." Kala could barely get the words out as she puked out a piece of her intestines.

Closing her eyes, she couldn't think clearly as she activated her teleportation. She had no idea where she was going to end up, but she needed to get out of there.

When she opened her eyes, Kala was staring at Roberta Turner.

"This is a nice surprise." Roberta smiled warmly.

DAY THREE

Chapter Seventeen

Kala was taken aback that her delirious mind took her directly to Roberta. Her body felt better, as if the torture she had just experienced never happened.

"You have blood all over your mouth and clothes." Roberta stood up from where she sat and headed to the bathroom.

Kala was in Roberta and Turner's bedroom. It was decadent and luxurious with lots of maroons and golds. She felt as if she had walked into a home design magazine, everything in its perfect place. Aside from the four-poster bed that she currently sat on, there was a chaise, a two-seater couch and a recliner. It was so far from any reality Kala had experienced in a long time that she wanted to crawl up in the blankets and never leave.

Instead, she sat waiting for Roberta to return.

Kala didn't have to wait long. Roberta brought in a small tray full of medical supplies.

"I just need the towel and some new clothes. I'm not injured," Kala reassured her. She must have looked like a mess with the amount of blood she chucked up.

Roberta handed her a wet white towel. It was warm against Kala's face. By the time she was done with it though, it was completely red.

"What happened? If you don't mind me asking." Roberta sat down in the recliner across from Kala.

"Apparently, I was in a non-human zone." Kala debated what to do with the soiled towel. It felt rude to throw it away.

Roberta picked up on her dilemma and gently took the towel out of Kala's hand and tossed it in the trash. "Blood never comes out anyway."

"Thanks." Kala attempted a smile.

"I thought you weren't human now?" Roberta was puzzled.

"It looks like there's still a part of me that is. I'm not sure what happened to me," Kala vented.

Roberta tossed Kala a pair of jeans and a light v-neck sweater.

Kala accepted the clothes gratefully. "Do you mind if I shower?"

"Of course." Roberta motioned to the bathroom.

Kala stood up and walked inside. It was just as decadent as the bedroom: all white marble and gold trimmings. Since her clothes were covered in blood, Kala made sure none of it touched the pristine counter.

Stepping into the steaming hot shower was quite possibly the best feeling Kala had experienced in a really long time. In fact, she couldn't remember the last time she had actually taken a shower, which was scary all to itself. The water was hot on her skin, relaxing her muscles instantly. Titan or not, Kala still felt stress and so did her body. Her brain didn't even want to comprehend what was happening to her *physically*. She was never one to have health problems, and panicking wasn't her either, but Kala was a Titan now. That was enough to send anyone around the bend. But part of her was human, too. Now that she wasn't puking up her intestines, Kala was slightly relieved that there was still enough human in her to react to the Grigori hideout.

Kala wasn't a worrier by nature. She was more of a problem solver:

find the conundrum, figure out a way to resolve it, and execute. This Atlas business wasn't helping since so much of it was entirely out of her control. That was why she didn't want to leave Zeus. He was a tiny shred of the control that she needed and now she had to rely on others to find out what he knew. Or, more importantly, what he could *do*.

As much as the shower comforted her, Kala reached her ten-minute tolerance. She never understood Jack's ability to stay in a shower for almost an hour. Sometimes she would join him…

Kala turned off the water and her memories at the same time.

Jack was gone.

There was nothing she could do about it.

Kala shrugged off surging emotions and quickly dressed herself. The clothes fit perfectly. Giving her hair a good towel dry, Kala walked out of the bathroom and sat down on the small couch next to Roberta.

Roberta had been on her laptop and closed it when Kala walked in. "Better?"

"Much, thanks." So much so, Kala didn't want to leave. She wanted to stay in Roberta and Turner's house and forget about everything. She had a weight on her chest that wouldn't go away. It twisted and turned and made her feel as if she was gasping for air, but she was breathing just fine.

"What brought you here?" Roberta was calm and patient. Curiosity gleamed in her eyes, but she seemed content to let Kala share *what* she wanted, *when* she wanted.

"It must have been our whole *head* connection. I just got out of there and showed up here." Now that Kala thought about it, she was surprised that she didn't show up at her old apartment or Jack's…

Roberta thankfully interrupted her thoughts. "Makes sense. I'm sure teleportation works similarly to astral projection. Our connection is the closest reference your brain has to the process, so you came to the source." Roberta was excited by the prospect.

"Sure. That's probably it." Kala wasn't that interested in the science of it. "I'm just glad I'm here. I *really* don't want to do my mission."

"I can't imagine it being worse than your last one." Roberta looked genuinely sympathetic.

"It isn't. But it's all relative. You're not going to like it, and neither is your husband." Kala felt the need to confess to someone. Telling Talan or Owen was like telling the parent that was going to make you do your chores no matter what. No excuses. Sympathy, yes. But the answer would always be to complete the task at hand. But Roberta and Turner were more *shades of grey* kind of people. And Kala really needed to hear something besides an *obligation and duty* speech, especially since she still hoped to get rid of the stupid curse before her time was up.

"Tell me," Roberta urged.

Seeing the curiosity and fascination in Roberta's expression, made Kala not want to tell her.

Roberta was not going to be happy.

"I'm supposed to destroy Fortski's cure for cancer," Kala blurted. She would have covered her eyes and peeked through her fingers if she had the choice, but Kala stared at Roberta straight on.

To Kala's surprise, Roberta's response was a simple raise of an eyebrow.

"That's it? You're not going to try and detain me or something?" Kala was a bit taken aback by the utter lack of angry-I'm-going-to-stop-you-if-it's-the-last-thing-I-do reaction.

"Cancer, huh?" Roberta repeated aloud. "He was told to drop that." Her voice was laced with annoyance.

Then Kala noticed something she hadn't noticed before: Roberta looked pissed. And not at the prospect of destroying a cure for the disease: she was mad at the fact that Fortski was working on it in the first place.

"You know a cure is a good thing, right?" Kala felt out of her element. Normally, she thought that any human being would be considerably upset that she planned to destroy the antidote to the most deadly killer on earth.

But Roberta appeared as if she would tear Fortski's head off. She stood up, furious. "If he releases this cure, all his other work will be put on hold!"

This whole conversation wasn't at all what she had expected. "What's more important than saving millions of lives?"

Roberta didn't even pause in her answer, "Saving *billions*."

Kala was confused. "So this other work he's doing will save *more* people?"

Roberta nodded. "Oh yes. It'll change the world. I know Fortski. If he releases the cure, he won't continue his other research." Then she paused, upset. "Not in time, anyway."

"What is he working on?" Kala wondered what could be so much more important. She had thought curing cancer was pretty darn big.

Roberta sat down next to Kala again, eyes filled with determination. "I can't tell you that. But Kala, you must do this mission. You *must*. I see how this curse of yours works. Destroying Fortski's research *is* for the greater good. I want you to trust me on this."

"Not you, too," Kala complained.

"It may not be what you want to hear, but I believe in your work. This will restore the balance." Roberta seemed desperate in her plea.

Kala couldn't take anymore. "I should go."

Roberta's face softened. "You don't have to. I won't push, but just think about what I've said."

"Oh, I will." Kala didn't want to think *at all*. She wanted to run out of this place, find a nice cardboard box and live there for the rest of her life. Maybe if she didn't complete the cycle, Cronus's little spell of protection-loss would never kick in and she truly would be safe.

Except for the fact that the world would end.

Just a minor hiccup.

Ugh.

There Kala went thinking again. She needed to stop that. It wasn't helping anyone.

"You wanted me to tell you not to do it," Roberta deduced.

"Yeah, pretty much." Kala leaned back on the couch and sighed heavily. "I have no doubt that my mission restores some kind of balance or whatever it's designed to do, but I don't want to do it. Who would?"

"I'll do it for you," Roberta volunteered suddenly.

That made Kala sit up. "What?"

"I have the access. I know where he keeps his research. I *know* why it should be done. I have no problems or reservations. I *want* to destroy it." Roberta's eyes were on fire with enthusiasm.

Kala was speechless.

Could someone else perform the Atlas duties? If the deed was done, the deed was done, right?

But if Roberta did it now, then Kala's clock would reset and she'd have to do something else horrible! She definitely was on board with Roberta taking on the burden, but she wanted a chance to break the curse first.

"I'm thinking, yes." Kala could hear the relief in her own voice. "But give me two days. I don't want you to reset the clock."

"You give me the word and I'm on my way." Roberta appeared positively elated.

Kala wasn't sure if it would work, but part of her needed to try. Maybe she could find people who *wanted* to do the horrible task. It would be a win-win for everyone, including the world! Kala didn't even want to tap into her Atlas memories to see if he had already tried this tactic. Somehow, she knew a weasel like Atlas would have thought of this long ago, making her a weasel by default. But after murdering Jack, Kala could handle being a weasel at the moment. The sane part of her mind knew it was too good to be true, but knowing that Roberta would do what Kala had no desire whatsoever to do lifted a huge weight off her shoulders.

Kala exhaled a large sigh of relief and stood up. "I really should go. I need to get back to my father and Talan, or at least get them to come to me." Her brain felt focused again, like Roberta's volunteering was why she had teleported to her in the first place. A part of a plan she could live with. "Are you sure you're okay doing this?" Kala wanted to make sure that Roberta was on board.

Roberta stood up facing her. "I've never been more certain in my entire life."

Kala knew she meant it.

Really meant it.

It surprised Kala a bit. Delving into other people's motivations and thought processes really wasn't her thing. So she just nodded and tapped her head. "I'll contact you when I want you to do it."

"I'll be here." Roberta leaned forward and embraced Kala.

Kala wasn't much for physical affection, but the hug felt nice. It reminded her that there was still a part of her that was human, as weird as that sounded.

Pulling out first, Kala smiled and gave Roberta a small salute. "Wish me luck."

"Good luck," Roberta replied encouragingly.

Kala concentrated on the location of Zeus. She knew she didn't have much time before she became a fountain of blood, but Kala had to know if Owen or Talan found out anything.

In and out.

Turner's house disappeared.

When her new surroundings came into focus, Kala was not in the mystical cave that housed the king of the Olympians.

She was in a hotel suite.

And from the neon skyline outside Kala figured out pretty quickly that she was in Las Vegas.

"Well, hello, gorgeous."

Kala turned around to see Asmodeus in a bathrobe holding a glass of champagne.

Really?

Chapter Eighteen

"**I** certainly wasn't expecting *you*." Asmodeus positively beamed.

"I have no idea why I'm here," Kala confessed honestly. "I was trying to get back to Zeus." The last place on earth she wanted to be was with Asmodeus. He was like dealing with a teenager in his constant need for affection and desire to get into her pants.

Asmodeus took a sip of his champagne and sat down on a leather armchair. "Where is the old bird anyway?"

"Wouldn't you like to know?" Kala wasn't about to spill the location of the *Titans Most Wanted* to their number one lackey.

Kala figured she might as well eat something while she was in Vegas, so she plopped down on the matching leather couch across from Asmodeus. "We ordering room service?"

"This is becoming a thing with us." Asmodeus grinned.

"Except the actual eating part. We never ordered last time," Kala reminded him.

The room was spectacular. The thing about Vegas was that they did everything big and gaudy. This suite was no exception. Space-wise, it was huge, well over 3,000 square feet and every inch of it was decorated and furnished. The color theme was brown, tan, and gold. It wasn't tacky like most of the Vegas abodes Kala had visited; the décor was tasteful, classy.

Seeing Asmodeus drinking champagne in a bathrobe started to annoy Kala. "Could you get dressed or something?"

"I can get rid of the robe," Asmodeus suggested.

Kala rolled her eyes. "Something casual will do just fine, thank you."

With a snap of his fingers, Asmodeus looked like a model again, with a black t-shirt and jeans. He still held the champagne glass, of course, but a second later one magically appeared in his other hand. Reaching across the gap between them, he handed her the drink.

Kala took it, thinking she could use a drink right about now. This was the third time she had tried teleportation, and it was the third time she had ended up in a place she hadn't expected.

But Asmodeus?

She couldn't fathom why her brain had sent her to *him*. Kala's only desire was to torture Zeus until he released her of the curse. Why would her mind send her to the one guy who had no idea where Zeus actually was? What could Asmodeus possibly do for her cause? It made no sense.

After ordering room service and pigging out on filet mignon and lobster, Kala felt more herself. Maybe this meal was the reason she had come here. It was almost worth it. She glanced at the clock.

1d 19h 21m 43s: 9:39 AM.

At least it was still morning. Kala was amazed at how much comfort that brought her. It reminded her of nights when she'd wake up thinking it was time to go to work, but really had five more hours to sleep. Kala tried to appreciate the little moments, since she rarely had them nowadays.

"So why are you here?" Asmodeus eyed Kala, suspicious but intrigued.

The guy was so readable. Kala wondered how any girl had ever fallen for his charms. But then she looked at him and shrugged. Because he was ridiculously sexy. It pained her to admit it, but there was no denying the fact that the king of Demons had some serious game. Kala just happened to be the kind of girl that was immune to *bad boy* appeal.

That was why she loved Jack so much. He was so *good*.

Her heart squeezed and she leaned back on the couch, closing her eyes.

Before she could open them, Kala felt Asmodeus sit next to her. "Did I upset you?"

Kala was ready to say something snarky when she opened her eyes to see Asmodeus looking genuinely concerned. It was the last thing she expected. "Aren't you supposed to be a Demon? You know Demons are evil. Why should you care if I'm upset?" Snark won out, she guessed.

"Haven't you figured it out yet? I'm entirely smitten with you, Kala Hicks. And now that you're a Titan… let's just say we aren't limited in our options anymore." His grin almost got her, he was so damn charismatic.

"You wish." Kala could always rely on her big mouth to shoot down a would-be-suitor. In this case, she was happy her attitude was running the show. Forget-all-your-troubles-sex was tempting and Asmodeus would definitely fit the mark, but Kala wasn't interested. Her heart always went back to Jack.

"There's that look again. What are you thinking about?" Asmodeus asked.

He was way too perceptive for his own good.

And Kala was too weak to fight it. She had to confess to someone, it might as well be a Demon. "I'll never forgive myself for killing Jack." Saying it aloud made it real. She wouldn't. The world would thank her if it could, but nothing could make her feel justified in murdering him. Nothing.

"You had to. It was your job. I would have preferred it if you hadn't, but that's because I *want* this world to end. Or at least be in chaos." He shrugged. "I'm a Demon, what can I say?"

"You're not helping."

Asmodeus tucked a piece of Kala's red hair behind her ear. "Did you really think I could? I am *evil* as you say." He smiled.

Kala shook her head at his sarcasm. "I don't know what to think anymore. I have no idea how teleportation works. I seem to always show up in the last place I expect. All I want is to go back to Zeus and make him destroy this curse. I can't even do that!" Her frustration was mounting by the second.

"And where is Zeus again?" Asmodeus asked gently.

"Really? I'm a soldier, Demon boy. I'm not going to slip, no matter how much charm you lay on. I'm the girl that doesn't fall for it, remember?" She appreciated his effort, but seriously.

"How can I forget? It's what makes you so fascinating." Asmodeus leaned in closer.

Kala stood up. "No more touchies." She had no idea where that word came from, but it seemed appropriate.

Asmodeus raised his hands in surrender. "No more touchies." He leaned back on the couch as if he didn't have a care in the world. "You won't tell me where Zeus is, and you don't want any of this." He waved his hand over his body like it was on display. "So, why are you here?"

Kala slumped down on the couch next to Asmodeus. "I told you, I have no idea. I focused on the last location of Zeus and I ended up here."

"I see." Asmodeus looked thoughtful. "Maybe he's in a place you can't go to?"

He phrased it like a question, but it jolted Kala that he might be correctly guessing where the Angel-gang was. Unfortunately, her *jolt* only confirmed Asmodeus's suspicions.

He grinned. "So they're in a place you can't go to?"

"I never said that," Kala defended lamely. "I was there before obviously." That was the only argument she could think of.

"True. But you're not there now, which means…" Asmodeus took a sip of his champagne. "It's a place where humans aren't allowed."

"I'm not human, remember?" Kala freaked out. He was way too close to figuring it out.

"Oh, but you are." Asmodeus's eyes lit up. "It's another thing that makes you a walking mystery."

Kala pondered this for a moment. It seemed like Asmodeus knew more about her than she did. She was less worried about Zeus's location in that second than she was in finding out what Asmodeus knew. "What do you mean? What am I?" Kala asked.

Asmodeus leaned in closer and Kala didn't fight him off, she just wanted answers. "It means: you're half-human, half-god. You swallowed Atlas, which is troubling the Titans to no end, by the way, but you're still *you*. No one knows what the consequences of that are yet, but the real question is: how *did* you consume him?"

Kala felt baited. He had designed the conversation to lead back to retrieving information from her, and not the other way around. She'd interrogated enough people in her day to recognize the tactic. Kala moved away from Asmodeus and gave him an exasperated look. "You don't know any more than I do. You're so transparent."

Asmodeus's eyebrows crinkled in utter surprise and disappointment. He wasn't used to people seeing right through him.

"Cronus," he began.

Kala cut him off, nodding. "Cronus wants to know how I almost consumed *him*, doesn't he?" She knew her leverage. "Well, you tell that big boy that if he tries to hurt any of my friends, I'll eat him too." That sounded bad even as it came out of her mouth, and of course, Asmodeus was enticed.

"You can eat me first, if you like?" he suggested.

Kala really hated that he was attractive. He was a Demon! Why couldn't he be butt-ugly with some kind of skin disease?

"We're obviously not going to divulge any of our secrets to one another, so do you want to go gambling?" Kala said, suddenly feeling the urge not to be in her own life anymore, and gambling seemed like the best solution.

Asmodeus shrugged. "Sure."

So a Titan and the king of Demons partied and gambled in Vegas in the early afternoon. It was fun and pathetic all at once. Asmodeus used his telekinesis at the roulette wheel and Kala used hers at craps. The best part of the whole experience was the fact that casinos had no clocks. No glaring reminder that she was neglecting her duty – and it felt amazing. By the end of it, Kala had over a hundred thousand dollars' worth of chips. She was so adrenalized by the rush of it, she turned to Asmodeus and kissed him.

Kala didn't know who was more shocked, Asmodeus or herself. She almost pulled away. But, dang! The boy could kiss! Apparently, it was so mind-blowing she couldn't think straight! His lips were forceful, but not in a smash-your-teeth kind of way. More like a desperate need to devour her.

When all the warning bells officially chimed their way back into Kala's sanity-center, she yanked herself away.

Asmodeus was positively grinning.

"Wipe that smile off your face. I was just happy I won." Kala tried miserably to play it cool.

"Of course, beautiful." He kissed her forehead and she let him, surprisingly. "It was everything I imagined."

Kala grunted and walked toward the cash-out booth. It wasn't as if she needed a hundred thousand dollars, but she wanted it anyway. And frankly, Kala wasn't interested in making eye contact with Asmodeus right then. What had she been thinking? She hadn't. It was that simple. Always impulsive. Always having a mess to clean up. Kala hoped Asmodeus wouldn't get any more ideas. That was a one-time kiss and she *never* planned to repeat it. No matter how good it felt.

"Kala," Asmodeus called from behind.

She wouldn't have responded except for the fact that she couldn't remember a time when Asmodeus had ever called her by name. He always used some kind of pet name for her.

The hairs on the back of her neck raised.

Cronus.

She could feel him.

Kala slowly turned around to face a man in an all-black suit standing next to Asmodeus.

In human form, Cronus looked like he owned the casino. He was a little over six-feet, short black hair, clean-shaven with the famous supernatural bone structure. If Kala were to guess, she'd say he was somewhere in his early forties, not the multi-millennia old fart that he was.

Asmodeus's demeanor was subservient next to the Titan. She couldn't really blame him. She had fought Cronus before and he almost demolished her. Not to mention the fact that he had chopped Talan into pieces. In human form, he might not be as powerful, but Kala had to assume he could still destroy her. She had almost beaten him in the 5th, though. Almost consumed him. But she had no clue as to how she did that, so a repeat of the act wasn't statistically looking so good.

So she decided to be deferent. "What are you doing here? I thought I taught you to leave me alone." Okay. Not so much. Submissiveness wasn't one of her traits.

"You will learn your place, Human," Cronus snarled.

Asmodeus gave her eye signals to shut-the-hell-up, but Kala ignored him. "You want to fight me in a casino?" She looked at him like he was an idiot.

Cronus's eyes glowed blue like Penny's had, but his were a lot more intimidating. "No. I want to *kill* you in a casino."

Great.

Chapter Nineteen

Kala concentrated as hard as she could to teleport herself out of there, but Cronus laughed.

"Not today." He grinned.

Right.

Soldier first.

Get to higher ground.

And hopefully before Cronus attacked.

Kala had no qualms about making a fool of herself as she ran in the opposite direction of the Titan and towards the staircase, poker chips flying everywhere. The last thing she wanted was innocent by-standers to get hurt or worse, killed. And Cronus wouldn't care if he took out most of the casino's inhabitants just to destroy Kala.

People swarmed like locusts, diving after the chips, which to them equated to free money. The crowd blocked Cronus and Asmodeus from following her right away.

Cronus was probably over-joyed at seeing Kala run, but she wasn't doing it to get away. She was trying to find a more defensible fighting area. The roof seemed like the best option, so Kala was about to see if her "god" side had enough stamina to run up fifty floors of stairs. With all the steps she had climbed with Derek in the Compound, Kala knew she was up for the task.

Here was to hoping, anyway.

Cutting her way through the gamblers, Kala reached the staircase and flew up the steps as fast as her legs could carry her. It felt amazing. Her body ran steadily upwards, but there was no exhaustion, no panting, just speed. It was as if she was the Bionic Woman or some kind of super soldier.

As she made her way up, Kala listened for any signs of pursuit, but she didn't hear anything.

Fine. She figured Cronus knew her end game and was already waiting for her on the roof. She needed the element of surprise to survive this fight. Even though Kala had been reassured that it would be near impossible to kill her, she didn't want to take any chances.

A few minutes later, Kala was at the roof entrance door.

She knew Cronus was behind it. Waiting for her. Smug. Expecting to see her spill out onto the roof and be *shocked* that he had beaten her there.

There was nothing like the present.

Kala kicked the door open and jumped to the right.

BAM!

A crack of lightning barely missed Kala as the doorway lit on fire.

Kala rolled behind an air-conditioner the size of a small car. "Isn't that your son Zeus's trick?" she yelled in the direction the bolt came from.

"It's effective," came Cronus's steady voice.

"Except that your aim is terrible." Why did Kala feel the need to antagonize? It came way too naturally for her.

CRACK!

And the air-conditioner was on fire.

Kala didn't have a plan yet, but flames weren't doing her any favors so she high-tailed it to the next mounted structure. It happened to be the base of a giant satellite dish. Her whole idea of getting to higher ground was feeling kind of fruitless.

What did she think she could do?

Her last fight with Cronus consisted of her being tossed around like a chew toy. It wasn't until the Titan dropped pieces of Talan at her feet that some kind of innate power started to spill out of her. She just needed to tap into that.

But Kala didn't want to.

She was scared that she wouldn't be able to control herself and end up chowing down on the leader of the Titans. If Cronus *integrated* with her brain, Kala was sure she'd turn into a schizoid. It was more terrifying than dying.

Speaking of which…

SNAP!

There went the dish, crashing next to her feet. The base was still intact, so Kala stayed where she was.

"You can't hide forever, Human." Cronus sounded amused.

Kala imagined him standing casually in his perfectly tailored suit, flipping his hand occasionally to drop lightning bombs on the lame half-breed.

"I'm more than human. You can't kill me," Kala baited. She wanted either confirmation of that or for Cronus to slip up and tell her something else she might not know.

"You are more human than Titan. And I can kill you just fine." Cronus sounded bored. "Now come out and face me."

"I really don't feel like being fried with lightning right now." Kala didn't budge.

BOOM!

Kala felt the metal from the structure she leaned against, push into her back, launching her forward to her knees. Behind her stood a twisted mass of metal. Cronus was going to destroy every piece of cover Kala ran to until there was nothing else to hide behind.

Feeling desperate, Kala ran to another air-conditioning unit.

She could feel the annoyance dripping from Cronus's tone. "Are we going to do this dance all day?"

"Considering it's my life, yes." Kala searched her surroundings. Could she survive jumping off a fifty-story building? Not likely. It was the whole *human* part that was unclear. The Supernatural was making her quite aware of the fact that, even though she was a Titan, there was still a part of her that was fragile.

Kala was about to throw caution to the wind and full on body slam Cronus when Asmodeus popped in next to her.

"I wouldn't do that." He guessed her intentions.

"I have to do *something*!" Kala wanted the confrontation to be over with at this point.

"Let me distract him." Asmodeus smiled.

"You work for him." Kala couldn't fathom why the Demon would help her. She had seen the terror in his eyes when he looked at Cronus.

"What can I say? I'm a sucker for a good kiss." And with that, he kissed Kala briefly on the lips and teleported away.

BAM!

Kala stood up. Her gut told her something was wrong.

And it was.

In the spot where Asmodeus must have teleported in to fight Cronus was a pile of dust.

"Did you *kill* him?" Kala was surprised at how much the thought of Asmodeus dying affected her.

Cronus shrugged. "Asmodeus is fine, but I sent him to a place where he won't be returning anytime soon. I won't tolerate disloyalty, especially not from a Demon."

With Owen sending Asmodeus to the 5th Level of Hell a few days back, the Demon had a nasty habit of being banished by his superiors.

Still.

Something felt off about the whole thing.

It was too easy.

Too *heroic* for Asmodeus.

Kala had an itching suspicion that she was being set up. For what, she had no idea. If she knew Cronus's end game, maybe she could figure it out.

Best to keep him talking rather than attacking. *That*, she knew for sure.

"No lightning?" Great. Provoke him. Half the time Kala wished she could divorce her mouth from her brain. They never seemed to agree with each other.

Cronus stared at Kala as if he were dissecting an insect.

She wondered why there was a sudden *lack* of attacking. He had been trying to roast her five seconds ago, but now that she was out in the open…

Nothing.

"Are you going to kill me or what?" Kala asked in a voice dripping with irritation. Kala was tired of constantly fighting and running and fighting and running. She wanted Cronus to make his move and maybe she could counter it.

"I could." He toyed with her.

"Really? Because you've tried a butt-load of times and I'm still here," Kala responded back.

Cronus paused, staring at her again.

"I really wish you supernatural beings would stop staring at me like I was some kind of unicorn. Has no one ever given you lip before?" Kala surveyed the roof while she kept Cronus distracted. A part of her seriously debated whether or not to jump. Maybe if she were far enough away from him, she'd be able to teleport again. Kala made a mental note to ask Rotoph about it later. If Rotoph was able to block teleportation from the Compound, he must be doing it the same way Cronus was now.

She never thought she'd actually want Rotoph by her side, but she could really use him right now.

In the mean time, there were more places to duck and cover, but that wouldn't get Kala anywhere.

Cronus looked like a baller in his black suit, watching Kala like a hawk.

"Seriously, what now?" She shrugged her shoulders. "You either let me go or try to kill me, but this waiting around is starting to bug me." There was nothing worse than a standstill. One of the reasons Kala became a soldier was because she needed action, the adrenaline rush. The only time she could handle sitting still for long periods of time was when she had a rifle in her hands.

Cronus's hands shot out before Kala could react.

CRACK!

Her body was completely engulfed with lightning.

Everything clenched: jaw, legs, arms, neck.

Kala couldn't move a muscle as the energy surged through her.

This is how I die? Struck by lightning from a Titan?

She couldn't accept that.

Not going to happen.

BOOM!

Not knowing how, Kala pushed the energy from the lightning out of her body like the blast ring of a nuclear bomb.

Cronus was knocked to his feet, shock in his eyes.

After a second or two Kala appreciated what she had just done. She looked up at Cronus. "Is that all you got?" She was definitely not feeling the bravado she spouted, but she figured she'd try to bluff as best she could.

Cronus slowly rose, dusting himself off, his expression full of fear and wonder. "I know what you are," he said.

Kala could see his eyes were welling with… tears? It scared her more than the lightning. "What do you mean?"

Cronus shook his head. "You're on the wrong side, Kala Hicks."

And he was gone.

It took a moment before Kala could move, afraid he'd pop back in and snap her neck. Not that it would kill her, but she didn't imagine it would feel too good either.

After she was sure Cronus was gone, Kala ran her hands through her hair.

What was that?

What did he mean he knew *what* she was? What *was* she? She had consumed Atlas and she had almost consumed Cronus. Was she some kind of God-eater? Did those exist? Where did she get *that* skill? From the dumpster her mother abandoned her in? And what about the skill of taking a lightning strike and turning it into a blast ring? She tried to wrack her brain for any memory of Atlas's that showed he could do this, but Kala knew it was fruitless. She could tell by Cronus's response that he thought she was something different.

But what? He looked so sure! It drove her nuts!

And where was Asmodeus?

Did Cronus really banish him?

Probably. She shrugged. It was for the best. What was she supposed to do with the king of Demons anyway?

Kala felt more alone than she ever had in her entire life. Being a foster kid, that was saying something. Standing on a rooftop in Las Vegas with a crushed air-conditioner and demolished satellite dish behind her, Kala couldn't move.

What had her life become?

Who was she?

What was she?

Talan's face suddenly appeared in her head.

A warmth spread through her that she couldn't explain.

Thinking of him gave her a strange sense of hope.

Of home.

Kala closed her eyes.

When she opened them, Talan stood in front of her.

Completely out of character, she hugged him tightly.

His arms gently wrapped around her. Kala almost cried it felt so good. She didn't even pause to think that she had finally made it back to the hideout. She didn't even care that the human part of her body was probably about to fall apart. Kala just wanted to stay in that embrace for as long as she could make it last.

Talan's voice whispered in her ear. "You can't be here. You'll hurt yourself."

Hearing the pained concern in his voice only made Kala want to stay more. She never realized how much she needed contact until this moment. A part of her had felt it with Jack, but she hadn't been ready to admit it back then. But his ability to make her feel safe and wanted was why he was the first man she had ever loved. Feelings she had always been proud that she never needed.

But she did.

"Kala, what is it?" Owen's voice came from behind.

She pulled away from Talan and faced her foster father. "Did Zeus tell you anything?" She didn't want to talk about Cronus yet.

Talan shook his head. "He just babbles. We can't get anything coherent out of him."

"Let me try." Kala started to move toward Zeus with determination. She planned on taking out all her frustration on the god.

Owen stopped her. "Kala, I know that look on your face. Something happened to you. Tell us."

Kala sighed heavily. "Cronus just attacked me again."

"You went back to the 5th Level of Hell? Why?" Owen asked worriedly.

"I wasn't in the 5th. I was in Vegas," Kala informed them.

Looking around to distract herself, she saw the rambling Zeus in a corner. Rotoph, Hephaestus, and Penny were at some kind of forge, clanking on metal. They barely noticed that she was back, they were so focused on their work. Kala figured it must be some kind of super weapon. Maybe something she could use in the future against Cronus? Her soldier mind wanted to go over and find out.

But the looks on Talan and Owen's faces stopped her.

"What?" Kala couldn't tell if they were upset she'd fought Cronus again, or the fact that it was in Vegas.

"Kala, Cronus hasn't left the 5th since the end of the war. It's been 2,000 years." Owen let that gem simmer.

Kala's head started to spin. It didn't help that Zeus began to repeat the word Cronus over and over again.

"Why would he come down for me?" She didn't want to admit it, but she already knew. Cronus had come to assess some theory he had about her and she had confirmed it for him when she pushed the lightning out of her system.

"To finish what he started in the 5th and destroy you once and for all?" Talan suggested.

"No," Kala sighed. "He was testing me. He said he knew what I was." She peered up into Talan's eyes and then Owen's, looking for some kind of recognition. Hoping beyond hope that they would know what Cronus saw and tell her *something*!

But they both appeared just as confused as she was.

After a moment, Owen nodded slowly. "We know something is different about you. The fact that you were able to destroy Atlas and infuse him into your human body without dying has never happened before."

"And you almost did the same with Cronus," Talan added thoughtfully. "The truth is, we don't know why you were able to do those things. There's nothing about you that makes you different from any other human."

"Thanks," Kala joked sarcastically.

"You know what I mean," Talan said.

Lurching forward, Kala was reminded why she couldn't be there. Blood spurted from her mouth before she could stop it.

"You have to leave." Owen placed his hand on her back to calm her.

Kala gently shrugged him away. "No, wait. I think I got this."

"It's physical, Kala, it's not mental. You may die." Talan seemed adamant to make her leave.

"Just give me a second." Kala moved a few paces off. The lightning incident showed Kala that she had powers she was not aware of. Physical or not, she had to try. Seeing mumbling-crazy-Zeus in the corner only inspired her more. Kala knew she could extract the information she needed from the god. Talan and Owen weren't motivated like she was. They weren't the ones that had to do horrific things every four days.

Wiping the blood dripping from her nose, Kala hid her face from the two worrywarts. After chowing down on Atlas, waking up had been an ordeal similar to this one. She almost didn't survive it, but Roberta had worked her mojo and helped her through it. The secret had been keeping calm and focusing on integrating with the warring sensations in her body. Having Roberta would definitely help right about now, but Kala knew she could do this herself.

Leaning forward, Kala relaxed her chest and head. Back to Yoga 101. Deep breaths, relaxing her mind, relaxing her body. She choked a large splattering of blood on the floor but ignored it.

Kala tuned out Owen and Talan, who were still trying to convince her to leave. Out of the corner of her eye, she noticed that Rotoph had walked over. Kala knew he sensed what she was doing. Even Zeus grew more and more excited saying the words, "tricky, tricky, fixy, fixy."

He was nuts, but it gave Kala a surge of confidence.

Closing her eyes, Kala used the same energy she used to push out the lightning to try to push out the human part of her that rejected the hideout. Another cough of blood threatened to break her concentration and will. She shook it off and kept focusing.

As her body started to collapse in on itself, Kala used the anguish she felt to motivate her. She had never felt such intense pain in her life. Integrating with Atlas hadn't been this painful. It was as if her veins were exploding.

Maybe they were, she thought with horror.

Shaking away the disturbing thoughts, Kala imagined pushing out the pain. Pain equaled death.

Blood puke.

Lovely.

She screamed.

Talan and Owen tried to grab Kala.

They were going to teleport her.

"Stay back!" she yelled as blood poured out of her mouth.

Kala stepped away from them, knowing that they wouldn't listen to her.

She just needed more time. Kala was close. She could feel it.

Kala reached deep within her body and mind. *Integrate. Integrate.* She repeated to herself.

Tuning out Owen's booming voice became harder and harder. Her body grew weak.

She was dying.

Kala was going to die.

No.

She wiped the blood from her mouth and cried out, delving into her power, that secret reserve that allowed her do things that were impossible.

Talan managed to grab her.

Kala physically felt her mind blocking his teleportation.

She was staying and no one would stop her.

Human side be damned, Kala wasn't going anywhere.

CRACK!

The sound reverberated through Kala's form. It hadn't come from outside.

It had come from inside her mind.

With one last spurt of blood, the agony disappeared.

Gone.

Kala wondered if she was dead, or if her plan had worked.

Slowly, Kala straightened herself.

Definitely alive.

She wiped as much of the blood from her mouth as she could.

Everyone stared at her. Even Hephaestus and Penny had stopped their work to watch *the Kala show.*

Their faces all had the same expression: shock.

Only Zeus moved. He acted like an excited baboon, jumping and clawing at the walls, his words nonsense.

"Could someone get me a towel or something?" Kala broke the silence. Yet again, she was covered in her own blood.

Talan was the first to respond as he handed her a small blanket. "This is all we have."

Kala took the proffered blanket and wiped her face, hands and neck as best she could. By the end of it, the material was almost entirely red.

Not wanting to talk about what just happened, Kala turned to Penny. "Do you have an extra shirt?"

Penny couldn't seem to snap out of stare-mode, but eventually she shook her head. "I didn't exactly pack."

"Right. Supernatural hideout. Why would you need clothes?" Kala saw the logic in this, but it still irked her. Wearing her own blood on her chest wasn't how she wanted to spend the day, but at least she was alive.

But Talan quickly came to the rescue by waving his hand over her body. All the blood instantly disappeared from her clothing and skin.

"You couldn't have done that earlier?" Kala glanced at the blood-soaked blanket, but she managed an appreciative smile. "Thanks."

"Can we talk about what just happened here?" Hephaestus still had a stunned look on his face. "This half-breed acclimated her human side to a god's station. *That's impossible.*"

"Now I know where Penny gets it from," Kala observed sarcastically.

"You and your *impossibles*."

Rotoph stepped forward. "How did you do that?" His eyes were calculating, as if he could gain some kind of advantage if he knew.

Kala felt like she was surrounded by paparazzi. She placed her hands up for everyone to leave her alone. "Look, I don't know how I did it. I just did. It was the same with Atlas, the same with Cronus and the same with pushing out the lightning."

"What lightning?" Owen asked, his face concerned. Kala remembered seeing that expression growing up when she'd stay out without his permission. She hated it then, she hated it now.

At the word lightning, Zeus's mumbling turned to screeching with glee.

Kala ignored him and told the others what she had done when Cronus attacked her.

Instead of talking to her though, they started talking to each other, as if Kala was some kind of circus monkey that had performed a radical trick.

When she heard Hephaestus say, "We should start testing her and see what she's capable of," Kala had to shut down the whole conversation right there.

"Whoa, whoa, whoa! You guys are supposed to be on my side! There will be no *testing*." Kala had had enough.

She walked away from them all, toward orangutan-Zeus. Time to get some real answers.

But she was surprised when it was Penny who stopped her. "Kala, none of us know what's going on. The supernatural world *doesn't change*, nothing is new, it's always the same ancient battle within the families. So when someone like you comes along, it's scary. If you haven't figured it out yet, we don't like change."

Kala sighed. She appreciated Penny's honesty, but it didn't change the current situation. Only Zeus could do that. "I get it, but one thing at a time. I want to get rid of this damn curse, then we can figure out why I'm different. Deal?" She eyed everyone in the room for confirmation.

Owen nodded first, but added, "Cronus claims to know what you are. That could be very dangerous. We'll back burner this for now but, Kala, in your case, knowledge is power. And Cronus has it all."

"Truer words were never spoken."

Oh no. Kala groaned to herself.

She turned to see Asmodeus standing over Zeus.

"I knew you faked that whole hero act," Kala grumbled in annoyance.

Asmodeus smiled. "I had to find this place somehow, and with your heart broken, I figured it was a good bet you'd jump here next."

"Don't flatter yourself. I could never be interested in a lousy kisser. Too much drool." It wasn't true, but she hoped it would sting.

It didn't.

"Being on the other end of that kiss, you didn't exactly pull away, but I understand. You don't want to upset your Angel-Boy over there," Asmodeus snickered.

Kala didn't want to look at Talan and his butt-hurt face. Kissing the guy who had stranded him in the 5th Level of Hell to be chopped up by Cronus was pretty awful even on a "friend" level.

"I hope you got everything you needed from Zeus here. I did give you a little extra time. If not, I'm sure the Malaks could help you." Asmodeus shrugged with a grin. "Good-bye, beautiful. We'll meet again."

Before Kala or any of the others could react, Asmodeus and Zeus disappeared.

Chapter Twenty

Kala felt a hand on her shoulder. She was sure it was Owen, since she figured Talan would be upset at finding out about the Asmodeus-kiss. But it was Talan's voice that spoke.

"Zeus wasn't going to help you. He can't. He's too far gone. We'll find another way."

Kala touched his hand softly and squeezed it. "There is no other way." She turned around. "I have to get him back."

Hephaestus stepped forward. "It's better that he's gone. As crazy as Zeus was, Cronus has always had a way of extracting information out of him. We hid our work while we were down here, but if he had been here when we broke the prisoners out? All would have been lost."

Owen nodded. "Our brothers and sisters can help, Kala. There are some among them who can track gods. We'll find Zeus once they are free."

Kala took a moment, then nodded. "Shouldn't we move somewhere else? Cronus knows where you are now."

Penny shook her head. "We can't. We've already established where the portal will open. We can't just move it."

"Then you better hurry." Kala only saw this ending in violence. If Cronus knew where they were, it wouldn't be long before he sent his family after them. She would. There was no way he'd let the Grigori return and, if he really could extract information from Zeus, he'd know what Hephaestus was up to and send the cavalry to stop it.

But the best part of this situation was the fact that Hephaestus told her that Cronus *could* obtain info from Zeus. And Kala intended to use that. Even if it meant swallowing Cronus whole. Heck, even if it meant swallowing Zeus whole and reversing the curse herself. She was too terrified to try either option, but more so with Zeus: because if it didn't work, she'd never break the curse. Then she'd be stuck with a crazoid in her head.

And she was afraid of losing herself.

Kala hadn't lost herself with Atlas, but it had only been two days! If Talan hadn't sectioned off her brain to stop her from passing out every time she had a memory, she probably would have been unconscious most of the last forty-eight hours.

Hephaestus and Penny went back to the forge, which apparently held *the portal*. This was all becoming too sci-fi for Kala. Rotoph and Owen followed to help.

Talan stayed with her.

Then Asmodeus's words echoed back in her head: *If not, I'm sure the Malaks could help you.* It had been such a throwaway line, as if he was mocking her, but maybe he knew something about the Malaks that she didn't. It wasn't beyond the realm of possibility that Asmodeus was throwing her a bone.

"What did Asmodeus mean about the Malaks helping me?" she questioned Talan.

"I'm not sure. They're the least powerful beings besides Demons. Ever since Atlas tricked the first human to take over his duties, they've been hunting the surrogates down trying to take over the job themselves." Talan repeated what Kala already knew.

"Are you sure they wanted to kill the *Atlas-surrogate* to gain the power for themselves?" Kala's mind was spinning. There was something there. She just couldn't seem to formulate it into a coherent thought.

"Why else would they want to be the Atlas? Every Malak I ran across always talked of humans being unworthy. Remember Grautlin?" Talan wasn't trying to shoot her down; he seemed to be rationalizing it through for himself.

"How can I forget? The guy tried to kill me *twice*." Kala recalled that Grautlin was pretty adamant about being the next Atlas. As if it were an honor.

But why would Asmodeus bring it up? Was he trying to distract her? Throw her off Zeus and onto something else? It was so hard to tell with the Demon. One moment he appeared to genuinely care, the next he was pretending to be a hero just so he could steal back Zeus, her only lead.

"I need to talk to one. Do you know any? Maybe someone high up on the food chain?" Kala decided it was better to go to the source.

"Aside from a select few, Malaks and Demons don't know the Grigori are back," Talan replied apologetically.

"You really are clueless, aren't you? Do you honestly think the last week has escaped the notice of the supernatural world? Rotoph roped in Malaks and Demons to attack us in the bar, remember? They didn't seem all that shocked to see him – or you. You underestimate the need to gossip. That's not just a human trait." Kala was surprised Talan actually thought that he was still a secret.

From the look on his face, the realization was dawning on him. "Then releasing as many Grigori as we can is our only defense."

"Defense? No one can touch you without the blades, and I *have* one at least." Kala touched the top of the hilt, making sure Asmodeus hadn't pulled any shenanigans.

Still there.

"There are eleven Titans who have the others, and only three Grigori here. We've managed to keep our three other brothers and sister out of this mess in case we fail." Talan spoke of the Grigori who had escaped with them centuries ago.

Kala had never heard Talan or Owen speak of the other Grigori on earth. "Okay. Well, you guys do your thing and I'm going to find some Malaks." She fully intended to leave.

Talan's eyes stopped her. "Kala. We need you. You can't leave now."

"Ten minutes ago you were telling me to get the heck out, so just pretend my *human* side is killing me and let me go hunt some Malaks."

"Ten minutes ago we didn't know how powerful you were. I didn't *want* you to leave. I wanted you to be safe. I understand your need to rid yourself of this curse, but don't you think it can wait until we get some backup?" Talan sounded irritated.

She had actually managed to piss Talan off. It amused Kala for some reason. He was always spouting his love and loyalty, but her one-track mind finally made him crack. "As soon as the family reunion is over, you're taking me to a Malak," Kala ordered.

Talan nodded. "I promise."

Kala smiled at him. There was an affection there between them that she couldn't deny. It felt as if they had been friends their whole lives. Kala knew Talan had no-no feelings for her, and she was definitely attracted to the guy, but no one could replace Jack. No one ever would. Friendship she could handle though. Friendship was safe. And Talan made her feel safe.

BOOM!

"It's starting! Talan, we need you!" Penny's voice yelled out.

Kala walked straight for the forge, followed by Talan.

It was one of the strangest visuals Kala had ever seen. It looked like a tiny tornado drilling a hole into the air itself, growing bigger every second.

Penny, Talan, Rotoph, and Owen clasped hands, then suddenly

Penny and Talan grabbed onto Kala's to complete the circle.

Penny shrugged. "I don't know what kind of abilities you have, but they're powerful and we need as much of it as we can."

Hephaestus stayed out of the ring and chanted some kind of spell.

The tornado grew bigger and louder with each passing second. The noise was so intense Kala wanted to snap her hands away and cover her ears, but she held on to Penny and Talan.

The center of the swirling wind started to open up and Kala could see the Heaven-prison Talan had shown her before. Even through a small opening, it was a stunning view, as if galaxies had collided in one spectacular moment. Why would Grigori want to come to earth when they could be there? Kala still didn't understand that logic, but she supposed if she had been locked up against her will, she'd want out too.

Penny's eyes widened with anticipation. "They're coming!"

Kala couldn't see anything so she assumed Penny had some sort of connection to the portal that allowed her to sense the Grigori on the other side.

KABOOM!

The swirling hole tilted almost two-feet sideways before it righted itself.

"HOLD ON!" Penny screamed. "DON'T LET GO!"

Hephaestus's voice grew louder as he chanted.

Kala held on with all her strength, but the force of the portal tried to pry their hands apart.

Then a person was visible from the other side: a stunningly beautiful woman with dark skin and pitch-black hair. It was a shocking contrast between the raging storm and the calm beauty of the angel.

"Antel!" Owen shouted. "Come through!"

The Grigori named Antel's eyes lit up when she saw Owen and she stepped through the swirling abyss to land safely inside their circle.

Antel yelled over the noise, "The others are coming!"

Penny screamed, "Join the circle! We need your strength!"

Antel nodded, taking Owen and Talan's hands quickly so the circle wouldn't be broken for long. Once their hands were clasped, Kala felt the power intensify. Surges of invisible energy flowed through her body and out through her hands. Angels and deities might be able to handle opening magical portals to angel prisons, but *half-human Kala* felt like her soul was being shredded.

After Antel passed through, a line of Grigori appeared in front of the growing tornado. It was now the size of a small car. One after another they came through, each one joining the circle, until it was ten strong. Five new Grigori already seemed like a lot to Kala; she wondered how many more there were. She tried to count the line of them waiting to pass through, but there seemed to be no end.

The next Grigori started to walk into the portal…

SLASH! SLASH! SLASH!

The portal closed with a loud CLAP!

The energy flow, dead.

Kala looked up and saw Owen, Antel and Rotoph drop to the floor from the blades that slashed their throats.

Three Titans stood behind them: Iapetus, Theia and Hyperion.

Kala saw red.

Even though she logically knew that Owen wasn't dead, seeing his throat cut sent her into a rage.

Deep within her being, Kala let the power that had consumed Atlas and almost consumed Cronus take over. It scared her, but her rage was stronger. It was as if she was awakening something ancient inside her that had always been there, but she'd never known how to connect with it – until Atlas.

Like before, Kala had no control over the words that came out of her mouth, "YOU WILL BE PUNISHED!"

The Grigori blades flew out of the Titan's hands to land hilt first into Talan, Hephaestus and Penny's hands.

Shock registered on every being in the room. Then Talan responded.

He slashed his blade at Hyperion.

The Titans didn't need the blades to attack, they were powerful enough all on their own.

Penny tried to attack Theia, but the Titan threw her across the room. It didn't stop Penny though. She used her ability to disappear from view and popped back in to surprise Theia with a stab to her chest. Theia screamed in pain, but still had enough power to backhand Penny to the floor.

Hephaestus was the most at home in battle. He'd been doing this a long time and it looked like he was enjoying himself as he stabbed Theia again in protection of his daughter. Being locked away to make weapons for the Titans for thousands of years had given him all the anger he needed to use the blade that *he* made.

Kala fought inside herself, trying to stem the power she had no control over. She had no idea what it was or where it came from and as a soldier, Kala's first rule was to always know what her weapon could do. A part of her wanted to use it, but the other part of her warned against it. Last time she let it have free reign, she had devoured a god.

Iapetus was suddenly in front of Kala his eyes curious. "Son, are you still in there?"

He was referring to Atlas, Kala assumed. "He's dead. I have all his memories, but his soul is gone. It's only me." Kala pulled out her own Grigori blade and stabbed Iapetus in the stomach. "You're not my father." She nodded to Owen's still form. "*He* is." Then she slashed Iapetus's throat. "Doesn't feel so great, does it?"

Kala started to feel normal again. Fighting like a human brought her back to herself.

Iapetus mended a lot faster than the Grigori, his gut and neck healing before her eyes. And he didn't even appear mad at Kala, only interested. "The Grigori is not your father no matter how many times you tell yourself that he is." He backed up before Kala could stab him again. "Whether Atlas's soul is inside you or not, he *is* inside you, which makes you a Titan. *My* son."

"Reality check, I'm a girl." Kala feigned an attack to the right. When Iapetus moved left to avoid it, she stabbed him in the heart. "It may not kill you, but it'll make you weak enough to imprison." She cut his ribs for measure. "I'll find my answers and take down every one of you to get them."

Though Iapetus's wound healed quickly, his body showed that the blows were slowing him down.

Seeing the gravity of his situation, Iapetus called out to his sister and brother. "Now!"

A second later, the Titans were gone.

But so was Hephaestus.

They couldn't re-open the portal.

"Well, that sucked," Kala groaned.

Chapter Twenty-One

It took a few hours for Owen and the other two Grigori to regain their strength. Kala didn't leave Owen's side. Seeing her only real dad have his neck sliced in front of her was something she never wanted to repeat.

The five new Grigori eyed her warily, not sure what to make of her. They didn't know her like Owen and Talan did, so Kala understood: they didn't have a reason to trust her. Seeing her rob the blades from the Titans had surprised everyone in the room, including Kala. She wanted to know where her strange wellspring of power came from, but at the same time, she wanted nothing to do with it.

Talan turned to Kala. "I'll take you to Lotun. She's the leader of the Malaks."

Kala was relieved to hear that Talan was willing to take her so soon. Especially since the portal was closed with no way to re-open it without Hephaestus. There wasn't much Kala could do for anyone there anyway. Talan had kept his promise by asking the other Grigori if they could track down Zeus, but none of them had that particular skill, so Kala was back to the Malaks, her only lead. This news made Penny a wreck. She could care less about Zeus, and had hoped they could find her father. She tried to convince anyone who would listen that their first priority should be getting Hephaestus back. Most of the Grigori seemed to be on the same page as Penny, feeling that their numbers were still too small to take on the Titans.

That was where this whole thing was headed: another war between gods and angels. And probably Demons. Seven days ago, Kala had no idea any of *this* existed and now she was a major part of it. She was a Titan. At least partially.

And something else.

Something that scared the most powerful of the gods.

The most powerful of the Grigori.

What was she?

Maybe the Malaks *could* help. It was a stretch, but Kala was running out of options. Asmodeus was a dick, but Kala knew as warped as his feelings were for her, they were real to a degree. To what degree she had no idea, but she didn't believe he'd mention the Malaks if they didn't have something to offer her.

And Talan? He claimed that only a few knew he was back. Kala knew that was a joke, now that the Titans and Asmodeus knew. They'd tell the whole supernatural world just to keep the feelers out so they could wrangle the Grigori back to their prison. But maybe this Lotun Malak knew Talan was around. Maybe they had some kind of a relationship or past. Kala found that she didn't like that so much. She didn't want Talan, but she didn't want anyone else to have him either. It made no sense, but Kala was okay with that. Most of what she felt didn't make sense.

"Let me say goodbye to Owen before we go," Kala said to Talan.

She walked over to her foster dad and placed a hand on his arm. He turned and hugged her. "You leaving with Talan?" he asked as he pulled away.

Kala nodded. "He's taking me to Lotun." She watched Owen's face for a reaction.

He didn't seem surprised. "If any of the Malaks can help you, she can. She'll know if Asmodeus was trying to trick you or not. She knows him better than anyone."

"Really?" Kala mused. Interesting. "Were they friends? Lovers? Enemies? What?"

"I'll let her tell you. I try not to think of Asmodeus," Owen stated flatly.

She felt a pang of guilt. Owen knew she kissed the Demon and she didn't want him to think less of her for it. But the gleam in his eyes when he looked at her told her that Owen would love her forever. "Tell *Mom* that I love her." She had only called her foster mother mom once and that was four days ago, but she wanted to get used to it. And the 'L' word was getting easier to say, at least when talking about her parents. Owen and Linda were her mom and dad no matter what Iapetus said. And the expression on Owen's face made it all worth it.

He squeezed her tight. "I will. I love you, Kala."

"I love you, too." She pulled away and headed to Talan.

Before she reached him, Antel stepped in front of her. She was truly a stunning woman, her dark skin and eyes to match. "May I have a word?" she asked politely.

"Sure." Kala wanted to leave, but was curious what Antel wanted.

"Owen told me some of the things you've been able to do," Antel started.

When there were at least ten seconds of awkward silence Kala prodded, "And?"

Antel smiled which made her even more beautiful. "And…I want you to be careful using your gifts. Atlas may have given you strength, but he was weak. A more powerful soul could kill you or worse, take over your body. I can see Atlas in you, but I also see something else… *someone* else."

"Who do you see?" Kala's interest was piqued.

Antel shook her head. "I don't know, but there is something very special about you, Kala. You are Owen's daughter and Talan's soul mate, so I will protect you with my life."

Soul mate? Kala didn't feel like arguing the matter, though. Disagreeing with Grigori never ended with convincing them of anything. Once they believed something, that was it. Kala thought she was stubborn, but Grigori were ten times worse. She simply said, "Thanks." Not knowing what else to say.

Did she swallow someone else, too, when she consumed Atlas? Or was the power that allowed her to swallow him in the first place from *somewhere* else? She needed answers. All she had was more questions.

She joined Talan's side.

"Ready?" he asked.

"As I'll ever be," she responded.

Talan's hand wrapped in hers and Kala felt the tingling sensation she always felt when Talan touched her. Which was why she had a *no touching* rule. But he was teleporting her, so they had to have contact. She shrugged inwardly. The Grigori may believe that she and Talan were soul mates, but she still knew that she had lost her true soul mate when she killed Jack.

Taking a deep breath, her surroundings turned to swirls of light as Talan teleported her away.

They arrived in the middle of a forest. Kala hated nature. Sure, it was beautiful, but it was full of bugs and creatures she wanted nothing to do with.

"Where are we?"

"Somewhere in France," Talan answered. "Lotun doesn't like cities. She prefers the forest."

"Of course she does," Kala grunted. It figured the one Malak that could potentially help her lived in the one place that Kala couldn't stand.

The ground was a thick layer of pine needles making it feel spongy as they walked.

After twenty minutes of trudging past endless amounts of trees, Kala grew restless. "Are we going to have to search the entire forest for Malakgirl?"

"You are the most impatient person I know." Talan appeared amused.

"Because you know so many people," Kala retorted.

"More than you think," he smiled.

Kala figured he was right. She knew practically nothing about Talan. Only that he was a Grigori who taught Turner and Roberta in disguise.

And that he had saved her… a lot.

Talan had showed her some of his past in a vision, but it didn't really tell her anything about him personally. What did he do in his spare time? Did he have a hobby? Owen was Grigori and he had seemed so normal. Owen being in the Navy was the reason Kala had joined herself. He loved Linda and they did what human couples did: eat, sleep, shop, watch TV, and go to the movies. Owen was a bit of a gun enthusiast, which in turn, influenced Kala to be one as well. So if her foster father had interests and hobbies it made sense that Talan would have them too. She just couldn't imagine him doing anything but stand there, teaching some kind of super-science-magic-trick or beating up Malaks or Demons.

She was about to ask Talan what his favorite color was, when a woman stepped out from behind a tree in front of them.

Damn these angels and their good looks, Kala eyed the woman who she knew was Lotun. Though her clothing made her look like an ordinary camper with dark brown khakis and long sleeve, fitted t-shirt, there was nothing ordinary about her. Her eyes were overly large in contrast to her small nose and lips. Everything about her was delicate from her lithe figure to her tiny hands. Kala guessed that Lotun was five foot two at the most. Being only five foot six herself, Kala still felt like a giant looming over a child.

Lotun's hair was long and pale blonde. It lay in perfect waves as if she had just stepped out of a shampoo commercial. Kala unconsciously touched her own auburn hair that she had tied up in a messy ponytail, feeling self-conscious in front of the Malak. She was over it in about a second when she realized she didn't care.

Lotun spoke, first addressing Talan with bedroom eyes. "My Grigori has brought me a toy?" She eyed Kala with a smile.

Talan went straight to business ignoring her flirtations. "Hello, Lotun. We need your help."

The Malak dismissed Talan's plea for help as she stepped up to him, tracing her finger over his jawbone seductively.

That was it.

Kala couldn't watch this a moment longer.

"Asmodeus sent us." She thought she'd tell a half-truth, just to see what Lotun would do. And, more importantly, so she'd stop touching Talan.

Lotun finally turned to Kala with interest. "Did he?" But her interest in Kala was fleeting; she turned her attention to Talan. "Everyone knows you've been back, you know."

"I told you." Kala couldn't resist. She loved being right.

Lotun focused on her. "Who are you?" Then she stared at Kala, really stared. Her eyes widened. "Atlas?"

At the sound of Atlas's name, Kala was transported to another memory. This one was a doozy, and she began to lose consciousness. Feeling Talan's hands hold her up felt as if it were happening to someone else. Kala was aware of his presence, but could do nothing to signal that she knew he was there.

The memory took over and flooded Kala's vision.

She stood in the same forest, which only added to the surrealness of being in two places at once. It was almost as if someone had projected two movies on top of each other.

Different stories, but identical location.

Lotun was there and she appeared very angry with Atlas. Honestly, it didn't feel all that different than the situation she was in now with Lotun. And Kala wasn't surprised that Atlas pissed off another being of power. The guy was seriously annoying.

Before the memory version of Lotun could speak, Kala heard the real

Lotun's voice. "Interesting. She's having a memory about me. Can you bring her back?"

Talan spoke. "Atlas shows her what she needs to see. She'll return to us when it's done."

Kala's mind reeled. *Atlas shows her what she needs to see? Atlas?* As if he was swimming around in her head, alive and well. She tried to tune Talan and Lotun and concentrate on the vision.

If a part of her subconscious was Atlas, then her brain was trying to show her information that could be valuable. Kala knew in the depths of her soul that Atlas was dead and not lurking in her head, but it was interesting that Talan wasn't so sure. He really had no idea what was going on. It made Kala feel a little better that she wasn't the only one in the dark. But at least she knew some things that no one else did. She liked secrets. It was one of the reasons she'd taken the job with Turner. Secrets usually kept you safe. The person that knew the most would often be the person with all the power.

The memory of Lotun screamed at Atlas. "This curse is a plague on us all!"

"Don't be so dramatic. I'm the one who has to do it." Atlas crossed his arms defensively. "Why did you bring me to this horrible place?"

On that Kala and Atlas could agree. Nature was pretty on TV and in coffee table books, but not in real life.

"Because I can break the curse of balance." Lotun's voice was full of determination.

That had both Kala and Atlas's attention.

Inside, Atlas's pulse raced a mile a minute and he was beyond excited, but his voice was steady as he asked, "How?"

Lotun wore a look on her face that Kala didn't like, but she could tell Atlas was clueless. She had seen that expression before a thousand times on the field when facing her enemies. It said: *I'm going to have to kill you now.* So she wasn't surprised when the Malak admitted, "The only way to break it is ancient magic. I know the ritual and *it will* release what Zeus did to you and return the fates to their natural order. But Atlas, you'll have to make the sacrifice."

Atlas was too self-involved to understand what she was telling him. "I'll make a sacrifice. What do you want? My children? Pleiades or Kalypso? Take them. They never did me any favors."

What a prick.

Kala almost wished Lotun *had* killed him at that moment, but then… But then her life would have been perfect! She would have been with Jack because he never would have trained to be the *Atlas-surrogate*, and she never would have shot the President.

Yeah, she wished Lotun had killed him then and there.

But this was only a memory.

Lotun set him straight. "No, Atlas, your children are safe whether you care or not. The sacrifice is *you*. You have to die for the ritual to work."

Atlas paused for a few moments before he spoke. He grew angrier and angrier the longer he stared at Lotun. "You want me to *die?*" he asked incredulously.

"To bring order back to the world, yes," Lotun spoke confidently.

"But I do that perfectly well *alive*." Atlas could not see how under any circumstances Lotun would ever imagine he'd agree to her idea.

"It's not about your job. It's about Zeus tearing balance from the universe itself and turning it into a curse. It's not natural. It needs to stop." Lotun wasn't leaving room for argument. "I'm going to do this, with or without your permission," she added.

Atlas teleported away before Lotun could grab him. Kala could feel his terror. It dawned on her that this memory took place right after the Titans had betrayed the Olympians and then Zeus had refused to free Atlas from the curse. Penny had kept Atlas in hiding, showing him how to trick humans into doing his job. Lotun's plan couldn't happen because she never found Atlas. Tricking humans really *was* his witness protection program.

Before Kala could read anymore of Atlas's thoughts, she was back in the present with Talan and Lotun.

She was on guard. "Look, before you try and perform that ritual on me, I'm trying to break this curse as well."

Lotun eyed her carefully. "You came to me. I *can* break this curse. And now you know how."

Talan's face showed his confusion, so Kala filled him in. "She has to kill me to do it."

Talan was all fury and fire. The Grigori equivalent of *puffing up*.

Even Kala was a little scared. He didn't look any different, but he radiated power like he was a nuclear warhead.

"If you touch her…" he began to threaten.

"Relax. I don't even know if it would work. She's part human and that may throw the whole thing off. I'll have to research it." Lotun didn't like Talan's *puffing* at all. It made her view Kala like competition.

Then something occurred to Kala. "Could you kill Atlas inside of me? I'd gladly sacrifice him to break the curse." If she could get rid of both at the same time… her heart surged with hope. She'd lose her superpowers, but that didn't concern her. She just wanted out of this struggle between gods, angels and Demons.

Lotun sighed. "Possibly. I'll see what I can find."

If this was possible, it was bittersweet. Only Atlas had known about Lotun's ritual, and he didn't tell Kala when she had begged him to get out of killing Jack. If Kala had known, she felt like she could have forced Atlas to do the ritual rather than swallowing him. Jack could have lived if Atlas hadn't been such a coward.

Kala didn't want to die either, but she would if it meant saving the planet.

She just wasn't there yet. Doing the job herself kept the world safe. If the ritual meant they had to kill her, the *universe* would take over her job. So, it didn't make the situation better, it simply shifted the responsibility back to the *fabric of space* as opposed to Atlas.

"You do that and get back to…" Kala's vision went wonky.

Everything blurred and she stumbled to catch her balance.

She felt Talan's hand propping her up, his voice etched with concern, "Kala, what is it?"

"I don't know," Kala answered.

She could see it now.

Lotun was inside her head.

Reaching, searching, reading her thoughts.

Kala lost her motor functions. She tried to warn Talan, but he obviously thought she was having another memory.

Trying to push Lotun out of her mind was impossible. She felt helpless as she heard Lotun's voice inside her body. "The cure for cancer, huh? Interesting. It could save so many lives, why would destroying it keep the balance?"

Lotun sounded like a scientist trying to figure out a formula that had been giving her trouble.

"What's this?" Lotun was like a kid in a candy store picking through Kala's brain. "Oh, how tragic. Killing the love of your life." Then her voice turned frightened. "The prophecy..."

It was too much.

It didn't bother Kala that Lotun found out about her mission, or even that she was the Fated One. It was the way she dismissed Jack, as if it were nothing.

But it was *everything*.

This time it was easy. Kala tapped into her hidden power and grabbed the very essence of Lotun crawling around inside her.

Lotun screamed. Not just in Kala's head, but outside as well.

Talan held onto Kala tighter and she could hear him asking Lotun, "What's happening?"

But Lotun kept screaming.

Kala squeezed the part of Lotun that was inside of her with all of her might until she heard a pop.

In an instant, Kala's motor functions were back in working order.

She was on her knees with Talan beside her.

Lying in front of her was Lotun, eyes wide in terror, staring at Kala like she was some kind of monster.

Lotun's voice cracked as she uttered, "You're the Fated One."

"Duh."

Chapter Twenty-Two

"We know this already." Kala quickly rose to her feet with a little help from Talan.

Lotun carefully stood up as well, her eyes never leaving Kala's.

"What happened?" Talan was completely at a loss.

"Such power," was all Lotun could say.

Kala had felt it too, but she had no idea where it came from. She explained to Talan, "I bumped her out of my head. Maybe it was something that I picked up from Roberta?" *Maybe it was,* Kala rationalized. Or at least, that was what she wanted to believe. Having an untapped power source wasn't what it was cracked up to be. It was like having an atom bomb stuck inside you without any idea when it would go off.

With a withering expression, Lotun asked, "Roberta Turner? Are you still teaching her your tricks, Grigori?"

Grigori. So impersonal. Guess she was mad at Talan now.

Talan ignored her, his attention never leaving Kala. "Are you sure you're okay?"

Kala nodded. "I'm fine."

A desperation filled Lotun's eyes. "I have to see more. I'm sorry I have to!"

SLAM!

Kala wasn't prepared for Lotun to smash into her brain a second time. She tried to tap into her wellspring of power again, but was too off balance.

Lotun's voice echoed in her head. "It *is* you. I'm sorry. I'm so sorry."

Kala had no idea what she was talking about. She only wanted Lotun to leave.

She heard Talan's voice. "I come in an act of peace and this is how you treat me? Invading Kala's head like she was yours to play with?"

SWOOSH!

Kala gasped for breath as Lotun left her mind.

When she looked up, she saw why.

Lotun was engulfed in green fire, sent from Talan's outstretched hands.

She screamed in anguish. "I'm sorry! I couldn't stop myself! I had to see! I had to!"

He twisted his hands and the green flames roared louder and touched the trees with their height, though the pine needles didn't ignite.

Lotun's skin wasn't burning, but her face was wracked in terrible agony. Her screams turned silent.

It was horrifying.

"STOP!" Kala yelled at Talan.

He glanced at Kala. Whatever he saw there made him extinguish the fire.

She ran over to Lotun's crumpled form and helped her to her feet. Kala looked at Talan, angry now herself. "We need information from her, not roast her like a marshmallow."

He was taken aback and she could see he was a little ashamed as well. "She was hurting you. She tried to read your most private thoughts. You couldn't seem to push her out. These things can't go unpunished, Kala. Not in our world."

Kala knew he was right. She hadn't been able to shove the Malak out the second time. "So you leap to burning her alive? Couldn't you have just knocked her on the head or something?" It was the extremity that bothered Kala. Seeing Lotun covered in flames… It wasn't something she wanted to see again. Ever.

"I'm sorry," Talan replied quietly.

Lotun's face went from pain to shock. "Grigori don't apologize." She was genuinely perplexed.

"Well, he did, so get on your feet." Kala helped the Malak stand. "What can you tell us about… me?" She hoped Lotun wouldn't clam up in resentment at the two people who'd just tortured her.

Lotun shook her head, not wanting to re-live the memory. "I've never seen power like hers before." She peered up at Talan. "She's more powerful than a Grigori. More powerful than *anything*. I…" The girl was reeling. "Of course she is… she's…" She shook her head, unable to comprehend her own words.

Kala didn't like where this was going. "I'm what? I'm just a human."

"A human that swallowed a god!" Lotun's eyes wouldn't stop widening as she gawked at her.

It irritated Kala. "Stop looking so shocked. That happened days ago."

Lotun turned back to Talan. "She's the Fated One, Talan."

"We know that already, Lotun. We've read the prophecies and it only talks about the person who will take this curse away. *The one who knows death.* Do you know who that would be?" Talan spoke carefully.

Lotun shook her head. The crazed glaze in her eyes worsened. "Pandora only has half of the prophecy. The Malaks have kept it hidden. There's more! The Fated One isn't just a person. Talan, the Fated One is…"

And she was gone.

Popped out of the forest like she was never there.

Kala and Talan stared at each other in surprise. He walked over to Kala and examined where Lotun had been.

"Did she teleport out mid-sentence, because that's really low." Kala was beyond frustrated.

"No. Someone teleported her out." Talan sighed. "Only one being has that kind of power."

"Let me guess. Cronus?" Kala could feel her eyes rolling.

"The master of time and space himself," Talan confirmed. His expression turned regretful. "I'm sorry if I disappointed you with my behavior. I don't like seeing you hurt. Especially by a Malak."

Kala sensed some angel prejudice going on, but she decided to let it go. "How are we going to find the other part of the prophecy? Would some other Malak have it?" Because Kala wasn't interested in having another brawl with Cronus. Now he had two prisoners Kala needed: Zeus and Lotun. He was starting a collection. Was he going to kidnap everyone who tried to give Kala information? Probably.

"I didn't even know more of the prophecy existed. I'll have to tell Pandora." Talan barely hid his worry.

"It sounds like the prophecy says who the *Fated One* is, but it's me. So what was Lotun talking about?" Kala hated having more questions. She hated having questions at all, but the more she delved into this new world of hers, the more out of her depth she felt. Words like *Fated One* belonged in fantasies not real life. Not her life.

Not knowing what to say, Talan stared at Kala sympathetically. Finally, he said, "Whatever she was going to tell us, Cronus didn't want you to hear. It must be what he concluded himself. The prophecy only confirmed it for him."

"You don't think he knew of the prophecy beforehand?" Kala wondered.

"No. If a prophecy doesn't involve him directly, he doesn't pay much attention to it. There are too many to know all of them. If Lotun kept the prophecies about Atlas hidden, then only the Malaks knew of it. And probably only a select few. We just have to figure out *which* few and track them down." Talan surveyed the forest. "You want to get out of here and go somewhere less…rural."

For some reason, Kala didn't. As much as she despised being outdoors, at that moment it felt good. She could tune out the rest of the world and not have to deal with any of her problems. "Can we just sit here for a bit?" Kala plopped down on the ground and lay on her back. The sun filtered through the tight branches, letting small pockets of light touch her face. Despite the dry ground and sharp needles poking through her clothing, it felt amazing. "What time is it anyway?"

Talan lay down next to her but made sure he didn't make physical contact.

Their arms were less than an inch apart, but Kala was aware of the heat radiating off his body. It made her feel connected to him. More connected than if they were actually touching.

"Before you react, everything is going to be fine," Talan began.

She didn't like the sound of that. "It's Day Four isn't it?" The sun looked high in the sky, but she was in France. Her countdown clock was tied to the time zone where she became Atlas, which meant east coast time. France was five hours ahead.

Talan sounded surprised to hear how calm Kala appeared. "Not quite. You have about an hour. It's 4:03 AM your time."

Instead of picturing a clock with the time on it, Kala only saw the countdown.

1d 00h 57m 00s.

A little over twenty-four hours before she'd have to destroy Fortski's research. Or before Roberta would. Her heart desperately wanted to believe that Roberta *could.*

"Talan?" Kala spoke his name softly. "My mission is to destroy the cure for cancer." It felt good to admit it, especially to someone who would support her no matter what she did.

He was silent for a moment, then said, "Why would it be to destroy something that would help so many?"

Relief flooded through her. "Right? That's what I thought. It doesn't matter anyway. I'm not going to do it."

Talan paused. "Do you want to see what will happen if you *don't* do it?"

Kala briefly thought about telling Talan that Roberta would do the deed for her if she ran out of time, but she decided she'd take a look through his *future eyes* first. "Yes."

Talan reached his hand over and clasped Kala's. The familiar tingle sent a shiver through her body. It also made her feel safe. She relied more and more on Talan and his unending support. It went beyond physical chemistry and the fact that he was beautiful to look at. Only Jack, Derek and her foster parents had ever made her feel as protected as Talan did. Kala had relied on herself her whole life. It was difficult for her to trust anyone. But she trusted Talan. She trusted him with her life.

"Ready?" he asked.

She nodded.

The branches above her shifted and swirled as the familiar sensation of *Grigori vision* commenced. She saw the scene that had repeated on every TV or screen where she was about to demolish Fortski's computers. Instead of destroying them, the Kala in the vision started to walk away. On the wall was a digital clock. Five seconds until the end of Day Four. She waited to see what would happen.

Kala's stomach turned when the ground jolted beneath Fortski and vision-Kala. The building started to collapse as giant cracks split the walls.

Not again.

She knew then that it didn't matter what her task was.

It would always end the same.

The world would implode on itself.

The nature of the curse was built that way. If Atlas didn't do the horrible act, the planet would collapse.

"Take me out," Kala instructed Talan.

He broke their connection by releasing his hand from hers. She wanted to hold it for support, but she appreciated his respectfulness.

"I'm sorry," Talan said softly.

"It's okay. It makes sense, I guess. If the world didn't end every time, Atlas would have slacked any chance he could. I don't know what else I expected to see." Kala stared at the branches above. As much as the pine needles beneath her itched and scratched, it was a peaceful moment. Reality wasn't something she wanted to face. "I don't think I can do it," she confessed again. "But it needs to be done." Kala sighed. "Talan." She needed to own up to her plan. "I'm going to have someone else do it."

"What do you mean?" Talan turned to her.

"Roberta said she'd do it."

Talan's eyes said it all. He was trying to think of a way to let her down easy.

"Don't tell me it's impossible. She's going to try. She *wants* to do it. I don't. It's the perfect arrangement."

"Kala, if Atlas could have made people do his dirty work, he would have. Tricking humans into taking his place was the closest he ever came. Roberta won't be able to," he told her kindly.

She stood up angrily, brushing pine needles off her jeans. Her hatred of nature came back in a rush as she pricked her finger on one of them. "Can we get out of here now?"

Talan stood up next to her. "Kala, I'm sorry, but you're missing the point here."

"And what's the point?" She crossed her arms.

"*Why* does Roberta want to help?"

Kala hadn't thought about that.

It suddenly made her stomach turn.

"Because she's helpful?" Kala volunteered.

"I've been teaching Roberta and Turner for years now, and the woman can be kind at times, but she never does anything without a reason. The one thing I don't have access to is Fortski's secret project. He doesn't share it with anyone, not even his most trusted assistant, namely me."

"You know what? I don't care why she wants to do it. She'll do it. In the meantime, let's try and figure out how I can break out of this curse in the first place. I need to find Zeus." Kala was so angry and so frustrated she didn't want to think about Roberta and what her reasons were. All she could think about was Zeus, Zeus, Zeus! Why would he create something so stupid?! Why did he have to be crazy?! Why couldn't anything be easy?! She wanted to punch the Olympian in the face so bad it made her heart squeeze.

A tree would do nicely. Kala swung as hard as she could.

PUNCH!

"Ouch. You do realize you just attacked an invalid?" Asmodeus's voice grated on Kala's last nerve.

She had just punched Zeus in the face.

It took her a second to figure out where she was.

Kala stood in front of Zeus in Asmodeus's hideout.

Score.

DAY FOUR

Chapter Twenty-Three

Kala saw Asmodeus sitting at a small wooden table drinking a cappuccino. He smiled. "Guess you're tuned into me. I'm flattered."

"Don't be." Kala didn't like the implication. "I was imagining punching Zeus in the face and I guess the universe agreed with me."

"You keep leaving that Grigori for me. He's going to take it personally someday." He took another sip. "But I don't mind. I never liked that guy anyway."

"I hardly noticed." Kala rolled her eyes.

The place was a decent-sized room in what appeared to be some sort of mansion, or at least a very nice house. The décor consisted of Victorian era antiques, from the ornate table and chair that Asmodeus currently had his rump parked in, to the floral couch, wooden roll-top desk, and the heavy curtains framing a window overlooking fields of green grass.

Kala decided she had had enough with Asmodeus. Grabbing onto Zeus, she tried to teleport out of there.

Nope.

Asmodeus smiled. "The boss man put a no-teleport spell on the guy. Sorry." He stood up and walked over to her. "Cronus wouldn't like it that you're here, either, but I have a soft spot for you."

He reached out to touch her cheek, but Kala swatted his hand away. "You go sit over there. I'm going to talk to Zeus-man for a bit."

Asmodeus did as he was told, adding, "I hear that you actually took my suggestion and talked to Lotun."

"Yeah, and your *boss* took her away just before she could tell me the good stuff," she complained.

"He tends to do that." Asmodeus pretended to sympathize.

"You wouldn't happen to know what Cronus figured out about me, would you?" Kala thought she'd try.

"Why do you think Ms. Lotun isn't here with Zeus? Because Cronus doesn't trust me when it comes to you. He knows I have a weakness for you." Asmodeus shrugged.

She had no idea why Asmodeus felt the way he did about her, but she wasn't above using it against him. The problem was he kissed like a pro. It was too damn tempting. She really didn't want to do the walk of shame because she had made out with the king of Demons. It would be too humiliating.

"Lotun has another piece of the prophecy about me. She was about to tell me what being the Fated One means," Kala admitted. The whole thing was frustrating.

Zeus rubbed his sore nose, but he perked up his head at the mention of prophecy.

"Prophecy, prophecy, prophecy," he cackled. "The one who knows death; she'll be the one who breaks the curse."

Kala focused her attention on Zeus. "Do you know *the one who knows death*? It's a she? Who is she?" Question him while he was making slight sense, she figured.

Zeus cackled and cackled to the point where Kala wanted to punch him again to shut him up. Instead, she spoke as calmly as she could.

"Please, Zeus, who is she?"

His eyes grew wide and he stopped laughing. "The daughter of the man who will sacrifice his life and his gift to save her. She is the one who knows death." He started to giggle again. "You don't have to wait long. She'll be born in three hundred years!" Zeus roared with laughter and began to babble incoherently again.

Kala froze.

Three hundred years?

"He's just messing with me." Kala spun around to Asmodeus. "Right?"

The Demon shrugged. "Could be, but to beings like us, three hundred years isn't that long."

Her heart dropped. "I'm in my twenties and I feel like I've lived a thousand years. I can't do this every four days for three hundred years! I can't!" Kala's mind felt like it was going to explode.

"Calm down, buttercup. Zeus is insane after all. He might be confusing prophecies or people or anything. No need to have a heart attack based on the word of a looney." He took another sip of his espresso.

Kala nodded. She knew Asmodeus was right, but Zeus's words felt true. Her deepest darkest fear was that she'd have to do horrible things forever. And three hundred years might as well be forever to her. As a human, she might have, at least, had some other Atlas wannabe kill her and take over. Morbid, but true. But since she was the full-blown Atlas now, she was stuck with the gig. For as long as the curse lasted.

"Even if it is true, at least you know the curse will be broken someday. That's positive, right?" Asmodeus shrugged his shoulders as if he was giving words of encouragement.

"But three hundred years?!" Kala tried to do the math in her head, but it was never her favorite subject. "That's... I need a calculator."

Asmodeus answered for her though, "It's 27,375 times if you wait the full four days every time."

Kala was stunned. "27,375 *acts of atrocity*!"

"See? That's not so bad." Asmodeus acted like this was proof that Kala was overreacting.

"Not so bad?! I'm going to go insane. There's no way. I'll be straight up evil by the end of it." Kala was beside herself at the mere thought. Every four days doing some vile, horrible thing. Sure, it saved the planet – but what about her? What about her soul? There was no way she wouldn't be destroyed by it. She couldn't even do her second mission, and if the world hadn't been crumbling beneath her feet, she would never have done the first.

"Evil is a bit strong. Jaded, maybe, but who isn't a little bit jaded?"

"You're not helping." She was tired of his positive spin on the whole thing. Especially coming from a Demon!

Kala took a deep breath.

She had listened to Zeus rattle on and on about nonsense. She was reading way too much into what he said. The god was crazy. Prophecy be damned, Kala wasn't one to abide by the rules anyway. Besides, she still was unclear as to what *the one who knows death* meant. Did the girl have some kind of relationship with the Grim Reaper? If all these gods, angels, and Demons existed, why couldn't there be a King of Death?

No more supposition. Kala reminded herself. *Think like a soldier. What's in front of me? What do I need to do right now?*

"I need to sit." Kala sat down on the old-fashioned couch. The cushion was hard but comfortable.

"Would you like an espresso? They're really quite tasty," Asmodeus offered.

She shook her head. "They remind me too much of my first encounter with Atlas."

Asmodeus snapped his fingers and a shot of tequila appeared in Kala's hand. "Your favorite."

She didn't argue. She drank it in one delicious gulp. It made her miss Derek terribly. He was always her drinking buddy in between missions.

She wondered if he was okay and what he was doing. "Thanks." Kala placed the shot glass down on the ground next to her foot.

"Wow. A thank you. Wonders never cease." Asmodeus laughed.

"Don't let it go to your head." She smiled, despite herself.

"Never." He put his hands up in supplication.

"What am I supposed to do now?" Kala didn't expect an answer. She merely needed to speak her worries aloud. "Interrogate crazy-pants here some more?"

"You're the one so desperate to track Zeus down. If Cronus knew you were here, he'd have me move him immediately, so I'd ask him while you can." Asmodeus nodded his head in Zeus's direction.

He was right. Kala had been a broken record claiming that all she needed to do was find Zeus, the god who was dumb enough to create her curse. And now he sat in front of her and he might as well be drooling. What did she hope to pull out of Zeus? What she *had* pulled out of him she didn't like very much. Kala just wanted him to get his brains back in order and reverse the damn spell!

The fact that Asmodeus had let her have this much time with Zeus was a testament to how much the Demon liked her. She had to admit, he was growing on her as well, in an annoying-brother kind of way. An annoying brother that happened to be ridiculously beautiful and a mind-blowing kisser. She didn't want to think about it. Kala was just grateful that Asmodeus allowed her to stay.

No time like the present.

Kala stood up and then kneeled in front of Zeus.

"Zeus?" She tried to stop his ranting.

After repeating his name a few times, the god finally went silent. Zeus stared at Kala with wide, child-like eyes. "I'll tell you something, but we have to be alone."

She looked over at Asmodeus, but he shook his head. "You know I can't do that."

"He can turn around, turn around, turn around," Zeus sang as if these were the words to his favorite song.

Kala pleaded to Asmodeus. "I'm not sure how long he's going to be coherent. Could you just turn your back or something?"

"Fine," Asmodeus sighed. He flipped his chair around and sat with his back to Kala and Zeus.

She focused back on Zeus. "Okay, he's turned around. Now what can you tell me? Can you break this curse?" She still didn't think she was above consuming him if she felt it necessary. Kala didn't want an insane Olympian stuck in her brain, but if it meant breaking the curse, she had to consider it.

Zeus motioned her forward. "Come closer. Secrets. Secrets."

Kala leaned in, her face only inches from his.

He whispered, "The prophecy. I know the rest of it. *He* can't know." Zeus nodded toward Asmodeus. "*He* doesn't want you to know. Neither does Daddy." He giggled. "But Daddy knows. He knows what you are."

Kala carefully took his hands in hers and their eyes met. "What is the prophecy? What am I?"

Zeus stared down at their touching hands. When he looked back up at Kala, his eyes were crazed. "Fix me now."

The words sounded strange to Kala's ears. She was about to ask him to repeat it when she felt an excruciating pain flood through her hands and to the rest of her body. She tried to move, but found that she was paralyzed. Not even her voice would work. With all her strength, Kala tried to scream out to Asmodeus, but Zeus had her locked in place.

His voice was barely above a whisper, "This won't kill you."

Small comfort.

The pain intensified. Kala tried to tap into the power inside her. To swallow him, to fight him, anything to stop the agony.

She found it right away. The spot where she had pulled her strength from before. But Kala couldn't touch it, couldn't use it, couldn't do anything with it.

Because Zeus was draining it dry.

The silent horror of what was happening made Kala feel completely useless. The pain started to wane, but so did her energy. She was losing consciousness. It was as if Zeus had tapped into her life-source. He was recharging. Healing himself. Kala could see it in his face. His eyes cleared up, his skin de-aged until he looked about thirty-something, his hair turned from white to brown.

And then Zeus had apparently taken what he needed, because he dropped Kala's hands. All of her functions returned to her, but she was so exhausted she could barely move a finger. She struggled to keep her eyes open. She wanted to stay awake. Zeus had used her. Sapped her. She was going to lose him.

Zeus cleared his throat to grab Asmodeus's attention. When Asmodeus didn't turn Zeus replied. "You really do have an affection for the girl. Such loyalty."

Asmodeus turned around at that.

Kala could see the terror and shock in Asmodeus's face at seeing Zeus fully restored and capable. Then worry and anger at Kala flopped out on the floor.

But Asmodeus was smart. He put his hands up in peace. "What did you do to her?"

Zeus laughed. Not the crazy-insane laugh like before, but an honest mirth at Asmodeus's words. "Nothing Ms. Hicks can't handle. She'll be back as new in a few hours."

Somehow that didn't make Kala feel any better. She could barely stay conscious.

"Asmodeus, you must choose. Me or my father?" Zeus put it to him candidly.

"Can't I be Switzerland?" The Demon raised an eyebrow with a hopeful smile.

"I don't understand that reference, but I'm assuming you don't want to decide just yet. I'll give you a few days to think it over, weigh your options. But know this: I plan on uniting everyone and everything against my father and if you don't stand with me, you will pay the consequences." Zeus's words were filled with power.

Kala tried to slap herself awake, but it was no good. Her body was completely depleted. She wanted to speak. To ask him questions. If he was at full strength he could break the curse. The obvious war that was coming didn't faze her. She didn't care about any of it.

Kala just didn't want to do horrible things anymore.

As if Zeus had heard, he peered down at her. "I'm sorry, little one. I'll need you on my side, so don't take what I did personally. My father will try and convince you to side with him, but you mustn't listen. He should not rule. He should never have ruled in the first place."

It took every ounce of strength for Kala to speak. "What… did you… do… to me?"

Zeus leaned down. Though his eyes were full of hope and kindness, Kala still wanted to punch him again if she were capable. "I'll let you discover that on your own. I'm sure my father will tell you as a way to gain your trust. You have something very old and very powerful inside you, Kala Hicks. Even before you consumed Atlas no supernatural being would have been able to harm you." He sighed and smiled warmly. "The Fated One. I never thought I'd see the day."

"What… about the curse?" she croaked out.

His face turned sad and he shook his head. "As crazy as I was, I was telling the truth. A girl born three hundred years from now will be the one who breaks it. I would if I could but, if truth be told, I don't know how I created it in the first place. It was born of anger and madness. I had no control. But this girl. She will be very special. Like you."

Kala wanted to cry. She didn't want to believe the Olympian. She wanted him to be lying. Three hundred years of doing the unthinkable. It hurt her so deeply she couldn't stay awake any longer.

She just wanted to be unconscious so she wouldn't feel the pain anymore.

So she wouldn't feel anything.

Kala closed her eyes and fell asleep.

Chapter Twenty-Four

T hat didn't work.

Kala woke up encased in dirt.

She could breathe, though, which quashed her initial panic. Figuring it was because of her Atlas-side, Kala tried to find a way out.

Maneuvering her hands and arms was easier than she thought it would be. The dirt was loose so she was able to dig in an upward motion. Even though her nose, mouth, and eyes were caked in soil, for some reason it didn't bother her.

Normally, the mere thought of being buried alive would have terrified her, but for reasons she couldn't explain Kala felt comforted. It was as if the earth was blanketing her from all the horror she had faced her whole life.

After a few minutes of digging, Kala stopped. She wasn't making any headway and the longer she stayed in the dirt, the more at home she felt. For someone who despised nature, this sensation was completely foreign. Breathing made all the difference. It made her understand that the real fear was suffocating to death.

Kala didn't have that.

She knew she couldn't die like this.

Kala had no proof, but deep down, she just knew.

The longer she stayed, the stronger she felt.

She was recharging.

It was such a strange notion that she almost dismissed it entirely, yet the more she thought about it, the more she knew it was true. She could feel it. Literally, feel the part of herself that Zeus had drained gaining strength, pulling energy from the earth, from the life within it.

Was this a skill that Atlas had? But her secret-power-source was the part of her that devoured Atlas, so it had nothing to do with him.

Why would lying inside the dirt heal her?

Kala hated dirt.

She hated bugs. She hated camping. She hated all of it.

Give her a city and the girl was happy. Take her out to the woods and she was miserable. It had always been that way.

Now, she was buried alive and… loving it.

A part of her wanted to stay down there. If the world ended, she doubted she'd feel anything. She could just sleep. It would be so nice to rest. Really rest.

But like all good fantasies, Kala awoke from hers as two hands yanked her out of the earth.

She could barely see because of the cake of dirt covering her face. The sun was so bright she had to squint to focus on anything. When her vision finally adjusted, she stared up at the man who pulled her from the ground.

Cronus.

Fantastic.

Kala replied warily, "Could you not electrocute me right now? I've had a very hard day."

"I'm not going to hurt you. I'm the one who buried you. To heal you." Cronus's voice was calm and what was worse… nice.

"Zeus said you'd be sucking up." Kala always used to feel jealous of powerful people because of the way everyone would always swoon and give them what they wanted. Now that the head Titan and the head Olympian were both vying for her favor: it felt gross. Fake. Annoying.

"You do feel better, don't you?" Cronus prodded.

She did.

Kala didn't want to give him the satisfaction though, so she cut to the chase. "What do you want?"

"Don't you want to know *why* you feel better?" Cronus watched Kala's reaction carefully.

Yes, she did, but she really hated it when people "fished." Lali used to do that. Of course now Kala knew her former team member was a Demon, so maybe it had been Lali's way of irritating Kala. Lali would always leave voice mails, such as *I have huge news, call me* or *You'll never guess what? Call me.* So the only way Kala could find out what happened is if she phoned back and asked. It was a serious pet peeve of hers.

Kala viewed her surroundings. An enormous mansion towered behind them. It looked like it was built hundreds of years ago, definitely European in its architecture. It reminded Kala of a BBC mini-series for a Jane Austen or Dickens novel. She had been buried in the back yard of this gigantic estate. The place where Cronus had pulled her up out of the earth ruined the perfectly manicured lawn.

"Well, don't you want to know?" Cronus lost his patience.

"You obviously want to tell me and I'm not going to beg." Kala shook her head. "I'm sick of being pulled back and forth between sides. I don't care what you people do to yourselves, just leave me out of it."

Cronus examined her with an unreadable expression.

Kala could tell he still wasn't used to her giving him attitude. She just hoped he wouldn't throw another lightning bolt in her chest.

"It makes sense, you know. Your attitude, your power, your abilities. I don't give much thought to prophecies unless they involve me, but I should have paid attention to yours," Cronus began. Then he motioned toward the house and a small garden area with table and chairs. "Would you like to sit?"

Kala glanced down at herself and comprehended how crazy she looked. She had a thick layer of mud and dirt over every inch of her body. "I think I need to wash up."

Cronus snapped his fingers. She was clean from head to toe.

"Nice," she approved. "Look, I've been dicked around since I met you and your little family. Just tell me what you know about me and the prophecy." She was tired of waiting. Tired of these *superbeings* lording over their knowledge. Knowledge about *her*.

Cronus nodded slowly. "Very well. I'll show you the prophecy and we'll see what you make of it." He waved his hand slightly and an old parchment appeared. Handing it to Kala, he said, "The complete prophecy."

Kala carefully took the parchment paper from him. The prophecy wasn't that much longer than Penny's, maybe a paragraph. But the last sentence that referred directly to her didn't make sense to Kala. It only confused her more:

One cannot live while the other one exists. A new Atlas shall reign and the potential must die. A beginning to the end and an end to the beginning. A new paradise shall be born. The Fated One will be the last.

The cost will be great, and the immortals will reign. The one that knows death will release the curse of balance. She will be born from the man with the power of death. He will sacrifice his life and his gift to save the balancer.

The Fated One is the first. The first of us all. The mother of us all, born into a human.

"What does it mean?" Kala peered up at Cronus.

Cronus smiled gently. "It means you were born with the power of Gaia."

Crickets.

"Who?"

Irritated, he accused, "You really don't know anything, do you?"

"I'm sorry if I'm not a history major. Just tell me who the hell Gaia is and why she's stuck inside me?" Kala felt a flood of relief, finally hearing some answers, but it was rapidly morphing into stress because she had more questions.

"Gaia is my mother," Cronus answered. "She's the Earth. As in *Mother Earth*."

Kala could see that she had stretched Cronus's every last nerve. "And I'm her?" This was going nutzoid fast.

"A part of you, yes. But my mother has been sleeping for thousands of years. She is still very much alive. So, no, it's not like when you devoured Atlas. She simply placed a part of her power inside of you. But it was enough to consume Atlas, and it would be enough to consume any of us. Gaia's powers are endless, even a small piece of it. But, Kala, she gave you her power so that you could save the world from the Grigori." Cronus was dead serious.

Kala shook her head. "Oh, no. You're not going to rope me into this little battle of yours. Owen is my dad and Talan is my... well he's my... friend. And he doesn't attack me with lightning bolts!" Cronus was a professional manipulator. Zeus had warned her and he was right. Cronus was trying to twist the prophecy so he could get her to do what he wanted her to do. It aggravated her immensely. "AND...the prophecy doesn't say anything about stopping the Grigori, so you're full of it!"

"It may not say it directly, but *it's implied*," Cronus argued. He didn't like the fact that Kala didn't automatically fall in line. She could see that he expected it of her.

"You haven't been around humans in a really long time. You need to brush up on your persuasion skills. It's *implied*?! That's ridiculous. There was nothing about the Grigori implied or otherwise in that prophecy. You're scared they're going to take your power away and you want them sent back to their prison. Just be straight with me, I'd respect you a lot more." Kala wasn't going to put up with Cronus's bull for a second. If he thought she'd turn against the only father she had ever known, or the one being who had her back at every turn? Forget it. "You're delusional," she added for measure.

"I'm delusional?" Cronus was taken aback. "*The immortals will reign,*" he quoted back to her. "Who do you think makes the immortals?"

"What are you talking about?" Kala wanted to slap some sense into this guy. "*You're* the immortals, all of you freakazoids, including me now that I wolfed down one of you. Grigori can't *make* immortals."

"Can't they? Let me show you what will happen if you *do* complete your mission." Cronus's eyes were full of fury and intensity.

It made Kala take a step back. "I don't want to see…" That was a lie. Kala desperately wanted to see *why* destroying the cure for cancer was a good thing.

Cronus cut her off. "You do. I can see it in your eyes. That pet of Talan's, John Fortski, invents something much more dangerous than a cancer cure. Because his research is destroyed, he has to start from scratch. It's because of that act that he discovers the formula that he's been working his whole life to make." Cronus's eyes were wide with dread. "Kala. He gives humans *immortality.*"

Kala knew this was supposed to horrify her, but it gave her a sense of relief. If humans were immortal then they'd be cured of *all* diseases. "That's kind of cool," was her honest answer.

"Kind of cool? That could be the end to true immortal beings, including yourself, and you think it's *kind of cool!*" Cronus was furious.

"Don't get your panties in a bunch. I'm pretty sure you'll be just fine. Zeus said I'd be doing my job for another three hundred years. Yay. So, I think we're all going to be okay." Kala felt like she was dealing with a serious drama queen. A suit-in-tie-Titan drama queen, but a drama queen all the same. So what if humans found immortality? They'd certainly been looking for it for a long time. And it made Kala feel a lot better about her job. She still hoped Roberta could do it for her, but if she had to do it, now she knew Fortski would invent something even better. Balance. It was finally making sense.

"Do you want to see this wonderful future you think you're going to be living in?" Cronus had a look on his face that pretty much told Kala she couldn't refuse him.

Kala had seen what would happen if she didn't wipe out the cure: mayhem and destruction. There wasn't anything that Cronus could show her that would be worse than that. But she hadn't seen the future of what would happen if she *did* destroy it. Her curiosity could never say no to a *future vision*, so it made it easy for her to say, "Sure."

Cronus held out his hands and Kala tentatively took them. Trusting the Titan didn't feel natural. Considering the only time she'd had contact with guy ended up in some kind of super-battle, she felt pretty justified in her wariness.

But he held onto Kala without zapping or attacking her.

As with Talan, the vision flooded over her like she was watching a holographic movie. As the years flew by it was like watching humanity on fast-forward. And Kala saw the real problem with immortality.

There were too many, more and more people, to the point where it almost made her feel claustrophobic. On the ground, in malls, in the sky with lane upon lane of flying cars, humans were everywhere. No one died. People kept reproducing. How long could the earth sustain it? What was the point of immortality if the planet you lived on wasn't big enough?

Apparently someone else had the same idea, because the rest of the images that flew by her were a horrifying blur: men in hazmat suits exterminating people as if they were cockroaches, serial killers with free reign to kill, executions, staged natural disasters, all in poorer areas, all people who the rich wouldn't miss or even knew were gone.

Population control.

She felt Cronus's hands slide away. The vision stopped.

He looked at her with a sad expression on his face. "Your precious Grigori are teaching the man who is responsible for all of that chaos. He will rule the world someday if you don't stop them."

Kala couldn't imagine anyone killing that many people, even if it was for the greater good. Whoever this man was, he needed to be stopped. "Who?"

"Who do you think? General Geoffrey Turner," Cronus spat.

Turner? How? Why? What could possibly turn the man she admired so much into a mass murderer? It didn't make sense. It couldn't be real. She needed to talk to Talan. She needed answers from someone other than Cronus.

The Titan shook his head. "I won't let you complete your mission," he added with determination.

"But then the world will end."

"I'd rather end it all than see the future we saw come to pass," Cronus said.

"What are you going to do?" she asked, not wanting to hear the answer.

"I'll stop you by any means necessary."

Ominous.

Great.

Kala grumbled.

Chapter Twenty-Five

In a blink of an eye, Cronus disappeared and Kala was alone on the manicured lawn. She had no idea where she was. It could have been anywhere really. This whole teleportation power was pretty handy when she could control it.

Kala figured she'd better concentrate on Angel-Boy since she had a flood of questions to ask him, the first of which was how on earth Turner could be responsible for what Cronus had shown her. Knowing the man and working for his elite military team had given her special insight into Turner's character. She knew him to be fair, and honestly, a very helpful human being. Kala never would have survived her ordeal with Atlas without Turner and Roberta. Even if what she saw was true, maybe it really was to save the planet. Look at what *she* was being forced to do to stop the world from ending. As terrifying and horrible as the vision was, Kala knew the wisdom of never judging unless you'd walked in the other person's shoes. And Turner had never judged her. Neither had Roberta. Kala couldn't imagine that they'd kill so many innocent people. Maybe

Cronus was lying, trying to turn her against them so that she would join his side.

She just didn't know.

Talan.

A second later, Kala was back in Talan's D.C. apartment.

At this point, it felt like home.

Talan was alone and sitting on his couch. When she popped in, he looked up, his face filled with concern. He stood up and met her from a respectable distance of about a foot. It felt like a mile. That was the problem with chemistry: you didn't have to be touching to feel it. Sometimes being across the room could be more torturous than holding hands.

Kala shoved her feelings aside. "I was with Cronus." Then she told him everything, from Zeus recharging his batteries, to the whole *Gaia* thing, to the future vision, to Cronus's threat to stop her from completing the mission.

Speaking of her mission made Kala glance at the clock.

0d 10h 33m 15s.

7:27 PM!

PM!

Before Talan could respond to her lowdown, Kala gasped. "I only have ten hours! What happened?!"

Talan gently touched her arm. He tried to hide his shock over everything Kala had told him. "You were probably in the earth for hours. Cronus was right, you needed to recharge after Zeus drained you."

It blew Kala's mind that she had rested comfortably in dirt for what must have been at least thirteen hours. Her life now was so foreign to her, Kala was surprised she could function properly. It had to be her training as a soldier. Take one step at a time and only focus on what was in front of you. Without it, she would have been bonkers by now.

"It explains so much." Talan shook his head. "Gaia." Apparently, this made him awestruck.

"I'm still not sure what all this means. Talan, the future I saw…" Kala began.

His far-off look turned back into super-focus. "If Fortski does invent a cure to mortality, then over-population is the natural order. But mass murder? I've seen Turner make sacrifices most people would never consider just to save *one* soldier. It would have to be a pretty desperate situation for him to resort to killing innocents."

"Is there any way we could see? Maybe Cronus altered the vision to make me side with him." Kala didn't want to believe Turner was capable of what she saw. "Or maybe it wasn't Turner at all. I never saw him in the vision."

"One way to find out." He held out his hand.

Kala took it gladly. She needed to feel their connection. The energy that always passed between them. It invigorated her as much as it comforted her. She closed her eyes and waited for the vision to start.

Colors swirled and took form. It was the same future that Cronus had shown her: humans multiplying like rabbits. But before seeing the mass murders, though, she saw roads being replaced by grass and trees, water recycling plants, paper and packaging laws – so many things that improved the world it made her dizzy. But the people kept coming. Growing in number, taking over every inch of unpopulated land.

Turner was there. He was a leader, in charge of population control. He appeared to be very powerful. He was being told that the trees and grass weren't enough: the world was running out of oxygen. He had to think of something. He was in charge of keeping the human race alive. Him. Only him.

She'd seen enough.

Kala took her hands away from Talan's to make the vision stop.

"I know what happens next. I don't need to see it again." Kala didn't want to watch the killings. Cronus had been right, but he'd only shown her the worst parts. Whether his goal was to manipulate her or not, Kala knew that the murders were true. Kill in small amounts to save the many. As a soldier, she knew that mantra well. It was something that Jack believed in more than anyone she knew. It was why he'd begged her to kill him.

To save the world.

"It doesn't look like he'll have a choice." Talan seemed to be processing what he had witnessed as well.

"Is this what we want for human kind? Sacrificing innocent people just so the rest can live forever? Is immortality worth that? This doesn't seem like balance at all." Kala's anger rose steadily. "Curing cancer sounds way better!" She was venting now. "But because of this stupid curse, I don't even have a choice! If I don't destroy it, the world will end anyway! It's like the universe is blackmailing me!"

Talan carefully touched her arm, trying to stay within his bounds. "You can't control what the world sees as balance, Kala. No one can. We may not like it, but that future is the one destined for mankind. If your curse didn't exist, the powers-that-be would have destroyed the cure for cancer some other way. It's destiny."

Kala shrugged away from his touch. "The Grigori are the ones that brought people into this new age. Maybe Cronus was right to imprison you."

She regretted saying it as soon as the words left her lips. Talan's face fell.

"I'm sorry," she started.

Talan cut her off. "No. You're right. We helped shape this future to come. But as horrible as some of it is, the marvels you humans have created and are going to create are miraculous. I don't regret what we did, I'm proud of it."

Kala didn't argue with him. She was simply upset by what she had seen. But she couldn't completely agree with Talan, either. Maybe Cronus was right; maybe the Grigori were too dangerous.

It didn't matter.

Kala was loyal to a fault.

Owen and Talan could be the devil themselves and she would still die for them. That was Cronus's big mistake, because he'd never be able to convince her to betray them. Having a childhood without any strong connections to anyone made Kala overly loyal to those she considered family. What could she expect from a Titan who would turn on his own father and then his own son? He'd rather let the world die than have a future where humans could potentially out-power him.

"You know I'll never turn against you, right?" Kala needed to say it aloud.

She could see from the expression on his face that Talan didn't know the extent of her loyalty.

She felt an overwhelming desire to comfort him. It was so strong she found her hand reaching out to touch his face before she could stop herself. "I know I can seem cold at times, and that I don't appreciate everything you've done for me, but I do. I really care about you, Talan." Expressing emotions was more difficult for Kala than being Atlas, but she wanted Talan to know she didn't take him for granted.

Talan reached up and held the hand that touched his cheek. Kala felt a thrill at his touch. Normally, she'd jump the guy and take out all her stress and aggression in wild, amazing sex, but she genuinely had feelings for Talan and she didn't want to ruin what they had. He already thought they were soul mates; having sex with him would just confuse things. Kala's heart belonged to Jack. She knew he was dead, but the emotional wound was still raw and fresh with pain.

But the longer he held her hand, the more she wanted him. It may have been pure chemistry and hormones, but Kala wasn't the poster child for restraint. Look at her kiss with Asmodeus.

Before she could think better of it, Kala leaned in and kissed him. Electricity raced through her as his lips answered her back in the most passionate kiss Kala had ever experienced. She could feel her brain turning to mushy-mush-mush as Talan pulled her in tight from the small of her back. Their bodies pressed against each other, Kala felt the heat between them like a living fire.

She didn't think she could stop.

She didn't want to.

Kala wanted to hold onto this sensation. It made her forget everything. It made her feel amazing. It made her feel alive.

She had thought Asmodeus was a good kisser, but Talan… It was so intense Kala's brain turned to jelly. Her mind could think of nothing else but his hands on her body, his lips on her mouth, and the ache in her chest only had her wanting more.

Kala could barely breathe it was so overwhelming. She took control and threw Talan on the couch so that she was on top. This only excited Talan more as he pulled her in close, grabbing on to her thighs as if he would devour her whole. His need for Kala fueled her passion.

As if coming to his senses, Talan pulled away slightly. "Kala, maybe we shouldn't…"

She shut him up by kissing him hungrily. She didn't want to hear logic or should we- shouldn't-we. Kala just wanted to lose herself in the physical pleasure she was experiencing. To forget everything and just be in this moment with someone that cared about her.

Deep inside Kala, she knew what she was doing was wrong. She cared about him, but she didn't love him. She only loved Jack. And he was gone forever.

To wipe the thought from her mind, Kala peeled off her shirt so she was only in her bra. She started to unzip Talan's pants.

Talan's hand gently stopped her. "You're not ready," he said breathlessly.

"You don't know what I'm ready for." She continued trying to take off his pants, but it was too late.

His words took over and jolted her into reality.

It hurt.

The pain in her chest squeezed and Kala couldn't stop it.

What was she doing?

So much had happened in the last four days, Kala hadn't had time to mourn Jack. Instead of dealing with it, she was trying to avoid it by using Talan and his feelings for her.

She didn't think she could feel any lower.

Kala was grateful that Talan had stopped them. Being with him would have made things so much more complicated. It was going to be bad enough from this make-out session alone. Was he going to turn all stalker-puppy on her?

Looking into Talan's eyes, she knew he wouldn't. She saw something in him that she had only seen in Jack.

He loved her.

It struck her like a bullet to the heart and she cracked.

"Don't look at me like that!" she yelled. But it was too late. She could feel the tears threatening to take over. Kala hardly ever cried. Only when she had killed Jack had she truly lost it. She learned early on that crying only led to more pain and never did her any good. Being a Titan – fighting gods, angels and Demons – those were close enough to being a soldier that Kala could deal. But *her feelings*? The flood of emotion threatened to drown her.

"I can't help how I see you." Talan reached out his hand and touched her cheek. "I know you don't feel the same, but I love you, even if you never love me back."

"Please, don't. I can't hear that. I…" Kala desperately tried to push down her emotions. "I miss him," her voice choked.

Talan held her and she fell into his chest. He stroked her hair as she took comfort in his arms. "I'm so sorry, Kala."

Normally, Kala would fight being held by any man, but she was tired. Tired of fighting, tired of her walls. As much as sex would have given her a momentary ounce of satisfaction, being with Talan and feeling him hold her close ended up being so much more fulfilling.

I've been waiting for your go-ahead, but time was running out and I happened to be in Fortski's lab… Anyway, I couldn't do it. I tried to smash his computers, but it was as if some kind of force field protected them. I thought they were Fortski's invention, but he looked just as shocked as I did… Hello?… Kala? Are you there?

It was such a shocking moment, having Roberta jump into her brain just then, that Kala forgot how to respond back. But Roberta's words started to sink in.

Kala sighed heavily.

Roberta couldn't do it.

Of course she couldn't.

Kala knew this from the beginning. She merely enjoyed living in denial for a while.

Where are you now? Kala asked.

Oh, thank God, I thought Clifton had found some way to shut down our communication. Kala, I'm in trouble. You're going to have to find Geoffrey.

A knot twisted in Kala's stomach. *What happened?* She asked with dread.

Fortski flipped out as you can imagine… Kala… Clifton has me in the Compound, and I don't think he plans on letting me out. Ever.

Kala's head hurt. This was all her fault.

I'm on my way.

Chapter Twenty-Six

$\mathbf{Q}$uickly dressing herself, Kala pulled away from Talan, a spring in her step. Missions. She liked those. At least the kind that meant saving someone and not doing something unconscionable.

Talan was alert. "What is it?"

"Roberta just *mind-melded* me and she's in trouble. Clifton has her prisoner for trying to destroy Fortski's lab."

"Did it work? Was she able to do it?" Talan seemed genuinely curious.

"No, Mr. Smarty Pants, you were right. She said it was like some sort of force field."

"Only the Atlas can perform the Atlas duty." He nodded as if this news confirmed everything he had ever thought.

Kala wasn't up for a round of I-told-you-so, so she laid out her plan. "Let's teleport inside the Compound, grab Roberta, then take her to Turner. I can worry about the mission in…" She glanced at the clock. "Nine hours, really?" The countdown began to crush her soul yet again, but focusing on Roberta's rescue helped.

"I'm with you." Talan clasped her hand.

Together they focused on the Compound.

Nothing.

Kala concentrated as hard as she could.

Still nothing.

Talan took his hand away. "Something's wrong. You don't think Rotoph is blocking teleportation again?"

A sinking sensation roiled in Kala's gut.

I'll stop you by any means necessary. The words repeated over and over in her head.

"Cronus," she said aloud.

Talan nodded. "He's blocking us from teleporting in."

"I'll have to do it the old-fashioned way, I guess." Kala shrugged. "Time to talk to Turner and Derek."

Talan was on board. He gripped her hand.

***

The next second they were in Turner's house. His living room, to be precise.

Kala eyes met Derek's.

A surge of warmth spread through her body and she felt as if her heart would explode where she stood. Seeing his beautiful brown eyes and dazzling smile made her happy beyond measure.

Derek ran over to her and picked her up off her feet in a giant bear hug. Kala enjoyed the moment as long as she could, which lasted until Derek put her down.

"I was worried about you," he said. His face radiated relief at seeing her alive and well.

"I'm kind of hard to kill nowadays." Kala bumped up against him playfully.

Turner stepped into view, seemingly amused at finding Kala and

Talan in his living room. "What brings you two here?"

Kala didn't want to be the one to tell him, but she needed his help. "Clifton is holding Roberta in the Compound."

Turner's face turned pale. "Why would Harry detain my wife?"

She could see the anger starting to boil inside Turner and she didn't want to admit the situation was her fault, but she needed him to know everything. "She was doing me a favor…"

Turner cut her off with his hand. "Is this about the cancer thing?"

Kala nodded. "I didn't know…" What didn't she know? She knew it was dangerous. She knew Roberta was risking herself. She knew it probably wouldn't work. But did she stop Roberta? Did she ever consider the consequences? She was ashamed to admit that the answer was *no*.

Turner was dialing his cell phone. He put it on speakerphone.

"Hello?" General Clifton's voice came through the cell phone in a casual tone.

"Harry? What on earth are you doing with my wife?" Turner accused abrasively.

"Excuse me? What are you talking about? What would I want with Roberta?" Clifton sounded irritated.

He put on a good show. If Kala hadn't known for certain that he had taken Roberta, she might have believed him.

Turner shook his head. "I know you have her, Harry. Let her go and I'll forget this ever happened."

"Where is this coming from? Why would Roberta be at the Compound anyway? I'm telling you the truth. I don't know where she is." Clifton's sincerity was flawless.

This guy was good.

Turner wasn't easily fooled though. "You're honestly going to sit there and lie to me?" He paused, not sure how to proceed. Then his anger erupted, "Deny it all you want, but I have my sources and I know you've taken her. If you harm one hair on her head, they'll never find your body." He hung up.

The fire in his expression was something Kala had never seen in Turner. It was murderous. He'd rip Clifton from limb-to-limb to save Roberta and wouldn't think twice about it. Seeing that look made Kala grasp that his love for his wife was the only motivation he needed to kill innocents in the future she'd witnessed. If Roberta's life was on the line, there was nothing Turner wouldn't do, of that Kala was certain. He had said as much when she asked him what he would have done if his mission had been to kill Roberta. *I'd let it burn.*

And he would.

Right now, Turner looked like he was going to burn Clifton to the ground.

"You're positive Harry has her?" Turner already knew the answer, but he needed to hear it.

"Roberta told me herself." Kala tapped her head.

"Well, you heard him. He's denying the whole thing. He's always been jealous and he's always wanted her for himself. He's going to try and keep her like a possession. The man is insane."

Kala wondered why Turner would have worked with Clifton for so long if he really felt that way, but power created odd bedfellows. Time could build up resentments, destroying the strongest of friendships. If Clifton really did have feelings for Roberta before Turner came along, it must have been pretty painful to watch another man swoop in and marry her whether it was his best friend or not.

"Can't you teleport in there?" Turner asked, his anger intensifying.

"We're being blocked again," Talan informed him.

"That's why we came to you," Kala replied. "We're going to have to break her out. Without magic."

Turner didn't seem fazed by this in the least. "I've got a bag of tricks Clifton knows nothing about." Focusing on Kala, his expression left no room for argument. "Roberta is the mission. I don't care about your *Atlas* thing, understand? Once Roberta is safe, I'll give you access to Fortski's lab and you do what you need to. Are we agreed?"

Being a Titan, Kala shouldn't have felt intimidated in the least, but the man radiated more power than Cronus. He really would rule the world. Kala envied the love Turner and Roberta had for each other. She had chosen the world instead of Jack. If Turner had been in her place, the earth would have crumbled by now. The thought stung in a way she never expected. Kala shook it from her mind and didn't bat an eye as she said, "Roberta's mission one. Agreed." Going after Roberta somehow made her feel better. As if doing this would make what she did to Jack hurt less.

"I'll let Mr. Echolls take you to my own personal Cog." Turner motioned for the two of them to go.

Kala's heart jumped in her throat. The Cog in the Compound was full of insanely advanced technological inventions designed solely for combat. If Turner had a Cog of his own, she was excited to see what toys he had.

Turner nodded to Talan. "You. I need your eyes. I have my own security cameras stationed around the Compound. If there are any of your angels or Titans around, you'll be able to recognize them, correct?"

Talan's eyes lit up. "Yes." He looked at Kala. "I'll gather the Grigori that passed through the portal and we'll take care of Cronus."

Kala was worried about whether or not the Grigori could do much to Cronus. Maybe their combined powers could at least distract him long enough for her to complete her mission and get the hell out of the Compound. Breaking in would be hard enough, but escaping would be so much easier if she could teleport Roberta and Derek to safety. "Be careful," she said.

"You too." Talan smiled, then walked with Turner to another room.

Kala turned back to Derek. He was grinning. "What's that look for?"

"That guy is in love!" He laughed.

"Shut up." Kala punched him in the arm.

"Have you beat him up yet? It seems to be a pattern with you," Derek teased.

"You seriously suck so hard right now. Can you just take me to Turner's Cog?" Kala smiled, but she wanted to change the subject. Even joking about Talan's feelings for her made her uncomfortable.

Derek picked up on her mood change right away because he observed, "I get it. I never thought I'd see the day when Kala Hicks actually had feelings for someone other than friendship."

Apparently, Kala's face was an open book. A thought struck her: Derek never knew about her and Jack. She had never told him and he had never picked up on it. Of course, after the rollercoaster ride of the last eight days, the subject of her love life never came up. Did Derek even know that Jack was dead?

Kala stopped him in the hallway. "Derek."

Seeing Kala's seriousness made Derek pause. "It's none of my business I was just teasing you…"

She shook her head. "Jack's dead."

He stared at her for a few moments, then nodded in acceptance. "These supernatural freaks take him out? Is that why you're so protective of me?"

"I'm protective of you because you're my family, but Derek…" Kala didn't want to tell him, she wanted to blame anyone else for Jack's murder. She couldn't bear to see the look of disgust on Derek's face when she admitted her guilt. Taking a deep breath, she charged forward, "*I'm* the supernatural freak that killed him." The catch in her voice was unavoidable. Saying it aloud to Derek hurt her more than she could have imagined.

"Was he *evil?*"

It was obvious that Derek had complete faith in Kala. He trusted her judgment and if Jack needed to be killed, then he needed to be killed. It made it all the more painful for her.

"No. It was my Atlas mission. If I didn't kill him the world would collapse. That earthquake you felt a few days ago? That was me not wanting to go through with it. I almost let the world end to keep him alive, Derek."

Kala shoved down her tears as much as she could. "I loved him."

Instead of the hate and disappointment Kala expected to see in Derek's eyes, she saw recognition and understanding. He could have condemned her right there, and she would have understood completely, but instead…

He hugged her.

It was the last thing Kala expected.

She clung to him, sapping out every ounce of comfort she could.

"You saved us all, Kala. Jack would be proud."

The words were meant to reassure her, but they slashed her heart in two. The image of Jack's lifeless body collapsing to the floor from *her* bullet would stay with Kala forever. And the hardest part to come to terms with was the fact that Derek was right: Jack *would* be proud of her. For some reason, that made it worse.

She pulled away, regaining her composure. Kala needed to keep her emotions bottled up if they were going to rescue Roberta.

But Derek wasn't ready to let Kala off that easy. "I'm sorry about Jack." He paused then shook his head. "I can't believe I never saw it."

"Lali saw it and she was a Demon." Kala's way of squeezing out of intense moments was with humor.

"She's a Demon?" That took Derek by surprise.

"*Was*." Kala understood he had no idea that Lali was dead either.

Derek's smile faded and Kala felt a swarm of guilt rush over her. In the span of two minutes she had told him that the other two members of their tight-knit crew were gone. Whether Lali was a Demon or not didn't matter. They had spent enough time together that the four of them were inseparable.

Derek was all she had left.

"I didn't mean to make light of it…" Kala was at a loss.

Derek processed his emotions the way Kala did. He took a few moments, then nodded. Slowly he cracked a small smile. "I can see the Demon thing. Lali wasn't exactly friendly."

Kala smiled back. "We're okay, right?"

His expression was serious. "We're more than okay. We're family. You're never getting rid of me."

Kala didn't bother to hide her relief as she sighed, "Good. Now, can we start this mission or not?"

Derek grinned as he led the way to Turner's Cog. "You're the one spilling her guts."

"Shut up." Kala couldn't help but feel happy. Derek always knew her moods – when to push and when to pull back. She rubbed her hands together, readying herself for the Cog. "Let's do this."

After a few more hallways, they arrived at a steel metal door with a DNA scanner next to it. Derek stuck his thumb in and with a KERPLUNK, the door slowly swung open. He turned to Kala before they entered. "This stuff is insane."

She was ready to see what toys they could use. Derek opened the door the rest of the way and motioned Kala inside.

The room was big and cluttered, not at all like the Cog in the Compound. Of course, that one was neat and orderly for secrecy, with every door sealed up, hiding what was behind it. Here, it was a free-for-all for gadgets and gizmos. The actual space was about the size and shape of a semi-truck, long and narrow. The more Kala examined the area, the more she noticed that what had seemed like a mess of wires and metal was actually a structured workspace.

"Do you know what all this stuff does?" she asked, a little jealous that Derek had free rein of Turner's personal technology.

"About a tenth of it. A lot of these devices are still in progress, but some of them would blow your mind." Derek smiled, then thought better of his statement. "Although with your *super powers* maybe it wouldn't." He shrugged.

Kala said playfully. "Ha, ha. Trust me, I'd rather deal with technology than my spotty teleportation skills. I kind of suck at all this stuff. I miss being a soldier."

Derek looked thoughtful. "You'll always be a soldier, Kala. Now you're just a soldier in a more powerful army."

"I guess, but I miss the days when everything was a little more black and white."

He sighed with a laugh. "So do I. Demons, angels, gods, Titans… seriously? And *you*. You're freaking *Atlas*. Now I know why you kept asking me if you were hallucinating. That's how I feel all the time lately."

"Well, I'm still not ruling out that possibility." She shook her head. "I'm glad we're together though."

"Me, too."

Derek knew his way around and led Kala directly to a metal workbench that had three pairs of goggles lying on it. The goggles were a spectacle unto themselves, they had so many tiny levers and buttons attached to them. It reminded Kala of the night vision goggles she'd used in the past, but more complicated and smaller. Next to each pair was an egg-shaped metal device the size of a thimble.

"Say hello to our eyes." Derek grabbed a pair of the goggles and handed them to Kala. "Put them on. Let me show you."

Kala placed them on, but all she saw was Derek standing in front of her. There was nothing special about the view through the lenses. "Should I press some buttons or something?"

"Hold on, Miss Impatience." Derek picked up one of the metal eggs, pressing a button that opened it up.

The egg appeared empty inside which made Kala want to say something, but she waited for Derek to show her what the device did.

"Okay, now…" Derek reached over and flipped a lever on the side of Kala's goggles.

Tiny pinpricks of red dots flowed out of the small egg.

"Nanobots." Kala recognized.

"Phase-nanobots." He grinned.

Kala looked up at Derek with surprise. "Like the suits?" If the nanobots were like phase-suits they'd be able to move through any wall, and being so small, no one would ever know it. She hated phase-suits with a passion. Walking through walls wasn't a great experience; her propensity for motion sickness didn't help much, either.

He nodded. "Those goggles not only control the bots, they're equipped with cameras as well."

"That's great for seeing what we need to see, but how are we going to break in?" Kala was thrilled with having eyes in the Compound, but without teleportation, she needed some way to get inside.

Derek gave her an apologetic shrug, motioning to the wall behind them.

Hanging off two hangers were the dreaded phase-suits.

"Fantastic."

Chapter Twenty-Seven

After changing into the phase-suits, Kala remembered the last time she wore one. The night she shot the President, who happened to be the current *Atlas surrogate*. It wasn't a pleasant memory, so she tried to focus on what lay ahead instead. The suit was a tight fit and every inch of her body needed to be covered. Body parts could be left behind if they were exposed, and Kala wasn't about to let that happen. She kept the hood off for the time being so she could see better. The thin mesh that covered the face allowed for vision, but it was still a bit cloudy. Her new goggles hung loosely around her neck. If anyone saw them, they'd think they were about to go swimming, since the outfits resembled wet suits, a detail that had saved their cover many-a-times before.

Kala and Derek joined Turner and Talan in Turner's surveillance room. The fact that this room existed in his personal residence showed Kala how paranoid the man was. Or, at least, how well-informed he was, depending on which way one looked at it. There were wall-to-wall screens, showing almost every angle of the Compound both inside and out. A long metal table with a single swivel chair was the only furniture in sight. Everywhere Kala looked, there was a different screen. With thousands of screens surrounding her, it felt as if she was inside a fly's eye.

"Why do we need the bots if we have all this?" Kala motioned to the mass of monitors.

Turner responded, "This is only half of the Compound. There are hundreds of rooms I haven't managed to slip a camera in. Clifton pretends not to know what I'm up to, but he's just as duplicitous. It's a game we play, and this time it's to my disadvantage. He has Roberta in one of his private rooms and we need the bots to figure out which one."

"What about Cronus? Did you spot him on the cameras?" Kala found it hard to fathom that, with all the screens she was staring at, it only showed half the Compound. She never knew how big the structure actually was.

Talan indicated one of the monitors. Sure enough, there was Cronus, dressed as a security guard, with no one giving him the time of day.

Turner pointed out, "I tried having him removed, but as you can guess, anytime anyone came near him they turned away, completely forgetting their task. Some even forgot who they were, so getting the Titans to leave won't be easy."

"Titans?" Kala didn't like the sound of that.

Talan specified three more screens showing Hyperion, Themis, and Kala's favorite, Iapetus. The three of them were spread out around the outside of the Compound. Though they were clearly visible on screen, their powers kept humans away from them. "Cronus is the strongest, so he's staying inside in case his brothers and sister fail. The Grigori will try and lure them to one place and attack. The Titans carry the sacred blades, but thanks to you we have three plus yours."

"And you outnumber them," Kala reminded him.

Talan conceded her point. "True, but they've been gaining power for the last 2,000 years while we've been imprisoned. I don't know how well we're matched anymore." Talan appeared worried. "We won't have to fight long in any case. The Titans are only here to stop you from completing your mission. If they can stall long enough for you to fail…"

"I won't fail," Kala interrupted, then faced Turner. "Roberta first, but as soon as she's safe I have to destroy Fortski's research."

Turner nodded. "You do what you please. I'm not interested in the world ending, so I'll give you as much leeway as I can after Roberta is safe and sound in my arms."

"I'm more worried about Cronus than Clifton and his men, but they are going to be a pain," Kala complained. She eyed the clock.

0d 2h 55m 33s: 2:05 AM.

"Less than three hours. We'd better get a move on." Kala's adrenaline was on overdrive. As horrible as destroying the cure was, it felt like any other operation at this point. It was nothing like killing Jack. Nothing ever would be.

Talan teleported away, back to Owen and the others. Turner gave Kala and Derek the rendezvous point where they were to deliver Roberta. Less than two weeks ago Turner was Kala's boss, now they were working together as equals. It was a surreal moment, but at least part of it felt familiar. It was nice performing a mission for Turner again. It almost felt like old times, except for the fact that she was about to break into her own headquarters and fight men she had worked beside for the last few years.

Derek seemed a lot less fazed by that particular aspect. After working solely for Turner, she noticed he had no problem fighting Clifton's men. Kala couldn't really blame him. There was always a bit of a divide between Turner's favorites and Clifton's favorites. Clifton surrounded himself with arrogant a-holes, while Turner gravitated towards the unique or the intelligent. Even through kidnapping Roberta and lying about it, she'd bet her life that the two of them would act as if it never happened once Roberta was safe. It was such a strange and demented relationship. It made Kala grateful for her own healthy friendships. Of course, most of hers were with non-humans, but she was grateful anyway.

Loading up in a Compound Jeep, Kala made sure she had two handguns strapped underneath her suit. Cronus had stopped anyone from teleporting in, but he may have put some kind of *no magic zone* in as well. She didn't even know if he could do that, but Kala wanted to have a way to defend herself. Prepare for all possibilities. It was her way of life before becoming Atlas. Now it was more vital than ever. Dealing with humans was one thing, but dealing with the supernatural? Best to be ready for anything.

They were silent as Derek drove toward their destination. He was taking back roads to avoid any contact with the public and more importantly, surveillance. Clifton utilized anything and everything, including traffic cameras, so they didn't want to take the chance of alerting him of their approach. Although covered by the darkness of morning and driving with no lights, made it easier to stay hidden.

After thirty minutes, Derek parked under an outcropping of trees about a mile from the Compound's warehouse front. Turner assured them that the phase-suits were capable of passing through the special black metal of the Compound, but Kala was a little apprehensive.

Derek went around to the back of the car and pulled out a round piece of metal two inches thick and about thirty inches in diameter. Kala wanted to ask what it was, but she figured she'd find out soon enough. With her phase-suit and goggles, what was another gadget to add to the undertaking? At least all these things were grounded in science. Magic and powers were still hard for Kala to wrap her head around. It probably explained her lousy success rate at teleporting. Tangible inventions were much easier to swallow.

"We have to stay low to the ground. There's some tree cover that will hide us." Derek didn't wait for a response as he led Kala forward toward the warehouses, holding the large metal circle under his arm.

Kala figured the device had something to do with reaching the walls of the Compound itself. Since there was about a half a mile of dirt between her and the first wall, the biggest problem would be getting down. Derek and Turner seemed positive that their way in wouldn't alert Clifton. She didn't know what a metal circle would do, but at this point Kala had to rely on trust. She had no choice. There was no other way. She really wanted to send a lightning bolt up Cronus's arse for being such a baby. The fact that the Titan was doing all this to make the world end because he was too scared of human immortality was such a pouty-toddler move.

But she couldn't think about that now. She needed to focus on finding and freeing Roberta. The Atlas mission was always lingering on the outskirts of her thoughts, but it wasn't something Kala wanted to think about. It was priority number two and as a soldier, she had to complete her tasks in order of importance. Roberta was number one. It occurred to her how stupid that sounded, since saving Roberta accomplished nothing in the big scheme of things, whereas destroying Fortski's cure would *save the world.*

It was amazing though, how her brain could rationalize why rescuing Roberta was more important. Atlas missions were too painful. Kala needed to feel the rush of doing something good. Something right. And saving Roberta would accomplish that. The woman had saved her life. She had taught Kala how to fight Demons and Malaks when she was a vulnerable human. Kala owed Roberta, and she wasn't about to desert her. Not now. Not ever.

"Here it is." Derek stopped about a quarter mile from the first building. They were in a section of trees that weren't as dense as the others were, but Kala still felt safe behind the large trunks, especially in the darkness. Derek had picked this location because it was one of the few blind spots of the main camera system that Clifton had access to.

He dropped the metal disc on the ground. Kneeling down, Derek touched its surface; a small keypad lit up. He punched in a code and the circle started to spin, making almost no noise. Then it dropped, fast, through the dirt like a silent missile.

Derek explained, "It has a sensor for the type of metal the Compound is made of, so it won't make a sound to alert anyone. The area we're above is mainly for maintenance, but we still have to be on our toes."

Within seconds, the device hovered back up to the surface and Derek pulled it aside, revealing a perfect thirty-inch diameter tunnel with a small cloud of smoke coming out, drifting into the wind. Kala could only assume that the dust was what was left of the dirt that had magically disappeared. Technology that could dissolve soil was pretty darn cool in Kala's book.

She was definitely impressed, but it still didn't answer the question. "How are we going to get down a 2,600 foot shaft?"

"Oh, ye of little faith," Derek teased as he threw her a black metal box.

"Ah, got it." Kala grabbed the box. She had used one once before, on a mission overseas, when she had to rappel down a castle wall. It was a dangerous escape and without this little gadget, Kala probably wouldn't have made it. It was small in size, only three inches tall on each side, housing a cable the circumference of dental floss inside. The box could attach to any solid surface and hold up to five hundred pounds of weight.

Kala turned to the nearest tree and placed the apparatus on the bark. Like superglue on metal, the invention stuck to the tree with no chance of pulling it off. The thin cable popped out with a tiny half-inch carabiner attached to it. She secured it to her phase-suit and was ready to rappel down.

Derek was already equipped and on the lip of the tunnel by the time Kala joined him. "Me first." He smiled.

"If you recall, I'm the one who has better recovery time with phase-suits." Then she smiled back. "And I am kind of a god now."

He moved aside and Kala started the lengthy trek down the rabbit hole.

It wasn't long before Kala's feet touched the smooth black metal of the Compound's roof. Never in a million years did she imagine she'd be breaking into this place. She honestly didn't think it was possible, not by mundane means anyway.

Being down in the cylinder of dirt, Kala felt the raw energy. At first, she thought it was her adrenaline pumping for the task at hand, but it was the earth itself.

Gaia.

She hadn't processed the whole Gaia-being-a-part-of-her revelation just yet. The only perk seemed to be shocking the hell out of all the big guns like Cronus, the Grigori, and… Zeus.

Thinking of him made her cringe. He was back and at full power. The god had drained her like a battery then left to do who-knows-what. Nothing good, of that, Kala was sure.

Derek hung above her head. The two of them couldn't stand next to each other in the small circumference, so she'd have to go in first.

Activating her phase-suit, Kala felt the familiar sensation of passing through a solid surface as if it were made of liquid. Teleportation was easy compared to this. Talk about something not being natural. The wall was thicker than she expected, well over four feet, so at one point most of her body was encased in the ceiling. Kala remembered to stay still and let gravity pull her the rest of the way through. It was more claustrophobic than being buried in the dirt by Cronus.

Finally, Kala dropped to the floor. She pulled back her hood, taking deep breaths to relieve herself of the side effects of phasing. A moment later Derek was by her side.

No one was in sight.

So far so good, Kala thought.

She just hoped she wasn't jinxing herself.

Chapter Twenty-Eight

Kala made a quick rundown of the space they were in. It was definitely some kind of storage area. The doors were closed, but marked with signs indicating what was inside. Mainly cleaning supplies and science equipment. Nothing that required surveillance or sentries. Turner certainly knew the Compound inside and out to drop them into one of the few areas that didn't have security. She was still on guard, though, never underestimating Clifton or her circumstances.

Derek wasted no time as he popped open the small metal egg filled with the nanobots and let them loose. "You can contact Mrs. Turner with your mind, right?"

Kala nodded, but internally she wasn't so confident. Head-jumping was still new to her and she didn't feel she could rely on it.

Roberta? Kala called out in her head. She felt like some kind of crazy person talking to her imaginary friend.

Waiting was also strange, as if a phone was ringing and no one was picking up.

Relief washed through her when Roberta's voice answered, *Are you in the Compound?*

Yes. We're on the west side. Do you know where Clifton has you?

No. I've never been here before. Harry is acting like he's keeping me for my own protection. He told me that Geoffrey is on a mission and may not make it out alive. I can tell he's lying, but I have to know: is Geoffrey safe? Roberta tried to hide the worry from her voice.

Kala remembered Turner saying that Clifton secretly wanted Roberta for himself. Maybe this was some kind of ruse to convince her that Turner was dead so she'd be with him. How pathetic.

He's completely safe. He's at your house watching from his surveillance room. The room where Clifton is holding you isn't on his radar though. Can you tell me anything about where you are? Kala knew the Compound as well as any soldier, which meant about a quarter of it. But anything could help.

Let me think. Roberta paused. *After his men took me from Fortski's lab, we went up at least one, maybe two flights of stairs, then we walked for at about ten minutes. I just don't know in which direction. I'm sorry I can't be more useful.*

No, that's a good start. We'll be there soon. Kala tried to comfort her.

Harry is treating me well. Tell Geoffrey not to worry about me.

And then Roberta was out.

Derek had waited patiently while setting up the nanos and adjusting his goggles accordingly. "Where we headed?"

He reached over to Kala and flipped a couple of levers on her goggles. She saw the tiny pricks of red light. They looked like microscopic ants, all legs, ready to invade.

"She's either one or two floors up from the lab. She said she walked for about ten minutes, but she doesn't know which direction. Any ideas?" Kala surveyed their area, making sure no one was coming.

All clear.

"There are only two ways they could go on the second and third floor.

We'll have to divide the nanos." Derek placed his thumb on the opened egg and a small holographic screen popped up.

"Whoa." Kala was fascinated. She had thought holo-technology was off in the future, but seeing now that Turner already utilized it made her understand just how advanced his research was.

"Pretty cool, huh?" Derek was amazed as well. He punched in a couple of numbers and the holograph turned into a flat map of the Compound. "We'll send them through these spaces here… and here." He pointed to a long line of rooms to the north and south of Fortski's lab on the second and third floor. "These are the areas Turner doesn't have eyes on. She has to be in one of them." Derek traced a line over the two sets of rooms.

Before Kala could react, the nanobots were off, moving faster than she expected. She could see both her perspective and theirs. Kala had to close her eyes because she was seeing double and it made her sick. It almost felt as if she was in an Atlas memory.

Derek apparently could see her discomfort; he leaned over and adjusted a lever on her goggles. "You can lower the opacity on the image. It won't be so disconcerting. I know you and your motion sickness." He smiled.

The image faded and now appeared as a light overlay. Kala's head cleared after a few moments of deep breaths. "I'm good."

More than good. The whole thing was fascinating. The nanobots traveled straight through every wall as if the surface was made of liquid. Kala watched what looked like a faded movie as the nanos raced through each room. She could see scientists, guards, soldiers, all working, none of them the wiser. If they only knew there were tiny robots crawling above their heads and flying through the walls.

"They're about to split. Keep your eyes out for Roberta," Derek instructed.

Kala and Derek stayed off to the side of the hallway so they'd be out of view from anyone who happened to pass by. Kala knew that once they found Roberta they'd be on the move. When the nanos moved in different directions, the screen in Kala's goggles divided in two so she could see both views. Staring straight ahead helped her to see both nano aspects objectively.

"Got her," Derek announced.

Kala saw Roberta a second later. She sat on a couch in a small room on the south side, two guards stood at the door.

Derek controlled the nanos through the metal egg device. He made both teams of bots join back together to survey the entire area.

Kala had to blink hard a few times to keep herself from succumbing to nausea. Being Atlas and having the use of teleportation was actually a boon to Kala, who had always turned a bit green when travelling by conventional methods.

Derek made the nanos seek out every possible way into Roberta's prison. The path of least resistance was through a couple of empty storage rooms coming in through the west wall, which meant at least ten more phases.

Kala had never done that many in one mission. Usually it was one wall and she was in. Being a Titan, Kala knew her body could take it, but she was more worried about Derek. "Maybe I should go alone. I don't want the phase-suit to wreck you," Kala volunteered.

"I'll be fine. They've been rated for twenty entries. This is ten." Derek left no room for argument.

So Kala didn't bother.

"Roberta doesn't have a phase-suit, so we can't go back the way we come in. Also, there are twenty soldiers between her room and the lab." Kala pointed out the obvious.

"That's why we're phasing into her room. There are *two* guards." Derek looked at her with a smile, but he might as well have said, *duh*.

"But we'll be recognized." Kala saw the genius in having the soldiers on the inside of the room so no one would suspect a switcheroo, but at some point somebody would identify two of Clifton's Most Wanted. They didn't exactly blend.

Derek tapped his chest. "I have another toy from Turner. It'll make us look like the soldiers we swap with. If anyone stops us, we'll just claim that we're moving the prisoner."

"Right. I'll just shut up now." Kala wished he had told her earlier about the magic-disguise gadget, but right now she was just relieved he had it. "Couldn't we just use it now and disguise ourselves?" Kala tried to think of all possibilities.

"Kala, seriously. You don't think I've thought of all this? We need to scan their faces and these two soldiers are Clifton's main guys. It's why they are personally guarding her. We couldn't get in pretending to be anyone else, except Clifton himself, and we don't know where he is." Derek's patience was wearing thin.

"Fine. You could have told me all this before we left, you know," Kala muttered defensively.

"I thought you'd trust me, Kala. I know I betrayed you, but I thought I'd proven myself by now. Think of how many times since then that I've blindly trusted you. I got this." Derek shook his head.

"I do trust you." Kala's pang of guilt was spreading rapidly. Yes, Derek had turned her in to Clifton and Turner, but he had thought he was doing the right thing. She had more than forgiven him. Derek had been through a lot because of her and had to *believe* a lot because of her. Questioning each other wasn't a part of their modus operandi. "I'm ready." No more questions. Whatever happened, happened. Kala vowed to be prepared for it and protect Derek at all costs.

Derek steadied the nanos like surveillance cameras, forming them into one group in each area where they were headed, creating thirty small screens in Kala's goggles. It was faded enough that she could still see well enough to move freely and comfortably. She kept the mesh covering of the phase-suit pulled back until they actually had to pass through a wall.

Pocketing the controlling metal egg, Derek led Kala through the belly of the Compound.

The path the nanos found was the path of least resistance, which Kala was grateful for. She didn't like hurting her fellow soldiers. They were only following orders, and if the situation had been reversed, Kala would do the same thing. As far as Clifton's men were concerned, the two of them were enemy invaders. If only they knew what was really going on. Kala barely believed it – and she was an actual Titan – so the possibility of explaining themselves was out of the question.

The first two phases went off without a hitch. Sneaking into empty rooms and avoiding hallways was the only reason why alarms hadn't gone off. It amazed Kala at how much of the Compound didn't have cameras. It only proved to her the distrust between Turner and Clifton. If anything happened to Roberta, Turner would obliterate Clifton. Saving her would only delay the inevitable, though. At some point, the Turner/Clifton relationship would come to a head. Kala just hoped she wouldn't be around to see it.

After the third phase Derek pulled back the mesh covering on his face and puked. It was so out of character for him, Kala didn't react right away. Then her protective instinct kicked in. "You're staying here. I'll get Roberta."

Derek wiped his mouth and shook his head. "I'm good." He placed the mesh back over his head and walked through the fourth wall before Kala could stop him.

Kala sighed in frustration, following close behind. She knew Derek long enough to know the guy wasn't going to back down.

After the eighth wall, Derek dropped to the floor. This time he puked up blood.

Kala rushed to his side, but by the time she arrived, he was already half-way to standing. "Derek, this is ridiculous. You're going to die. Stay here and I'll come for you when I can teleport back in here," Kala pleaded.

Derek shrugged her off with his hand. "No. I can do this."

"The blood-vomit on the floor disagrees with you." Kala was tempted to knock him out and come back for him later, but she was afraid it would injure Derek more. This must have been how Owen and Talan felt about her when she was in the god hideout.

Then she remembered when she first encountered Asmodeus and

the Malak, Grautlin, had shot her. Asmodeus had healed her. He was a Demon, not a Titan, but maybe Kala had similar powers. She had to at least try. "Let me try and heal you." She motioned Derek to come to her.

Derek's face was skeptical. "You can do that?"

"Honestly? I have no idea, but before your guts come out of your mouth, I suggest you let me try."

He nodded and moved next to her. Derek always appreciated Kala's bluntness and, by the greenish pallor of his dark skin, he would be willing to try anything.

She mimicked what Asmodeus had done to her, placing her hands on his body, one on Derek's chest and one on his stomach. Then Kala concentrated as hard as she could. She imagined healing Derek from the inside out. Since there wasn't an actual *wound* to focus on, she had to center her thoughts on his entire body.

"Anything?" she asked hopefully.

"I still feel like shit," Derek said weakly.

Kala felt like an idiot, standing there with her hands on Derek. She always used to make fun of faith healers she'd seen on TV. It made her wonder if they were really Demons using their powers to squeeze money out of people. She guessed, if they were curing people of their ailments, it wasn't a bad trade-off. But if those people knew they were being healed by Demons it might screw up their whole *faith* thing.

Kala was about to write-off her attempt to fix Derek as impossible when she began to feel warmth under his skin.

He responded in turn. "I definitely feel that."

A surge of motivation flowed through her and Kala concentrated harder. The heat grew in intensity and her hands began to burn. A part of her questioned if she should continue since she had no idea what she was doing, but the other part of her wanted to fix her friend.

"Kala." Derek's voice was small and choked. Something was wrong.

She tried to pull her hands away…

But they were stuck.

The burning grew more and more intense.

"Kala!" Derek screamed.

She yanked and yanked, but it was as if her hands were glued to his chest.

In a bright burst of white light, Kala was thrown backwards, finally separating her from Derek. Quickly rising to her feet, she raced over to him.

He stood in the same spot where she'd left him… and he was smiling.

"Are you okay?" Kala was terrified that she had caused him permanent damage.

Derek slowly nodded, then flexed his hands open and shut as if he had just injected himself with adrenaline. "I feel… amazing."

Relieved, Kala examined him more thoroughly, but there was nothing really to examine. "You really feel fine?"

"Better than fine. I feel like I could run up Mt. Everest barefoot. Whatever you did, it worked. A lot."

The last time Kala had seen Derek like this was when he drank ten espresso shots on a dare from Lali. "Well, I guess it worked." Kala was happy, though part of her knew she had done more than heal Derek. Burning hands and bright flashes of white light were never good, especially when she had been making it up as she went. She glanced at the clock in the room.

0d 01h 02m 43s: 3:58 AM.

An hour and two minutes. Her heart sank. "Let's get Roberta and get out of here."

Derek was so full of energy he saluted and leapt into the ninth wall. Kala followed and they were in the final room before Roberta's. The phase hadn't effected Derek at all this time. Even as a Titan, Kala experienced some disorientation from phasing, granted a lot less than she had as a human, but still. He appeared as if running through walls revitalized him. She couldn't worry about what she might have done or not done to Derek, they needed to figure out what their next move was going to be.

Derek's eyes were wide with drive. "We won't have much time before Ron and Jim try to signal the alarm. Do you have any crazy powers that could help us?" He seemed juiced to see more of what Kala could do.

She wished she could appease him, but Cronus may have put her other powers on lock-down as well. "We should rush them. You seem pretty amped up. If you run through the phase like you just did, I think we should be able to catch them completely off guard. I'll try and use the whole telekinesis thing, but I'm kind of hit or miss with my new skill sets."

This was good enough for Derek. "On my mark. One, two… three." He ran like a bull through the wall. His body even made a popping noise, he moved so fast.

Kala ran after him. The phase jolted her insides and she almost barfed when she entered the room.

Derek already had Ron in a headlock.

Jim reached for the alarm. Kala sucked up her feelings of discomfort and jumped at Jim's feet, tackling him to the floor before his hand could reach the alarm. She was about to punch him out with her Titan strength when a lamp smashed over his head.

Roberta stood over the two of them, a satisfied grin on her face.

Derek made quick work of Ron and the two guards were now unconscious lumps on the floor.

Roberta held out her hand to help Kala to her feet. "I'm glad you could make it."

Derek pulled out two small disks the size of pennies from inside his suit. Activating them made a beam of light shoot out of each disk. With Ron and Jim side by side, Derek scanned their bodies with the devices, then tossed one to Kala. "Keep it on you and press the red circle."

He pressed down on the disk he was holding. With a flicker of light, Derek's body transformed into Jim's. Kala did the same and she was now Ron. When she looked down at her own hands, she saw the exact same hands that were lying on the ground in front of her.

Derek and Kala tied up Ron and Jim's unconscious forms and left them on the couch.

"We move quickly." Derek opened the door and the trio was off.

The plan was to go to Fortski's lab. Derek knew a secret way out from there and he would lead Roberta to safety. Kala would stay behind to complete her mission.

Simple.

She just hoped it actually would be.

By the time they reached the last hallway leading to the lab, they had passed fifteen of Clifton's men. They were questioned every time, but everyone bought the story that they were moving Roberta to a safer location.

Kala thought they had almost made it when they turned the last corner and came face-to-face with General Clifton.

His eyes widened in shock at seeing his most trusted men moving Roberta from her prison. "I gave you strict orders!" he screamed. "Take her back to her room!" His eyes met Roberta's and he stumbled a bit in his speech. "I promise I'll send word as soon as I find out Geoffrey's status."

Kala made a quick surveillance of the hallway to make sure no one was there. With one Titan-packed punch, Clifton's body hit the ground hard. "He should be out for a while."

Even as Jim, Derek's smile was his own. "Nice. I only wish I could have done it."

"Me, too," Roberta echoed.

Derek was amused by that, but they were running out of time. He led them down the hallway and into Fortski's lab.

It appeared empty, just like the last time Kala had been through there.

Derek deactivated his disguise, Kala following suit.

"You take Roberta back to Turner. I have to stay here," Kala instructed him.

Before Derek could respond, Cronus teleported in behind him.

"You shouldn't be here. Now for your punishment," he scolded Kala.

Cronus snapped Derek's neck.

Chapter Twenty-Nine

For a moment everything froze.

In slow motion, Kala watched her best friend in the entire world fall to the floor, lifeless.

Out of the corner of her eye, Kala saw Roberta's eyes turn black. Then she began to speak, and the words that came out her mouth were ancient and powerful.

Cronus reached over and touched Roberta's arm; she collapsed onto the ground. "She's not dead, but she will be soon enough. She and her husband would have been key players in the future I'll never let happen."

Kala stared at Derek lying on the floor, his head twisted in the wrong direction.

She was in shock.

She couldn't move or speak.

And Cronus kept acting as if they were having a casual conversation.

As if he needed to teach her a lesson.

As if he could justify killing Derek.

Fury pumped through her like fire. She stared at Cronus and deep within the well of her being, she cried, "YOU KILLED HIM!"

Cronus withered in fear. "Now, don't blow this out of proportion. Your friend is fine…"

Rage and wrath consumed Kala's soul. "I WILL SWALLOW YOU WHOLE!"

Cronus took a step back. "He's alive! Remember the white light? Instead of healing his wounds, you healed him *forever*. He can't die!"

Kala heard him, but his words weren't enough to calm her ferocity. Seeing Derek dead in front of her was too much for Kala to comprehend. She needed to end Cronus once and for all.

Cronus appeared to sense this as well, but instead of moving away from her, he shifted toward her. "I can't let you complete your mission no matter what you do to me. I'm taking you to the 5th."

He touched her arm and Kala felt the familiar sensation of teleporting. It only enraged her more. There was no way she was going to the 5th Level of Hell. And there was no way she was going to let Cronus dictate whether or not she would complete her job.

When their surroundings came into focus, they weren't in the 5th.

They were above ground, almost a mile from the main entrance of the Compound. It was where Derek had taken them when they had escaped the structure days before.

It was enough of a shock that Kala was jolted out of the intense anger that threatened to overwhelm her. She peered up at Cronus, whose face betrayed his own surprise as well.

Kala could tell they were both thinking the same thing: that she was responsible. How else could the leader of the Titans fail to teleport the two of them to his desired destination? In her fury, her powers always grew stronger, so it made sense. But, now that she had calmed down a bit, there was nothing stopping Cronus from taking her to the 5th.

He seemed to have the same thought because he reached over to touch her arm again.

Nothing.

Cronus grabbed her tighter.

Nothing.

Kala removed his hand forcefully. "Sucks, doesn't it?"

Cronus tried to reach for her again, outrage and shock visible in every expression line on his face. "How are you doing that? You're not stronger than me! No one is!" His temper was palpable.

"I AM." A large booming voice reverberated in the air.

Before their eyes, Zeus materialized.

"Hello, Father." Zeus smiled. He wore a suit like his dad, but his tie was loose around the neck. Being a few inches taller and wider than Cronus, Zeus was a lot more daunting.

The father-son duo radiated power, staring at each other. Kala suddenly wanted to duck out of their line of fire.

The big *uh-oh* moment for Cronus happened next.

In a line behind Zeus were Penny, Talan, Rotoph, Owen, Antel and the other four Grigori whose names Kala didn't remember. But the one who sealed the deal, and made even Kala take a step back was Hephaestus.

Somehow, Zeus had managed to find and rescue his son. Kala knew with certainty what they planned on doing next.

Open the Grigori portal.

Kala knew who the winning side of this battle was going to be.

Cronus didn't flinch. "You'll be dead before that portal opens," he sneered.

The Titans: Hyperion, Themis, and Iapetus teleported in behind Cronus.

"Now, Hephaestus!" Zeus roared.

In response, the Grigori, Penny, and Hephaestus formed a circle and Hephaestus began the chant that would open the gateway.

Cronus and his Titans stormed past Kala, charging Zeus and the ring of power behind him.

With an audible CRACK, the Titans slapped against an invisible wall protecting Zeus.

The Olympian laughed at his father. "I've been renewed with the power of Gaia! Your days are done, Father! Even as we speak, I have my Olympians taking over your precious 5th and destroying every molecule of that decrepit place! You tortured and imprisoned me for thousands of years, now I intend to do the same to you!" His eyes glowed purple with power and rage.

The *Gaia* part of that conversation left Kala feeling a little responsible. She was the one that had fallen for Zeus's little battery-suck tactic. But the expression on Cronus's face said it all.

He was torn. Torn over whether to stay and fight, or to go to the 5th and save his home.

As an observer, Kala made a few realizations about Cronus over the last few days. He loved power and he loved being feared. He was always trying to assert his authority by *punishing* the beings that *wronged* him. Throwing pieces of Talan's body at Kala's feet, snapping Derek's neck: they were all moves designed to exert his dominance. But as soon as he saw that Kala would kick his butt, he'd backtracked and tried to make nice. He liked being safe. He wanted to be the bully from the next room, unless he was assured of a win, then he'd confront his victims directly.

She could tell Cronus wouldn't stoop to sucking up to his son, so Kala wondered what his next move would be.

When he spoke, his voice dripped with force and intimidation. "I am the god of time itself. Your puny barriers can't stop me, Son." Cronus threw his hand out at the barrier.

BOOM!

Iapetus was the first to react, throwing himself at Zeus and tackling him to the ground.

Hephaestus's chant grew louder and louder.

The portal began to open.

Kala felt out of place. She watched as this crazy supernatural battle unfolded in front of her, with no idea what to do. She wasn't a part of the circle so she couldn't just join in the middle. And something held her back from using her Grigori blade against the Titans. It was almost as if Kala was witnessing a family squabble and she wanted to stay out of it. Granted, the family was made up of super-powered gods and angels, but the maturity level was about the same as any normal human family. Meaning nil to none.

The ground shook violently beneath her feet.

Zeus held back all four Titans as they clawed and scratched to reach past him and pull even just one person from the circle.

Kala was impressed and she knew she should give him some help, but her feet remained locked in place. Why couldn't she move? Zeus was alone and helping the ones she loved. It was something deep inside her. Remembering the future Cronus had shown her. A dark, bleak future full of murder and secrets. He claimed the Grigori were responsible.

And this was the moment.

The moment where she could either stop it or help its coming.

She wanted to do neither.

The ground shook again.

Kala watched in fascination as the portal opened to eight times as large as the previous gateway. Good or bad, Grigori flooded out of the gates and swarmed at Cronus and the other Titans.

Cronus knew the battle was lost.

He briefly made eye contact with Kala, his voice speaking into her head, *Don't let this future come to pass.*

Then he was gone.

The other Titans disappeared with him.

There was still chaos as hundreds of Grigori poured through the portal. Zeus joined the circle and the gateway grew to the size of a house.

Kala had seen enough.

The ground shook once more.

That was when she knew it wasn't the opening that caused the shaking.

It was the end of the world.

Kala hadn't been paying attention to the time.

If she didn't complete her mission, this new future wouldn't exist.

A part of her was tempted to let it burn.

But, if she did that, Jack would have died for nothing.

Kala knew then that she'd never refuse an Atlas mission, no matter how horrible. She couldn't do that to his memory. He'd died to save the world. Kala had murdered him. She needed to hold onto the shred of justification that she had.

Cronus was gone.

She could teleport again.

Kala left the mayhem in front of her and arrived in Fortski's lab.

Derek sat on a stool next to Roberta while Fortski took a sampling of blood from his arm.

Kala nearly cried in relief. She raced over to him and practically shoved Fortski out of the way, hugging Derek fiercely.

"I'm okay. I don't know how, but I'm okay," Derek assured her.

Roberta added, "His neck cracked back into place right in front of us. John is taking a sample of his blood to analyze."

Cronus had been right.

"Congrats, Derek. You're officially death-proof." Kala didn't want to let him go.

When the earth shook again, she knew she was running out of time. Glancing at the clock, she shuddered.

0d 0h 01m 04s.

One minute left.

"Derek, take Roberta out of here." He saw the determination in Kala's eyes and nodded.

When they were gone, Kala turned to Fortski. She didn't have to ask which computers held the answers to a cancer cure. She recognized them from her vision.

"I'm going to destroy all your research on cancer," she told him.

Fortski appeared more surprised that she knew what he was working on rather than the threat. "How did you… I haven't even told Geoffrey…

What do you mean?"

The ground shook.

"You feel that? If I don't do it, the world ends." Kala only had thirty seconds left.

Fortski stepped toward her threateningly. Kala pulled out her gun and held it level, but she wasn't aiming at Fortski, she was aiming at the computers.

She shot the three computers containing the cure, destroying the hard drives, and pretty much turning them into a pile of mechanical mush.

Fortski grabbed a pile of papers off the desk and held them in front of him as if they were the Holy Grail.

The papers from her vision.

Kala played her part.

She leapt forward and grabbed the papers from his hand.

Fortski screamed, "Please! You can't! That's the only copy."

"I know. I destroyed all the hard drives," Kala reminded him. "I have to do this. Trust me. It's for the best."

"No, please!" Fortski pleaded. "Do you know how many lives I can save with that? Thousands! Millions even!"

Kala shook her head. "I have to."

"Didn't you ever know anyone with cancer? You can save them! You'll be destroying the cure! Do you understand?! You're destroying the only copy I have! I can't memorize equations like this! Turner will kill you for this!" Fortski was in a total panic. Just like she remembered.

Kala finally felt the calm that she saw in her face when she witnessed the vision. "No, he won't." Kala took her lighter and set the papers on fire.

Fortski shrieked and jumped at her. Kala pushed him away with ease. She had almost forgotten that the push would make Fortski soar clear across the room and crash against the wall. His cries tore her up, but she also knew he'd be inventing something far greater in the future.

Something that would cure humans of more than just cancer.

It would make them immortal.

The prophecy repeated in her head over and over for better or worse.

The immortals will reign.

03d 23h 59m 59s.

THE UNDERWORLD

DAY ONE

Chapter One

3d 23h 59m 58s

John Fortski huddled in a ball, sobbing. He was a mess and Kala couldn't blame him. She debated whether or not to try and explain why she had destroyed his life's research of creating the cure for cancer, but, ultimately, Kala decided against it. It would only upset him more.

Kala surveyed her surroundings. She was still in the Compound's laboratory and had just set aflame Fortski's cure. Not something she thought she'd ever fathom doing. But, as Atlas now, it was either that or watch the world end. Black or white choice. No compromises. Do what her vision told her or…

Or civilization as the world knew it was gone.

And this time Kala's vision told her to kibosh John Fortski's brilliant discovery of how to wipe out cancer.

Yeah. Being Atlas was a real hoot so far.

"Don't move."

The click of a gun sounded directly in Kala's ear.

She recognized the voice. It was General Harry Clifton. Her ex-boss, and not someone Kala particularly liked.

Even though Kala knew she couldn't die, being shot at by Clifton wasn't high on her priority list.

"You know you can't kill me, right?" Kala didn't even try to hide her condescending tone.

"We'll see about that!" The confidence in his voice was infuriating. BAM!

"Ow! Son of a…" Kala felt the bullet crash through her skull and it stung worse than she would have imagined. Still, as the bullet harmlessly popped out of her head and clattered to the ground, Kala took the opportunity to snatch Clifton's gun and level it at his chest.

His eyes were wide and round at witnessing Kala's bulletproof body. Being a Titan definitely had its perks.

"How did you… Some new technology…" Clifton couldn't seem to complete a sentence.

"I don't think you want to know," Kala sighed.

Clifton's poor little brain was on overload. He'd seen too much over the last eight days that he couldn't explain and it was finally causing his brain to fry. "Please, tell me," he asked carefully.

"I'm the one holding the gun, General. Not sure if you should be making any demands, especially after kidnapping Roberta. I'm also pretty sure you planned on offing her husband." Kala eyed Clifton knowingly; she had ruined his perfect plan by rescuing Roberta, General Geoffrey Turner's wife, and Clifton knew it.

Even with a gun pointed at him though, Clifton managed to calm himself. He nodded. "You can't be killed. You and your friends can teleport in here like it's the Starship Enterprise. Eight days ago you were one of my best soldiers. What the hell happened?"

"Long story." Kala was oddly relieved to finally be able to speak to Clifton in a somewhat civilized manner. She never had any affection for the guy, but she had respected him as her boss. And to have him try to execute her for the last eight days had been both annoying and strangely hurtful.

"Long story, huh? Let me guess: you don't have time to tell me." Clifton nodded to the gun. "Can I have that back? It's not like I can do any damage."

Kala handed him the weapon with a shrug. Clifton's ability to adapt to any situation was a trait Kala admired in the guy. Knowing he was at the disadvantage, Clifton simply accepted it.

Besides, Kala knew that if she could fight and beat Cronus, leader of the Titans, General Clifton was just a flea. He couldn't harm her, so handing him back the gun only proved how powerless he truly was.

It was at this moment Clifton noticed John Fortski crying in the corner. "What did you do to him?"

Fortski felt the need to join in the conversation at this point. "She destroyed my research! I had the cure to cancer, General! And she burned it all!"

Clifton raised an eyebrow. "Is that true?"

Kala holstered her own weapon and nodded. "Didn't really want to, but yeah."

Clifton put his gun away as well. "Turner will go after you for that."

"He knows. He was kind of pissed that Fortski was working on the cure in the first place. He supposed to be focused on some kind of immortality drug." Kala was testing Clifton, to see his reaction.

Clifton chuckled. "Age-pro. A fool's dream, though admittedly the trials have shown some interesting results having absolutely nothing to do with anti-aging. Turner should have been happy with the cancer cure." He tilted his head toward the destroyed computers. "So this mission was Turner's? Rescue Roberta and destroy the cure?"

Clifton was fishing as much as Kala was. It made her realize how alike they were. Soldiers to the end. But it only benefited Kala to be on civil terms with Clifton. Having to deal with his elite soldiers coming after her while at the same time fighting Titans… It made her job as Atlas a lot more difficult than it needed to be. She didn't think she and Clifton would ever be friends, but maybe they could leave each other alone. Plus, she had no earthly idea how Turner was going to handle the whole you-kidnapped-my-wife-you-bastard scenario either. But from what she knew of both the generals, they'd most likely continue as they had: as if nothing ever happened. Theirs was a relationship she did not pretend to understand.

Kala decided to tell Clifton enough to satisfy his curiosity, but she wasn't going to elaborate any more than she had to. "Saving Roberta was my mission from Turner, yes, but destroying Fortski's research was my own mission. Different agenda. Let's just say my new super-keen powers were given to me once I agreed to work for my new boss." Vague, but Clifton understood Kala wouldn't give away too much.

"I see." Clifton touched the watch on his wrist. "NOW!"

Within seconds, the room was filled with over fifty soldiers aiming automatic rifles at Kala.

Clifton snarled as he spoke, "You just admitted to me that you no longer work for the U.S. government! Was your first order to kill the President?!" He motioned to all the guns pointed at her. "Do you think you can survive hundreds of thousands of bullets? Because I don't think your special armor will do that!"

Kala sighed. He still didn't get it. And how could he? His mind needed to have a scientific explanation for what Kala could do. She chastised herself for using the term, "new boss." That *did* sound like she had changed loyalties.

Teleporting out of there seemed like the best course of action, but Kala didn't want to be on the run from Clifton while she was trying to accomplish her Atlas missions. She wanted to bring him to her side – or at least to some kind of understanding.

And –

Kala needed to show the General that she was indestructible so he'd stop attacking her.

"Listen, General, my new boss is still the United States. It's just not your unit anymore." Which was true in the sense that being Atlas meant she was saving the world and that included America. "Do you really think General Turner would have anything to do with me if I was working with another country?"

"I can't take that chance." Clifton made a sweeping motion with his hand. "FIRE!"

Wow. That was loud.

Fifty guns sent bullets thumping into Kala's body all at once. The force of it was so shocking that she barely felt the pain. She had thought her skin would tear to pieces, then reform, but it was more like she was made of water. As each bullet broke through her skin, her body rejected it and pushed it out again. It went on like this for almost five minutes – until Clifton ordered his men to stop with a wave of his hand.

Staring at him with an apologetic smile, Kala shrugged. "I'm telling you, we're on the same side. And this time *believe me*. You can't kill me."

Clifton eyed Kala, trying to decide how to proceed. He came to some sort of conclusion in his head and addressed his men. "Report to section ten."

With confused expressions at what they had just witnessed, the soldiers followed Clifton's orders and left the lab.

Out of the corner of her eye, Kala saw Fortski uncover his ears. The poor guy had been through a lot in the last ten minutes.

After a moment of contemplating his options, General Clifton held his hand out –which she cautiously shook. "I won't send my men after you… for now." He motioned to the thousands of bullet casings littering the floor. "Waste of bullets anyway. But you agree to keep me in the loop as much as you can?"

Clifton's men weren't exactly a problem for Kala, but she didn't like hurting fellow soldiers simply because they were following orders. Having them off her back was worth throwing Clifton a bone or two every once in while.

"I can live with that," she agreed, "as long as you leave Lieutenant Derek Echols alone as well." At this point, Derek couldn't be killed either thanks to Kala's misuse of her healing powers. Still, she didn't want him having to constantly watch his back either.

"I consider you two one and the same. We're good on my end." Then, to Kala's surprise, Clifton saluted.

The salute brought her back to a time when she had been so sure of who she was in the world. She was a sniper, a soldier, a part of an elite team that saved the world from bad people. Clifton's simple gesture reminded her of what she had become in the last eight days: a god, burdened with doing unspeakable acts in order to stop the universe from collapsing.

Kala saluted back and for once in a really long time she felt normal.

Fortski finally stood up and pulled himself together after realizing that Clifton wasn't going to help his cause. He wiped his cheeks dry and walked over to Kala and Clifton, trying not to trip on the shell casings.

"If you two would please leave my lab, I have work to do," Fortski said coldly. "And have a team brought in here to clean up this mess," he ordered Clifton.

Clifton didn't seem ruffled by the barking. "I'll send a team immediately." He nodded a good-bye to Kala, "Lieutenant Hicks."

She nodded back, "General."

Clifton left the room, leaving Kala alone with Fortski.

Fortski held back his rage as he repeated, "Leave my lab now."

Before she teleported out, Kala tried one last time to reassure him. "If I hadn't destroyed your research, the world would have been destroyed. No lives would have ever been saved by your cure. And this way you're destined to cure *everything*."

A glimmer of understanding crossed his features, but his defenses quickly replaced it. "Please, Lieutenant, just go."

Kala didn't want to upset him further, so she teleported out of the Compound.

When she landed at her destination, relief washed through her. She was home, at her dingy one-bedroom apartment. Kala almost wanted to hug the strewn out clothes on the floor that made her place such a mess. She hadn't set foot in here since her human self had to escape from... Asmodeus.

Asmodeus.

It seemed almost funny now that she had been so terrified of the king of Demons coming after her. Now she would actually appreciate his company. Until Asmodeus picked a side though, Kala knew she wouldn't be seeing him any time soon. He'd either stay with the Titans or join the Grigori and the Olympians. Either way, Kala knew she could handle Asmodeus. He was so very predictable in his self-serving ways. Everyone else, on the other hand, was a hassle. Even the good guys. They all had their agendas and Kala wanted nothing to do with any of it.

Being at home gave her a sense of comfort. Unlike before, Kala knew she could defend it now. Consuming Atlas, a Titan, had made her immortal. And finding out she had within her a part of Gaia, the mother of all gods meant she could consume any god she wanted. It was an advantage that kept her enemies at bay for the moment. Even Cronus was scared she'd vacuum-up his soul. Not that she would. Why add yet another life's experiences when having Atlas's memories bounce around in her head felt schizophrenic, to say the least. Talan had at least fixed Kala's brain so she wouldn't black out every time she flashed back to some crazy moment in Atlas's life. If she added any others to the mix, Kala doubted she'd be able to stay conscious.

Her favorite plushy green armchair greeted her like an old friend. Walking over to the ratty monstrosity, Kala plopped down into its soft goodness. For once in a really long time she actually smiled in happiness. She missed that chair.

Not bothering to turn on the flat screen resting on crates in front of her, Kala tried to ignore that the TV even existed. She knew that once she turned it on her new mission would play repeatedly. That was another "perk" of her new job as Atlas: all screens showed her a vision of what she was meant to do to prevent the world from ending, except computer screens apparently. So at least she could numb her mind Internet surfing if she so pleased. But her days of binge watching television were over.

The reason the green chair was so comfortable was because of all the time she'd spent in it between her Special Forces missions, planting her butt right in this chair either watching TV or playing a lot of video games. Part of her wanted to get rid of the Atlas curse just so she could play Mass Effect one more time.

Kala closed her eyes and took in the silence, feeling the peace of the moment. She knew it wouldn't last long but was determined to enjoy it as long as possible. Sounds of her neighbor clanking dishes, a car starting in the carport, a siren blaring in the distance… They made Kala feel normal. As if all she had to do was open her eyes and everything she'd experienced in the last week would be a dream.

But when Kala opened her eyes…

It was still only the blank screen of the television that greeted her.

And the overwhelming sense of foreboding seizing her chest. Things weren't the way they used to be. They never would be again. No more Jack, the love of her life. She was forced to kill him as her first Atlas mission. No more human life. She was Atlas now and she needed to complete her missions. The faster she accepted this reality, the better.

Kala had felt an inner calm when finally deciding to complete her last Atlas task. She wanted – no, *needed* – Jack's death to have some meaning.

So the sooner she turned on that TV, the sooner she'd know what to do next.

Yeah.

Not yet.

Kala listened to the everyday noises of life happening around her a little longer. Life that was able to continue because of her. Because she did what needed to be done. Still a soldier. Still with a purpose in life.

Besides, Kala knew, this moment of respite wouldn't last long. At any moment she fully expected some form of visitor, spouting "End of days," or "We can only do this with your help," or "Please help me kill my (insert relative here)." As for the coming war between the Titans, the Olympian gods and the Grigori, Kala wasn't sure if she even wanted to take sides. Now that she knew the mother of them all, Gaia, was inside of her somehow, a part of her wanted to let the *children* figure it out on their own.

Taking a deep breath, Kala decided to rip off the emotional Band-Aid, feel the pain, get it over with, and face it all without help. She'd rather watch her vision alone than have someone like her adoptive father, Owen, who (it turned out) was a powerful Grigori angel, standing over her shoulder supportively. Or Talan, another Grigori (with his gentle, caring eyes) asking how he could help. It was painful having such loyal, sympathetic people in her life. Kala didn't want to justify her actions; they were too atrocious. So to have her loved ones encourage her actions "For the greater good," made doing the unthinkable worse.

Nope. At this point, Cronus would be a better companion by her side. He'd simply tell her to ignore the whole task and let the world burn. At least she could beat the Titan senseless and feel good about it. Kala had to admit, she'd loved seeing Cronus squirm when he thought she was going to consume him.

Grabbing the remote, Kala turned on the television before she could chicken out.

The vision played on the screen in front of her, but she wasn't quite sure what she was seeing.

It was a dark place, like some sort of cave or underground cavern. A grotto. Every surface was made of craggy rocks soaked with moisture. Constant dripping sounded all around, convincing Kala that this place must be under a body of water or waterfall.

Vision/Kala stepped into view and placed her hand on a large stone lying in the center of the grotto.

The scene was peaceful and calm. Almost as if the world wasn't about to end like it had in her other visions.

Vision/Kala took a deep breath and almost appeared sad, but determined. Her hand began to glow on the stone.

And it moved.

Kala watched the television more closely and realized that it was a man lying at Vision/Kala's feet, not a rock at all. He coughed and sputtered, until his eyes met Vision/Kala's.

"Hades." Vision/Kala nodded in solemn greeting.

"Who are you?" Hades asked.

"Atlas. My mission is to wake you," Vision/Kala replied calmly.

"That's unfortunate," Hades sighed. "For you, anyway."

Hades reached up and touched Vision/Kala's forehead.

Kala watched in horror as Vision/Kala dropped to the cavern floor with a small thud and she knew with certainty…

She was dead.

Chapter Two

Kala turned off the television. She didn't need to see her own death on repeat.

Dead.

As in, what?

If Kala died, did that mean Hades became Atlas? Kala tried to rationalize what she had just witnessed. No it couldn't mean that, because when Kala consumed Atlas she had destroyed the Titan's ability to trick humans into doing his job. Essentially, the way it worked before was that whoever killed the acting-Atlas *became* the acting-Atlas.

It was how Kala snagged the gig in the first place. The Atlas surrogate had been the President of the United States and Kala had been forced to shoot him. Her commanding officer (and aforementioned love of her life) Jack, unbeknownst to her, had been training his entire life to be the next Atlas, so the kill should have been his. But Kala was the sniper of the team and she had a clear shot…

But…death?

How could that be?

What would that mean for the planet?

Would the curse end? Zeus had been the god who created the curse. He had ripped the balance of the universe and placed it inside Atlas, making Atlas responsible for committing one act of atrocity every four days in order to keep the world stable and safe.

So would this mean that balance might go back into the fabric of the universe where it belonged?

The next time you complete the cycle, you will be stripped of all your protections, and we'll see how you fare against everyone you've wronged.

It was from one of her flashbacks from Atlas's memory, when Cronus had announced that after Atlas's next mission, he'd strip the curse of all its protections. She had already completed that mission. It had been to destroy Fortski's cure for cancer.

So, apparently, by taking away her protections, Kala was going to die?

But what about the prophecy? She was some sort of *Fated One* or to be exact *the* Fated One. According to Zeus some girl three hundred years from now was going to break the Atlas curse for her. If Kala died performing this next task, then the prophecy meant nothing. It didn't make any sense. *All* sides: Titans, Grigori, Malaks, Demons and gods, believed this prophecy was real.

The Fated One will be the last and *The Fated One is the first.* Those two lines always seemed to conflict with each other in Kala's mind. Which one was she: last or first? Could this prophecy be spelling out her death?

The only way Kala was willing to risk death was if it meant the curse would be gone for good and that the world would be safe.

But she'd have to complete her mission regardless, wouldn't she? If she didn't wake Hades, then the world would end anyway. It was looking like her death was inevitable no matter which way her mind went.

And Hades!?

Hades!?

From Kala's recent research on her family tree, Hades was the Olympian god of the Underworld. There was really an *Underworld?* She guessed so. It wasn't that far out of the realm of reality considering her father and Talan were Grigori angels who had been imprisoned in the *5th Heaven.* And Cronus had been hiding out in the *5th level of Hell.* It was starting to look like every mythos actually existed. Either that or Kala was in some sort of psychiatric ward living in a delusional dream-state.

Shrugging, Kala figured if that was the case, maybe when she died after waking Hades, she'd be brought back to sanity. Jack would still be alive. She'd just be a soldier. And Kala could go back to getting into bar fights like a normal human being. It sounded so perfect she almost wished it was true.

But she knew it wasn't.

Kala was Atlas and she needed to wake Hades. No matter what the cost.

The only problem was, she had no clue as to where the cave in the Vision was located. And what was worse, she didn't know how to find out. Four days seemed like a minuscule amount of time!

With her last two missions, she recognized both locations as at least being on Earth! Kala was soon realizing that a location involving a supernatural being, especially a sleeping one, meant the cave could be anywhere. As in, not on this planet.

There was just no way to be sure.

Four days had felt like four years trying to stall on completing her missions. And she had managed to wait to the very last second for both. But now? Now she didn't know if it would be enough time to a) locate the place and b) figure out how the hell to get there! Kala hated to admit it, but she needed help.

Maybe Talan would know something.

"What do you need?"

Kala jumped out of her chair, seeing Talan standing in her living room. "How the…"

"I heard you ask for me, so I came right away." He seemed genuinely concerned.

And completely unaffected by the fact that he had read Kala's mind!

It was hard not to see the beauty in Talan. The guy was an angel, so being stunning came with the territory. With his short, cropped hair, chiseled face and body, Kala found it hard to rein back her hormones. She wanted what she wanted and in the past Kala would have simply taken the guy. But after falling in love with Jack, then having to kill him for her Atlas mission… It kind of took the thrill out of any kind of romantic connection she might have been considering.

In one of her darkest moments, Kala had turned to Talan to help her forget. It had been Talan who pushed her away, not wanting to take advantage of her emotional state. What could she say? The Grigori was a gentleman through and through. Kala genuinely cared about him; she didn't want to jeopardize their friendship. Even though Talan believed the two of them were soul mates, Kala reserved that title for herself and Jack. Dead or not, she didn't think she'd ever love anyone again.

"I don't like you poking around in my head. If I need you I'll call you," Kala said defensively.

Talan was used to Kala's behavior toward him though. "You *did* call me. Which is why I came."

Did she? After thinking about it a moment or two, she guessed that, in the supernatural world, she *had* actually called him. Telepathy, teleportation and telekinesis, all the tele's came wrapped-up in the Titan package. Kala just wasn't used to them yet.

"Well, I didn't know I was calling you. There's a difference." When Talan stood there patiently waiting for her to continue, Kala finally caved, "I saw my next mission."

Talan took a small step toward her, cautious of her boundaries. "Whatever it is, Kala, I'll help you through it."

Hearing Talan be so supportive made her defensive. "Didn't all the Grigori return like twenty minutes ago? Shouldn't you be with them?"

The quiet of her apartment had made Kala momentarily forget that she had just come from the epic confrontation between Zeus and his father, Cronus. Cronus couldn't stop his son from opening the portal that freed all of the Grigori angels from their prison. Kala wasn't even sure how many Grigori there were. Before she had left to destroy Fortski's cure, it had looked as if there had been hundreds, maybe even thousands of Grigori pouring through the gateway.

"I have plenty of time to be with my brethren. *You* are the most important. Besides, Owen will take care of them. He's better at that kind of thing," Talan explained rationally. "Now tell me how I can help you."

Kala wasn't so sure he'd want to help after he heard what her task was, but she plowed ahead anyway. "I have to wake up Hades, and when I do… he's going to kill me."

Talan froze, his face unreadable. He simply stared at Kala as if every one of his cells was about to explode. "That's impossible," he said finally.

Kala shrugged. "Pretty possible. I'd show it to you if I could, but basically, I wake the guy up and he kills me with one touch."

Talan began to pace. Not something Kala had ever seen him do. She knew she should be flattered that the thought of her dying made him so nervous, but it only amped up her adrenaline. Like she could defy the vision and find a way to survive…?

"Why would he do that?" Talan ran his hand through his hair.

"I don't know. But you know I have to do it. There's no other way to save the world from exploding in on itself." Kala walked over to Talan and placed her hands on his arms to stop him from moving. "Talan, you're the one who constantly reminds me that this my duty. Maybe it means the world will be back in the universe's hands if I die. That's a good thing, right?"

Talan's eyes flashed fury. "NO, it's not a *good* thing!"

"Well, the whole thing is moot anyway because I have no idea where Hades is and have even less of an idea of how to find out." Kala let go of Talan's arms.

She knew how he felt about her, but seeing Talan's temper flare at the thought of losing her reminded Kala of how strong their bond had become in only a handful of days. Going to to Hell and back – literally – had bonded them in a way she couldn't describe. She might not be able to allow herself to fall in love with Talan, but she cared about him deeply. That was hard to admit, but Kala was tired of being so closed off. It was exhausting.

But Talan's anger was now replaced by determination. "You may be misinterpreting your vision. From what I know of the curse, just killing Atlas won't stop it, it's more complicated than that. I have to talk to Penny —"

Kala didn't really want to focus on the whole "death" aspect of her mission. She wanted to figure out where that grotto was located. "My first priority has to be finding a way to accomplish my task. I can't think of the consequences." She made sure their eyes met. "Okay?"

It took Talan a few moments to finally nod in agreement. "Okay." He stepped away from her, walking toward the window as if making eye contact was too painful. "What did the place look like? Every detail. If it's supernatural I may be able to recognize it."

Kala sighed, exasperated. "I'm telling you, it looked like a cave. A wet, craggily cave. The amount of moisture down there makes me think it's under a waterfall or lake or some kind of body of water. But that's about it." She walked up beside him and they both stared out the window.

"What does 'craggily' mean?" Talan asked.

"You know, lots of bumps and dents and rough surfaces," she tried to explain.

"But no stalactites or stalagmites?" Talan turned to face her.

Kala looked up at him as well. "No, none. Does that mean something?"

Talan's expression was thoughtful. "Usually near any kind of moisture, stalactites and stalagmites form naturally. That's why they're calling dripping stones. They're formed from years of water running over inorganic material."

"Okay, Mr. Science, so what are you saying; because there weren't any stalactites and stalagmites, that could be some kind of clue as to where this place is?"

"Yes, it could be a very important detail. I just wish I could see it to know for sure."

Kala moved away from the window and grabbed a bottle of water from the cupboard in her kitchen. "Cronus would know. He's the one who imprisoned all of the Olympians after the war." She took a sip of water. "You don't think he'd tell me where he put Hades, do you?"

Talan gave her a look that suggested she was out of her mind. "Cronus didn't want you to complete your last Atlas mission. Now he has the singular power to prevent you from accomplishing your next one? I think you know the answer to that question."

"Yeah." Kala plopped back down in her comfy chair. "I just wish there was a way for you to see the place. Can't you just plug into my brain or something? You've fiddled in there before, shown me potential futures, blocked out memories, etcetera etcetera."

Talan appeared bashful, as if he was hiding something from Kala. He finally fessed up, "I admit, I have tried to tap into the memory of your visions, to help you. But it's blocked off. Only the true Atlas can see. It must be a part of the curse. I can show you the future of what will happen if you don't accomplish your mission, but that's about it."

"What then? Should I Google 'caves'?" Kala suggested sarcastically. "I have no idea where to start."

Kala looked to Talan for help. He looked severely conflicted. "What's that face?" she asked. "I've never seen *that face* before." Talan seemed as if he were having a full on battle inside his brain.

"I hesitate to even suggest it…" he began.

Kala stood up. This must be good. "I'll take anything at this point."

Coming to some sort of conclusion in his head, Talan sighed deeply. "Asmodeus may know where Cronus took Hades. His help had been integral to the Titans' plans. It's quite possible that Asmodeus was the one who hid Hades."

Asmodeus, the king of Demons. The last Kala saw of Asmodeus he was being given an ultimatum from Zeus after the god had used her like a battery pack to restore himself. Asmodeus was pretty narcissistic. She figured he would weigh his options and pick whichever side he thought would win. To be honest, even Kala was curious as to what the Demon's opinion was on that particular topic.

"How do I contact him?" Kala knew Talan was right. Asmodeus was the best lead they had.

Talan didn't appear pleased by Kala's quick acceptance to his proposal, but he shrugged. "You're the one who seems to find him. How did you do it in the past?"

True though it was, Kala could see that it hurt Talan to admit she had some kind of connection to the Demon. She couldn't explain it, but before she had control over her teleportation, she tended to *pop* up wherever Asmodeus was located. Kala supposed it was because Asmodeus had a care-free type of attitude that she needed in her dark moments. Granted, he was probably *care-free* because he was a selfish, soulless Demon, but sometimes Kala's life was too overwhelming to handle, so not caring for a while had been the best medicine she needed at the time.

Kala just wished she hadn't kissed the guy. Sure, it was mind-blowing: the Demon was unnaturally stunning and had had thousands of years to perfect his kissing technique, but it was a mistake she didn't want to repeat.

Not wanting to go into too much detail, Kala answered Talan's question. "I hadn't been in control of my teleportation yet. So I guess since you and Owen were in the supernatural-beings-only hideout, my brain took me to someone familiar. I didn't do it on purpose. And the second time, I was technically trying to find Zeus. It was only a coincidence that Asmodeus was with him."

Kala tried to downplay any kind of connection she had with Asmodeus. Talan had never once tried to make her feel bad or guilty about kissing the Demon, but she could see it in his eyes that it hurt.

Talan quickly tried to mask his emotions as he responded, "It's okay, Kala, you don't have to deny it. You have a connection with Asmodeus, it's that simple. So why don't you try calling him in your head, like you did with me."

Kala knew that was difficult for him to admit, especially if it worked. It would be further proof to Talan that Kala and Asmodeus truly were bound in some way.

Speaking carefully, Kala said, "I'll give it a shot."

She closed her eyes and concentrated on trying to picture Asmodeus: his tall stature, perfectly straight nose, sandy brown hair and his signature sexy-pout. Kala was about to call out to him in her head when…

"Hello, my lovely," Asmodeus's voice was right in front of her.

Kala opened her eyes, relieved it only took seconds for the Demon to arrive. She was getting good at this telepathy thing.

But surveying the room, Kala's heart dropped.

Yet again, she hadn't summoned Asmodeus to her – she had teleported herself to Asmodeus.

Her chest squeezed in sympathy for Talan. She imagined him standing in her apartment watching as the woman he thought was his soul mate disappear to be with the king of Demons. Kala cared enough about Talan to know it was a mean thing to do, purposeful or not.

Kala switched into soldier-mode before she allowed herself to feel any worse. The mission was all that mattered.

"Don't call me lovely," she chastised sternly.

But Asmodeus only smiled. "How did you find me? I've been cloaking myself from all supernatural beings since our last encounter."

Kala was at a loss and didn't really want to come up with theories. It would only encourage the Demon and that was the last thing she wanted to do. "Who knows? I need your help, I tried to send some sort of telepathic message and I ended up…" She examined the room they were in. "…Where is this place?"

It was a fairly large room with leather furniture and wood floors. But what made it spectacular were the wall-to-wall shelves filled with thousands of books. Not just any books, but old, ancient tomes, bound in leather with gold plating. Kala was never much for libraries, but this place had a warmth to it that made her want to curl up in one of the plushy leather chairs and read all day.

Asmodeus eyed the room with a hint of pride. "This is my safe place. No one knows it's here. No one except *you*. I guess I'll have to kill you now." He reached out and brushed his hand against her cheek.

The tingling sensation Kala felt only made her more determined to stay away from the Demon. She took a step back. "If only you *could* kill me. Immortal, remember?" But she knew he hadn't been serious, Kala simply wanted to create a slight distance between them.

As usual, Asmodeus was unfazed with Kala pulling away. "So, what can I do for you?"

Kala jumped right to the point. "I need to locate Hades."

Chapter Three

Asmodeus raised an eyebrow with curiosity. "Hades, hmm? Did Zeus ask you to find his dear brother?"

Kala knew she needed to tell Asmodeus the truth. He had the ability to see through her anyway, so why bother trying to hide it. But she decided she was only going to tell half of what she saw in her vision. She wasn't sure how Asmodeus would respond to her dying. If she were to guess, he'd probably sabotage the whole mission. It was no secret he was fascinated by Kala. Plus, she wasn't exactly sure where he stood on the whole *world ending* issue as well. The first go around with the Demon he had wanted her to fail her task so the planet would be plunged into chaos. He had said it was a Demon-thing, but the more Kala learned about Asmodeus, the more she knew that was just for show. He was a survivor and the Titans were the ones that wanted Atlas to fail. He did what they commanded to keep himself alive. But now?

"I haven't talked to Zeus, but I'm sure the next thing on his agenda will be to find his fellow Olympians that are missing. Honestly, I really don't care what Zeus, Cronus or any other deity wants. I need to find Hades because I have to wake him up. It's my new Atlas mission." Kala walked over to examine the books. Some of the titles were in languages she didn't recognize. She wasn't even sure they were human. "What kind of books are these?"

Asmodeus went to her side and pulled out a large black-leather book with no writing on its spine. He opened it up and handed it to her. As Kala took the ancient tome, the strange lettering inside began to glow and pulse at her touch.

Smiling, Asmodeus gently took the book from her hands and placed it back on the shelf. "I've been collecting these over the years. Mostly they're harmless, but the book you just held is the original text of Gaia and Uranus. I wanted to see what it would do when *you* touched it."

"So I can make a book glow. Is that because I have Gaia in me?" Kala wished someone would tell her more about who she was and how she had a piece of a goddess inside of her.

"Most likely. I recovered it from Cronus's personal library and replaced it with a fake. I figured it might be useful some day," he confessed.

Kala was curious. "I can't read it, though. Is it magic?"

Asmodeus shrugged. "Oh yes, there's magic in there. Unfortunately, I have no way to access it. I was hoping you might be of some help in that department." He turned to face her, his eyes probing. "But that's for a later date. Now: Hades. You have to wake him up, but you don't know where he is, yes?"

Kala hated admitting she needed help, especially from Asmodeus, but she nodded. "I was hoping you knew where he was located."

Asmodeus stared at Kala for a few moments, and then shook his head. "No idea. Cronus didn't trust me enough to tell me where he hid the Olympians." He grinned. "Crazy, huh?"

"Insanity." Kala felt compelled to smile back, but her heart sank. How was she supposed to complete her task if she didn't know how to find her target? "Could one of these books help?" she asked, desperate for any aid.

Asmodeus viewed all four walls of the floor-to-ceiling shelves. "Sorry, beautiful, nothing here that could locate a sleeping god. I can ask around though. Over the centuries there have been plenty of supernatural beings that have tried to track down the Olympians. Cronus did his job a little too well."

"You don't think Cronus would tell me…" Kala thought she'd ask Asmodeus his opinion, but his expression was identical to Talan's.

He laughed. "Keep dreaming, sweetheart. Cronus doesn't want any more gods mucking up his plans. He's the one who put Hades to sleep in the first place. And you know he wants you to fail, so why ask?"

"I don't know. I'm kind of his mother in a weird way. Maybe I could scare it out of him. The guy tends to buckle under pressure when he thinks I'm going to kill him." Kala knew she was sounding desperate. But she was. Desperate. She was positive none of the Atlas surrogates had ever had to find an unconscious *god* and wake him up. It was as if the universe couldn't wait until it had the real Atlas back, no longer an acting-Atlas, but the Titan itself, to do the really hard missions.

Kala searched her Atlas memories for any indication as to where that damn cave was, but came up with nothing.

"Cronus knows you won't consume him if you have a choice. It's the uncertainty that you'll lose control and kill him out of raw emotion that scares him. You tend to give into your rage if you haven't noticed. It's how you became Atlas in the first place."

Kala wasn't sure if she liked the fact that Asmodeus's observations were ringing true. But he was right, the only times Kala ever considered devouring Cronus was when she was enraged and lost control. "When did you get so observant? It's disturbing."

Asmodeus slightly brushed his hand against hers. His hand was gone before she could swat him away, but a part of her didn't want to anyway. She found a strange kind of comfort in Asmodeus. His blunt and sometimes brutal outlook helped her work out her problems. Maybe he could jog her mind into figuring out what to do next.

The Demon sighed heavily. "I can't believe your mission is wake up Hades. The guy is a total dick."

Kala laughed. "Coming from you, he must be bad."

"Me? I'm a perfect gentleman." Asmodeus mocked offense.

"Yeah, I'm sure the king of the *Demons* is all heart," Kala joked back.

"Better than king of the Underworld, believe me." Asmodeus turned thoughtful. "Hades was the first god to be taken in the war. Cronus needed to get Hades out of the way fast since he has a knack for controlling dead things. Cronus didn't want to be fighting both the living and the dead."

"So where would Cronus hide him?" Kala wondered aloud, sharing her thoughts with Asmodeus. "It's some sort of cave, under a body of water. That's all I can tell from my vision."

Asmodeus was at a loss as well. "That could be anywhere. Might not even be on Earth. But, as I said, I'll ask around."

Kala couldn't help but feel awkward. It was as if they were *friends*. Something she never thought she'd say about any *Demon*, let alone Asmodeus. But he had proven on more than one occasion that he could be trusted – to a degree. It was all the other degrees she was worried about. "So what about you? Have you picked a side yet?"

Asmodeus slowly nodded his head. "Actually, I have."

Kala would be fine with his choice either way. Even when he was on Team Cronus, Asmodeus still helped her out. It would be more difficult since Kala would always side with her father, Owen, which meant by default she was on Team Olympus and Grigori. But that didn't have to get in the way of whatever *arrangement* Asmodeus and Kala had made between themselves.

"So, which side did you pick?" she asked.

Before Kala could stop him, Asmodeus leaned down and gently kissed her. When he pulled back he smiled, "Yours."

It threw her off to the point where she decided not to kick him in the nads for his surprise-attack kiss. "Mine?"

Asmodeus nodded. "One thing I've learned lately is that *you* tend to win, unlike your namesake." Then he laughed, "Besides, I never really liked Cronus anyway. He was just a means to survive."

"And now, *I'm* that means?" Kala suddenly felt overwhelmed by the confidence Asmodeus seemed to have in her.

"Everything in life is a gamble, but over the last eight days you've shown you're nearly unstoppable. Anyone that can scare Cronus is an ally I want." His eyes bore into her with intensity. "And I'm an ally *you* want as well."

Kala couldn't seem to look away, but finally she spoke, "Whether it's in my best interest or not, I *do* consider you an ally… of sorts." She didn't want his head to blow up from an over-sized ego, so she added that last part.

Asmodeus clapped his hands together. "I'll take it." He glanced at a clock behind him. "I better get to it. I'll find you when I learn anything."

And just like that, he was gone.

Kala was left in his personal hide-out-library, with a strange feeling in the pit of her stomach. That conversation was the most "real" conversation she'd ever had with Asmodeus. Usually they flirted, tried to play each other, spoke in disguised innuendos, but nothing like that this time. It made her feel guilty for some reason. He was the king of Demons after all. But what did that really mean? Honestly, the Malaks she met were just as nasty as any of the Demons. In fact, her former soldier-in-arms, Lali, was a Demon. Before Lali had tried to kill Kala, she had fought beside her in their elite team. Lali had even saved her life on a few occasions.

The more immersed Kala became in the supernatural world, the more she realized there really wasn't much of a line between good and evil. It was simply whose side you were on.

Aside from wanting the world to end, Asmodeus could be a decent guy.

Kala shook her head from the absurdity of that sentiment and racked her brain, trying to figure out what to do next.

She spent the next few hours going through any book she thought could help. Half of them she couldn't read. After a while, though, her Atlas memories kicked in and some of the texts became legible.

None of it seemed to help. Most of the books appeared to be written-down spells and magic. That wasn't a total loss: Kala knew that Roberta would be chomping at the bit to read some of these tomes. Kala might just have to smuggle a few of them to her. Roberta would probably have more luck translating them than Kala.

Kala glanced at the clock.

3d 20h 22m 15s: 9:38 AM.

Five hours had gone by since she'd destroyed the cure for cancer. It felt like five minutes ago.

Putting away another book, Kala plopped down in a leather chair. The problem was trying to convey to the others what that stupid cave looked like.

If she could just *show* her vision to Talan, Owen, Asmodeus, Turner – *anyone* her vision, maybe they could locate Hades.

Turner.

With the kind of technology General Turner had access to, he could probably use satellites to find the place. If the cave was anywhere on Earth, he'd be able to find it, if he could just *see* it. Or have a snapshot of it! It was so frustrating. Describing it meant nothing. Maybe a sketch artist would help? Anything to share what she saw.

Maybe there was something that could pull it out of her mind somehow…

Turner's prototype machine. It scanned her brain. It was where Kala and Penny talked about her first mission. All inside her mind.

It had recorded her brain waves, telling Turner and his scientists how her noggin worked. And that was before she had devoured Atlas. Maybe it could capture the vision and show it in real time?

It was her only lead. She had to try.

Closing her eyes she concentrated on Turner. When she opened them again she was back in Fortski's lab, staring at Turner and Fortski.

"Oh, hi," she said lamely. Considering the fact that she had only left the Compound hours ago, Kala didn't think Fortski had forgiven her yet.

General Clifton, though, had been a man of his word and cleaned up the floor of shell casings his shooters had left behind. The place was spotless.

Kala focused her attention on Turner. "I need to talk to you."

Fortski eyed Kala like a disease. Kala was very familiar with that look. Before she had become Atlas, Kala had received it on a nightly basis whenever she'd reject some poor schlub at a bar.

Fortski whirled back on Turner. "Do I really have to continue to humiliate myself by standing in *her* presence."

Ouch.

Turner sighed, shaking his head. "You need to learn when someone has done you a favor, Fortski. This girl has basically guaranteed your success with Age-pro, now take Lieutenant Echols's blood sample and get to work."

"What's he going to do with Derek's blood?" Kala didn't like the innuendo that Derek could be a lab rat.

"I should take some of *hers* as well." Fortski appeared downright happy at the prospect.

Turner grimaced with disapproval. "Later. You have enough to research for now." Turner focused on Kala. "If your vision of the future is right, then Lieutenant Echols's blood may be the key to unlocking immortality."

Kala simply nodded. She didn't want to tell him the rest of her glimpse into the future, where Turner was responsible for killing thousands of people. She was still having trouble stomaching it herself. It was the part of her Atlas duties that she didn't understand: how her last mission had been to destroy the cure for cancer, which could save millions, because ultimately Forstki would create a drug that would cure *everything* and save billions – only to have the world become overpopulated, forcing Turner to kill thousands. She pushed the thoughts away and tried to be at peace with the fact that it went beyond her understanding.

Fortski gave Kala one last glare of disgust before leaving to the other end of the room to continue his work.

After he was out of earshot, Turner gave Kala his full attention. "Now, what do you need from me?"

"Do you think that brain machine of yours could record memories?" Kala asked.

Turner seemed intrigued by this idea. "Possibly. Why would you need to see memories? Or are these Atlas's old memories you want to look at, since you can't remember everything at will."

Kala hadn't even entertained that possibility. She couldn't simply access her Atlas memories since Talan's mind-mojo kept them hidden until she *needed* to see them. If she could record those memories and store them digitally, that might prove helpful in the future. "That's actually a good idea but, no, I need some immediate help figuring out where my next Atlas mission is. I figure if I could show it to you and my other allies we have a better shot at finding the location."

Turner nodded, obviously interested in the idea of taking another crack at Kala's brain. "I see. It's on the black level, but I've heard that won't be a problem for you to access anymore. Harry told me of your truce."

"And you've forgiven Clifton, even after taking Roberta?" Kala pried.

Turner shrugged as if the matter couldn't be helped. "Harry and I have a complicated relationship. Roberta is safe, that's all that matters, and I've taken steps to ensure he can never kidnap my wife again."

Kala didn't even want to ask what those steps were. She was sure they involved some kind of dark magic.

"Let's do this," Kala steered the mission forward.

Turner nodded and walked toward the door that led to the inner sanctum of the Compound.

With one last glance at Forstki, Kala followed Turner out of the lab.

Traversing the many twists and turns of the underground facility had always felt like a giant labyrinth to Kala. It was only once she became Atlas that she was able to go to the different branches of the Compound. When she had been a soldier, Kala was limited to one small area that included The Cog (where all the tech resided), the ready room (where her team would suit up) and the infirmary for whenever a teammate was injured. The walls were made of a special black metal that prevented any enemy's radar detection.

Before Atlas, Kala had been certain those were the only threats to her country and the world. Now she knew that with the snap of a finger any one of the supernatural beings could teleport in. She wondered if Rotoph, a Grigori with a knotty past of disloyalty to his brothers, was preventing Cronus and the other Titans from entering the Compound. He had done it before; she just didn't know if anyone thought the facility needed protection. How would the Titans even know she was even here?

It took almost an hour of walking before they reached the room that held the machine. Just as Kala remembered, a chair sat in the middle of the room with a single headpiece that had hundreds of wires attached to it, all strung to the ceiling, then back down to a computer terminal.

"We don't have Dr. Rosen with us this time," Turner said, "but I know how to work the machine. I'm just not very good with keeping the volunteer safe. I'm afraid we've had two coma cases so far. But since you're immortal and a Titan no less, you'll be fine." Turner didn't seem worried at all.

"You're saying you could put me in a coma?" Kala wasn't reassured in the least.

"I don't think so, no." Turner began to set up the computer terminal. "Not deliberately at any rate."

"Comforting," Kala said with a sarcastic tone that Turner ignored. "Oh, and FYI: Dr. Rosen was Pandora, not a real doctor." Kala felt the need to inform him.

"*The* Pandora?" Turner looked like he had received another treasure.

"Yes, *the* Pandora. So the only reason my brain probably didn't fry was because I had her help." Kala began to doubt the sanity of her decision to hook into the machine for a second time. If she went comatose, she wouldn't be able to complete her mission and the world would end. But if she didn't try she might never find out where Hades was sleeping.

Turner grunted, exasperated. "You're a Titan, for heaven's sake. I'll send for Talan if anything goes wrong. He'll be able to pull you out if needed. But you won't need him, I'm sure of it. Now, do you want to do this or not?"

Kala stared at the monstrosity of a machine for a moment longer, then nodded.

Here goes nothing.

Chapter Four

Kala was surprised at how calm she felt after the seventh hour of being strapped into Turner's device. They had made some progress initially, which gave her hope that they'd be able to put her vision to video. But the few images they managed to pull out from her memories were the same images seven hours later. She was conscious through the whole experience unlike the last time when Penny *aka* Pandora took the opportunity to talk to Kala's subconscious.

Kala and Turner communicated with each other the entire time as she guided him through what he called "brain mapping." She worked well with Turner. He'd become a vital ally throughout the upheaval her life had become. It was difficult for Kala to imagine the man helping her today would be a mass murderer in the future. Even for the sake of population control, it didn't seem like something he'd do. But time and circumstances could change a person. Kala had seen it before on a smaller scale – but after living for hundreds of years? Maybe human beings became more closed off about life and death. She'd certainly seen indifference in the immortal beings she'd met so far. All they wanted to do was destroy each other, and they didn't care about the millions of humans that could end up as collateral damage.

Life *should* matter. Coming from an ex-sniper, Kala felt like a hypocrite, but the simple idea that killing one person *saved* lives allowed her to live with herself. If it was senseless murder. Kala could never be a part of that. It was one of the reasons she wanted nothing to do with the whole Titans versus Olympians war that was coming. They didn't care who they hurt as long as they demolished the other team. For what? Power? *To rule?* Rule what? Humans didn't even know the gods existed. What exactly were they going to *rule?*

"Are you okay in there?" Turner's voice cut through her train of thought. "The wave lengths from your memories that are showing up on the screen are going crazy. I keep seeing snippets of you pummeling Cronus."

Kala pulled off the headpiece and massaged her forehead. "I need to take a break."

"Of course." Turner helped Kala to her feet. "Come look at this." He led her over to the computer's monitor screen.

"I'm not sure if I'll be able to see anything. Screens usually equal *Vision* for me, but I am able to use the computer, so maybe it'll work the same way."

Upon examination of the monitor, Kala happily found that she was able to see the results of the scan. It was fascinating, as if someone had taken a camera and attempted to film her memories. The images were shaky, full of static and slightly blurred, but the pictures were there. "This is incredible. Do you think we'll be able to clean it up?"

Turner's face was alight with excitement as he spoke, "I'm not sure, but even what we have so far is more than we've ever been able to achieve on our volunteers."

Volunteers? Somehow, Kala doubted anyone actually *volunteered* for this machine, but she kept that distinction out of her mind and was highly impressed with what Turner had managed to record. "Can we scroll through this?"

Taking control, Turner fast-forwarded through the footage he'd managed to pull from Kala's head.

And there it was.

Maybe.

"Okay, stop there," Kala instructed Turner.

The cave. Hopefully.

Yes – it was. The image was distorted, but the cave was almost clear, as if someone had taken a picture in the dark.

"That's the place!" Kala cried in triumph. "Let's focus on cleaning this one up. Maybe someone will be able to recognize it. What about your satellites? You think the location can be tracked down?"

Turner shrugged, unsure. "We only have two satellites that can scan underground and they're a bit glitchy, but we can certainly give it a try." He began typing in commands. "Let's see how much we can clean this up first though. The more information we give the satellite, the better."

For the next few hours, Kala and Turner worked on trying to analyze and clean the footage they had. Kala knew she should be worried about the countdown deadline, but if she didn't know where she was going, then the mission was impossible anyway. Not wanting to, Kala glanced at the time.

3d 07h 10m 33s. 10:50PM.

Kala's heart jumped in her throat.

"What is it?" Turner noticed at once Kala's change in mood.

"Nothing. It's just, there's only seven hours left of Day One. If we don't figure out where Hades is…"

Turner interrupted by placing a hand on her shoulder reassuringly, "We'll find him. We're so close now and the day's not even over." Then Turner's eyes lit up. "I wonder if Roberta could do a locator spell for Hades."

Kala perked up instantly. "You think she could do that?"

"I really have no clue, but we've got to try everything, right?" Turner picked up his phone and left the room to call his wife, leaving Kala to work on the image of the cave.

She was using a program that was created for cleaning up security footage with low pixilation, and it was definitely helping, but not enough. She wondered if this would ever work in time. Maybe Roberta *could* help. Too many maybes.

Glancing up from the screen, Kala almost thought she was hallucinating as three people suddenly appeared in front of her. But it was no illusion. Kala groaned inwardly, Olympians. Great.

Zeus, Hephaestus, and Talan apparently had felt the need to track her down to the Compound. Talan she was happy about, but the other two Kala could do without.

Talan seemed cautious as he approached Kala. She knew it was because he was unsure what had happened with Asmodeus. She decided to try and set his mind at ease : "Asmodeus knew jack shit, but he's going to ask around. Turner hooked me up to his machine and we managed to grab some images from my vision. Come look."

Kala didn't want to ask why the other two Olympians were there, so she pretended as if they were all there to help her. It wouldn't last long, but she would enjoy the delusion while she could, and maybe she could get an answer.

Talan came around first, examining the still image of the cave. "I don't recognize it. Zeus?" He motioned for the god to look.

A flicker of recognition from Zeus as he studied the screen. "It seems familiar, but I'm not sure. Definitely Earth, though."

"That's something." Kala didn't want to sound too grateful, but she couldn't help but feeling a stirring of hope.

"Would you like me to try?" Hephaestus offered. "Machines are my specialty."

"Have at it." Kala stood and let Hephaestus sit down at her chair. Instead of typing though, he placed his hands on the monitor screen.

"I can see the missing pieces," Hephaestus announced. "I'll put them together." In less than a few seconds, Kala was looking at her vision.

She was so shocked by the ease at which Hephaestus put the whole thing together it made her feel stupid she didn't ask for his help earlier. Of course, he'd be good with computers. He had forged the twelve blades that could injure all supernatural beings, why not electronics?

Before the vision began to play, Turner returned to the room. His only reaction to the new guests was a slight opening of his eyes.

"Hephaestus got it to work. Check it out." Kala needed as many eyes on her vision as possible, and she trusted Turner a lot more than she trusted Zeus and his son.

They all gathered around the screen to watch. When Zeus recognized Hades, Kala heard him mumbling under his breath. She was sure she'd have an earful after everyone was finished with the viewing party. Talan had to turn away when Vision-Kala was killed – whereas Turner immediately stared at her.

"I didn't think you could die," Turner voiced his thoughts. "Maybe you should sit this mission out."

"It doesn't work that way. If I don't do it, the world ends," Kala explained.

"Well, it looks like if you *do* do it, the world will end too. The next cycle won't be complete. Isn't that the way it works?" Turner countered.

Zeus guffawed and rolled his eyes. "She won't die. At least not permanently." He focused on Kala. "We didn't come here to see your vision, or help you complete it. We came here because we need you on our side against Cronus."

Changing the subject back to his own problems. Typical.

"What do you mean I won't die permanently?" Kala decided to steer the conversation back to her mission.

Zeus looked as if she had asked him to eat nails. "You're not going to help me until I answer, are you?"

Kala knew there were a few ways to answer that question: diplomacy, deception...

"Nope." Kala went with honesty.

Zeus acted as a child would, by crossing his arms defiantly. "You really shouldn't wake my brother. He's not exactly someone you want to have around."

"I don't have a choice in the matter," Kala pushed. It was one thing for Asmodeus not to like Hades, but for *Zeus* to have such a bad opinion? It made Kala wonder again how her Atlas vision was actually a "good" thing.

Zeus grumbled, "Since Atlas tricked you humans into taking over his job, I've never heard of an Atlas mission that had anything to do with a god or a Titan. It became a job for human existence, not immortals. Waking up Hades only puts you little apes in danger. And since my brother's only goal is to consume as many souls as he can, he'll *want* you to fail…" Zeus suddenly broke off, as if an idea had just come to him.

"What?" Kala didn't like that look.

"That's why he kills you. So you'll fail you're next task. It's a trap. You can't go," Zeus announced with authority.

"But I have to." There wasn't a choice. Go, or world go boom. "And you still haven't answered my question. What do you mean about me not dying permanently?"

Zeus sighed as if Kala was an idiot he had to explain things slowly to. "Hades can't kill an immortal. But he can send them to the Underworld."

Oh.

"So it *is* real, then." Kala knew the Underworld existed, since seeing Hades in her vision, but it was nice to have confirmation.

"Of course it's real. What did you think?" Zeus acted as if she was absurd for even doubting.

Being trapped in the Underworld sounded way better than actually dying. But if she couldn't find a way out, then she'd end up there forever anyway. "Is the Underworld how they describe it in mythology books?" Kala asked.

"More or less." Zeus shrugged. "But you won't be able to get out without help, and I won't help you unless you help me fight Cronus."

Now it was Kala's turn to feel like she was dealing with a child. "Really? You're giving me an ultimatum?"

Talan made eye contact with Kala. His whole demeanor toward her had changed. The news that she'd be in the Underworld and potentially be able to come back to life had obviously put the pep back in his step. "I will get you out. You don't have to do anything you don't want to."

Zeus laughed. "You? Tell me the last time a Grigori entered the Underworld?"

Seeing the blank expression on Talan's face, Zeus acted as if he were vindicated.

"Exactly." He dismissed Talan from his attention and turned back to Kala. "The only way out of the Underworld is through an Olympian and the Olympians obey *me*. So, are we making a deal?"

Kala envied Turner, who could remain silent through all this. Even Hephaestus was trying to stay out of it, quietly watching and re-watching the video of Kala's Atlas vision. Talan was always in her corner, of course, but how could he argue with Zeus? From the look on the Grigori's face, it was clear that he had no idea how to escape the Underworld, let alone enter it.

Though she wasn't quite convinced yet enough to make any deals with Zeus, Kala decided to placate him anyway, to see where his intentions lay.

"What do you want from me?" she asked – then before he could respond, Kala added, "And don't think I'm going to consume Cronus, either. Because that's not happening. Ever."

Zeus appeared appalled. "Why not? It's the best way to defeat him."

Kala groaned. "I knew it!" Shaking her head, she responded, "Are you serious? You really thought I'd agree to that? You are more insane now than you were in that prison."

Hephaestus calmly entered into the conversation. "With Gaia in you, you'd have complete control of yourself."

Kala whirled on him. "You know that for sure, do you? I'm still partially human and even having a single memory of Atlas made me pass out. As in, zero consciousness."

"But *he*," Zeus nodded toward Talan, "fixed all that."

Talan joined in, "Atlas was a lesser Titan and it was a difficult process. If Kala consumes *Cronus*… I'm not sure I'd be able to help. He could be strong enough to take over Kala's body and then you'd be dealing with the power of your father *and* your grandmother."

"And Atlas." Kala somehow felt the need to defend the Titan she'd swallowed. He might not be the biggest heavyweight in the Greek pantheon, but he was at least in the ring. "Look, I don't want any part of your inbred war. I have to do my job and that's to wake up your stupid brother and apparently plan a prison break out of the Underworld. So unless you want to help me complete my mission, I have no use for you."

Zeus looked miffed. "If you can't consume Cronus, then you can at least help us find my other Olympians. I told my father they were destroying the 5th level of Hell in our epic battle if you remember? I lied. And now Cronus has the safety of the 5th to protect him. The Olympians are lost to us and if we can't find them, there won't be a war. Cronus will come after me with all he has and I won't be able to fight him off."

"Am I supposed to feel sorry for you?" Kala was appalled. "You do remember you drained me like a battery to get your mojo back, right?" She waved at the screen. "And I can tell you where at least *one* Olympian is, if you can figure out the location of that cave."

Zeus glanced at the screen and its repeated sequence of Kala waking up Hades. "Not *that* one. I would be perfectly content to go through the rest of eternity without my brother mucking things up."

"Well, I'm not letting the world end for your brotherly grudge, so you better get used to the idea of a family reunion. Besides, don't you have the whole of the Grigori to fight beside you? I thought that was the deal when you freed them." Kala addressed the question to both Zeus and Talan.

Talan nodded. "Yes, the Grigori will help Zeus and all those that side with the Olympians, but finding the other Olympians could tip the balance."

"Pressure, much? How on earth am I supposed to help you find your people if I can't even find this stupid cavern!" Kala was at her wits end.

She glanced over at Turner, who seemed to be eating up this entire conversation. If it hadn't been for physical proof of Kala being a Titan, he'd probably think this whole lot was insane.

It was then that he decided to come to Kala's aid. "We'll get the satellites on this footage and see if we can find a location. If it's on Earth like Zeus says, then we'll find it." Turner smiled when he said Zeus's name, probably because of how surreal it sounded aloud.

Zeus's demeanor turned serious as he addressed Kala. "My grandmother runs through your veins. Her power could decide the war."

Exasperated, Kala took a deep breath. "Then why don't you go and find her? I only have a piece of her inside me. I think the real deal would be much more powerful."

Hephaestus said almost sadly, "Gaia's been lost for three millennia. No one knows where she is. You're the first we've seen of her."

The sentiment struck Kala as sad for some reason. Gaia was Zeus's grandmother and Hephaestus's great grandmother and being close to Kala made them feel closer to Gaia. It was a little warped, but made a strange sort of sense.

"Look, just let me find Hades and wake him up. If I'm going to be in the Underworld for a while, then maybe Hades knows where your fellow Olympians are. There's not much more I can do," Kala admitted.

Turner's eyebrow rose. "Actually, my wife said she could do a locator spell if she had a personal item from any one of the beings in question."

Zeus and Hephaestus shared a look of interest, but it was Zeus who spoke, "I can get you something from Poseidon and Hera, but the others, Cronus kept anything of theirs hidden."

Hephaestus directed his comment at Zeus. "Poseidon and Hera may be all we need, especially if we could talk Hades into working with us."

Zeus said to Hephaestus, "He might be angry enough, since Cronus put him to sleep for so long."

"So you'll help me find Hades?" Kala asked.

Zeus turned his attention to Kala and nodded slowly. "We'll take *your human's* aid and we'll help you find Hades."

Kala wondered at how one of the most powerful men on the planet liked being referred to as *her human*, but Turner didn't seem to mind. He actually appeared eager to help.

Kala shrugged. "Let's get to it, then."

Chapter Five

Before Kala could do *anything*, however, five more beings suddenly arrived by teleportation. Four Grigori and Penny to be precise. The only one Kala cared about was her adoptive father, Owen, a Grigori angel himself. He was supporting Antel with the help of Penny since Antel was injured and couldn't stand on her own. Antel was a beautiful Grigori with dark skin and even darker eyes. Next to them was Rotoph and another male Grigori Kala didn't recognize. Antel seemed to be the only one hurt.

Turner was the first to speak, "For a high security building, people do tend to pop in whenever they like." He was more amused than angry.

Owen was out of breath as he said, "I apologize. We had to move fast and Rotoph and I both focused on Kala. We didn't know she'd be here."

Kala ran over to him and took Antel from his arms. "Is she okay? What happened?"

Antel's voice was weak, "I'll be okay. Cronus gutted me with one of the Grigori blades, so it'll take some time to recover."

Kala remembered all too well what a Grigori blade could do. She was first introduced to one when *Rotoph* stabbed Talan in the back, literally and figuratively. Rotoph had sided with Cronus during the war and forged the blades with Hephaestus. Hephaestus thought the blades were being made to immobilize the Grigori to enable the Olympians and the Titans to imprison them.

But Cronus had had other plans. He directed Rotoph to engrave the weapons with a spell that not only stripped the Grigori of their powers, but would drain any supernatural being that wielded them. When Cronus handed the twelve blades over to the twelve Olympians, Zeus and his fellow gods were drained of their power, allowing Cronus to imprison the Olympians along with the Grigori.

Hephaestus had been duped. Rotoph had done it all willingly. He betrayed his family to serve Cronus.

Then, as of three days ago, Rotoph had proved he regretted his actions by helping Zeus and Hephaestus free the Grigori. Nevertheless, Kala could tell that Owen and Talan still had their doubts. If Rotoph betrayed them once, he could do it again.

Kala's second introduction to the blades had been when Cronus had cut Talan into a pile of body parts. She had thought Talan was dead, but Owen was able to put him back together. That was the moment when she realized Grigori really couldn't die. Or, if they could, becoming kibble apparently wasn't a deal breaker.

And so it was now, apparently, with Antel: seriously wounded by a Grigori blade, but recovering. Kala led Antel to a chair for her to sit. When the Grigori was comfortable, Kala hugged Owen tightly.

"Where's Mom?" she asked as she pulled away from Owen.

"Safe." Owen alleviated her fears. "Your mother is the reason we're here. Cronus tried to take her. He brought five Titans with him. We barely made it out. Antel managed to create a distraction, but it left her vulnerable. Rotoph and I were the only ones powerful enough to teleport everyone at once and since we both have a strong connection to you…"

Kala eyed Rotoph with disdain. "I do not have a connection with that guy."

Owen chuckled. "Well, he thinks you do and apparently thinking it made it so."

Rotoph waved his hand. "I'm right here." He turned to Turner. "I put a *no teleport* dome over this place. Not even Cronus can break it."

Zeus joined in, happy at that news. "I bet it's driving him mad not being able to get in here." He glanced at Kala. "Especially, if he knows you're here with me."

Kala rolled her eyes. "Yeah, I'm sure." Then she sighed in frustration. "So Cronus went after *Mom*? Did he really think I'd be okay with that?"

Owen shook his head. "Cronus can't convince you to join him, so he'll try to persuade you by force and use leverage against you. He knows how much Linda means to you. I hid her where he can never find her."

Kala didn't exactly like the sound of that. "And where is that?"

"It's better if you don't know." Owen placed his hands on Kala's shoulder. "But she *is* safe, Kala. Trust me."

She did.

Kala nodded to the monitor. "Check it out. Turner managed to capture my Atlas vision."

Hephaestus seemed miffed at her statement. "I'm the one who made it playable."

Kala wanted to laugh at all the fragile egos. It made her realize humans had thicker skin than gods.

Penny hugged Hephaestus in greeting. She was so happy to have her father back after years of imprisonment by Cronus.

The new arrivals watched the footage. When Hades touched Kala's head to kill her, the unfamiliar Grigori nodded and spoke for the first time: "We'll have to come up with an escape plan to get you out of the Underworld. Hades won't let you leave easily."

Kala was impressed. Until now, not even Talan knew what Hades had done in that vision. And from the look of relief on Owen's face, neither had her foster father.

Owen asked the Grigori. "So it's possible to get Kala out?"

Zeus puffed up his chest. "Grigori can't go into the Underworld." But Kala could see he didn't really know that for sure. His leverage was falling apart before his very eyes and Kala was enjoying it immensely.

The new Grigori gave Zeus a look of incredulity. "I hope you're joking. You do know the Grigori helped *create* the Underworld, right?"

From the expression on Zeus's face, he did *not* know that.

"Who are you?" Kala needed to know. Anyone that could verbally bitch-slap Zeus was a friend of hers.

"I'm Ashliel." He nodded with a smile. "And I'm very pleased to meet you."

"Feelings mutual." Kala smiled back. "So, you can get me out?"

"Of course. The issue will be finding you first. Talan has the closest connection to you. He'll be able to find you the fastest." Ashliel's blue eyes met Talan's for his nod of confirmation. The new Grigori's features were soft, as if he hadn't lost his baby fat, making him look forever twenty. His body was lean though and Kala could see from his arms that he was in good shape.

Talan didn't make eye contact with Kala when he said, "She has a connection with Asmodeus as well. He should be brought into the plan. I may not be strong enough."

Kala knew how much that admission hurt Talan, but like always he put her safety above his pride.

She knew Talan was right, though, and she added, "He's asking around to see if he can find where the cave is located. He'll find me when he has information."

Owen did not look happy at the prospect of involving Asmodeus in anything to do with his daughter's safety, but he kept it to himself. "If Talan thinks we should bring him in, then I trust his judgment."

Kala noticed Owen didn't say he trusted *her* judgment, but she knew Asmodeus was a sore spot for her foster father since he'd found out Kala had kissed the king of Demons. Plus, Owen had banished Asmodeus to the 5th Level of Hell after all. It probably annoyed him that it had been Kala and Talan that set the Demon free.

Ashliel obviously sensed the awkwardness. "Asmodeus is a good choice. He should know the Underworld well."

Kala smirked at Zeus. "Looks like you're useless again."

Zeus smirked back. "Apparently, you don't need Hephaestus to find this location for you."

Hephaestus shrugged. "Oh, I already found it."

That brought every eye in the room to the Olympian.

"Where is it?" Kala spoke first.

Hephaestus and Zeus shared a look, then Hephaestus focused solely on Kala. "Help us with Cronus."

Back to the ultimatum.

But Kala didn't want to wait around for Turner or Asmodeus to find Hades. If Hephaestus knew where the grotto was located now, then she had to know. "I said I'd help. What else do you want?"

The tension could be cut with a blade it was so thick.

Penny eyed both her father and Zeus and actually stood up for Kala. Shocker. "The Atlas mission is what matters above all else. If Kala agreed to help, then she will. She's given you no reason not to trust her."

After a moment, Zeus nodded, then motioned to his son. "Tell her."

Hephaestus didn't need to use a mouse or keyboard, he simply touched the monitor and a view of the satellite feed popped up on the screen. A simple tap and the camera zoomed down to earth. Instead of moving toward a landmass, however, it plummeted into the middle of the Atlantic Ocean. Deeper, deeper, deeper… Kala didn't think many humans had seen this part of the ocean. It was almost pitch black the further down the view went. When the camera only picked up black, Hephaestus switched it into infra-red mode. Large rock formations appeared all around. The sea life swam ahead, not knowing that a group of gods, angels and humans were watching.

The screen went black for a few seconds as the view passed through rock at the bottom of the ocean floor.

And there it was.

The cave.

With Hades lying on the floor, sleeping.

Turner chuckled slightly. "The Hadal Zone. Someone has a sense of humor."

Only Kala knew that Turner was referring to the deepest, darkest part of the ocean named, the Hadal Zone. *Hadal* referring to the "mythical" god, Hades. Leave it to Cronus to be on the nose.

"What is this *Hadal Zone*?" Antel spoke up. Her pallor grew healthier each minute that passed and she wanted to be a part of the plan.

"Only a handful of people have ever gone that deep. It's named after Hades," Turner answered. "I have the equipment to get you there. I'm just not sure how to puncture through rock without letting all the water in."

"Can't I just teleport?" Kala felt like she should at least try. "Now that we know where it is, why don't I just jump in?"

Rotoph inspected the cave on screen, shaking his head. "Cronus has a spell surrounding the outside that won't let you. I can see it through the infrared. I might be able to break it, but not from here. We have to be right above it, which means I'm going with you."

Owen and Talan's leeriness of Rotoph's suggestion was obvious to anyone who had eyes. Talan stepped in at that point. "I'm going too. The closer I can be to you, Kala, the better chance I have at following you to the Underworld."

Ashliel glanced at Zeus. "You think Oceanus guards the location?"

Zeus nodded to Ashliel. "I wouldn't doubt it," then turned to the others. "Oceanus won't let anyone near that location. You need me *and* Poseidon to open it. Rotoph might be able to break the teleportation-blocking spell, but we're the ones you need to break through the protection barriers Cronus has put up to hide Hades."

"Forgive my lack of mythological lore, but Oceanus is a Titan, I assume?" Turner asked.

Zeus responded, "Yes. And one of the most vicious. He was responsible for taking down my brother, Poseidon. He sided with the Olympians in the first war, but he was the first to attack us in the second." He eyed Turner pointedly. "I have something for your wife that belongs to Poseidon." He handed Turner a small charm made from coral.

Turner took it gently, then replied, "I could have a car pick her up now, but I feel *your* mode of transportation is faster."

Talan took a step closer to Turner. "I'll get her."

Kala knew Roberta had had less than a day to recover from her kidnapping, but she also knew the woman was strong and she'd do anything to help. Talan was the best man for the job, too, since he had been teaching Roberta and Turner advanced science and magic when he was disguised as someone they trusted. Kala wasn't sure how Turner felt about the matter, though, since technically Talan's deception had been a betrayal of trust.

But Turner didn't seem fazed when he responded to Talan's offer, "Bring her to this room and prepare her for who's in here."

With a slight nod, Talan disappeared.

It would take a few minutes for Talan to explain to Roberta about the supernatural mash-up she was about to enter into.

Turner pulled Kala aside. "Harry is in charge of undersea research. He has the kind of vehicle you'll need to get to the bottom of the ocean safely."

Kala had had a feeling she'd be working with General Clifton again, she just didn't think it would be this soon. "Bring him in," she sighed in resignation.

Turner kept his focus on Kala. "Should we tell him *everything*?"

"He still thinks that all that he's seen is technology-based," Kala answered, shaking her head slightly. She was incredulous at Clifton's failure to believe his own eyes. Then she continued, "I won't hold anything back, but I'd rather not explain everything to him. Let him believe what he wants."

Turner shrugged. "Knowing Harry he'll try and use the information to his advantage somehow."

Zeus, who had obviously been listening, interrupted. "Who is this *Harry*? If he's a problem, I can eliminate him. It would be no trouble."

Turner sighed with a slight smile as if debating the idea, then shook his head. "As tempting as that may be, I need Harry. I won't always have gods and angels backing my plays and he has a particular set of skills that I don't have."

Kala couldn't imagine what those "skills" were, and frankly, she didn't want to. "Is General Clifton still in the Compound?"

"I'm right here." Clifton entered on cue.

Turner quickly explained to the others, "I called him as soon as you gave the go-ahead." He nodded to his watch.

"That was sixty seconds ago," Kala responded.

"I'm efficient," Turner replied.

But Kala suddenly didn't care about Harry's arrival – because right behind him was Derek. She ran over and he squeezed her in a giant bear hug.

Clifton said, "As promised. Not a scratch on him. I figured you'd want to use him on whatever it is you're calling me up here for?"

Kala pulled out of the embrace and gave a slight nod to Clifton. "Thanks."

Derek's expression was one of surprise as he confided, "When General Clifton tracked me down I thought I'd be in for a fight. I know you said I can't die now, but I really didn't want to test that theory."

"You can't die. That's a fact." Antel spoke from her chair. Her pallor was looking better as her wounds healed rapidly. "Not even decapitation would take you. Your body will simply regenerate."

Kala motioned to Antel. "That's Antel. She's Grigori."

"Ah, like Talan?" Derek inquired.

"Pretty much." Kala smiled as she watched her friend take in the room. She knew Derek already had three escape routes developing in the back of his mind, all involving taking Kala with him if need be. Always the soldier. Even though he'd been working in her elite government team with Turner for the last few years, Derek still looked like a marine with his shaved head and muscled build, his dark complexion only accentuated his flawless features of angular cheekbones, full lips and brown eyes.

Kala kept one eye on Clifton, too. He was watching the room, taking in all of the players. Whether he knew or believed in the supernatural yet, Kala had no idea. General Clifton was the kind of guy who would be very hard to convince that magic was real.

Kala glanced around and made the introductions. "That's Zeus. That's Hephaestus and the rest are Grigori. And you both know Penny as Dr. Rosen."

Derek mouthed, "Zeus?" He knew all about the Olympians and Titans, but aside from Cronus snapping his neck, Derek hadn't been properly introduced to any of them aside from Penny, and he had thought she was a neurologist.

"Yup. And we're just waiting on Talan to return with Roberta so we can find out where Poseidon is." Kala wanted to laugh at the absurdity of this conversation. She felt like at any moment a couple of orderlies would cart her away to the loony bin.

But it just showed how far both she and Derek had traveled in their lives these past several days because he simply said, "Okay then."

Clifton, on the other hand, was in complete denial of gods, angels and demons being "real."

"Zeus, Hephaestus, Grigori? Are those their call signs? What government do they work for? Ours?" Clifton asked in general, but his eyes rested on Turner. As strange as their relationship was, they still had an unexplainable bond.

Turner didn't hesitate. "Yes, those are their code names and they work for America. As for Roberta, she's going to be performing a locator spell. You know Roberta has been delving more and more into Vodun and black magic? You've seen the results from my labs."

Clifton nodded, but Kala couldn't tell whether or not he was entirely on board. At any rate he didn't argue. No doubt he was running through his options in his head.

Turner pointed to the screen playing Kala's vision. "Lieutenant Hicks has to reach this location in the Hadal Zone."

Clifton examined the video of Kala's vision and went into mission-mode.

"You'll need the XV-4250 to get to those depths. And phase-suits if Lieutenant Hicks needs to leave the ship. We've adjusted them for deep water pressure." Clifton smiled at Kala. "We wouldn't want your head exploding."

The Titan part of her wouldn't have that problem, but the human part would most definitely pop like a balloon. And, immortal or not, Derek was all human: she really didn't want him feeling the sensation of a brain bomb. So, as much as she hated phase-suits, she'd have to put one on one more time.

Antel's eyebrow raised with curiosity. "What's a phase-suit?"

Kala explained how the suit allowed the wearer to walk through any surface: wood, cement, steel, anything.

Ashliel responded, "If Rotoph can bring down the teleportation blocking spell and Zeus can take out the protection barriers, it'll be just rock between you and Hades. You could just teleport."

Kala answered, "If Zeus and Rotoph fail or if they can't break the spells in time, maybe a phase-suit can get me through to that cave whether or not Zeus and Rotoph succeed. Science may beat magic in this instance. I hope, anyway."

Phasing wasn't Kala's favorite thing on the planet. She sighed heavily. "Let's just get this over with."

DAY TWO

Chapter Six

Kala watched the clock as it counted down.

2d 23h 22m 33s: 5:38 AM.

It was day two already and Kala was raring to go. The entourage had moved to the science lab downstairs. It had only been a day since Kala had confronted Fortski and destroyed his work, but a lot had happened in those twenty-four hours.

In the middle of the room at one of the long tables Roberta was preparing her tracking spell with Talan. She had the coral charm that Zeus had given her and was coating it in a kind of powdered mixture. Talan was helping with some of the details. In the past, he had been training her disguised as an old Voodoo priest; now that Roberta knew his true identity, Talan didn't bother hiding who he was anymore.

Clifton appeared to be treating this situation like any other mission, despite the oddity of Roberta's magic preparation. Kala knew Clifton had feelings for the woman, so there was probably a part of him that believed Roberta could do no wrong. Turner and Kala privately discussed at length whether or not to confide the truth about gods, angels and Demons to Clifton, but Turner didn't think Clifton would believe it anyway. The final decision had been to let Clifton see what he sees and have him make his own conclusions.

At the moment, Clifton was privately conferring with Fortski in the corner, which didn't settle well with Kala. But she wasn't exactly the person that should step in to stop it. Since Turner didn't seem to mind, she left them alone. Fortski had taken several samples of Derek's blood after the discovery of his newfound immortality.

It was an odd sight seeing a couple of Olympian gods, a handful of Grigori, and humans all in the same room. Even at that, though, each group kept to its own kind except for Owen and Ashliel, who were talking with Zeus and Hephaestus.

Kala stayed with Derek, slightly away from everyone. Even though they were now "more than human," it felt like they were soldiers again. Especially since Clifton wasn't trying to kill the both of them.

Derek nudged her shoulder affectionately. "You thinking how weird this all is?"

"Pretty much," Kala confirmed.

"I still can't wrap my head around it. I mean… I can't die. Does that mean I won't age either? What do I tell my family? I know I look good," he smiled, "but after a while they're going to know."

Kala thought about the drug she saw in the future that Fortski was going to invent. "You won't have to worry about that for very long."

When Derek gave her a look of amused puzzlement, she told him, "In five years Fortski is going to invent a pill that will make *all* humans immortal. Not like you where you could be chopped to pieces and regenerate, but the kind of immortality where they'll never grow old. They'll still be fragile as far as humans go, but they can't die from aging." On seeing the surprised expression on his face she added, "So you'll fit right in. No one will ever know how bad ass you really are."

Derek shook his head in amazement. "I thought this world was crazy before." Then he genuinely lit up. "I was so worried I'd have to see my parents and brothers die while I lived on forever, but now I won't have to." In a sudden burst of emotion he leaned down and hugged Kala.

Then he pulled away, serious. "I can't say I'm happy about what's happened to me, but I'm glad I'll be seeing your mug for the next… God, how many years? I can't even comprehend it."

"Don't think about it. It'll drive you crazy. I'm still dealing with a weasely Titan's memories from the last however many thousands of years."

Then Kala eyed him, solemnly. "But you saw my vision. When I wake up Hades, he is going to send me to the Underworld. I may not be able to die, but I could get stuck there… If I do, and I can't complete the next Atlas mission, the world may end sooner than we think. And that future of humans becoming immortal will never come to pass."

Derek cocked his head to the side. "Well, let's just make sure that doesn't happen. I've got your back, you know that. And now your little supernatural friends will let me tag along since I'm not a *fragile* human anymore," he added with a grin.

Roberta motioned Kala towards her, breaking up the conversation with Derek. They walked over to Turner's wife. Roberta's spell preparation looked as if it was one of Fortski's laboratory experiments, with bubbling beakers, Bunsen burners and Poseidon's charm resting at the bottom of the glass container moving with the flow of boiling water.

Kala liked Roberta. She had an air of confidence about her that Kala respected, and she was always willing to do whatever was necessary to help Kala complete her Atlas tasks. Roberta and Turner had been the first people to help her fight Demons and Malaks with weapons that actually worked. Roberta was a powerful woman who harnessed magic like she had been born a supernatural being. Added to Turner's scientific advancements, the two made a formidable pair. A pair that would rule the world someday if the future Kala foresaw came to pass.

Roberta nodded toward the beaker. "It'll be ready soon, but now that we know you have Gaia in you, it would be helpful if I could harness some of your energy. I can only assume Poseidon is a powerful god if he lives up to his mythology, so the more mojo the better."

"Of course. What do you want me to do?" Kala hoped Roberta wouldn't drain her Gaia-battery like Zeus had, but she trusted that Turner's wife would know when to pull back.

"I can channel your power through touch." Roberta smiled. "All you have to do is hold my hand," she glanced at Talan knowingly, "and Talan's. We'll form a circle."

Roberta wasn't blind. She could see Talan's loving eyes every time he looked at Kala. And from the expression on Roberta's face, she apparently thought Kala should feel the same way.

Kala refrained from commenting either way; she simply took Roberta and Talan's proffered hands. Kala was starting to understand the power of a circle. Her only previous experience had been when Hephaestus first tried to pull the Grigori through the portal connecting this world to the Grigori prison. The sensation felt almost the same. A feeling of surging power traveled through Kala's entire body, as if the three of them completed an electrical circuit.

Roberta closed her eyes and began chanting. Kala recognized the language as some dialect of Latin, but couldn't understand what Roberta was saying. Kala watched Poseidon's pendant flail in the bubbles of the mucky water, which then began to foam and spill down the side of the beaker.

Roberta's voice grew louder and more intense. The murky liquid responded in kind. Until….

CRACK! The beaker exploded!

To Kala's surprise the shards of glass flew up to the ceiling rather than out and around as she had expected. The water that had been inside the beaker kept its form for a few seconds, then dropped down onto the Bunsen burner, extinguishing the flame. The tiny pieces of glass quickly followed, falling down from above, harmlessly, and forming a small pile.

Magic. Roberta must have known that the beaker would explode, so she had created a spell to keep everyone protected. Kala respected the woman's talent.

When Roberta opened her eyes, they were solid white.

It jolted Kala so much she pulled her hands out of the circle.

Roberta's eyes instantly cleared and her face was awed. "I know where Poseidon is," she said in wonderment.

Kala jumped when Zeus's voice rumbled beside her. She hadn't even noticed him joining her side. "Where?" His stance was aggressive as if he'd throttle the answer out of Roberta for no reason except to prove his power.

Turner immediately stood behind his wife, his hands resting protectively on her shoulders. He couldn't do much against a god like Zeus, but that didn't stop him from exuding an air of intimidating confidence. Even as a human.

Roberta patted one of Turner's hands affectionately, looking up at him. "It's alright, Geoffrey." Then she turned to Zeus with a look that gave Kala shivers. "Zeus can't hurt me." The way she said it…

Kala knew it was true.

And so did Zeus.

It made him take a step back, his expression reevaluating. He had never seen humans as a threat before. The idea must have been so foreign to his way of thinking. Yet even Cronus had expressed a fear of humans taking the gods down. It was the reason why he wanted Kala to fail at her Atlas mission.

But Roberta acted as if her veiled threat hadn't even happened as she warmly addressed the room: "Poseidon is in the Underworld."

Zeus seemed pleased by this. "Fortuitous. It seems your Atlas mission is siding with me. Now we can all get him out."

Roberta cocked her head, thoughtful. "Your father was no fool. Even I *can* sense the protection spells he has guarding the Underworld. Tell me, Zeus, have any of you ever tried to see if you can get inside?"

It was obvious from the expression on his face that the answer was no.

Penny motioned to Zeus. "I suggest you try now, to be sure she's right. If we can't enter the Underworld then the only way we can get in is to either break the spells or through Hades touch like Kala will have."

Zeus nodded. Closing his eyes, his face tensed in concentration. This went on for a few more moments until he finally shook his head. "I can't get in."

Then understanding flooded his features as he explained, "This was why Cronus put him to sleep, so we couldn't reach Poseidon."

Roberta pointed her finger to correct him, "Not just Poseidon. Other Olympians are there: your siblings. Trapped. Stripped of their powers daily with a Grigori blade by their mother, the Titan, Rhea. Correct?"

Kala was impressed with Roberta's knowledge of Greek mythology. But from the confidence in her tone, it seemed like the tracking spell itself gave her these specific facts.

Zeus nodded, "Yes, Rhea is my mother and mother to the first six Olympians. But what about the others: Athena, Ares, Hebe, Persephone and Dionysus? Are they there too?"

Roberta shook her head. "No. They must be imprisoned somewhere else."

"Or hiding," Penny blurted out.

Zeus turned to her angry, "Why would my children hide from me? They would want to fight the Titans."

Penny shrugged. "A lot has changed since you were chained up. If Cronus isn't holding your children, then chances are they made a deal with him for their safety – or are hiding until the war is fought and over."

Zeus sighed heavily. "Too much time has passed. I can't worry about the weaker Olympians now. We have to focus on my siblings." His eyes were distant as he said, "When my mother conspired to save me from Cronus, I thought she'd always be on my side…" He shook his head. "Never mind."

Zeus turned to Kala. "You may be our only hope after all. Hades is leading you directly to where you need to be to save my family."

"The briar patch," Kala mumbled.

Zeus was confused. "I don't understand that reference."

Kala shrugged. "It means what you just said. But how in the hell am I supposed to get out of the Underworld if no one can get in to help me escape?"

Talan's eyes met hers. "I'll get in." Then he elaborated, "Once we figure out how to break the protective barriers surrounding Hades, the walls to the Underworld shouldn't be too dissimilar."

Zeus's stance grew more and more angered as the situation sunk in. "We'll tear down that spell and bring an army to get you out. I won't let my brother and sisters spend another day in Hades's domain."

Kala didn't want to argue with the god, since he seemed so determined, but she wasn't sure that what he wanted was possible. She had to think strategically, which meant she'd have to devise a plan that didn't include a rescue party. There was no way she could plan now though since Kala didn't have any clue as to what she'd find in the Underworld other than what she'd read in books. And how accurate could those really be? She'd have to figure out the lay of the land once she was inside.

Speaking of which, "We should get going. It looks like Hades might know what he's doing when he sends me to the Underworld."

Zeus was the only one who didn't seem convinced of that statement.

From her Atlas memories Kala knew Zeus didn't have much trust in his brothers, especially Hades. She guessed brotherly rivalry ran in gods families as well as human ones. It didn't matter anyway. She wasn't going to shirk on her Atlas duties, so the vision would come to pass if she had anything to say about it. It would be the first time she ever considered finishing the mission before her four-day mark. But Kala knew escaping from the Underworld would be a daunting and difficult task. She needed the full four days to find out her new mission, break out of the Underworld and accomplish the new task. Thinking about it too much would drive her mad though, so she focused on the present situation.

Breaking up the meeting, Kala headed toward the exit with Derek to prepare for their journey. As Kala opened the door, she felt a hand on her arm. It was Penny.

"Can I speak with you for a moment?" Penny asked, almost timidly.

Penny's tone startled Kala enough to motion for Derek to go on ahead without her.

"What is it?" Kala said.

Taking a deep breath Penny spoke with a slight catch in her voice. "You'll be going to the Underworld."

"Yes," Kala prodded, confused at Penny's obvious statement and the girl's apparent emotional state.

Penny paused as if unsure of how to proceed. Then she continued, "Jack will be there."

Kala froze.

Her brain, her body… everything: frozen.

Seeing Kala's paralyses, Penny plowed forward. "Don't worry, his body is just a shell housing a soul, his mind won't be there. It's the way the Underworld works. He'll be in the Fields of Elysium. It's reserved for heroes." Penny paused, trying to regain her composure. "I just thought you should know, in case… you see him."

Too many feelings warred within Kala's heart and brain, but finally she found her voice. "How do you know he'll be there?"

"Because he was to be the next Atlas, and he was willing to sacrifice himself for you to complete your mission. It's the way your world works. Your body and soul go to the mythos you believe in while living." Penny paused, holding back tears. "Anyway… I didn't want you to be blind-sided."

Kala saw in that moment that Penny had been in love with Jack, too. Kala had never acknowledged it before, but it had been obvious from the very start. Penny had desperately wanted Jack to be the Fated One and not Kala. The way Penny looked at Jack…the devastation in her eyes when Kala had shot him…

It somehow bonded them in that moment, something Kala never thought would happen. Slowly, Kala nodded. "Thanks for telling me."

Penny forced the wisp of a smile. "Of course." Sighing deeply, Penny switched back to her familiar colder tone, distancing herself from Kala. "Good luck on your mission."

"Thanks," Kala responded.

As she watched Penny walk away, Kala stood in place, determination washing over her. Kala had one more goal when she entered the Underworld.

She was going to find Jack and bring him home.

An hour later they were standing on a military loading dock ready to depart. Kala surveyed General Clifton's ship, or, more accurately, his super-submarine. That was the only way she could describe it. As she was recently a part of the Clifton/Turner elite unit, Kala was used to seeing technology beyond what the public knew existed, but even this ship blew her mind. Clifton called it the XV-4250. She never knew the reasoning behind the naming of all Turner and Clifton's gadgets, but Kala was sure it had been cataloged in a very specific way. The two of them didn't do anything by *accident*. The stealth plane Kala's old crew used was an XV-350, so she figured the XV must stand for something.

Entering through the top hatch, Kala climbed down a metal ladder that led to the belly of the beast. The interior of the sub was made from the same undetectable black metal as the Compound's walls. Kala wondered if this applied to gods? Would Oceanus see them coming from a mile away? Probably. But at this point it was up to Zeus to hold off his uncle.

The entire control center was holographic, which Kala had limited experience with. Derek seemed more adept to it, probably because he'd had free run of Turner's personal Cog for the last week. As amazing as Kala thought having supernatural powers was, on some levels Turner and Clifton had the gods beat when it came to their gadgets and devices.

There were six of them on board: Zeus, Rotoph, Ashliel, Talan, Derek and Kala. Zeus appeared confident on the surface that he'd be able to break the protection spells hiding Hades, but Kala sensed he was a little wary of the idea as well. However, after Rotoph volunteered to help Zeus after he was finished breaking the teleportation spell, Zeus appeared to relax a little. The Olympian would never admit he needed help, but it was obvious he was relieved to have it.

Kala didn't know *what* to expect. Being at the bottom of the ocean was already an unnerving concept, let alone the thought of some ancient Titan attacking them.

Only Ashliel had been the surprise tag-along. But someone needed to run the sub and he seemed to have the same knack for computers and technology as Hephaestus. Zeus didn't want Ashliel on board though, arguing that he felt outnumbered and that Hephaestus might be able to help him break the protections spells. In the end, however, they both agreed that Hephaestus needed to stay on land to keep a handle on the Grigori. Zeus didn't want to lose his new allies. If no other Olympian was above ground to remind the Grigori who had rescued them, Zeus was afraid they'd abandon his cause. Then he mumbled something about angels and Malaks being flakey and Ashliel volunteered to come.

Kala was starting to like the Grigori. So far, Kala's experience with the Grigori had been two types: the calm, reasonable type like her father, Talan and Antel; and the rebellious fire and brimstone type, like Rotoph. She felt Ashliel was somewhere in between. He definitely had a cool and collected side, but every once in while Ashliel would verbally take Rotoph down a notch and put him in his place. It was entertaining, and that kind of wit always impressed Kala.

She closed her eyes and took a deep breath. Her motion sickness had kicked in the moment she stepped foot on board the vessel. Being underwater, she couldn't exactly look out at the horizon to steady her equilibrium, either.

Derek's hands soon found their way to her shoulders as he began to give her a massage. She instantly relaxed and closed her eyes. "I still feel like barfing, but that makes it better. Thanks."

She could hear Derek's soft chuckle, "You're the toughest girl I've ever known and even as a god you still get motion sickness?"

"Ha, ha, laugh it up. We all have our things. Mister *cockroach*."

"Okay, those things are foul. And remember our mission in Florida?! Those things flew! Flew! I can take on bullets any day, but flying cockroaches?! Forget it," Derek laughed.

"I *did* see in my vision that if I don't complete my task the world will be taken over by cockroaches. Just saying," Kala teased.

Derek stopped massaging her and eyed her seriously. "Please tell me you're joking. Cuz I'm going to live through whatever apocalypse may come if you screw up. I can't live in a world overrun by those little suckers."

Kala shoved him affectionately. "Thanks for the confidence, dick."

Derek's smile returned and he nudged her back. "Any time, princess."

The ship traveled through the ocean and slowly moved further and further down for hours.

No one spoke. Everyone was too wrapped up in their thoughts of what was to come.

Ashliel's voice finally broke the silence. "We're almost there." He turned to Rotoph. "You sense the teleportation blocking spell yet?"

Even though Kala planned on using a phase-suit to find Hades, Talan needed to teleport to her once she had located the body. More precisely, he needed to try and teleport directly to the Underworld once Hades killed her.

Rotoph nodded, then added, "It's one hell of a spell too. It may take a while."

Ashliel barely acknowledged Rotoph (to his annoyance) as he turned to Zeus. "What about Oceanus? Anything on your radar?"

Zeus shook his head. "Maybe we'll get lucky."

Famous last words.

SLAM!

The ship jolted hard right and everyone that was standing toppled to the ground.

"I think your uncle Oceanus found us." Kala directed her comment to Zeus as she tried to stand, but fell down again ungracefully to the floor.

Ashliel gained his bearing back first and steered the craft downward, then stopped. "Better strap on those phase-suits, because we're right above Hades's cave."

Chapter Seven

After several minutes of General Clifton's XV-4250 being thrown around like it was Oceanus's plaything, Kala was finally suited up and ready to go. The phase-suits practically looked like scuba gear anyway, so she'd fit right in at the bottom of the ocean. With the gear adjusted for water pressure and temperature, Kala could at least be assured that her body wouldn't explode or freeze when exiting the ship. But swimming in the blackness of the ocean… knowing that a Titan was waiting to tear her to pieces… It didn't exactly make her feel confident.

Feeling selfish that Derek was right beside her, ready to go, Kala suppressed a wave of guilt. He was immortal, yes, but she still didn't like putting him in danger. Yet he was the only person she truly trusted. Sure, her father and Talan were a close second, but whether or not they wanted to admit it, they had to think of their people first. They may claim that Kala was their one and only, but if they were put in a position where they had to choose between the entire Grigori race and her, Kala wouldn't blame them if they didn't pick her.

With Derek, he'd pick Kala every time. Even in the past when he had thought she was crazy and had handed her over to Clifton. Once Derek had realized Clifton wanted to kill her, he risked his life, his career, *everything* to save her. She'd never doubt him. Loyalty was what Kala valued the most. She'd never betray her best friend and he'd never betray her. It was that simple.

Derek handed her a handgun that appeared to be made of some kind of plastic or resin. "Turner gave me a few toys from his Cog," he explained. "Thought we might be able to use these." He placed an identical gun inside his phase-suit.

Kala took the gun, but couldn't hide her doubts. "I don't think a gun will help us down here. Even if it shoots, bullets don't hurt Titans."

Derek smiled knowingly. "It's no guarantee, but these might. Roberta said she studied your Grigori blades and carved some kind of magic-mojo-something-or-other into the bullets. She's pretty sure it'll at least do *something*."

Kala strapped the gun into her suit, grateful. "I'll take something over nothing any day."

The ship swung violently to the left. Kala and the crew were used to the jolts by now and managed to stay on their feet.

Calling back to Zeus, trying to hide her annoyance, Kala yelled, "I thought you were here to take care of that guy?" She turned to Derek, holding her stomach. "I'm seriously going to vomit."

Derek eyed Zeus, who was throwing Kala irritated glances. "You guys really *are* like family," he laughed. "And for the king of the gods or whatever, Zeus is a whiner."

"Right?!" Kala was glad someone finally saw that too. The Demons, Malaks and Grigori all had a certain element of understanding not only their powers, but where they fit in the world, whereas the Titans and Olympians just seemed like big babies that cried when they didn't get their way. Kala's only regret was the fact that by her swallowing Atlas, she had brought all of the Titans and Olympians back to the surface. Life would probably be a lot better for everyone involved if Cronus and his siblings had stayed in the 5th Level of Hell and Zeus had remained on the crazy train rendering him harmless.

However, as Kala's Atlas visions were showing her, the universe obviously wanted these upper beings back in the game, otherwise she wouldn't be on her way to wake up Hades and prison-break the rest of Zeus's siblings in the Underworld.

Derek led the way to the decompression chamber and the ship's exit. Kala was impressed with the durability the XV-4250 exhibited, considering the constant beating it was currently receiving. After a particularly large jolt, Kala grabbed the wall to steady herself. She was surprised she hadn't vomited yet from all the lurching and jerking.

Zeus followed close behind, Rotoph on his heels.

"Do they need suits?" Derek asked Kala, not bothering to talk to the two supernatural beings directly.

Zeus answered though. "I am a god, *human*, I don't need a *suit* to be underwater. I just wish Poseidon were here. My powers come from the air and sky, not… ocean."

"Well, he's not. So do you think you can break the protection spell *and* fight Oceanus?" Kala was in no mood for negativity.

Zeus's face said 'no,' but he nodded. "I'll break that spell."

Rotoph added, "And I'll break the teleportation field."

Two protection spells that needed to be broken. The hardest part for Kala was that Zeus and Rotoph were the ones she depended on to break them. Not two of the most reliable beings in creation.

Rotoph nodded toward the door. "Let's just get in the chamber with your…" he nodded awkwardly at the phase-suits, "…rubber clothes." He turned to Derek. "After she's in, you'll have five minutes to return to this ship. That's all the time Ashliel thinks he has to keep your General's contraption together before Oceanus destroys it beyond reckoning. With your immortality, you won't die if you don't make it, but it will be a very long swim back to shore considering we're in the middle of the Atlantic."

Derek's nod was barely perceptible. "I can do five minutes."

Rotoph nodded back. "Good." He turned to Kala. "I'll need to get as close to the chamber walls as possible to destroy the blocking spell. Grigori aren't great underwater."

"Do you need an oxygen tank? We're using these." Kala showed him the small lipstick-sized mouthpiece that had enough oxygen in it to last a few hours. The size was important because it fit snuggly underneath the hood of her phase-suit and every part of her body needed to be covered by the suit in order to move through walls. She didn't want to leave any body parts behind.

Rotoph shook his head. "I'm Grigori, we don't need to breathe, we just like to. No, it's more of the swimming and seeing that will be an issue. Oceanus will target me if he finds me."

Zeus breathed in deep, trying to pump himself up. "Oceanus won't find you. I'll take care of him. When you're done, signal me and we'll take down Hades's protection spell together."

"Two spells. You sure you guys got this?" Kala surveyed them both.

Rotoph shrugged. "The universe seems to think you can perform this mission, so we must be the reason you do."

It made logical sense, but Kala hoped the outcome would be favorable for everyone. It was one thing if they managed to break both the teleportation spell and the protection spell, but entirely another if they mortally injured themselves in the process.

There was nothing else to be said.

It was now or never.

Derek sensed this as well. He shut the door to the decompression chamber, sealing the four of them inside. Kala and Derek placed the small oxygen tanks in their mouths and pulled their hoods over their faces, securing themselves inside their phase-suits. Walking to the holographic wall, Derek punched keys floating in the air like he was playing with lasers in a laser show.

A loud sucking sound filled Kala's ears as she felt her body squeeze from the pressure. There was no pain, but it didn't exactly feel great, either.

Derek nodded to the three of them, then typed in the final code.

Water rushed into the chamber from a slot above them next to the hatch that led out. As the water level rose, its icy touch made Kala shiver. She wished it would pour in faster, but having three tons of water rush in at once at these depths would snap the ship in two. It took a few minutes for the entire room to fill with water.

Derek took the leadership position, being the only one familiar with the ship and its technology. The holograph controls were still visible and useable even in the darkness of the ocean-filled chamber. He swam up to the hatch and typed in a code on the holo-keypad. The door swung downward.

Kala saw only blackness through the hole. To counter that, she and Derek were equipped with specially made glow sticks that would give them a few feet of light. Rotoph and Zeus would have to rely on Kala and Derek's light or whatever supernatural powers they could muster. Searching Atlas's memory banks for any kind of advantage the Titan may have underwater resulted in nada. Kala would have to rely on Turner and Clifton's gadgets to get her down to Hades in one piece.

Kala swam away from the XV-4250. Its dim lights cast barely a blip in her field of vision. One thing she did notice: the ship had stopped moving. The ocean currents buffeting it had ceased.

Oceanus knew the power-hitters were no longer inside.

Now that they were outside the ship, Kala swam past Derek and took the lead. Around her wrist was a holographic GPS marking the exact coordinates of where to enter the cave.

Glancing back at Zeus she noticed he had a thin layer of air around him like a second skin. Rotoph had the same and it made Kala wonder if it was some kind of spell she could perform for the future. Not that any of the gods were forthcoming on spilling trade secrets. Also, she'd learned that Atlas had been pretty much useless his entire life, so she wasn't finding out much from culling through his memories, either.

Pulling out her gun was an odd sensation, being that she was underwater. Kala had used rifles that worked in water before, but never a handgun. And with Roberta's extra mojo, she wondered what kind of effect it would have on a Titan. A small part of her wanted to test it out on Zeus just to make sure it worked, but she didn't think the Olympian would appreciate it very much. Besides, Kala may actually need the guy, considering they were about to face the deity *the ocean* was named after.

As if on cue, Kala barely made out the dark swirling whirlpool heading straight toward her. Aiming her gun, she looked around trying to see any sign of Oceanus. Kala wasn't exactly sure what to look for, but all the supernatural beings had appeared human, so she searched for some kind of human silhouette.

First things first, she had to avoid the cyclone of blackness about to swallow her whole.

In her mind she heard Zeus say: *Move aside and let me take care of my uncle.*

Within Zeus's bubble of air, lightning traveled up and down his body. He looked like an electric eel, but ten times more terrifying. The closer the whirlpool traveled the larger Zeus's lightning bolts grew, until he lit up the blackness of the ocean within ten yards of where he swam.

The light helped Kala see her destination with the use of her holo-GPS. Only fifty feet away.

As much of a show as Zeus's lightning was, the spinning chasm of water still drilled its way toward them.

Zeus slammed his entire body into the vortex. Lightning shattered the whirlpool to pieces.

A shock wave crashed into Kala and Derek and they were pushed farther away from their target.

Upon impact, Zeus's lightning was snuffed out, leaving them in darkness once more.

Kala could hear Rotoph chanting in her head. He was using telepathy as well, to let her know when he broke the teleportation block. Since that was just the first of two spells that needed to be broken, Kala worried that – with Zeus busy occupying Oceanus – the protection spell might not be broken any time soon. And that was the most important to her, since she planned on entering the cave with the phase-suit.

Using the intercom system with Derek, Kala said, "I've got to help Zeus if he's going to take that second spell down."

Without hesitation Derek responded, "Let's do it."

Kala didn't argue with him to save himself. She knew it was useless. Derek would use up every one of his immortal lives if it meant he could help. It was just who he was.

Swimming toward the newly generated sparks of lightning was the only way Kala could tell where Zeus was located.

Oceanus had all the advantages. He was a water god, at one with the ocean, able to control it to his will, while Kala was an ex-human, now second generation Titan, with some kind of earth-force Gaia mix in there. If anything would help her at the moment, it would be Gaia, but she had no idea how to tap into that part of herself.

So she swam blindly into the battle, gun ready, hopeful that the mixture of Roberta's magic combined with the science of Turner's technology would take out Oceanus long enough for Zeus to destroy the protection spell.

THWAP!

Kala flew back at least a hundred feet, faster than she thought was even possible considering she was underwater. It felt as if she had been hit by a wrecking ball straight to the chest. Unfortunately, the impact caused her to drop her glow stick, leaving her stuck in the blackness.

"I guess that was Oceanus," she said through her com-link to Derek.

"You okay?" he asked.

"Yeah, can't see anything, but hopefully I'm on my way back." Kala tried to shake off the pain as she swam blindly back to the battle.

Zeus's voice screamed in her head: *I said stay out of this! Go to the location and wait!*

Kala concentrated on Zeus and hoped he could hear her as she thought: *I need you to break that protection spell and you can't do that if you're fighting Uncle dickface.*

Radio silence on Zeus's end.

Kala didn't have the time to figure out if he heard her or not, she swam as fast as she could once she saw Derek's light stick glowing in the distance.

Then she saw Oceanus.

He was enormous.

It was the first time Kala actually felt as if she was seeing a *Titan*. Well over the size of a house, Kala could only see the silhouette of the god. Definitely man-shaped on top, but instead of legs, he had a fish tail. She could only imagine what Derek must be thinking. Two former soldiers staring at a gigantic merman. It would almost be funny if it wasn't so terrifying.

Quickly joining Derek's side she ordered, "If you can, get behind him. We'll try out these guns of Turner's."

"Copy." He swam away, carrying out Kala's orders.

A lightning bolt hit Oceanus in the eye, but he batted it away like it was a pesky fly. As the lighting flared again, Kala made out Zeus in the near distance. He looked tiny compared to the Titan but, to give him his credit, he held his own.

No time like the present. Kala unloaded her entire clip of bullets into the god. She could feel more than see Derek doing the same from behind Oceanus.

The Titan reeled back, causing an enormous wave of force that pushed Zeus and Kala backward.

Zeus's angry voice screamed in her head: *I told you to stay out of it!*

She called back in her mind: *At least it did something.*

The god's tone was dismissive: *It won't last. The ocean is his domain. He can recharge in a matter of seconds.* Then he sounded at a loss: *I'm not strong enough to defeat him. Not in his territory.*

Which is why Cronus had him here as a guard dog. Only Poseidon had a fighting chance and he was imprisoned in the Underworld.

Zeus was right. Kala could make out the shadow of Oceanus swimming toward her, free of the temporary sting of bullets and charging at her with a vengeance.

Oceanus's voice reached her mind. It was deep and powerful, giving her goose bumps even under her phase-suit. *Cronus warned me about you, Kala Hicks, skinwalker of Atlas and devourer of gods.*

The way he said *skinwalker* made Kala shiver. He didn't speak like the other Titans and Olympians she'd met so far. Being in the ocean away from man had made him distant, detached from humanity. Oceanus didn't see Kala as Atlas as the others did, he saw her as a meat-suit that encased a Titan. She accessed as much as she could about Oceanus from Atlas's memories and could find only one thing…

Fear.

Atlas was terrified of him.

Like Atlas, Oceanus had switched to the Olympians side in the first war. After both wars Atlas received disdain and dismissiveness from both the Olympians and the Titans, whereas Oceanus was still feared by all. He was a recluse who drew his power from the biggest entity on the planet: water.

Kala spoke to him through telepathy: *Let me through to Hades. I won't fail my mission.*

His voice raked on her every nerve as he said: *What do I care if your world ends? The ocean will always remain. The human scourge will finally be eradicated.*

Not to be dramatic or anything.

A blast of water shot Kala back, farther from her destination and nearly shoving her oxygen mouthpiece into her jaw.

Lightning bolts slammed into Oceanus from Zeus, but it didn't even make Oceanus budge at this point. He was absorbing the lightning now, turning it into energy.

Kala yelled at Zeus in her head: *How the hell do we get rid of this guy?*

Zeus sounded just as exasperated: *If I knew that I would be doing it! This is why I said we needed Poseidon!*

Well, we don't have Poseidon! Kala shouted the obvious. Then she signaled her com, "Derek, you still breathing?"

"Not a scratch. Guess I'm not considered a threat. I'm out of bullets though, not that they did much good." Derek's voice was soothing in the chaotic darkness.

"Copy. How close are you to the cave location?" Kala glanced down at her holo-GPS. She was at least a half a mile away at this point.

"Right above it. Rotoph is still working his mojo. I'm just a lookout at this point."

"Just stay there and do what you can. Hopefully, we can – " Kala began.

Kala was interrupted by Oceanus's open-hand to her chest. The fact that his hand was the size of her body propelled Kala even farther from Hades's location.

And Ouch!

Lights flared from behind Oceanus, and it wasn't Zeus's lightning.

It was…

Lasers.

The XV-4250 apparently had some firepower and was using it on the Titan.

Talan's voice sounded in her head: *Not sure how much longer we can stall him, but you should swim back to the location.*

Instead of relief, Kala only felt dread as Oceanus went after the ship.

She screamed at Talan: *That's Derek's only ride home!*

He can't die, Kala. He'll be okay.

He can die, over and over and over. He just keeps coming back to life and he'll drown a thousand times over before he gets to safety! Kala's mind reeled at the thought of her best friend being tortured for days by an endless cycle of drowning, then waking up only to drown again.

She couldn't let that happen.

Kala *wouldn't* let that happen.

The fury in her grew, so intense that Kala was beginning to lose herself again. To the rage. To the fear.

To Gaia.

And the voice that came from deep within her, projected itself with searing rage into Oceanus's head: *If you draw your power from the water, then I will take the ocean away from you!*

Kala shot her hands out and swirling tornadoes of air formed from her palms. Bigger and bigger the cyclones grew until the water began to push away and form a cavern of air.

The light from the XV-4250 gave an eerie cast to Oceanus's face as he stopped his pursuit of the ship and turned to see the spectacle Kala was creating.

It was exactly what she needed.

Kala pushed her cyclones even farther, surrounding Oceanus, pulling him into the stadium-sized cavern of air she had created.

In just seconds, he was cut off from the water. From his power.

And Kala had created the domain Zeus would need to defeat his uncle.

Air.

Zeus's face lit up at the terror he saw in Oceanus, now on the muddy ocean floor with Kala and Zeus.

The Olympian spoke to Oceanus, but Kala could hear him, too: *You're going to wish she had consumed you.*

Zeus threw a raging boulder of lightning at Oceanus and it hit with frightening impact. It was as if Zeus had thrown a toaster into a bathtub and Oceanus was frying. Kala could see every detail as the glow from the Titan's electrocution lit the entire area. Oceanus couldn't move, his bluish skin rattled and spasmed as each shock to his system brought him more pain. Finally, the Titan lay on the ground, motionless.

Oceanus looked like a large beached whale under a dome of black water.

Kala's mind slowly became her own again and she expanded her field of air to include the entrance to Hades's cave.

Unzipping her phase-suit hood, Kala spit out her oxygen mouthpiece and turned to Zeus. "Take down that protection spell."

Zeus didn't argue.

Kala could see in his eyes that he feared her.

Good.

Chapter Eight

Kala ran over the rocks and mud to Derek and Rotoph and the XV-4250 that had landed next to them.

By the time she reached them Rotoph had completed breaking the teleportation block. "Now Zeus and I can take down the protection spell together." He stared up at Zeus, who had just joined them.

The Olympian nodded and the two of them began chanting.

Talan and Ashliel exited the ship to join them. Kala whirled on Talan, angrily. "How could you put Derek at risk like that?!"

Derek interrupted before Talan could answer. "Whoa. Kala, I'm a soldier. I knew the risks. It was always a possibility I'd miss the boat."

"Not if I could help it." Kala wasn't letting the matter drop. "I had things under control."

Ashliel peered up at the blackness of the ocean above them in awe. "That's putting it mildly." He turned to Talan. "You said she was special. I thought you were exaggerating."

Kala didn't like praise. It made her feel uncomfortable, so she turned back to Talan. "Well? Anything to say?"

Derek stopped Talan again before he could speak, walking over to Kala so they were face-to-face. "Kala. Stop. I might have been fragile before, but I'm not now. And guess what? Even if I *could* die, I still would have come, because dying for a cause I believe in is what I signed up for. So stop treating me with kid gloves. Trust me, I really don't need it."

Kala's temper began to fade and the true emotion she had felt replaced it: terror. "The thought of you drowning over and over…"

Derek nodded. "It would have sucked. Yes. But I've been through a lot worse."

Kala guffawed, "Ha! Like what?"

"Like eating your chicken picatta." Derek smirked.

Shaking her head and cracking a small smile, she responded, "That *was* pretty bad."

"Yeah, undercooked chicken with an unmentionable sauce. I was puking capers for three days." Derek laughed. "Now, no more yelling at lover-boy over there, got it?"

Kala gave him the stink eye and lightly punched him in the gut. "I'll drown you myself, dick."

Talan finally chimed in, "I saw you were in danger and I just reacted. I'm sorry."

A pang of guilt washed over Kala. Talan was always looking out for her and she always seemed to be chastising him for it. But it had been only days since Jack died. Since Kala murdered him. So, to have another man be completely in love with her, made her angry. She couldn't explain it, but it was how she felt.

BOOM!

The ground shook from the noise. From the expressions on Zeus and Rotoph's faces, it appeared the protection spells had been demolished.

Zeus confirmed it as he said, "It's done. You can use your little suit there, but you can teleport now."

"I'm not good enough at it yet and I don't want to teleport into a rock or something," Kala said in offhanded dismissal of Zeus's nagging. "We needed to break the spell in case I need back up – which I won't – but it's nice to have the option."

Turning to Derek, she gave him a look that stated quite clearly she didn't want an argument. "Go back with Ashliel and the boys. Talan will try and teleport to me once I'm in the Underworld."

Derek shook his head in wonder. "I'm still not used to you using words like 'Underworld' and being serious." He reached down and gave Kala a hug. "Take care. And get out of there as soon as you possibly can."

"Oh, I will. I don't plan on staying." Kala hoped that was a true statement.

Walking over to Talan she tried to reassure him with a small smile. "You think you can find me?"

Talan held his feelings back as he nodded. "Yes. I've put the word out to Asmodeus as well. My sources say he'll help."

Cryptic, but Kala knew it was hard for Talan to talk of Asmodeus. She didn't want to admit it in front of Talan, but it gave her a measure of comfort that Asmodeus might show up in the Underworld. If anyone could get her out of an afterlife, it would most likely be the king of the Demons.

"Well, then, let's do this." Kala used her holo-GPS to locate the exact place of entry that coincided with Turner's satellite projections. She nodded to the black dome of water above them. "I have no idea how I did that, so I have no idea how long it's going to last. I'd get back inside the ship if you don't want to suddenly have a hundred tons of water fall on top of you."

Without another word, Kala pulled the tight hood back over her head and zipped it up. Activating her phase-suit, she dropped into the ground. Once her body was inside the rock and sand, Kala had to mimic swimming to pull herself down farther since there was no momentum otherwise. Before her eyes was a blackness even darker than the ocean had been. She had no idea how far down the cavern was but, surprisingly, a part of her was enjoying this time in the ground. Kala had learned that as a result of having Gaia in her veins, being immersed in the earth rejuvenated her. The phase-suit felt like a barrier separating her from her true home.

She realized then that that was how she had created the giant bubble of air in the ocean. Kala had drawn from the earth and created a pocket of it in the depths of the ocean. Though water covered over seventy percent of the earth's surface, there was still ground beneath, which made Kala strong as long as she was on the planet.

But the Underworld? That was a different story. She didn't know how her Gaia powers would work there, if they'd work at all.

Kala broke through the ceiling of the cave without notice, dropping ten feet to the ground. It wasn't a graceful landing, but at least she wasn't injured. She pulled off her hood, letting it rest behind her neck.

Surveying her surroundings, Kala was definitely in the right place. She could tell by the lack of stalagmites and stalactites in her vision. But, since there was no sign of Hades, she was obviously in the wrong part of the grotto.

It was a large cavern, moisture covering every surface of its rough-hewn rock and walls. There were over a dozen openings leading to different parts of the cavern. Kala wasn't sure which one led to Hades. Walking over to a tunnel on the far left, Kala marked her spot by placing a small rock in the middle of the entranceway. If she was going on a hunt, she'd need to remember where she had been so she wouldn't re-trace her steps.

The tunnel walls were like the cave, wet and cold rock with crags and crevices that Kala was sure some kind of deep-water critters lived within. Not that creepy-crawlies bothered her; she just didn't feel like having anything jump out at her at this particular juncture in life. It was bad enough that she was lower than the deepest part of the ocean searching for an Olympian god who had been given Titan-anesthesia for the last few millennia.

Reaching the end of the tunnel happened quicker than Kala expected. It opened to a small five-foot by five-foot space with no sign of the sleeping god. Backtracking to the original cave took even less time. Kala repeated this process, searching each corridor and marking them with rocks as she went. It was difficult not to become frustrated after exploring her eleventh tunnel. She had held a bit of hope on that last one since it had been at least half a mile long. But it only opened out onto a small pool of water that seemed as if it belonged in some kind of treasure hunting movie where Kala would find the lost jewel of something-or-other.

Only three more corridors to go. Kala knew that this place must be some kind of Titan-hideout, and it amazed her to fathom how much of this world Kala knew nothing about. Even before learning about the supernatural, Kala had always found it fascinating that so much of the planet was unexplored. Of course, she hadn't expected to be the one exploring it, but in a way, Kala was glad she was. She still wasn't ruling out the possibility that she was in a coma somewhere and this was all a dream.

Returning to what Kala referred to as the main cave hub, she noticed all the rocks she had used as markers were gone. It took a few seconds to process, then Kala was instantly on guard. If she didn't move them, someone else had. Someone who either didn't want her finding Hades – or just wanted to mess with her. When it came to supernatural beings, it could be either. Not one to dwell on changing circumstances and the fact that she had no way to remember which way to go, Kala surveyed the room with a soldier's eye.

If someone was there, they could be lurking just out of view in any one of the tunnel entrances. Kala moved to stay close to the walls so she wouldn't be an obvious target.

Even though her gun was empty of bullets, she pulled it out from her phase-suit and carried it as if it was locked and loaded. Only Kala needed to know that she had no ammunition. Sidling the walls, Kala examined the tunnel openings one at a time, leveling her gun as she faced each entrance.

Nothing.

Just as Kala was about to relax and explore what she thought were the last three tunnels, a woman's voice came out from behind her. "Hello, Kala."

Spinning around with her gun in hand, Kala aimed the firearm at a woman standing in the center of the cave. She was stunning, with long auburn hair that rested all the way to the small of her back and a face with strong, angled features that made her appear Native American. The woman dressed in a deep forest green pants suit and looked as if she could both run a fortune 500 company while at the same time blend into a forest as if she were half elf.

Kala jiggled the gun in the woman's direction. "Just stay right there. Who are you?"

Probably another Titan, Kala inwardly groaned. But as she wracked her Atlas memories to recognize this lady, she was coming up with nothing.

The woman examined Kala knowingly. "You can put that *toy* away. It's not loaded and Roberta's bullets wouldn't hurt me even if it was."

Dropping all pretense, Kala holstered her weapon inside her phase-suit. "Are you with the Turners? How did you get down here?" As soon as the words spilled out of Kala's mouth, she knew it was a ludicrous idea that any human could be down in these caves.

"You know who I am." The woman eyed her with a slight smile.

Kala was about to say that this lady was crazy, but instead found herself saying, "Gaia."

Gaia nodded, impressed. "You're the first being I've let see me in thousands of years."

Gaia.

Standing in front of her.

Real.

Mother Nature herself.

Instead of saying something profound and meaningful, Kala muttered, "Everyone thought you were asleep." Such intelligence.

Gaia raised an eyebrow in contemplation. "It was easier to let them think that. The truth is, I despise them all and wanted nothing to do with any of them."

"I can definitely relate," Kala agreed.

Gaia laughed. "I know you do. That's why I'm showing myself to you after all this time. You're special, Kala Hicks. The only one of my children who has any sense."

"Wait. What?" Kala did a double take. "Atlas is your grandson not your child."

Gaia stepped up to Kala and placed her hand on Kala's cheek. "Atlas is my grandson, but *you* are my child."

"But… dumpster," was all that came out of Kala's mouth.

Gaia let her hand drop and her eyes were distant from the memory, seemingly full of regret. "That was unfortunate, but human waste was the best way to hide my scent on you. I couldn't let Cronus find you or even know you existed. I'm sorry for that."

"But I was human." Kala couldn't seem to wrap her head around what Gaia was telling her.

"Yes. Because your father is human. I rather like your kind. I've been living among them since I separated from my children and grandchildren. As stupid as humans can be, it's nothing compared to my offspring." Gaia wasn't holding back her feelings about her family, Kala noticed — then Gaia's eyes met hers again and they were alight with pride.

"I'd never been able to have a human child before you. It was quite a surprise. I knew I couldn't keep you, but I made sure someone found you in that dumpster. It took years, but eventually your essence beamed like a beacon to anyone who was looking. Fortunately, only the Grigori were looking." Gaia sighed. "That's their job, finding extraordinary humans and bringing them to their full potential. Owen saw your light and found you." She smiled. "I was so happy it was Owen. He was always one of my favorites. When Rotoph helped the handful of Grigori escape two hundred years ago I was pleased that he was among them."

Gaia's words flew over Kala like butterflies she couldn't catch.

Kala knew she had a piece of Gaia inside of her, but she had just thought…

What *did* she think?

Kala realized in that moment that she hadn't thought about *how* Gaia was in her at all. She had just accepted it and used Gaia's powers whenever she could. But her *mother*? It was overwhelming. Emotions threatened to boil over. Not only had she found her mom, but Gaia was the mother of all the Titans and grandmother to the Olympians!

Kala's regained her composure – then scrunched her face in disgust. "So, Cronus is my *brother*? That's awesome." She couldn't hide the sarcasm if she tried. Then another thought hit her, "And Zeus is my nephew? No wonder I want to punch him all the time." Kala continued her rant, "And what does it mean that I swallowed my other nephew?"

Gaia gently touched Kala's arm to focus back on her. "You're only *half* related to them, if it makes any difference. You're still half human as well."

"Even now that I took over Atlas?" Kala was happy to finally ask someone who had answers. Devouring Atlas may have made her immortal, but if Gaia was her mother… maybe she always was.

"You'll always be half human no matter how many of my offspring you consume. But I don't recommend it, it can be an uncomfortable experience. Uranus forced me to consume my children, but eventually I let Cronus free and he… took care of my husband."

"Wait a minute. Stop right there. Are you saying I can *un-consume* Atlas? Like spit him out or something?" Kala's head was reeling. Could that really even be a possibility? Letting Atlas out like the annoying gnat he was? Even before she heard the answer, Kala already felt a pang of devastation. If she could have released Atlas in the beginning, then Jack died for nothing.

Kala was surprised that she felt instant relief when Gaia shook her head. "You are my daughter, but you're not me. No. Atlas is dead, you can't spit him out. But his memories and powers are inside you for good. When I look at you, Atlas *is* you." Her eyes twinkled with amazement. "You're something new, Kala Hicks. That's why I had to see you."

More thoughts raced through Kala's brain. "So, my father is a human?" When Gaia nodded, Kala responded, "Can you tell me who he is?" Being in a cave under the ocean talking to her mother for the first time, who happened to be the mother of the gods and asking about her father, was beyond surreal for Kala.

Gaia took a deep breath and slowly shook her head. "I'll tell you someday, but not today."

"Do I know him?" Kala asked.

"No. But he doesn't even know you exist and he knows nothing of who I really am. I haven't seen him since I found out I was pregnant with you. I was so shocked and scared of who you would become I took you as far away from him as possible. As you've figured out, I don't exactly have a great track record with having decent children." Gaia tilted her head in thought. "But that might have more to do with Uranus being their father. Your dad was a good man and seeing who you are today, I may have gotten it right this time. I just need you to be patient. Can you do that?"

The need to know who her parents were was never a strong impulse for Kala, especially after Owen and Linda found her. Being lost in foster care was a difficult childhood, but somehow Kala always felt she was destined for something greater. In hindsight, maybe it was the fact that she was half-god. The thought was too insane to consider. It solidified for Kala that her destiny was always to become the next Atlas. To be a part of that crazy prophecy. Linked to the Atlas missions until some girl three hundred years from now frees her from the burden.

And as always, Kala's soldier mind took over. "Why are you here?"

"Ah," Gaia acknowledged. "Right to the point."

"You're not going to try and stop me are you? Because I need to do this." Kala really didn't want to have a smack-down with her newly found mother if Gaia wanted the world to end, and she certainly didn't think she'd win, but she'd fight to the death if she had to.

"No. I love this earth the way it is, and as unfortunate as it is that you are now forced to do the unthinkable, it *is* necessary." Gaia eyed Kala as if she were inspecting her. "I came here to tell you that the war between the Titans and the Olympians as it stands now is a foregone conclusion. I can't stop it. I've never been able to stop them. But *you* might. There's something about you that both sides want desperately. They know there's a piece of me inside you, but they don't know I'm your mother. I'm not sure how either side would respond to that." Gaia placed her hands on Kala's arms. "I need you to be careful. Stay close to Owen and please try and open yourself to Talan. There are some things you must trust, and his love for you is one of them. Jack was a good man, and he would have made a good Atlas, but that wasn't his fate."

Kala cringed at the mention of Jack. "No, his fate was to be murdered by the woman who loved him." She shrugged Gaia's hands off her. "You're not exactly telling me anything I didn't know. Except for the you-being-my-mom thing," Kala qualified. "I'll always be on Owen's side, but I want to stay out of a war. I just want to do my job and keep this globe spinning. If Cronus and Zeus get in my way, then I'll deal with them, but I'm not fighting anyone."

Gaia nodded. "It's more difficult than you think. But that's what I wanted to hear. I think it best if you don't tell anyone we met. My offspring can be very petty and jealous and it may turn against you."

"I'm not really into sharing, especially with any of your offspring." Kala surveyed the cavern with exasperation. "Do you happen to know where Hades is?" Might as well ask.

Gaia nodded, smiling at Kala as if she wasn't going to see her for a while. "I hope we meet again some day," she said.

Before Kala could respond, Gaia reached up and touched Kala's forehead.

The grotto walls blurred, then came back into sharp focus.

Kala wasn't in the larger cave anymore.

Sleeping at her feet was Hades.

Chapter Nine

Stepping into one of her Atlas visions was something Kala never thought she'd get used to. This was only the third, but it felt as if she were in a virtual reality déjà vu.

This was it.

Kala would wake up Hades and he'd send her to the Underworld.

It didn't exactly scare her, but it wasn't something she wanted to rush into either. Maybe she could just sit there for the next two days and let her four-day time limit run to the last minute like the last two Atlas missions.

But Kala wanted to get started on the next four days: to find Jack, get out of the Underworld, bring home the Olympians and complete her fourth Atlas task.

There was nothing for it.

Kala slowly played out her vision and reached down to wake Hades.

Before her hand could touch him, the familiar grating sound of Cronus stopped her. "Can't we talk about this?"

Well, *that* never happened in Kala's vision. She pulled her hand away, knowing it still wasn't quite time yet to fulfill her duty. "What are you doing here?" She almost didn't want to ask, for the simple reason of not wanting to hear Cronus speak again. It wasn't as if she didn't already know the answer.

But still.

Kala didn't want Cronus to stop her from waking his son.

Turning to see his annoying face, Kala gave him an impatient glare. "Well?"

Cronus was still having trouble with how Kala addressed him. Being the god of everything pretty much guaranteed that anyone around you showed deference.

But, yeah, Kala could care less.

Now, knowing Cronus was her half-brother, made her grateful she was raised as an only child.

She hadn't quite yet processed the news of being Gaia's daughter, though. Why *didn't* Gaia's other children inherit their mother's powers? They had powers of their own. Kala only had Gaia's. Was it because she was half-human? Was Gaia's power the only thing that transferred out of the womb? It wasn't as if Kala had grown up thinking she was *different*. She never had any Harry Potter moments where she accidentally performed some kind of magic trick she couldn't explain. Jumping from one foster home to the next, Kala had developed survival skills that were completely driven by her fists and kicking ability. There were plenty of situations where she could have used some Gaia mojo, if only to scare the living crap out of the kids that bullied her.

Not knowing her father's identity was also an itch Kala couldn't scratch. She respected Gaia's decision not to reveal him, but it only reminded Kala of how gods loved to have their secrets. Not that Gaia was lording it over her, but it still equated to the same thing: closed lips. Owen would always be her true father; it would just be nice to finally know who her biological dad really was. According to Gaia, he didn't even know Kala existed.

Looking over at Cronus, she saw that he wore the same tailored black suit he had on the last time Kala saw him, with his distinguished short black hair and Titan bone-structure that most people would kill for. Cronus was older than dirt, but he looked to be a man in his forties.

His voice was calm, almost sincere as he pleaded, "You're here to wake Hades, aren't you? You'll start a war, you know."

There was that word again.

War.

"Keeping the Olympians in the Underworld won't last. Zeus knows they're there. He'll find a way to get them out. Stopping me won't prevent that." Kala broke the news.

Cronus couldn't hide the shock from his face. "How did you find out?" was all that came out of his mouth.

Kala shook her head. "Really? It wasn't that hard to figure out after seeing my vision."

"Your vision?" Cronus stared at Kala with venom. "You're saying your Atlas task is to wake up Hades?" He didn't seem convinced.

Kala wished Cronus would just go back to whatever hole he had crawled out from under, but she was stuck with him. "Yes, and he takes me to the Underworld where I spring out your kids." That wasn't exactly what the vision told her, but Kala enjoyed watching Cronus squirm. "Apparently, the universe thinks rescuing the Olympians is bringing balance, so if you want to fight the universe…"

"Are you on Day Two now? I thought you were waiting until the last minute so you wouldn't have to be tortured and all that," he said dismissively.

"Waking up your son didn't seem so bad," Kala taunted. "Besides, I still remember Atlas's memory of when you said to him how on his next cycle, you'd drop the protections on Atlas. Which means I'm pretty much fair game to all the supernatural."

Cronus waved her comment away. "You can take care of yourself. You have Gaia in you and I saw what you did up there." He pointed at the ceiling, indicating the dome of air Kala had created to best Oceanus.

"My brother isn't easily defeated. It's such a waste that you're on the wrong side. There's so much I could do with you!" His face suddenly lit up, animated, excited at ideas only he could see. "If you'd only join me! I could teach you how to use your powers. No one could stop you. Not even me!" He acted as if he admitted something he shouldn't, but Kala saw right through it.

"Listen, *Darth,* I'm doing fine on my own, thanks. And I can stop you any time I like. The one power I *know* I have is to swallow you whole," Kala quipped.

Cronus laughed. "You couldn't contain me for long. I'd take over your body and Kala Hicks would be gone forever. Your naivety will be your downfall."

"Your ego will be yours. Now, if you'll excuse me. I have to wake up your kid." Even though the moment didn't match her vision, Kala didn't know what else to do. She knelt down next to Hades and as she reached out...

WHACK!

Cronus threw her across the grotto, smashing Kala against the wall. The wind was knocked out of her, but instinct and training involuntarily moved her muscles and she jumped to her feet in a crouched position. When it came to brute strength, Cronus had her beat, but one thing she learned from her mother: even though the Titans were half-Gaia as well, they didn't have access to Gaia's powers, only Kala did. She wasn't just Mother Earth's daughter, she was something more. None of her other half-siblings could do what she had done, which was why they assumed Kala had somehow inherited some kind of Gaia-battery hard-wired into her being. If they were to learn that Gaia was Kala's mother, who knows how they'd react.

At the moment, Kala didn't care.

Jumping to her feet, Kala decided to play defensive: Cronus needed her to attack him, then he could toss her around like he had before.

Sure enough, Cronus, stayed rooted where he was, hovering over

Hades like his protector.

Kala circled him, keeping at least twenty feet between them.

Cronus seemed amused.

Without warning he tossed a lightning bolt from his hand. Kala moved quickly and the jolt of electricity barely missed her.

"Not very original, are we?" Kala mocked the Titan. She knew how fragile his ego was.

And like clockwork, Cronus's face scrunched into a scowl. "I'll show you original, runt!"

He had certainly gained some confidence in his ability to beat Kala since the last time she saw him. Cronus must have convinced himself that Kala would never devour him, and that even if she did, he could gain control over her. Maybe that was what he wanted. Maybe he thought Kala's abilities would give him the edge to win the war before it even started.

Not having any leverage this time, Kala stayed calm within. Trigging her Gaia-juice only seemed to happen in extreme moments, and unless Cronus planned on killing Hades so she couldn't complete her mission…

Kala's blood froze.

That was exactly what he planned on doing.

Her gaze met Cronus.

Panic flashed in his eyes. "You can't stop me!" he screamed.

Cronus reached down to grab Hades.

Kala ran full speed into Cronus's body, tackling him to the ground and away from his son.

The Titan tried to throw her off, but Kala used his momentum to smack him back down on the cave floor.

Cronus flipped his body over, attempting to drag himself toward Hades. Kala held on tight to his legs. It would almost be comical if Cronus's intent wasn't so dire. Elbowing the base of Cronus's spine caused the Titan to scream in pain. Yet again, Kala wished she had a better grasp on her powers, more specifically what she *could* or *could not* do. Kala hated the fact that she had access to a treasure trove of internal weapons that her own mind restricted her from.

Kicking his feet, Cronus managed to land his heel across Kala's cheek, causing her to lose her grip. Taking advantage, he leapt toward Hades, his hands wrapping around his son's neck.

Could a Titan strangle an Olympian?

It seemed too easy and absurd, but Kala didn't have time to wonder logistics. Reaching behind Cronus's neck, Kala tried the same tactic herself, using the full force of her Atlas strength, squeezing Cronus's windpipe. He let go of Hades's throat to clasp onto Kala's forearms and their vise-like grip.

At least it prevented the Titan from hurting his son.

Kala thought that all the commotion might have been enough to wake Hades, but the god still slept soundly on the cave floor. At this point she almost wished Hades would open his eyes on his own if only to help her fight Cronus.

An electric surge jolted Kala clear from Cronus. Every nerve in her body felt as if it had just been lit on fire. It took a few seconds before Kala had any sensation in her limbs. Her jaw unclenched from the pain.

Cronus threw his hand out toward Hades. Yellow fire poured from Cronus's outstretched palm and engulfed Hades's body in a ball of crackling flames.

Still the god didn't awake.

Without thinking, Kala lifted her arms, pointing to the dripping ceiling. Water poured down from seemingly nowhere to extinguish the deadly fire.

A twinge inside her.

That feeling she experienced when being buried in the dirt came back to her tenfold. Kala was connected to the earth. Before it had simply *recharged* her battery, but now…

On instinct, Kala imagined holding onto a piece of rock from the wall, then pictured it flying at Cronus full speed.

The rock lazily fell to the ground.

That didn't work.

Cronus saw the rock and laughed. "Was that you?"

Kala was about to deny it out of sheer embarrassment, but she nodded. "I'm still learning, and you make a great guinea pig."

Cronus stayed his distance and rubbed his neck from where Kala had tried to choke him. "Why are we fighting?" he sighed. "We can be on the same side. It's *you* who's deciding to be stubborn."

"Stubborn? Because I don't want the world to end? You are so delusional." Kala shook her head in amazement.

"It won't *end*. Nothing ever ends. It'll just be different." Cronus pleaded for Kala to see *his* reason. "And *we* will be in charge. We've lost our power in this world. The humans own it now with their technology and science. And I showed you: it's only going to get worse. Yet you continue to align yourself with the very man responsible for it all."

He was referring to Turner, of course. Kala had seen the future and Turner's role in it: killing thousands of people to keep the population down. Was that a future Kala could really get behind? The doubts still lingered.

But side with Cronus? Where *billions* of human lives would be lost if she didn't complete her Atlas task? No. Cronus's way gave no thought to humans. And Kala was human, partly anyway. At least Turner's future actions were for the greater good, no matter how despicable.

"Just stop talking." Kala brushed him aside.

"Atlas is still in you and I *know* he'd hear me out," Cronus seethed. "He'd side with his people, not humans."

"I may have Atlas's memories, but he's gone. It's just me in here. I hate to blow your little theory on consumption, but it doesn't work the same way as when your mommy hid all you kids inside her by eating you whole. I can't spit the guy out. He can't take over my body. He's dead and I inherited all his mojo and knowledge." Kala loved proving Cronus wrong, just to watch him squirm.

"You don't know that for sure," Cronus fished.

Kala leveled her gaze at him. "Yes. I do."

Before Kala could react, Cronus leapt forward and grabbed her arm.

Instant paralysis overtook her entire body and a surge of heat traveled straight to her brain from his touch.

Cronus was inside her head, probing, trying to find anything that would help him figure out who or *what* Kala was – or more likely: what she was capable of.

It was worse than when Lotun, the leader of the Malaks, jumped inside Kala's brain. Even though Kala had been physically paralyzed that time, the pain wasn't this intense. It was as if Cronus had taken a heated fire poker and jammed it in her ear. And unlike Lotun's intrusion where Kala knew exactly what the Malak was seeing, Cronus was able to hide his discoveries from her.

Kala concentrated as much as she could, though the searing heat thwarted most of her efforts.

His voice was like breaking glass as he soothed, "Don't fight it. It'll only make it worse for you."

But he was wrong: the pain only fueled Kala. She wasn't the kind of girl who gave in. The fire only made her want to fight harder. Yes, fighting made it hurt worse, but Kala was trained to withstand torture. As an elite soldier, Turner and Clifton had to rely on their men not spill national secrets. Pain be damned, she wasn't about to let Cronus violate her like this.

The pain became an isolated thing, like a button in Kala's brain. She switched it off. Pain meant nothing. Only destroying the source mattered.

Pulling from deep within, Kala took her free hand and grabbed Cronus's neck.

Shock registered in his expression. She relished it for only a second as she squeezed with all her strength.

As Kala pressed harder into his throat, this time the Titan didn't budge.

He was desperate for what was inside her head, positive Kala must be hiding something from him.

And now she was.

Kala didn't want him to know that Gaia was her mother.

Yanking at Cronus's neck did nothing. The heat still burned her insides, though her training kept the sensation at bay.

"ENOUGH!" A woman's voice echoed through the cavern.

All at once, the burning was gone. Cronus was no longer touching Kala and Kala was no longer clutching Cronus. Their bodies were forced apart by an invisible hand much stronger than the two of them.

Gaia stepped forward, her face a mask of rage.

And Kala saw something she never thought she'd see.

Cronus.

Cowering.

"Mother?" His voice was timid as he stared at Gaia in disbelief.

"I will *not* let you destroy this world, Cronus. You *will* let Kala do her job." Gaia scolded her son as if she had just seen him yesterday and not the thousands of years it had actually been.

"But the humans, Mother. They must be stopped." Cronus slowly recovered from the shock of being face-to-face with Gaia.

Gaia took a step closer to her son, her expression still livid. "Our time is through, Son. We've had this planet long enough. You had your chance, but you and your siblings wasted your lives hiding in the 5th Level of Hell terrified someone would steal your power. The very thing that you did to protect yourself ended up fulfilling your worst fear: the world went on without you. And now the humans are growing more powerful that we ever were."

Cronus sounded like a three-year-old as he argued, "That's the Grigori's fault! They taught them everything, just like we thought they would!"

Gaia lifted her arm to stop him from speaking and he complied immediately. Kala cocked her head in appreciation. She wished *she* could shut Cronus up that easily.

Gaia spoke more calmly. "It is no one's fault. It is just the way destiny works." She turned to Kala. "Now go. Wake up Hades."

Kala gave one last wary glance at Cronus then walked towards the Olympian's sleeping figure.

Cronus screamed in fear and rage and leapt toward Kala as if to tackle her to the ground. Kala crouched in a defensive pose, ready to thwart the Titan's attack, but before his body could reach her, Gaia suddenly reappeared between Kala and Cronus. Just as Cronus crashed into his mother instead of Kala, Gaia said to her daughter, "Be safe."

When Cronus's hands hit Gaia, they both vanished.

It took Kala a moment to take in what had just happened. She had no idea where Gaia took Cronus, but Kala didn't want to waste a second of her own time. Who knew if Cronus had back-up ready to stop her from completing her mission.

Just like in her vision, Kala took a deep breath and reached down to wake up Hades. Her hand glowed brightly.

And the Olympian moved.

Since she had already seen these same events play out, it was no surprise when Hades coughed and sputtered as he finally awoke from his long slumber.

"Hades." Kala nodded in greeting, playing her part.

"Who are you?" Hades asked.

"Atlas. My mission was to wake you," she replied calmly.

"That's unfortunate," Hades sighed. "For you, anyway."

Kala knew what was going to happen next. She almost wanted to mock Hades and tell him she already knew what he intended, but Kala simply let Hades reach up and touch her forehead.

Dropping to the cavern floor with a small thud, Kala felt the darkness surround her completely. Her last thoughts were of Jack, wondering if his death had felt the same and hoping she'd see him soon.

Time seemed to vanish and lose its grip on Kala's reality.

And she knew with certainty that she was truly dead.

DAY ONE

Chapter Ten

"You're as beautiful dead as you are alive."

Kala heard Asmodeus's voice in the blackness.

She opened her eyes. Nothing felt quite real. It was almost as if she was in a dream: surreal, slow, her focus slightly off.

And gray.

Everything was gray: from the dirt below, to the sky above, to the forest of trees in front of her, to the sluggish river behind. All gray.

Kala slowly sat up, trying to gain some kind of bearing. Jumping slightly at the sight of her own gray skin, Kala noticed that even her attire – loose drawstring pants with a tank top – was the same gray color. She wondered who dressed her, or were these even real clothes? It was better than being naked, but eyeing her skin again and flinching at the gray and pasty texture that looked like everything else around her except...

Asmodeus.

Crouching next to her with his usual grin, Asmodeus stood out like a rainbow lollipop in the middle of a rain cloud. Everything about him was bright by contrast. His skin looked so full of color compared to her own.

Out of curiosity, Kala pulled a piece of her hair to examine it. Normally, auburn red, it was now just another shade of charcoal.

Kala knew she needed to adjust quickly. More importantly, she needed to focus. She was dead. What had she expected really?

"How did you get here?" Kala asked the Demon.

"I used to be on Team Cronus, remember? He apparently hasn't changed the locks on me yet." Asmodeus surveyed the area with some disdain. "I try to stay away from here, as you can imagine. It's not really my design ascetic."

"Is it all gray like this? I feel like I walked into a black and white movie." Kala stretched out her arms and legs, carefully getting to her feet. Asmodeus stood with her and even offered his hand to help up Kala the rest of the way. "And why are you in full Technicolor?"

Asmodeus's smile seemed extra bright in the grayness. "I'm not dead, silly." Then he motioned at the scenery. "I'm afraid the entire Underworld is all this same varying form of drab, the only exception being the Fields of Elysium."

The Fields of Elysium.

Kala had managed to keep her secondary mission hidden from everyone. She had tried not to think about it too much after Penny told her where to find Jack, in fear that Talan or Zeus or even Asmodeus would hear her thoughts.

But ever since Penny revealed Jack's location…

She was going to get him back.

"Do you know where the Fields of Elysium are?" Kala asked without making eye contact.

Asmodeus cocked his head to the side thoughtfully. "Talan told me about your plan to rescue the Olympians. They aren't in the Fields."

"I didn't ask where the Olympians were. I asked where the Fields of Elysium were." Kala flashed Asmodeus a determined glare.

The king of Demons stood for a moment, apparently trying to figure out Kala's intent. After a long pause he sighed deeply. "You're going after that human of yours."

His words infuriated Kala. "I have to try. I don't give a crap about this Titan-Olympian war. Jack didn't deserve to die and I'm bringing him back with me!" She knew she sounded like a child, but her frustration and pain were too deep to care.

Asmodeus raised an eyebrow. "I'm all for screwing over the gods, but I'm not sure you've thought this one through." He tried appealing to her logical side, "What about your Atlas mission? Have you changed your position on the world ending as well?"

"I'm still going to do whatever it is I'm supposed to, but I can rescue Jack too. I'm a great multi-tasker," Kala defended her position lamely.

Asmodeus didn't say a word.

Kala could only handle five seconds of the silence. "Just tell me where the damn Fields are."

He couldn't hide his amusement at her explosive temper. "Your wish is my command." Asmodeus nodded toward the gray pine trees in front of them. "The forest is the safest route around here. You might want to avoid the rivers."

Kala tried to access Atlas's memories for any information about the rivers of the Underworld as her own knowledge of Greek mythology was a bit sketchy. But aside from the River Styx and the Ferry Man of Death, Atlas didn't know many details about this place.

"What's up with the rivers?" As a soldier, Kala couldn't let Asmodeus's comment lie without finding out more information.

Asmodeus seemed pleased to talk about the subject. "Well, there are five of them surrounding the Underworld and they can be quite useful in taking down your enemy, but also dangerous to you in your current form." He lifted his hand and ticked off each finger as he listed every river and what its waters could do.

"There's Acheron, which gives new meaning to the word 'depression.' One drop from that river will bring you to your darkest place. There's

Cocytus, which does kind of the same thing, but not as bad. The river Lethe makes you forget everything. Phlegethon we'll see from miles away – as it's *made of fire*." He let that sink in before continuing, "And Styx, the water that if you could bottle it up, I'd suggest doing so, since it makes any mortal or god have to keep their promise to you if they make an oath while touching it."

"That does sound like a good one," Kala mused. "I could make Cronus and Zeus promise to play nice."

"I'd start thinking of the wording now. There's always a way out of an oath if you're creative enough." Asmodeus sounded as if he'd had experience in that department. "But, yes, a little bit of the river Styx and a good oath from a god can go a long way. Trust me on that." He smiled slyly.

Kala didn't even want to know. But knowing about the rivers was useful information to have, especially the Styx. Any tool she could used to manipulate Tweedle-Dee (Cronus) and Tweedle-Dum (Zeus) was a good thing.

Walking side-by-side with Asmodeus through the muted landscape still didn't feel real yet. Part of her knew that going after Jack first was wrong. The other part didn't care. She was just surprised that Asmodeus wasn't arguing with her. It probably amused him to some degree. Kala was simply a fascination to the Demon; pretty soon, she knew, he'd lose interest. Then she'd really have to be on guard. Asmodeus wasn't a supernatural being Kala wanted on her bad side. She could still remember the screeching sound of his scream when he first hunted her after she became the next Atlas surrogate. It had chilled her to the bone. Even Penny had been scared.

As they entered the thick grove of trees, Kala could see in full detail each pine needle, and their varying shades of gray.

She was dead.

As in dead.

Kala was glad there wasn't a mirror around, she probably looked like a zombie minus the rotting skin. She wondered if *that* was next on the list.

Her heart skipped a beat as she thought of seeing Jack again. Never thinking it was possible had given her a sense of purpose in her Atlas missions, as if she was doing it in his name so his death would have meaning. But, now... knowing that she could find him in the Underworld and potentially break him loose? Kala couldn't ignore an opportunity like that. She had to try.

As if reading her thoughts, Asmodeus glanced down at Kala. "Even if you find him, he's not what he was on earth. He's just a shell now."

She didn't want to hear it. "Yeah, yeah, Penny told me already. I'll take the shell. I don't care. It would still be him."

Asmodeus countered delicately, "True. He still has his soul, but he won't recognize you. He won't even be able to speak. It'll be like he's in a walking coma."

If Kala could cover her ears and scream, "*Nanana, I can't hear you,*" she would have in that moment. Instead, she fumed in silence. "You don't know the bond we have," she defended herself lamely.

Her next Atlas mission.

It tugged at her consciousness. It was easy to forget responsibility when you were *dead!*. But when she awoke Hades, her last mission was completed – and a new one was born. It didn't matter if she was dead. That wasn't the way the curse worked.

It'll be like he's in a walking coma.

Why did Asmodeus have to say that? Couldn't he let her live in her delusion for just a little while? Because that was what she knew it was: a delusion.

No.

Kala hurried her steps and Asmodeus caught up quickly. "You don't even know where you're going," he reminded her.

"Is it far?" She heard her voice crack. Emotion surged through her. All Kala wanted to do was to see Jack. Just one more time. Even if she couldn't save him. Even if he really didn't know who she was. Just once.

Asmodeus gently stopped Kala with his hand and forced eye contact with her. "Yes, it's far."

"Can't you teleport us there?" she asked desperately.

He shook his head. "You can only teleport in, not out and not around. Not even I can break that kind of mojo." Asmodeus's eyes were full of concern. "You're thinking too hard, beautiful. Jack is gone. You need to mourn him and move on."

Kala shrugged his hand away and stormed off further into the trees, yelling over her shoulder. "It was less than two weeks ago! I shot him! I can't move on! I don't want to!"

Asmodeus ran immediately to her side. "Were you really *that* in love with the guy, or is this just the guilt of killing him talking?"

Kala grunted in anger. "You're such a dick."

He didn't look like he'd argue that point. "I *am* a Demon."

Whirling on him, Kala shouted, "Of course I was in love with him! And of course I feel guilty! It's both okay?!"

And it was. It was truly both. The love she felt for Jack was like nothing Kala had ever experienced. The guilt for killing him was equally as strong. The two emotions constantly collided inside of her. Kala couldn't mourn his loss because she was responsible for it. As a result, both emotions threatened to destroy her.

"I thought I was in love before, but not like you were with Jack," Asmodeus suddenly confessed. "Even when I wiped your brain and put in new memories of me as your boyfriend, you still couldn't let go of him." He tilted his head as if conceding a point, "It was probably because of the Gaia in you, but still…" He paused. "You're either obsessed or you truly love him." Asmodeus's fascination with Kala only seemed to grow from his observation by the way he looked at her.

Kala stopped and turned to him, thoughtful. "You thought you were in love?"

Asmodeus shifted on his feet, which suggested that he wasn't comfortable at the direction this conversation had taken. "That's not the point. The point is: I've never seen anyone as focused as you on being with one person."

Kala couldn't help but smile. "Oh, I think finding out who the king of Demons was in love with is *exactly* the point. Who was she?" Kala had to know.

Moving away from her, Asmodeus traversed through the gray trees, trying to avoid Kala's gaze.

That only enticed Kala more. This time she was the one hurrying to catch up. "You have to spill now," she pried. "Come on. I'm dead. Who am I going to tell?"

"I'm sorry I brought it up," Asmodeus mumbled under his breath.

It was such a shock seeing him like this. Normally, he was all shark, never the prey, but now? He almost seemed... vulnerable.

Kala touched his arm reassuringly, no longer teasing. "Did it end badly?"

Asmodeus shrugged with a masked smile. "Let's just say she was interested in someone else."

The concept of supernatural beings having relationships was still foreign to Kala. It was hard to imagine a Demon like Asmodeus going out on a date, or grabbing a drink, or... anything else Kala seemed to reserve only for *human* behavior. And this girl he was in love with could have been thousands of years ago. What did people do back then? After a moment's thought she figured they probably drank back then, too. Not much had changed in the wooing department. But was it the same with Demons? Angels? Gods?

"Was she human?" Kala asked delicately.

Asmodeus finally caved, "She was a Malak, and it was thousands of years ago."

A Malak.

Then it hit Kala.

She cringed. "It wasn't that annoying twat, Lotun, was it?" Kala hated the leader of the Malaks since she'd jumped in Kala's brain and read all Kala's private thoughts. To give Lotun her due, the Malak had been much better at mind-reading than Cronus at least.

Asmodeus laughed, almost relieved at Kala's insult. "Yes. She's not so bad when you get to know her."

Kala remembered how Lotun wouldn't stop flirting with Talan, implying that they had a past together. "Oh, man, was Talan the other guy?"

Eyes flashing with anger, Asmodeus nodded. "We tend to have the same taste in women." His expression turned thoughtful. "The funny thing is, I had only *heard* of Talan before I saw him in that alley on your first mission. Lotun told me of her feelings for the Grigori, which is why I knew him by name, but I had never seen him before. Owen too. The only Grigori I had ever laid eyes on was Rotoph, and trust me, I could have done without."

With a sudden certainty, Kala blurted aloud, "Is that why you sided with the Titans and imprisoned the Grigori? Over a girl? And over *that* girl?"

"I thought if he was out of the picture…" Asmodeus didn't bother denying the accusation.

"It must eat you up that out of all the Grigori to escape a couple hundred years ago, Talan was one of them. No wonder you guys hate each other," Kala surmised. Then she laughed knowingly. "So that's why you like me! Because Talan does. It all makes sense now." She shook her head in amusement. "Boys and their caveman competition." Kala wasn't offended, she saw this kind of behavior all the time, especially, in a male-heavy line of work. When one guy started to like a girl, suddenly all the guys started liking her. She always figured it was because of some kind of residual caveman DNA where *getting the girl* became a competition.

Asmodeus stopped her again with his hand, this time not so gently. It was so abrupt she immediately thought they were being attacked.

But when her eyes met his, she was even more shocked to see the hurt in his expression.

"This is not a competition. I may be all jokes most of the time, but I feel something for you, Kala Hicks. And, if you recall, I felt it before you even met Talan, so don't brush it away like it means nothing."

His intensity made her stomach churn. Kala liked their flirting and Asmodeus's *no strings attached* attitude. But this? This was real and it only made her feel conflicted and miserable, like she had to make him feel better or something. Like she had to *admit* feelings she didn't feel. Or did she?

Kala closed her eyes, as if not seeing Asmodeus in front of her would somehow make her feel better about the situation. A moment later she opened them. "I don't want you or Talan, okay? I just want to see Jack."

Asmodeus stared at her for a long second and then nodded, some of his roguish smile creeping through. "Follow me."

They walked in silence after that. It wasn't awkward or weird, it was actually nice. It was almost as if a layer of fakeness had been lifted between them. Their constant banter was an easy way to relate without getting too deep. But after Asmodeus's admission, their dynamic had changed slightly. They were becoming friends, Kala realized, and then thought of the horror Owen would feel when he found out. And Talan – though Talan already knew. He was the one who contacted Asmodeus in hopes that he'd help Kala. And Talan had been right. Asmodeus came running the moment he heard she was in danger.

Passing through the small forest, the duo entered a landscape of gray desert that appeared to go on for miles and miles. The terrain was rough, cracked clay with sporadic tumbleweeds rolling by like in a Spaghetti Western. One of the Underworld rivers wound down the middle, gently lapping its murky waters against the thin shore.

Kala broke the silence. "Which river is that?"

"Lethe. The one that makes you forget," Asmodeus answered.

It was almost tempting for Kala; to jump into the water and forget everything. It might not make her happier, but it would at least destroy the pain she felt for Jack and what her life had become.

"We'll use the Lethe as our guide," Asmodeus said. "It eventually spills out to the Fields of Elysium." Asmodeus walked to its edge and began moving north.

Kala quickly followed and peered down at the river's surface as they traveled toward their destination.

Her breath caught in her throat.

Kala could see images in the reflection of the waters.

She knew instantly what they were.

Kala was seeing her next Atlas mission.

Chapter Eleven

Kala stopped in her tracks to watch the vision. She didn't want to. She wanted to ignore it and keep heading to the Fields of Elysium. But even dead, Kala's soldier instincts were there. Her crazy mind wanted to grab Jack, snap him out of whatever stupor Asmodeus seemed to think he'd be in, and then Jack could help her on her new mission. It would be like it was supposed to be. Jack had trained to be the Atlas his whole life. He could teach her a few things. The prophecy was wrong. Jack and Kala *could* exist together: both of them being dead, then coming back to life… That could be a loophole.

The absurdity of Kala's logic tried to creep its way into her brain, but she swatted it away. One step at a time.

"Why are we stopping?" Asmodeus said, finally noticing that Kala hadn't moved.

She nodded toward the flowing surface of the river Lethe. "I see my next mission in the reflection of the water."

"Please tell me you have to kill Talan?" Asmodeus appeared hopeful.

Kala didn't bother responding. It was important now to focus all her attention on the vision. Difficult to see at times from the movement of the current, she concentrated and the images became clearer.

A large room. Maybe in a basement or warehouse. It was hard to tell. In the center were two of Turner's brain machines: chairs with wires seemingly growing out of the ceiling, draping down and connecting to a computer and monitors.

The room was far from empty. Vision/Kala was there with Turner, Cronus, Hades, Gaia and Talan. Seeing her mother made Kala realize that Gaia's return would not be a secret for too long. Kala's battle with Cronus in the cave – and the possible war between her children and grandchildren – must have forced Gaia to come forward and reveal herself.

That was the weirdest part about these visions. Witnessing what was to come made Kala try to figure out what events would lead the players to their final destination.

Hades and Cronus began to back away from Vision/Kala, their eyes full of terror.

Please don't tell me I have to consume them both, Kala repeated in her head. Having to integrate with Atlas was hard enough, but to add King Titan and the Death God? No thanks.

Gaia nodded to Vision/Kala and Talan. "Now."

Hades and Cronus screamed as Vision/Kala, Talan and Gaia threw their hands toward the pair and white fire charged out of their fingertips.

Hades and Cronus were consumed by the bright flames, writhing and uselessly trying to break free. Vision/Kala, Gaia and Talan used the fire to control the gods, making them each sit down in one of Turner's brain machines.

Turner ran onto the scene and quickly attached the wires and leads to Hades and Cronus's heads, the white flames not hurting him at all.

"It's done!" Turner exclaimed.

Vision/Kala, Gaia and Talan stopped the onslaught of fire.

With another slight nod of Gaia's head, Vision/Kala walked over to the two gods and touched their wrists and ankles. A purple glow formed around the areas where she touched, locking them into place.

Kala shuddered in horror when she saw the blank stares in Hades and Cronus's eyes. They were trapped. Not only physically, but mentally as well.

Before Kala could truly comprehend what she had seen, the vision began to repeat itself.

Asmodeus stood next to her, waiting patiently for Kala to finish her viewing party.

Prying her eyes away, she shook her head, not knowing what to say.

"What do you have to do?" he asked, curiosity etched all over his face.

Considering his wishy-washy allegiances, Kala wasn't sure how much she wanted to share with Asmodeus. And what she saw…

"I have to process it before I talk about it, okay?"

Asmodeus cocked his head to one side, confused. "I'm here in Dead-world to save you and you still don't trust me?"

Kala knew she had to throw him a bone, if only to stop him from hounding her. "Let's just say, as messed up as it is, it'll end the war between Titans and Olympians." Kala wasn't exactly sure that was a true statement, but what else could it have meant? The leader of the Titans and the god of death were locked into Turner's machines. Trapped. And if what Kala had previously been shown of the future was correct, then Turner would live forever – which meant he could keep them prisoner forever. Would any of the other Titan's retaliate? From accessing Atlas's memories, she didn't think so.

Kala tried to shake the memory of Hades and Cronus's empty eyes from her brain. As much as she hated Cronus, she felt horrible at what she'd have to do to him. It didn't feel right. But what Atlas mission did?

The look on Asmodeus's face was a mixture of curiosity and amusement. "You really aren't going to tell me, are you?"

After a moment, Kala shook her head. "It was only a few days ago you tricked me into thinking you were dead, then tracked me down so you could steal Zeus. So, sorry, you haven't reached BFF status yet."

Asmodeus nodded, conceding her point. "Fair enough. But I fully intend to reach 'BFF status'. Maybe even something more than that?"

"Keep dreaming. You're lucky I even left the BFF category open to you." Her easy banter with Asmodeus was comforting at the moment.

Kala still wasn't sure what locking Hades and Cronus into Turner's brain machines would accomplish, but she was tired of trying to figure out everything before it even happened. It was more exhausting than actually performing the duty itself.

Priority one: "Can we just get to the Elysium Fields?"

"I'm not the one taking breaks," Asmodeus answered playfully. "Come on. Let's get you to your human."

Steering clear of the riverbank this time, Kala walked next to Asmodeus, letting him stand near the water. Seeing her vision on repeat wasn't exactly appealing to her at the moment.

A sudden thought struck her and she quickly glanced at her wrist.

No GPS watch.

If her clothes hadn't transferred to the Underworld, why would her gear?

The only question it begged was: how was she going to know how much time had passed? Kala didn't think there were any clocks, or sundials, or anything else to show passing time in this gray world, and without them she'd have no idea if she'd make the four-day countdown. The world could end and Kala wouldn't know. Cronus had to know this. He'd probably try and keep her here in the world of the dead until time ran out. Maybe he knew about her mission, too? Maybe some other prophecy told him he'd be imprisoned? Kala just didn't know.

Gathering reinforcements was her best option. The easiest way out would be to unite the Olympians trapped down here and get them to help her escape. She knew everyone in the living world thought that her *only* plan was to go after the Olympians, but Kala wanted to be selfish for once and find Jack first.

Shrugging, Kala took a deep breath of determination. Four days. She had four days. After rescuing Jack, she'd go after the Olympians. Just thinking the thought made her feel surprisingly relieved. Kala hated being deceptive, especially to people she cared about. Zeus could join her in the Underworld for all she cared – but what about Talan? Owen? Derek? She wanted to keep her promise: free the Olympians and let them fight their way out. Yes, they would be weak from the Grigori blades, but hopefully a few hours would bring them back to semi-fighting strength. Kala would just have to take down Rhea and steal the dagger. She had no idea how difficult that would be. Jack could help though. He used to be her commanding officer and he was always better at strategy than she was. Yes. Jack first, Operation Olympian-Rescue later.

A woman appeared in front of them. The landscape was so bleak, to have a beautiful lady suddenly materialize twenty feet away was jarring. With eyes of ice blue, her hair was long and black, falling down her shoulders in loose waves. Kala found it hard not to stare at the stunning contrast. Even the woman's skin was a perfect cinnamon brown, completely flawless with full naturally red lips. In juxtaposition with their gray surroundings, the lady was like a star in the darkness. Though Asmodeus was the only other creature in color, even he didn't come close to her striking figure.

"Rhea," Kala said before thinking. The Atlas part of her brain recognized the Titan immediately.

Rhea smiled, though there was no lightness to it. Her demeanor was defensive, as if she expected an instant attack. "I'm not sure what to call you, so I'll call you *thing*." Then she turned to Asmodeus. "You're not welcome here, traitor." Waving her hand, Asmodeus's body flew up into the sky as if he were being sucked into a giant vacuum cleaner.

In less than a second, he was gone.

Kala froze.

If Rhea could dispose of Asmodeus that quickly, what could she do to her? Kala was dead after all and she wasn't sure how much, if any, of her power she could tap into in this state.

Turning back to Kala, Rhea's smile became cruel. "Well, *thing*, you've come to try and take my children from me?"

Kala chose her words wisely. "I was thinking about it." Or not.

"You must think me heartless keeping my children here bereft of their powers. I cut them with the Grigori blade every hour of every day for the last two thousand years. Believe me, *thing*, I am more tortured than they are. But I do what must be done to protect them. And I won't let you destroy everything I've worked for!" Rhea hissed in anger.

Thinking about Rhea cutting her kids with the dagger every hour for two thousand years sounded like the worse kind of hell Kala could imagine. Not because Rhea had to hurt her children, but because of the repetitive behavior. It meant Rhea had had to keep track of time for that long. It reminded Kala of her own predicament, and that as long as she was cursed with the Atlas missions, she would have to keep track of every minute for all eternity! Unless Zeus was right about the prophecy and some girl in three hundred years would free her. But even three hundred years… it made Kala's head spin.

"You've been down here two thousand years slicing up your kids and you think that's a good thing?" Every time Kala tried to say something that could possibly calm Rhea's anger, something else entirely would come out of her mouth. "And you can call me Kala."

It occurred to Kala that she was talking to her half-sister and Cronus's main squeeze. From her Atlas memories, she knew that Cronus and Rhea were parents to six of the Olympians; Zeus pretty much fathered the rest of them with Hera and Demeter. The incest was astounding. Since Rhea referred to *her children*, it was officially confirmed that only Hestia, Poseidon, Hera and Demeter were in the Underworld.

Which led to the question: "Where are Athena, Ares, Hebe, Persephone and Dionysus?" It never hurt to ask.

Rhea tilted her head to the side in reflection. "I don't care where Zeus's offspring are. They mean nothing to me. I only agreed to keep *my* children safe. Cronus wouldn't give me Zeus. And Hades was sleeping soundly until *you* woke him up, *thing*."

Rhea wasn't going to let go of calling Kala *thing,* so Kala gave up on trying.

One good thing about Titans and Olympians though, they sure loved to talk. Kala came from a top-secret military background where torturing humans for information was actually a difficult task. Most soldiers didn't crack. But these supernatural beings? Once confronted, they spilled their secrets with no fear of the consequences. Maybe it was because they were gods? Or, maybe it was because they had no social skills. But either way, Kala was going to take advantage.

"Waking up Hades was my Atlas mission, so yeah, couldn't be helped. But he seems fine. Killed me, if it makes you feel any better," Kala said, stalling. She analyzed the terrain out of the corners of her eyes so Rhea wouldn't notice. Not much around to use as weapons, so she'd have to rely on her physical skills and possibly any of her Atlas strength or Gaia mojo. She just hoped death didn't mute those powers.

Rhea, like her husband, did seem to perk up at the expense of Kala's misfortune. "It does a little." Her stance tightened once again though. "But I still don't know *why* he killed you. Hades wanted you here for a reason. He hates his brothers and sisters, so I can't imagine he'd want you to save them, but that doesn't mean his motives won't conflict with my plans. He's here in the Underworld somewhere and my spies can't find him."

"This *is* his domain. Just because you've been hanging here for a couple millennia doesn't mean you own the place." But Kala filed away what Rhea said. His own mother didn't know why Hades had sent Kala here. If it wasn't to help free his brothers and sisters, then why would Hades want Kala in the Underworld? It gave her a small chill down her spine. Motives for the god of death didn't seem like they'd end well.

Nodding to the sky, Kala inquired, "So, is Asmodeus okay?" She tried to distract Rhea so she could move closer to the goddess.

Kala's biggest and best weapon was the river Lethe flowing beside her. If she could just throw the goddess in, Rhea would lose all her memories. Kala could possibly convince Rhea to be an ally. She'd have to get closer to the Titan first. She'd try reasoning first, and if that didn't work, Kala would provoke a fight. She was good at both, but she hoped her words would win in the end; she didn't have much confidence in her fighting skills at the moment.

"What do you care of the Demon King? He cares nothing for you or anyone else. Asmodeus only looks out for himself," Rhea spat.

Didn't like Asmodeus. Good to know. And not surprising, Kala didn't like him half the time, either. But one thing she did know: as self-obsessed as Asmodeus was, she couldn't deny the fact that she cared about him on some level. He was like the friend that gets on your nerves, but somehow grows on you eventually. If Asmodeus hurt, Kala wanted to know about it. "That may be true, but I still want to know."

Rhea shrugged dismissively and grunted, "He's fine. I simply revoked his invitation to the Underworld."

Kala slowly took small steps forward while she talked, so as not to alarm Rhea. "Look, can I be honest with you?"

Rhea watched Kala carefully, her face appeared confused as if Kala wasn't what she expected. Finally she nodded, "Speak, *thing*."

"We're probably on the same page here. I *had* to perform my Atlas mission or the world would end. So, I'm stuck here. Zeus is the one who wants me to free his siblings. I could care less. I told him I'd try, but I honestly don't feel like going through the trouble." Kala tried to be as convincing as possible. At this point she had every intention of freeing the Olympians just to piss off Rhea and Cronus, but she wanted Rhea to let her guard down long enough for Kala to push her in the river. "I just want one favor. I want to bring back Jack Norbin. He's in the Fields of Elysium. I had to kill him for my first Atlas mission, but now that we're both dead, I think we can exist together in the outside world without it ending and all." A part of Kala wanted to see what the Titan would say. Maybe as Hades's mother she could free Jack and send him back to earth.

Rhea actually looked sad for Kala. "No. He's the potential and you're the Fated One. You're still a *thing* to me, but you are the one from the prophecy, even I cannot deny that. Your lover has to stay in Elysium for all eternity: he won't be allowed to reincarnate, not with you alive. It would tear the world to shreds. Not even Cronus wants that." Rhea sighed, "No Atlas mission will have as vicious consequences as your first. If you don't complete your next mission, the world will crumble, but it won't *end,* unlike your first mission, which was a part of the prophecy. If you hadn't killed your lover, the very earth itself would have torn itself apart and there would be nothing left for anyone. Not even the gods."

In Kala's stupor at hearing Rhea's words, she hadn't even noticed that the goddess had closed the distance between them. The Titan was inches away.

Rhea continued, "You're a dangerous woman, Kala Hicks. I can't have you destroying everything because you miss your boyfriend."

Before Kala could reach out to throw Rhea into the river, Rhea's hands were already clasped around her arms.

In that moment, Kala realized that Rhea had the same idea as her.

Feeling the air beneath her, Kala was surprised that she felt a sudden relief.

It would all be over soon.

And Kala could be at peace.

With a resounding splash, the water flowed over Kala's body and all her memories washed away with it.

DAY TWO

Chapter Twelve

The woman woke up on the shores of the river Lethe, dry and tired. For a moment, she felt a surge of panic when she couldn't remember her name, but it passed when she realized she didn't care very much. In fact, she couldn't remember anything. She didn't even know where she was, except that the water flowing next to her was dangerous. She didn't know why, she just knew it was true.

Examining her clothes and body thoroughly, she made sure that she was completely dry. A drop would be enough to hurt her, somehow she knew that as well. The gray landscape didn't bother her, either, for it was peaceful in its own way. Part of her sensed that it was somehow wrong, though, that there should be…*colors*.

The word sounded strange in her head. What *were* colors?

A moment later the thought had dissipated.

It wasn't important to her. *Nothing* was important to her. And that somehow felt very good.

Slowly, she stood up and tried not to look at the water. Her instincts screamed at her to stay away from the river. But a sideways glance betrayed her and she saw something strange on its surface.

Though she knew it was dangerous she stared at the water regardless, curiosity winning over safety.

Images formed of two women and four men in some big basement. One of the women she thought she recognized, but couldn't quite place. White fire came out of the hands of three of them, encasing two of the men. The two men were then strapped down in wired chairs and locked in by the familiar-looking woman. The images repeated after that in an endless loop. She stared at it for hours, not able to pull her attention away.

Over time she began to see similarities in the familiar woman from the water to her own body. Legs, arms, hands, feet, they matched exactly. She realized that the woman must be her. She admired how the woman shot out white fire from her hands and wondered, if that was indeed her, where she had learned how to do that?

Was this the past or the future? Should she be worried? Should she figure out why she couldn't remember anything?

She found that she didn't want to know, and the longer she watched the images, the more distraught she felt.

Finally, the woman yanked her head away and began walking away from the river. It was much calmer now, walking amongst the dry shrubs and cracked ground. There was nothing to focus on and that felt right. It felt peaceful.

She must have walked for miles and miles, but her feet didn't ache. It was good to walk. It gave her a strange sense of joy. As if she had a purpose.

A mission.

The word stuck in her brain and she couldn't seem to let it go.

Mission. Mission. Mission.

She battled her own mind: the more she tried to push the word out, the louder her head would scream it.

MISSION.

It was as if her brain was telling her to do something that she had no understanding of. It surprised her that she knew the meaning of the word. She knew how to speak, she knew what things meant, she just simply couldn't remember who she was or what she had done in her life.

"Kala?" A man's voice sounded from behind her.

She turned to see who had spoken. It surprised her at first to see the man. He was in full color, which made her instantly know what colors were. Looking down at her own gray skin she found herself envious of his bright, flushed cheeks. Then she realized that he had called her a name. Was she "Kala?" Did he know her? As she examined the man, she realized he was one of the men from the vision she saw in the river. He was tall and nice to look at with light brown swoopy hair, blue eyes and a bone structure that accentuated every one of his perfect features. There was also a warmth about him that she immediately felt attached to. She must know him, especially if he was in her vision. How could she feel such a connection with a stranger?

"Do I know you?" she asked, hoping the answer would be yes.

As he stepped closer to her, she found that she wanted him to embrace her. It was such a powerful sensation the woman almost grabbed the man to pull him close, but as she didn't know who he was, she decided to hold back.

His voice was soft and low, which comforted her even more, "Kala, it's me, Talan. Don't you recognize me?"

"I saw you in the river," she said trying to be helpful. "But I don't remember knowing you. Is my name Kala?"

The man called Talan reached out tentatively then pulled back as if he were overstepping some boundary. "Yes, your name is Kala. We're friends."

Kala.

The woman rolled the name around in her head. Yes. She was Kala. That sounded right. "I'm Kala," she repeated. Then to make the man

Talan feel better, Kala reached out and touched his face affectionately. "And you're Talan."

Talan seemed surprised by her affection. "The Lethe really wiped your brain, didn't it?"

"The river Lethe is dangerous," Kala said the only thing she was certain of. The only true memory she had.

Talan took her hand and held it with both of his, making sure his eyes met hers. His touch sent shivers through her and she wanted him to kiss her. "The water took away your memories. We have to get them back."

She pulled her hand away. "No, that doesn't sound right. I don't think that sounds right." Maybe this Talan wasn't good after all. One thing she was certain of, she didn't want to remember anything.

Talan put his hands up as if declaring peace. "That's a part of the spell the river puts on you. It makes you *want* to forget." He gently took her hand in his again. "And Kala, you of all people deserve to forget. I wish I could wipe the pain away from you forever, but you have a mission."

There was that word again.

"Mission?" Kala liked the way Talan's hand felt in hers, soft yet strong. It helped her erase the pull of trying to remember.

"Yes, Kala, you have a mission. You've been in the Underworld for two days now, and if you don't return to earth and complete your mission, the world will be destroyed." Talan made sure she heard every last syllable. "You only have four days to complete it. Do you know what it is yet?"

She remembered the images in the water and knew instantly that this was the "mission" Talan spoke of. "In the reflection from the water I saw some men in chairs. You were there and we attacked them with white fire. It kept repeating." It felt good to say what she'd seen aloud after watching the loop for hours and hours.

Talan nodded, but his face was disturbed. "White fire? Did you recognize these men?"

The woman shook her head, "No, but they seemed really upset."

"That's your Atlas mission. You only have two days left to complete it and we have to get you out of here. We have to rescue a few friends as well, but we're going to need to you to get your memories back."

The more Talan talked, the more he made sense. She didn't like what he was saying, but her mind kept tugging at her to listen.

"How do I do that?" she forced herself to ask.

"I might be able to help. You just have to trust me." Talan squeezed her hand slightly and she wanted to kiss him again.

So she did.

Talan pulled back at first, but the sensation became so intense he pulled her in close and his lips pressed against hers as if he could never stop. And she didn't want him to. Nothing had ever felt so right. Even without her memories, she knew down to her soul that she was meant to kiss this man. They belonged to each other. It was almost as if they were one soul when they touched.

"This isn't right." Talan yanked himself away.

"But it feels right," she answered, confused.

Talan's eyes bore into her with an intensity that made her knees weak. "Let me give you back your memories."

She could only nod. If Talan's kisses felt this way without her memories, she could only imagine what they would feel like with them.

Talan placed his hands on top of her head and she could feel heat radiate off them. As his grip tightened, the burning grew. In a flash Kala was Kala again. She still had no memories, but she knew who she was. Kala. Talan finally released his hold, shaking his head. "The water from Lethe surrounds your memory cortex. I can't remove it."

"I'm Kala," she confirmed.

Talan's eyes were hopeful. "Yes. Do you remember anything else?"

Kala shook her head. "No."

Talan sighed, defeated. "I don't know how to fix you."

"How did you make your hands burn?" Kala wondered how he knew there was water in her head.

"I'm a Grigori angel," he explained. "I've helped you with your memories before when you first became Atlas."

Kala liked the sound of Talan being an angel. Better than a Demon she supposed.

Or a human.

Something inside of her stirred at the thought of a human. She was human, wasn't she? What else could she be? Kala needed to know.

"Am I human?"

Talan nodded. "But you're something more as well. You have a Titan inside of you." His face grew concerned. "I'm just afraid he'll break through the Lethe water first and take over your body."

Kala shook her head. "Gaia said that couldn't happen. He's dead now."

Talan and Kala both stopped.

"How did I know that?" Kala wasn't sure where her statement about Gaia had come from. She tried to follow the memory to recall anything from it, but it was as if she had nothing to draw from, just a big empty space.

Talan's face lit up. "You've always been able to do things that no one else thought you could. Maybe you can find your memories on your own." His expression turned awe-filled. "Did you speak with Gaia? She hasn't been seen in thousands of years, before I was imprisoned."

"You were imprisoned? I'm so sorry." Yet Kala didn't feel sorry. It was the strangest thing, so she voiced it aloud. "Why don't I feel bad for you? Shouldn't I feel bad for you?"

Talan laughed and it made Kala's heart warm at the sound. "You've expressed on many occasions that I whine too much about my prison. It was in the 5th Heaven, which is quite beautiful." He brushed his hand against her cheek and Kala could see the love in his eyes. "Your mind is fighting the water. You're remembering emotions rather than solid visions of your past." Talan kissed her forehead, which sent a thrill down her spine. "Now tell me about Gaia," he prodded.

"There's nothing to tell. I don't remember," Kala confessed. "I don't know why I said what I said. Who is Gaia?"

"A part of her is inside you and gives you great power. Like I said, she's been gone for a long time, if she came to you, then she must believe things are dire. And she must believe in *you*." His eyes shone with pride.

"She's my mother." The words came out of Kala's mouth as if someone else spoke them.

Talan's face paled. He didn't move. He didn't speak.

It scared Kala. "Is that bad? Is Gaia evil? Say something."

Kala couldn't remember the meeting with Gaia, but she knew she was Gaia's daughter. And she knew she needed to tell Talan. She just didn't know he'd respond this way.

Talan snapped out of his stupor. "Kala…" he paused, then continued, "That changes everything." He ran his hand through his hair in worry. "I just don't know if we can rely on what you're saying. What if Hades tainted that water to make you believe certain things? It could be part of his plan to throw us off."

"Rhea threw me in, not Hades." Kala shook her head in surprise. "Maybe your little angel hocus pocus is helping me unlock some of this stuff. I don't know where it's all coming from."

Talan shook his head. "I couldn't get past the water. This is all you."

Kala wanted to kiss him again, but instead she asked, "Are we in love?"

Talan didn't answer right away. After a moment he finally replied, "*I* am. Your heart belongs to another."

Kala couldn't imagine feeling more intensely for someone other than Talan. It was as if her mind and body were being pulled to him by a force she couldn't control. The mere concept of being in love with another man was… heartbreaking. She wondered if, when her memories came back to her, if she was secretly in love with Talan and hadn't told the other man. If so, she felt bad for whoever it was she was supposed to be in love with.

"Who is he?" By asking, Kala could see that it hurt Talan to talk about and she instantly regretted it.

Talan took a step back from her, keeping his distance.

It killed her in ways she didn't expect. All Kala wanted to do was close the distance between them and feel his body against hers again. The sensation was so overwhelming, she almost did it, but she waited to hear Talan's answer.

"His name is Jack Norbin," Talan finally admitted.

Hearing the name sparked a deep pain inside Kala. The sensation was so powerful she began to collapse.

Talan was there to catch her before she fell to the ground. When she had regained her balance, he moved to step away, but Kala stopped him with her hand. "Don't go." Pulling him in, Kala kissed Talan again. This time he was quick to respond, his hands drawing her into his chest.

The force of their passion left her breathless, yet she couldn't seem to get close enough to him. It was as if the more they kissed, the further away he became. Her desire for Talan grew fevered and obsessive. She needed him more than anything she'd ever needed before. She knew this even without her memories. Kala kissed him harder, as if she could devour him whole. Talan's energy seemed to fill her up. The more she kissed him, the more she felt them becoming one.

"Kala," Talan choked.

With sudden terror, Kala pulled away as Talan dropped to his knees, his face pale, his body weakened. She covered her mouth with her hand in shock. "What did I do?"

Talan breathed in deep, trying to regain his strength. Kala knelt down next to him, touching his face, kissing his forehead. "I'm so sorry," was all she could say.

Though Kala had no memory, she realized what she had done. She had almost consumed Talan like she had done with Atlas.

She remembered.

Standing on a beach, the Titan Atlas cowering in fear, Kala being so angry, so full of rage... why?

Jack.

Kala had to kill Jack and Atlas was making her. All she could see was red. All she could do was destroy. She wanted to make Atlas suffer. She wanted to make him go away.

So she did. She swallowed him whole and he died inside her, becoming a part of her, integrating into her soul.

Kala snapped out of the memory and her heart squeezed with shame at what she had almost done to Talan.

He must have seen the horror in her eyes because he said, "I'm okay. You stopped in time."

"I can't control it," Kala confessed in misery.

Talan reached out and cupped Kala's face with his hand. "It's okay, Kala. I'll be fine. At least we know you still have your powers down here. That's a good thing."

"I almost devoured you whole and you're telling me it's a *good thing*?" It only made Kala want him more, but she reined in her self-control for fear of destroying him. "It's just, when you said that name… I didn't want to hear it. It was too painful. My connection with you was strong enough to make me forget." Kala sighed and stood up. "He's dead, isn't he?" She knew the answer before she asked the question.

Talan nodded, then motioned around the gray landscape. "We're in the land of the dead, though. I think that's where you were headed before Rhea threw you into the river. You needed to see Jack. It won't be him, Kala. He'll …"

"He'll just be an empty shell," Kala finished, not knowing where the words came from, but they were true, like the others. "I know." She shrugged. "I guess it's good I don't remember him since I don't feel the need to find him now."

Talan stood with her. "We have to get your memories back. You're too dangerous without them." He seemed fully recovered as he sighed in frustration, "You don't know how hard it was for me to get in here, not even Zeus could enter. I'm it until the others can figure out a way to break Cronus's protections spells."

His words didn't mean anything to Kala except that she'd have Talan to herself for a while and that made her happy.

But Talan obviously had other plans. He took a few steps away from her, calling out, "HADES! I know you can hear me! We need your help!" Talan gave Kala a smile. "Let's see whose side he's on."

"I'm on no one's side, Grigori."

Kala and Talan turned to see a man dressed in a black suit with long black hair to match. His skin was sallow, almost as gray as Kala's, his body thin as if he was a skeleton with skin painted on.

Hades grumbled in irritation. "Now what do you want?"

Chapter Thirteen

Kala stared at the god Hades. There was something familiar about him, but she simply couldn't place it. Maybe she knew him? He definitely seemed grumpy.

Talan addressed Hades first. "Your mother dumped Kala into the river Lethe."

"Very clever," Hades laughed, which was actually quite terrifying, enhanced by the deep lines creasing his cheeks. His amusement faded after a few moments, though, and his face reverted back to an expression of annoyance. "What do you want me to do about it?"

"I can see the water swarming inside her head, but I can't take it out," Talan admitted with frustration.

"And you think I can?" Hades demanded.

"I know you can," Talan responded with confidence.

Kala watched the exchange silently. The entire conversation was about her, but she had no attachment to it. Part of her wanted her memories back because her instincts were screaming that she needed them, but another part of her brain was enjoying the silence. Her life was already becoming complicated and she had only been wiped memory-free for a short time.

Hades shrugged. "Of course I can, but why should I? From everything I've heard of Kala Hicks, keeping her muted seems like a brilliant idea."

Talan's anger flared, "She's Atlas now, did you forget about that? She only has two days to complete her mission!"

"And?" Hades appeared unfazed.

"*And* the planet dies!" Talan was appalled at Hades's lack of concern.

"We can always start a new one," Hades sighed. "I don't even know why I came when you called. You Grigori are so righteous and *this one…* I thought I could officially meet the girl who woke me up, but she's useless, too."

"Why did you send her here then? You must have had a reason." Talan sounded exasperated.

Kala found that she wanted to know the answer to that question as well.

Hades shrugged. "I was feeding on her life power, you idiot. Taking her life gave me the strength to come back home." Then he smiled. "And when she told me she was Atlas… well, the whole thing just seemed too serendipitous to ignore."

Talan nodded as if he had just understood some giant revelation. "You want her to fail her next mission. That's why you brought her here. You don't care what happens to the world above us because you want to collect the billions of souls that will die if Kala fails her Atlas task."

Hades didn't deny it. "So?"

Talan was appalled. "You'd side with the Titans?" he asked incredulously.

Hades's own temper rose at the accusation. "Well, what have my brothers ever done for me? We fought the Titans and won, then we fought them again and I've been taking a nap for two thousand years. I'm weak, but a couple of billion souls would do just the trick to perk me up." He calmed himself once more. "I hate the world anyway. I *want* it to end."

Kala found the exchange fascinating. The world. Hearing Hades say he wanted it to end stirred a rage inside of her. Another image formed in her head of a man… Jack. The man Talan said she was in love with. The man who died. The memory was of Kala pointing a gun at him and he was begging her to kill him. Her head squeezed in pain as she saw the memory of her pulling the trigger.

Kala fell to her knees. When she looked up, Hades's attention was focused on her. Talan knelt by her side.

"Did you have a *memory*?" Hades inquired in shock.

Kala wasn't sure if she should lie or not, so she told the truth. "I've had a couple." She turned to Talan. "My life is painful, isn't it?"

From the expression on Talan's face, she could tell that he didn't want to answer. Finally, though, he nodded. "But there are good things as well."

Hades hadn't moved as he continued to stare at Kala. "That's impossible. You shouldn't be able to have any memories."

Talan turned to plead with Hades. "I'm telling you, she's different. Even if you don't want to side with your brothers or the Titans, side with her. She's going to change everything. She's the Fated One from the prophecy." It was so heartfelt Kala was a little embarrassed that Talan was referring to her. He made it sound like she was some type of leader or something. Not that Kala was opposed to the idea; it was simply that she was enjoying not having any responsibility.

"Please," Talan implored, "just give Kala back her memories."

Hades shook his head, fear in his eyes. "No. I just saw my mother for the first time in 2,000 years and I thought she was being paranoid, but she was right. Kala Hicks is too dangerous." His demeanor was determined. "I'm keeping to my plan: she stays in the Underworld. If you want her to be happy, stop trying to get her memories back. Rhea did her a favor."

A familiar voice sounded from behind Kala. "Sorry to disappoint, but she's about to get her memories back *without* your help."

Kala saw Talan's face first. His reaction to whoever was behind her was one of horror. She was almost afraid to look, but Kala's curiosity won out.

Two men stood next to each other. One was tall with brown eyes and sandy brown hair and looked like a supermodel and the other one was …

Jack.

As if watching a movie in fast-forward, Kala's memories suddenly flew through her mind at frightening speed: her birth, her life as a foster kid, being adopted by Owen, training as a Seal, her military operations, Turner, Clifton, falling in love with Jack, becoming Atlas, killing Jack, fighting Cronus… It was too fast to keep up!

In less than an instant Kala remembered everything.

She was thankful that she was already on the ground or she would have collapsed from the impact. Water from the river Lethe poured out of her ears in small waterfalls. She didn't think that her head could hold that much liquid.

She was Kala Hicks, daughter of Gaia, raised by a Grigori angel.

The pain was too much to bear. Remembering everything was more of a curse than being Atlas. She almost wished she could dunk herself back into the river Lethe. The river's amnesia had been quiet. It had been safe. It had been calm. Now responsibility, pressure and anguish all threatened to pull her down into a dark abyss.

But seeing Jack so close to her…

Rising to her feet and brushing past Asmodeus, Kala raced to Jack. She wrapped her arms around the only man she ever loved. It took her a moment to notice Jack hadn't moved to embrace her back. Her heart sank as she pulled away and looked into his eyes.

Blank.

Everyone had been right. Jack was just a shell housing a soul. A soul that could never exist with hers in the world of the living. Only in the Underworld could they stand like this, together. It was unbearable to look at him. Staring straight ahead with no expression was excruciating to witness. All his personality, his memories, his life: gone. Tears filled Kala's eyes as she reached up to touch Jack's cheek. He was still so beautiful, even in death.

"Jack," she said aloud, as if saying his name would revive him somehow.

"What were you thinking?" Talan accused Asmodeus angrily.

Asmodeus acted as if he expected this kind of reaction from Talan. "She has her memories back, doesn't she? You're welcome."

"By bringing her pain?" Talan was furious. "She would have remembered all on her own. She doesn't need you! Did you take him from Elysium?"

"Of course I did. It's not like he knows what going on," Asmodeus added, defending his actions. "And I've had to walk all day with this zombie since I can't teleport in this place, so I don't want to hear it."

The last thing Kala wanted to hear was bickering, but at learning what Asmodeus had done... "Did you just rip him from Elysium? Can you take him back?" Her heart squeezed in pain at the thought.

Asmodeus shrugged guiltily. "Possibly? But I really don't particularly want to make that trek a second time."

Kala whirled on Hades, who she now noticed was staring at her with a mixture of fascination and fear. "Can *you* take Jack back to the Fields of Elysium?"

Hades seemed to be processing what he had just seen, so he ignored Kala's question. "No one has ever released the waters of River Lethe by themselves. No one."

"What can I say? I'm full of surprises. Now, can you take him to Elysium?" Kala was desperate. She had been fighting so hard to find Elysium and rescue Jack, but when Rhea had told her that the prophecy still stood – that Jack and Kala could never be on earth together without it shattering – Kala had decided she'd settle for just seeing him.

But, now, Asmodeus had torn Jack away from what was essentially heaven. Kala was terrified her own selfishness would doom Jack to wandering this crappy gray desert forever.

"Tell me how you did it, and I'll consider taking him back." Hades tried to bargain.

"I don't know how I did it," Kala answered honestly, though internally she wanted to smack the god. "I saw Jack and BOOM, everything remembered."

"You lie. You won't tell me," Hades accused. "If you refuse to confess, I'll send your precious Jack to Tartarus where he'll be imprisoned and tortured for all eternity." Hades had a satisfied grin plastered to his face from his threat.

Kala didn't like threats.

"You ungrateful dick," she began to fume. "I woke your ass up after 2,000 years of lying in a cave at the bottom of the ocean and you bring me *here*," she motioned to her gray surroundings. "Your mother throws me into a memory-erasing river and now you're threatening to throw the love of my life into the worst prison system in the universe?" Kala shook her head, appalled. "Are you kidding me?"

"No?" Hades appeared confused. "Was that a question?"

Kala was sick and tired of these gods and Titans who acted like children. "No, it was not a question. You *will not* take Jack to Tartarus, you *will* take him to the Fields of Elysium, where he will be treated like a king until the end of days. Do you understand?" Enough was enough.

Hades puffed up, angry. "How dare you talk to me like that in my own realm. I don't care who you are, I'm sending you all to Tartarus!" Then he grew. A lot.

"We should probably run," Asmodeus suggested.

"No way." Kala was just as livid as Hades.

The Olympian laughed. "I was warned about your powers. You won't get anywhere near me." Hades threw his hands up and with it hundreds of rotted arms burst through the cracked desert floor, pushing their way to Kala, Talan, Asmodeus and comatose-Jack. In a matter of seconds they were suddenly facing an army of zombies.

"*Now* do you want to run?" Asmodeus suggested again, with a little more urgency in his voice. "We could leave these two as distractions and make our getaway."

Kala didn't even dignify the Demon with a response. He knew very well that she would never abandon Talan and Jack.

But more than that, she was seriously pissed at Hades.

Sliding very comfortably back into soldier-mode, Kala made a quick head count of the decrepit army now facing her: somewhere around fifty. It was the most foul spectacle Kala had ever witnessed. The bodies ranged from slightly rotted, to goopy, to almost full-on skeleton. Logic said the ones with less meat would be easier to take down.

Keeping her eye on the puppet master, Kala was surprised to see that Hades simply watched his army move forward without using any kind of controlled movements. It was as if he simply brought them all back to life and they could function on their own. Each zombie moved at its own pace, with its own gestures. It wasn't as if they had their own personalities or anything, but they definitely acted of their own volition. Apparently Hades had made them alive just enough to act as individuals, but dead enough that he could still steer them to his means.

Which, at this moment, happened to be attacking Kala.

The first wave of dead soldiers tried to grab at Kala's throat.

Kala wondered if she could die again in the Underworld, but she knew she couldn't. This fight wasn't about killing, it was about capturing. Hades wanted the four of them in Tartarus and he was too afraid to grab Kala for fear of her devouring him.

Fighting the zombies was harder than she thought it would be. No matter how many times she slammed a body to the ground, it would jump back up as if it had merely tripped. If she wasn't careful the minions would swarm her like a puppy pile minus the cute and cuddliness.

Having a Demon and a Grigori at her back helped, but they seemed just as frustrated at the corpses' ability to bounce back. Kala lost count of how many arms she had ripped off, but the zombies kept coming, as if losing a limb was always a part of the plan.

She needed to get to Hades. He may have let his reins loose so the corpses could fight on their own, but he was still the man in charge. Stop the master-controller, stop the army. The last thing Kala wanted to do was consume the god of death, but she'd have to get close in order to scare him.

Kala tried to trigger her ability from afar, but from Hades's relaxed manner, she could tell it wasn't working. She needed to be close to touch him, to connect physically. She had to try.

"We have to clear a path to Hades," Kala called out to Talan and Asmodeus.

Hades had taken control of Jack, leading him to his side, but Kala had no intention of letting Hades control Jack permanently. Plus, in a fight, Kala had to prioritize, and Jack in a coma made him easy to keep track of.

Asmodeus screeched his battle scream and it made the hairs on Kala's neck stand up straight. She hadn't heard him do that in a while and, as the sound penetrated deep into her eardrums, she realized how thankful she was that she hadn't. The scream made the zombie soldiers clasp their ears in pain, some clawing the flesh from their heads to make it stop, others trying to yank out their eardrums themselves. Lovely, but effective. Kala almost wanted to do the same, but she managed to tune most of the sound out to focus on her goal.

Hades.

Talan stepped to her side and the two of them tossed aside each minion that dove into their path, lurching their way toward Hades body by body. Mowing them down, actually, sometimes two or three at a time. It was invigorating! Kala's Atlas strength surged through her and even though each soldier in the zombie army snapped back into place, endlessly renewing the assault, Kala and Talan flung them away again and again.

Slowly, she grew closer to Hades.

In the past, Kala hadn't known what she was doing when consuming a supernatural being. If she was being honest with herself, she still didn't know how to trigger that part of her powers. At this moment, though, she had no choice: it was either take down Hades or get thrown into Tartarus. A place that had terrified Atlas.

Kala searched his memories for any sign of visiting the Underworld prison, but apparently it was the hearsay that Atlas feared. Not a surprise, considering how the god had hidden himself from the Titans for thousands of years, but Kala knew better than to risk it. From Atlas's memories, even Cronus was fearful of Tartarus and Cronus had made the 5th Level of *Hell* his home.

So, yeah. Kala wasn't about to let herself be taken.

With a renewed sense of purpose, Kala pushed ahead with confidence. She was going to take Hades down in his own world. Zombies flew hundreds of feet in the air at her touch and the path to the Olympian grew shorter and shorter. Kala reveled in the fact that she could see real fear in his eyes the closer she came.

Only five corpses left. Four. Three. Two…

Jack stepped in front of her, eyes alive and angry. "You killed me, now I'm going give you what you deserve!"

Kala froze.

A zombie ran toward her, but Talan now fought for the both of them. He tried to get through to her. "Hades is controlling Jack. Those are not Jack's words, Kala! Don't listen to him!"

But she couldn't move. She stared at Jack in horror.

Jack continued his hateful rant, "If you had truly loved me, you never would have pulled the trigger. You would have let the world burn for me. For us!" He grabbed her arms and shook her. "And now you come to the Underworld and take me from my reward? I was in the Fields of Elysium, Kala! I was at peace! Now, I'll be sent to Tartarus to burn for all eternity!" he screamed. "Because of *you!*"

All Kala's worst fears tore at her chest as if one of the zombies had clawed her open. Everything Jack said was true. This *was* him. He meant every word.

Talan screamed as he ripped minion after minion apart. "Kala! Jack would never say those things to you! He loved you! Hades is tapping into your head!"

His words made sense, but Jack's made more. Kala *did* kill him. Even Turner had said he'd let the world burn to save Roberta and Kala could see in Turner's eyes that he meant it. Did Kala not love Jack enough to make that sacrifice?

Jack answered her, "No. You didn't love me enough. You're not capable of it. You took a gun and shot me in the head. *You* deserve to be punished not me."

"Kala! I can't hold them off much longer!" Talan screamed.

Asmodeus's screeching grew closer and Kala could see he was coming to help Talan keep the soldiers off her.

She heard his voice from behind. "Please tell me she's not actually listening to Hades's puppet?"

His words struck her hard. For some reason Asmodeus's sarcasm managed to weasel into her subconscious more than logic ever could.

All Kala's pain – the blame, the guilt, the devastation – manifested itself in Jack. That was why his words were so easy to believe because that was how she felt. Kala *did* kill him. She *did* pick the world over Jack. She loved him, but she had made the right decision. And the first person who would agree with her would be… Jack.

The real Jack.

Kala focused all her strength into the palm of her hand and hit Jack square in the chest. His body flew into the air and landed a few hundred feet away. She needed him out of view. Kala couldn't have him distract her from her target.

Hades.

Slowly, her eyes met his.

And Kala grabbed his arm, pulling Hades's face down to hers.

"You'll pay for making Jack say those things," she threatened.

All the rage Kala felt at being manipulated and emotionally torn to threads, she poured into Hades.

And she fed.

Hades screamed in terror and pain.

Kala had never felt so much power, not even from Cronus. Hades was in his realm and being asleep for thousands of years hadn't weakened him at all. He had lied. He wanted the world to end, but not to recharge his batteries. Kala didn't have time to ponder any more questions. She would know soon enough after she devoured the Olympian whole.

Hades roared in horror, "STOP! PLEASE! I'll take you to my brothers and sisters! I'll send Jack to Elysium where he'll rule for all of time! Please! Don't kill me!"

Kala didn't care what he had to say. She only wanted to feed. The god was intoxicating. All the zombies around them dropped to the ground, rotting instantly, until all that was left were piles of bones. Kala could see the color slowly come back to her skin.

Suddenly, she was yanked away.

Her connection to Hades dropped.

In a rage she turned to see who had pulled her from her meal.

Asmodeus stood there with a chastising expression. "I won't let you swallow that asshole."

Kala snapped back to herself at his words, instantly relieved. She had almost consumed Hades! It had felt so right at the moment, but now Kala wanted to vomit. But she regained enough of her composure to put on an angry face for Hades.

"Where are the Olympians?" she demanded.

Hades didn't flinch. "They're across the River Styx on the edge of the Underworld. You have to get across the river on Charon's boat or you won't be in the same dimension as the prisoners. The Demon knows where Charon is."

Asmodeus nodded. "I can take us there."

Hades straightened his suit, his hands shaking with nervousness. "I'll just go return your boyfriend now." Jack had made his way back to Hades, comatose once more. "He'll have his own palace in the Fields of Elysium and will be treated like he was my own son."

Before Kala could respond, Hades disappeared with Jack in tow.

Talan rested his hand on Kala's shoulder supportively. "Are you okay?"

Kala nodded, but she was far from okay. At this point, though, all she wanted to do was leave the Underworld. "Let's just get these idiots and get out of here."

Talan turned to Asmodeus. "Lead the way, Demon."

"At least one of us is useful, *Grigori*," Asmodeus smirked. "Follow me."

DAY THREE

Chapter Fourteen

It seemed to Kala as if they had been walking for months, but according to Talan it had only been a full day. That put her into Day Three on her Atlas timeline. It was frustrating not knowing the exact time, but she trusted Talan to know where she was in the countdown.

The two boys had said nothing to each other the entire time, and Kala found she had very little to say as well.

Fighting Hades hadn't exactly been fun. Kala never wanted to fight dead things again as long as she lived. *If* she was ever going to live again. The more she learned about Hades the more she thought her vision might not be such a bad thing. The two main culprits in wanting the Atlas mission to fail and leave the world in chaos were Hades and Cronus. It made sense to lock those two down, otherwise Kala would be fighting them every four days until she could find an end to this curse.

It still rubbed her wrong though. Their blank stares reminded her of Jack's. It would be easier to think Jack was just an empty shell, but knowing that his soul was still inside him was heartbreaking. And now, she'd be doing the same thing to Hades and Cronus: trapping them inside their own bodies.

Jack's painful words echoed in her head. She knew Hades had put them in Jack's mouth, but it still hurt to physically see Jack say all those hateful things. But it was still better than her last living memory of him. Kala would rather Jack scream obscenities and hateful words at her than have to remember blowing his brains out, any day of the week.

In a way it was almost cathartic, though. So many unresolved emotions rolling around inside her. Even hearing the worst of her fears somehow made her feel lighter in a sense. As if, for once, Kala might be able to move on someday. It gave her hope.

Talan tried to catch her eye, but she turned away.

Without her memories she had pretty much fallen all over the guy. It embarrassed her and she didn't want to discuss it with him, especially in front of Asmodeus. But she couldn't deny that when her brain was wiped, Talan had felt like he was… what? Talan threw the words soul mate around like it was going out of style, but Kala despised those words. If anything, she owed that sentiment to Jack, but he was gone now. Truly gone. Even so, Kala wasn't ready to move on to someone new. She didn't think she ever could.

Kala's love life was the least of her problems, though. She was about to take on Rhea again, but before that the boat guy, Charon. Two things she was not looking forward to. She wished she could use that whole white-fire trick from her vision. Kala had zero clue as to how to activate that skill set, but she'd figure it out soon enough, she guessed.

In a little over 24 hours.

The thought churned her stomach. Kala wished she could teleport out of this place. She hadn't realized how used to the whole teleportation she had become. Now, having to walk for miles and miles and being stuck in this drab, gray landscape, Kala remembered what it was like to be human.

The last hour the terrain had changed considerably, however, shifting from desert to soft grass, leafy bushes and an occasional outcropping of maple trees. Everything was still gray, but the change in scenery lifted Kala's spirits somewhat.

After her fight with Hades, Kala noticed that she had a little more color to her skin, making it a grayish pink rather than stone cold corpse gray, which also made her feel little better. All-in-all, having a sense of purpose and destination kept her focused and sane.

Asmodeus's voice cut through her thoughts and the silence of the Underworld. "Just past those trees," he announced.

Kala viewed the aforementioned trees to see another river in the distance. The River Styx. The river that could be used as a weapon by forcing the victim of its waters to make an oath. Kala wished she had a bottle to store some of it for later. Aside from the brief River lesson Asmodeus gave her upon entering the Underworld, even Kala had heard stories about the River Styx before her personal involvement in the supernatural world. She hadn't heard much, just that some guy had a boat or raft or something and took the dead to the Underworld. If the spirits were anything like coma-Jack, then Charon had a relatively easy job. She wondered how difficult it was going to be to either convince him to take them across *the other way* or commandeer his boat. A breakout of the Underworld. Surely people had tried. Then, thinking of Jack's condition once more, maybe they hadn't.

Talan stayed quiet as the trio approached the river. Though Kala appreciated the Grigori not bringing up her previous behavior, now his silence was beginning to drive her mad. He was hurt, she could see it in his demeanor, but she had no way to console him. She knew in his mind that Talan believed Asmodeus had saved Kala and not him. Which wasn't true. It was a combination of both their words that had snapped Kala out of her Hades-torture-stupor.

Since there was nothing she could really say to make him feel better, Kala opted for keeping her mouth shut. In hindsight, it was probably making things worse, but what else could she do?

"There he is." Asmodeus pointed. "Charon."

A couple hundred feet down river was a flat square of wood floating in the water with what looked like a man steering it with a large pole.

Finally Talan spoke, "I've heard things about Charon. Do you know him, Asmodeus?"

"Like *personally*?" Asmodeus nodded. "On a few occasions, I guess. Not much of a talker." He raised an eyebrow in thought. "Charon picked this gig for himself. It's not a punishment or anything. He *wants* to spend all eternity going back and forth and back and forth and back and… you get the idea."

The way Asmodeus conveyed his point showed his disdain for even considering that kind of life. And Kala had to agree. What type of supernatural being would opt into motoring dead souls back and forth forever? She just hoped Charon was reasonable.

Talan seemed to be on the same wavelength as he asked, "Do you think he'll let us cross on his boat?"

It was annoying that they needed Charon's raft, otherwise they would have crossed the river miles back without the guy ever knowing. It made sense though. Cronus always tried to have several back up plans.

"Do I think he'll *let* us use his boat? No, of course not. But between the three of us I'd be embarrassed if we couldn't get by Charon." Asmodeus headed towards Charon without waiting for a response.

Kala and Talan made brief eye contact before following the Demon. She wasn't sure what she read in Talan's expression, but this was no time to try and figure it out.

As they approached Charon, Kala had a better view of the… creature? He didn't look quite human, which was a bit of a shock for her. So far in her brief encounters with the supernatural they had all been human-ish. But this guy? He was exactly what she'd expect the Angel of Death to look like. His face was grotesque as if he had been clawed evenly down each side, then sewn back together with a staple gun. He had solid black eyes and his skin was the dark brownish-gray a corpse would have that had been rotting for a long time. Wearing only a long black robe, Kala could see his taloned feet planted on the raft. His veined hands were all that poked out of his draping sleeves and they clutched a long wooden pole that he was using to control the boat.

The river at this point was about a hundred feet wide; Charon was halfway across the water, heading straight towards them.

"Well, at least he's alone," Kala said to no one in particular. She didn't really know if that was indeed a benefit, it just seemed like the right thing to say.

"Charon is half-Demon, half water-nymph. He's no match for us, but if he won't let us on his little ship there, it will definitely be a good fight," Asmodeus informed them. "Let me talk to him first."

Kala and Talan didn't argue. If Asmodeus had *any* kind of relationship with Charon, then they had to try the simplest form of getting across: asking.

After an agonizing wait, Charon's raft met the shore in front of them. He eyed them over carefully, as if trying to figure out why they were there.

Asmodeus didn't make Charon wait long. "Hey, Charon. Long time, no see."

That was casual.

Charon couldn't hide his disdain. "Yes. I was hoping for a few hundred more years before your next visit."

"So cold." Asmodeus acted offended, but Kala knew the Demon could care less what Charon thought of him. "Listen, we need to get across using your boat."

"Right to the point, as always." Charon rolled his black eyes. From what Kala could surmise, Charon knew Asmodeus pretty well, which was a big *uh-oh* in their current predicament. "The answer is *no*, Asmodeus. You know how to leave the Underworld, just take your friends out that way." Charon lifted the pole. "Now, if you'll excuse me, I have work to do."

"You still think you're better than everyone else, don't you?" Asmodeus grabbed the end of the raft with his foot, preventing Charon from moving it.

Charon hissed at the Demon. It made him look like a human lizard and it was a little intimidating. "Let go of my vessel!" he roared.

"Your *vessel?*" Asmodeus laughed. "It's a flimsy raft!"

This wasn't going well at all. Before it could escalate further, Kala stepped forward. "Please. We just need to use your *vessel*. Those are the rules. How you wish us to accomplish that is entirely up to you." Kala wished she could have said that nicer, but years of military interrogation techniques had kicked in instead.

"Who are you to threaten me?" Charon straightened his chest in defiance.

Kala had to admit: the guy was one scary looking individual. But, having just fought an army of rotting zombies, one Demon-nymph or whatever he was, didn't scare her half as much as it probably should have. "I'm Kala Hicks slash Atlas slash some kind of Gaia mojo in me, this is Talan. He's a Grigori angel, so you might not want to mess with him, and of course you know Asmodeus, king of the Demons, which aren't *you* half Demon or something? Shouldn't you be doing what he says?"

Charon seemed the most offended by Kala's last statement as that was the only part of her rant he chose to respond to. "He may be king to the Demons, but he is not *my* king! I am the gatekeeper of the Underworld and he doesn't scare me!"

"So, Grigori? Atlas? Gaia? Still a no?" Kala really didn't want to fight Charon, but it was looking as if it was a foregone conclusion.

"No!" Charon shoved Asmodeus's foot off his boat and pushed away from the shore before anyone could stop him.

Kala was about to jump in after him, but Asmodeus warned, "Don't get any water on you! You're a god and he can make you promise something! This is the unbreakable oath river, remember?"

Being Atlas and half Gaia made the River Styx a big no-no for Kala, but she couldn't let Charon go. She needed that boat and Kala wasn't about to let it float away without a fight. Taking a deep breath, Kala ran and jumped with all of her strength. She landed square in the middle of Charon's raft, not a drop on her.

Charon was more baffled than threatened: apparently no one had ever *jumped* on his boat before. Before he could gather his wits, Kala took her opportunity and threw him into the water. With a loud SPLASH, Charon was gone.

She waited a few moments to make sure. After a while, when Charon hadn't re-surfaced, Kala glanced at Talan and Asmodeus with a surprised but happy smile. "That was easy."

Kala took the abandoned pole and began to steer the raft back to the shore to pick up Talan and Asmodeus.

Asmodeus cringed, "I'd watch out if I were you."

BOOM!

Uh, oh.

Out of the river, lifted on a geyser that would rival Old Faithful, Charon stood, pointing at Kala. "You *dare* attack me on my own vessel!"

Kala wished he'd stop using the word *vessel*. She agreed with Asmodeus, this rickety, wooden, moss-covered, floating pile of crap could hardly be called a boat let alone a *vessel*.

Despite the fact that she was now facing a monster on an explosion of water, Kala calmly responded, "I told you: we just need it to get across. I promise I'll give it back to you."

Yeah, that would work.

Charon waved his hands at Kala and she suspected something was about to shoot out of them so she rolled to the side. White fire, like her vision, seared the spot where she had just been standing, burning a hole in the raft.

Screaming in rage, Charon accused, "You ruined my vessel! I *will* destroy you!"

"Technically, you're the one who busted a hole in your little raft here." Kala knew she was making things worse, but couldn't stop herself. "And any chance you could teach me how to do that white fire thing?"

Charon's answer was another blast of white fire. This time, Kala was singed slightly on the shoulder, not being able to roll away in time. Another hole damaged the boat. Oddly, no water was flooding through. Being as it was the boat of the dead, it must be unsinkable.

Dodging both Charon's fire and water from the River Styx was becoming quite the impossible feat and Kala was determined not to get a drop on her. She wasn't even that concerned about Charon using the water against her, forcing her to make an unbreakable oath. It was the thought of Asmodeus using the river that worried her most though. The things he could force her to promise… She shuddered to think where his mind would go.

Kala needed to figure out a plan. And that plan was to get to the other side on this Swiss-cheese boat any way possible, preferably without getting wet.

Ducking and rolling yet again caused another gaping hole in the boat. With each new injury to his raft, Charon screamed as if he had shot himself. "Stand still, *human!*"

He saw her as human. Interesting. So far everything about Charon screamed loner. Even though Kala had told him she was Atlas with a sprinkling of Gaia, he was too self-absorbed to care. He just wanted his boat back and for Kala *and friends* to go away. She'd almost feel sorry for him if… nope, the guy was a baby. She had no sympathy lately for babies.

"If you'd just let us use your damn boat to cross, you wouldn't have to blow holes in it!" Kala shouted, trying to reason with the creature.

Charon screamed in rage, making the grotesque streaks down his face appear even more hideous. "Why can't you just go *away*?!"

"I'm trying! I have fifty feet to go, asshole! Stop attacking me and just push me the rest of the way!" Kala had no patience for stupidity.

"Never!" Charon raged.

"Is it a pre-requisite of the supernatural to be stubborn *and* stupid?" Kala groaned.

This only seemed to anger Charon further. He leapt from the twenty-foot geyser to land in front of Kala with a sneer. "Prepare to die, *human*."

"I'm already dead, moron." Kala punched Charon across the jaw. Normally, she'd go for the privates, but seeing as she wasn't sure a half Demon/half water nymph actually *had* privates, she settled for what was in front of her.

Charon barely moved from her blow.

Ducking, Kala dodged Charon's arms as he tried to grab her. She turned to *Laurel and Hardy* on the shore. "Some help would be good here, guys!"

Not waiting to see what the boys would do, Kala returned her focus to Charon.

When the monster flew at Kala again, she used the force of his jump to gain the upper hand by grabbing his arms and throwing Charon back into the water once more.

This time, though, Kala knew he'd be back.

TUG!

Charon's hands wrapped around her ankles and pulled her down into the river.

The water covered her completely and Kala found she was more panicked about the fact that whoever talked to her first would be able to make her promise anything they wanted, than the thought of drowning.

First things first, though: Charon's hands were still wrapped around her ankles, drawing her down into the depths of the river.

How deep is this thing? Kala wondered in amazement. It felt as if they had been sinking for hours. No matter how hard she kicked, she couldn't break loose from Charon's grip. The need for breath didn't seem to be a problem, she noticed. It wasn't as if she were breathing in water, she just wasn't breathing. In the midst of fighting off the *ferry man* from the Underworld, it was good to note that it appeared as if she could hold her breath indefinitely. Like she had when she had been buried underground. Originally, Kala had thought it was because of her Gaia connection, but apparently, it was more of a "god" thing.

Deeper and deeper.

Kala reached down and tried to pry Charon's hands loose from her ankles, but his fingers might as well have been made of steel.

Seriously! This river had no bottom!

Then, through the murky grayness, Kala saw a gigantic shadow swim in front of her – and Charon let her go. Whatever creature had helped her, Kala was grateful as she began to swim up to the surface. With frightening speed, Charon and the enormous shadow zoomed past, fighting in the water, the shadow yanking Charon like he was a tiny pebble on the shore.

Kala hurried as fast as she could, wanting to see what creature had attacked Charon.

Still far away, she could see up above the perfect square of the raft with its round holes looking like eyes staring down at her. It gave her a surge of inspiration and she pushed harder for the surface.

Almost there.

Just as Kala burst through the surface of the river, Talan's hand reached into the water and dragged her onto the raft.

His eyes met hers and there was an urgency that she'd never seen before. "Kala Hicks, you must make your oath to me." Her heart sank in betrayal. She had never expected that Talan would take advantage of her in this way. It was painful as she felt the power of the River Styx forcing her to agree.

His next words, though, almost made her cry with relief. "You can never make any oath to Asmodeus, Charon or any other supernatural being or human from this moment forward. Do it, Kala, now!"

Kala didn't have a choice. The power of the River Styx grabbed hold of her and made her say the words: "I give you my oath."

It was a horrible sensation being forced to promise something you had no control over, but Talan had known her fears and anticipated them. Feeling a surge of gratefulness, Kala pulled Talan in, embracing him while sprawled on the boat's floor. "Thank you, Talan." Then realizing her soaked body had gotten him wet as well, she returned the favor. "Make your oath to me: No supernatural being or human can force you to make an oath from this moment forward."

His hand brushed her cheek and he smiled, "I give you my oath."

Charon and what Kala could now see was some kind of creature burst through the surface in mid-fight. The beast was at least twenty feet tall and five feet wide. He was basically man-shaped, but his skin was a deep blue with scales the size of plates all over his body and black leathered wings the span of the entire river. Green glowing eyes bore into Charon with hatred. His black taloned claws ripped at Charon's throat, but Charon fought back, trying to pull the creature under the water.

"Is that some kind of river monster?" Kala asked Talan, then searched for Asmodeus. "Where's Asmodeus?"

Talan simply nodded at the blue creature.

Kala stared in shock.

"It's his Demon form," Talan explained, obviously not bothered by the sudden change.

Asmodeus was both terrifying and exotically beautiful, like a human dragon. Kala always knew he was a Demon, but seeing as he always had the same *GQ* model shape, she just assumed that was what he always looked like. She had been naïve, apparently.

Kala stood up, preparing to help Asmodeus in the fight, but before she could leap in, Asmodeus took both his taloned claws and ripped Charon in half.

Each half flew to either side of the river, lifeless.

Standing in shocked silence, Kala could barely register Asmodeus flapping his enormous leathered wings and pushing the raft to the opposite side of the shore.

Once safely on the other side, Asmodeus transformed back into his human body, completely naked.

As Kala continued to stare, Asmodeus smiled his wicked grin. "It seems I need some clothes."

Chapter Fifteen

With a snap of his fingers, Talan had Asmodeus clothed in an instant. Kala didn't think Talan wanted her seeing a naked Asmodeus any more than the Grigori wanted to.

The Demon inspected his t-shirt and jeans with some disdain. "What? Did you get these from The GAP?"

Still reeling from witnessing Asmodeus in Demon form, Kala didn't even crack a smile at his joke. "So…" was all that came out.

Asmodeus was highly amused at Kala's reaction. "Pretty magnificent, aren't I?"

"I was going to go with 'terrifying,' but you definitely got the job done." Kala stepped over the lower half of Charon's body for emphasis. The creature's guts were strewn across the shore, a deep purple against the gray sand. It was mildly repulsive, though Kala had seen worse. Kala had *caused* worse.

"I can live with terrifying." Asmodeus examined his clothes again. "Though I don't think I can live with this polyester blend. It's itchy."

Kala rolled her eyes. "I think I prefer the non-talking Demon form better."

Talan joined in matter-of-factly, "He should stay in his human form if we're to face Rhea."

"I wasn't serious," Kala muttered. Talan took everything so literally. "Do you think she's close?"

Asmodeus closed his eyes, concentrating, then opened them quickly. "She's close, though I can't pinpoint her." He focused on Talan, "She carries one of the Grigori blades. Do you think you can track that?"

Talan simply nodded. His eyes began to glow a soft blue, then flared bright white before finally returning back to normal. "He's right, she *is* close. Follow me." He stepped forward, leading the way.

"Um, guys, shouldn't we have a plan or something?" Kala didn't like entering a fight without a tactical approach if she didn't have to. To be fair, most of Kala's battles had been on the fly, but if she could help it, it would be nice to have *some* kind of strategy.

Talan shrugged, "Rhea already knows we're here, so there's no chance of catching her off-guard. We fight. That's about it."

Kala sighed in resignation. "Good plan."

Asmodeus was still futzing with his t-shirt as if it were crawling with ants. She knew his irritation was more to do with the fact that Talan had supplied the clothes and less with his discomfort, but Kala kept her mouth shut and ignored the Demon's complaining.

Kala also noticed that Asmodeus hadn't even tried to force Kala into making an oath on the River Styx. There was no way he could have known that Talan made that feat impossible, but it showed Kala that Asmodeus could be trusted on some level. She had thought for sure he would make her vow to be his sex slave for all eternity, but was pleasantly surprised that it didn't even look like the thought of using the river had entered his mind.

"Does that mean there's no more Ferry Man in the Underworld?" Kala wondered aloud. Being ripped in two didn't exactly bode a favorable outcome in terms of living.

Asmodeus answered, slightly annoyed, "That lizard? He'll be back. Hades has probably pieced that creep together already. Charon always was one of his favorites."

"So some of you supernatural beings can die, but some can't?" Kala saw this as an opportunity to possibly learn a few things about her new world.

Talan responded, "No one really knows. We weren't even sure Atlas was dead until you confirmed it."

"What about me? I'm part human," Kala asked.

Asmodeus nodded, "But you're more god now than human. I'd say that puts you in the hard-to-kill category. Being *immortal* isn't literal, not if there's someone stronger than you."

"But Cronus and Hades? Can they die?" Kala kept thinking of her vision. The thought of putting her enemies in a coma, strapped to one of Turner's machines for all time, was harsh by anyone's standards.

Asmodeus laughed, "That's pretty specific."

Kala didn't say anything. She hoped neither one of them would draw any conclusions about her query.

But Asmodeus shrugged, "No, Cronus definitely can't die. And Hades? He's the ruler of the Underworld. Why do you think Cronus put him to sleep? If he could have done so he would have killed Hades and Zeus and been done with this little family squabble."

Hades had been asleep for 2,000 years and now Kala was basically going to do the same thing to him again – but forever this time, although, Cronus probably had intended Hades to *sleep* forever as well. Still, it didn't make her feel any better.

"So how do we defeat *any* of them?" Kala asked.

Talan responded first, "The Grigori plan on making them call a truce. Or locking them in another dimension. It's up to them, really."

"Oh, gee, that sounds easy," Kala countered sarcastically. But it *did* make her feel better. Locking them in another dimension was the equivalent of putting them in a coma. Wasn't it? They'd be trapped, but conscious, awake, able to live… She brushed the nagging thoughts from her mind. Kala never thought she'd feel bad about doing anything to Cronus, but those machines…

As they walked, the terrain changed drastically. It went from shrubs and tree patches, to full sized boulders and rolling hills. Kala could see why Rhea chose this area: it was full of hiding places. Slipping into combat mentality, Kala kept her eyes peeled for any movement.

So far, nothing.

Kala was about to order the three of them to split up to cover more territory when a familiar figure stepped out in front of them.

Rhea.

She did not look happy.

Her eyes only met Kala's, as if Asmodeus and Talan weren't there. "Hades told me how you managed to break the spell of the River Lethe."

"And how I was kind enough not to consume him?" Kala put as much confidence in her voice as possible. The truth was, she had no idea if she was a match for Rhea or not. The Titan was Cronus's better half, and mother to half the Olympians. The woman had to be strong. At least Kala knew her devouring-mojo was still in action down in the Underworld. She didn't want to use it for fear of not being able to stop herself, but she trusted Talan and Asmodeus wouldn't let it go that far.

Rhea was careful how she phrased her next sentence. "Was it kindness or lack of control that you failed to consume him?"

Kala didn't let Rhea's insult affect her in the least. "For your sake, you better hope it was kindness. You wouldn't want me to *lose* control, would you?"

Rhea wasn't fazed. "I think I can handle a *thing* like you. My son is weak from sleeping so long. I won't be such easy prey."

And… now what?

Kala tried to discreetly search for the Olympians she had come to rescue, but with all the rocks and hills around they could be anywhere.

At least there weren't any mystically-powered rivers. That was one less thing to worry about.

The situation now, though, was becoming awkward at this point. After all their fronting no one was saying anything. It reminded Kala of a spaghetti western showdown without guns.

Kala had to break the silence. "Are we going to fight or something?"

"Your move," Rhea prodded.

As a sniper, Kala wished she was perched on some nearby rock with one of her rifles right now, with her super-aim skill that appeared to have been enhanced by becoming Atlas. She would definitely have made Rhea think twice about messing with her.

A sudden thought occurred to Kala.

Her super-aim skill hadn't just been about being able to hit a fly on the top of the Washington Monument (which was awesome), it was about the fact that she could see that far. Kala could use that now to find the Olympians. To do that she needed to jump to higher ground.

She cast a brief glance at Talan. He nodded. Talan might not know what Kala was planning to do, but he understood she needed him to create a distraction.

Kala made sure Rhea's eyes were on her, she used the good old-fashioned *human* technique of body-checking the Titan, feinting multiple frontal attacks. Kala almost wanted to laugh when Rhea fell for it each time, darting a foot or two backward in anticipation of Kala attacking.

Talan took advantage of Rhea's focus on Kala and shot out a wave of black fire at the Titan.

How many colors of fire are there? Kala wondered as she leapt behind the largest boulder she could find. As she climbed the craggy rock, she saw the advantage of black, as Talan's fire wrapped around Rhea like a dark fog, preventing the Titan from seeing in front of her.

Catching on to the diversion plan, Asmodeus joined the fight. He screeched his terrible scream and Rhea covered her ears from the sound.

Rhea shouted, "I will not lower myself to fight with a Malak and a

Demon!" She threw her hands out to rid herself of Asmodeus and Talan, but the black fire prevented her from aiming correctly. She apparently didn't know Talan was a Grigori, which was only to their advantage. Malaks were angels, but not nearly as powerful as the Grigori.

Asmodeus grabbed a softball sized rock and chucked it at Rhea's face, hitting her square in the nose. The Titan reeled back from the shock of the blow.

The Demon shrugged, "Rocks work too."

Talan did not look impressed. "Something a little more powerful, please?"

While the Hardy Boys had Rhea covered for the moment, Kala reached the top of the boulder. Taking a deep breath, she concentrated her eyesight as she had that day with Talan and the fly.

Sounds of battle threatened to break her focus, but Kala forced herself to ignore them and slowly rotated her body, making her eyes take in a panoramic view of the surroundings. Within seconds Kala saw further than her human eyes could ever have seen, miles and miles in every direction. She searched every rock, cranny, hill, tree or bush until…

Kala saw them.

The Olympians were huddled over a campfire like vagrants over an oil barrel. Kala's Atlas memory recognized them immediately: Poseidon, Hera, Hestia and Demeter. The last four of the Cronus and Rhea hook-up. She had no idea where the rest of the Olympians were (i.e. Zeus's brood, the god certainly did get around) but Rhea had made it quite clear that Zeus's kids were not her problem. She was only concerned about her own children. (Though, from the look of them, it didn't seem like she cared all that much.) Even from this distance, the Olympians appeared weak and downtrodden, all hunched backs and bowed heads.

Their location was less than a mile away behind a boulder almost the size of the one Kala stood on.

Olympians found, the Grigori blade that Rhea possessed now became Kala's first priority, since it was the reason the Olympians were weak and stranded in this place. If she could steal the knife away from Rhea, then maybe the gods could regain some of their strength to help in their escape.

Kala just needed to find it…

There it was.

Rhea had resorted to making a swing at Talan with the knife. Apparently, though, the black fire was harder to extinguish than the Titan had anticipated. Not bad for a "Malak."

Asmodeus jumped directly in front of Rhea, attacking with his Demon strength, then leapt away before she could swipe him with the blade.

It was time for Kala to join the fray.

The boulder was twenty feet high, so jumping didn't seem like a feasible option. As quickly as she could manage, Kala clambered down.

Asmodeus showed up next to her. "So, the blade, right? We need it?"

Kala nodded, appreciating the fact that Asmodeus already knew what was needed to escape this place. "Rhea has the Olympians hidden a mile north of here."

"Considering the ocean is our way out of this place, all we need is Poseidon. The others will be useless." Asmodeus flinched when Talan was almost nicked by Rhea's swing.

"Poseidon will be pretty useless if we don't get that blade back," Kala answered, stating the obvious.

"Plan?" Asmodeus eyed her hopefully.

"Get the knife."

"Good plan." Asmodeus took a giant leap. He landed directly in front of Rhea and sucker punched the Titan. Rhea flew back ten feet, almost dropping the Grigori dagger.

Kala took her shot and ran over to the fallen Titan, grabbing at the knife.

Rhea was too quick. She rolled away while trying to swipe the weapon at Kala.

Contorting her body backward, Kala was fast enough to evade the blow.

Impressed at the Titan's apparent fighting skills, Kala relied on her modern day combat training to help her gain the upper hand.

Rhea acted as if she were in a bar brawl, all instinct, no schooling. Kala was good at both being as she used to have a bar fight almost nightly – plus her two black belts, in Aikido and Tae Kwon Do. Fighting was all about knowing and learning about your opponent.

Disarming Rhea was the goal, but she held onto the Grigori knife like it was her lifeline. Maybe if Kala could turn the blade on Rhea…

It would require hand-to-hand battle, but Kala had no choice.

Baiting Rhea, Kala yelled, "For someone who claimed a Demon and a Malak weren't even worth your effort, you can't even manage to hurt one of them!"

Rhea screamed in outrage, "They're like gnats! Too small to swat, but don't do any damage."

Kala tilted her head, disagreeing, "You *did* just fly back ten feet. I've never seen a gnat do that."

Rhea did what Kala hoped.

She charged.

Using Rhea's momentum, Kala easily flipped the Titan on her back. In a quick succession of hand movements, Kala had Rhea pinned to the ground.

"Grab the knife!" Kala shouted to either Asmodeus or Talan.

Asmodeus leapt in front of her with a smile and reached down to grab the blade…

A sharp pain hit Kala's side.

When she blinked her eyes, Rhea was somehow standing next to her, holding the bloody Grigori dagger, grinning triumphantly.

Blood poured out of Kala's gut and the magic of the knife flushed through her, weakening every muscle in her body.

"You fight like a human not a deity," Rhea scolded.

Asmodeus kneeled next to Kala instead of attacking Rhea, his hand resting on her wound. Asmodeus healed her immediately, at least the bleeding part. There was nothing he could do about the magic of the blade, though. Recovering from that only required time. Being officially *dead*, Kala wasn't sure if it would take longer for that process to happen.

And time was something she didn't have.

It was strange that Talan wasn't instantly by her side. He was normally so overprotective, like Derek. The Grigori had made a habit of putting himself in peril just to see if Kala was okay.

Meanwhile, Rhea was into the bragging thing, laughing at Kala's struggle to stand. "Even if you had Atlas's full power, you'd still be nothing to me, *thing*. You and your Demons and Malaks can buzz around me like flies, but that's all you'll ever be! I am the mother of the Olympians! Malaks and Demons are just pawns. I am the queen!" Rhea loved hearing herself speak, which fortunately only meant more time for Kala to think of a way to get that knife. Rhea continued to gloat, "You may have a piece of Gaia in you, but it means nothing! I will *never* be afraid of you, *thing. I* am the devourer! Your powers are immune to me!"

"Well, yeah, now that you took them away," Kala had to interject. Though a part of her was relieved she didn't have to test that theory.

"Even if I hadn't…" Rhea began.

"*Even if I hadn't…*" Kala mimicked.

Rhea stood there, stunned. Apparently childish mimicking hadn't been invented 2,000 years ago when she volunteered to slash her kids down here in the Underworld. The Titan didn't know how to respond.

Physically, Kala had never felt worse in her life, not even when she'd had the stomach flu in basic training for three straight days of mud runs. Mentally, she kept her wits about her, trying to see any angle she could.

Rhea finally responded, "I'm not stupid. You'll probably find some way to weasel out of the blade's weakening spell. So just to be certain…"

Without warning, Rhea swung down with the dagger.

Kala was too weak to fight it off. Asmodeus was suddenly in front of her, trying to block the knife from hitting Kala. The dagger sliced his forearm to the bone.

"Damn, it," Asmodeus grumbled. Now, neither one of them could use their powers.

It only excited Rhea. "Two down. Now where is that little Malak?"

"Right behind you, Titan," Talan's voice boomed with power.

Kala looked over to see a line of at least twenty Grigori facing Rhea.

Kala's heart soared when Owen stepped forward from the middle of the line-up, rage in his voice. "And we're not Malaks, we're Grigori."

Rhea's face turned ashen in fear.

Kala never got tired of seeing that kind of reaction.

Chapter Sixteen

Owen's hands glowed purple, bright against the gray landscape.

Kala had never seen him so angry, not even when she had snuck the car out and drove it to the beach when she was fifteen. He had definitely been irked then – but now? She could almost see his eyes turning red.

"Get away from my daughter!" Owen commanded.

Rhea was still reeling from the fact that she was now facing a phalanx of Grigori. "I didn't believe it when Cronus told me," she gasped. "You're not supposed to exist anymore."

Owen apparently wasn't really in the mood to hear Rhea monologue: he pushed a stream of purple fire straight into her chest. She screamed in anguish as the fire wrapped itself around her arms and legs until Rhea was hog-tied with the flames.

Asmodeus couldn't resist. He pushed her, making her fall hard on the ground.

The more the Titan struggled, the more flames were created. Within moments, Kala stared at a purple cocoon made of fire, Rhea's screams silenced by the encasement.

Owen reached Kala's side, hugging her tightly. "Are you okay?"

Her movements were sluggish from the power of the blade, but having Owen's arms around her instantly made Kala feel better. "I am now." They pulled away and Kala saw the rest of the Grigori ready for action. Rotoph, Ashliel and Antel were among them, already walking over to greet her with Talan by their side. This group was becoming Kala's Grigori core of five. "How did you guys get down here? Talan said it was hard enough for him to get in here alone."

Ashliel answered, "The Grigori united and we battled against Cronus and the other Titans. Zeus punched a hole in the Underworld's protections and with Talan's help we managed to bring in twenty-three Grigori."

It suddenly made sense where Talan had disappeared to. "What about Zeus?" Kala wanted to know why Rhea's favorite son hadn't bothered to show up for his siblings' breakout.

"Zeus and Hephaestus didn't want to risk entering Hades's domain," Antel answered. "They still don't trust their brother."

Owen added, "And I don't trust Zeus and Hephaestus, so it worked out perfectly." He surveyed the area. "Do you know where Poseidon and the others are?"

"A mile north of here. They don't look like they're in good shape." Kala motioned to her weakened state. "In fact, they look a lot like Asmodeus and I do right now."

Owen glanced at Rotoph who nodded.

The Grigori appeared to be in a great mood. Kala figured it was because he was being let into the inner circle more and more. The fact that he was the one responsible for their imprisonment was something Kala wasn't sure any of the Grigori would forgive, but since he was also the one responsible for helping them escape, they seemed to be giving him a second chance.

Rotoph pulled out a red marble the size of a tennis ball. Its surface was covered in runes similar to the ones etched on the Grigori blade. He showed it off with a smile. "A little remedy for your ails," he said roguishly.

Being that Rotoph was the one who created the Grigori-power-sucking-blades with Hephaestus, it was one more thing on the long list of things he had to make up for. He placed the ball-like device in Kala's hand.

She was surprised at how light it was. Kala had expected it to feel like a paperweight from the look of the marble-like material it was made from. A moment after the red ball touched her skin, the runes flared a bright yellow.

As if downing five Red Bulls in a row, Kala's body surged with energy. She was more than fixed…

Kala was *alive*.

No longer in the muted gray tones of the dead, Kala was once again in full color.

Rotoph grinned in what Kala realized was an attempt at humbleness, but he had too much of an ego and failed miserably. "I added that resurrection rune just for you."

He might as well have winked like a used car salesman, but Kala didn't care. She felt so good, so alive, that she hugged Rotoph, which shocked everyone, including Rotoph.

"You're welcome," Rotoph said as he pulled out of the embrace. Looking down at the red device, he nodded toward Asmodeus. "May I?"

"Please do." Asmodeus's whole demeanor had perked up at seeing Kala cured of the Grigori blade's effects. Kala handed the ball over to Asmodeus and watched as the runes came to life. His face flushed from rejuvenation and the wound on his forearm sealed shut. "Much better, thank you."

No one replied back but Kala hadn't expected them to. They tolerated Asmodeus because Kala had some kind of strange relationship with him. If she let Owen have his way, he'd have sent Asmodeus back to the 5th

Level of Hell and thrown away the key. After Kala had set him free, Owen left any and all punishments of Asmodeus up to his daughter.

She had to give the Demon props for standing between her and the dagger and taking the blow. Frankly, Kala only found out less than two weeks ago that Demons, Malaks and gods existed, so she didn't really know all that much about their true natures. Being raised in a world where people's faith made it black and white – Demons were bad and Angels were good – Kala admittedly had a bit of a bias when it came to Demons. Though pretty much most of them had been dicks who wanted the world to end, and Asmodeus wasn't much better in terms of his philosophy of life, he *had* proven to be a friend to her. At this point that was all that mattered to Kala.

Asmodeus handed the device back to Rotoph. The Demon looked slightly uncomfortable standing among a large group of Grigori, especially with a writhing Rhea-cocoon at their feet.

Owen glanced down at Rhea. "That fire won't last long. We have to make this quick."

Kala decided to take the reins. "Let's get that device to the Olympians and find our way out of here then."

Talan was the first to respond, following Kala at her side while she led the army of Grigori through the Underworld. She kept her guard up. Rhea might be taken care of, but there was still Hades to contend with and Kala somehow doubted he'd let them escape without a fight. At least she had more back up this time.

Without incident, however, Kala and the others arrived at the Olympian's hiding spot. They were even more downtrodden than Kala had seen from a distance. Poseidon stared at the small gray campfire as if it possessed all of life's secrets, not even noticing the large group of Grigori suddenly standing before him. Hera, Demeter and Hestia at least acknowledged their presence by slowly glancing up at them. The Olympians' skin was so pale it was almost gray, like the rest of the Underworld, their clothes ragged. Kala noticed that they still managed to look like hungry supermodels though. Shocker. The supernatural world tended to produce ridiculously gorgeous specimens.

Examining them more closely, Kala saw the slashes on their arms that their mother had given to them over the years. It was no surprise that Poseidon had almost twice as many as the others. According to Zeus, Poseidon was the strongest of his brothers, so it made sense that he had probably tried to break free from time to time. Rhea would have had to deal with him much harsher than the others.

Hera was the first to speak, her words slow and forced as if she hadn't said anything in a long time. "Who…are… you?"

Kala chose to be the voice of the group. "We're the ones getting you out of here."

Hera's eyes lit up, though her speech was still sluggish, as if drunk. "But we're so weak."

"Not for long." Kala nodded to Rotoph. He stepped forward with the red-runed ball, placing it in Hera's hand.

The magic of Rotoph's cure took longer with the Olympians than it had with Kala and Asmodeus, probably because they'd been slashed with the blade for so long. But when all four gods were back to themselves, Kala stared at them in wonder.

Hera was the most beautiful woman she had ever seen, starting with her with long, flowing, black hair and dark black eyes to match. Hera's skin was a golden brown, bestowing an almost Egyptian look about her. Demeter and Hestia were also stunning, though not in the same way as Hera. Demeter was of smaller stature, with long red hair and crystal blue eyes, her small nose and freckled face made Kala almost think of her as human, she was so cute. Hestia was long: long face, long nose, long limbs. Out of the three girls Kala found Hestia the most interesting looking, but knowing that Zeus had hooked up only with Hera and Demeter simply solidified Zeus's shallowness. And they were his *sisters*.

Kala planned on never telling any of the Titans or Olympians she was their half-sister/aunt for fear of them coming on to *her*.

Poseidon was last to rejuvenate and his recovery took the longest. Watching as life was given back to him, Kala was stunned at seeing the Olympian. Poseidon looked the way Kala imagined a god to look. No more of good-looking humans in suits like Zeus or Cronus. Poseidon was almost seven feet tall and all muscle. His body was sculpted as if he had been chiseled in marble and his skin had a bluish teal tint to it that only emphasized that Poseidon belonged to the ocean. But it was his eyes that affected Kala the most: a deep green that bore into Kala as Poseidon stared down at her.

The ocean god sighed in contentment at being fully restored, and then examined all the people standing before him. "Where is Zeus?" he asked carefully.

Owen answered, "He was worried Hades would trap him down here with you, so *we* came to help."

Poseidon placed a hand on Owen's shoulder with affection. "It's good to see you, Owen."

Owen smiled. "You too, my friend."

Kala knew she shouldn't be surprised that Owen and Poseidon knew each other, but it just struck her as odd, especially since the Olympians had tried to take the Grigori down all those years ago. It just showed that some things in the supernatural world were simply about power and not personal relationships. But even stranger for Kala was remembering growing up with what she thought was an ex-Navy Seal, living a normal life, now to see him as a Grigori warrior pal-ing it up with the God of the Ocean? It made her head hurt.

Owen motioned to the east. "We'll have to leave through there."

Poseidon nodded in understanding. "It leads to the ocean, yes." He surveyed the area. "Where's mother?"

"I have her wrapped in Grigori fire for the time being, but she's strong." The urgency in Owen's voice was enough to put Poseidon in action.

Poseidon turned to Hera, Hestia and Demeter, "Sisters, let's leave this place."

Demeter paused, unsure. "But Brother, this could be a trap. We *were* responsible for imprisoning the Grigori. They could be leading us to our death."

Kala understood Demeter's hesitation. Supernatural politics didn't make much sense to her, either, but they needed to get out of there. "I get where you're coming from, but we're running out of time and standing around a campfire getting stabbed by your mommy every hour has to be better than death."

Demeter eyed Kala carefully, as if trying to translate her words. Eventually, she nodded. "I will trust my brother's decision."

Poseidon shared one more look with Owen, as if weighing whether or not to give into Demeter's warning. After a moment he began to walk east. "We're leaving here now."

Everyone appeared to agree with this consensus and the large group moved east with Poseidon.

Hera turned her head, sensing something that wasn't there, then said, "Hades is back." She glanced up at her brother, "Do you think he's on our side?"

Poseidon barely shook his head in the negative. "If I know my brother, he'll side with mother."

Demeter was incredulous, "Even after being put to sleep for 2,000 years? And after his sisters and brother have been tortured just as long? I can't believe it."

Hestia gave her sister a look that suggested Demeter was insane. "You can't? You *do* know Hades, right? He'd never go against mother."

Kala didn't want to join in the family squabble, but she thought she'd give them the information she had. "Last time I saw him, he was definitely on Team Rhea. He tried to stop us by setting an army of the dead on us."

Hera snorted in irritation. "Hades is a fool and always has been." Then she focused on Kala, curious. "I recognize the Grigori and the king of Demons, but who are you? You seem *human*." The idea obviously confused her. "And you're *alive*," she added even more befuddled.

All the Olympians' eyes were on Kala. She suddenly felt exposed. Kala would never tell them that she was half-Gaia, only Talan knew the truth of that, so she decided to go with what everyone else knew. "I *am* human. I got roped into the Atlas gig by accident and somehow I ate him." That wasn't vague at all.

Owen chimed in at their shocked faces, "I raised her, though she didn't know I was Grigori. Kala has always been special."

Such a dad.

Hera wasn't letting it go, though. "*How* did you eat him?"

Kala shrugged. "Apparently, I have some Gaia-mojo inside me, but I really don't know for sure. It seems to be a skill I have when my emotions run high. I almost consumed Cronus twice and Hades, too, when he turned my dead boyfriend into a puppet."

Hera and the others kept to themselves after that. Kala could tell that they were processing the information and rating her threa*t level.*

Poseidon was the first to talk, "You were raised by Owen?"

"Yes." It was hard for Kala not to feel as if she was on trial.

Poseidon nodded, though, as if coming to some sort of conclusion in his head. "Then you're trustworthy." And that was all he said.

As far as deities went, Kala decided she liked this crew the best. Of course, she hadn't seen them in a fight yet, but it already seemed they were a notch above Zeus and Cronus's style of the *nanny-nanny-poopy-pants* variety.

Suddenly Kala was flying through the air at lightning speed, then slamming hard against a boulder.

Ouch.

Speaking of fights.

Kala was on her feet, whirling around to see whom her enemy was.

Rhea and Hades.

Apparently, they had targeted Kala and Owen as Kala saw that her father had been thrown against a boulder a few rocks down from her.

Take out the most dangerous first, she guessed.

Not that they needed to.

Kala almost gulped when she saw hundreds of dead soldiers charging the Grigori and the Olympians.

It was already a full out battle.

Rhea and Hades were busy with Asmodeus and Talan fighting side by side. Something Kala would probably never get used to. It still amazed her that Hades could puppet so many dead bodies without having to concentrate directly on them. The zombies fought as if they had minds of their own. The Grigori were making quick work of them, but the dead's sheer numbers kept the battle going – and their resilience to losing body parts.

Owen joined her side.

Kala instructed, "You take Rhea. I take Hades."

Her father nodded, already in combat-mode. Not only was he a Grigori, he was also a Navy Seal and Kala put more value in the latter at the moment.

Poseidon had joined in Talan's fight against Hades while Asmodeus tried to take down Rhea. A small part of Kala felt bad for Owen as he'd now have to fight by Asmodeus's side, but she didn't have time to worry about her adoptive father's feelings.

Hades was the one that controlled the army of dead and Kala needed to take down the source.

Just as Kala and Owen arrived, Hera and Demeter launched themselves at their mother, clawing and ripping at Rhea, taking out a couple millennia of rage.

But no matter how many supernatural beings came at mother and son, nothing seemed to affect them. It was as if they were protected by some kind of force field cased around their skin.

Owen shot out his purple fire at Rhea once more, but this time she laughed and swatted it away as if it were nothing. It didn't stop Owen, though; he jumped into the fight using his black fire to try and blind

Rhea. But nothing anyone did was having any affect.

Before Kala jumped in herself she yelled her observation over the chaos. "They're protected by something!"

No one acknowledged her, too wrapped up in tearing the enemy to shreds.

Kala knew she was alone on this one, but her knowledge of the supernatural was weak. How would she be able to figure out how they were shielding themselves? Wracking her Atlas brain was no help, big surprise. The Titan had stayed hidden most of his life, like a sniveling coward, so he almost knew less than she did about Hades and the Underworld.

Then something the Grigori angel Ashliel had said to her echoed in her brain: *You do know the Grigori helped create the Underworld.*

He may know something.

Kala fought her way to Ashliel's side. He was at the center of the army of the dead, throwing black fire from his hands, popping zombie heads off like dandelions.

When Ashliel saw her he nodded toward Hades, yelling over the mayhem. "Shouldn't you be playing with the big boys!?"

Kala had to shout back as she shoved and tossed soldiers aside to reach him. "Rhea and Hades are protected! You said the Grigori helped build this place. Any ideas on how to *un-protect* them?"

Ashliel continued to make heads fly as if he was having fun doing it, but his expression was lost in thought. Taking down any attackers that stepped too close to Kala, she batted them away in annoyance.

Finally, Ashliel nodded his head. "They're using 'The Veil' as their own force field."

"I'm sorry: *The Veil?*" Kala had no idea what the Grigori was talking about.

"What separates the living from the dead. The Veil was here long before Cronus's protection spells. They probably figure they'll finish with us quickly and restore what damage they may have done to The Veil after they're done," Ashliel grunted as a zombie lunged at him. He made quick work of the corpse, lighting the whole rotting body with black fire.

Kala kicked a dead soldier into a swarm of incoming zombies, giving her a little more time. "So what are you saying? We take down this *Veil* or something?"

Ashliel couldn't hide the horror from his face. "I don't think *that's* a good idea. Removing the one barrier between the living and the dead would have colossal effects on the *living* world. But we might be able to disrupt it, long enough to capture Hades and Rhea and make our escape."

Looking back at Rhea and Hades and their lack of injuries, made the decision a no-brainer. "We have to try," Kala said desperately.

Ashliel nodded and signaled to Antel, who wasn't far off. The female angel was holding her own against the zombie army, but even in the chaos she turned at Ashliel's call. He pointed up, shouting, "Hades and Rhea are using The Veil for protection!"

The female Grigori instantly knew his intentions and nodded. Antel motioned to five Grigori, and then to Kala, yelling over the noise of battle: "We Grigori have to combine our powers to do this, so you'll have to keep the dead off of us. No distractions."

Since Antel was a distance away, Kala stayed with Ashliel and two of the Grigori while the other three set up a perimeter around Antel.

Giant beams of yellow fire burst out of Ashliel and Antel's chests, shooting straight up to the Underworld's gray sky.

It was hard enough fighting off the army of dead before this started happening, but the instant the yellow fire hit the wall of the Underworld, the zombies flew into a frenzy.

Kala could see Hades and Rhea scream in panic at seeing the columns of flames. *They know what it means*, Kala realized with certainty.

And they weren't about to let it happen.

Corpses climbed over each other, trying to reach Antel or Ashliel. Kala fought with every ounce of strength she could muster, tearing off legs, arms, and heads, anything that would slow the attack.

Talan and Owen caught on before the others and charged their way toward Antel and Ashliel to try to protect them. The other Grigori followed their leads. Before Kala knew it, her small circle of three had become an army of ten. The other half of the Grigori did the same for Antel. Even Asmodeus was quickly by Kala's side, screeching and causing the zombies to cover their ears long enough for Kala to decapitate them.

The only ones who didn't abandon fighting Hades and Rhea were the Olympians. For them it was personal. But as the fire began to turn a bright white Hades and Rhea knew they were in trouble. Turning away from the fight, the duo tried to shake off Poseidon and his sisters.

Kala heard Ashliel's voice scream, "NOW! OWEN! THE PURPLE FIRE!"

Owen's hands shot out and Hades and Rhea were encapsulated with the purple flames of their prison. Within seconds of struggling to free themselves, they were locked in the Grigori cocoon once more.

All at once, the zombie army dropped, their puppet master no longer connected to them.

The white fire came flying down to disappear in both Antel and Ashliel's chests.

From the deafening roar of combat to the eerie silence of the Underworld was jarring in its juxtaposition.

Poseidon was the first to recover. "Let's move."

Following in line, Kala, Asmodeus, the Grigori and the Olympians went with Poseidon to what Kala could only refer to as the "Ocean Exit," since no one seemed to want to elaborate.

At a spot that didn't seem different from any other place in the landscape, Poseidon stopped. He turned to Kala, "You're the only one with human in you. Can you breathe underwater? I can give you a second layer of skin that will make it possible for you."

Looking around, Kala realized she was the only one who wasn't *all* supernatural, which meant she could potentially drown. But, after her experience in the River Styx, she knew she'd be okay. Shaking her head, Kala responded, "I'm alright. I was able to hold my breath indefinitely in the River Styx."

Poseidon nodded in acknowledgement and turned to the sky. "Get ready to swim."

Talan was by Kala's side and said to the group, "As soon as we're out of the Underworld we can teleport back to the Compound."

Since some of the members of their team had no idea what *the Compound* was, everyone had to hold hands.

As serious as the moment was, Kala couldn't help but wonder if they were breaking some kind of world record for the most people teleporting.

Poseidon locked hands with the end of the train and used his free hand to perform the spell that would let them escape. Saying words Kala barely recognized, she didn't have time to wonder what they meant.

The sky of the Underworld cracked and broke as if made of glass. A giant tidal wave of water rushed through at terrifying speed, slamming down on the small group. It felt as if a skyscraper had landed on Kala's head, but being more than human made it possible for her to survive.

It took a moment for Kala to appreciate the fact that the water was being dumped into an invisible cylinder the circumference of her party size.

Poseidon had punched a hole in the Underworld directly under the ocean.

Once the tube was filled, the water pressure subsided and the army swam up through the opening.

The darkness of the ocean was strangely vibrant and colorful compared to the grayness of the Underworld. Though Kala had already been resurrected, she felt a flush of energy soar through her as she swam in the icy waters. The sensation was invigorating.

Kala was on earth again.

She was home.

Chapter Seventeen

Talan didn't waste anytime. As soon as their army had passed the borders of the Underworld, Talan tried to teleport them but…

Nothing.

Being in the ocean, Kala knew the only way to communicate was through telepathy. *What's happening?* She asked Talan.

His response was immediate. *Something is blocking us from teleporting.*

Cronus, Kala guessed.

The large group kept swimming, hands still clasped together. Kala thought what an odd sight it would be to see a couple dozen people holding hands in a line at the bottom of the ocean.

Luckily, just like when she was immersed in the River Styx, Kala was able to hold her breath endlessly. Not even the water pressure bothered her. She may be part human, but being Gaia's daughter obviously protected her from "science."

Rotoph! Kala called out. *You're the teleportation-blocker expert. Do something.*

I'm… trying, Rotoph responded. His voice sounded strange, as if he was rattled by something more than being stuck at the bottom of the ocean. Then he added, *If it's Cronus, he's hiding himself well.*

Or someone *else* was hiding him, most likely Oceanus.

Kala mentally prepared herself to face Oceanus. At least they had Poseidon with them this time. She hoped that would make a difference if they had to fight.

Then she saw them.

All of them.

Eleven Titans. Only Rhea was missing, trapped in the Underworld with her son.

Oceanus was front and center.

Kala felt very small in that moment.

Even Poseidon looked dwarfed compared to the twenty-foot Titans. Apparently they could grow in size, Kala observed with annoyance. Cronus was no longer in his sharp black suit. Like his other siblings, he now wore a traditional Greek tunic embroidered with designs and symbols, though the details were lost in the ocean darkness.

Swimming in a group with the Grigori, the Olympians and Asmodeus didn't give Kala the confidence she thought it would. Her Atlas memories must have been infiltrating themselves into her consciousness because seeing the giant Titans in front of her actually made her afraid.

But it also made her angry.

After everything Kala had just been through in the Underworld, to be stopped by the Titan Brigade was… annoying. Why couldn't they just mind their own business? Kala was losing her sense of guilt about her mission to trap Cronus by the second. In fact, she was almost looking forward to it.

Cronus spoke to them all through telepathy, *Surrender now and we won't harm you.*

Owen's voice was low and angry in Kala's head as he responded to Cronus, *You are not capable of harming us, Cronus. Not any more.*

Kala wondered if Rotoph had more than one magic red-ball-of-renewal for any supernatural being that was sliced by a Grigori blade. She also wondered if at any point they were going to stop holding hands. The action was bordering on absurd considering the circumstances.

We'll see, Cronus answered with venom.

Oceanus sent hundreds of spinning whirlpools in Kala's direction.

Bracing for impact, Kala released her hands from Talan and the other Grigori angel next to her.

Before the whirlpools hit their party, Poseidon swam faster than any fish or vehicle Kala had ever seen. His body absorbed all of the swirling drills of water, then he pushed back with his hands creating a vortex so large it looked like it would consume all eleven Titans in one blow.

But Oceanus was ready for the attack, he held out his arms and the vortex dispersed into harmless bubbles.

Kala had the sneaking suspicion this battle would take a while if left to the two ocean gods to fight it out.

Though no Titan, Grigori or god had full power when immersed in water, that didn't stop them from joining in the fray.

Green, purple, white and black fire burned through the ocean's depths on both sides.

Not one to be overshadowed, Asmodeus turned into his true demon form matching the Titan's size, his deep blue scales reflecting all raging fires around him. Using his black leathery wings like fins, Asmodeus took on Cronus himself and the two of them tumbled further down into the ocean's depths.

Kala had no idea how to access her fire skills, though from her Atlas vision, she knew she'd be learning soon. Since no one seemed likely to offer her a tutorial at the moment, however, Kala had to do her own thing.

This was becoming an impossible task, though: Poseidon and Oceanus were moving the water surrounding the battling groups at impossible speeds and force. Kala was hit by an underwater wave the size of a truck, knocking her backwards. She fought off motion sickness, almost gasping for air out of habit. Luckily, she remembered where she was, but it was difficult holding her breath when being bounced around so violently.

What was becoming more and more obvious to Kala was the fact that she had no idea what she could do. Brute strength seemed pointless since it was almost impossible to throw a punch in water, fire was out because she had no idea how to use it, and the dome-of-air trick she'd used before would hold Poseidon back as well. And since Poseidon seemed to be the only one doing any damage to the Titans, Kala didn't want to ruin a good thing.

So, she ended up treading water, watching the battle unfold, feeling completely useless.

Surprising her more was the fact that with all the brouhaha over how much of a threat Kala was, none of the Titans were paying her any mind. Not even Cronus appeared interested in a confrontation; he was too focused on trying to annihilate Asmodeus. It only showed Kala that this war was ancient. Ancient and petty. There were thousands of years of resentment between all parties: The Grigori for their imprisonment, the Titans for the betrayal of their children, the Olympians for the betrayal of their parents and Asmodeus for… well… for being his Demon-y self. The bitterness ran deep and the human part of Kala wanted nothing to do with it. Ironically, neither did her Atlas side.

Think strategically…

The Atlas-mission countdown clock was ticking and Kala knew they had to get back to the Compound. The only way to do that was to teleport. Cronus was preventing it. Rotoph was the only one who could stop him.

Trying to find Rotoph amongst the chaos was a challenge. It was only after scanning every silhouette and supernatural being through the darkness of the ocean that, on the brink of failure, Kala finally spotted the Grigori. Rotoph was fighting off Atlas's father, Iapetus, along with Clymene and Theia. Three-on-one. These Titans definitely knew Rotoph was the key to their escape plan.

Kala swam through the blazing fire that lit up the water in small spurts of colors. No one seemed to notice her as she made her way toward Rotoph.

As she neared the Grigori, though, his voice called out to her inside her brain, *Kala, leave me. I can take care of this.* Rotoph's voice was insistent.

You look like you could use some help. Kala wasn't sure why the Grigori would refuse her aid.

Rotoph barely evaded the yellow fire bursting from Iapetus's hands as he swam to the right. *I mean it, Kala. I've run from my destiny long enough. It's time.*

Kala remembered what Rotoph had said to her once: *I had a destiny I didn't want to fulfill, so I banished my own people.* She had always wondered what he meant by that. What had caused him to work with the Titans to imprison all his brothers and sisters? Kala was about to find out.

I find it hard to believe that fighting Titans in the ocean was the reason you sent your people to prison. Kala ducked as a beam of yellow fire was chucked at her by Theia. Kala had been noticed at this point and the Titan looked more than happy to try and take her down.

Rotoph sent his own bolt of blue fire at all three Titans, but only one shot found its mark. Blue fire must have been some kind of freezing magic because, hit by Rotoph's fire, Theia stopped in her tracks and began to sink to the bottom of the ocean.

Kala, please. Just let me do this. Go take on Cronus if you want to help, Rotoph pleaded.

I'm going to help you whether you like it or not. Kala didn't like the tone of Rotoph's voice. He sounded defeated. *We need the teleportation embargo lifted and you seem to be the only one who can do that, so I'm going to kick Atlas's dad's ass. Trust me, I'm satisfying both parts of my personality here.* Kala swam as fast as she could at Iapetus, landing her fist on his ten-foot chest. To her disappointment, the impact only shoved Iapetus back a few feet. He was definitely more annoyed than injured, but at least Kala could move the Titan away from Rotoph. Then Rotoph would only have to deal with Clymene, and Kala was sure the Grigori could handle her solo.

Besides, Kala was tired of all this *destiny* talk. Ever since *prophecy* and *destiny* entered her life, it had gone to the crapper. She didn't need Rotoph to do something crazy because he thought it was his fate. *She* was the Fated One, after all, and she was just fine shouldering that burden alone. Rotoph might be annoying, but Kala had grudgingly grown fond of the angel since he had joined her side. She wasn't going to let anything happen to him. *Rotoph, just take down that teleportation block and let me handle the rest.*

Rotoph wasn't answering her anymore; he was busy trying to evade Clymene as she swiped outward with a Grigori blade. With all the fire being shot around like it was a flamethrower convention, Kala had barely noticed that most of the twenty-foot Titans were also carrying the crippling blades. She had also forgotten that she held one herself. Pulling out the knife she'd taken from Rhea, Kala swam down as Iapetus launched a round of yellow fire at her. Her arm was nicked by the flames and searing pain shot through her body. Seriously. Ouch.

Yellow fire equals pain: check.

Kala took advantage of Iapetus's moment of triumphant gloating from actually hitting a target and sliced the Titan's thirty-inch sized toe.

It was enough.

Iapetus tried to send more flames in Kala's direction, but the blade's magic rendered him powerless.

PUNCH!

Iapetus's giant fist made contact with Kala's face and she flew back through the water at a sickening speed. Iapetus may not have magic, but he still had brute strength.

The one good thing about Iapetus's attack: Kala grabbed Clymene's hair as she passed by, pulling the Titan away from Rotoph. Clymene was so surprised, her arms flailed in the water, trying to gain back control. Taking full advantage of Clymene's disoriented state, Kala reached down to the Titan's barrel-sized neck and sliced it open with the Grigori blade. Blood poured into the ocean, making it even blacker than it already was. Clymene's body went still as Kala released her, sending her down to the bottom of the ocean to join Theia.

Iapetus roared in rage. Even though it was muffled by the water, it was still terrifying. Kala used her smaller size to her advantage and swam underneath Iapetus's legs to reach his backside. Slicing throats seemed to be the only way to stop a supernatural being, at least temporarily. And Kala needed Rotoph free so they could all teleport out of there.

Just as Kala reached out to cut Iapetus's neck, Iapetus reached behind and grabbed Kala in one hand, tossing her away from him.

I could use a little help, please, Kala directed her thoughts at Rotoph.

But Rotoph had moved away from Kala's battle with Atlas's dad. At first Kala was relieved, since this meant he could break Cronus's teleportation block in peace, but when Kala saw Rotoph floating in the water with a blank stare on his face she knew something was wrong. She'd seen that look on many soldiers before: frozen from fear and unable to fight.

I said leave me alone. Rotoph's voice was small and scared.

Every cell in Kala's body told her she needed to do something to help him. There was no logical reason why. Experience told her that Rotoph was reverting back to his true self: a coward. Faced with eleven of the twelve Titans, the boy had snapped. That was the logical explanation.

But Kala knew it wasn't true. Whatever Rotoph's *destiny* was, it was paralyzing him.

Since Iapetus was the only Titan in her way, Kala needed to get rid of him fast if she were to truly help Rotoph. It helped that Iapetus didn't have any of his magic, but the Titan was still five times her size, not to mention the fact that he was lightning fast and supernaturally strong. And she couldn't use stealth: the Titan was staring right at her. Kala was just grateful all the other Titans were occupied fighting her team, but she needed help.

Asmosdeus. Kala called out to the Demon. *I need you to distract Iapetus. I'd take care of him myself, but I think something's wrong with Rotoph and I need to get to him right away.*

On my way. The Demon's voice sounded all too eager to help, swimming back up from the depths of the ocean.

Kala kept Iapetus focused on her, making him believe she planned to attack him full-on. Out of the corner of her eye Kala could see Asmodeus swimming towards Iapetus. Kala swam toward the Titan, forcing him to keep his attention on her.

Just before Kala reached Iapetus, Asmodeus's demon form plowed into the Titan, dragging him into the water's depths.

Thanks. Kala projected.

My pleasure, buttercup. Just make sure that Grigori gets us out of here. I really hate water.

Kala swam over to Rotoph, who was floating listlessly as if he were in some kind of coma. She grabbed his arms to get his attention.

Rotoph!

The Grigori didn't respond.

Rotoph! What is wrong with you?

With all the chaos behind her, Kala was more afraid of the look in Rotoph's eyes when he stared at her.

It's time, Kala. His face was ashen even in the darkness of the ocean. *I'm scared.*

I don't understand. Just get us back to the Compound, Kala tried to reason with him.

This is it, Rotoph smiled wanly. *You're not the only one who is a part of a prophecy.*

Screw prophecy. Let's get out of here. Kala didn't want to hear of another prophecy!

It's why I sent my brethren to the Fifth Heaven. I was a coward. I wanted a way where we could all survive. I don't want to die, Kala. Rotoph stared at her, desperation in his eyes.

But Kala wasn't having it, not after surviving the Underworld. *Grigori can't die.*

"*The Grigori with the power of runes will sacrifice himself in the battle of the ocean. Titans against all others to save The Fated One. To save the Grigori. To save the world." It's pretty clear.* Rotoph's expression was growing more and more miserable. *I've been running from this for a long time. Everything happens when it's supposed to though, right?* He looked at her with sadness. *I couldn't have even fulfilled the prophecy years ago when I helped imprison my brothers and sisters. You weren't born yet. And I know with every fiber of my being that you truly are The Fated One, Kala Hicks.* He paused, then looked at Kala, resolved. *I'm scared as hell, but you're worth dying for. Just don't make my sacrifice pointless.*

Rotoph, we can get around this. Just break Cronus's teleportation block. Kala was desperate to stop Rotoph. If she could help him defy his prophecy, then maybe she could defy her own.

Kala, look behind you. We're losing. Oceanus is the ocean. Poseidon is strong, but he's been weakened in the Underworld for hundreds of years. And the Grigori? We're being overpowered by the blades I made, and we're not really the underwater type.

What about that red ball of healing you used on me and Asmodeus? Kala needed to find a way.

What? I'm just going to swim up to everyone and hope they have enough time to regenerate themselves? You know that's not possible. Rotoph smiled, his sadness replaced by resolve. He reached out to touch Kala's hand. *Without you, Owen and Talan would never have given me a chance to prove myself. Thank you for that. Tell them I'm sorry.*

Rotoph, we can find another way. Kala knew her arguments were falling on deaf ears. Rotoph had made up his mind.

He pulled his hand back and took out two red runed marbles. *I'd swim back if I were you.*

Rotoph. Kala didn't want to move.

Move now, Kala. I made this to affect Titans only, and you're part Titan.

It won't kill you, but it will hurt.

The runes glowed yellow as they had when healing Kala. Then the light grew brighter and brighter until it turned white.

Kala knew a ticking time bomb when she saw one. With one last nod of respect to Rotoph, Kala swam away. Away from the light. Away from having to witness another prophecy come to pass. She swam straight for the raging battle in front of her. Both sides looked beat up, but Rotoph was right: the Titans were winning.

BOOM!

A wave of white light washed through Kala like a tidal wave of pain. Every nerve ending screamed in agony; Kala felt as if her insides were exploding into tiny pieces. She focused on her human side, on her Gaia side, anything to siphon away the torment away. Her movements slowed from the amount of concentration it took to overcome the pain. Even then she still couldn't shake her excruciating misery.

The only up side was seeing the Titans in even more pain than she was. The battle had stopped as the twenty-foot Titans writhed in tortured anguish. Kala knew it wouldn't kill them, but it would take them down for a while.

Within seconds, Talan swam up next to her, taking her arm and leading her back to where the other Grigori, Olympians and Asmodeus were gathering. Asmodeus was back in his human form again and, when he saw her barely able to move, he helped Talan by taking Kala's other arm.

Did Rotoph make it? Kala asked through the pain. But she already knew the answer.

Talan shook his head. Kala could see the sadness in Talan's eyes. He may have been at odds with his brother, but knowing that Rotoph sacrificed himself to save them meant everything to him.

As if on autopilot, everyone clasped hands once more. Watching Cronus's body writhe in unnatural jerked positions confirmed that he was in no position to keep the teleportation block in place.

Talan took the lead and teleported them all into the Compound.

Chapter Eighteen

Kala, the Olympians, the Grigori and Asmodeus landed in Fortski's lab.

The man himself, John Fortski, jumped in surprise at the sudden appearance of over twenty supernatural beings showing up in his workspace, all sopping wet, creating large puddles on the pristine tiled flooring.

"Oh, well, hello," Fortski greeted them nervously. "I'll just call General Turner then."

The little guy disappeared after that, running to fetch Turner.

Owen was doing a head count, while the Olympians stood there dumbstruck.

Being in the Underworld for 2,000 years, they had never seen technology before. To stand in Fortski's lab, which was more mad-scientist than scientist, was overwhelming.

Asmodeus was the only one who looked out of place. And to be fair, he was. Kala walked over to him, not sure what she wanted to say. "So, thanks," was what came out.

Instead of pulling a typical *Asmodeus* move like trying to kiss her or touch her in an inappropriate way, he simply smiled and tipped an imaginary hat. "Call if you need me."

Then he was gone.

Kala couldn't blame him. If she had a choice at the moment, she would teleport herself out as well. But her Atlas vision… and Rotoph's death… His words echoing in her head: *Don't make my sacrifice pointless.*

Kala thought of her Atlas mission to keep her mind focused. It was in a big room like this one, but it had been empty except for Turner's two brain machines. Kala couldn't imagine Turner having another location for his precious machines, so she assumed that the location was somewhere inside the Compound. Since Turner was in the vision, she figured she could ask him.

Feeling a hand on her shoulder, Kala turned around to see Owen, wet hair plastered to his face. "How you holding up?"

Kala shrugged. "Is Rotoph really dead?" She didn't want to believe the Grigori was truly gone.

Owen sighed, "We don't know. His body evaporated after he activated the runes, but maybe someday he could reform…" He shook his head, pain in his expression. "I was just starting to like the guy again."

"Me, too," Kala admitted.

"He believed in you," Owen said quietly.

Kala nodded. "He wanted to tell you and Talan he was sorry."

Owen didn't respond. Kala knew him well enough to know that he was compartmentalizing his emotions.

Kala took a deep breath, letting him off the hook. She went right to business, glancing at a clock behind Owen.

1d 07h 10m 22s: 10:40PM.

"I have less than 8 hours in Day Three of my Atlas mission. We have to find the location." Kala didn't elaborate aloud. She planned on telling a select group of people, including Owen, but now wasn't the time.

Owen seemed to pick up on that, nodding, "We'll find somewhere private to talk."

Generals Turner and Clifton entered the room, Fortski trailing timidly.

As Kala made her way to confer with the Generals, it almost didn't register that she had bumped into another person. Just as her brain was registering that this person hadn't been there a second before, Kala recognized that it was Cronus who stood in front of her. His body looked wracked and broken, his skin covered in large, gaping blisters oozing with white puss. And he looked pissed.

"You'll *never* complete your next mission. After the world crumbles I will skin you alive and make sure you stay that way for all eternity." Cronus touched Kala's forehead.

"Bitter, much?" Kala was about to attack the Titan just to make herself feel better, when the room began to spin uncontrollably. "What did you do to me?"

"It's just a little coma, *human*," Cronus laughed.

The sound of yelling and people running toward Cronus and Kala echoed loudly in Kala's head as her knees gave out.

Cronus de-materialized as Talan's arms wrapped behind Kala to catch her fall.

Her eyes met Talan's worried ones as he whispered in her ear, "I'll wake you up, just hold on."

Kala reached up and touched his cheek. Then everything went black.

***

Looking around the black space, Kala was reminded of her time in Turner's brain machine. For all she knew, that was exactly where she was, though before she had felt she could wake up. Now Kala felt stuck. No Penny to visit her this time either.

Last time, Penny had snapped her fingers and the place lit up, but after snapping her fingers forty times, Kala decided to give up and get used to the darkness.

Kala could see her own body, that was about it. She hated to admit it, but Kala almost missed the Underworld. At least that place had scenery.

Not sure what she should do, Kala mentally tried to wake up. It sounded so easy, but when you look and feel awake (even passing the pinching her forearm test), the feat appeared impossible. She wondered if her coma was the same as Hades being asleep. Would she wake up a thousand years from now to a world that didn't exist anymore? Kala had a little over a day to complete her task and the only person she had told it to was Talan when she'd had her memory wiped, so Kala could bet he had no idea what to do.

With frustration threatening to overwhelm her, Kala decided to walk. If she were walking in her head, then maybe she'd run into something eventually. It was a long shot, but she was desperate to escape the darkness.

The more she moved, the better she felt, and Kala started to think about what she was going to do. Remembering the prophecy, Kala almost laughed at the thought that she was supposed to be some kind of *Fated One*. What kind of Fated One gets put into a coma by her enemy while standing in front of an army of her allies?

A dumb one.

Good luck, world, if I'm the one keeping you safe, Kala grumbled to herself.

"The cost will be great, and the immortals will reign. The one that knows death will release the curse of balance." Kala repeated the last part of the prophecy in her head.

Zeus had told her that *the one who knows death* was some girl three hundred years in the future. But now that Hades was awake, it seemed more logical that it could be referring to him. And if that was the case…

Maybe Hades was the one who would take Atlas's curse away. Maybe that was why Kala and the others had to imprison Hades and Cronus in the brain machines. Maybe that was how the curse would be broken.

It gave her a sense of hope she hadn't felt in a while.

The more Kala thought about it, the more it made sense. Zeus probably made up the girl just to throw her off so she wouldn't figure out that Hades…

"Um, hi?" A female voice sounded in the darkness.

Kala squinted her eyes, trying to see who was speaking. The voice didn't sound like anyone she knew. She half expected Roberta to jump into her brain to try to wake her up. The woman was amazing at that kind of thing. No matter how hard she tried, though, Kala couldn't make out who was in front of her.

Probably a figment of her imagination.

"How are you making it so dark in here?" The voice asked.

Figment or not, Kala had to explore every avenue of breaking out of this coma, so if it meant talking to an imaginary friend, then, so be it.

"I don't know how to make it light," Kala admitted.

"Yeah, but you're the one *making* it dark."

Kala didn't know how to respond to that, so she simply said, "I'm not doing it on purpose."

"Oh. Phew. You scared me for a second. I got this, hang on." The voice sounded like a teenager, Kala realized. Maybe she was about to face a teenage version of herself. It made sense. She was fifteen when she met Owen and Linda, and they had changed her life. Was that what this coma was going to be? *This is your life, Kala Hicks.* She certainly hoped not.

Suddenly an entire landscape appeared all around Kala, from utter darkness to standing in a giant oak forest. It was stunning, filled with rich colors of greens, browns, yellows and blues. Kala could actually feel the heat from the sun as it filtered through the leaves on the trees. This was quite an upgrade.

But what struck Kala as odd was the fact that she'd never been to this location before. Why would her mind invent an oak forest?

Standing in front of her was indeed a teenager, but she was definitely not a younger version of Kala. Kala had never seen this girl before in her life. She stood about Kala's height, with chestnut brown hair and gray eyes, and didn't look older than seventeen or eighteen. She was very pretty.

Something about the girl made Kala pause. The girl had power. Kala could sense it immediately.

And, in that instant, Kala knew she wasn't talking to an imaginary friend, she was talking to someone real. Someone like Roberta who had the ability to head jump. Someone even more powerful than Roberta, it seemed, since Turner's wife hadn't shown up yet.

Out of military habit, Kala was immediately on the defensive.

The girl viewed her "oak tree" landscape handiwork and smiled. "This place always does the trick."

"You've been here before?" Kala asked carefully.

The girl nodded as if reflecting on a familiar thought. "My grandmother taught me how to create environments like this when I'm in a dreamscape. This one in particular helped me out in a really hard situation."

"Coma?" Kala inquired.

"Buried alive," she answered.

"Yeah, that's worse," Kala acknowledged.

The girl shifted awkwardly. "So, you're in a coma I'm guessing?"

Kala sighed, starting to feel at ease with the girl despite her military training. "Yeah, can't seem to snap out of it."

"I'm Chelsan, by the way," the girl said, holding out her hand. Kala shook it.

"Kala." When their hands made contact, Kala almost jumped back from the shock. Images raced past her, too fast to comprehend. It felt as if Talan was showing her a future vision or his memories. Kala tried to slow down the pictures so she could translate what she was seeing, but no matter how hard she tried, she couldn't do it.

Chelsan yanked her hand away with a shocked expression, too.

"Whoa."

Kala stumbled a bit from the sudden disconnection. "What was that? Are you a Grigori or something?"

"A what?" Chelsan eyed Kala with confusion.

"It's a type of angel. Are you a Malak then? Or Demon? Or god?" Kala was sure the girl had to be some kind of supernatural being to not only have the power to visit Kala's head, but to make her see visions like that.

"Um…" Chelsan appeared very uncomfortable at where the conversation was going. "You know none of that is *real*, right? And I've never heard of a *Malak* either."

Examining Chelsan's expression, Kala was reminded at how she had felt when first confronted by Atlas. Kala had thought it was all a dream. Whoever this Chelsan girl was, she obviously had never had contact with the supernatural world.

"Malaks are another kind of angel," Kala explained. Then she shook her head. "I didn't believe it at first either," she began carefully, "but if you're not supernatural, how are we seeing each other?"

Chelsan appeared to be weighing her answer. "I guess I'm a little supernatural, but it came from science and magic, not gods and angel stuff." Then, without judgment, she asked. "Are you telling me *you're* one of those things?"

Kala nodded. "I'm Atlas." It felt weird to say to a stranger, but somehow Kala knew it was the right thing to do.

"As in the Greek god who holds up the earth?" Chelsan clarified. "But you just said your name was Kala." She seemed genuinely confused.

"I'm both. I became Atlas." Kala shook her head at the absurdity of her statement. "You think I'm crazy." Kala didn't blame the girl. She'd have thought she was insane, too, if their places were reversed.

Chelsan shook her head. "No. If I told you about my life, you'd think I was crazy too." Then she asked thoughtfully, "So what does that mean, you're 'Atlas?' Are you supposed to be in the North Pole keeping the planet spinning or something?"

Kala sighed in frustration. "I wish it was that easy, although thinking about it, that probably wouldn't be that easy." She re-focused. "I have to keep the balance of good and evil in check or the world will literally crumble."

"Whoa. I thought my life was hard," Chelsan replied.

There was no sarcasm or disbelief in the girl's tone, which made Kala realize that Chelsan must have had it pretty rough as well.

"Why do you think you're in my head?" Chelsan genuinely wanted to know Kala's thoughts on the matter.

"What do you mean?" Kala was confused. "You're in *my* head."

Chelsan eyed Kala as if to see if she was serious… Then she understood that Kala was telling the truth.

"Nope," she said, "you're in mine. And that's saying something. I have blocks up the yazoo that my grandmother taught me and she's pretty good at this stuff. Maybe it's because you're Atlas? I've never had to block out a *god* before."

Kala was still reeling from the fact that she wasn't in her own brain. It made a strange kind of sense. If she was in a coma her spirit was free to roam anywhere it wanted. Apparently, it wanted to jump into some poor girl's head. "It sounds like I need to meet your grandmother." Kala thought the next best thing would be Roberta. Maybe she could teach Kala more about this whole *head-jumping* process.

Chelsan's face revealed that she wasn't quite sure if Kala meeting her grandmother was such a good idea. "Um, my grandparents are an acquired taste. Are there more of you? Gods, I mean?" She seemed curious.

"Unfortunately. Zeus and Cronus are dicks, and so are the Titans, but some of the Olympians don't seem as bad." Then Kala added. "I'm sorry I hijacked your head. I have no idea how that happened."

Chelsan seemed impressed at the mention of the Titans and Olympians, then she turned thoughtful. "Well, usually, the way it works is: you have to think of the person whose head you want to jump into."

Then she shrugged. "But you don't know me, so I'm not sure, either."

Kala considered it for second. "That's so strange. I was thinking of Zeus."

Chelsan shrugged. "Well, I'm definitely not him. What *exactly* were you thinking about him?

Kala contemplated, "I was thinking about how he had lied to me about a prophecy of a girl…" She froze.

"What is it?" Chelsan picked up on Kala's sudden mood change.

"This might sound weird, but would the phrase *the one that knows death* apply to you at all?" Kala asked, scared of the answer.

She didn't need Chelsan to respond. Kala could see from the paler shade of white Chelsan's face turned that the phrase definitely meant something to the girl.

"I control dead things," Chelsan confirmed. Her voice was small, as if admitting this to Kala might put her in danger.

Kala was terrified to ask her next question, but she plowed ahead despite her fear, "What year is it?"

Chelsan hadn't been expecting that. She tilted her head to the side and replied, "2321."

Before Kala could respond, she was being pulled out of the forest at lightning speed. Trying to hold onto anything she could, Kala grasped only air as her body flew into the darkness once more.

If Kala hadn't died already, she would have thought she was dying now since she saw a light at the end of the black all around her. Instincts kicking in, Kala steered herself toward the glowing beacon, knowing it was the right thing to do.

The closer she was to the light, the brighter it blazed, until Kala was on top of it. Not stopping for a second, Kala jumped as if she were leaping into the sun itself…

DAY FOUR

Chapter Nineteen

Kala woke up gasping for air. Her head yanked to a halt as she realized she was hooked up to one of Turner's brain machines and the wires had been pulled taut from her leaning forward.

"We got her!" Turner's voice beamed beside her.

Finally catching her breath, Kala ripped off the suction cups attached to her head and took a moment to view her surroundings.

Derek, Owen, Talan, Roberta and Turner were with Kala in a small room that housed the brain machine and a small computer station next to it.

It was comforting not having a ginormous group of Grigori and gods hovering over her.

And these five were the people she trusted most in her life right now.

Derek was the first to help Kala unhook the rest of the equipment fastened to her. As soon as she was free her arms wrapped around her best friend in a tight hug. "I missed you too," Derek chuckled softly in her ear.

Kala pulled away, smiling. "You have no idea." Then she asked Owen.

"Where are the Olympians? And how the heck did Cronus get into the Compound? Especially after the damage Rotoph caused him."

Owen answered, "The Olympians are here and secured. Ashliel is trying to help them locate the rest of their brood. No one seems to know where Zeus's offspring are. Cronus used whatever strength he had left and took advantage of our massive teleportation, essentially hitchhiking in with us. But there's no way he can get in here anymore. Hera is making sure of that."

Roberta added. "We were quite worried about you. I tried to travel into the machine to pull you out, but you weren't there. Your essence was somewhere else. We were afraid Cronus hid it somewhere and we'd never get you back."

That thought was frightening. "He could do that?"

"We honestly didn't know," Turner answered. Obviously, we were mistaken."

Roberta added, "It wasn't until Talan tried to reach you that we were able to pull you back."

Kala's eyes met Talan's. "Thank you." Then she addressed the group. "I somehow managed to jump inside the head of the girl from the prophecy." Admittedly, Owen and Talan were far more impressed by this news than the human side of the room, but seeing as *prophecies* were new to Derek and the Turners, Kala wasn't surprised.

Talan asked, "From the future?"

Kala nodded. "She said she could normally block out people from jumping in her brain, but somehow I got through."

This idea seemed to excite Roberta. "I've been trying to perfect that technique for years, but there are still flaws. I'd love to pick her brain."

"Considering she's three-hundred years in the future, I don't think that's possible," Kala said.

Owen stepped forward, taking over the conversation. "We'll have to talk more about this later. You only have an hour to complete your Atlas mission."

"What?!" Kala's head flew up to see the clock.

0d 0h 59m 34s.

"Holy crap!" Kala's heart raced. "I don't even know where it is! And Cronus and Hades are supposed to be there! As in already *captured*! How is that going to be possible?"

"Slow down," Talan tried to calm her. "Just tell us about the vision and we'll help you."

Kala knew that Talan already had some knowledge of the task since she had described it to him briefly when her memory had been wiped by the River Lethe. Carefully, Kala told the small group every detail of her vision. She didn't want to leave anything out, hoping that someone would pick out an aspect that Kala may have overlooked.

After she finished, Kala asked Turner, "Do you think that room is here in the Compound?"

Turner looked as if his brain was moving a mile a minute. "We need to keep this between the six of us. Harry can never hear of it."

Kala was not expecting that kind of reaction. She knew Turner didn't trust Clifton and neither did she, to be honest, but the way Turner had just expressed himself led Kala to believe he had a motive she wasn't recognizing. "Not a problem, but why the secrecy?"

Turner looked over at Owen and Talan as if he was unsure if he could confide in the Grigori.

Kala tried to assure him, "You can say anything in front of them."

Turner did not seem convinced. "I have an idea of why your vision showed us strapping Cronus and Hades to my machines, but I'm not sure your Grigori friends would agree to let it happen."

"They don't have a choice. If it's the Atlas mission, they *have* to accept it or the world ends. Tell me what you're thinking." Kala could see that Turner held the answers and she needed to know them.

Owen confirmed, "Kala is right. We would never question the mission."

Tilting his head sideways as if he found that hard to believe, Turner answered, "'Never' is a strong word."

Kala could see that Turner was having a real struggle trusting that Talan and Owen would be on board with whatever was rolling around in his head, so she suggested, "We can talk privately if you want, but they'll eventually find out."

Talan stepped forward. "You're talking about harnessing Cronus and Hades's powers to use for your own purposes."

Turner had the expression a child who was just caught stealing a candy bar.

Talan had been disguising himself as Turner and Roberta's mentor for years now, so he knew the couple better than anyone. Now Talan nodded in understanding. "Roberta has been able to raise the dead, but you don't want to be tied down to spells to keep them animated."

Roberta and Turner's faces went pale at the accusation, but they didn't deny it.

It took a moment for Kala to process. "What?"

Owen slowly appreciated the situation. "Remember, Kala, when you came here to the Compound to reassemble Talan and Turner's two assistants? You were worried about them talking to General Clifton and I told you they could be trusted."

Kala vaguely remembered the moment. "I guess."

"Those were walking corpses, so there was no threat of them turning sides." Owen asked Roberta. "If you aren't controlling them, who is?"

Roberta answered cautiously, "I have a handful of warlocks in a secured room. They keep the corpses animated during the day, but it takes a lot of energy. We can only control a handful at a time. They can't function on their own."

"And why on earth would you do this?" Kala seemed to be the only one disturbed by this news. Then she glanced over at Derek. His dark skin almost appeared pale at where the conversation had headed.

Turner wasn't fazed at the disgust in Kala's tone. "For security and control. If I control everyone around me, I can never be betrayed."

Remembering the vision Cronus showed her of the future, Kala realized that this was probably the first step in Turner's journey to becoming the most powerful man in the world.

Power of the dead: Hades was able to control corpses, but they could also perform tasks on their own.

If Turner could harness that ability…

"If you control Hades, you control the dead," Kala concluded.

Slowly Turner nodded. "On a grand scale. One I could never achieve with just magic."

"But how could this restore *balance* to the universe?" Kala was at a loss.

"I don't just want an army of the dead, Kala. The balance that your mission will bring is what I *need* to do with Hades's power," Turner admitted. Then, addressing Owen and Talan, he explained, "You two know even more than Kala and Derek that we humans will destroy ourselves in the next twenty years, thirty if we're lucky. Things have to change for this world to survive and this Atlas curse or whatever it is, knows that. And, it knows, *I'm* the only one who knows *how* to stop it."

His eyes now turned to bore into Kala's. "Everything happens for a reason. Tell me, you've seen the future. I can tell by the way you look at me. Do I make the world a better place?"

Kala paused before answering, then clarified, "The *world*, yes, but the people…" The images of people being murdered to maintain population control.

Turner didn't seem fazed by her implication. "Your curse isn't about balancing *people*, it's about balancing the planet. As long as the planet survives, then humans will, too. The curse doesn't care if the thousands of lives Fortski could have saved with his cure for cancer die. It only cares that we stay on our path. Our path leads to survival."

Turner said it with such conviction Kala believed him. She could see the man from the future now. Hard, cold, evil even – but doing things for the greater good of the planet. Like her.

And his words rang true. Kala had always thought about the Atlas curse saving lives, because she was a soldier and that was what she was trained to do. But it wasn't about that at all. It was why a horrible act had to be committed every four days. The planet didn't see it as being an act of atrocity at all, it saw it as a necessity for survival. It was about saving the earth itself, weighing its options and deciding on a path that led to its continued existence. It didn't matter who or what lived on it as long as the world stayed intact. That was the balance.

And Turner was the man to do it. Kala remembered all the good things about the future: no more roads, just grass and trees, fuel cell cars that recycled water so there was no such thing as droughts, no waste or garbage, just clean. Clean air, clean water, clean soil. It was a Utopia of sorts. Only Turner and Roberta would know what the trade-off was to obtain this healthy world: culling the population by any means necessary, but not so much that the public would notice. Take out the unwanted and blame it on a natural disaster. No one would question it. They'd only say a silent prayer in thanks that the world wasn't too overpopulated to live in.

Seeing Turner's future laid out for him, Kala felt a deep empathy for the man. They weren't that far apart in their missions. Kala had to perform the unthinkable for the greater good as well.

Their goals were the same: protect this world by any means necessary.

It was as if Kala was renewed. Maybe this was what it meant to be Gaia's child. Maybe that was why she was destined to be Atlas, to be the Fated One. Her first priority had to be the earth, because without it, *no life* could exist.

No more needed to be said. Kala looked at Talan and Owen, searching their faces for approval or disapproval. She almost wanted to laugh, because the same expression was in both their faces: trust. They were leaving the decision to back up Turner to her. Glancing over at Derek, Kala saw that he was shocked by everything he had heard, but his loyal eyes were with Talan and Owen.

Kala had never felt more connected to anyone than these five people in her entire life. Even more than Jack, and that was a hard thing to admit.

To Turner, Kala said, "I don't need to know the details. I trust you."

"And you know why Harry can never find out about what we're doing?" he asked of the room.

Kala responded, "Because he'd try and steal the power for himself and use it to get rich and powerful, not for the greater good."

Turner sighed in relief, "Precisely. This Atlas mission has to stay between the six of us. No one else can know."

But Gaia was also a part of her vision… It was time to fess up. Only Owen would be shocked since Talan already knew her secret. Turner, Roberta and Derek might find it fascinating, but only Owen would truly understand the ramifications of what it meant to be Gaia's daughter. "Remember, Gaia was in my vision as well. We have to tell her. I don't want to spring it on her when we're in the room. After all, we are going to capture and harness her son and grandson for all eternity."

Roberta was thoughtful. "She was on board in your vision though, correct?"

Kala nodded. "Yeah, she was with us. Being that she's *Mother Earth*, I don't think she'll have a problem with our motives. I just have to figure out how to contact her."

Talan glanced at Kala, unsure, and she took that as her cue. "I should tell you something else before we proceed." All eyes were on her. "Gaia visited me when I was in the caves under the ocean." Kala paused, trying not to sound dramatic as she confessed, "She told me I was her daughter."

As she predicted, only Owen was taken aback, but then his eyes lit up and he touched her cheek with his hand affectionately. "I always knew you were special."

This was getting a little too dad-like in front of the crowd, but Kala didn't mind. She loved the fact that Owen would always see her as his daughter and she'd always see him as her father.

Turner cleared his throat. "We *are* on a time crunch here." He motioned to the clock with his head.

0d 0h 45m 23s.

Kala's heart jumped in her throat.

"I still don't know how we're going to track down Cronus, Hades and my mom and get them to…" Kala eyed Turner for an answer as to the location.

"Los Angeles," he replied simply.

"Los Angeles? Are you freaking kidding me? Where is this place?" Kala was more than shocked to find out that the location of her vision was clear across the country. Luckily, teleportation was on the table, but still… she was running out of time.

"Not even Harry knows about this place in LA," Turner answered. "It's an underground site like this one, but it houses only *my* people. I let Harry think all my best scientists and engineers are here in the Compound and, by keeping Fortski here, there's no reason for Harry to even suspect I have another facility."

Kala supposed Turner was right, since Fortski was considered the smartest man alive. General Clifton would assume that Turner kept his best people with him and not in another location. "How can you be sure that the room in my vision is in this Los Angeles facility?"

"Because the only two brain machines that would work on beings as powerful as Cronus and Hades are in the Los Angeles headquarters," Turner explained. "If I concentrate on the location, can you teleport me there, if you've never been?"

"I have no idea." Kala suddenly saw a whole new set of problems. "If Turner is the only one who's been to the location, then how *are* we going to teleport there?"

Talan answered, "Turner is right. All he needs to do is think of the location and I can take us all there."

"We should go now, to make sure it's the right place," Turner suggested.

"Just the three of us." Kala motioned to Talan and Turner. Then she turned to the others. "We'll be right back."

No one seemed pleased by this notion, but no one argued either.

Roberta focused on Turner. "Be quick."

The grin on Turner's face showed how excited he was to teleport and even Roberta had to smile back.

Owen nodded his approval and Derek gave a small salute.

With everything in order, Talan stepped forward and touched both Kala and Turner's arms.

In a millisecond Kala stood in the room from her vision, Talan and Turner by her side.

Turner almost stumbled from the jolt of teleportation, but a smile was still plastered to his face. "Remarkable," he uttered, his voice awe-filled.

Talan ignored Turner, keeping his attention solely on Kala. "Is this the place in your vision?"

"Yeah, definitely," Kala confirmed.

The overwhelming sense of déjà vu took her aback. Everything was identical to her vision. They were in some kind of basement with slate walls, floors and ceilings. In the center of the space rested Turner's famous "brain machines." Kala suddenly wondered if they actually had a name. Turner seemed like the kind of guy who would label his devices, especially ones like these that he revered so highly. Hundreds of cables and wires grew into the ceiling like vines and hung loosely over the metal chairs, ready for Hades and Cronus to be strapped into. Seeing the cold metal seats, Kala had a sudden pang of sympathy for the deities, knowing the kind of pain they'd have to endure sitting on such a hard surface until the end of time.

Or until someone woke them up: that was always going to be a fear and a possibility.

Kala had awakened Hades after 2,000 years. She bet Cronus had never planned on anyone doing that.

Shaking the thought from her mind, Kala instructed Turner. "Let's go back and get the others so we can come up with a plan."

Turner grinned, which indicated to Kala that he was on board. Talan shook his head in amusement and touched the two of them so they could travel back to the Compound…

Nothing.

He tried again.

Nada.

This was never a good sign, and Kala was running out of time.

Immediately on guard, she kept her eyes open for any sudden attack.

"I can't let you leave."

Whirling around, Kala found herself face-to-face with Gaia. When their eyes met, Kala knew that this was supposed to happen.

These were the three allies from her vision.

"It's you." Kala felt an instant sense of purpose. "You're the one who is going to bring Cronus and Hades here."

Gaia nodded slowly, "Yes, I am."

Chapter Twenty

Upon recognizing Gaia, Talan hugged her immediately. Gaia had mentioned that she knew Talan when Kala had met her before. Seeing them embrace only solidified their affection for each other.

When they pulled away, Talan addressed Gaia in a serious tone. "You know what we plan to do?" He motioned to Turner. "What *he* plans to do?"

Gaia talked as if Turner weren't in the room. "I've been keeping my eye on this man. He has the right kind of soul to do what needs to be done."

The way she said it made the gooseflesh on Kala's arms rise. Kala knew Turner to be a good man, but he had a dark side, a side she had seen in her vision of the future. But, in order for the world to survive, that was what was required.

Turner didn't seem offended at all by the implication; if anything, he appeared pleased that the mother of all gods was not only agreeing to their plan, but helping it come to fruition.

A moment passed between Gaia and Talan. They were in complete agreement.

Kala began to feel like a third wheel between the two of them, and if *she* felt that way, she could only imagine how Turner felt.

Even though there wasn't a clock in the room, Kala knew they were running out of time. "How do we do this?" she asked. "In my vision, white fire came out of my hands and I have no idea how to do that." She was actually nervous, as if she might fail in her performance because it was magic and not brute force like she was used to.

Gaia focused on Kala and touched her daughter's hand. A warm sensation flushed through Kala's body, and all her cells tingled. As if there were pieces of a puzzle inside Kala's brain, abstract thoughts began connecting together, without her control and without her understanding. It should have been frightening, but Gaia's touch soothed Kala's anxiety.

After a few brief moments, ideas began to take shape. Kala could see where her powers resided in her head. Like the Grigori, Kala had access to white fire, purple fire, green fire, blue fire, black fire, yellow fire – and the longer Gaia held on to her, the more Kala learned about herself and about what she could do. It was as if her mother was downloading YouTube tutorials on being a supernatural being straight into Kala's brain. Connections that weren't there before were suddenly as obvious to Kala as if she had known what to do her entire life.

By the time Gaia pulled her hand away, Kala was rejuvenated. She had an entirely new arsenal in her head. One that she had complete access to and didn't require physical weapons. It was invigorating, empowering. Before she had fought with gods, Demons and Malaks blindly, winning because she had tapped into something inside her that she had no control over.

Now Kala knew every single power she was capable of. As strange as it sounded, it was exhilarating to know what each color of fire did: white was for control, purple was for capturing, green was for pain, blue was for paralysis, yellow was to destroy, black was to blind or hide and red was for resurrection. Kala almost wanted some Titans and Demons to show up so she could try each one out.

And gone were the days of *accidentally* devouring a supernatural being. If Kala wanted to consume, she could. Gaia had been right before, though, Kala couldn't *spit* the deities out like her mother could. If Kala ever chose to consume another god, she'd be forced to integrate them into her and, in turn, kill them. They could never take over her body as she had feared, but all their memories and powers would become hers, and her half-human brain wasn't likely to accept the changes very well. There was the possibility that Kala could lose herself and her sanity. Definitely, not worth the risk, but Kala didn't have to let anyone *know* that. It was always good to inspire a little fear in her enemies, especially when they interfered with her job.

With all this new knowledge of her capabilities, Kala was ready.

Kala ordered, "Just stay back here, General Turner. We're going to need you to hook Cronus and Hades up to the machines. Your cue will be when they're seated."

Having foreknowledge of what was about to take place, however, didn't make Kala feel any more confident. She didn't have faith that everything would work out the way it played in her visions. Yes, Kala believed that she would accomplish the Atlas mission, but a part of her worried she'd have to think on her feet and complete it another way.

Now all they needed were the players.

Gaia knew her part well as she made eye contact with each person in the room to make sure they were prepared for what she was about to do. When she seemed satisfied by what she saw in every person, Gaia's eyes rolled back in her head, the sockets turning a deep purple.

Not even realizing it, Kala was already crouched in a defensive stance.

Cronus and Hades were no joke. Her vision could have been the tail end of a very long battle. Just hopefully not longer than thirty minutes, since Kala was pretty sure that was all the time she had left on the clock.

Gaia's eyes turned back to normal – and Cronus and Hades stood before them. Their expressions were the same: anger and hatred.

Cronus was almost completely healed from Rotoph's rune-bomb, which made Kala more angry than she cared to admit. But she wasn't going to let Rotoph to have died in vain. If Rotoph couldn't kill Cronus, then Kala would imprison him.

Cronus and Hades saw Kala first and not even seeing anyone else in the room, Cronus lunged at Kala. "How could you possibly break the eternal sleep spell?!" His fist smacked into Kala's waiting arm as she blocked Cronus's blow with ease. She never would have guessed how martial arts could be such an advantage against deities. Apparently, when it came to physical harm all they knew was hit, punch, tackle and throw.

Kala was about to continue the fight when Cronus was thrown back by invisible hands. Gaia's hands.

When Hades saw this, he scanned the room. His eyes went round with shock when he finally saw his grandmother. He froze.

Cronus was too livid from being tossed aside to notice though, assuming that Kala had flung him backwards with her own magic. He began to charge her again –

– and, just as suddenly as before, Cronus fell to the floor when his whole body smashed into an invisible barrier. He was on his feet almost instantly, ready to renew his attack despite the obstacle.

"You will cease your fighting!" Gaia's voice echoed in the large room.

Cronus whipped his head around to see who spoke. And, like his son Hades, Cronus stared at his mother in muted astonishment. Cronus had known his mother was back since their confrontation in the cave beneath the ocean, but he hadn't expected to see her here, with Kala. Again.

Finally, he found his voice. "Mother."

Hades suddenly went into a panic, explaining, "It was all his idea, Grandmother. He wanted the Atlas mission to fail. He's the one who wants a new order –"

Gaia's raised hand silenced him immediately. Not because he chose to quit talking, but because she had used her power to stop his vocal chords from working. "Enough."

Her attention went back to Cronus. "I wish I could save you, my son, but you've proven too many times to be a danger to this world."

There was a mixture of fear and defiance in his tone as Cronus answered, "I did what I thought was best for this world."

Gaia's hand slashed down in the air. A long gash opened on Cronus's chest and he grunted from the pain. But wounds were only minor inconveniences for gods: his skin was immediately knitting itself together. But Gaia had made her point. "You did what was best for *you,*" she accused.

"I didn't. I swear…" Cronus began.

Another slash of the chest shut him up.

Gaia continued, "You've made your choices and they've brought you to this place where *I* have to tidy up your messes." Her attention finally went to Hades. "You followed your father blindly and now you'll have to pay as well."

Cronus threw a scathing look at Kala. "You would work with *her* over your own child?!" His rage was palpable.

Gaia answered with such intensity that Kala felt herself shiver. "Kala *is* my child."

Gaia might as well have killed Cronus right there. The expression on his face was one of horror and disbelief. "No…" was all that came out of his mouth.

Kala would have joined into the conversation at that point, but she was resolved to let Gaia take the lead. Besides, witnessing how her mother punished her children for speaking out, Kala didn't want to find out the hard way if she could heal as fast as Cronus.

Hades was in full suck-up mode at this point, his vocal chords returned to him. "Grandmother," then he smiled awkwardly to Kala, "Aunt…" he moved on quickly, "I only sided with father out of fear. I had just woken up thanks to…Auntie… here. I was scared Cronus would put me back to sleep."

Gaia shook her head and Hades clammed up. "It doesn't matter why you chose Cronus. What matters is that you *did* choose him. Yes, my children and grandchildren will always fight and there will always be wars, but none that will destroy *my* lifeline." Her rage grew overpowering yet again as she faced down Cronus. "I *am* the earth, my son! Tell me, when you conspired to destroy the world, did you even care that you'd be murdering your own mother?"

From the look on his face, it was obvious it hadn't even occurred to Cronus. He tried to explain lamely, "You've been gone for so long, I didn't even know if you *were* alive."

"If the earth exists, I am alive. You knew this, but you didn't care. You only thought of yourself and your own power. Just like your father," Gaia spat.

The last sentence destroyed Cronus. "Mother, how could you say that?"

Kala would almost have felt sorry for Cronus if he wasn't… Cronus. He kind of had it coming.

And, true to character, Cronus went from hurt to hate in a split second. "You're no mother of mine," he growled. He waved his hand dismissively at Kala. "And if you would side with this half-breed, then I *want* to destroy you. I'll revel in it!"

Hades did not like the way this was going. "Father…"

Cronus turned his angry eyes to his son, "You have something to say, Hades?"

The coward that was Cronus's son, quickly shook his head.

Sneering with delight, Cronus focused back on his mother. "I guess I'll just have to kill you now."

Purple fire burst out of his hands, blazing toward Gaia.

Kala and Talan stepped forward to help, but Gaia needed no aid: the purple flames were snuffed out before they even came within a few feet of her person.

Only a flicker of disappointment registered in Cronus's face before he tried for a second attack of white flames, but Gaia thwarted that as well.

The colored fires and their meanings clicked in Kala's brain once more: purple to capture, white to control. Cronus was doing anything he could to take charge of his mother. It was interesting to Kala that he chose not to hurt Gaia with green fire.

Gaia had had enough.

As her mother turned to her, Kala heard Gaia's voice in her head. *Don't do as I ask, but make them believe you will.*

What?

Kala had no idea what Gaia was talking about until her mother said to her. "Kala, consume them."

If Hades could have squawked like a chicken he would have. And, after having every one of his attacks blocked by Gaia, Cronus's face turned white with fear. Cronus out of all the gods knew what it felt like to almost be devoured by Kala.

But Gaia's words made sense now: *Don't do as I ask, but make them believe you will.*

So Kala stepped forward as if she were about to eat them whole.

The moment became clear. She was in her Atlas vision now. It suddenly made sense why Hades and Cronus began to back away from Kala, their eyes full of terror.

And when Gaia nodded to Kala and Talan, this time Kala knew what her mother wanted. "Now," Gaia commanded.

Hades and Cronus screamed in fear as Kala, Talan and Gaia threw their hands toward the pair, white fire charging out of their fingertips.

The fire that controls.

Hades and Cronus were surrounded by the bright flames, struggling like fish caught in a net. The white fire felt so natural pouring out of Kala's outstretched hands, as if she'd performed this task a million times. Even though Gaia and Talan summoned their own fire, Kala was connected to them both through the power of the magic. It was as if they thought with one mind, knowing exactly what had to be done.

Time to puppet them to the chairs.

In that moment Kala felt the enormity of what she was doing: saving the world from two of its biggest enemies – and sentencing Cronus and Hades to an eternity of prison. Worse, Turner would be able to use them like they were his very own god-machines. It was vile and left a bad taste in her mouth.

But it had to be done.

Kala was surprised at the ease in which they controlled the gods, making them put one foot in front of the other, maneuvering each to sit down in one of Turner's brain machines.

There was no more fight in either of them. Their faces transformed into expressionless drones, almost as if they were lost souls wandering the Underworld, as Jack had been. Kala could see Gaia's power at work, wiping Cronus and Hades's brains of any individual thoughts or feelings. It was Gaia's last gift to her offspring. The balance of the planet depended on the two gods being imprisoned forever, but Gaia had the decency to ease their minds from the horrific burden of caring.

Once Cronus and Hades were seated, Turner hurried over, quickly attaching the wires and leads to their heads. He had waited in the wings patiently just as Kala had asked him to do. Turner couldn't hide the excitement in his eyes at the prize he just inherited. Now Kala understood why the white fire didn't affect Turner as she had seen in her vision. The flames were harmless upon touch, only used to control.

"It's done!" Turner exclaimed.

Kala let the magic drop from her hands, as did Gaia and Talan.

Gaia nodded slightly to Kala. Understanding what her mother wanted this time, Kala walked over to the two gods and touched their wrists and ankles. A purple glow formed around the areas she touched, locking them into place.

Not needing to see a clock, Kala could feel the Atlas clock reset. She was in tune to everything supernatural inside her body now. There was no one like her, part human, part Titan, part Gaia. It didn't make her feel special, it made her feel capable and Kala had missed that feeling.

Kala knew who she was and what she could do.

Standing next to Turner, staring at the empty gazes of Cronus and Hades, part of Kala was relieved. These two wanted to make her fail at her missions. They wanted the world to end. The curse of balance found a way to stop them. And, yet again, it involved General Geoffrey Turner.

The man was already tweaking the nodes and leads to his liking.

Harnessing the power of Cronus and Hades…

She knew he would use Hades to control the dead, but what would he do with Cronus?

Kala turned to Gaia and Talan. She didn't really want to talk. She didn't really want to do anything. "We should get back to the others. They'll be worried by now."

Turner interjected, "I should stay here."

Gaia answered, "No. You need to return, too. You were right, Harry Clifton can never know about what we've done here. Understand?" Her expression left no room for argument.

Since Turner had already forced everyone to make that same promise, he was more than pleased. "I'll take it to my grave."

Gaia shook her head. "There will be no grave for you, Geoffrey Turner. This is your burden for eternity."

Turner seemed both pleased and scared by this statement, but he bowed slightly. "I won't fail you."

Kala had never seen Turner act with such deference. But he *was* talking to Mother Earth, and Gaia had just given him everything that he wanted.

Gaia motioned to Talan. "Take Geoffrey back to the Compound. Kala and I have things to discuss."

Kala wasn't sure she liked the sound of that, but maybe she could find more answers from her mother. And, considering Gaia had already disappeared once for a few millennia, Kala wasn't sure if she'd ever see her again.

Talan didn't argue with the goddess, which only proved to Kala how much he trusted Gaia. If one thing could be said of Talan, he lived to protect Kala. If he even thought for a second she'd be in danger, he would have never agreed.

Turner looked as if he had just received a shiny new toy and was being ripped away from it, but he walked over to Talan without argument.

Before they left, Kala gave Talan a hug. "Thank you for everything."

Talan's arms squeezed back, but he didn't try to kiss her or do anything inappropriate, always respectful. Pulling away, he nodded a goodbye to Gaia and then disappeared with Turner.

That left Kala alone with Gaia. She turned to her mother, wondering what Gaia would say to her.

Reaching out and taking Kala's hands, Gaia said gently, "It's time for a proper good-bye."

Chapter Twenty-One

Before Kala could ask what Gaia meant, her surroundings blurred and shifted and Kala knew she was being teleported somewhere.

When everything came back in focus, Kala had to blink back the intensity of the colors invading all her senses. An onslaught of blues, greens, reds, oranges, yellows and purples from every type of flower imaginable was laid out before her for miles and miles. Long winding cobblestone pathways twisted and turned throughout, making this the most stunning garden Kala had ever witnessed.

"Where are we?" she asked of Gaia.

"The Fields of Elysium," her mother answered softly.

A lump formed in Kala's throat. Why had Gaia taken her back to the Underworld? Though this was at least *the nice* part of town so-to-speak. But this was where Jack was supposed to be. Kala wasn't sure she could bear to see him again, with his lifeless eyes, wandering the Underworld forever because their souls could not exist together on Earth.

Kala finally found her voice, "Why are we here?"

"I thought you could say good-bye." Gaia's face was kind and caring, but seeing Jack would be torture. He didn't even know what was going on around him. But maybe that was okay. Maybe Kala just needed to say the words so that *she* could heal.

Nodding her head, Kala genuinely meant it when she replied, "Thank you."

"Kala?" Jack's voice froze Kala instantly.

Only her eyes moved as they locked with Gaia's. Her mother smiled gently. "I gave him back his consciousness." Then Gaia spoke in Kala's head so Jack couldn't hear. *Now that Hades is no longer the ruler of the Underworld, I'm placing Jack in charge. He's a good man and will do well. But since he can never be reincarnated on earth again as long as you're alive, you have to say your final good-bye now.*

For both your sakes, I'll wipe all remnants of your romantic life together, so he can be happy here, and so you can move on. But he needs to know who you are and remember your life together as soldiers so that he remains loyal. Upon seeing the pained expression in Kala eyes, Gaia continued to explain, *He'd never let you go as long as he remembers his love for you. You know that, Kala. But be content, Daughter, there is one that loves him as much as you do and if his affections for you hadn't been real, Jack would have returned her feelings. She has volunteered to stay here with him.*

Penny.

Kala knew it without Gaia mentioning her name. Always in the way Penny spoke of Jack, the way she looked at Jack, Pandora was in love. It twisted Kala's stomach with envy that Penny would be able to be with Jack for all eternity, but she knew Gaia was right. She wanted Jack to be happy. He *deserved* that.

Nodding her agreement, Kala turned to face Jack.

He looked almost angelic, standing amongst the flowers, his brown eyes full of life and joy at seeing Kala in front of him. "Jack," she choked out.

Two steps later, Kala was in Jack's arms and he was kissing her.

Knowing this was the last time she'd ever kiss him again, Kala was determined to make it count. Even though it had only been days, it had seemed like years since his lips were on hers. Her heart squeezed in both anguish and contentment. Being with Jack felt right. Where she was meant to be.

Pulling away, Jack smiled at her and spoke between kisses, "I missed you so much."

"I missed you too," Kala smiled back. It was the first time in a long time when she had felt an ounce of happiness – though it was laced with heartbreak at what was coming next.

His lips pressed against hers again and Kala lost herself in the moment.

Then it was time.

Time so say good-bye.

Kala pulled away from Jack, but kept her hands holding his as they faced each other.

"You're not mad at me?" Kala had to ask him.

His expression was incredulous. "For what?"

"For… killing you."

Jack sighed as if Kala was insane. "Mad at you? Are you joking? No. I would never be, nor will I ever be *mad* at you. You completed your mission and saved the world. I was a small price to pay."

"Don't say that," Kala shook her head. "You meant everything to me."

"Which is why it was a sacrifice. That's your job now, Kala. You have to make horrible choices for the greater good. Penny trained me to accept this from an early age. I was ready to die." He held Kala's face in his hands lovingly. "I will *never* blame you for doing the right thing."

Though it should have brought her relief, it raked her soul with guilt. Then Kala wondered aloud, "Do you remember what happened here in the Underworld… before Gaia brought your consciousness back?"

"You mean when Hades made me say all those awful things to you? Yes, I remember, and none of that was me. That was all *him* trying to break you." Jack kissed her forehead. "We can be together down here, though. You can complete your Atlas missions at the end of the four days, but spend the rest of the time here."

And there it was.

An offer Kala didn't want to refuse.

But she had to.

It was no life. Not for either one of them.

Gaia was right. Jack needed to be wiped of any romantic feelings he felt for Kala. It was the only way he could be truly happy.

And Penny loved him. As ornery and annoying as the girl was, she would love Jack with all her being.

Just like Kala did.

It was time to let Jack go.

Kala reached up and touched Jack's cheek. "I want you to know: you're the first man I ever fell in love with and I will always be eternally grateful for that."

Jack took her hand and kissed it. "I love you, too. And we'll have all eternity to be together. Not bad, huh?"

Kissing him one last time, their lips finally parted. Turning around to Gaia, she nodded.

Gaia's hand barely moved, but when Kala's eyes met Jack's again the love that she once saw there was replaced by affection and respect. In less than a second Jack went from seeing her as his lover to seeing her as his friend.

It hurt.

A lot.

But it was the right choice.

It was the first time in a long time that Kala actually felt like she had made a good decision.

Jack had a slightly confused look on his face. "I'm sorry. What were we talking about?"

Kala forced a smile as if she were teasing a friend. "We were talking about how Penny will be joining you down here. You have to be pretty excited about that." Every word of that hurt Kala to the core, but one thing she was good at: hiding pain. Something she learned to do growing up.

Jack blushed slightly as if thinking of Penny made his heart soar. "Ha, ha. Well, I'm stuck down here since you and I apparently can't exist together in the real world. Might as well live in paradise with my girlfriend."

Fighting back emotion, Kala laughed to disguise the hurt. "If you're going to be spending *all of time* down here, you should probably marry the girl."

"Do gods marry?" Jack asked genuinely perplexed. "That seems like a human thing."

"Well, you're human," Kala teased, hoping Jack wouldn't sense her sadness.

"A *dead* human, thank you very much." Then he mock-straightened himself up as if he were royalty. "And now that Turner's got Hades hooked up to one of his machines, I'm technically King of the Underworld." He tried to hide his laughter.

It was so Jack that Kala had to smile with him. "King of the Underworld, huh? Well, you'll be good at it, like you were at everything else when you were alive."

"Aw, gee, thanks." Jack joked sarcastically. Then his eyes lit up as he saw something behind Kala.

Turning around, Kala saw Penny standing next to Gaia.

Never seeing her happier, Kala motioned for Penny to walk over to them.

Cautious at first, Penny moved to stand next to Kala. "Are you sure you're okay with this?"

Kala nodded, not wanting to elaborate, afraid she might either break down and cry or punch Penny in the face. She knew that wasn't fair, but it was how her brain worked.

"Come here, you." Jack pulled Penny into his arms and kissed her. When they parted, Penny didn't make eye contact with Kala and that was probably a good thing.

"Well, I'll let you two get to it. Gaia and I have other places to be." Kala didn't know if that was true, but she couldn't be there anymore.

Jack reached down and hugged Kala. Like a friend. But she'd take it.

When they ended their embrace, Jack saluted Kala. "You and Derek have to come visit us sometime."

Us.

Jack and Penny.

"I'm sure Derek would love the Underworld," Kala laughed.

Jack laughed, too. *Genuinely* laughed.

And with everything that had happened, the sound made Kala sincerely happy.

It was time to leave.

Walking over to Gaia, Kala waved one last time to Jack and he waved back with his all-American-boy smile.

Though painful, Kala was grateful that her last memories of Jack had been replaced by happier ones. Even if he didn't remember his love for her, Kala *would* remember and be content that Jack was happy now.

Upon her mother's touch, the scenery disappeared. Transporting again.

When they reappeared, the two of them were in Kala's apartment. It was smaller than she remembered, but it was home.

"I thought you'd want to go somewhere familiar," Gaia explained.

"This is good, thanks." Kala looked at her mother. "So you're probably leaving now?"

Gaia nodded. "I have to see to my other children and grandchildren. They must know I'm back and what I sanctioned."

"You think anyone will try and break Cronus and Hades out of there?" Kala couldn't imagine the Titans and Olympians taking this lightly.

Gaia's confidence was unshakable. "They will do as I ask, but I've made sure the room Cronus and Hades are in is protected."

Protection spells could be broken. That was a lesson Kala had learned several times on her last two missions. But she decided she didn't want to think about it anymore. If Gaia said they were locked up for good, then Kala wanted to believe that.

"When I was in the coma, I met the girl who is going to break the curse of balance. Did you make that happen?" Kala hadn't had time to really think about the enormity of talking to someone three hundred years in the future. Now that she did, Kala wondered if Gaia was somehow responsible.

But her mother shook her head. "Your mind is more powerful than even you know. And the girl must be very strong as well if she were able to receive you. You two are bound."

Kala nodded and glanced at her old beat-up green armchair calling her name. Then she glanced at the turned-off TV and sighed. "I'll never be able to watch TV again, will I?"

Gaia shrugged apologetically. "Maybe in three hundred years?"

"I'll have to do some serious binge watching," Kala joked.

And that was when Kala noticed it. Her burden was lessened slightly. She actually felt normal for once in a really long time. Yes, Kala was still Atlas and she had another three hundred years of having to do the unthinkable, but now she had a better understanding of how the universe worked. And with having the chance to truly say good-bye to Jack, Kala felt like she was ready for anything.

Gaia hugged her daughter. "Good-bye, Kala. We'll see each other again."

"I hope so." Kala meant it.

And, with that, Gaia was gone.

It took a few minutes for Kala to move again: when she did, she plopped down in her plushy chair. She should really talk to Talan and Owen and give them a heads up on everything that she knew, but it could wait.

Glancing at the clock, her countdown was already three hours in.

Turning on the TV, Kala watched her new Atlas mission unfold in front of her eyes.

Shaking her head in amused disgust, Kala muttered aloud. "Well, this one's going to be fun."